UNSAFE

THE SCRIPT of ONE-ZERO-THREE

Initially a prize-winning writer of TV and cinema commercials and documentaries, Paddy Carpenter has enjoyed a long career in film production, during which he has fulfilled most rôles at one time or another, working in 30 countries with many major figures of the cinema.

As an assistant director, location manager, production manager, producer, director and writer – even, on rare occasions, as actor, he has contributed to and been responsible for the shooting of feature films, TV series, documentaries, commercials and pop promos, collaborating with a formidable, perhaps unsurpassed, roll-call of acting, directing and technical talent.

A pilot for 30 years, he has been a partner in a flying club, is an event commentator for air sport and has written on aviation safety. He has managed a pop group and penned song lyrics. He is a specialist in transport in most forms and writes on aspects of social history.

UNSAFE – The Script of One-Zero-Three comes about as a result of his love for the serenity of flight and his profound distaste for injustice.

UNSAFE

THE SCRIPT of ONE-ZERO-THREE

Paddy Carpenter

"Your government and mine know exactly who is responsible for the bombing and how they carried it out, but they will never make the facts known. Much of the wilder speculation that's been in the press is true, but no one in authority will acknowledge what is true and what's not."

Member of the President's Commission on Aviation Security and Terrorism to one of the British Lockerbie bereaved.

"I love my country. But I fear my government."

Dr William Chasey. A subsequent American victim.

To the victims of Pan Am Flight 103, both the dead and the living; and to justice and truth which, even before the aircraft had left the earth, were already casualties.

Also to the memory of the passengers and crew of Iran Air Flight 655, whose destiny was so tragically intertwined and whose loss tends to be much less remembered.

Acknowledgments

This project would never have begun without my becoming aware of the dedication and courage of journalists, editors and film-makers John Ashton, Ian Ferguson, the late Paul Foot, the late Allan Francovich, Ian Hislop, David Johnston and John Pilger, to all of whom I pay every possible tribute.

The work of other authors and commentators has been invaluable in piecing the background jigsaw together. Professor Robert Black, Wifred Burchett. Duncan Campbell, Tony Collins, Merryl Wyn Davies, John H Davis, Jim Garrison, William Goldman, David Ray Griffin, Jill S Haldane, Paul Halloran, Mark Hollingsworth, Mark Lane, Peter Laurie, George Monbiot, Henshall Morgan, Michael Moore, Greg Palast, Julian Pettifer, Gareth Peirce, Clive Ponting, James Risen, Alexander Rose, the late Anthony Sampson, Ziauddin Sarder, Graham Smith, Stanley Stewart, Joe Sutter, Antony A Thompson, Kenneth R Timmerman, Andrew Weir, Geoffrey Wheatcroft and Bob Woodward are prominent among those who in their own areas of expertise and research have tried to 'put history straight'. People who shine lights are due the thanks of all of us.

I owe personal thanks, among many others, to David Ashwell, Bert Batt, Phil Beer, Keith Boreland, John Burrows, Carlton Campbell, Martin Campbell, Justin Cartwright, Ben Challis, Mike Challis, David Comer, Ray Corbett, Nick Darke, Rob Davis, Maggie Evans, Geoffrey Forster, Ron Fry, Mike Godsell, Harry Green, Laurie Greenwood, Jim Harrison, Tom Hawkins, Sam Hipperson, Ian Hislop, Harry Hodgson, Paul Hudson, Roger Inman, Adrian A Jackson, Bernard Jones, Steve Knightley, Ted Lewis, Hilary Lissenden, Roger Lunn, Macdonald Martin, Barry Matthews, Jimmy Mullins, Les Parrott, John Pritchard, Bethany Porter, Miranda Potter, Geoffrey Randall, Amy Rigg, Charlie Sargent, Chris Sargent, Safaya Salter, Audley Southcott, Terry Stone, John Swain, David Tondeur, Clifford Haydn-Tovey, Richard Walker, Betty Weekes, Jim Weekes, Bridget Wheeler, Ken and Jane Wilson, Mike and Chris Woodhouse and Davey Woods.

Contents

Help with Reading the Numbers

Unless you are familiar with aviation, you may need a little assistance with numbers. As far as aircraft types are concerned, I was going to spell them out in the text as spoken, but aviation people thought it looked silly. Well, it did, but it's easy for them, because they know through familiarity how Boeings and Cessnas and so-on are dealt with. This is for everybody else.

Aircraft   Starting with Boeings, as they feature most in the story. People refer to them as follows:

207 Seven-O-Seven That's the letter 'O', **not** Seven-Zero-Seven, Seven-Nought-Seven nor, of course, Seven Hundred and Seven.

727, 737, 747 etc. Seven-Two-Seven, -Three-Seven, -Four Seven and so on. Except that Americans and others speaking American English may use Seven-Twenty-Seven etc. I don't think there's a 720 in the book, but if there were, everyone says Seven-Twenty.

For some reason, Airbus designators are pronounced the American way:

A300   A-Three-Hundred, on its own, then

A310, A320, A330, A340 are always: A-Three-Ten, -Twenty, -Thirty, -Forty and so-on upwards.

A319 , A321 become A-Three-Nineteen and -Twenty-One, as a rule.

Douglas aircraft are all prefixed DC, for Douglas Commercial. I think the only marks mentioned are the DC3 and 4, no problem there, and the DC10, which was always the DC-Ten, **not** DC-One-Zero. The US Air Force always have their own designations and for them the DC3 became the C47, pronounced C-Forty-Seven, reasonably enough.

A Convair 990 is mentioned. That would be referred to as a Nine-Ninety. I don't think the text specifies which size of ATR Ray flies on, but if it did it would be the Forty-Two or the Seventy-Two.

Three other military aircraft get a mention. The B52 is known world-wide as the B-Fifty-Two. Well, it has bombed most places in it. The other US bomber, the F111, is rendered as F-One-Eleven. The Boeing 707-derived tanker, the KC135, is, I think, referred to as KC-One-Three-Five.

Of the light aircraft in the story, the Cessnas are the C172, that's C-One-Seven-Two, and the C150 Aerobat is spoken of as the C-One-Fifty; while the Piper, the PA28, is always the PA-Twenty-Eight. Just to be sure, the Warrior II is Warrior Two, not Eleven. Typefaces can confuse anybody.

Radio I've set messages out in full, so there should be no problem about how call-signs, times, headings, runways and so-on are spoken. When you see "tree" and "fife" and "niner" these are not misprints; this is how controllers and pilots are supposed to pronounce 3, 5 and 9 for better clarity, not that they always do. Controllers are more likely to be meticulous than pilots in this respect, and the British probably more than other nationalities. "Niner" was ruthlessly parodied in the film *Airplane*! Among many conventions, "thousand" is supposed to be rendered as "tousand" and the figure 0 should always be "zero", thus the call-sign, Clipper One-Zero-Three. But because "O" is easier and quicker to say, it's not at all impossible that One-O-Three might be used at times by a pilot, but almost certainly not by a British controller. Away from the radio and the flight deck, most people and certainly passengers would refer to PA One-O-Three – so where PA or Pan Am 103 appear in the text, the choice is yours.

Airports and Runways Los Angeles International Airport is widely known by its 3-letter designator, which is pronounced L-A-X and **not** Lax, although having said that there are probably Californians who just **have** to.

And in case runways confuse the hell out of you, just as they do new pilots, they are designated by their magnetic heading, rounded to the nearest 10 degrees, with the final 0 knocked off. So a runway pointing more-or-less east, say 094 degrees, is rounded to 090, becomes written 09, pronounced Zero-Nine. Used from the other end, the same strip of grass or concrete has a heading of 274°, so comes out as Two-Seven. Simple? In America, they drop any first zeros -- Runway Zero-Nine there becomes Runway Nine. Ah, well!

And the Freeways It's Highway One-O-One and Interstate Four-O-Five. Both O as in "go".

Does any of this matter? Unless you are reading aloud, probably not, but then again . . . Years ago a journalist wrote a good book about a very serious incident involving a police car in London. He titled it *No Answer from Fox-Trot Eleven*. The trouble was that when it was published no person in the capital had ever heard of such a vehicle. In the convention followed by every unit since the city's first wireless cars had gone on the road, the car had been Fox-Trot One-One. Not the happiest of book-launches, probably.

Introduction

This is a work of fiction, about a work of fiction, which focuses on a real-life event. That may sound complicated, but isn't, even though there is a widespread view that the public account of the event has itself been fictionalised. I hope the book makes it clear where invention stops and truth starts, and so helps the reader to decide if the facts in an endlessly fascinating and crucially important case have indeed been officially tampered with – and if so, how and why.

Twenty five years after the event, the Lockerbie bombing can still generate headlines and stir passions. Among those for whom the memories will never recede there are some who believe that the 2000 trial offered a measure of justice and others who feel it merely produced a scapegoat for an angry world. Even the first group would have to admit that justice was far from complete; one man could not have been responsible for the entire plot. Evidence of other conspirators has been suspiciously absent, meaning there are other parties not yet brought to trial. The case is thus, by definition, open. In this respect the two groups have more common ground than they may tend to believe.

This book has been gestating since 2001. Its own progress from then to now is a story in itself but has no place here. In successive forms and variations though, one aim has been paramount. Convinced that the victims and both groups of bereaved have been denied meaningful justice, I have striven to present the full range of facts in the hope that the opportunity for the public-at-large to re-evaluate and balance what they understand of Lockerbie may result in a much more widespread acceptance of that view. The truth is known and potentially available; all it requires is enough people to demand it.

In the dispelling of myths and even in the simple retelling of the tragic story, some raw nerves will inevitably be touched and for this I apologise. There is no alternative other than silence – and giving voice is done with the best of intentions.

Because any novel involving itself with history by nature encompasses both fiction and fact, I have included a bibliography, in the spirit of "If you find what is written here unbelievable, see what the real experts say." I thoroughly recommend all the authors and works listed.

It is worth underlining, because Lockerbie is patently an ongoing story, that UNSAFE is set in 2006 and takes no account of any developments since that time. I hope that when the time is right to revisit the subject and consider what revelations the intervening years have brought, there will significant progress to discuss.

Paddy Carpenter   Gloucestershire UK June 2014

Foretaste

This is no night to be flying.

Hail clatters on the windshield, not that the pilot is expecting to see anything at all helpful through that for another minute at least. Ray Scriver's concentration is entirely given to the instruments on the panel, trying to counteract every lurch and swing of the needles. A fearsome, gusty crosswind is determinedly trying to push the aircraft away from the two invisible electronic beams he is relying on to lead him through and down out of the blackness. He's in the dark heart of the boiling, turbulent clouds which alternately seem to drag the aircraft back and earthward as if enmeshed in a net; then up sharply as though an unseen mighty crane has hooked into the fuselage. That's it, he thinks; the plane is a fish, being played by an enormous angler. It must be God, or more likely St Peter, in monolithic waders.

Every time he restores order and gets the indications of seven different pointers almost where they need to be, the big fisherman has another tug at him and he has to make corrections all over again, through the yoke with his left hand, the throttle with his right and the rudder pedals with his feet. But every correction, every input, affects all the other balances and imbalances, each one changes the picture relayed by the dials and needles behind the circular glasses. If he weren't holding the controls his limbs would appear to be performing a slightly mad, out-of-beat dance, one that on a night like this won't end even when the aircraft breaks cloud and he sees the runway lights. That's if he does. Conditions are marginal. If the lights aren't visible when he reaches his pre-calculated decision height, the rules say he must stop the descent, abandon the approach, climb and transit to his alternate airport thirty miles away, where he should reportedly be able to break cloud legally and safely – just!

Bang! The craft shudders as if punched by a giant fist. Turning more into wind to stay on the localiser beam sees the rate of descent increase sharply, so power has to be added, power that very quickly takes him higher than he should be; he's found an express lift of an updraught. Ray is sweating with the concentration. As he juggles the needles and the dancing artificial horizon and direction indicator into brief compliance he momentarily considers, as he often does, the absurdity of accepting this level of challenge by way of recreation.

He is very close to that decision height. If he breaks cloud in time, the rest of the approach and the landing too will still be very demanding in such foul weather. A pulsating yellow light on the panel and some Morse-like tone through the speaker tell him he is crossing the middle marker, a simple radio beacon around a half-mile from the airport's threshold. As the bleeping and flashing cease, and at the very instant that the still-distant high intensity runway lights start to burn through the finally thinning cloud, Ray becomes aware of another alert tone; one that for a moment he can't place and has trouble reacting to. He finally comes to resigned realisation, moves the mouse to the pause button at the corner of the screen and scans his cluttered office to discover the whereabouts of a housephone handset.

For some reason Eve insisted on programming all the phones in the rambling house to ring with a different tune, so it's an infernally jangly rendering of *Jesu, Joy of Man's Desiring* that has interrupted this strange choice of activity for a few minutes of after-work relaxation. He thinks it must be her, until he looks at the clock and realises the time – going on for two. E knows that he likes to write late, but even she wouldn't call at this hour, barring something serious. But then, given recent events, is his wife really likely to be phoning at all?

Probably not.

If the timing of the call has been calculated, as he will soon come to suspect, then he could reasonably be expected to be asleep. A woman's voice, American, strident, forceful, of indeterminate age, asks for him by name. When he confirms it, she gives him hers, adding,

"You don't know me."

He fails to catch what she says it is, but he knows she's right; they haven't spoken before; nor is it, he thinks, a name he's heard – something that later on will reinforce the suspicions which will soon take hold. Before he can ask her to repeat it, she's off, leaving no pause for interjection, already the intensity rising with each phrase. The volume though, stays constant giving an impression of someone on the edge; just in control, but also to a degree threatening.

"I'm calling you," she says, "because I lost someone murdered in the Lockerbie massacre. I understand that you're planning to deepen my grief and reopen the wounds of all the relatives and friends by making a movie about it. I'm calling to ask you not to; to ask you if you think it's fair to make an entertainment out of the suffering of those that were lost and those that are left behind? Don't you think that they and we deserve to have some peace, not to have the whole thing dragged up over and over, this time for what – prurience; profit? Don't you feel guilty at cashing in on their suffering and our misery? I don't understand how you can live with yourself. I speak for so many others who think the same way. To us you people are like vultures. Why don't you leave us alone?"

For the first time, Ray is able to get into the conversation, if only temporarily.

"I'm sorry; I didn't catch your name."

She repeats it, but the combination of the small phone handset and her accent render it incomprehensible. "And may I ask who it was you lost?"

"My best friend."

"And may I know their name?"

This, he thinks may help identify the caller, without having to ask her a third time, which he doesn't really want to do.

"It doesn't matter. They're dead. It's no business of yours."

"I think it does matter," Ray says. "I am very sensitive to – as conscious as anybody of the devastation that the . . ." He gets no further.

"You can't be," she cuts in. "You couldn't begin to understand. You've no idea or you'd realise how terrible it is for us every time it's raked through afresh. If you had you wouldn't think of doing what you're doing."

"What I'm trying is to bring the awful story of what happened to your loved ones to a wider audience so that maybe we can all get nearer the truth of why they died." He feels the need to say it, though he is already convinced that she's not interested in hearing his views.

"We know what happened." The woman is now close to shouting, but more angry, he feels, than upset. "We had a trial. We heard it all. We know who did it. We got a verdict."

Suspicious now that she is trying to bully or even provoke him, Ray tries to respond slowly and calmly.

"Which a great many people think was sad miscarriage of justice. There were tainted witnesses, unsound testimony; the judges accepted a theory that the flimsy evidence didn't in any way prove . . ."

"There we go," she barges in again. "You think you know more than three judges, to say they were wrong. Who the hell do you think you are to

3

say that?"

"Just a concerned outsider taking the facts at their face value; someone under no pressure to give a verdict that virtually everyone apart from the defendants was desperate for."

"It was a fair trial." She effectively **is** shouting now. "They were guilty. One managed to wriggle out of it, but they did it. They killed all those people. At least one is paying for his crime."

"So you're agreeing with me, that judges can get it wrong and you're saying that they did so in Fhima's case. So why not in Megrahi's? The trial wasn't remotely fair. The defence spent half the time with their arms tied behind their backs. Where's the justice in that? That was the only way there was even one guilty verdict."

"Defence lawyers will say anything to get evil people off," the woman says.

"Their job is to get acquittals if they can, but their remit is also to stop innocent people being convicted and they could have done that, but it's hard if they're stopped from presenting a full defence by dirty tactics."

"That's your opinion. You sound like you would let anybody off, any no-good terrorist who didn't give their victims any chance, any justice, but then expects to be protected by the legal process – and supported by people like you."

"It's not me, it's the law that says you have to let people go, guilty or not, if there isn't conclusive proof, and that can sometimes be really bad, but I'm totally convinced those two Libyans had nothing to do with it. They were just fall guys."

"How can you say that? So your film will say they didn't do it and come up with some far-fetched story – tell me who **you** think did it?"

Ray can't believe she's asking a non-rhetorical question; that she's actually inviting him to speak, although he has no intention of giving an answer now, and later will be glad that he doesn't.

"I can't pre-empt the film, but I can promise you that it'll respect the memory . . . " She's climbing all over him again.

"Respect nothing. I suppose you're another of those soft liberals, undermining the values of decent . . . "

It's Ray's turn to butt in now. If this is bait he's taking it.

"Look madam, you couldn't be more wrong. You know nothing about me, but I'll tell you what I believe. I think it's offensive to the memory of those who died, and I would have thought offensive to all those in your position . . . " She tries to interject with another comment about his having no concept of the reality of her position but he just presses on. " . . to have justice denied by there having been, at nearly twenty years on, just a flawed show trial and a single token figure of guilt. How can anyone be content that all that effort and the millions that the investigation and the prosecution cost, can give us – you, so little? No more names, no facts, no details, no corroboration but yet lots of basic unaddressed questions, the answers to which your government and mine have fallen over themselves to cloak in official secrecy. Logic says that's completely inappropriate, if the story is as they claim. But of course the secrecy can only be to hide an alternative story, which is the one that would tell us what really happened. That's what I would have thought all the victims, the dead ones and the living ones would want to be heard. Not a badly-concocted fable served up to give you someone to hate!"

"I can't believe your arrogance. I'm going to do all I can to stop your film being made, and if it **is** made I'll do my utmost to persuade people not to go see it. I hope you never make a cent out of it."

"Well, I've worked five years on it and it's cost me a small fortune to get this far, so you've every chance of being granted that wish, and arrogance works both ways, but I hope your support for censorship fails at least."

"It's not censorship, Mr Scriver. The world doesn't need your movie, or you. Good afternoon." And she's gone.

Phew! Ray has always known that he has to expect at least some pressure on the lines of that he's just experienced, but that was really unsettling, and being in the middle of the night didn't help. She said 'Good afternoon' which puts her somewhere towards the US west coast, he presumes. He finds a pen and scrap of paper, and dials 1471 just in case, but the schoolmistressy voice intones 'The caller withheld their number,' so there's no clue to be had there.

Suddenly he goes cold as the potential of what's just occurred can almost be felt moving about like an animal in his cranium. At dawn it will be a week, virtually to the minute, since he touched down after carrying his script a full circle of the earth. But in theory only a handful of people actually got to see it, plus perhaps a similar number who were made aware of its subject. How did this woman find out about it? What's worse, how much has he now said to her? What has he given away? He's been so cautious up to now about discussing the work, especially on the phone, and suddenly, because he thought he was talking to one of the bereaved, someone vulnerable, a woman still apparently blinkered by grief nearly twenty years on, he's let down his guard. Is she really who she claimed to be? Did she ring in the small hours deliberately to wrong-foot him?

The more he thinks, the worse it gets. This mysterious woman in California not only knows about *One-Zero-Three* but has also got his home telephone number. Or did she say 'Good afternoon' to mislead? Where else could she be? Was she calling from the UK, even? She could be sitting in a car up the lane. He runs through the conversation. If she was playing a part she did it pretty well; enough to get through that shell of protective caution that he's been trying to grow over the last months.

Within two minutes Ray has convinced himself that the woman wasn't in the least who she said she was.

Damn!

He thought he was up to this game and he's just failed at Level One.

–ooOoo–

Of course, that night wasn't at all when the story really started. Why would it be? One of the hardest things about their craft, Ray or any other screenwriter will tell you, is deciding the place to begin.

–ooOoo–

1 Morning is Broken

Ray hasn't been up this early for a good while. For years a 4am alarm call was a regular event in the Scriver household, but lately there has been little need to rise from bed at the hour of the lowest ebb. Until this morning there's been perhaps a year, or even two, for him to forget how easy it is to drown in negativity in the fifty-five minutes or so that it will take him to get out of the house. It's England and not that far off midsummer so it will be getting light in a few minutes. But the old demons come flooding back, just as if it were the depth of winter, with ice to scrape off the car. The strange thing is that when the early rising was routine, the palpable depression was always rampant, even when the day was full of promise. It didn't seem to matter whether its schedule presaged boredom, relative drudgery and difficult people or whether the hours were to be spent in the company of favourite souls and absorbing work. And whichever of the two extremes had been on the cards, once the car was started and pointing in the right direction he'd always been exhilarated at being up and about at this privileged time of day. Today is no different. As he moves around the kitchen, making the tea, cutting the fruit, spooning the yoghurt, the darkness that is for now beyond the windows throws a black drape over the breakfast, the journey, the day and the future.

The news doesn't help. Already he's heard a summary on the clock radio that crashed into his unconsciousness at 3.59. You shouldn't do that, he decided long ago. You need to choose what to wake up to. Nobody can expect to cope with headlines in their head about 30,000 earthquake deaths at four in the morning. He'd forgotten this rule, but it shouldn't be a factor because today should be different. Tonight he'll be in Los Angeles and he's been looking forward to it for days: the last thing he expected to be feeling, at the moment before setting off, is indifferent, inadequate, fearful and mildly suicidal.

Today there's no one big debilitating disaster on the bulletins; just a sequence of run-of-the-mill low-grade stories whose common theme is that if there is a wrong, illogical, dangerous, unfair, damaging decision to be taken, on any matter, anywhere – someone will usually take it. Under normal circumstances Ray keeps his end and his spirits up by hurling abuse at the radio. According to some theories, he has shouted for a living, and certainly has a variety of tones and volumes to suit all occasions. Occasionally a news item will require a serious response, when there's something really absurd to be pointed up and exploded. That means a letter to an editor or even a 600-word article. Ray has always been a better writer than he is a speaker. His off-the-cuff berating of the newsreader would not for a moment convince anyone of the soundness of his argument. His written prose, his accounts suggest, is moderately more coherent and persuasive than his breakfast snarls.

But at 4.10am there's no fight. The food he's preparing is probably contaminated by agrobusiness pesticides and escaped GM genomes. He's almost certainly got something terminal and hasn't long to live. The roads beyond the hamlet are full of half-trained drivers oblivious to their own and others' mortality; people who would never get near a steering wheel if there were any form of psychological or aptitude check. To get to Heathrow alive will be a miracle. If he does, there hasn't been a serious air disaster for some months so one must be due and it's highly likely to be today. And with the way the country and the world are going in 2006 – democracy an illusion, the economy doomed, society edging towards meltdown and chaos, with war either intermittent and informal or hot and regular seeming virtually inevitable, you're probably better off dead, so a plane crash might not be the worst of all options. At this time of day his respect for politicians of all levels and shades is zero; his hatred for the mechanics of state authority total; his confidence in the intelligence and trustworthiness of just about everybody else in the world completely missing. He wants to go back to bed; forget New Zealand, not bother with Pinewood, the airport and the motorway. He'd like either to die in his sleep or to wake up at a more congenial time.

In 45 minutes he will be counting his blessings and feeling he's the luckiest man in the world.

2 It's History – Man!

In a rare instance of not leaving things to the last moment, all the bargain IKEA timers were put in place yesterday, set for 5am, awaiting only this morning's throw of the rocker switches at the sockets to begin their elaborate sequence. For the next 552 hours (is it really that few?) the combinations of lights seen through the cottage's numerous windows during the minimal hours of darkness will suggest an occupant indulging in an even odder and more nocturnal pattern of wakefulness than the eccentric-enough norm. The switchings-on and off will suggest very late work in the upstairs study, with occasional visits to the kitchen and lavatory; a progress to the sitting room and finally to the master bedroom, via an excursion to the attic; a sort of dummy existence lived by an unseen protagonist who can work lights but not draw curtains. Ray is reminded of trams on a new system or route not yet opened, running a full 'ghost timetable', sometimes for weeks on end, humming into stops with doors opening and announcements Tannoyed, with eerily no passengers whatsoever to be seen.

He flicks a tumbler on a socket built into one of his many bookshelves. A favourite section this; one that would be labelled something like 'Political Mysteries and Scandals', if he went in for labelling. Ownership of the innocuous-enough titles displayed here ensures that, though he is avidly patriotic, he will never, ever be granted any form of official security clearance. There is an irony that behind these particular volumes, the ones that salaried burglars will doubtless photograph and catalogue (assuming they haven't already), lies the hidden recess into which, also last night, he inserted a back-up hard disc and a pair of large notebooks. The IKEA-facilitated son-et-lumière (a transistor radio is also included in the switching plan) may persuade everyday robbers to try elsewhere. The best he can hope for in the case of those breaking and entering while simultaneously looking forward to generous government pensions is that their nasty, invasive work might be briefly delayed.

–ooOoo–

Ray has had a highly-developed concern for fairness and justice for just about as long as he can remember. He cannot forget being scandalised when an RI teacher (in the days when it was religious instruction rather than education) gave him a detention for advancing a perfectly arguable opinion. In the intervening years, the sheer number of injustices that can be found lurking in every newspaper page, TV bulletin or current affairs programme has come to suggest to him one of those giant snowballs roaring down a steep slope, growing larger with each revolution and threatening to engulf everything in its path. In fact, Ray and his contemporaries were encouraged to believe that in certain other countries, injustice was the default situation. Not too many of them would come to decide, as he eventually did, that it was actually the norm in a far broader swathe of states than the 'officially designated' ones, and that it was in many respects just as prevalent in the UK as the Ukraine, for example. In fact most people lose the militant idealism of youth as life requires them to concentrate on matters of more immediate concern like career, a home, family responsibilities. Many never regain it. Ray can't say he thought overmuch about the world ills and unfairness when his career was booming; there was no spare time or energy. It's only since becoming more interested in history and through that, fascinated by his present project, that the blazing indignation of teenage years has resurfaced.

Which is why he has no objection to being called a conspiracy theorist; in fact he rather enjoys it. For one thing, it can often signal that his discoveries are pretty much on the right track. People who use the term (which Ray shortens to CT) think they are using the ultimate pejorative, deploying the conversational weapon of mass destruction – the put-down so complete that it ends the debate instantly and for all time by dismissing out-of-hand not only the question that has been raised, but along with it the fitness of the questioner to so much as take part in any discussion, on any subject.

Its users fall into two categories. Those in the first simply utter the phrase as a conditioned response when they don't want to be bothered to use their brain – when they've lost the intellectual curiosity to think anywhere approaching even the edges of the box; to look for the holes in what the powers-that-be ask us to believe – even when, as so often, the official line conflicts with reality. Ray believes that far too many of us have given up the practice of thought on anything more than an occasional basis. The second batch, though, are the ones to worry about, because when they spit the words CT they have an agenda, involvement, vested interests; they are complicit; they actually are or they represent those same powers-that-be, even if they don't always completely realise it. The first group don't want to think about something that might be unpalatable; the second group don't want **anyone** to think about something they **know** is unpalatable and in many, many cases all too true.

With most people, the very idea that the concept of CT exists and that the two words are floating around above a discussion waiting to be plucked out of the air and used like a sharp weapon are enough to keep them quiet: the threat works. As a label, 'conspiracy theorist' is so damning that the majority of the population will these days accept any cock-and-bull story trotted out by officialdom rather than risk being tainted by this description. Unfortunately, use of the term to smother debate is helped by the existence of CT junkies, attracted and addicted to each and every wild suggestion that surfaces, however devoid of logic and factual basis they might be. The net of disdain that easily ensnares them is handy to cast wider with the intention of suffocating bigger, more cerebral and more inconvenient fish, Ray knows.

High-level CT users have had a pretty clear run since 2001, because they've had an extra card in their pack, the one with a flag on it. 'If you question whether we are telling you the truth,' they say, 'it is not only too fanciful to be countenanced, but in the light of present circumstances it is an act of hideous disloyalty to your country to even think of disbelieving us.' Thus armed, plus now being possessed of the power to be able to suggest quietly that the career prospects of media people can be instantly and permanently blighted by displaying such lack of patriotism, 'they' managed to persuade nearly all of America's and most of Europe's investigative journalists, with a few very honourable exceptions, to remove the word 'investigative' from their job title. Today's media climate rewards pliant columnists and prefers reporters who re-hash press releases rather than look behind the words spinning across the pages.

Ray rationalises that the CT epithet is just another way of saying 'historian'. In ten years of reading, researching and writing more and more history, it didn't take him a fraction of that time to appreciate that if you read a dozen pages about the past you are likely to encounter a dozen conspiracies. Real ones: no theory involved. Human history, he's come to understand, is all about individuals or groups of all sizes banding together with others, always initially in secret, with the aim of benefiting themselves and disadvantaging those not in the grouping. If that isn't a definition of conspiracy, he tells his friends, what is?

The object is always to gain control of something, whether it's land, resources like food, minerals, or people as slaves or workers; but ultimately increasing the participants' influence, power and wealth by taking from those currently in possession. The means can range from unfair legal contract, through bribery and threat all the way up to all-out war. Except where the bad-news truth has, for a while, been obscured by enthusiasts for closed government, every page in the annals of every country, from the earliest and most patchily recorded hand-scribed document to the most recent e-mail, will reveal evidence of closed pow-wows, meetings, conferences and convocations at which decisions, treaties and pacts lead to action in the form of invasion and battles, annexation and appropriation, pacification and exploitation – decade on decade, century after century. In countries calling themselves civilised and democratic the action is more likely to take the form of bad laws, dubious fiscal policies and the awarding of contracts or patronage, all of which are just as effective at making the insiders more prosperous and usually everyone else worse off than they were previously.

Ray has a pet theory that most if not all the problems of the world can be put down to empire-building of one kind or another. From international politics, to the workplace, to family and personal relationships, people seek power and control because it is seen as bringing benefits, whether Imperial pomp, a bigger office, or better presents and toys.

The scale of the plotting, the scheming and the measures taken in history to achieve these goals is mind-boggling; many of the results would, if predicted, have been dismissed as fantasy, beyond belief, the work of overactive imaginations. Express the aims of the Holocaust and the aspirations of the Third Reich in a couple of sentences and the point is made, but consideration of any of the other episodes of genocide, both attempted and carried through, or examining a selection of the world's great empires of any era (including our own) will demonstrate the principle beyond any doubt. People conspire, massively. It's endemic to human beings. They always have. They still do.

The upshot is that no sequence of events, however apparently fictional or wildly inventive it may sound, can be rejected as too unlikely or far-fetched to be a real possibility, because it or something like it has taken place over time in different settings, often with frightening regularity. Ray knows that the entire fascinating interconnected cavalcade of history demonstrates the prosecution of conspiracies, large and small.

It is little else.

Why should we believe, he argues, that human habits and particularly the instincts of the currently powerful, have suddenly and miraculously changed? Show him, he says, a politician, a banker or a business leader and he'll show you a conspirator.

–ooOoo–

3 Risk Assessment

There's an odd line that people use to try and reassure those who are frightened of flying – or train travel, or boats, or car journeys. 'It's very safe,' they say. 'Remember you could step out of your front door and a roof tile could fall on your head.' So it could. A few days before the beat-the-traffic attempt on London that's about to begin, Ray was walking in a wood with Ogre, the dog, and had to run for his life when a substantial section of an otherwise perfectly healthy tree cracked loudly apart above his head and crashed down, hitting the path exactly where he'd been two seconds before.

Of course there's a risk to doing anything. But staying at home is no answer if the statistics are right. Home, they tell you, is the most dangerous place you can be. Going anywhere else apparently should be a whole lot safer. People (and Ray is a veritable addict in this respect) love those lists that put activities in order of hazard. With modes of travel, flying commercial is always made to sound spectacularly safe, but that's because the figures are given in passenger deaths per million kilometres. As airliners travel such huge distances, that distorts the picture impossibly. If you plot the fatalities according to the number of passenger journeys, rather than by distance or hours travelled, the mathematics aren't so comforting, as only motorcycles prove to be more unsafe. Ray long ago bought Andrew Weir's *The Tombstone Imperative* and read of the tricks that the air transport industry plays with the numbers; and the risks that the vested interests, airlines, plane makers, regulatory bodies and governments let us take; and the things they could do for our safety but don't, because to do them would hurt too many balance sheets.

We know from those lists that the acts of mounting a cycle, getting into a car, or boarding a train have a degree of probability attached to them; that to travel is always to a greater or lesser extent to play Russian Roulette – chancing the odds. Ray knows it, for goodness sake, because he doesn't only fly a simulator but he's been a private pilot for years and in his more reflective moments thinks that it's a pretty strange activity to have as a hobby. To do something for relaxation where, if you do just that – relax – and happen to miss something or make a small mistake, you are very likely to kill yourself, is not particularly sane behaviour. Which probably means that it's something that most weekend pilots don't really think too much about – explaining why their safety record is well down the list, whatever units you measure it in, although they, unlike motorists, almost never kill third parties. Whatever scare propaganda anti-airfield campaigners put on their leaflets, light aircraft almost never wipe out innocents on the ground.

—ooOoo—

Ray has been in love with airports since a time when one of London's was still just a very big grass field and he and friends used to bicycle up after school and watch the flights through the chain link fence. It really wasn't that long ago. Soon one of the boys on bikes was flying from there with his ex-RAF father. Not long after that the friend had a licence himself and used to cut classes and fly aerobatics over the school, earning himself the name 'The Mystery Flyer' in sensationalised reports in the local newspaper.

These days, airports are mostly like shopping malls. Although in many places in the world, departing or arriving at one remains a bruising, chaotic experience, and even at the organised ones, weather or something man-made can intervene and gum up the smooth running, in general they offer one of the more civilised and orderly means of starting a journey, by public transport at least. Certainly airside, after security, there is normally an atmosphere of almost unbelievable calm. Under the surface an unknown proportion of passengers killing time in any waiting area may be anxious in the extreme, but most manage to affect a convincing nonchalance.

Nevertheless Ray is always aware — and wonders how many of the brains ticking behind the composed faces around him are in time with his, realising it's all a question of that damned roulette — that it's just a game of numbers. Which of them is pondering the fact that every so often, a departure lounge like the one they're in empties and a mass of people stand up and disappear down a walkway, not knowing that they're taking their last few paces and using up their final precious hours or minutes on this earth?

—ooOoo—

4 Friends – The One Where He Meets the Big Producer

There's another, far less troubling way in which the principle of random chance impacts airports: you run into people that you know. There seems to be a rule that, even if you only fly occasionally, when you do you will stand in a queue in front of a stranger who turns out to live near you, or you sit next to someone who shares a mutual acquaintance. And most likely of all, you glance across the check-in or the duty free shop and spot a friend that you haven't seen for 15 years, or possibly someone that you were working with a fortnight ago. It's happened to Ray to the extent that no one would believe it if he reflected the frequency of such coincidence in a screenplay. 'Life just isn't that convenient,' would be the readers' first complaint. Ray isn't complaining. This morning in a trolley jam waiting to squeeze into Terminal Three he will find himself jockeying for the inside track with DB Hollingsworth.

Thomas Raymond Scriver and David Barclay Hollingsworth go back a long, long way; they first worked together in the late 1970s. If you are a free-lance film technician, or certainly if you were one then, the people you worked with were your friends – all those that you didn't actively dislike, that is. Not to say that they were friends in the sense that you socialised beyond the particular assignment with all of them, but you liked them, you enjoyed working with them and you were pleased to see them when they turned up on another job (and the chances were strongly that they would in those days – when the industry was small). You would generally, pre-breathalyser, repair to the pub with some of them at the end of a studio shoot or a daily location.

If it was an away location, while it lasted you would work, laugh, eat, drink – and let's be honest, some people did also occasionally sleep – with other members of the crew. It was not unknown for a clapper-boy or a focus-puller to get a quiet tap on his hotel room door from a nubile young production assistant wanting to 'check something on the camera sheets' (an unappreciated euphemism) or for an assistant director to help an actress deal with the insecurities of the job, away from the reassurance of home. Members of a film unit can easily imagine themselves a troupe of strolling players, self-contained, a family of hard-working nomads with their own internal affections, loyalties and bonds. There was that convenient phrase 'Doesn't count on location', implying that temporary liaisons might be pursued without involvement and without upsetting pre-existing relationships elsewhere. Of course they rarely could and often did. The Sunday lunch scene in the film of *The French Lieutenant's Woman* shows to perfection the misery lying-in-wait when location carries over into reality; when what seems to make perfect sense, in the heady atmosphere of vibrant company seemingly insulated in a distant and atmospheric place, becomes something very difficult to manage on return to normal life and everyday domesticity.

On location people can become close, and they can do the opposite. Gerald has always said that if a shoot lasts more than three weeks, you've identified the individuals you can't stand on the unit and spend the remainder of the film tolerating them at best.

Crewmembers that you worked with longest or most often and didn't end up despising, were the ones most likely to graduate to becoming real friends, kindred spirits you would make an effort to see 'outside' work, as opposed to greeting them with what was genuine affection when they were next encountered. However, anyone can lose touch even with real friends, and that's all the more likely when life is a semi-constant progress through a sequence of assignments that are always demanding and normally in the company of a different unit – a this-week's or this-month's group who are also in the main counted as buddies and, as usual, share most if not all of your waking hours.

Having met on commercials, Ray and DB also worked for 9 months on the same TV series in the early eighties, so became friends by any definition. Later DB and Lillie came at least once to stay in Wiltshire and Ray took them flying, a dubious pleasure he inflicted on all but the most obstinate of his weekend guests. On the programme Ray was the first AD or assistant director, running the set on behalf of the producer and the director. He always defines the job as organising the chaos that is a film set to get the director's vision into the can within the timescale and budget of the producer. (That's the film can, not the American sort, although it can come to the same thing.) It's a largely impossible, generally thankless, hugely undervalued and grossly underpaid task of which the simplified description above is but the tip of a huge growler that Ray could probably expand upon over several hundred anguished pages. One of the problems of the job is that if you're doing it well – and if everyone else is doing their job attentively – and if nothing else intervenes to upset your plan – the set can run so smoothly that it can look as if you do nothing but call for quiet and start the rehearsal, or the camera for a take.

Two things then happen. Firstly: people get the idea that anyone can be an AD and they certainly don't need paying much. Secondly: producers and others, including sadly some assistant directors, think that if the first makes their presence more assertive, with a lot of unnecessary noise, the shoot can be made to go faster and more efficiently. 'Building up the part' in its popular form involves haranguing and picking on crew members' faults and failings in the mistaken notion that individuals will concentrate harder in order not to be bawled out in front of the rest of the unit. Watching the ghastly first assistant character in the Burt Reynolds movie *Hooper* made Ray for a while almost ashamed to admit to what had become his most regular job-title. 'Crack the whip,' producers say, in the expectation that sergeant-major-like barking alone can raise a crew's game. It's a big mistake. Technicians put under extra, unnecessary pressure can get nervous and make more errors. They can also get turned off, and become hostile and resentful. The work actually moves more slowly.

Ray taps the side of his head at parties and will tell anyone unwise enough to show interest in what he has done most of for his living: 'A good first uses all he can of this, and (pointing to his mouth) not too much of that.' DB hasn't heard Ray's theories on assistant directing as they haven't met or spoken for 20 years in round figures.

–ooOoo–

On the series, DB had been one of the location managers; a key rôle but slightly lower in the pecking order than the first assistant. The hierarchy of the film set is a mysterious one. Ray always says that the most important person on a movie is the person who drives the mobile toilets, in that if the actors needed in the scene are bursting to go to the loo, nothing worthwhile is going to happen until the so-called honey wagon arrives. It's a tongue-in-cheek way of conveying that most people from the apparent highest to the apparent lowest on a film unit have a vital function, on which the entire operation depends, so really everyone is as important as everybody else.

This is not a view that goes down with those who adhere to the 'auteur' theory of film-making which tries to elevate the director to a position of supreme creator. To this concept Ray and most first assistants would tend to respond with 'Let the bloody auteur try and make a film on his own and see how far the prat gets.' They regard the idea of 'A Film by Sardo Flannery' as something of a joke, especially when, as often now, it can be attached even to a director's debut movie. Filming is of course the branch of the arts that has to be the most collaborative of all, totally opposite from the painter or writer alone in the proverbial garret. The sheer number of people necessary to make a film – people who then by definition affect the finished product, directly or indirectly, in a terrifying number of ways – has driven many a director to climb up the walls of the set. In this context, the idea of authorship is hardly convincing.

Someone, and that someone is the first AD, has to keep minute-to-minute tabs on all these individuals (a word Ray uses quite deliberately) and make sure they are all on the spot to do the necessary, whatever that may be, at the appropriate moment. In a studio they may be scattered, working or lurking in a multitude of hideaways; on location they can be doing the same across whole counties.

The AD's contact with all aspects of a location is the aptly-titled location manager. If a director suddenly decides to change a plan and do a shot requiring the whole circus of actors' caravans and make-up and wardrobe trailers to be moved away thirty feet or half a mile, first the AD would try to dissuade him or her, by pointing out the delay involved, and on failing would ask the location manager to action the move. If directors come to the set not knowing what they want, or are naturally disorganised, or – heaven help us – genuinely want the spontaneity of making things up with the actors as they go along, the first assistant and the location manager share the pain.

Some say that the director's job is as close to being impossible as it gets, largely based on the existence of that huge number of people and the spanners that every one of them holds ready to toss into the works, plus the massive number of required decisions that they generate. This theory implies that the director has to become a something of a megalomaniac or a martinet to achieve anything. Some do. Ray has done a little directing and likes to float another theory – that the director has the easiest job on the unit, simply because all he has to do is ask for something, and if he's chosen the right crew for the job, it happens. It helps of course if what the director wants is within the bounds of possibility; is achievable within the laws of science and nature. Ray has worked with directors who, King Canute-like, behave as if the tide will not come in, or the sun won't go down – at least not until they've finished their sequence. If the director's expectations are unrealistic, it's bad news for everybody – and the budget. The first AD is the individual who now and again has to drag perhaps just one of the director's feet back into the real world.

Assistant directors, especially the first, by definition permanently inhabit the battleground between the two worlds, the two existences, the physical and the fantasy. The location manager undoubtedly inhabits the first, waiting at its margins, hoping to avoid any director-dragging but ready to add weight when it can't be avoided.

–ooOoo–

5 Controlled Descents

The journey that Ray is about to start is to visit one of his **favourite** directors, Gerald Logan. It's going to be very long trek and overall he won't see home for more than three weeks. And home is looking particularly appealing at present. When he walks out of the house he feels a need to stop for a moment and drink in the silence. It's one of those days when it's highly likely that deer will be grazing in the field at the back, on the edge of the wood that drops off into the valley. Already the sun is coming up and the cloudless sky is starting to turn blue. He looks up, not for the purpose of avoiding that statistical falling roof tile, or something detached from an aircraft – a frozen lump of toilet overflow or a piece of metal flap track, debris of the sort that killed first one Concorde and then, by extension, the rest – he just needs to enjoy a few seconds under the infinity of the sky. Soon enough he'll be up in it. Even as he watches he spots movement. High above and unheard, the first overnight jets from the States to Europe are powering overhead, sometimes lasers of light reflecting the low sun in the east – what Julian Pettifer called *Diamonds in the Sky*. Later will come the squadrons bound for London. They'll be lower and can usually be heard; sometimes it will be so quiet in his valley that Ray can actually hear the throttles coming back in the descent. By the time those come over today he'll be nearly at Heathrow himself.

Starting the return to earth is the phase of flight that he enjoys most as a pilot. It doesn't matter whether the cruise is at 1,500 feet in a light aircraft or thirty-something thousand in a jet, airfields invariably look impossibly small. For any captain there is always the slightest moment of doubt that there will be somewhere long enough to land and stop, but this feeling always goes in an instant, dismissed by the memory of experience and by the litany of tasks that have to be followed to manage the descent. Speed and height must be lost in the correct ratio; the checks, the radio calls and other actions have to be carried out at their proper place on the descent profile, with the aim of positioning the aircraft at the end of the runway in the right configuration. This, at its most basic, means wheels down and the low-speed landing aids – the flaps – set for touchdown. To manage this without the passengers being aware of the changes in height, speed and pitch, and to top it off with a 'greaser' landing, is one of the biggest recurring buzzes Ray has ever felt.

There is an intoxicating magic about captaincy; about operating controls skilfully; about making complex procedures look easy; about finding your way confidently and delivering your charges safely. Ray's grandfather was a chauffeur and had driven cars and motorbuses almost as soon as they existed. Ray wanted to drive things from his very first ride on a bus. There was a circular piano stool at his parents' home. It was adjustable for height by rotating it, so it made a perfect steering wheel for pretend cars and charabancs made from rows of dining chairs. He never learnt the piano but he hadn't really needed to be taught to drive. He'd even got double-declutching worked out by watching and when the time came he did it first time.

But people trusting you to drive them in car is a world removed from allowing you to take them somewhere so alien and potentially hostile to human beings as the sky. Every pilot remembers their first instruction flight and their first solo is a big moment, although generally too riven with anticipation – and concern to get back on the ground without mistake – for much of it to stay in the memory bank. But the first time they take up a non-pilot passenger, someone who doesn't have the knowledge and necessary skill to take over if the captain makes a pig's of it; that's probably the largest milestone of the three, the first time they really feel like a commander. Only then do you, the fledgling pilot, begin to believe that 'Self' in the Captain column of your logbook really means something. Someone has put their faith in you to take them to another dimension; one that can be at once fabulous and fearsome; and then bring them back safely to earth and normality.

Ray loves being a captain. He did at one time consider the idea of training for a commercial licence: not because he particularly wanted to be paid to fly, but for two other reasons. One: he thought to study more comprehensively, assimilate more knowledge and become more competent would be undoubtedly good for his flying and for his passengers. The second reason he wouldn't admit to many people, but he thought it would be good fun to be able to check in at hotels as Captain Scriver.

A successful flight, like the electricity supply in a film studio, has three phases. The first is take-off and climb; the second is cruise or the en-route phase; and the third is the approach and landing. There is a hoary old aviation joke that says ideally pilots should record the same number of landings as take-offs. Where the logbook registers a discrepancy, the aviator is either extremely lucky or deceased.

–ooOoo–

6 According to Rank

He's looking round for the last time, reluctant to break the mood. The house felt odd and lifeless last night. No Eve, obviously, but with Ogre already gone to friends, he's not unhappy to leave the stones and wood. In the summer the house feels less important anyway. Mostly summer is about outside. Finally he sits into the Saab and shuts the door, but still feels the need to open a window to have a final sniff of the air. He performs the seatbelt routine. In the microseconds it takes, he always deliberately wonders if he will finish the journey unharmed. Ray thinks that by being aware of the negative possibilities, he is more likely to drive cautiously and avoid incident. Eve thinks the reverse and calls his approach 'conjuring up catastrophes', which he really dislikes. He's ready. Taking the same care that he devotes to starting up a Piper with its noisy and threatening propeller, he turns the key. After a short interval to respect the cool metal in the engine, he selects first gear and moves away. Loose gravel from the unswept lane pings and patters in the wheel arches; applause for the opening of perhaps an epic adventure.

True to earlier prediction, now he's in the car, on the move, he feels good. As Steve, the builder's mate with the entertaining range of malapropisms, would have it: 'He's in his elephant'.

—ooOoo—

The neighbour of a past girlfriend of Ray's had been the captain of an RAF Nimrod search and rescue aircraft. These were old de Havilland Comet airliners, recycled at monstrous expense to the British taxpayer. The odd thing was that this fellow had never been a pilot; he was a navigator by trade. Ray could never quite come to terms with the idea of there being a captain, someone in charge and responsible for the flight, but not flying the aircraft. It's true that sea captains don't generally steer the ship; they have a coxswain to man the ship's wheel; but it's very different standing next to someone and giving them a heading to steer and ordering the engine revolutions you want, from sitting behind someone hoping that they're going to bring your aircraft, your command, down safely. You can hardly sit there saying, 'Left hand down a bit – Oops watch the drift! – Catch the sink.' – when you're not actually qualified to do what they're doing. And how about those Eastern bloc airliners from the Soviet era with multiple flight crew members on even a small passenger airliner? Ray once talked his way into such a cockpit, on a film charter flight, and was astonished to find five people, of a variety of nationalities, visible with difficulty through a thick fug of cigarette smoke. Was that flying by committee, and if four disagreed with the captain, what happened? He also remembers, as a paying passenger, a night, instrument arrival to Moscow Sheremetievo in an Illyushin 62, an aircraft with a far from unblemished safety record. That was noticeable for the alarming variations in engine note, which seemed to continue for about ten minutes. The four rear-fuselage-mounted engines Kusnetsovs kept going from something near idle to climb power and back to idle, as though the large crew on the flight deck was arguing amongst themselves about the throttle setting required.

On a film set, the command structure is far from straightforward and in some ways similar to the navigator captaining the Nimrod. Actually, in the seniority respect, that overworked sergeant-major analogy can prove quite helpful. Ray likes to tell the story of the RSM at the Royal Military College, Sandhurst addressing a new intake of officer cadets, who have the nominal rank of second lieutenant and therefore actually outrank the sergeant-major, despite his years of soldiering and vast experience, usually involving real combat and possibly killing. His speech goes: 'Gentlemen, when I address you individually, I shall call you "sir". Likewise, when you address me, you will call me "sir". The only difference is that **you** "sirs" will bloody well mean it.' The RSMs do indeed run the parade ground, the classrooms, the assault course and the firing range. Some would argue that they run the whole college – and most of the army as well.

Just as the RSM's word is law on parade, despite the presence of senior officers, the first assistant controls the set. He or she runs the shoot and is the boss, even if they aren't – really. Everybody knows that they're outranked by the producer, who may be on the location or the stage, or not. Some are always; some rarely. Some you only ever see at the end-of-picture party, for producers of course don't often now come in the singular. Over time they've multiplied until there are usually half a dozen or more on the credits. As to what, if anything, they all do and how all the 'producing' is workshared, few in the industry, Ray included, have any idea.

With the exception of a handful of rare directing partnerships, there is only one director and the director is always on set. The respective job titles couldn't make the director / first assistant relationship any clearer, so why then don't directors run the set? Because they don't have time. Occasionally they try, which can be disastrous. They might do it for either of two reasons; one if a director is way sharper and can consistently out-think their first, when it means big trouble because someone's chosen the wrong first. The other arises if the director is concerned more about his image than about the job. To the uninitiated casual observer, watching a set function for the few minutes before utter boredom sweeps over them, it's the assistant who looks like the director – the one giving instructions, waving arms, pointing, controlling, using the radio and the megaphone. This can distract someone who's vain or insecure sitting in the chair with 'DIRECTOR' on the back. 'All these people must be thinking that Roger is the director, but it's me – look it's me, I'm in charge really. I think I'll ask for the bullhorn and give some orders.' Ray's advice is never, ever give a director a megaphone.

The function of directors is to visualise what they want on the screen. This gives them an endless stream of creative decisions to make, of which those relating to the performance to be coaxed from their actors are the most crucial. They are, or should be, far too busy achieving their vision to concern themselves with the co-ordination of dozens of people, not all of whom are permanently on set; or with preparing for the third shot after next or the location move this afternoon; or tomorrow's dance rehearsals, or any one of a thousand important considerations, none of which they need to be distracting them when the pressing question is should the star cry in the next shot, or just look terribly sad?

This is why there is a first assistant to deal with all the other stuff. Some questions maybe have to be answered by the director urgently, and the experienced first will filter and prioritise those so as not to overload his boss. Directors are best advised to let the AD deal with the real world and the nitty gritty, and concentrate firmly on the fantasy. They have plenty of other help. Many of their creative decisions can be delegated to, or at least shared with, a whole troop of department heads, numbers of whom also outrank the first assistant, certainly if salary is taken as an indicator of importance in the pecking order. Yet on set they defer. Otherwise that pernicious enemy, chaos, will quickly establish itself.

And chaos is costly, wherever it prevails. It has an insatiable appetite for resources and reputations. Unchecked it can ruin lives and even, in the worst case, take them.

–ooOoo–

7 Traffic News

As the car threads through the lanes on the way to the M4, contrails and points of silver light appearing above call Ray's attention again to a procession, almost a formation, of those eastbound jets – more of those celestial diamonds. On the in-car stereo there's a favourite Show of Hands CD, *Lie of the Land*. As the screen clicks up to Track 5 and the intro starts, he's reminded that he long believed part of this haunting song to be about the very road he'll be joining in a few minutes, and has only recently learnt that it in reality refers to the M3. But the verse of Steve Knightley's lyric he reacts to most tells of piloting a passenger plane at daybreak.

> High above the earth hours before we land
>
> Morning slowly breaks and dawn is lifting
>
> The only one awake is gently in my hand
>
> I trace a hundred lives through darkness drifting
>
>
> I will bring you back, I will hold you
>
> My arms are strong, they will enfold you.

And the title is *Captains*. Damn these coincidences!

Ray gives a lot of thought to coincidences in fiction and in life. They can be a nuisance, but you wouldn't want to be without them. After all they're really only chance meetings, concurrence in time and place of people and circumstances, fortuitous or otherwise. And on such things all our lives turn.

–ooOoo–

He has driven this motorway a million times. He hasn't really of course, but a sufficient number that justifies that stock phrase more than the majority of its instances. And it doesn't get any more fun. In fact it's one of the many things that he's glad he doesn't do so often now. He's seen it in all weathers, at all hours of the day or night, deserted and heaving, free-flowing, contraflowed, stationary. Not that it's often quiet these days. At this time of the morning he used to have the road largely to himself and pass an occasional heavy. Now, thanks largely to Mrs Thatcher and her contempt and hatred for railwaymen, the nearside lane carries an uncannily train-like procession of huge trucks. Even the continuous grooves their wheels make in the tarmac echo the worn stones of the old freight-carrying horse tramroads that were the immediate antecedents of the railways. The ever-heavier monsters forced by the new European dictatorship onto our fragile infrastructure constantly render all attempts at resurfacing futile, by furrowing the inner lanes, ready for endless ribbon-lake puddles to form every time it rains. Given the physics, it could not be otherwise.

It was reading about the politics of the railways that relit the fuse of Ray's passion for the fair and logical; the self-evident deception of privatisation that brought his idealism, his distaste for official duplicity, out of its long abeyance, leading eventually to his present quest and this journey. He has increasingly found incompetence, the misuse of power, covert influence and apparent corruption in almost every area to which he's turned his attention – but the catalyst for his search was the transparent claim of John Major and his ministers that the break-up of the rail network into, eventually, dozens of private companies would be to passengers' advantage. Not only was this pure nonsense for reasons evident to even the most minimally informed observer, but this fanciful outcome was being predicted at a time when the government plainly hadn't the first idea how they were going to undertake it – let alone what the results might be.

Even the most knowledgeable commentators were surprised at the extent of the unmitigated farce that ensued. The only members of the travelling public to benefit were those who happened to be lawyers, accountants, uniform, livery and logo designers, company directors and shareholders; categories that in the main avoid train travel. All that the average passenger tended to find were new paint schemes on old trains that were often shorter, more crowded and more expensive to ride on and that frequently no longer connected with each other in a sensible way. Things that had been simple, like buying the best-value ticket, or obtaining a complete timetable, suddenly became virtually impossible.

Encouraged to read further back into railway history had only made Ray more hot under the collar. Thatcher's anti-rail bias was extreme all right, but it was only an overt version of what had been going on for years. Without the railways, World War II could not have been won, but flagrant underinvestment and pegged charges in the following years pitched rail into an unequal struggle against road transport which would have made the steel-wheel mode look uneconomic even without manipulation of the figures, and there was plenty of that, he'd discovered. Under Harold Macmillan, who everyone thinks represents an age of gentlemanly politics when Westminster and Whitehall played by the book, there were two covert teams set up within the British Transport Commission. The task of one was to 'make an economic case' for the wholesale conversion of railway trackbeds into 'Motor Roads', and that of the other to produce figures to 'prove' that the rail network required substantial reduction to render it less expensive to run.

Helped by the skewed statistics that the civil servants cooked up, the rail network quickly began to shrink, piecemeal, well before Dr Beeching was brought in to perform the major surgery for which he is known and widely reviled. Operation of the rail network cost public money, while the newly denationalised road haulage companies could undercut as they were paying no more than a token amount to use the roads. When people pointed out the discrepancy, no one wanted to listen. Meanwhile road budgets began to fatten out of all proportion, encouraged by the effective lobbying of bodies such as the British Road Federation and the Road Haulage Association, to which the oil companies added their considerable weight and resources. The ultimate aim of the whole exercise – the break-up and sale to private enterprise of the nationally-owned railways and their assets, including ferries, hotels and of course land – did come about, although it took far longer than Macmillan and his 1950s Tories hoped, and the railways remained publicly-owned in all for nearly fifty years. Given the starvation and neglect, it was perhaps surprising that there was much left to sell.

Now the gargantuan trucks wriggle out of their grooves across to the middle lane in county-long overtaking manoeuvres causing conflict and disarray behind as cars and vans travelling at sensible speeds are bullied, barged and cut up in an ill-tempered rolling roadblock by others that don't want to. "Where are the cuffing police?" Ray groans as yet another Sprinter or Transit roars past at 100 mph in the outside lane, muscling through insanely close to the car in front, defying any principle of 'wait your turn'. Over 20 plus years there have hardly ever been police to be seen at this time of day, even though now every five minutes there's enough plainly visible dangerous driving and assorted lawbreaking to fill a dozen notebooks. The traffic officers, Ray knows quite well, are safely in their canteens or service area cafés, having their free or subsidised bacon and eggs before ambling gently in their expensive patrol cars to a vantage point commanding a view of a road with an unnecessarily low speed limit, where with their speed cameras they will target motorists, most of whom will be driving completely reasonably and safely. They will only be interrupted in this pointless but quota-serving exercise and tempted to visit the motorway when someone on a mobile phone, someone with a serious personality disorder or simply someone with an inability to concentrate and appreciate danger, does something to create an incident. One person's lack of self-discipline and official indifference will then have combined to cause the principal interconnector between the West of England and London, the conduit for all the activity of commerce and life for millions of citizens, to come to a shuddering halt at a combined cost of thousands of pounds per second. Upon such unstable foundations is our economy balanced. No wonder it's in permanent danger of upset.

Ray's friends in the police wouldn't like his conclusions, but its impossible to deny that there's too much soft-target, Government quota-led policing. Preventive policing, the original function of the uniformed branch, is now mostly a memory, replaced by a response, fire-brigade, style of service. And the covert resources that could bear down on the dangerous, criminal drivers threatening his life this morning will be out in force later catching headmistresses and vicars committing technical offences.

–ooOoo–

8 Treating the Subject Lightly

Once on the road, even in the dark of winter, Ray can generally cope with the radio news. He passes a point on the route that he will ever identify with an item that made him more astonished and angry than most. It was a couple of years ago, as he headed for a day's filming in a DIY superstore, that he heard that the Government had announced the formation of the Serious Organised Crime Agency, touted as a British FBI. Ray was veritably horrified, and remains so, for good reason. What has happened to this country? He knows a little about the early days of the British police.

With our modern perception it's hard to imagine a nation without a police force, yet Ray is always surprised to remember that the UK has only been policed in its entirety for 150 years. That's only 50 years longer than the extended period taken, before that, to get the principle accepted and implemented. It's a very British and in one way slightly comforting story that could see it take a hundred years to get forces fully deployed in an era when there had long been a growing, indeed desperate, need for them. In the towns lawlessness was pandemic: crime was the only means of survival for many. The streets were unsafe, the turnpikes beset by highwaymen, and yet parliament debated and agonised endlessly about replacing the patchy, inefficient and sometimes corrupt system of parish constables, watchmen and beadles with something better organised and effective. As always, there were vested interests in play, but there was also overriding and genuine concern about the danger posed to civil liberty. The British establishment was only too aware of the blood-spattered events in nearby France and the sinister part played by the police there. Very reasonably, there was suspicion, reluctance and caution about introducing such a body to our soil. The legislators continually resisted any moves by voting them down.

In Ireland there was a city police force in Dublin from 1786. In 1814 Robert Peel was Chief Secretary for Ireland; he tried to form a police force but had initially to make do with a response unit, the Irish Peace Preservation Force, until he was able to introduce a full-time armed 'Constabulary Force' in 1822. But Ireland was treated like a colony; much of the population was considered little better than savage and people would put up with what they were given. The mainland was a harder nut to crack. Some burghs in Scotland introduced more modern-style forces under local powers, as did the City of London, but nationally the argument dragged on. Peel, now Home Secretary, had numerous reverses and when he eventually succeeded with his Metropolitan Police Act of 1829, it virtually crept under the wire and might easily not have been passed. It then took a further 27 years for police forces to cover Great Britain, with the much more peaceful shires resisting and complaining to the last that they didn't need and couldn't afford them (although social change in the countryside too was breeding sporadic outbreaks of disorder).

The important point in Ray's view – indeed the crucial one, he will argue, for the British population, now as then – is that the system adopted was specifically designed to be a compromise to accommodate the fears of centralised power. Policing would be local, town and county based, not countrywide in any way, and it was to be independent of national politics and – as far as anything could be in England – free too of local politics and class interests. In short, parliament saw to it that the French experience was avoided and that the new police would not become agents of the state and threaten personal freedom – although, realistically speaking, true personal freedom was at the time enjoyed by only a small minority of society.

Ever since then, everyone connected with government has eyed with fervent distaste the independence of police forces, which was vested in Chief Constables whose autonomy was particularly notable in the counties. The control of the British police by or through the political and administrative axis has been a long-cherished ambition, assiduously pursued and achieved progressively through barely-noticed measures. As a result, the well-founded fear of a government police force that so occupied the politicians of the 1820s has been quite forgotten, and their eloquent speeches urging caution erased from memory as if they had never been made.

One hundred and eighty years on, the New Labour administration that morning announced on Ray's car radio, as he drove to Reading for a few days of Homestore commercials, the formation of a national investigative force without having so much as mentioned the fact in the Houses of Parliament. It's true that of course there was at some later point a token debate which few attended; no one listened to any of the issues raised and a pointless vote was taken which endorsed the measure by a massive majority. Of true consideration and overview by the elected parliament – of the traditional checks and balances, there was no sign. Government is now presidential, virtually dictated by decree. Parliament is a sham. Members of Parliament are largely wasting their time and our money. And it's still only 5.40am!

Does the United Kingdom need an FBI? To answer that you'd have to look at the record of the American original. Numbers of the books on his shelves, not to mention the document that Ray has stowed in his computer bag on the seat beside him, conclude that one of the consistent functions of the FBI over time has been to obstruct justice, sometimes grotesquely, rather than to further it, so **his** answer at least would have to be emphatically 'no'.

−ooOoo−

There is a place, about 15 minutes after Ray joins the slip road, where more ghosts than usual must haunt the littered embankments. You could still see the short stretch of replaced road surface for years. It was a scene of one of those horrific motorway accidents in fog, which often forms on the hills and in the river valleys of this high section and rolls across the motorway unpredictably, in banks, sometimes hidden in less dense outer swirls. The new 'Special Motor Roads' hadn't existed for long before there was an incident of what the press coined 'Motorway Madness', a multi-vehicle pile-up in poor visibility. They've happened with tragic regularity ever since, always from the same causes; drivers going too fast, too close together and ploughing into something in front of them; either an existing accident or just someone going at a more suitable pace for the conditions. Academics have endlessly studied the phenomenon; there have been reports and advertising campaigns, and still these events continue. This one in March 1991 involved 51 vehicles; a major fire broke out and raged through the wreckage. Ten people died and 25 were injured, some trapped and burnt alive in their cars and vans. It was news for 48 hours and then forgotten, except of course by the injured and the families and friends of the dead. Ray remembers a commercials director who lived in the West Country at the time and regularly travelled up and down at high speed in the outside lane in his Bentley, which must have weighed two tons or more. He claimed his policy was actually to speed up in fog so that if he hit something, he wouldn't know anything about it. Ray has never been able to get this mad and chilling image out of his mind after that, and when fog is likely won't go near a motorway if he can possibly avoid it.

He recalls the burnt-out cars on the A74 just by the Lockerbie crater, and how for some time it was thought that the missing occupants were dead, vaporised by the massive heat of the exploding Jet A1 in the 747's fuel tanks. Then it was found that the vehicles hadn't been travelling along the dual carriageway at all, but had been blown there from their parking places on the Sherwood Estate.

Between Reading and Slough, Ray spots the first low airliner of the morning, crossing from left to right, coming from the Bovingdon radio beacon near Hemel Hempstead, on what's called its base leg before making a left turn onto its final approach to Heathrow. The sight of such craft, under radar control, being expertly positioned in this precision manner

31

provides a vision of order and professionalism that contrasts increasingly with the amateur grand prix on the road below. But with more people learning to fly light aircraft, Ray has noted a regrettable tendency for the pushy and inconsiderate habits of road users to start translating to the sky.

Overseas carriers' airliners have long played one-upmanship games on the ground when they could get away with it, to the consternation of fair-play imbued Brit pilots who would get terribly upset and even complain to their passengers over the public address about being deliberately baulked on the taxi to take-off or the stand by a TWA, an Air France or an Aeroflot. Some of the British eventually started to retaliate, with maybe a little more style and subtlety, but in domestic light aviation at least, gentlemanly and considerate behaviour was the rule for years.

The last time Ray flew, a few weeks ago, he was cut up in an airfield's circuit by a character who then compounded his lack of airmanship by two absurdly unprofessional and dangerous manoeuvres on the ground and then had the nerve to berate and blame Ray at the Flying Club counter. With people like that in the air, Ray thinks it's possibly time to turn in his licence.

–ooOoo–

At any time of the year there can be those fabulous days like today, when the atmosphere is dry and the details of the countryside stretching to distant horizons sing out with almost unreal sharpness and clarity. Even Ray can take decent photographs on such days. Sometimes you can just point and shoot and get gold. But on every film set there is someone being paid to make beautiful frames whether they're getting any help from God or not. This is the technician known variously as the cinematographer or the director of photography. An older title now fallen out of favour, for obvious reasons, was cameraman or lighting cameraman, and the latter provides a clue to the rôle. Totally responsible for the quality of the photography and how everything from star's close-up to rainswept landscape looks and feels on film, cinematographers adapt natural light, filtered with giant silks or reflected from all sorts of portable surfaces. They introduce artificial light using lamps ranging from the massive to the tiny. Their mobile generators can be the size of buses; their equipment trucks can be juggernauts. They will have a crew of electricians of a number appropriate to the task, headed by a gaffer, the chief electrician, assisted by the number two – the best boy. Ray has lost count of the times he's been asked in the kitchen at parties about the duties of the mysterious best boy, gaffer and grip.

If Ray had his time in the film business over again, he would have headed straight for the camera department for sure. Knowing what he does now, he thinks it unlikely that he'd have blundered into the production department. Starting as a clapper-loader, progressing to follow-focus camera assistant and probably sticking at camera operator; that would have suited him fine. Most of Ray's close friends in the industry, apart from other ADs (those who mentored him and those who later assisted him, but generally not, for obvious reasons, his contemporaries and competitors) have been in the camera department, mostly focus-pullers and operators. That's probably because, along with the AD and in most cases the DP, they are the people who have to, or at least should, concentrate one hundred percent for the entire working day with absolutely no let up or time for even a few moment's inattention. They are the ones who end each long day absolutely wrung-out and exhausted. If they are doing their job properly, and the vast majority of them do, they are worth every penny of what they earn, and they're far less likely to be bored than most of the others on set, because they're busy.

Being an assistant director tended to provide job satisfaction once a job was over, rather than enormous enjoyment while it was going on. There were some great days and good times, but other departments had more fun, less constantly-pressing responsibility and more recognition. Organising something extremely complicated can be elating, but that can be tempered later by the finished result. ADs can work themselves to a standstill and perform miracles, but the film can still quite easily be mediocre. There is no direct correlation. And it's perfectly possible to put into a project massive effort that goes unappreciated and unrewarded. Sometimes you really don't understand how much of a good job you did until your efficiency has hastened your return to unemployment. Then sometime later you learn (if you didn't suspect already) that the film is a turkey. You can do a few like that and find that six or eight years have flown past, with very little to show for it except a few highlight memories.

Apart from some sadness at not seeing that band of friends on an irregular basis, Ray is quite glad that he doesn't really seem to be an assistant director any more.

–ooOoo–

9 Aluminium Rain

If there's a wind blowing from any direction in the east between north and south, and if the day is clear, a London-bound driver on the M4 may, as Ray has earlier, start to see aircraft being manoeuvred for their approach to Heathrow at any point from Reading onwards. Broadly speaking, the busier it is, the further west aircraft will start to be lined up by the controllers. Thus the closer to the airport, along what are known as the runways' extended centrelines, the more likely it is that aircraft will be passing overhead – at intervals that are far too regular for most of those whose homes lie below the progressively lowering flightpaths. This effect is more apparent when westerly breezes (which predominate) dictate an approach to Heathrow **from** the east, as opposed to towards it, and the aircraft are descending, not over the relatively open fields of Buckinghamshire, but above the serried rows of 20s and 30s housing that make up Hounslow and district. There the passing of an aircraft every ninety or so seconds, seemingly just over the chimney pots, is an unwelcome fact of life that is captured graphically by news crews every time there is a reporter's 'piece to camera' about some Heathrow item to hurry onto tape.

Ray once worked on a four-part series; one of Gerald's, where virtually every location chosen was dotted along those eastern approaches in places like Wandsworth and Barnes. Hours were wasted trying to fit the recording of dialogue scenes between the stream of passing aircraft and the producer jumped up and down about the speed of shooting on a daily basis. Ray has often wondered since why the location manager offered such obviously noisy places. He himself has always lived under flight paths of one sort or another, and with his fascination with all forms of transport, quite enjoyed it. His parents lived strategically placed for two of the radio beacons that surround Heathrow and Gatwick. With the wind from the west, airliners would leave the stack over the one called Ockham near Ripley and usually begin the turn onto the ILS or Instrument Landing System localiser beam for final approach, not far from overhead the house. When easterlies blew, 707s, Tridents and other ground-shakers departing east would seem to fly along the street at maybe three thousand feet, climbing noisily towards the one identified as 'BIG', on the airfield at Biggin Hill, the famous wartime RAF fighter station.

Despite all this activity, even in times when aircraft were less reliable than those of today (he remembers DC4s and Lockheed Constellations, among others), there was no local apprehension, as far as he can recall, that an engine failure or a collision might cause one to fall on the neighbourhood.

Such an event is inevitable yet London has been extremely fortunate in this respect, considering the truly enormous numbers of aircraft that have criss-crossed the sky above the packed buildings and clogged streets of the capital since Heathrow opened for business in 1946. There are few first-rank city centres where a procession of arriving aircraft has been such a regular, observable feature of daily life. The worst accident of the type, the departing Trident crash at Staines in 1972, astonishingly killed no one on the ground, although had the flight lasted only a few more seconds, the doomed aircraft would have fallen on houses filled with weekending families; the open ground it providentially impacted lies less than half a mile in a direct line from the main shopping street and the railway station. In the early days, some passenger aircraft ended up perched spectacularly on semi-detached rooftops, but Britain has so far escaped the appalling disasters sadly seen in many cities in the world. Even when an Argonaut on approach to Manchester crashed into the heart of Stockport in 1967, with terrible loss of life among its occupants, there was no casualty among people on the ground in the busy centre of the borough.

On the morning after Lockerbie, the very inevitability that commercial aircraft, at some time or another, will kill people going about their normal life in towns was unfortunately articulated by the Duke of York, delegated by the Palace to visit as his ship was docked in Edinburgh at the time. Pressed by the media for comment, and no doubt thrown off-guard by the scale of the horror that he had just been privy to, what he said was entirely valid, but was forever labelled insensitive by the grieving inhabitants.

The British became used to death from the sky, especially in the Second World War. Londoners were scandalised when the US Ambassador, Joe Kennedy, Jack's father, who famously thought that Britain was wrong to oppose Hitler, moved out to the safety of Sunningdale to escape the blitz. Death from the air can effect major attitude changes. Pearl Harbour certainly did, bringing a reluctant United States into that war. Those that radiated outwards like seismic shock from America after 9-11 mean that the world will probably never be the same again. The rain of death on Lockerbie, by contrast, altered next-to-nothing internationally, except to cement the suffocating power wielded by dealers in secrets.

–ooOoo–

For all its fancy Metroland gatehouse and art deco administration building, beyond the façade, Pinewood, England's Hollywood in Buckinghamshire, is a factory – a factory that just happens to make films. Ray had taken a temporary job in the main works of a large building company before gratefully escaping to the film business and remembers being struck, on his first visit to a major studio (the one at that time called ABPC Elstree), by the great physical similarity between those two premises of quite different purpose and output – drains and dreams. Pinewood is much less cramped than ABP and retains, with its old mansion and gardens, a few more trappings of the past, but also has not a few areas that border on the squalid. Film studios may be fantasy factories and magic may truly be created under their lights, but the concrete-block reality of the places can be sometimes brutal and is often untidy. The notion of creating wonderful visions from blandness and chaos is not in the least an exaggeration. Jean-Luc Godard said that 'Photography is truth. The cinema is truth 24 times per second.' Ray would argue the reverse. A long-time colleague of his has developed an after-dinner speech under the title *The Camera Always Lies* on the premise that whatever beautiful or spectacular image is presented on screen, just out of frame there will be in reality a myriad of untidy distractions that the paying customer would never expect or wish to see in a million years.

Despite awareness of this extremely utilitarian underbelly, driving into any studio, and perhaps Pinewood most of all, remains enduringly an adventure. There will inevitably be at least a few old friends to greet (if they can be recognised with the passing of time) but the main attraction is the buzz of who's there doing what. Not that you're going to get to see what's being done on any stage except those on which you have business or an invitation; things are much more secretive these days with 'Closed Set ' signs prevalent and even ID badges for all and security staff at stage doors not infrequent facts of life. The AD is of course the one person on a unit least likely to be able to take advantage of an invitation to go calling on another stage, being fully occupied in the workings of his or her own, which includes keeping tabs on all the comings and goings, authorised or not. Generally firsts have to be content with the wonders, if any, being conjured in the brown-insulated film cathedral under their own control. And wonders there will often be, for the skill and inventiveness of production designers and their army of associates genuinely seem boundless. Given enough time and a sufficient budget, anything and everything that can possibly be imagined may be brought into being, or to a state that is as near 'being' as is required to satisfy that most demanding of visual interrogators, a Panavision lens.

Swinging the car quietly and thankfully into a parking place on this sparkling and promising morning, Ray wonders if any of the ungainly white boxes of stages around him may, in a few months' time, witness the building of a section of Boeing 747 *Clipper Maid of the Seas*, or the bridge of the *USS Vincennes*, the back room of an Amman shop, or any one of well over a hundred sets mentioned in the document on the passenger seat. No one has yet started analysing the pages to make lists of elements like sets, but if and when one is drawn up it will include several highly detailed accurate scale models of a small Dumfries-shire town.

–ooOoo–

10 The Cutting Edge?

'Left on the cutting room floor' is a phrase that has made it into everyday use, which means that the public-at-large understand the place's concept. Some people will confidently assert that it is where films are really made, to which Ray's response tends to be a quizzical 'Oh, really?' not usually bothering to add, 'So I wonder what I've been doing all these years'. In the days when Ray spent a lot of time in cutting rooms, the editing process was dramatically low-tech and slow, and editors needed to have particularly dextrous fingers as they physically chopped lengths of printed film and stuck or 'spliced' one to another before trying each edit in a viewing machine. If it worked, they'd move to the next cut: if it didn't they would have to unpick the tape and try something different. Now it all happens on hard disc. The editor sits in front of two large video screens and uses a special computer with dedicated editing software; what took minutes can now be achieved in seconds.

Ray has always been amazed at the difference in atmosphere that exists between the set and the editing room. Even if the studio or location has an appearance of calm, it will in reality be seething with uncertainties below the surface. Will the plan for the day work, or more likely, at what point will it be scuppered by someone's not being ready, or an equipment failure, a weather issue, or just something taking longer to achieve than has been foreseen? Finishing something more quickly than allowed for can equally introduce those metaphorical spanners. Confusion and its constant companion, delay, lurk malevolently behind the flats and black drapes of every film set, waiting for the slightest opportunity to slip out like a villain in a Restoration tragedy and stab the assistant director. By contrast the editing suite always appears to be the repose of total organisation and absolute order. Ray accepts that no doubt there exist pressures and time constraints of which he is not in any way aware, but imagines that these are insignificant beside the relentless awareness of seconds ticking away that he has lived with for every minute of most hours of a career largely spent fending off the in-built anarchy inherent in actually shooting film.

He always thinks that the set can be likened to the passenger cabin of an airliner, initially a scene of total muddle as the 'self-loading cargo' (as some pilots arrogantly but not inaccurately call their charges) find their places, stow their possessions and finally take their seats. The cockpit is the equivalent of the cutting room or editing suite – what goes on there is orderly and apparently unhurried, the tranquillity is the antithesis of the pantomime taking place beyond the door behind the flight crew.

There is another difference between set and suite. The exposed negative that is sent off to the labs each night contains images that have had the capacity to be infinitely variable. They are the result of thousands of creative decisions taken during the day or in preparation for it. Yet even if the shots required have been meticulously planned or drawn out on storyboards, to the extent that the results can be closely predicted, there still exists a massive chance for variety in the details – of the staging, in the camera work and the acting, to name just three of many. Circumstances may conspire to provide some images that are less impressive than the key technicians hoped for – say the weather is unkind or an actor has trouble playing a scene. Equally chance may provide unforeseen bonuses that make the images actually more effective than ever anticipated – perhaps a flock of wild birds arrive and add another dimension to a sequence, or a chance remark by someone around camera, during rehearsal or set-up, sparks an idea that totally changes the way a scene is structured. So by design or happenstance, the set of images that go for processing at the close of the day's shoot are unique, could never have been totally anticipated and always have the potential to have been quite, quite different in almost every respect.

So if the set is all variables and permutations of possibility, the cutting room is all about known quantities and certainty. What is delivered to the editor by the laboratory is absolute. Whatever variations may or may not be present within its contents, it is the full extent of the material provided by the director and unit for editing into those scheduled scenes. Digital manipulation aside, it cannot be altered; it can merely be assembled using, if required, all the tricks of the editor's trade, such as using the picture from one take and the sound from another, in search of the perfect result. One step beyond that notion of films being truly made in the editing room is an even more extreme school of thought that says you can create a whole different movie there from the one that was in the screenplay or the one that was shot on the floor. Ray has never understood that, simply because the material that comes back from the laboratories is so finite, and so specific to the director's interpretation of the script at the instant of shooting. It seems to make no sense to try and make one film from the material intended for another. Far better, he thinks, to write the best screenplay that the story requires, plan for achieving it, film as closely as possible what is needed to interpret what is written, neither shooting too much nor too little, which should leave the editor with not a great deal to do but join the best takes together. This is Gerald's philosophy. Gerald is great at telling the story with the camera, often using shots several minutes long, with complex camera moves following the action as it develops, rather than making dozens of separate cuts. Actors love this, if they've learnt their lines! He refuses to waste time filming masses of cover shots that he doesn't need and doesn't plan to use; he might allow for one or two as a safety fall-back, but generally there aren't too many ways to assemble a rough-cut scene for a Logan movie.

Sometimes when Ray can't sleep, he plays a game where he re-edits sections of his own life as if it were a film. It's revealing to do that, imagining that you have the opportunity to go back and re-shoot sequences, incidents and episodes that might have gone a different way, if you'd spoken other words or made alternative choices. It's not something he does too often. His life story is not short of wasted opportunities and the list — of extra scenes needed and dialogue that he'd like to re-script — can appear in the night to stretch formidably long.

–ooOoo–

11 Let Us Proceed In Peace

Like traffic policemen, Ray and Tom erode their way relentlessly through mountains made of scrambled eggs, potato cakes, fried bread and sausages. Around their table, in the Pinewood studio canteen, lounge members of Tom's cutting room team. Unlike the older duo, they're not attacking the more-than-full English but are making do with coffee, doughnuts and other competitively unhealthy fare.

"Sophe'll run you over to t' terminal in 'er car when you need to go," says Tom, in a pause before tackling a Striding Edge of bacon, laced with a scree of tinned tomatoes. "Zat OK Sophe?"

Ray has an excuse to take in Sophe for the first time. The only girl at the feast, she is strikingly attractive in the school of understated English or possibly Scots; certainly there is some red in the blonde. She nods and Ray smiles in thanks.

The plan is working. Ray had written freelance commentaries for documentaries, mainly of a motorsport nature, in the 70s and Tom had been a film editor at one particular production house. They'd often worked together and some of the films they constructed from the sometimes unpromising footage brought back by the directors and cameramen had eventually and much to the surprise of all, won prizes at some sports film festivals. For a long time now, Tom Couper has been a very sought-after feature editor and he is currently cutting a movie here at Pinewood. Ray has bribed his old collaborator, with the promise of a large breakfast, to look after his car, to save the horrible airport charges. Tom can use it, and also move it if some shooting requires a cleared section of car park, as happens frequently. Ray will take a spare key on his trip so he isn't reliant on his friend being at the studios when he returns, although he might have to search a while for his car! Now Tom, the idle sod, is ducking out of the trip to Heathrow, but the bonus is that Ray is going to get a lift to the airport from a lovely young National Film School editing graduate. Oh what a beautiful morning!

Ray had been in the car park a good ninety minutes before the time arranged with Tom, just as he used to for most studio or location calls. It was the only way of ensuring, as far as humanly possible, that you were never held up, failing earthquake or nuclear attack. He would always recline his seat and have a nap, secure in the knowledge that he now couldn't be late. As on the motorway earlier, from here you can see the procession of airliners on the middle stages of Heathrow's final approach to Zero Nine

Left. Ray had watched a few descend, right to left, through the climbing eastern sun before closing his eyes for an hour.

—ooOoo—

"Ya gonna show it me, then?"

Ray and Tom have repaired to the cutting room to attempt to wash down the gargantuan breakfasts with more coffee. Tom's direct South Yorkshire approach leaves Ray with no choice. He hadn't planned to let anyone view the script before he sees Gerald, but there's no good reason to refuse without offending his old collaborator. He picks up his computer bag, unzips it and carefully takes out one of three copies of a thickish screenplay. He wipes imaginary dust from the title window and passes it across with two hands.

"*One-Zero-Three* — was that the flight number?"

Ray nods.

"The radio callsign was Clipper One-Zero-Three. I've thought about using that."

"Nah — that sounds like one of those sailin' ships carryin' tea." Tom is always quick with a decision. "By — it's a biggie. Hav'ya timed it?" he goes on, referring to the length of the work.

"About 2 hrs 50," says Ray deliberately knocking off ten or fifteen.

I thought more from 't feel of it." Tom opens it at the title page. "I like that. 'I love my country, but I fear my government.' Where's that from? Who's Doctor William Chasey?"

"He's one of the people whose story shows just how paranoid and nasty the American establishment got over Lockerbie."

"Ooar?" says Tom, instantly interested.

"He was one of their own — ex-military, republican — a Capitol Hill lobbyist. An American company brought him a job, to represent Libya's point of view in Washington, when Libya was under UN sanctions after the Lockerbie indictments. He thought long and hard before taking it, but even though he wasn't convinced at all of Libyan innocence, he signed up to represent them and declared his affiliation to the US authorities, as required by law. No sooner had one arm of government allowed him to register, than another told him he had broken sanctions and would face criminal charges. Then the dirty tricks began. Like Will Smith's character in *Enemy of the State* they froze his bank account. He was sure he was bugged and followed. Then he was fined $50,000 without even a court case. But worst of all, the FBI visited some of his clients and told them that he was under investigation for fraud."

"Oh! Very nice." Tom says. The Yorkshire accent is particularly good at sarcasm.

"So they deliberately ruined him, an honest, upright, patriotic American, just so the Libyan case shouldn't be heard on Capitol Hill. And this was someone who, up to then, hadn't questioned the official version of what happened. Others who did – Pan Am's lawyer, their insurer, the legal team's investigator and some US Government people who broke ranks and blew whistles – they really got the treatment; threatened, set up, dragged through the courts on bogus charges. Went to prison, some of them."

"F'kin hell. It's a bit heavy this then. How about you? **You** gonna be all right?"

"I don't know. I mean, plenty of people have written books, run websites, made documentaries and so on, putting out alternatives to the official story, and they haven't all been silenced, so we'll just have to see what happens. I'll have to be, won't I?"

And you say you couldn't just've e-mailed it to Gerald?"

"Nor post or DHL or whatever. I won't risk it being intercepted and opened."

"I thought you were being a bit paranoid, Raymond, till you told me all this."

"Probably am. That's why I won't even talk about it on the phone."

"Don't they have to get a warrant to tap your phone?"

"In theory, yes. That's what we're always told and what the law says. But in practice you find that the Yanks have been routinely scanning all our international calls, at a place in Yorkshire actually, since the 1960s – and eventually they got access to everything domestic too. No wonder we can't keep any trade secrets. And God knows what MI5 and GCHQ are doing now. For years they've been a law unto themselves; not properly accountable to anybody at all. Because they can plug into Menwith Hill, which is foreign, they can get round British law and listen to anybody that takes their fancy."

"Anybody that reads the *Guardian*, is it?" says Tom. "I remember Edward Heath said the spooks were f'kin bonkers, years ago, when he was supposed to be in charge of 'em. Didn't 'e say they thought everyone who read the *Mirror* was a commie who needed watchin'?"

Although Tom seems to be engaging in this conversation he's already moved on, turning pages rapidly and scanning them. His slow speech and unsophisticated air belie one of the sharpest brains Ray knows. Having him even glance at the work is probably a good thing after all.

"Where's the crash?"

"Which one?"

"You got more than one?"

"One was the cause of the other."

"Oh yeah," says Tom, with a questioning intonation, but it isn't really a question. Ray understands that Tom wants to read what is so often referred to as the 'disaster' to see how he's dealt with it. Everyone will. For much of the population at this remove there are but two things they remember about Lockerbie — one is the classic picture of the nose section of *Clipper Maid of the Seas*, on its side, like a dead animal, merging into the soft grass of Tundergarth; the other is a conviction in the back of the mind that 'the Libyans did it'. He is all-too-aware that numerous people will be happy if those twin impressions lie undisturbed and the carefully-conditioned link between them rests permanently unchallenged. The way he handles the actual event in the screenplay will probably determine whether they do or not. To him, every page of the screenplay is as important as any other, and indeed there are shocks and revelations dotted around in it that he hopes will impact an audience more than the depiction of a basic fact that they'll already have grasped — the jet disintegrated and fell to the ground. But the writing of that sequence alone will be the most crucial in selling it, in getting the picture made. Tom knows that too, so his opinion will be very much worth having. Ray doesn't usually change his mind so completely, so quickly, but he has today.

"Start at page 15," he says. The explosion is several pages on from 15, but Ray has written a sequence, a building of scenes, places and people that he hopes will express everything he needs to get across in a simple and gripping way. He's about to learn if he's on the right track. It is also, as he's implied to Tom, the second airliner destruction in the picture, and so inevitably needs a treatment different from the first.

He sips his coffee, watching Tom's eyes travel down each page. He knows the sequence by heart. He goes through it in his head, the shorthand found there only bearing a passing resemblance to the words actually typed on the neat, organised pages, where they're dragooned under headings with data into a conventional format.

Shock cut of fierce dog's mouth barking.

Wider of dog, quietens at unseen man's command.

Wide of sheep farmer, sheepdog, sheep and old Land Rover on high pasture with dusk approaching. Not far above, scudding clouds with breaks to reveal mainly clear, cold-looking sky with light in the west. There is falling drizzle or at least its promise. Apart from the wind, the occasional sheep bleat and the cries of hungry, circling birds there is absolute silence. Man and dog look up.

Farmer in close-up.

His point of view. High above and somewhat to the west, a jet passes south to north, its navigation lights bright, its noise now just perceptible.

Another wide shot as Land Rover door slams and vehicle sets off down bumpy track. Sound is of freshening wind rather than the car. In the distance the lights of a town are already on.

Closer on town. There is a little traffic seen but no people or sound. It's unearthly quiet. It almost has the feel of one of those deserted settlements in the westerns.

In an unremarkable street of semi-detached bungalows, a woman carries plastic shopping bags from a parked car to her home. A church bell rings once.

A striking architectural profile of a church in the
town as the bell rings again.

A full-screen close-up of a large, much deeper and
louder church or cathedral bell striking at the same
interval. The sound carries over as:

A priest coming through an ancient gate, with an
overcoat over his robes and carrying his service books and
notes, looks at his watch and glances up at his cathedral
tower, as floodlights are switched on.

Priest in close-up.

Ray is perspiring slightly now. He feels that Tom's long-honed editor's
instinct will have already seen half a dozen ways of improving this bit, if not
the whole sequence. This is standard screenwriter insecurity kicking in.
Tom says nothing and turns a page.

As if it were the priest's POV, but this is a
minaret of a mosque in Amman, Jordan. It's fully night
here, but this tower too is floodlit, although badly.

"You gonna 'ave the old call to prayer, boomin' out over t' speakers?"
Tom asks. Ray has thought about that one.

"Too corny," he replies. "Obvious."

"Right," says Tom.

They are keeping pace. Ray continues to track the cutter's scan.

High angle from the balcony of the minaret of the
town's rooftops and bustling streets below.

Down in the busy and noisy market, the women in
burkahs there too are carrying plastic shopping bags.

In a room leading almost directly off the market, two
Palestinian men we have seen before sit motionless,
watching television. The street clamour is heard but

46

artificially dimmed. They are in another place.

The cheap electric clock on their wall sweeps on.

A car boot closes in close-up. The shot widens. It's the woman in the quiet Scottish town with the last of her shopping. Some of these are Christmas bags.

As she goes up the garden path for the last time, the shot includes a Christmas tree and lights in the front window. There is the sound of normal domestic life in the home, in contrast to the deathly quiet of the street. She shuts the front door . . .

Shock sound cut to hammering on another. A man that the script calls Dalkamoni is shouting in Arabic and beating on the steel of his police cell.

Outside a German policeman responds to the commotion and opens the slider.

The prisoner demands in English to know the time and the officer tells him and slams the hatch shut again.

Another boot closes. This shot develops in a different way to reveal that the setting is the drop-off parking at Heathrow Terminal Three Departures. Cheerful passengers from the car head towards the welcoming entrance.

In the seasonally-decorated terminal some faces we know pick their way through the crowds in the general direction of the Pan Am check-in. The camera majors in on a large group of students, travelling together . . .

"You need to skip the scene with the American guy getting the upgrade," Ray advises, "and go to the cases on the conveyor, or the cathedral cloister really."

He could have told Tom to start there but he wanted him to read the earlier part to get a better idea of the build-up.

In the centuries-old cloister, the priest we saw earlier quietly chats with other clerics, the sacristan cross-bearer and senior members of the choir, as the younger members assemble and form up in a procession, prodded and tidied by an assistant choirmaster. The voices are hushed, respectful, expectant.

In the Terminal Three departure lounge familiar faces, shop, drink coffee or maybe something stronger.

A Pan Am crewbus drives on the Northern Perimeter Road as an El Al 747 or some-such aircraft lifts off spectacularly in the background.

In the crewbus, the film's female lead, playing Tanya, a Pan Am flight attendant, has a short, inconsequential, amiable scene with her colleagues, the point of which is to show the absolute normality of today. All is routine. Nothing marks out this winter evening from a thousand others.

If the flight attendants are relaxed, the flight crew in briefing are positively demob-happy, all looking forward to completing for what should be, for at least one of them, the last flight before a Christmas break. They don't skimp on their preparations, but from their dialogue at least part of their thoughts are plainly elsewhere.

In the Clipper Class lounge the three Americans who pretended not to know each other in the check-in scene Tom skipped now have similarly light-hearted banter with a fourth who has joined them. There is a certain wariness in the dialogue about what will happen when they arrive back home.

Tom doesn't seem to pick this up; at least if he does, he doesn't ask about it.

In the gate lounge at Heathrow the camera tracks along the rows, lingers on faces and moves on. Fragments of conversations are heard as we pass. Intercut with this is the activity in the cockpit as the pilots and flight engineer work through their check lists, and also the preparations in the galleys as the flight attendants prepare their stock and make everything secure and ready. On the apron outside, the baggage loaders are transferring the few remaining luggage containers from trailers into the capacious holds of the 747.

Close on container AVE 4041PA, sliding into position in the forward hold, on the left side, adjacent to the aircraft's outer skin.

In the corner of the gatelounge, by the airbridge door, a ground attendant leans towards the microphone on her lectern. The screen fills with her hand as it moves to the microphone switch on its base.

Close on the speakers on the Amman mosque's minaret.

Close on a hand striking a tuning fork. It is the assistant choirmaster. He gives the note to a choirboy soloist; steps back and raises his hands to count in the unaccompanied choir. The boy begins to sing and the procession moves sedately forward. In the nave of the cathedral the silent, standing congregation strains to hear the distant notes of the traditional start of the Anglican Service of Nine Lessons and Carols.

"Once in bloody Royal David City. Love it. F'kin marvellous."

Tom chortles. He seems to like it and he doesn't know the half of it yet, thinks Ray, very relieved.

So far so good.

—ooOoo—

12 Final Clearance

The procession winds across ancient flagstones under mediaeval arches, stunningly photographed.

Must remember, Ray notes in his head, to delete that two-word statement of what might justifiably be regarded as the 'bleedin' obvious'.

Still the treble soloist alone carries the familiar hymn as the clergy and choir near the cathedral proper. The other trebles and the tenors take up the second verse:

'He came down to earth from Heaven'

Their voices are indeed heavenly.

Unexpectedly we cut back to Heathrow. People in the gatelounge are forming their own procession. In slightly slow-motion, their queue to have their boarding passes checked and their progress down the airbridge mirrors exactly the pace and the gait of the religious counterpart.

A new image, sheep again. These are processing too, also in some degree of slow motion, down a tunnel very similar to the airbridge. Their cries are not heard, although their distress is more than clear. We don't see what awaits them at the end of their tunnel, but we know that they're going for slaughter.

Back in the airbridge, the faces are there. We see that the cheerful quartet of American men have separated. The young Palestinian man from Bekaa who's in the script before Tom's start point; the one who was sweating so much when he checked in at Frankfurt, is among the last to board. We see him when the choir is singing about *'the poor, the meek and the lowly'*.

51

For some reason Ray is pleased with that touch, although he isn't quite sure of the reason.

The singing continues but the quality of the sound has gone. So has that of the picture. We find out why. The sheep farmer is having his supper at his kitchen table. The cathedral service is being televised. The picture is on his none-too-new television.

The Border Collie sleeps in a basket in the corner of the kitchen. In close-up its eyes open and once again it looks heavenward.

Outside, in low shot, the farm is a black silhouette with one lighted window. The clouds remain dark and threatening, but through gaps the sky above them is lit by an almost-full moon which picks out a contrail from a jet powering its way north. Only the dog has heard it above the television.

In the Scottish town the car still stands in the street. Different music fades up as we crane towards the house. Inside the house the woman with the shopping and her family are also watching TV.

In the kitchen a teenager shuts the fridge door with natural sound and goes out of the back door. We crane up and away as he walks down the empty Sherwood Crescent, munching a chocolate biscuit.

On the Heathrow apron the baggage hold door closes firm. The sound is heightened.

Close on a hand clicking fast an airline seat belt, again with exaggerated sound.

In the wide passenger cabin, the flight is far from full. Passengers and attendants are stowing the last items

in the lockers. More doors slamming, including the final
cabin door. Everyone is now sealed on board.

In Damascus, Ahmed Jibril has just passed through an
arched doorway, guarded by a man with an AK47, and is
walking down a dimly-lit, narrow corridor to his quarters.

Back in Clipper class, two of the four Americans,
referred to as Gannon and McKee are seen, sitting apart
from each other. Each has been served with a drink and the
flight attendants are preparing to give their safety
briefing to the passengers.

As the senior purser fingers the PA microphone, in
the cockpit the co-pilot, Raymond Wagner, presses the
transmit button on the control yoke.

"Clearance this is Clipper One-Zero-Tree, stand Kilo
one-four with information Lima. We're requesting start."
In his free hand he holds a pen to copy the reply onto the
flight log clipped to a board also attached to the yoke.

"Good evening Clipper One-Zero-Tree. Cleared to
start for Kennedy, Daventry one-fox-trot departure, squawk
zero-tree-fife-seven and call one-two-one decimal nine for
push."

In the cabin the charade of the safety demonstration
is under way. Most of the passengers are paying no
attention.

Outside, the engine fan of No 4 begins to turn. It
is the first and only engine to be started at this stage.
The co-pilot is on the radio again.

"Heathrow Ground, good evening. Clipper One-Zero-
Tree on Kilo one-four is ready to push." Back comes the
reply.

"Clipper One-Zero-Tree, good evening. Clear to push to face south-east."

The plane's giant bogie wheels begin to turn in close up as a giant but low-to-the-ground Douglas tractor propels its massive weight backwards.

The feet of the ground engineer in close, moving across the tarmac. These shots are ominous, portentous. The hooded figure walks alongside the noseleg with its twin wheels, his ear-defender headset connected by flexi-cable to a port on the mechanism.

In the cockpit switches are thrown and held as the other engines come to life in the order 1,2,3, evidenced by the various temperature and pressure gauges on the instrument panel starting to climb.

The ground engineer disconnects and coils his cable and walks away to the front and well clear to the left, where Captain Jim MacQuarrie can see him. He raises his hand to indicate that there is nothing to obstruct the aircraft's moving off.

"Ground, Clipper One-Zero-Tree's ready for taxi," the co-pilot advises.

"Clipper One-Zero-Tree, clear taxi via the inner for two-seven right."

The 747 begins to taxi forward past the end of Pier 7. From a vantage point, probably a window in the empty gate lounge for stand K14, in which the lights have been switched off, two figures watch it pass and disappear.

Seen closer, they have smart suits with identity badges and cropped grey hair. They watch intently and impassively. The impression, helped no doubt by music, is that these are not airline people.

In the tourist cabin Tanya is involved in the ongoing ritual: "In the unlikely event of a landing on water, life jackets are to be found under . . ."

In the back of the Amman shop, the two Palestinians continue to wait. Their expressions betray nothing.

There's a shot in a dark Beirut office that won't mean as much to Tom as it could, moving from a perspiring Caucasian man to a telephone. We think it's going to ring, but it doesn't.

Back to the 747 taxiing, making slow progress in a long queue of other aircraft all trundling haltingly to the holding point near the threshold of the runway.

In his Damascus rooms Ahmed Jibril drinks tea and looks at his watch.

Back to the carol service as the congregation sing. Now it's the turn of:

"Angels from the realms of glory, Wing your flight o'er all the earth . . . "

In the Heathrow control tower, airfield visual controller, Richard Dawson, clears the 747 onto the runway.

"Clipper One-Zero-Tree. After the departing British Airways seven-fife-seven, line up and hold, two-seven right."

The large aircraft turns tightly left to line up on the runway, tyres scrubbing across the asphalt and its large white-painted designator 27 R. Beyond a link fence is the airport's perimeter road. Parked just off it, in a position to observe the departure, is a dark GMC 4x4, containing two more men with cropped hair.

The cathedral organist's hands and feet on the keyboards and pedals combine to produce the roar of the organ.

"Clipper One-Zero-Tree's cleared for take-off, two-seven right. Surface wind two-four-zero at twelve knots."

The captain's right hand advances the four throttles on the centre quadrant.

In close-up, the engines turn at take-off power but the sound is the organ.

As the 747 starts to accelerate down the runway, intercut with the faces of passengers and crew, the congregation sings the chorus:

"Co . . . . . me and worship, Worship Christ the King

"Co . . . . . me and worship, Worship Christ the new-born King."

The aircraft lifts into the air.

An air-to-air shot looking down on the jet as it climbs up over the fields and villages of Buckinghamshire, before plunging into thick grey stratus. The carol continues.

"Shepherds in the fields abiding, Watching o'er your flocks by night

God with man is now residing, Yonder shines the infant Light."

The sheepfarmer and his dog are at his door. They take in the night sky and move towards the Land Rover.

"The captain has turned off the seatbelt sign and you are now free to move about the cabin. However, we do recommend that for your comfort and safety . . ."

"Clipper One-Zero-Tree, take up a radar heading tree-fife-zero and recleared to flight level one-two-zero and contact London on one-two-eight decimal niner-zero."

The camera roams around the 747's cabins for a short while, catching snippets of conversation and all the normal activity as passengers settle into the flight and the cabin crew busy themselves with their routines. The flight time is ticking away.

In Clipper class, the American called Gannon is getting up from seat 14J. He turns in the aisle and exchanges the slightest of glances with the one referred to as McKee, seated in 15F, as he walks back towards Economy class. There he winks as he passes the first of the two others in his scattered party, Lariviere, in 20H, next to the aisle, and makes the tiniest face at the similarly-placed O'Connor, five rows behind. Tom won't know that he is Matthew Gannon, CIA Deputy Head of Station in Beirut, but the description of the way he moves purposefully conveys an impression of assurance and power.

He is scanning the faces of the passengers looking for someone.

He spots the person he's searching for. It's the young Palestinian, the only one on the plane. He's referred to as Jaafar and he sits reading in window seat 53K just two rows from the rear toilets and servery. The look of fear on his face, when he looks up at Gannon's approach, speaks volumes.

"Khalid Jaafar. Do you mind if I sit down?"

Now the choir is singing *"Oh little town of Bethlehem, How still we see thee lie"*

A slow-moving aerial shot drifts over Lockerbie. There is virtually no movement on the ground.

Which a producer will like, Ray thinks, as it's going to be a model shot and the fewer moving elements, the cheaper it will work out.

On the flight deck the altimeter, green annunciator lights, the strange automatic moving of the control column and spinning of the trim wheel indicate the Clipper's levelling at 31,000 feet, confirmed by Raymond Wagner's radio transmission:

"Clipper One-Zero-Three's level three-one-zero."

"Roger Clipper One-Zero-Tree, contact Scottish on one-two-six decimal two-fife, good evening." Wagner repeats the new frequency and signs off. He's already set it on standby so with the practised click of one rotary switch he's able to talk to Scottish Control at Prestwick, where Alan Topp sits in front of two green-glowing radar screens.

The cross-cutting continues — the cabins - Beirut - Captain MacQuarrie pushes his seat backwards and to the left. He unclips his seat harness with "Gotta hit the boy's room. Take her a minute, please Ray. You have . ." Wagner responds automatically with "I have control". Flight Engineer Jerry Avritt makes room in the tight cockpit space as MacQuarrie eases out of his left-hand seat and exits past him.

Sheep on hills, Damascus, the Cathedral, Amman, Sherwood Crescent. All calm, quiet. Only the flight attendants and Wagner are active. He calls for the oceanic clearance, monitored by Avritt. Relaxed professionalism.

"G'd evening Shanwick, Clipper One-Zero-Three for oceanic." A different controller, without radar screens, Tom Fraser, replies. The flight powers on.

Illuminated by snatches of moonlight a lone teenage fisherman on the English side of the Solway Firth is about to witness something he will never forget. Engine noise penetrates the cloud. Briefly the glow of lights.

Back in the radar room at Scottish Alan Topp watches his displays. The camera moves in on one to show the read-out, PA0103, with its position illuminated like a tailed comet with each rotation of the radar head.

Cut to the radar scanner at Great Dun Fell, revolving against the night sky, once every eight seconds, regular and dependable. The image dissolves to a not dissimilar-shaped cross in the Cathedral, where the priest is now giving a sermon. As he speaks, earnestly and sincerely, the camera moves round the cathedral, focusing on the congregation, the architecture and the sacred artefacts and symbols.

"You know every year we hear this story of Advent, of the coming of Christ and of Christmas. And every year the Christmas message inspires us to start afresh, to start over with new hope for a better world and with new determination to make that world a reality beginning with ourselves and our own relationships - say by being nicer to our neighbours, and perhaps even our family." There is restrained laughter from the congregation. "But does it last? Those very real feelings of peace and goodwill to all people can sometimes seem to be forgotten even before the Christmas decorations come down. So we should from time to time take stock and look back and ask if anything in this world of so much schism and conflict has actually

improved since we last celebrated Christmas and last spoke
of the benefit of its divine message. Has anything
changed? Has anything got better? Are the world's
problems any more resolved than they were when we were
telling the same inspirational story, and going through the
same joyous celebrations last year? I have to say I think
we have some cause for hope – that in some ways they are."

In the house in the quiet street the family is still
watching television. Another programme is about to start.
The announcer and the signature tune identify it as the
popular and in this instance heart-rendingly titled series,
This is Your Life.

Back in the passenger cabins of the 747, all is
normal for a few agonising seconds. In the cockpit, Tom
Fraser's voice is in the headsets, confirming the requested
oceanic clearance. He speaks it all, but the two men on
this flight deck will never hear the whole of it.

We feature a row of passengers, before the camera
eases away from them, down to the carpet of the left-hand
aisle. It descends through the floor into the semi-
darkness of the baggage hold below. Its movement
continues, towards and into the metal baggage container AVE
4041PA, through the bronze Samsonite suitcase, into the
Toshiba radio cassette player, past the atmospheric
pressure capsule and the attached transparent jelly-looking
timing device. We follow its wire to the silver pencil-
like detonator stuck into the polythene bag containing the
ugly yellowy-brown plastic explosive.

–ooOoo–

13   That Passeth All Understanding

Ray has wrestled long and hard with the moment of detonation and its depiction. Even now he's not entirely sure that his treatment is right and thinks it might change somewhat in coming drafts. What unfolded in the seconds after the explosion in the baggage hold, just under the feet of those ordinary, innocent, unsuspecting passengers in rows 12 and 13 has been painstakingly pieced together and the mechanics are well-understood, although the physics seem surprising, at least to the non-specialist. But what it was actually like to be there, experiencing or observing the effects and reactions, no one can ever truly know.

There remains with him the major question of whether it is right to show what can only be speculation, however carefully and responsibly such speculation might be researched. He has considered what and how much those who died that evening might wish to be known of their last moments of awareness, for awareness of a terrible wrong there would definitely have been, for every man, woman and child on board. Without doubt the preoccupying feelings would have been shock and fear, but Ray imagines that bolts of indignation and anger would have flashed across some minds, while others would have burned for a moment with the question 'Why?' and the fleeting hope that the outside world would learn the truth behind their lonely and terrible predicament.

He has come to realise that there were two crimes, not one. There was the over-riding crime of murder, indisputably, but the knowledge that everyone on board survived the detonation and undoubtedly lived on, for varying lengths of time, aware of the aircraft breaking apart around them, means that there has to be an additional count of mental torture. Forcing a group of people to look certain death square in the face adds another and even more wicked dimension to murder, as the later crimes of 9/11 demonstrated in the most graphic ways.

He notes that the families of many of the victims on Flight 93, 'the flight that fought back' on the never-to-be-forgotten day in 2001, agreed that their loved ones' last hours and minutes should be speculated about and reconstructed in two films. They didn't consent, he's sure, with the intention of providing popular entertainment, but rather as a celebration of the passengers' courage and resolve in responding to an unprecedented act of aggression. Attempting to put himself in the place of those on Clipper 103, Ray has come to the conclusion that although circumstances were different – in that the length of time that these unfortunate human beings will have had to recognise their fate was measured in units of seconds – the same logic applies; namely that an impression of what they suffered can justifiably be presented. The aim is similar: to explain and to present for the first time to a wide audience, the full barbarity of the crimes perpetrated against them.

Whatever the popular perception, Flight 103 was not blown to smithereens at 31,000 feet. Hollywood and action films in general have propagated a myth, in pursuit of what is imagined to be impressive and spectacular, that, for example, a car need only encounter the most modest of incidents to erupt in a massive fireball. It can happen, but mercifully it rarely does. On celluloid, objects having but the remotest propensity for flammability can be seen, not only burning but exploding, with excessive and unconvincing vigour. The break-up of 103 could not accurately be portrayed in this manner traditionally beloved of film special effects technicians and the directors whose wishes they serve. Ray hopes to be able to insist that they hold in check their natural over-enthusiastic tendencies in this instance. For this film, building a model of a 747 and destroying it with a large measure of black powder and petrol will not do. It's true that a Jumbo could blow up like that, even without a bomb, from a cause as mundane as an overheating air conditioning pack, as a TWA example tragically proved eight years later. But even when the heat-seeking guided missile hits the Airbus on page 6 of this very script; though it describes a blast of an entirely different magnitude – one that had been overkill in every possible sense – it would be still be wrong to represent it in this conventional fashion.

According to the pathologists, no one on 103 died as a direct result of the actual detonation of the device. That is to say, no one was at that moment blown apart; no one had shrapnel injuries; no one was burned by explosive gasses. If a number of passengers seated near the bomb's location suffered blast injuries, they would have come from the deformation of the floor below and although possibly significant and agonising, in the way of broken limbs and other serious wounds, evidence is that they would not have been, in themselves, life-threatening.

The evidence from the recovered bodies and the wreckage of *Clipper Maid of the Seas* means that properly conveying the death-throes of that aircraft will tax the story-telling abilities of the director, and require technical expertise of the utmost subtlety and of the highest order of innovation from the special effects and visual effects personnel. The process will potentially be complex and time-consuming. It will require experimentation and it will doubtless be relatively expensive.

The size of the explosive charge in the real event militates against any big-bang solution in its screen depiction. The relatively small amount of plastic explosive that could be fitted in the limited confines of a modified radio cassette player placed a limit on the destructive power available. An experienced bomb-maker like Marwan Khreesat, with both successful airliner kills and also failures on his CV, would know that one can be brought down by a relatively modest blast and that the Toshiba bomb could be sufficient to start the process – in favourable circumstances. That said, it seems unlikely that he would have himself chosen a radio of that limited size for such a large aircraft and more plausible that the decision came from others. He claims not to have known the target, and denies the bomb was his – but then, to quote (correctly for once) the famous line of Mandy Rice-Davies, he would, wouldn't he?

The aim of his bomb, or as officialdom categorises it, IED, standing for Improvised Explosive Device, would be two-fold; firstly to puncture the outer skin and cause explosive decompression. The latter would not, in itself, necessarily be able to enlarge the hole to the extent that the structural integrity of the fuselage could be compromised, even when the effects of the slipstream due to the aircraft's velocity were added to the loads on any weakened portion. But the second aim would be to destroy sufficient of the control runs and circuitry to make the aircraft unflyable, so that if it didn't break up initially, it might do so ultimately by performing uncommanded aerobatic manoeuvres that could themselves overstress the airframe, whether already weakened or not, to the point of failure. If this didn't happen and the aircraft stayed basically intact but uncontrollable by the unfortunate flight crew, the net result would be the same. Had the plotters known, N739PA was potentially a bad choice. It was one of 19 early 747s retrofitted with a heavier duty main deck floor as one of the modifications for incorporation into the Civil Reserve Air Fleet, (CRAF), available for military cargo and passenger use in times of national emergency. As it happened, the strengthening would make no difference.

When the underfloor control lines to the movable tail surfaces – that's the elevators, the stabiliser trim and the rudder – are broken or otherwise put out of action, there is little hope of survival, as was so graphically demonstrated in the case of a Turkish Airlines DC10 between Paris and London in March 1974. A faulty baggage-door latch gave way at 11,500 feet. The door detached and the decompression caused the main rear passenger floor to collapse, ejecting six passengers, jamming or breaking the cables and hydraulic lines and so rendering the pilots' controls useless. The nose dropped 20 degrees and the aircraft banked left, accelerating beyond its speed limitation. It was nearly full with 346 souls on board. Surprisingly the pitch reduced, the rate of descent lessened and the speed stabilised, but the aircraft remained banked 17 degrees left though not turning, now travelling at 430 knots until, 77 seconds after the latch opened, the huge aircraft hit a forest. The impact was unimaginable and the destruction total. It was the first disaster to befall a widebody airliner, and the heaviest ever loss of life in an aviation accident to that date.

With controls and flying surfaces either immobile or unconnected, aircraft will eventually hit the ground at a totally random speed, angle and attitude; the only question being whether it makes landfall in numerous pieces or basically one. In 1985 a domestic 747 circled around in Japanese airspace for about 40 minutes after a decompression resulted in a total loss of hydraulic power, uncontrollable but remaining basically on level keel, until it hit a mountain. Another DC10, that ultimately crashed on landing at Sioux City with many survivors, was brought back to earth with locked controls only through some degree of good luck and the supreme skills of three pilots and a flight engineer, using just differential power from the three engines to balance and manoeuvre the aircraft.

The three flight crew of Pan Am 103 had cumulatively something approaching 31,000 hours total flying experience, with nearly 11,000 hours on 747 aircraft, yet were utterly powerless in the face of a deadly ally of Khreesat's that was on board N739PA that evening. The bomber's friend is a complex and still only part-quantifiable law of physics that, in simple terms, causes the initial shock wave from an explosion, where and when it is reflected from a surface, to be amplified to a level beyond its original force. With its new strength, it can be transmitted around any available space, especially, it seems, confined ones, and any time it is reflected back into itself or meets part of itself reaching the same point via a different route, its energy is intensified. It's something like a nuclear reaction, constantly growing until it finds something on which to dissipate its extraordinary force.

The initial blast in the radio, within the suitcase, within the metal luggage container was not enormous. In the open air it would have produced a sizeable bang. In a container stacked with other bags, full mainly of fabric in the form of folded clothes, it might be expected that its force would have been attenuated. Indeed it almost certainly was. But the cases and their contents that could have absorbed much of the energy were largely inboard of the detonation's epicentre. Whether by pure chance or, as must be suspected, by someone unknown's deliberate placement, the Samsonite was positioned near the floor and sidewall of the container, as close as it could possibly be to the aircraft's aluminium skin. This would enormously aid the conspiracy's cause. The blast was directed along the route of least resistance, which was down and rearward, straight at the in-curving body side. The first shockwave made an initial 2ft square jagged hole in the lower left side of the aircraft. Such a hole is more than survivable.

Ray remembers the astonishment and rejoicing when an Aloha Airlines Boeing 737 landed safely, suffering but one fatality, with a large portion of its roof missing due to structural failure, many passengers sitting in the open air, in a sort of bizarre flying convertible reminiscent of an early motor char-a-banc.

But the Pan Am's shockwave was far from dissipated yet. Reflected from the skin and amplified by more gas coming from the chemical reaction taking place in the container, a re-invigorated blast twisted the stringers and ribs holding the skin together near the existing hole, helping to pop the rivets holding a much greater area of skin, which split in star-shaped bursts of metal, that despite being pushed out into 540 miles per hour of airstream, still curled over on themselves like flower petals. Now a few milliseconds after the detonation, the 2ft hole had grown to around 15 feet long by 7 feet deep, with further sheet metal being unfastened along or parallel to rivet lines at each passing instant. One crack ran forward and downward; one rearward and downward and one just slightly rearward and downward, but this one passed under the Clipper's belly and up the right side to the level of the main passenger deck floor.

There was worse. Blast was, as described, now reverberating through and pumping itself up in a whole complex of cavities that are an inevitable part of an aircraft's normally unseen structure, and irregular pieces of exterior aluminium were being forced off their retaining formers in numerous places when the shock waves combined at particular, seemingly random, places. Random or not, their combination was sufficient to be loosening a large area of the upper fuselage skin, generally above the original point of the explosion. But any definition of what was normally unseen, or indeed normality itself, was already meaningless. Now perhaps less than a second after detonation, strapped-in passengers would have been aware of an enormous bang that could have damaged some eardrums, as well as other tearing, screeching noises as metal split, curled over or broke away. Almost simultaneously, blast and gas entered the main deck cabin through the side, floor-level ventilators, followed by the sound of rushing outside air, quickly followed by incoming jets of freezing draught, together rumbling and buffeting round the disintegrating cabin. Undoubtedly some of the plastic inner cabin liner and window surrounds would have part-collapsed inwards, to reveal the bare metalwork of the structural formers behind – where they were still in place. Certainly at the left front of the aircraft, in the worst affected area of the enlarged hole, there was little below the main deck window beltline but open space. Soon the same would apply to the roof and, for those experiencing this horror, things were about to get considerably more awful.

To achieve the second, or back-up hope of the aeroplane bomber – the freezing of the control surfaces – the same physics had worked their evil. The deformation of the main deck floor, despite the CRAF strengthening, had indeed affected the mechanical connections, and some severe control inputs had been applied without the wishes of the only pilot at the controls. Co-pilot Ray Wagner was powerless to prevent or to counteract these movements, even if there had been time. There were two extremely abrupt changes in the aircraft's attitude; one, a strong pitch nose-down and the other, the start of a roll to the left. The changes were so violent and so absolutely unexpected in magnitude that enormous forces were imposed on the turbojet engines, such that the spinning turbine blades were forced into impact with their casings, causing large witness gouges, the friction enough to act as a brake on their turning. These four large Pratt and Whitneys, developing 43,500 pounds of thrust apiece, thus went from cruise power to zero effective thrust in under 5 seconds. The engines were becoming quiet, if nothing else was.

Decompression of an aircraft cabin causes a number of effects. One is that condensation may cause the formation of mist in the cabin. Given that electrical power in the aircraft failed totally a few milliseconds after the explosion, Ray has assumed so far that this would have reduced the cabin to total darkness. This plus the fact that any concept of the cabin as an airtight entity was already evaporating, the mist would probably not have become a significant factor. If the cabins had been plunged to pitch-black, and this he still has to confirm, the already off-scale levels of panic and terror could only have been ratcheted-up, dread of the unseen being one of the most primitive of human fears. Seeing though, would provide little comfort in this predicament. Any lack of engine noise probably went unnoticed amid the wholly understandable human screams coming from people mortally frightened.

Depressurisation's second effect is that anything light and unsecured may be sucked out into the open sky, if there is an aperture large enough, or even if it really isn't. This has applied in the past to people and to blocks of seats together with their occupants. It is certain that this process will have begun the moment that Flight 103 was holed. Anyone unsecured in the region of the stripped fuselage was liable to have been bodily ejected into thin air at 31,000 ft, ripping themselves wickedly on the jagged aluminium and plastics in their final contact with their would-be tomb. Many of the Lockerbie victims were found to have sustained injuries of this type.

But immediately following the decompression, the violent attitude changes, especially the pitch down, would have piled agony on agony. Extreme manoeuvres can be massively uncomfortable even for experienced pilots wearing full seat harness. Those known to have been experienced by *Clipper Maid of the Seas* would have been, for ordinary passengers secured by the minimal airline lapstrap, unimaginably distressing and disorientating. For those who had been standing, such as the flight attendants, all of whom would, at nearly 40 minutes into the flight, have been busy with the bar service and dinner preparation; for those passengers who were moving about the cabin or standing up and for those who had simply elected not to follow the 'comfort and safety' advice – the result would have been simply hideous. Effectively weightless they were thrown bodily, like dogs' toys, into the roof of their respective cabins, where they were joined by all the unsecured items in their vicinity – trolleys, hot coffee pots and hand luggage items including the inevitable bottles of duty-free.

Whatever injuries they sustained from their impact with the roof lining, or other items, or other people, they potentially then added to by falling back down onto the irregular and dangerous rows of thin headrests, belonging to seats both occupied and empty. Here legs, arms, necks, backs and skulls, of both the falling and the fallen-upon, would all have been susceptible to fracture. That's if these unfortunate individuals had time to fall back to the floor, for other factors were busy at work. Even now, less than two seconds had elapsed since the noise of the explosion, accompanied by this appalling lurch, like a huge encounter with turbulence, had conveyed to everyone a first intimation of their vulnerability.

Assuming that it was possible to see any of this, which seems unlikely, and that there was such a thing as a 'safe distance', which there wasn't, a strapped-in witness would normally have only a limited period of consciousness left to them unless they managed to secure a working passenger oxygen mask, which should have dropped automatically from emergency panels in the ceiling immediately following depressurisation. Without the life-giving gas, the process of death by oxygen starvation would begin, and at that altitude unconsciousness would occur in around 90 seconds. In a 'normal' depressurisation, the cabin crew has the task of taking portable equipment to people away from the reach of a mask and to assist those in their seats but unable physically, or perhaps emotionally, to avail themselves of this vital lifeline. Under these totally different, far from standard, circumstances, where the likelihood of the oxygen system working as expected would have been extremely remote, it could be argued that any who slipped quickly into oblivion were the fortunate ones – the ones spared awareness of the deeper horrors to follow.

Sadly, those demons were already at the door, and the lack of functioning oxygen masks, and indeed the sudden shock of biting cold, would have little influence. Those few who had become unconscious through one cause or another were indeed the recipients of a small measure of the priest's 'God's mercy', but with this compacted timescale, even for those on the point of passing out from the pain of broken limbs, the release would have in most cases come too late. Events were overtaking them with such rapidity that most by this point will not merely have suspected that their hour had come, but known it for a cast-iron physical certainty. And the majority of the human beings of all ages on 103 will not have been overcome by welcome narcosis. There wasn't going to be a sufficient number of seconds for it to take effect. Most people would remain awake and aware.

What happened next was of no great surprise, considering the progress of the 'skin-stripping' that the airflow around the fuselage had willingly exacerbated. The damage moved outwards from the major hole on the left side. The fault line passing under the keel of the aircraft linked up with some sporadic exfoliation on the right-hand side. As the rigidity of the left-hand structure began to fail, the air under the nose, which was descending and canted in a bank to the left, obviously tried to push the nose up and to the right, relative to the rest of the fuselage. And it succeeded. The left side and underside structure became increasingly compromised to the point of rupture, at which point the whole massive nose section of the aircraft simply pivoted, almost as if hinged, slightly up but mainly right, around the still more-or-less-intact right fuselage side, but of course tearing apart at the top. For one incredible instant the angle of attachment was in excess of 90 degrees, so that the right side of the fuselage impacted the front of the right inner engine intake, normally situated far behind it, just ahead of the wing. The engine tore from its pylon and fell away independently.

So, almost unbelievably – because we think of an aircraft as a strong and solid entity – at sometime under a mere three seconds from zero, the front section of the fuselage – that familiar shape containing the cockpit, part of the upper passenger cabin and the first rows of the lower, main deck – separated from the remainder of the *Maid of the Seas* and disappeared into the terrible blackness.

–ooOoo–

14   The Perils and Dangers of this Night

Since he first read how the front section of that Jumbo just twisted, hinged and broke away, Ray has never been able to prise the top from a boiled egg without thinking about N739PA cracking and coming apart, with live human beings no doubt falling out of both sections as it did so.

It's clear that slow motion will be the only way to begin to get across the details of what befell this mighty aircraft.   In reality, everything had happened so ridiculously fast that the sequence of events could never be comprehensible unless the timescale was expanded over and over, with plenty of double, triple, quadruple action and more.   Ray proposes an on-screen digital counter to give the timing of groups of shots from zero and so make the true compression clear.   It goes without saying that the choice of images will prove absolutely crucial to the clarity.   He thinks that the hardest part to get across up to this point will be the blast racing round in the aircraft's bowels, gathering the strength at odd, hardly explicable, places to deform the stiffeners and exfoliate pieces of aluminium skin.

The other big unknown is how to show what is happening if the passenger cabins and cockpit are now pitch black.   In theory this will be the DP's problem, but it could become an important decision, if for example the only way to photograph it is to introduce perhaps some emergency lights that would not have worked in reality during such catastrophic failure. Whatever is presented as film drama, there will always be experts on every aspect of any subject that is touched on, and directors who really care about what they do don't relish getting 'Sorry, but I must point out' letters from any of them.   Ray has drawn heavy circles round 'Check Emergency Lights' in the 'To Do' list in his work book.

If what had taken place in the first seconds is a matter, in dramatic terms, of making a familiar place instantly become sinister, threatening and increasingly insecure, the parting and what followed it comes straight from the tradition of horror fantasy, except that this was not fantasy.   It has the characteristics of a nightmare invention, like a devilish adventure ride in a perverted theme park, yet it happened to real people, who were alive and in the main, conscious, it even now being under five seconds from zero.

Ray can only begin to imagine the heart-stopping terror that confronted those in the remaining cabin of the aircraft, but especially those near to the break where the nose section had been.   They were in a tube that was now largely open at the front end, admitting a wind of perhaps 550 miles per hour, the like of which humans never, ever encounter and which equates to being hit by a solid wall. Crouching behind the seat in front, if there was one, would be the only way to avoid some tiny fraction of the pummeling pressure and part of the random shower of high-speed debris. Even then breathing would have been near to impossible, the ears assaulted, eyes would have streamed; and it's unlikely that the seats themselves could have resisted the airflow for more than moments before ripping from their tracks and flipping backward. No one would dare or be able to look into the wind, the rain or the missiles but yet it would have been impossible not to be aware.of the open void and the fact that without the missing section, both the controls and the personnel had gone that could have done the remotest thing to improve the situation. This was deteriorating by the second, for as the fuselage lost forward speed, it was also pitching further down, rapidly moving towards the vertical. Moreover, the noises of metal snapping, tearing and flapping, if they could be heard above the airflow, or awful vibration if they couldn't, would have telegraphed that the integrity of the remaining fuselage was about to become a thing of the past.

At some point before the final vertical plunge began from 19,000 feet, there had been damage to the tail surfaces caused by debris, including whole loaded containers ejected from the cargo deck. The damage contributed to a yaw, a sideways skid which imposes extra strain on an aircraft's structure. Here massive, way beyond design parameters yaw took place, evidenced by the fact that the pylons attaching the three remaining engines to the underside of the wings were subject to bending forces sufficient to snap them off, allowing the hot but essentially now inert engines to join the rain of debris effectively dive-bombing the unsuspecting citizens of Lockerbie.

With thick metal pylons being bent and severed like balsa wood, the flimsy, much battered, already stressed and partially disintegrated fuselage tube was many times more susceptible, indeed totally. By 9,000 feet any vestige of pretence of being an aircraft had deserted the *Maid of the Seas*. She was now a collection of falling heavy pieces and drifting smaller ones, and many of her passengers were no longer attached to her but like the *Maid*, hurtling to earth, either singly or strapped into seats or rows of them.

To anyone able to look into the awful wind, the streetlights of Lockerbie would have been visible below them. In some small sense the familiarity of the ground could have seemed welcoming despite, the knowledge that arrival there would, except in the most extraordinary circumstances, mean death. It took 47 seconds from the moment of detonation for the heaviest and speediest portion of wreckage to reach the surface. The other main sections and free-falling individuals will have taken many seconds longer. The pathologists say that in a high proportion of cases, hearts are known to have been beating all the way down and even in some cases subsequent to arrival. Some years later it was revealed that two victims had indeed, by some stroke of fortune, had their fall cushioned and arrived at ground level with relatively minor and treatable injuries. They had however succumbed to exposure and blood loss during the night because they weren't found in the exceptionally foul weather conditions.

It was assumed early on in the evening that the accident had not been survivable. Even many of the intact bodies that were visible were not readily accessible, so not all could be checked for signs of life. Virtually all of the corpses and body parts that were found were left in place where they had fallen, awaiting recovery and logging, following the early and correct assumption that this was a crime scene; at around 900 square miles, the largest in area there has ever been.

The detached front section and especially the cockpit would theoretically have had some tiny degree of advantage. Captain MacQuarrie had not had time to return to his seat, so only First Officer Wagner and Flight Engineer Avritt were in the small space. If each was secured by his full seat harness, behind the windscreens and assuming they had remained conscious, they would potentially have had a less uncomfortable and perhaps marginally less horrifying experience than others just described, but this is only to differentiate between mere degrees of sheer terror, with awareness of the same inevitable outcome.

Behind them on the upper deck and on the section of main deck below them, passengers, flight attendants and Jim MacQuarrie would have been more aware of their violent detachment from the rest of the craft and the open abyss just behind them. The bodies in the nose section were described as being particularly badly mutilated. Despite this, a stewardess was reported by rescuers as having been alive when found, but died very shortly afterwards. That portion is calculated to have hit the ground at 120 knots or 138 miles per hour, while those unfortunates in the front of economy class who remained tethered to their seats over the strong wing-spar centre-box section by their two-inch bands of lap-belt webbing, eventually riding the wings more or less in the open air, are said to have made landfall at 440 knots. That's 538 miles an hour or about 790 feet per second. Ten passengers, eight with seats allocated in this area, were never located. They were caught in the monstrous explosion that did eventually take place, but on the ground, caused by the presence in the wings and central fuselage tanks of the aviation kerosene being carried to fuel the whole Atlantic crossing, a load in excess of 200,000 pounds.

–ooOoo–

Revenge is a bad counsellor. The obscene ordeal and hideous death that the occupants of Flight 103 were forced to suffer was a calculated and procured act of retaliation, one of a series of murderous tit-for-tats that could be traced back at least to 1930s Germany. Scholarly specialists could very likely take it further. Revenge is seductive, seeming to offer answers, when all it does is repeat more plaintively the question, 'Why?' Just as the survivor on TV after 9/11 spoke for many, no doubt, when he said that 'somebody has to be bombed for this', Ray has been tempted. Spending so much time imagining that terrible three-quarters of a minute; plunging in the cockpit, surfing the wing, feeling the night sky over and over again, sharing with these ordinary people their last unspeakable moments of earthly experience, has made him increasingly angry that they should have been denied any meaningful justice, for reasons of shabby politics and grubby power games. The temptation is to wish that all those complicit and those brazen enough to promote the cover-up could be themselves dropped from 31,000 feet. As this is not going to happen and would be inappropriate – that is not to say undeserved – if it did, he tries to focus on more worthy and achievable aims. One of these is to make his contribution towards securing a review of the case, and with it the release of the man incarcerated in Her Majesty's Barlinie Prison who in the next act of revenge became the token, sacrificial patsy.

–ooOoo–

Because of the speed of events, including loss of electrics, the flight crew had been unable to take any emergency action whatsoever before the instant of separation. Had there been any power to the radios and any time remained, they could not readily have sent a Mayday, because they were in the process of receiving a message – the one containing the flight's oceanic clearance – at the very moment that the bomb exploded. To overcome the problem of not being able to transmit because of the incoming speech, a crew member would have needed to select another radio box or re-tune the one in use to 121.5 or another monitored frequency. Neither action was feasible under the disorientating circumstances; nor, tragically, would either have been in any way useful.

Ray has listed the angles from which he needs to show the explosion; the director may well produce a different list. The writer proposes the view from another aircraft that was just a few miles away at the time, using the same airway at a higher level; he wants to view it from the ground, from the viewpoint of the young fisherman, with of course the teenager's reaction; he needs that model shot, with a properly scaled blast, and he wants to cover the radar return fragmenting into many separate returns on controller Alan Topp's green screen. He requires the looks of realisation on the faces of some key people on board, including the handling pilot, Ray Wagner; the fictional flight attendant, Tanya Oaken; and the real Major Charles McKee. And he definitely needs at that moment to cut to a few people many miles away from the scene, but acutely involved there, most notably Marwan Khreesat. He also realises that he must show the debris and passengers falling through space, unconscious, dying or dead. But as to those scenes in the aircraft at the instant and in the seconds following the bomb blast, he isn't totally sure.

He's written them, and they're in the copies he's taking with him to New Zealand, but they may not stay. It might be just as effective to cut from the close-up of the mechanism in the radio-cassette to Khreesat, before going to the distant shots and the falling sequence. Or maybe going back to the cabin after the casette player and just cutting to black, which then becomes the night sky with the distant explosion. As he thinks through this question for the umpteenth time another voice in his head whispers, 'It doesn't matter what you write. The bastards will change it anyway.' He chases the thought away. This is a day for optimism, and there is a hell of a lot of day to go. Eight hours more than normal, to be absolutely precise.

–ooOoo–

15   "A Country Far Beyond the Stars"

Ray returns from the daydream, suddenly aware that Tom is speaking.

"What's this music?" the Yorkshireman is asking.

"It's a choral piece – Hubert Parry – composed in the gloom of the First World War, although the words are seventeenth century. It's beautiful."

Tom does something unexpected.

"Julian," he shouts through to the next room. "Can ya find *My Soul, There is a Country* by Hubert Parry for me?" There is a vague sound of acquiescence from behind the half-open door.

"If it doesn't come up, try *Songs of Farewell*," Ray calls out to the hidden Julian.

"It's great, you choosin' the music like this," Tom says.

"Seems to work. It just came to me. And the idea of the service, that would have been going on exactly that week at the right sort of time – it points up all sorts of comparisons."

"I can see that – s'nice." 'Nice' from Tom verges on a rave review.

"So you've got people fallin' t' their deaths in slow motion to church music?"

Ray has known for months that he's going to have to justify this over and over again. He hopes he's ready.

"I think we have to show things just as they were. Obviously some people were dead at this stage, or more likely unconscious for various reasons, but it seems the majority would have been alive and aware. Most would certainly appear to be moving because of the wind and the dynamics. For those that are already dead, religious music has a real relevance. And people who've been close, you know – come back from the dead, been resuscitated – they say that dying might be uncomfortable but being dead is serene and a beautiful experience. I'm sort of trying to make it awful and peaceful at the same time, if that makes any sense."

"But you're also saying, why's God allowing this to 'appen?"

"That's certainly one of the things."

"Got it, Tom," comes a shout from the next room. "Shall it play it through?"

"Well done Jules, go on."

And in seconds blissful voices are filling the workroom, flowing in soothing waves from hi-fi speakers round the walls, the words a setting of a poem by Henry Vaughan, who lived from 1622 to 1695.

My soul, there is a country, Far beyond the stars,

Where stands a winged sentry, All skilful in the wars:

There above noise and danger, Sweet peace sits crowned with smiles

And One, born in a manger, Commands the beauteous files.

He is thy gracious friend, And, O my soul awake

Did in pure love descend, To die here for thy sake.

If thou canst get but thither, There grows the flow'r of peace,

The Rose that cannot wither, Thy fortress and thy ease.

Leave then thy foolish ranges, For none can thee secure

But One who never changes, Thy God, thy life, thy cure.

Sir Charles Hubert Hastings Parry lived from 1848 to 1918, and is best remembered as the composer of *Jerusalem*. *My Soul, There is a Country* was written less than four years before his death when he was burdened by sadness and depression, much to do with the war. Somehow though it is intensely glorious and hopeful music, despite the title of the whole group of six motets – *Songs of Farewell*. Parry heard each of the motets performed only once in his life and never saw a performance of the whole group together. That would not happen until his memorial service in 1919.

As with most music, almost no one would have had access to this stunning piece for much of the first half of the twentieth century unless they were one of a tiny few fortunate enough to attend a rare recital in a major church or concert hall. Ray thinks himself incredibly lucky to be able to walk into HMV or Virgin and buy virtually any musical work that has ever been written, but for it to be available on demand like this in seconds, to an audience comprising a sizeable percentage of the population of the earth, is simply mind-blowing. Enough perhaps, to have given even Parry some optimism. Ray recognises the recording from its matchless weight and phrasing as that by the choir of Trinity College, Cambridge, conducted by Richard Marlow; the best version he knows.

The quality of the recording and that of the hi-fi combine to dim all sense of the editing room. Ray closes his eyes and is in Trinity Chapel on a December evening.

Tom carries on reading the harrowing slow-motion scene as people large and tiny, some recognisable to the audience only by their clothing, tumble alone, in seats, in rows, attached to or enwrapped in other debris, a monsoon downpour of metal, foil, wire, pipes, cables, containers, cases, handbags; pieces of every shape, size and composition.

The man who has lived with them and shared their fall almost daily for the past five years listens to the sublime music and, like its composer before him, thinks about death.

Death is the constant stock-in-trade of the movies, and in 99 cases out of 100 it's trivialised. Brought up on Cowboy and Indian, Saturday Morning Pictures, Ray grew to hate the casual and sanitised loss of life that was presented as entertainment. Then later there was 'gore for gore's sake', but the casual aspect, if anything, multiplied. Now the fashion for internet video clips of real deaths – people being run over by buses or touching live overhead railway cables – appals and depresses him. To him, every innocent, undeserved demise is a tragedy and if it has to be shown in the course of a story, should be portrayed very much as such. If he can construct a narrative without showing it, he will, but in this one he has no option. Much as he would like to deal with the outrage and its aftermath without representing the last moments of a group of people who really lived and whose relatives may see his film, he knows it's vital to re-create the sheer inhumanity of what happened to them. They were in a place that to people of our time seems as normal and secure as their own living rooms, but in an instant they were catapulted, sucked or ripped out into an environment that to a human being is the ultimate in hazardous and patently unsurvivable in numerous ways. Ray knows that his script has to portray this if he wants to bring the probing light of history to bear on the callous criminals who were responsible for these people's terrible end – and on the other guilty who ordered history rewritten as though truth was an inconvenient irrelevance.

He comes to his decision. He will keep the scenes in the Jumbo as it disassembles around its occupants. There is no choice. He must.

'Thy God, thy life, thy cure.' As the voices crescendo, the largest piece of debris, the strongest structure on any aircraft, the centre fuselage and wing roots complex, which also contains those thousands of gallons of highly flammable Jet-A1 aviation kerosene, falls obliquely to the ground, just avoiding the dual carriageway of the A74 trunk road, but instead incising the housing estate where the woman's car is still parked. The explosion, that engulfs the entire area and the dwellings in it, **is** of the traditional Hollywood screen-filling variety.

Ray recalls that the first time his typing reached the line about the woman's car, his laptop went blank and shut down for no apparent reason. Something or someone made him re-do an hour's unsaved work.

He is still above Lockerbie, looking down on the monstrous fire-ball without realising that the music has finished and Tom is handing back the screenplay.

"Well done, mate. I wanna read the rest, soon as I can 'ave a copy. Now I've got 'is nibs comin' at half-eleven and I better 'ave summat to show 'im." A cue, as pilots say, to file and depart.

Tom must be the only film editor in the world to refer to his current director as 'his nibs'.

Ray stands up and prepares to leave. 'Well done, mate' and 'I want to read the rest', coming from Tom, will do very nicely. This means just one down and many, many dozens to go. But the beautiful morning, despite the inevitably sad preoccupations, just got rather better.

–ooOoo–

16   Sophe's Lack of Choice

When he'd shut his boot leaving home this morning, it was the only sound to be heard for miles apart from the faint rush of a nearby brook. As he slams it at Pinewood now he realises that he is surrounded by noise. There's hammering and drilling from set construction on the studio lot behind him; to his left there's the constant roar of the M25, not half a mile away; while in front of him the whistles of the jets at approach power, five miles away but seeming much closer, merge in a general, measurable urban buzz. So much for the tranquillity of the green belt. This car park is so familiar, for a very good reason: he'd effectively lived in it for ten weeks in a harsh winter in the mid 90s. He'd been doing a massive space film and to save three hours of driving each day, he'd bought an old motor caravan and hidden it among the actors' trailers and the other mobiles parked round the Bond stage. The electricians had hooked up a feed from the stage supply, and with a blower heater on a thermostat his little kingdom was always welcoming after a 14-hour day. It didn't matter that the water tank had frozen: there were showers and loos in the studio. But coming out of the unit office and instead of facing a long icy drive, climbing into bed with a hot soup and a large scotch – that had been the acceptable face of film-making, for once. Having this car park as home for those bitter weeks could have saved his life. You can never know these things.

Like his motor caravan escapade of ten years earlier, Ray figures that the Pinewood authorities would frown on today's plan so he transfers his bags to Sophe's car with a certain degree of low-profile and affected nonchalance. Sophe's car! While the girl herself is apparently effacing and has an almost clandestine beauty, her car is brash, outrageously curvaceous, wildly overstated and a triumph of style over purpose. And she loves it, hence her delight at accepting her boss's suggestion of this extra chance to drive it during the working day.

They have barely left the main gate before Ray decides that this will be a ride to remember. In another quarter-mile he has also come to terms with the realisation that though she clearly lavishes a great deal of attention on this astonishing bubble, she has never given the business of driving a single thought since the day she burnt her L plates. It isn't just that she's spending twice as much on petrol, tyres and brake linings as she needs; many drivers fall into that category. This is worse; she doesn't seem to see or react to any events unfolding around her with the remotest comprehension and until the last possible moment. She is intelligent, enthusiastic and articulate. Indeed, she's holding an involved conversation about the benefits of working with a talented editor like Tom; a conversation to which Ray is only a half-hearted party as he is literally in fear of his life by this time and certainly doesn't wish to distract her further from the road. Yet the fact that she is nominally in charge of a device that can easily kill them both in an instant seems not to come anywhere near her consciousness. She turns her head when she speaks to him, gesturing with a spare hand for emphasis while following inches behind one of the giant battered tipper trucks of which that part of Buckinghamshire has more than its fair share. Its driver needs only to lift his foot from the accelerator a fraction and the bubble and its occupants will be underneath it and its formidable load of scrap metal. Ray remembers his dark broodings of earlier this morning and wonders if this really will be the day he meets St Peter.

He's never been one for fairground rides and theme parks, but remembers from filming them that even the most extreme and uncomfortable experiences tend to settle down to a tolerable degree after an interval. He wonders if this will happen but then reminds himself that those rides are calculated and controlled, even if they don't feel it. This is completely free form, like aerobatics flown by someone without any instruction or understanding. You don't know when the wings will come off; you can just be sure that at some point they will. His fear-inspired monosyllabic answers have clearly somewhat offended Sophe so she turns her attention to her music system, followed by the GPS and then on cue, she takes a phone call. Hands-free it is, but the difference isn't that noticeable as she weaves from lane to lane on the motorway, overtaking, undertaking, cutting and thrusting. Yet they aren't remotely late. They figuratively have all the time in the world, but at any second they could run out if it – totally.

Ray feels very sad. The system, the government, the Department for Transport, the driving schools, the car manufacturers, *Top Gear* – they all fail young people like Sophe. 'Pass this ridiculously basic test,' the message is, 'and then you know all there is to know. You can go anywhere you like without ever needing to consider anything other than not being caught for a traffic offence.' When Ray learnt to drive, if you didn't drive round a corner properly, you wouldn't come out at the other end but instead end upside-down in the hedge half-way round. Now because cars can go round most bends at most speeds without waving their wheels in the air, drivers think they have a God-given right to do it. Things don't generally go horribly wrong until they meet something unexpected like stationary traffic or a nervous horse just out of sight.

Even sententious Alastair on *Police, Camera, Action* doesn't help, with his 'We would never do anything as stupid as that, would we?' approach. Kids are turned loose with no sensible advice onto roads they've never practised on or even been told about. 'How do you go round a bend?' 'I dunno. I just, like, steer round it, I suppose.' As with 007, whose Pinewood stamping ground Ray and Sophe left nine minutes ago, they're licensed to kill, and they do, several times a day, clocking up Lockerbie-sized death tolls in the UK alone every few weeks.

Ray remembers that it was a young Alastair Stewart who first gave the news of Lockerbie to the ITV audience. There was one of those heart-stopping, 'We're going over to the newsroom' announcements that almost always forewarn us that death has visited unexpectedly and probably in multiple. Shortly after the story broke, Royal correspondent-in-waiting, Nicholas Witchell, did the same for BBC2.

It's funny about *Top Gear* and *Police, Camera, Action*, or actually not funny but curious. Years ago, hating the tone of the police clip programme, Ray had devised a show that promoted good driving and safety by using a light and humorous approach, and employed three presenters and a live audience. With tongue firmly in cheek, it had been called *The Bexhill Drivers' Club*, the south coast seaside town being a known hot-spot of driving incompetence. Not being remotely accomplished at selling and promoting his own work he gave it to a friend of a friend, who had 'connections' at HTV West. Nothing more was ever heard. Then a few years later, *Top Gear* appeared in a new format, with humour, three presenters and a live audience. It wasn't even worth asking the question, but it was somewhat ironic that here was a show promoting speed, competitiveness and motoring hooliganism and the reverse of safety and consideration, using his bloody format! Getting inwardly angry about motoring programmes, especially one he can't help loving in spite of himself, passes the remainder of the fraught journey and makes it just about bearable.

Sophe leaves him at the drop-off point and he watches the bubble squeal and wobble away towards a snagged gaggle of tour coaches. As the reddish-blonde hair disappears from sight he knows for a fact that she'll never live to be a mother; that she'll never pass on those fabulous Anglo-Scottish genes to beautiful children. She's doomed, just as the young people on Flight 103 were condemned. In theory she is in charge of her own destiny, a captain, and they had been mere passengers, carried along unstoppably. But to Ray this morning, Sophe is a victim too, because like the Syracuse students and all the others, her fate is sealed, and no one is going to say so.

He gathers up his bags and picks his way between jockeying hire cars and taxis towards the terminal, taking the selfsame steps towards the very doors that, not an hour ago, he was visualising 103's passengers cheerfully entering.

–ooOoo–

17   Opening Bids

Whatever the ultimate outcome, Ray will always look back on this morning's chance re-encounter with David Hollingsworth as one of those identifiable pivotal moments that changed everything. If Sophe hadn't driven like a dervish, or her departure had been delayed by a cordial exchange, the meeting could so easily never have happened. Its taking place still didn't guarantee that there would be any of those results that slowly began to unfold. If the conversation hadn't gone a certain way, with the right things mentioned and a happy progression of question, reaction and response, Ray and DB could still effectively have passed like the figurative ships in the night or jets out over the grey Atlantic.

In fact the odds, given the setting and the special circumstances, were heavily stacked against things panning out the way they have. In the first place, however experienced anyone is as a flier, the level of underlying tension that exists at an airport until they are successfully checked in and have passed through security tends to mitigate against serious consideration of anything peripheral to getting onto the flight. It was part of the coincidence that both parties were more than comfortably early and the terminal was not especially busy, which provided the opportunity for the exchange of more than a few predictable semi-banalities. In the second place, the very nature of their lapsed relationship gave instant grounds for a degree of awkwardness. On sight, each went through a frantic series of mindsearches. Why did we lose touch? Whose fault was our failure to keep connected? Does he perhaps not like me as much as I always thought? Was he slightly concerned that his girlfriend and I got on so well? For Ray there was another and a major cause for insecurity. DB, once very much a contemporary and of approximately the same relatively insignificant standing in the industry, was now hugely, but hugely, successful. You can never tell what success is going to do to someone. Ray remembers working with one comedy actor who, when starting out, was open and friendly but who became horribly withdrawn and self-obsessed on becoming a household name. Ray is always prepared for the worst. No wonder the conversation took a few moments to get going.

The icebreaker was the fortunate discovery that they were both actually booked on the same Los Angeles flight. There was the immediate and fleeting prospect for both of sitting next to an amiable companion; a human being on the same wavelength with things in common to discuss, instead of taking part in the seat allocation lottery. Any known quantity is probably better than finding that your neighbour, for what stretches ahead like an eternity, has perhaps a disinclination to acknowledge even your very presence, or a total lack of manners and consideration, or a predisposition to belabour you with stridently expressed opinions diametrically opposed to your own, or is possessed of ghastly personal habits. This brief window of hope was immediately closed by the realisation that they would inevitably be travelling in different classes. But already DB's old natural way was back and his plan for a solution was enough to roll back the years and dispel any remaining awkwardness.

"You grab a place in your queue, but keep an eye on me and I'll try to fix an upgrade. If I can't, too bad, but I'll have a go."

Whatever frequent flyer credentials were encoded on his ticket or his documentation, or whether he just used his long-polished location manager's charm, it worked like magic and soon he was flashing a discreet 'thumbs up' across the terminal. There were people behind him in the business class queue, so he signalled to Ray to stay in his own line. By the time Ray was at the desk, DB was hovering nearby to hear the check-in clerk welcoming him with the news of his good fortune. They'd walked together towards the security lane with an understandable lightness of step, although Ray couldn't forget that Major Charles McKee also had been pleased to get an upgrade at Heathrow.

–ooOoo–

"So." DB takes a sip from a large tomato juice. "What are you doing in LA?"

"Just catching up with a few people really. I'm only there a few days before I head down to New Zealand to see Gerald . . . "

"What, Logan?" DB interrupts with a sort of delighted chuckle.

"The same."

Gerald Logan was the director on the long series they did together. At that time he was just getting on the ladder, and he, like DB, had climbed it. Not all his films had been well received, either by the critics or at the box office, but he'd made up for that with some scorchers. And even the ones that didn't make it were well directed. Logan is an action director *par excellence* and he also brings the best out of actors. He is a great storyteller. The problem has been that he hasn't always had the best of stories to tell, or in some cases, studios haven't 'got behind' a film (as the jargon has it) with the promotion it deserved.

"Didn't I read that he's had an accident?"

"Horse. He was quite badly hurt and he's going to be few months out."

"He won't like that."

Ray nods in agreement. Gerald's energy is legendary. Sitting in a wheelchair and doing physiotherapy will drive him berserk.

"So you just visiting the patient? Long way to go," DB fishes.

"I've got a screenplay to show him. Catching him while he's a captive audience and can't get away. Not a chance anyone normally gets."

DB lets his eyes roam around the departure lounge for a beat before he comes back.

"About?"

There is a pause while Ray does exactly the same only more so, looking left and right before half-leaning forwards and almost mouthing the word rather than speaking it out loud.

"Lockerbie."

DB gives a long, slow, non-committal nod. People in the film industry do that a lot. Or they say 'Right' in a way that could mean anything from 'Interesting' to 'You've got to be joking'.

Screenplays are the lifeblood of film producers, and that is what DB Hollingsworth has had on his visa applications for many years now. Every producer is looking for the right script, around which he can build a package of directing and acting talent, a promising combination that will draw the money out of investors hoping for that elusive international blockbuster. There are not too many of that sort of script around, of course and they're hidden, needle and haystack-like in mountains of screenplays that don't have that potential. In London's Wardour Street, every other person is writing one, while in Los Angeles, bartenders supposedly have all got one in a plastic bag under the counter. Ray remembers, when Gerald was contracted to shoot commercials for a London production house, seeing a pile of feature scripts on the floor reaching the level of his desk top. There is no justice. Fine work can remain forever unread at the base of such piles, while less worthy writing can be selected and have time, money and blood lavished on it, but all the gloss and production value in the world will never disguise a poor script.

But if a film that gets everyone talking is the holy grail every producer craves, it's one that a big producer needs on a recurring basis. Once a reputation is won, there is intense pressure to repeat the alchemy, to find another mix of elements that will combine to give that elusive, unpredictable and unstable compound, audience appeal. It's easy to go back to being run-of-the-mill but no one wants to do it, once they've tasted the champagne of success. And DB has tasted as much champagne as anyone.

Ray guesses, rightly or wrongly, that DB has got three or four screenplays in his bag, just to go through on the flights out to LA and back. They'll have come pre-screened by a trusted reader, but even so it's unlikely that the man will actually himself read every word of all or perhaps any of them. All sorts of things can cause a producer, a director or a film executive to close the card covers and not reopen them – perhaps the subject matter doesn't resonate, the concept is flawed or not credible, or the writing is lumpy and awkward. Everyone knows that writing can be polished and improved, so dubious quality may not be terminal, but if the pages fail to carry the reader along, eager to know what's next, it's not going to get as far as a rewrite because its potential will remain unappreciated.

At this moment the coming journey takes on a second new dimension at the back of Ray's head. Not only is he going to spend the next twelve hours in far greater comfort than he ever expected; now he begins to nurse a hope that DB will, as a result of it, get to read and perhaps even like some of his script.

All this has taken a micro-second. He wants to see behind DB's mask, to know how the idea of a film on that topic goes down, but will he get a clue?

"Difficult subject."

Well, that's better than Gerald's reaction when Ray first mentioned the idea to him a couple of years ago. Gerald had said 'Isn't Lockerbie a bit old hat, really?' Difficult subject it is – that's perfectly realistic. But how old hat can Britain's biggest-ever mass murder be, when it's a subject that no one to date has tackled in a feature film? It's not as if there have already been two or three lacklustre versions doing the rounds. Anyway you couldn't get any more old hat than, say, Sherlock Holmes or Robin Hood but that doesn't stop endless reinventions; even some occasional good ones.

"Absolutely. That's why it's taken so long to find a format to tell the story, or the stories, I should say, because there are so many conflicting and intertwined possibilities in the exact method used by the bombers." Ray is instantly aware that he could have put that a great deal better. Fortunately DB gives him the chance to come back and offer a tidier explanation.

"So do you have an answer?. Do you know what happened?"

"We still don't know to the last detail, solely because those who do know – and there are plenty of them – continue not to say, for a variety of reasons. There are alternatives at every turn, but what we do know is that the version of events that was accepted at the trial and used to convict just one of the two Libyans accused – and acquitting one and not the other was a piece of lunacy all of its own – is one of the least likely of all the possibilities."

"Because?"

"Because overwhelming logic and at least as much evidence points to other scenarios, plus there are massive indications that certain parties able to influence the investigation wanted a particular result from the prosecution and did their damnedest to procure it by fair means or foul."

"So the story is about a deliberate cover-up."

"Yep, one of the most comprehensive there's been, with all sorts of levels from Presidential level downwards."

"President being . . .?"

"Reagan was still in office when it happened, but Bush, Senior, took office a month later. Within another two he had a late-night phone call with Margaret Thatcher, as a result of which the guilty party, a Palestinian faction linked to Iran and Syria, which had already been briefed to the press as responsible, was quietly removed from the frame and Gaddafi and Libya eventually moved into it."

"And they weren't anything to do with it?"

"No. I mean, the last thing I want to do is defend the Colonel. How did Reagan describe him in his characteristically statesmanlike prose, 'flaky and shaky'? He's an exploitative dictator and his regime is as odious as most of its type, but that's no reason for people to blame it for something it didn't do, just to suit someone's agenda. Libya had certainly given plenty of support to terrorist organisations, like the IRA, and had **previously** helped fund the group that perpetrated Lockerbie – that is true, but the fact is that

Gaddafi's importance and potential threat was always much exaggerated, not to say manufactured; even encouraged. That began in Ronnie's time with Al Haig and the usual military-industrial lobby, because to suit them, America always needs a bogey man or bogey country to justify the incredible level of defence spending and keep the tax dollars flowing their way. If there's no threat, they have to provide one, and Muammar Gaddafi filled the bill when there was a lull – he was antagonistic, he was eccentric, he was militarily-minded; and in real terms he was effectively harmless, he could be pushed round and even bombed with very little fear of any retaliation. He couldn't really have been more perfect for their purposes. It was mainly hype. Oh, and he had oil, which always interests America."

"And how about the people who you say really did it? You mentioned Iran and Syria. Why were they allowed off the hook?"

"Well, one, there was the question of Western hostages held in Lebanon by people close to Iran. If there had been moves against that country, then those people may never have come out alive. Secondly, America came to want re-established relations with the Syrians, because she was going to need their help to get at Saddam Hussein, a bigger fish offering an even more promising war; and third, there were vested interests in the US that didn't want some cats to come out of the bag – like how the explosives actually got on the plane, and who knew that they were on there, or might have been on there, and did nothing about it."

"Hold on. Are you saying that you think some people knew Lockerbie was going to happen? Does that mean they **let** it happen?" Clearly DB has not, in common with many people, heard any of this before, or perhaps he has but rejected it as CT, or maybe it's just become lost, forgotten like most of the tsunami of news that engulfs most of us every day.

"It seems an inescapable conclusion that a few Americans, some in the Middle East and Europe, and possibly one or a few in the States, knew it was going to occur but thought of it as collateral damage –the inevitable result of things that they had going and didn't want to upset. Whether these things were remotely in the interests of America or whether they had become corrupted is a big question, but put it this way: there are many, many more times reason to conclude that an American, for some reason, said effectively 'Let it go,' than there ever has been to connect any responsibility to the Libyan al-Megrahi."

"Holy shit!"

"Holy shit!" Ray agrees.

"I mean," Ray picks up the baton again, "there are so many unanswered questions and blank denials and dirty tricks that there's no way of getting everything in, but you just have to select some of the threads. For instance, a very early one: the aircraft was brought down at about three minutes after seven in the evening. But within a couple of hours, Lockerbie, which is not really near any very major town in England or Scotland was seeing the arrival of American, CIA, agents and by late evening an FBI man had set up shop."

"This is fascinating. I've got to find a gents. Be right back." DB jumps up and excuses himself, departing in search of something that for the duration of the next few days Ray will have to remember to refer to, against all his instincts, as 'the bathroom'.

—ooOoo—

18   Spooks Loose Aboot

Ray's mind drifts back to the start of it all, when he, like everyone else, thought that the downing of Flight 103 was just another terrorist event, if there can be such a thing. Of course it was a particularly awful one because of the high death toll, but no one thought at first that it was anything but a continuation of a series that had rumbled on for approaching twenty years. In the 70s and 80s people had become used to Irish terrorism and Palestinian terrorism and, if they thought about the matter at all, tended to put both in the same pigeon hole. Ray remembers telling Carl, his political neighbour:

"It's the same in both cases – you've got basically naïve and volatile people having their grievances inflamed by your lot; it turns into a campaign and there's plenty of volunteers to do the dirty work because it gives them a purpose in life – throwing stones or setting off bombs is much more attractive to some people than doing nothing or having a boring job, assuming there is one to have."

Looking back, Ray always feels acutely embarrassed at summing up the two of the world's major terrorist situations in seventy words, but at least pleased because not too many observers at the time would have acknowledged the existence of valid grievances. To many it was a question of black and white, good and bad, us against them. The universal 'them' at the time was the extreme left – Carl's 'lot', seen as being behind everything, supported by Soviet resources.

Carl and Ray had been friends from schooldays, and had for maybe thirty years now lived next door to each other, but ideologically they were streets apart. Carl had been brought up in a strongly Marxist household; Ray's father had been quietly and conventionally left, a Labour voter; no more. Ray had progressively developed a distaste for all party politics, but especially those of the extremes, so his exchanges of views with Carl became very interesting over time. While Carl was far from a champagne socialist, his property-owning country lifestyle was at such a great remove from the workers' struggle that Ray enjoyed debunking his extremism as hypocrisy; an accusation that his friend could never quite handle. But there were many issues, like human rights and oppression, where some of their opinions travelled parallel if not identical tracks, even if Carl had selective vision, tending to note the abuses committed by the West and its allies while overlooking those of his ideological homeland. Other points of common ground would occasionally come into focus.

Ray had observed in his father, a man who essentially disliked everybody who didn't come from the south of England, a particularly profound suspicion of the United States, which Ray hadn't really understood until relatively recent times. It was only then he realised why his childhood had been in fundamental ways blighted by the austerity following the Second World War. Throughout Ray's youth, America was clearly way ahead in standard of living, in income and opportunity, and even the defeated countries quite quickly rebuilt their infrastructure and their economies in a fashion that the UK was quite unable to match due to a dire financial position resulting from the global conflict. Her recovery was snail-paced. Although material wealth was not the be-all-and-end-all, certainly the horizons of his whole generation were narrowed to a considerable degree by the lack of money for education, sports and travel.

But there was more. Looking back, Ray realises something that escaped him at the time: numbers of his contemporaries had been undernourished in the womb or as small children, as a result of poor wartime and post-war austerity diet, and suffered from visible and hidden deformities as a result. When viewing photographs of his schoolmates years afterwards the effects of unsatisfactory early nutrition had become startlingly obvious.

To Carl, immersed in the doctrines underpinning Soviet Russia, America was an enemy, and although Ray did not then know enough of the necessary history, he was himself sufficiently conditioned by his father's attitudes not to embrace the USA with the uncritical enthusiasm that was officially encouraged to prevail. Often, therefore, Carl would find a not-totally unsympathetic sounding-board in Ray when he discovered a stick with which to beat the Yanks.

It was inevitable that when items started to appear implying there were questions to be answered over Lockerbie, and that some of these involved the behaviour of US government agencies, and secret ones at that, Carl would appear in Ray's kitchen, park his bottom on the rail of the Rayburn and flourish a photocopy of an article from some newspaper or other. But it was probably only in response to the 1995 showing of Allan Francovich's documentary *The Maltese Double Cross* on Channel 4 that things really moved up a gear.

Carl's pitch had gone along these lines:

"If a British aircraft crashed in America, is it conceivable that someone could walk into the police control centre off the street, announce that they were from Scotland Yard, and be allowed to set up a desk and observe and listen to everything that went on? Or that virtually before the dust had settled, a group of MI6 officers would have arrived from nowhere to start searching the bodies and moving and taking away evidence? Or that by the following day the streets of the town would see groups of British detectives in blue windcheaters and with chequered band POLICE-lettered baseball caps? If any of that had happened in the United States, everyone involved would have been rounded up, confined in the local police station and promptly deported. Everyone, from the police officers on the ground, to the President himself, would have said that this shouldn't be happening, and taken firm steps to prevent it, and would probably have been right to do so."

This last was a rare, but probably a tactical, concession from Carl. Normally he wouldn't recognise the Americans' right to do anything.

He was on a roll. Actions observed in the stunned town and the littered countryside amounted to illegal tampering with evidence, he'd said. They defied Scottish law and compromised any prosecutions and verdicts that might ensue – as well as usurping the jurisdiction of the police, a number of whom were so incensed by what was happening that they'd alerted journalists and even contacted at least one Member of Parliament.

Ray took all this on board. As always, a story of bullying could get his hackles rising but he was really engaged by what followed. He likes to rile Carl by tossing in inflammatory insults of the 'You're sometimes quite perceptive for a rabid communist' variety, but there is no denying that his neighbour's analysis is quite often seriously revealing. Ray isn't aware of any commentator having even asked the question that Carl raised next, let alone had it answered.

"OK. People have raised concerns, wanting to know what these goons were up to and how they contrived to get to a remote place so quickly. But the thing **I** want to know is, what were they doing in Britain in the first place? Why should there apparently be large groups of full-time CIA agents and FBI based in the UK? Do we have similar groups of MI6 and Special Branch detectives permanently on stand-by in the US awaiting something affecting British interests to occur? I doubt it, nor would we be allowed to, I suspect. And the supplementary to that is, who are these foreign spies and counter-intelligence people spying on and investigating in **our** country, as their day-job, when there isn't a Lockerbie to occupy their time? In theory they would be acting in the interests of the US, but who would be defining those interests and ensuring that the people targeted posed any threat to them?" Ray instantly took the point, but Carl wasn't finished.

"We know that as secret organisations grow better funded they get more independent and more difficult to control, and all the time the urge for empire-building pushes them to snare greater numbers of people in their surveillance net – to the point where they're watching ordinary members of the public on the most tenuous of pretexts."

"Well, you should know. Your friendly neighbourhood KGB led the world on that," jumped in Ray. "I agree that it's always going to mushroom, but a state must, I suppose, have the right to keep tabs on anyone who wants to overthrow it undemocratically, I mean, you for a start: if I was MI5, I'd want to know what you were up to, and my reasons wouldn't be all that tenuous." Carl, with his full portfolio of protest activities, including civil disobedience, could hardly do anything other than concede that one.

But Ray knew that his activist neighbour was right; that his argument had been proved regularly by our own authorities being found to keep files on a whole swathe of citizens of impeccable character and record. A coalition of people of very moderate opinions had been long forced to question whether our much-proclaimed 'free' society, which we are encouraged to celebrate, is actually very much less spy-ridden and watched than the Soviet system that we had been taught, not unreasonably, to despise. Carl was continuing:

"It's virtually inevitable that this targeting would in no way comply with the requirements of British law, so the standard response of our government would be to deny that it was occurring. The answer to what these spooks might be doing in the UK may have considerable implications for our national sovereignty."

This was too much. Ray had to challenge this.

"I can't believe you're talking about our national sovereignty. You've never cared a cow about our national sovereignty. I mean, I'm coming to the conclusion that we gave it away years ago, but I can't believe that you're seriously raising it as an issue. You would have flown the red flag over Buckingham Palace from the time you were sixteen. Or was all that about being an interesting political animal and you're really one of us at heart?

This sort of discussion had gone on for thirty years and with luck would go on for another thirty.

Carl had already done some degree of research on the Americanisation of Britain, as opportunities presented themselves, as a consequence of his general anti-establishment attitude. Back in those pre-internet days such information was not easy to come by. Few people were brave or tenacious enough to try peeling back the thick layers of secrecy, but what was exposed when they did was shocking beyond belief. Ray's father always said that Britain was 'treated like the 51st state' and yet he knew nothing of what people like Duncan Campbell would eventually unearth. No one had access to even the barest details for many years: they certainly didn't appear in the *Daily Herald* or on the *BBC Radio News*; the old man's sources. Snippets may have been published in the *Daily Worker* but nobody, apart from its tiny readership of Carls, saw or believed a word of what was written in that.

Ray is brought back to 2006 by an enormous bang, the reaction to which, by those seated around him, betrays the tension concealed below the nonchalant masks of today's travellers. A very large man, not old, but encumbered and unsighted or distracted by his hand luggage, has tripped after catching the edge of a table, twisted and fallen heavily. A few people cluster round and assist him. He proves to be uninjured and the false tranquillity returns.

It was undoubtedly his neighbour who had originally kindled Ray's interest in Flight 103, for which he remains grateful, and who helped keep the subject alive by wandering in with new nuggets of information. Ray never forgot the anomaly that Carl had picked up, although for a long time he failed to appreciate its full potential bearing on Lockerbie. It took several years of intermittent background reading, leaving and returning to the matter, before he had realised that the behaviour of the secret agents there had to cast into doubt everything we have ever been told about the case.

The odd thing was that the more he researched, the more he felt his feelings of cynicism and disbelief begin to outstrip anything ever expressed by Carl. Here was Ray, the moderate, gradually being forced, as he accumulated knowledge, to take a standpoint far more critical of authority and altogether more radical than any occupied by his ultra-left friend.

If there is one thing that has come to fire his anger, beyond the barbarity of the act itself and the boundless duplicity in the cover-up that followed, it is the image of the white helicopter. In the days after the crash, a mysterious unidentified machine intermittently prowled over the debris trails, warning-off and chasing people – including landowners and bona-fide searchers – away from certain areas. That might just have been understandable, except for one aspect, which was intolerable and symbolised an assumption that was now taking hold and would continue in respect of Lockerbie for years to come: an unidentified man sitting in the open doorway of the craft was holding a rifle to reinforce his yelled instructions. For Ray, with the carrying of that gun, without explanation or consent, Scotland had lost control of its affairs. This was the Wild West.

–ooOoo–

19   Background Action

Some good while later, Ray had tried his conclusions on Carl in the pub.

"The reason we're given for needing secret security services is to counter threat. The theory that these organisations live by – along too, incidentally, with the military and the police – is that the more money spent on guarding against threat, the more secure society becomes for its ordinary citizens. So it should follow that where the most is spent on intelligence, the real bad guys have the hardest time, because there are massive resources allocated, trying to nip their nasty activities in the bud. If this is true, then how is it that atrocities like Lockerbie get to happen?"

This conversation of course predated the Omagh bombing, New York's 9/11 and London's 7/7; all events in which it was later proved that security services were in possession of knowledge that should have forestalled them, yet despite all the expensive apparatus of state surveillance they still were allowed to go through to their awful conclusions. 'Were allowed to' is a simple construction of words implying passivity, a mistake – but in every case there has been enough doubt to lead a significant number of people to at least ask if 'allowed to' could have been in the active sense: 'permitted to occur'.

When he advanced this as a possibility in the Lockerbie instance, Ray was astonished to hear his friend the Marxist, the apologist for Stalin, the admirer of the system that developed what is always thought to be the most invasive and ruthless secret police apparatus ever known, make the statement that followed. It was as if the Lubiyanka prison and the Siberian Gulags had never existed.

"You're saying that people in official positions at some level take actions that threaten, in fact take, the lives of fellow citizens in cold blood?"

"I'm saying that it looks to be the case, but I'm also saying that it only seems surprising because we've been conditioned to thinking that we, in our advanced democracies, don't do that sort of thing – that it only goes on in banana republics and in those dinosaur communist states you love so much."

"Well, yes, you know me, I'm as ready to believe bad about the West as readily as anybody, but because our society is less locked down, I can't believe that anyone could expect to get away with it here – not in the long term."

"Well, I'll tell you what's happened – our lot have learnt from your lot, over the years, that if you brazen it out for long enough, deny something often enough, you can get away with anything. You know – like Kruschev, just say 'niet'. Because usually people forget; other things come along to occupy their attention and worry them and they just let things slip. It takes something really unusual to get them out protesting in the streets, and when they do it's often about something trivial, a sideshow, rather than a vital issue. There are so many injustices on every TV news bulletin and in every newspaper that no one has time to remember them all, let alone follow any of them up. What's that brilliant Richard Stilgoe song that goes 'Shock! Horror! Today's front page, tomorrow's on the bottom of a budgie's cage? Politicians, ministries, government agencies, they can all talk complete codswallop. If any journalist actually has the nous to point out the extent of the codswallop, they can be sure that, even if it gets printed, it will be old news tomorrow and be forgotten for good in a week – but their own stepping out of line possibly won't be. Unless the press, which means the newspaper owners, really have it in for someone and actually do take them on, like a dog with a bone, people are generally fireproof and they know it so they don't seem to give a toss."

Carl seemed to have taken the point, so Ray continued.

"Watch the news any night to see that in pursuit of power, the vaunted sanctity of human life is a regular casualty; that governments routinely sacrifice people in all sorts of ways to further their own aims. Having their armed forces fight unnecessary wars is a constant feature of history, and it's still happening as we speak. How many Americans died in Viet Nam – 58,000? They weren't killed by the North Vietnamese Army or the Viet Cong; they were killed by the decision that took them there. Ten million people died and twenty million were injured in the First World War essentially because the German Kaiser was a damaged individual who liked dressing up and playing soldiers. Those in control have always been more than ready to see people killed for the so-called greater good, and if the concept of greater good becomes subverted by narrow and factional, even personal considerations, they have all the motivation they need not to notice. And anyway, their populations are wont, spectacularly in the case of that war, with its pals' regiments and white feathers, to participate almost willingly in the deception and suffer its outcomes."

They'd digressed for a while into the causes of some better-known wars before the subject returned to the question of complicity in terrorist outrages. Ray had a question for Carl.

"When an atrocity takes place, is it good or bad for the security services?

"You'd expect it to be bad because it would point to their inefficiency, but you're going to tell me that it's to their advantage for some reason. They get more funding?"

"Exactly. What should look like a failing is actually made to work in their favour, because they can say that it happened because not enough was being spent, that their resources were insufficient and that they need more of everything. So their empire grows. Security services that are in control of threat, to the extent that no attacks occur, are in fact old news, and aren't going to get more resources and more money pushed their way. In a horrible irony, security authorities, or groups within them, need the occasional 'successful' outrage to convince everyone from public to government that they face a serious fight and need more weaponry. How often and at what level such attacks are permitted to succeed in the interests of some perverted notion of 'a greater good' is a question that has, at least, to be voiced. From 'leaving the back door unbolted' to full-scale false flag operations, security agencies, most notably the CIA, have been shown over and over again to have manipulated events in very devious and ruthless ways. I have to say that I now take a very askance look at every terrorist success in terms of: 'Is it really what it seems to be, or does someone just want us to think the obvious'." Ray would later encounter people who had formed such a view on Lockerbie. For now, it wasn't often that Carl could be reduced to silence, but Ray seemed to be managing it on this occasion.

"Because recently I've realised that your original point, way back when we first talked about this raises a very interesting supplementary. If those spooks and G-men weren't based in the UK in the normal way, but were brought in for a special reason, what reason was it? In theory their assignment could have been nothing to do with the specific attempt on Flight 103, because they were clearly in the UK before it happened, so speedy was their reaction time. So were they flown over in anticipation of an incident? Well, the official line – although that, like so much else, has been demonstrated to be quite false – is that there was no credible warning pointing to the likelihood of an attack on an American airliner flying out of Europe: now we know that there were several."

Ray had gone on to remind Carl about the Helsinki warning, the one that came to be circulated round the US community in Moscow. That alert's having been made public, if only to a limited degree, had to have contributed to the flight's departure from London with 159 empty seats, with only three days to go to Christmas Eve, when it should have been virtually full. There is an obvious inference to be drawn that a lot of people avoided it. At later dates, the two neighbours would discuss other warnings that were not shared with the public, including one in the possession of the US State Department, that also specifically mentioned Pan Am, but which was never communicated to the airline — and concealed for more than six years after the bombing.

Ray had continued with his analysis.

"So if the official determination was that the Helsinki warning was a hoax, that didn't prove no threat existed, given the other alerts in the system. Credible threats could reasonably justify secret agents and FBI operatives being drafted in, if they were. But why were they apparently on call and ready to travel to a remote part of the country with suspicious promptness? Astonishing as it may sound, was the downing of an airliner actually expected? Is that why the crash location was quickly crawling with 'investigators' when you would expect any spare personnel to have been deployed to ensure the flight's security **before** it took off from Heathrow, where in fact protection was laughable?. If a crew of spooks was brought to Europe in response to perceived danger, they don't appear to have done anything to counter it; just waited until it manifested itself. The flight was given no extra screening, unlike the preceding one at 11am. I mean, this was madness, when the route had specifically been threatened, yet security was virtually non-existent. If the Lockerbie horror was expected the question that inevitably follows is was it then allowed to happen? That process of thought in turn logically introduces the word 'facilitated' to the discussion."

"Hmm," Carl had said. "I still think the goons were here all the time, spying on the British public. I don't go along with the idea they were brought in specially. As to complicity, I tend to believe more in inefficiency. I would expect that Lockerbie happened because all the people in government departments, in intelligence, in the airlines, were just happily collecting their salaries for putting in the minimum of effort and thought, looking forward to their Christmas holidays and trusting that if something went wrong, someone else would get the blame." When later Ray's research became serious, he would discover that there was much to support his friend's assumption of laxity, but that would only have assisted any complicity, rather than ruling it out.

Flight 103 was not expected to fall on a Scottish town: that was excessively cruel fortune only compounding the tragedy. But for those who had a vested interest in the aircraft's demise the wreckage falling on land was almightily inconvenient. For their purposes the bomber did a less-than-perfect-job. The aircraft should have gone into the sea, beneath which any embarrassing items on board would have sunk forever, to evade questioning eyes. As it is, the nature of the items that the agents looked for so feverishly and removed so heavy-handedly must go a long way to explaining what Lockerbie was about.

–ooOoo–

Ray looks around, aware that DB's simple errand has taken a surprisingly long time. He can see no sign of the producer's lean figure amongst the passengers and staff criss-crossing the departure lounge, where the pair have settled, forgoing the business class facilities. He watches the complex patterns for a moment. Setting the background action, instructing the extras in what to do and when to do it, is an important part of the first assistant director's work. For years Ray has enjoyed watching the real choreography of the streets, parks, shops and transport terminals to see how people actually move and behave, with the aim of making his direction look believable. Unfortunately much of what can be observed in life can't be used on film because what the extras do mustn't distract the audience from the foreground action; their activity has to look natural but neutral, as well as work compositionally within the shot. One day, when Gerald and Ray were shooting two characters in a long dialogue scene in front of a location representing the Kremlin, Ray, bored with the time the setting-up and lighting were taking, for amusement staged the changing of the guard at the gate behind the actors. When Gerald saw a full rehearsal he snorted and repositioned the camera and actors fractionally, so that Ray's elaborate high-stepping ceremonial took place just off-screen.

Much later still, Ray had had another thought on the subject of the Lockerbie spooks. The function of secret agents is to gather information useful to the state by covert means, usually to provide forewarning of developments rather than investigating after the event, which is the job of detectives. In this light, one can then possibly allow some degree of legitimacy to the FBI agents who arrived in the town if they had worked in support of the obviously overstretched Dumfries and Galloway Constabulary, and had followed their direction and assisted within the requirements of Scottish law. Officially these early arrivals were to assist with the identification processes of the American victims. Legally the FBI could not be involved in an investigation until the occurrence had officially been determined a crime.

The CIA agents were a different matter. They didn't wear lettered baseball caps, just cream trench coats, apparently – that is, those who weren't pretending to be Pan Am engineers. Their being involved in and even controlling aspects of the investigation process was quite bizarre, especially given that they were observed to be acting in defiance of the precise Scottish rules of evidence-gathering. If they were not there doing police work – and they weren't – they were in attendance for another reason, and that had to be connected with their normal line of business. But since there was no incident to forestall, as the outrage had already taken place, their presence could only have been to prevent something else. And that had to be the escape of information. They were there to restrict understanding, rather than assist in the discovery of truth.

According to a Dumfries and Galloway police superintendent – whose home was in Lockerbie, not far from one of the main impact sites – agents of Mossad, the Israeli intelligence agency, also attended in the aftermath of the crime.

People think that the American Constitution enshrines the principle of 'America First'. It doesn't, but custom and practice over time mean that it might as well do so. Excessive emphasis on patriotism induces that mind-set, and national policy and attitudes certainly tune into that concept. Yet the history of both the CIA and indeed the FBI reveal plenty of instances (some would argue a total policy) where that perceived obligation has become blurred with the interests of first, the agency or the bureau, and second, the interests of individuals or groups within either of those organisations. One need do no more than whisper 'J Edgar Hoover' and research soon throws up other well-known names. And when entities are well-resourced and allowed to act covertly, even more so when they are given licence to operate outside the law and granted immunity, distanced from government by the practice of deniability, it's almost inevitable that abuses will occur. History shows that extreme powers are dangerous enough when deployed in a state's legitimate interests but can become utterly toxic when misapplied in areas that do not fall into that category.

Ray accepts that what is in the national interest can perhaps just occasionally be misinterpreted innocently through over-enthusiasm, but the misinterpretation is far more likely to be deliberate, which inevitably makes it, to some varying degree, corrupt. Action based on such skewed perception of the greater good can take place at the instigation of political leaders, or with their connivance, or can be completely unknown and unapproved by them. But there is a common factor in what follows, usually because top politicos, presidents or ministers, feel that they need the security services on their side to maintain their own political position and possibly even their own personal safety. So they help cover up, or look the other way. This places them firmly under the influence, even control, of their own security apparatus. If they weren't 'in the know', and already compromised anyway, they soon are because the moment they agree to one cover-up, they're trapped for good with their freedom of action limited. John Kennedy was a prime case of someone finding himself in such a position over Cuba and Castro. Ray is totally convinced that Thatcher's agreeing to the fake Lockerbie story has done as much for the office of British premier. Since 1988 the establishment from PM down has given barely one straight credible answer to a myriad of entirely reasonable questions. Even if the people 'in power' want to be open and honest, they are 'advised' not to be. The tail wags the dog.

He actually believes that politicians enjoy keeping secrets. Their belief in having justification to dissemble combined with having the power to do it becomes intoxicating. Being an insider, in the loop, is exciting in its own right: seductive, addictive. What gets Ray so fired up is the arrogance that the US and UK governments exhibit, not seeming to be the slightest embarrassed about their clumsy and obvious complicity in deception. They appear totally brazen and contemptuous as they ignore questions and trot out platitudes. It seems it is of no concern to them that people know they are lying as long as no one gets to discover why. It's all very Eastern Bloc.

Ray loves America, and has any number of American friends that he is very fond of. He has no quarrel with the vast percentage of the people of that great country, but that doesn't mean he won't object with his dying breath to the fact that **his** seems apparently subject to the dictates of American law and the US president, or more realistically the wishes and the agenda of those who undoubtedly control **him** – and he's not talking about the electorate. He suddenly remembers the fact that the very place in which he is sitting, Heathrow Airport, can, in common with what has at times been a list of more than 160 other installations in the UK considered vital to American interests, be occupied and fortified by their armed forces at the stroke of a president's pen. He had, until this moment forgotten Carl's discovery years ago of the existence of a presidential order which apparently can be invoked to assume 'legal' ownership of and clearly sovereignty over much of our once proud nation's infrastructure and territory in times of international tension – that's merely tension, not even war. He can't recall which of our great patriotic Prime Ministers buckled down to that one, assuming he was informed about it, which all evidence suggests he wouldn't have been.

His consideration of the question is ended by the return of DB from the lavatory, various shops and the duty-free, all of which fortunately appear to remain at present under nominal British control.

–ooOoo–

20   You Couldn't Make It Up

DB flops back into his seat. Right, thinks Ray. This is it. If he doesn't mention the script again and just makes small talk, then the idea hasn't grabbed him. Maybe the departure to the loo was a way of terminating the discussion. Ray determines not to broach the subject again until the producer does, or at least until there's a wide-open opportunity to do so. There won't be long to wait before finding out.

"So, if there are various theories, how are you going to deal with that? Have you just chosen the one you find most convincing, or do you present alternatives? Then that must get complicated?"

Ray has trouble suppressing a smile. It takes him a second to breathe and then he comes straight back.

"Exactly. That's why it's taken a very long time to come up with a format that works as a feature, but still allows the different versions. Another thing has been to decide how many of the sub-plots to include and to choose the most telling ones – there are stories of things that have happened to some people as a result of becoming involved in the investigation or in legal cases, whatever, that would make complete films in their own right: things that would make your hair curl. It's been very hard to select and to leave many of these out completely, but I've had to because there just wouldn't be screentime. And weaving any of the sub-plots around the main story without obscuring it has been a major headache. **And** where to start, because there are all sorts of options and even where to finish, because the story is far from over yet."

"It sounds really complicated – almost impossible to do."

"Well, I always thought Stone's *JFK* achieved miracles in getting a whole range of possibilities across as well as pointing up a lot of things that couldn't have happened, but I reckon this has been several times more of a challenge. Obviously, I don't know whether I've beaten it or not; that's for others to decide. But it hasn't been for want of trying."

"Is there a copy that I can look at, maybe, once we're on the plane? I'm very keen to see how you've managed it. It sounds really interesting."

Bingo! thinks Ray. 'Really interesting'. Compared to 'old hat', this is way up the scale! Just for a second, the idea crosses his mind that maybe he doesn't need to go and see Gerald after all.

—ooOoo—

On Wednesday 21st December 1988, Pan American Flight One-Zero-Three, Boeing 747-121 N739PA, ceased to be a single identified blip on controller Alan Topp's radar screen in Prestwick at 1902 hrs 50 seconds. It had been in the air for 39 minutes and 45 seconds and for about 7 minutes had been at its initial cruise level of Flight Level three-one-zero; that's 31,000 feet or approximately 6 miles high. Since starting work on this project and absorbing such details, Ray can never be on a commercial flight without checking his watch at around the 40-minute mark and saying a silent prayer for the flight he's on and for the souls of 103.

Today they've used the opposite runway direction at Heathrow, but beyond that, once clear of the London area, this flight has taken up a similar routeing, flying up the backbone of England. They, just like 103, must be using airway Upper Bravo Four or Upper Alpha One and will shortly themselves be transiting not far from overhead Lockerbie. The perfect weather over the south and west of England has given way to frontal conditions around Birmingham, and the flight attendants had to return to their seats for a few minutes, delaying the drinks service, but by Manchester they were above the cloud tops and both men have taken delivery of a welcome miniature of champagne. Ray hardly ever drinks at lunchtime; not since his very first day's work on a feature film, when his boss had whisked him into the pub, as was the custom then. Just one half of bitter coupled with the warmth of the afternoon had left him feeling slightly less than on top of his game for the rest of the day's shoot and he vowed never to drink while working again. It wasn't just in himself he'd noticed the effect; later in his early days as a first assistant he became very aware that the alertness and enthusiasm of some of the crew could be markedly different after lunch. He makes exception to his personal lunchtime rule only for weddings or other very special occasions, and today, meeting DB and the general feeling of optimism seem cause for a small celebration. Looking down now there are just a few holes in the cloud, but unless he spots Morecambe Bay, or some distinctive feature of the Lake District, or a piece of the Solway Firth coastline, Ray isn't going to be able to locate Lockerbie for DB, who anyway is on the inner seat and probably won't want to stretch across to peer uncomfortably downwards.

Ray breaks into their animated chat about the crew, the cast and the incidents of that job of 25 years ago. He has resorted to the elapsed timer on his watch.

"I was hoping to identify the town for you, but we can't see anything – there's too much cloud, but I know we're more or less over the spot." He lifts his glass. "So here's to all the victims, including of course, truth. May the truth come to be known, somehow. To the truth of Lockerbie." DB joins him in the toast.

"Perhaps it's appropriate to drink to your script, too," he says.

So, for the second time today, Ray unzips his computer bag and withdraws a pristine copy of the screenplay. They each place a hand on it and lift their glass in the other. DB looks at the title window.

"To *One-Zero-Three*," he says. "May it achieve everything you wish for it."

"To *One-Zero-Three*."

DB puts his glass down. He takes the book in both hands and opens it on his knee.

When Ray sits at the computer, he expects surprises. He types something at the top of a blank page and usually has no exact idea where inspiration will have led to by the time the page is full. But even he is astonished at the turn of events appearing on the blank page of this particular day. At 0410 this morning all it had on it was the briefest outline of a journey, like notes in a diary. Now, it's not even lunchtime and his script, the focus of his recent past, his present and he hopes, his future, has been opened with almost reverent ceremony at close to the exact co-ordinates in space that the crucial event that forms its subject actually took place. And the man opening it is one of the very few people in Europe, the world even, who could single-handedly turn the 109 pages of A4 paper into screen reality, if he wanted to. Was it Morecambe and Wise who used to say, 'You couldn't make it up'?

DB points to William Chasey's quotation on the title page.

"Who's he?"

That's two in a row. Ray will have to get used to this sort of déjà-vu. He explains briefly about Chasey, and how he wasn't even questioning the official line but was destroyed anyway, as a warning to others to keep away from the case. He mentions others, more involved in probing the cover-up, like Pan Am's lawyer, James Shaugnessy; Juval Aviv, the private investigator and some insiders who broke ranks when they suspected foul play, such as Lester Coleman and Joe Miano. He ends the summary with words he'd thought to use about four hours earlier to Tom, but hadn't got out. That often happens in conversation but it's rare to get another chance so quickly.

"The victims weren't just on the flight and in the town, and their loved ones, and those who had to see and deal with the horror. And in a wider sense, because of the cover-up, you could argue that we've all lost. We've all been bereaved."

DB's reply mirrors Tom's response to the revelations of reprisals:

"So, if all this has gone on, isn't it dangerous for anyone to get involved – like you – to be exposing it, as you are?"

"It could be. All I know is that in a society that's supposed to be open and free, the apparatus of the state should be used to hunt the guilty rather than shelter them, and that powerful people shouldn't re-write history for their own benefit and damage lives on a whim for their own ends. If it happens and we don't do something about it, it will only get worse, as indeed it has been doing for years. The more people who know about what goes on and question it, the less they can get away with it. They can't murder us all or ruin everybody, not yet at least. I take some comfort . . . it was the same over Kennedy – they killed him, they eliminated others who had been involved and some witnesses, but it didn't stop people like Mark Lane and Robert Groden writing books and Oliver Stone making his film, and he's still alive, so there's some hope of survival for inquirers into foul deeds. And despite all the high-level effort put into the cover-up, more and more people all the time are looking at the evidence and asking awkward questions."

For all that, Ray has been conducting the exchanges in an extremely low voice.

"You say 'they' almost as if 'they' are the same people?" DB notices.

"That's probably a conversation for another day."

–ooOoo–

Even though he's worked on a major space film, the genre is noticeably absent from Ray's list of favourite movies, and he can't remember ever watching one all the way through. There is however one thing that he loves about them and that's those spaceship shots where they thunder past camera, lights ablaze in the dark loneliness. He's chosen to start the film with some shots of that ilk, except that the spacecraft is a Pan Am 747, and it's not deep space but a dark night sky and some of those twinkling stars and galaxies are English towns like Stafford and Crewe, nearly six miles below. Every 500 mph pass of the aircraft is punctuated by a huge blast of engine sound. DB has turned to the first page and is already reading the next section aloud.

"'Opening Credits appear during a montage charting a relationship which develops in the course of a long-haul night flight. Involved are businessman, Daniel WEISS, 45-ish, British, a man who knows who he is, but with no set plan about where he's going, and TANYA Oaken, a Pan Am flight attendant, who doesn't do relationships with passengers and is absolutely astonished to find herself reacting to this one in a way she always thought impossible. Beginning with friendly asides and accidental eye contact on the first pass of the bar trolley, reinforced during the evening meal service and backed up with the issue of pillows and blankets, they start to talk during the long quiet hours when most passengers are asleep, and he goes to her servery to stretch his legs and get a glass of water. There is however no dialogue heard, but just the title music.' So these, I guess, are victims?"

"**She** is. He isn't — well, he is, but he doesn't die on 103."

"So this isn't it. I mean, there were no survivors; were there?"

"No. You're right. This isn't that flight. It's the year before. See, it says 1987, there."

"Got it. And are these real people?"

"They represent real people; Tanya obviously someone on the flight and he someone who's left devastated and wants to know why she died. There's no one real person who has sufficient involvement in different areas of the story that would allow them to fulfil his function in dramatic terms. I had to create him. I didn't want to invent anything, but I had to. I don't think any of the victims' survivors would anyway want to be portrayed to that extent. It would be too intrusive, even now. Weiss stands for all of them in a way, even though they've disagreed a lot."

"Really?"

"Inevitably I suppose, some latched on to the official line and the trial because it gave them what everyone now wants to call 'closure' and they cling on to that. Others remain deeply sceptical, not surprisingly as you're beginning to see."

"I like those shock aircraft cutaways."

"They sort of grab the attention, don't they? The idea is to emphasis the hostile environment out there, just like space. We couldn't exist the other side of that window, yet we're here in shirtsleeves."

"Shut up Scriver! You could make me nervous."

"We should be."

"What goes over all this – just music?"

"Yeah, a good strong title theme, but it's got to have a 'something nasty's going to happen edge, because as far as the audience is concerned, until they land this is 103 itself, and it's a real release of tension when they get down safely and everything is normal."

"Oh yes, here we are. We're on the ground. They've exchanged phone numbers and he's calling her in New York? Do you think you can get all this over in a title sequence?"

"Absolutely! You used to do commercials. I always argue that you can tell a life story in 30 seconds; Logan claims he could pretty well do *War and Peace* in three minutes."

"'Now a more romantic theme accompanies the later credits, as they get to know each other, become an item. We still go back to the 747 exteriors, but without the jet noise, to indicate that she's still flying, but it's routine, it's part of their life. He lives in London, she in New York but they meet in both places and anywhere else that the budget allows them to go.' That's very decent of you to consider the old producer. Most writers **I've** worked with recently haven't shown much interest in keeping down **my** budgets," DB laughs.

"So they're desperately in love and the future looks great – a good standard starting scenario. What's this? 'The title sequence approaches its end, cutting to the its final scene: Exterior Beautiful Bay – Isles of Scilly, England Brad's Yacht Magic Hour (3 Jul 1988). Weiss and Tanya relax on the deck of the yacht with friends Brad and Lisa as the sun goes down.'"

"That can be anywhere, as long as the sea's blue," Ray explains. "The Bahamas would be better than Brighton, but it's whatever fits in and we can afford."

"Who's this we?" DB jumps in. "Have you shown this to someone already?"

"No – figure of speech," Ray backtracks, thinking 'Twit, be careful!'

"I mean there's no way I can do this, even if I love it. I've got work backed up for two years. I need you to know that."

"Oh I understand absolutely. No, any thoughts, criticisms that you have will be . . . very welcome. It's very good of you to look at it."

"Well I'd rather read this than watch any of the movies, that's for sure. Have you seen what's on?" Ray admits that he hasn't looked. He doesn't say that he never watches movies on aeroplanes because the headsets and the sound drive him berserk.

"Don't bother, is my best advice." DB starts reading again. "'Brad moves to the bows and drops the anchor into the sea. In close-up the metal hits the water with a massive splash and the director's credit appears over. Dissolve through the rippling water to the straight grey bow of a different vessel which cuts sharply through blue waves. In an aerial shot, pan and track to find an American flag and the vessel's name, *Vincennes*. Pulling back reveals a battlecruiser steaming fast across rolling, sparkling waters. Fade up titling to read: *3rd July, 1988 – Straits of Hormuz – Persian Gulf.* Here we go then – Showtime!"

–ooOoo–

21   A Short Engagement

Ray will always believe that what DB reads in the these first few minutes is what hooks him. He notes that, unlike Tom earlier in the day, the thin, still-youthful-seeming producer doesn't turn straight to the crash, but works his way into the script from the first page. Perhaps it indicates a more serious and thorough approach, or just simply the fact that Tom didn't have several hours to while away. But first Ray has to explain something.

"There are several places that I could start; things that sowed the seeds for what happened to 103 or that are really wrapped up in the story, but I think this is the right one. What happened on this day was the trigger, even if the gun was already loaded, as it were. It certainly makes a powerful beginning."

"I recall something about the *USS Vincennes*, but I can't think what." DB flicks over a couple of pages, scans them and turns them back. "Oh yes, I remember now; you've got to have this!"

Screenplay pages, because of the conventional format used, have a sparse, fairly austere appearance. This is compounded in the text itself by an odd tendency of screenwriters in general to include minimal descriptions of both settings and characters. It's almost as if they vie with each other to convey the information using the least number of words. There is a well-known story, perhaps true, that the script for some early sailing-ship sea epic contained the minimalist stage direction 'The two fleets join and give battle.' One seven-word line there stands for what could well have filled several minutes of screentime, would have taken weeks, if not months, to shoot, and would have cost a small fortune.

There is nothing at all wrong with brevity and there are some sound practical reasons for keeping description short; heavy, cumbersome scripts are unpopular with everybody, because they're a nuisance to carry and use, they're expensive to produce and distribute and are more awkward to update. Updating is crucial: physically it's very fiddly and time-consuming. It's hard enough to make sure that cast and crew actually insert script revisions into their copies when there are a small number of new pages, but when there are reams of them, it can be overpowering. Many people on a unit will write notes on their script and certainly don't want to transfer their jottings to new pages and throw the old ones away any more than can be helped, especially not just for reasons of minor changes of dialogue. But if scripts don't get updated it leads to actors learning the wrong lines and all manner of problems when some members of the crew are using superseded versions. Ray worked on one movie where the formidable lead actress rewrote forthcoming sections of the script in her hotel room each night, leading to the issue of several pink pages affecting later scenes on almost every day of shooting.

It's clear that the fashion for abbreviated description transferred from the stage play, which traditionally is mainly dialogue with usually very little in the way of stage directions, of which Ray's favourite has long been 'Exit, running, chased by a bear'. This writer tends to kick slightly against the convention, certainly in his early drafts; firstly in the interest of conveying the atmosphere he hopes for in a scene, and secondly because he feels that a writer is possibly short-changing the director and actors if the settings and characters are too thinly fleshed-out. As DB, silent now, reads the first page of the sequence, Ray hopes he's got the balance right. Glass of champagne in his hand, he looks across at his words on the page:

```
INT USS VINCENNES-BRIDGE-STRAITS OF HORMUZ-DAY (3 JUL 1988)
```

The exact dialogue and technical commands and actions will be derived from the available transcripts and existing documentary material. Initially CAPTAIN WILLIAM C ROGERS III and his OFFICERS are seen on the bridge looking intently for radar targets off the Iranian coast. The concentration and tension are at high levels, but there is also a feeling of aggression in the air; a feeling that this is a ship looking for a fight. Not for nothing do other commanders in the fleet nickname it "RoboCruiser".

Cut to:

```
EXT BANDAR ABBAS AIRPORT - IRAN   DAY (3 JUL 1988)
```

An Iran Air Airbus 300 taxies from the terminal towards the holding point for departure. A caption identifies the location.

"Bandar Abbas Airport - Southern Iran"

Cut to:

```
INT IRAN AIR AIRBUS - PASSENGER CABIN   DAY
```

The aircraft is very full, mainly with poor Iranians going on pilgrimage to Mecca. They sit tightly-packed, too hot, with far too much hand luggage, including bulging woven plastic carrying baskets. Many, unused to flying, are praying vigorously, counting on their Misbaha beads. There are a large number of children, in excess of 20 per cent of the passengers, on the flight. Perhaps that "something nasty" music begins. Better, maybe, if it doesn't.

Cut to:

INT IRAN AIR AIRBUS - FLIGHTDECK DAY

A totally different atmosphere. Many degrees cooler, the
three crew are comfortable, relaxed, professional. This is a
routine short hop across the Gulf to Dubai. The FLIGHT
ENGINEER and the CO-PILOT read through the checklists as the
CAPTAIN taxies the aircraft.

These are not shots but scenes, and a scene can comprise just one shot or more likely a sequence of them. Screenwriters will only write shots in especially important places. In general, how to film a scene, in terms of the choice of shots, angles and sizes, is the preserve of the director, and some screenwriters give the director more steers than others, but they'll very often be ignored. With these four scenes, Ray has set up the situation on that warm day in the Straits of Hormuz, and it will be up to the director to visualise weaving a sequence of shots together to show that the men and women on the cruiser's bridge are destined to interact with the crew and passengers on the Airbus.

Everything about the departure of the Airbus is absolutely normal, and Ray uses the calm radio messages between the control tower at Bandar Abbas and the aircraft to portray this until the aircraft is climbing away. These exchanges may well be in Farsi, with subtitles; Ray still hasn't found out, but he's written them in English for now, not that he could do anything else. Meanwhile on the *Vincennes*, a radar trace has been spotted that may signify one of the 'hostile' Iranian gunboats that the cruiser has been harassing. Orders are given that see the impressive vessel turning sharply and speeding off on a new heading. Now we cut to the source of that radar blip. It is indeed an Iranian gunboat but it isn't being at all hostile. The crewmembers think they have shaken off the aggressive cruiser and are virtually dozing in the hot and humid day. Cutting between the two, the cruiser bears down on the tiny enemy until at last a sailor sees her coming through the haze and screams an alarm. As the *Vincennes* opens fire, the Iranian vessel turns tail and heads at full speed for the coast and what should be safety.

Somehow the gunboat, by tacking and jinking, avoids the scatter of ordnance emanating from the US ship and the chase continues. On the bridge the navigating officer warns the captain, 'One mile to Iranian waters.' Rogers orders no change of course, merely 'Continue engagement'.

Now a new element enters the story. It's another US ship, a frigate, the *USS Sides*, and a caption states that she is 20 miles away. She is cruising sedately, a picture of calm, which is confirmed by a totally different atmosphere on her bridge. Her captain, David Carlson, is alerted by his Electronic Warfare Officer to radar and radio traffic showing the *Vincennes* entering Iranian waters. While they discuss this far-from-uncharacteristic event, Carlson notices another radar blip. They don't know what it is; only that it appears to be heading straight for the aggressive cruiser. Cutting to the still-climbing Airbus tells the audience something that both US ships have yet to find out.

On the *Vincennes*, chasing the gunboat like a sheriff's posse is forgotten when the Anti-Air War Officer announces to the whole ship the presence of an unidentified aircraft that forms a potential threat, perhaps an Iranian warplane. Rogers makes tactical course changes for evasion and minimising target and orders his Radio Officer to attempt contact with the unidentified threat on Iranian military frequencies. The portent of the message is simple. Alter course away from our position, or we shall engage you with lethal force.

Hearing the messages from the *Vincennes*, the team on the *Sides* realise that the aircraft could be civilian and that the cruiser has not called on Civil Air Traffic frequencies. *Sides* immediately transmits a warning of danger on the International Distress frequency, which the airliner should be monitoring. There is no response. While the atmosphere on the cruiser's bridge becomes more and more tense and preparations continue to launch sea-to-air heat-seeking missiles, on the Airbus everything remains normal. As the scene shifts between aircraft and cruiser, on one visit to the cockpit, Ray has to specify a shot to tell the chilling story. While the Airbus crew chat relaxedly in Farsi, the camera moves in on the tuner heads, the indicators for the communications radios. As it grows ever closer to the one showing 121.50, the international distress frequency, its volume knob is turned down too low. Very faintly and distantly, the *Sides'* warning message is being repeated, but the Iranian crew is fated never to hear it.

In the *Vincennes'* Electronics Warfare Room, the Anti-Air Officer announces decision range. Ray reads his words again on the open page on DB's lap:

```
INT USS VINCENNES - ELECTRONICS WARFARE ROOM    DAY

The ANTI-AIR WARFARE OFFICER counts down the range of
the radar target.

                    A.A.W.O.

     Threat now approaching range six miles.  Two
     missiles have lock on target and await firing
     order.  Target now bears Zero-Zero-Seven, heading
```

One-Eight-Fife. Still unidentified. Elevation
Two-One degrees. Range six miles. Decision range.

INT USS VINCENNES - BRIDGE DAY

Without hesitation, ROGERS gives the order.

                    ROGERS

    Fire missiles! Hardastarboard! Countermeasures
    go!

Move into his eyes as his orders are repeated by others,
and repeated and repeated, ever more distant and slowed
down. Choral voices each singing one individual single
sustained note in disturbing dissonance fade up and
build, and continue throughout the next sequence, rather
like a piece by Henryk Górecki. Cut to:

EXT SEA - STRAITS OF HORMUZ (MODEL SHOT) DAY

Looking down on the Vincennes as the two missiles leave
the launchers and roar up and past camera. The voices
continue their notes in crescendo.

INT IRAN AIR AIRBUS - PASSENGER CABIN DAY

The flight continues, the passengers mercifully unaware
of events below. The vocal accompaniment continues to
grow louder.

EXT SEA - STRAITS OF HORMUZ (MODEL SHOT) DAY

Air-to-air of missiles streaking skyward. The voices
continue.

EXT SKY OVER STRAITS OF HORMUZ - (MODEL SEQUENCE) DAY

Air-to-air shot of the Airbus, still climbing, but this
is slow motion. The notes being sung sharpen a tone to
give a painful discordant chord as a missile inches
towads the nearer, starboard, engine, from head on and
below. At the second of impact the voices cease. There
is complete silence. The engine vaporises and the wing
folds back and tears away, leaving just an inboard
stump. The port engine is still giving thrust and the
wing producing lift, so the aircraft rolls to the right
and yaws in the same direction. The second missile
flashes harmlessly by. The nose of the Airbus drops and
still rolling to the right, it's soon tumbling over
itself, briefly travelling roof first before the
negative g rips off the elevators and much of the
tailplane, some left connected by wiring and so

flailing. The good engine, having gone through the
vertical downward and caused major loss of height, now
spins the wing and fuselage flat-inverted like an odd
helicopter blade for a few rotations anti-clockwise.
This proves too much for the rudder which breaks away in
two sections, while the fin deforms and the panels
exfoliate, pieces being flung outwards under the
centrifugal force of the rotation. After two rotations
some debris enters the surviving engine and it explodes,
causing damage but not collapse to the remaining wing.
The forward motion has almost gone following the
tumbling, and without the engine thrust to provide
rotation that too rapidly slows. Which means that
gravity takes over and that the predominant direction
becomes increasingly direct downward nose-first, 45
degrees from the vertical with the fuselage inverted.
With the acceleration seaward there is further
deformation and exfoliation of the fuselage, but broadly
speaking, what remains of the aircraft holds together
until it hurtles into the glassy sea, where the fuselage
forward of the wing roots folds under on impact. The
wing and aft section disappear in the giant splash. As
the surface of the sea restores it is already littered
with a hundred thousand pieces of pitiful debris.

290 human beings have gone from contented, expectant
life to a state of obscene flotsam in fewer than 15
seconds.

INT USS VINCENNES - ELECTRONICS WARFARE ROOM   DAY

The ANTI-AIR WARFARE OFFICER, sweating, looks into his
master screen. He breaks into a relieved grin.

                    A.A.W.O.(through ship's PA)

    Threat is down.   Confirm threat is now down.   We
    toasted it!

INT USS VINCENNES - BRIDGE   DAY

Pandemonium breaks out with ROGERS, OFFICERS and ratings
punching the air and whooping as if celebrating a football
goal.

DB closes the script and lets out a long breath.

"I feel I need another drink. How long before they found out?"

"Just a few minutes. It didn't stop them all getting the Combat Action
Ribbon and Rogers was decorated. George Bush senior, president-to-be,

went to the United Nations and told a pack of lies about the Iranian gunboat attacking a neutral vessel. We know what he said was invented because the other captain, Carlson, pieced all the evidence together. The *Vincennes* was in Iranian territorial waters and fired first.

"Then four years later Admiral Crowe, who had at the time been Chairman of the Joint Chiefs of Staff but by then retired from the Navy, confirmed it to the House Armed Services Committee. The chairman of that committee, Les Aspin, was keen to investigate, but shortly afterwards both Crowe and Aspin got plum new jobs in the Clinton administration and surprise, surprise, no inquiry ever took place. I call it 'promoting silence'. A lot of it goes on."

"And you're saying that episode began the whole Lockerbie thing?"

"There's no doubt about it."

–ooOoo–

22   That's Lunch Everybody

The producer catches the eye of a stewardess and top-ups are ordered. While they wait for them to come, he has a suggestion.

"Now listen. I'm sitting here saying 'What's this? What's that?' and you're giving me fascinating answers, which is great, but I'm probably posing darn fool questions that'll be answered further into the script and I'm never going to get through it. I suggest that I keep quiet now and just read it through as I would normally, and I can make notes and anything unresolved that I don't understand at the end, I can ask you about."

"Sounds good to me." agrees Ray.

Having David Hollingsworth read even a few pages is such a bonus, that if the man asks him to sing the script in the style of a Hebridean ballad or a Gilbert and Sullivan Operetta, Ray will comply readily. He looks out of the window for the first time for a while and observes that they are now out over the North Atlantic, having left the comfort of the Western Scottish coastline and islands.

It's slightly strange to think of the presence below of mountains and bogs and tiny fields as somehow secure, and being over the sea as more hazardous. Without the nearby existence of at least a mile and a half of strong, wide, straight, empty concrete or tarmac, the land has nothing to offer a large passenger airliner in the way of welcome. An emergency landing on the sea is exceptionally hazardous, but still preferable to alighting on almost any variety of UK landscape other than an airport.

Now he has the problem of how he is going to occupy the next couple of hours. He is so fired up, immersed in the screenplay and its labyrinthine plotlines that it's going to be practically impossible to concentrate on anything else. What did Kylie sing in that song that has made an old friend of his comfortable for life? 'I can't get you out of my head. Boy, it's more than I dare to think about.' Now he understands what the apparently contradictory lyric of Rob's hit was perhaps intended to mean. He can't escape being constantly aware of the subject but feels that if he doesn't focus on something else for an hour or two, his head will burst. He needs to give DB the impression that he's totally relaxed and enjoying the travel experience as he would on any old flight. He should read something or maybe try to jot some thoughts for his next project – play it cool. At least lunch is on the way to distract him, except that he has far from recovered from the Pinewood mega-breakfast and feels not one little bit hungry.

He's brought two books in his bag. If he hadn't been in the trolley race with DB he would have probably picked out another at the airport and now be deeply immersed in one of them, squashed into his seat in tourist class. What he's actually got is a Justin Cartwright novel, *Leading the Cheers* and *A Forest Beat*, a book rarely found for sale that he happened to come across recently second-hand at a car show. It tells the story of policing the Forest of Dean. He was planning to read it on one leg of his journeying, and note any references in it that might be usable in a TV series he's working up. Try as he might, he can't imagine for a moment that today he can settle down and be sufficiently distracted by the rigours of daily life in rural Victorian police stations. On any other day he would have found the harsh details fully absorbing. This morning, his thoughts are on law enforcement 127 years on from Sergeant Samuel Beard's bludgeoning to death by a gang of sheep rustlers; 93 on from another murder, that of Sergeant William Morris. For those early policemen even the most beautiful area, such as the one where he himself lives and thinks of as unusually safe, could be a sinister place – frequently the haunt of people equally as violent and venal as could be found in the cities and towns.

Nor will the Cartwright cut the mustard on this occasion. You have to read him slowly and concentrate on the elegant phrases and the flashes of insight that are expressed with such economy. Today even Cartwright's prose would struggle to hold at arm's length the demons of 103. There will be a strong temptation to look across to see which sequence DB's practised eye is scanning. A glimpse of any scene heading will engage the whirring mainframe that is the writer's memory bank, throwing up anxieties like those annoying messages that demand attention on the laptop.

'Error!   You have failed to explain this point satisfactorily.'

'Error!   The position this character takes is inconsistent.'

'Error!   This scene is total cobblers.'

–ooOoo–

It's obvious that film units come in all sizes. These days, lightweight electronics mean that a news crew has been pared down to just a journalist and a cameraperson while a major feature can number its personnel in the hundreds – as many people will have observed from the interminable credits on most modern films, where it almost seems that someone who once sharpened the director's pencil can get a name check. The complement varies according to the type of film and its budget. That too is clear. What is less well understood is that however many a unit comprises on any particular day, most of its number will be thinking about lunch.

The old adage that an army marches on its stomach is even more apposite to a film unit. Not that film units go in for much marching, especially these days. Out exercising the Ogre and himself, Ray recently came upon a period drama series being filmed in the next valley. When they broke for the midday meal, which was taking place no more than two minutes' walk from the set, every single person climbed into chauffeured cars and minibuses, a process that occupied far longer than taking a few beneficial steps.

To a film équipe, food and drink aren't just the raw fuels, the energy which enables its footsoldiers to plunge, or at least gravitate gently, back into action. Well-prepared food has long held an almost mystical place in the business of putting moving images on a screen. The first act of a young production assistant, on being promoted to trainee producer in a commercials production house, will be to go out and buy a copy of *The Good Food Guide*, always assuming that they don't have one already. However complex and intense the day's shoot might be, on an away location a small section of most members' consciousness will be reserved for contemplation of the where and what of the evening's fare. Within the shooting day on any set there are two repositories of the sacrament: the tempting refreshment table and the serving hatch of the mobile kitchen truck, a magic vehicle that is apparently able to issue far more food than it could ever physically contain.

The sustenance provided at these places of worship has other far-from-obvious functions. Film food is both a measure of time and an important palliative for boredom. The meals supply the punctuation marks for the shooting day. However much or little is being achieved on set or recorded on camera; however much or little individual members are being called upon to contribute to the output; the tea and biscuits, the breakfast or the morning rolls, the three-course lunch, the afternoon tea, the evening meal if one is needed, even the arrival of a fresh urn of coffee, are like the sounding of a town hall clock. They mark the passing of the shooting hours, chopping the long and for some the tedious day into manageable, bite-sized sections. From the assistant director's overly cheerful 'Good morning everyone' to the final, sometimes unbelievably welcome dismissal, 'It's a wrap!' the anticipation of the next intake of food is a spur for many and can seem to represent the entire focus of the day for some.

Any casual observer, member of the public or visitor seeing for the first time a film unit in action, or more likely inaction, will often have as their first questions: 'Why are there so many people and what do they all do?' and 'Why does it all seem so slow and why does nothing appear to be happening?' This latter sentiment will often be shared by many members of the crew, who may be unaware what's causing any particular wait. Because waiting there always is, even when things are going perfectly to plan. This is because lighting, the physical manoeuvring of cable, stands, reflectors and lamps is heavy work requiring great energy and strength and yet also great finesse. There are fast DPs and slow DPs, and electrical crews too can have variable work rates. Nevertheless to light a shot well will always take a certain minimum of time during which everyone except the DP, the electricians and the lighting stand-ins need to keep out of the way. Everyone else needs to be within call, but during this cooling-of-heels period between line-up and rehearsal, the catering area assumes a particular attraction.

Often only a couple of people on the set, one of which has to be the AD, may know exactly what job is delaying the progress to the next rehearsal or take. A good assistant will however make a point of keeping the cast and crew informed as to what's going on so that they are focused on at least the approach of a call to action. There's nothing worse than, say, after 'prepping' and lighting a set-up for half an hour, with all the cast sitting round on set, to be ready for a rehearsal only to find that someone needed for the scene has chosen this worst possible moment to slip off unseen to their dressing room or the loo.

Patrick, a friend of Ray's, tells a story rooted in working when young with Bette Davis. (The name was pronounced Betty, but a memo to the unit before shooting began forbade its use by all except those whom 'Miss Davis' personally invited.) He describes how the star was ultimately professional in her dealings with the assistant directors, always coming to set the moment she was called and religiously telling one of them any time she needed to leave the stage. Many years later the man was the first AD on an American mini-series in Europe, and one of the leads was the delightful Brooke Adams. In the settling-in period, he tried to convey his need to be told when artistes were departing the set for any reason and the actress slightly resisted this. One day she exclaimed: 'Gee, Patrick, do I have to tell you every time I go to the can?' Patrick was not normally one for the quick retort but adrenalin was clearly flowing that day for he came back, in a flash. 'Brooke, if Bette Davis could do it, you can do it.' Apparently, Miss Adams happily checked with the ADs for the rest of the shoot.

When your job is to try and avoid the waste of every single second, the fitting in of major hot meals like lunch or supper – which film caterers can manage to keep in tip-top condition for a surprising amount of time, but which don't stay perfect for hours – is a major task for the first assistant. If there is more time pressure than usual – say on location when weather is deteriorating – DPs and directors become desperate to achieve as much as possible before taking the meal break. You can lose the goodwill of an otherwise amiable director by insisting that lunch be taken. The no-man's-land between director and crew can be a perilous place to occupy.

When Ray first worked on features and TV series, there was rarely a decision to make. Working hours and the time of lunch were as rigid as in any factory: only the morning rolls and afternoon tea were flexible. On a big scene with many extras, having those served without excessive loss of time was an artform, but 'the trolley' has always been a trigger to set more volatile directors fuming. In the old days film technicians worked almost the same civilised hours as the general population and they could have a normal home life. The coming of TV commercials changed all that, with the process completed by Mrs Thatcher's anti-union legislation. That condemned film-industry working practice to revert to the standards of Victorian mills, mines and machine shops. Now if they want to work on a feature film, technicians often have to sign a secret contract, agreeing to ignore any small inconveniences like the European Working Time Directive. While most people in the country work a basic week of 36 to 40 hours, film personnel will generally work 66. Many of the 'In Memory of' dedications on movie credits refer to crewmembers who fall asleep while driving home.

–ooOoo–

Ray is in a sunny Herefordshire orchard. The cast and crew are napping after their lunch, a banquet on trestle tables, which is now being attacked by birds and giant insects. Unable to find his second assistant or his Motorola, he is trying to get people back on set. But they don't want to get up. Any of them.

"Where's Sue?" he asks a soundman.

"Over there!" The man languidly points through the trees. Ray sets off but can make little progress and keeps finding precipitous ravines to descend and cliffs that he has to climb with his fingernails, agonisingly slowly with time slipping away. If only he had his radio, he could call Melvin. They will all be back on set by now and wondering where he is and why the actress for the scene isn't ready. Where is she? Simon said she was this way. He drops down onto a railway track and fortunately a train is coming. It stops and Ray climbs up into the driver's cab. One of his old bosses, Roger, is in there giving the driver instructions for a shot. Roger is in charge. Ray doesn't need to worry any more. He goes through a door at the back of the cab and sits down. Except that this railway carriage is half-train, half-aircraft and his actress is dressed as an air stewardess and serves him another lunch, but he cannot, for the life of him, tear off the foil and cellophane coverings and get to any of his food . . .

"Mr Scriver. . . . . Mr Scriver!" A female voice with a pleasant southern hemisphere twang is saying his name. He opens his eyes. The dark-haired flight attendant called Lorna is touching his arm.

"Sorry, sir, but Mr Hollingsworth said it would be all right to wake you up. He said you wouldn't want to miss lunch."

"Mr Hollingsworth knows me very well. Thank you." He looks at DB who is smiling broadly.

"You're obviously not as used to early mornings as you were."

"Do you know, I've cat-napped at lunchtime for years working – ten or fifteen minutes after eating before going back. It can be surprisingly restorative. If I watched rushes I'd have to take my assistant with me to nudge me if I nodded-off and snored."

DB laughs.

'Mr Hollingsworth knows me very well.' They both know that's not true; how could it be after 20 years? It's just the sort of thing you say to a third party when you're feeling confident. Did they really ever know each other that well? Maybe – maybe not, but it's not something Ray intends to spend too much time worrying about. Carpe Diem! Onwards and upwards!

–ooOoo–

23   Eating Up the Miles

Ray is not a great one for talking while eating. A naturally slow consumer of food, he takes even longer if conversation intervenes in what to him is the serious business of appreciating and enjoying tasty fare. At dinner parties he's very happy to join in, declaim and even be sometimes slightly entertaining between courses, but when there is grub on a plate he prefers to listen and his neighbours at table aren't going to get too much out of him. He can't abide working breakfasts and business lunches; they give him indigestion and he used really to resent the fact that his second assistants would inevitably have to take advantage of the lunch break to get decisions from him on the call sheet – the programme for the following day's work.

He remembers being in Los Angeles for a few days after location-scouting in New Zealand for Gerald. One evening they went to a superb Japanese restaurant with an LA friend of the director's, one clearly as movie-obsessed as Gerald himself, if such a thing is possible. A near-banquet of food was ordered and when it arrived the conversation abated not for a second. 'Is this or that new release worth seeing?' 'Who's rumoured in-line to direct what upcoming project?' 'Did you hear that so-and-so was fired from this series or that movie?' Had the friend seen the new Steve Martin picture? Ray was party to little or none of this relentless Hollywood insider chat and was quite happy not to have to contribute, nor did he care that Gerald's friend addressed not one single question to him during the whole meal. He happily listened, savouring the excellent cuisine, attempting to try a good selection of the numerous dishes. He didn't get very far. The talking pair managed to eat almost subliminally, seeming completely unaware of the feast they were ploughing through, while exchanging their industry updates at an equally fast rate.

Soon they had eaten sufficiently and seemed to notice Ray almost for the first time since they had sat down, but only as a mild obstruction to the relentless rush of Los Angeles existence. He would have been quite happy to sample the remaining array of food, enough for at least another couple of people, and could have chomped away for maybe another ten minutes. But their body language indicated an impatience to progress to coffee, so Ray ruefully had to watch dishes of exciting untried specialities being cleared away by the waiters. They were in and out of the restaurant in not much more than 40 minutes. Today though, if DB wants to talk Lockerbie while they deal with their airline trays, Ray is going to be very happy to put his preferences to one side.

DB does.

"In general terms, how accurate is the script? I mean everything that I've read so far seems to be fairly precise about who did what. I know you said there are alternative possibilities, and things that haven't been admitted so can't be proved at the moment, but what I've seen up to this point shows no sign of that sort of uncertainty." He was clearly reading very carefully.

"You're absolutely right, but if you notice, there is some ambiguity in the way I've suggested the odd few scenes be shot, people in darkened rooms and so on. They don't always seem to be ambiguous when you read them because the characters are named —obviously they have to be in the screenplay context, so everybody knows which actor is involved in a scene – but the audience won't always necessarily recognise exactly who is doing what. I'm not talking about doing this a lot; just here and there, where there's no alternative. Later on, when the Daniel Weiss character starts trying to unravel the unknowns, the alternative theories are voiced. Some of these early scenes you'll see revisited, with Weiss or someone else asking, was this person A or B, or did this happen in this way or differently?"

Ray pauses, eyeing his meal, torn between tasting one of the minuscule roast potatoes and making another crucial point. He briefly wonders whether these tiny vegetables are grown on special miniature farms by pint-sized farmers. The need to state the point prevails.

"The aim has been very firmly not to make anything up. I mean, obviously any writing about an historical event, whether presented as a factual documentary or as a piece of pure drama, automatically contains invention; nobody knows what Elizabeth I and the Earl of Leicester actually really said or did to each other, so every writer who tackles the subject has to speculate on how their moments alone together would have gone. The important thing is to make it as faithful as it can be. It doesn't always happen. You know; we've had series that have presented Henry VIII in the style of *East Enders*! But in this case, I think it's particularly vital to build everything scrupulously on the known facts."

"But sometimes those are going to be very thin on the ground," DB advances.

"Absolutely! I mean, it's very ironic: there are people – probably quite a few of them – who could clear up all the uncertainty at any time by telling the world what happened. It's only because they won't that people are forced to evaluate different possibilities and theorise. Officialdom then takes a high moral tone about invention and speculation, conveniently ignoring that it's official addiction to unjustifiable secrecy that makes them necessary."

Ray applies himself to the duck breast, in the hope that he has covered all the bases for the time being. DB, he is gratified to note, falls silent for a decent interval.

The food is quite acceptable; the portions adequate, and he again for a moment considers, as he often does, the incongruity of being served a four-course meal six miles above the North Atlantic Ocean, in a thin-skinned aluminium tube moving at 500 miles per hour.

–ooOoo–

Ray looks in disbelief at the vast omelette, so large that with its salad garnish it obliterates all evidence of the shape and the margins of the plate that it buries. Eating on an airliner, as he feels he's been doing for some days, is not unlike undertaking keyhole surgery. Getting to grips with this real-world dish, on the other hand, poses a genuine physical challenge. 'A light meal,' he'd asked for. Fat chance of that in the old US of A. He doesn't really need dinner anyway; he's lost track of how many times he's eaten today; let alone how many hours he's actually been awake. He'd planned to go straight to his hotel and lock his bedroom door with a 'Do Not Disturb' sign outside, but DB clearly wanted to prolong the day as if to cement their rekindled friendship. The limo had dropped Ray off at the Belair Sands with the producer insisting that he'd return in an hour and a quarter and that they'd catch a quick bite.

Now he's here in a restaurant on Melrose with a thick Greenland Ice Cap shape of eggs that he hardly dares look at; much less start quarrying. As if the prospect of chewing his way through an entire Danish Crown Dependency is not daunting enough, he still needs to stay alert – to maintain the image of a switched-on, happening screenwriter for DB's benefit. Ray fears that the very choice of vocabulary summoned by his tired brain to define his assumed status probably means that he is impossibly far removed from being switched on and happening – or deserving of any of the more modern expressions implying the same, which he can't think of right now. But he mustn't show any sign of that uncertainty to his friend.

Worse, it being Los Angeles, he and DB are not dining alone. There should, oh horror, have been two of his host's acquaintances joining them at the too-small table. In the event one has cried off through some minor domestic crisis, which probably means he had a better offer. Ray can't decide whether one or two extra diners would have suited him better. As it is, the one who has arrived, Hal (who's some sort of studio executive) and DB can trade news and gossip with only occasional token polite attempts to include Ray in the conversation. Had the other one – who Ray thinks is called Ned but who might be Red or Ed – had he turned up, either of them might just have wanted to engage Ray in a one-to-one exchange, which would have been the last straw. Alternatively Red/Ned/Ed might have joined in the *Variety* news review with the other two and let Ray concentrate on the egg-mountain.

There is more than a little touch of déjà-vu about tonight. It has echoes of that long-ago Japanese meal with Gerald and friend, with the extra ingredient of fatigue thrown in. However, there does exist one great antidote to tiredness, however extreme in form, and that's being asked about yourself, even if you don't expect it.

"Ray's over with a screenplay."

This is not something that he particularly wanted to have publicly discussed; certainly not tonight anyway. He likes to acclimatise and do one thing at a time. Too late.

"Oh, yeah," says Hal, making a reasonable impression of interest, at a circumstance he clearly encounters several times a day.

"I read it on the way across. It's very good." Ray watches Hal making a U-turn from more-or-less dismissal to desperate need-to-know. It's remarkable how the three-word opinion of someone like DB can bring about such a shift.

"What's it about?" Hal stabs at Ray, turning **his** three words into one.

"It's political. Can't really say too much as it's sensitive. Quite a hot subject." Ray chooses his words as carefully as a man who's been awake for nearly twice around the clock can manage.

"Can't you give us a clue?" Six into two this time! Hal is now virtually drooling with enthusiasm.

"I'm afraid not, really. If I say more you'd probably guess and I'd have to kill you." Ray notices that the thin joke, which generally goes down quite well at home, passes straight over Hal's head. Not a glimmer. Hal turns to DB.

"You gonna do it?"

"I might," he replies.

Ray is instantly wide awake, but has to become so without showing any external evidence of a massive change of awareness. He doesn't recall ever having had to suppress so much excitement before. After all, DB is a friend and a sensitive being. There is no way he would say what he has just said, if he wasn't at least considering the idea of taking on *One-Zero-Three*. Surely he would never raise such a possibility just as banter to get a reaction from Hal, who doesn't seem to be a particularly close friend, but just one of the Hollywood faces, and a fairly bland one at that. Ray adopts what he hopes is a relaxed, matter-of-fact smile as DB continues.

"There's a lot going for it. I really like it. I just don't know how I could fit it in." Well, there's his get-out clause, Ray thinks. He stated earlier that he's got work lined up for two years. His brain is now spinning. What is DB actually saying?

"Ray's heading down to New Zealand in a few days, but I hope we can get together before he goes, to see if maybe we can think about working something out." DB flashes Ray a really warm smile, as if to close the matter for tonight.

"What'ya doin' down there?" Hal rattles out.

"Visiting friends, holiday mainly, bit of a break, few meetings but really social."

"You know Gerald Logan? You know Logan, don't ya D? He's down there in the hospital." Ray, in passing, wonders if Hal really thinks that there's just one hospital in New Zealand, which truly proves how tired he is. Astonishing that this guy should pluck Gerald's name out of the air.

"Yeah, DB and I worked with him way back. I'll be seeing him while I'm there."

"He gonna do your picture?"

'Shit,' thinks Ray. 'The way this guy's firing questions it'll all be in *The Hollywood Reporter* tomorrow: "Logan to shoot Lockerbie Exposé".'

"I doubt it," Ray says with truth. "I don't think it's his subject." Even as he says it, all his instincts are screaming, 'but it bloody well should be'.

"Why'sat?"

126

"Gerald likes a bit more action, I think."

"So what'ya got? A psychological drama?"

"Not quite. Just not the rip-roaring stunt-fest that Gerald excels at. It's a bit more . . ."

"I think you should let Ray off the hook for tonight." DB comes to the rescue, finally. "It was wrong of me to have mentioned it. Relax mate. Eat your supper. – Hal, have you seen the new Steve Martin picture?"

–ooOoo–

Perversely, after the near agony of staying awake through the meal and the blur of the ride back along the winding western extension of Sunset Boulevard in DB's Cadillac, Ray can't sleep. The last twenty-four hours have been astonishing by any standards and there are sections of the day that he needs to go over to check if they really happened.

During the remainder of the ritual of the airline lunch they had made no more reference to the script, confining themselves to reminiscences of long-passed days and of mutual colleagues and friends, a disturbing number of whom had wrapped for the final time. After the meal, DB had been encouragingly ready to return to his reading, leaving Ray back in excited limbo. To avoid looking as if he was wasting time, he'd taken out a reporter's pad and pen and pretended to be making some notes, punctuated by long spells of staring out of the window, something that he enjoys anyway, although there's only so much inspection of the grey, empty North Atlantic that a man can take. Eventually one return to the window revealed the coast of Greenland and Ray's eyes scanned it for signs of settlement, little realising that he'd be eating it later in the day.

Already he's forgotten just how he managed to pass those couple of hours, for the flight was well into Canadian airspace before DB finally closed the coloured covers. He had read very slowly and carefully, stopping and putting his head back and closing his eyes tightly at times, seemingly to indulge in the images conjured by the words on the page. Ray had stopped trying to follow the producer's progress; it was almost impossible anyway without obvious neck-craning, so he could only guess at those scenes that had caused his old friend to take time out for reflection. He hoped this was a good sign; indeed, that his interpretation was correct and that DB wasn't taking his breaks through boredom, or to think of ways to tell him gently that he hated the script. He need not have fretted.

"I think it's remarkable," DB said, probably somewhere over Baffin

127

Island, replying to Ray's unspoken question. "I feel shattered just reading it. It's such a powerful story. I had no idea about – well, any of it really. You remember a few basics, but until someone puts everything together as you've done, you're completely in the dark, you don't really know anything." He paused.

"The way they like it," said Ray, to fill the gap. DB nodded sadly.

"Obviously there's a film there and a damn good one, but whether it's viable, whether it would cover its costs or turn a profit, that's the eternal question."

"Bums on seats."

"Bums on seats," DB repeated. "I think they'd come in, but the man who can predict for sure isn't born."

"I thought you were that man."

"I've been very lucky. Look, I'd like to think about this some more, quietly, and maybe talk to a few people; get one or two other opinions from people I trust. Would that be OK with you?"

"I'd be delighted, David – really grateful for any advice."

"Can I hang on to this?" He had gestured to the now not quite so pristine booklet.

"Of course."

It had been as short and as sweet as that. The positivity had been elating but the brevity of the exchange had been somewhat anti-climactic. Ray had been bracing himself for hours of further discussion and questions; of justifying the inclusion of scenes and matters of structure and characterisation. Now, somewhat surprisingly, DB seemed content to shut the play and go off to consider it in isolation. Ray had no option but to comply and the episode was neatly punctuated by the serving of afternoon tea.

'High tea', Ray was inspired to call it in his state of mild euphoria, and Lorna the flight attendant laughed good-naturedly, as though she hadn't heard that one a thousand times.

For a moment Ray had found himself in a Hugh Grant movie.

–ooOoo–

In his hotel bed, Ray takes a reality check. How could he have felt disappointed when David Hollingsworth had been complimentary about his work and offered to take it away and discuss it with other players? 'Get real, Raymond!' And that was before the producer's even more exciting expression of interest over dinner. Thank goodness he went to the meal, against all his inclinations, or he wouldn't have heard that.

"Go to sleep for goodness' sake!" He actually says it out loud.

He can't. He continues to go over the events of the day.

DB had said that he needed to read something else before arrival at LAX, so once again Ray was left to his own devices in a strange unreality; a somewhat different one from his situation earlier, but just as disorientating in its own way. He had pulled out the book on the Gloucestershire Constabulary and tried to read some of it, dividing his time between the exploits of Superintendent Edward Chipp and the cabin window. Chipp, posted to take charge of the Forest of Dean in 1871, found it in 'a most lawless state' and his attempts to restore the Queen's peace and the rule of law were not welcomed, with his life being threatened on several occasions. He only survived a professional assassination attempt, targeted on his solo night patrols in his pony and trap, by changing his routine and going quietly on foot, using lonely forest paths, one passing the site of Sgt Beard's murder ten years earlier. What bravery! Ray looked down at other forests below him – the jurisdiction of the RCMP – the Mounties. How courageous they too had been, usually one single lawman alone in thousands of square miles with no real means of summoning assistance, open to attack from wrongdoers, disgruntled natives and wild animals. That combination made even the violent 19th century Forest of Dean seem relatively benign.

As the flight traversed Canada, he noted, as he always did on this route, how the seemingly endless and empty wilderness became progressively marked with more and more evidence of mankind's influence. Now and then there would be a wide spear-straight line, cleared through the forest as far as the eye could see. From this height it was virtually impossible to see whether it was for pylons or a pipeline. The very occasional dirt roads could have been railways – or vice versa. But he knew that soon, maybe in the next couple of hundred miles, tracks would be seen winding up to every summit and penetrating the heart of each forest and following all but the wildest and most rugged of the river valleys. They are testimony to the unstoppable power of the caterpillar bulldozer, the giant road-grader and the tipper truck, but Ray always wonders what all these accesses, apparently hundreds of miles from any settlement, are actually for. Why is it necessary to inflict these disfiguring scars on the face of the earth? Why do countries – these two, Canada and the US in particular, followed blindly by most others – treat land and the sublime beauty of the untouched earth as if they were infinite and inexhaustible? Is there a mindset derived from the early days of settlement when a limitless paradise seemed there for the taking? Did that enter the collective psyche as a belief that however much land is consumed by the mediocre or plain ugly, there will always be plenty more? Could it also be true that because the heavenly, abundant landscape was wrested by force from its established owners, North Americans have become conditioned to feel entitled to take control of the rest of the world – and even of space?

The mindset is not entirely transatlantic. He can't remember who it was remarked that seventy years ago, the British countryside was almost entirely beautiful, but now there remain merely beauty spots. Ray thinks even these showplaces are threatened and dwindling in number, blaming government as the arch-vandal with industry as the second accused. The third culprit is the ordinary populus. There is little doubt that when most of the landscape was owned by the grand estates of the aristocracy, it was largely kept immaculately. It's an uncomfortable truth for an egalitarian to accept, but the more land is subdivided, parcelled up and passed into the hands of everyday citizens, an ever-growing proportion comes under the control of individuals with no respect for its treatment and appearance. This sadly seems to include many of today's farmers. They will blame the untidy, even squalid, state of their holdings on the poor economics of present-day agriculture, but as Ray has challenged one or two of his acquaintance, how much can it cost to pick up escaped plastic sacks, string or sheeting, unwanted wire or redundant fence posts?

People react automatically to beauty and are equally unconsciously diminished by exposure to ugliness. Ray remembers something a South African friend heard Archbishop Desmond Tutu say: 'What we inflict on the earth, we are actually doing to ourselves, which means that with every day that passes, we're committing suicide.'

–ooOoo–

24   Crossing That Fine Line

If there's one thing Ray dislikes it's a queue. When he was growing up, the English queued for everything. In the war, before he was born, it had been a necessity and then in the early post-war austerity it became an ingrained way of life. He saw the same in Russia, on a visit many years later. But he could never become reconciled to the sheer waste of time. If there's something worse than a queue, it's an unnecessary queue, and if there's something worse than that, it's one you suspect is intentionally created. There, someone is sending the unfortunate queuers a message: 'We could deal with you more quickly, but we won't, because we want you to know that we are in control and can do what we please.' Immigration lines in all-too-many countries provide evidence of this phenomenon. So often the channels for domestic passport holders are well-staffed and deal speedily with returning residents while, mysteriously, foreign nationals face closed desks and interminable waits in a minimal number of open lines. There is always a feeling that to dare to complain about staff sitting idle, watching while one or two colleagues deal with the best part of an entire Jumbo-load of passengers, would be to invite even more delay, or perhaps worse. It's odd that governments spend millions promoting tourism, assuring would-be visitors of a warm welcome and pleasant experiences, while at the same time funding departments who seem to view their function as ensuring that those visitors' moment of arrival is the very antithesis of welcoming.

Of course no one wants people to be allowed into their own country without being carefully checked, but this can be done in advance on application for visas. If the checking at the port of entry is so important, then why are those entrusted with doing it placed under the pressure of dealing with long lines of impatient travellers? The irony is that when you've actually gained admission to many a country, the people you tend to meet first, hanging round the arrivals hall with all sorts of spurious offers, are the very types that any sensible society would do well to exclude.

Ray is well aware of the sound practical reason for subjecting immigration queues to extended delay. Arrivals areas are closely surveilled by cameras and one-way windows. Passengers' behaviour is closely monitored for signs of nervousness, which may indicate that they have something, like contraband or counterfeit identity, to worry about. The give-away signs are easier to spot when the targets are slowed down or stopped; the body-language of a waiting individual reveals far more than that of one in motion. Also, the longer the delay, the more a suspect person is likely to become tense and unknowingly draw the watching experts' attention. The practice

131

inevitably nets plenty of people who aren't smuggling or wanted, but are simply nervous about missing an onward connection, being late for a meeting, or just worried that their bags are being stolen from the luggage carrousel; but the authorities (several different agencies may be watching) find that slowing down the immigration line can pay dividends in identifying those who might be worth questioning or a search.

Ray seethed inwardly, pondering these questions at Los Angeles International, as he made painfully slow progress towards the red line on the floor and the head of his queue, which was inevitably moving more haltingly than all the alternatives he could have joined. DB had tagged onto the next-door file and disappeared through to the baggage hall some ten minutes earlier. Ray always at this point wonders what you have to do to get onto the watch-list, into the computer that used to be a massive black book, containing names of all those who, for various reasons, the Land of the Free declines to welcome to its bosom. What are their crimes, all those people, and how do they differ from many of the citizens who are happily living there, holding US passports? It isn't as if there are no undesirables, individuals of every shade of badness, comfortably resident already in the States. Everyone has seen gangster movies; it isn't exactly a secret. How much worse are these thousands they are determined to keep out? There couldn't possibly be in the entire world as many people with the potential of posing a serious threat to US security as appeared in those thick black books of old, let alone in today's expanded electronic version.

He has always assumed that the bulk of the entries relate to people who are suspected of being opposed in some way, perhaps very minor, to aspects of the American way of doing things. Most likely, many of the listed names would belong to people who had found cause for disapproval of something that America or American commercial interests had perpetrated in their own countries. To join, for example, an environmental group concerned about a pollution issue, or a labour organisation taking a stand on employee rights, would likely secure a note on the computer's listings, although not necessarily automatically invite a ban on entering the US. Membership of any one of a whole host of political parties and groups thought to have leftward-leanings would doubtless assure an individual of a higher-rated mention in the rankings. People known to have written material critical of American institutions would most certainly find themselves added to the targets, especially where those named institutions believed themselves to be specially tasked with the defence of the nation and its proclaimed values. If they were allowed in, Uncle Sam's boys would want to know they were there.

The closer the flight had approached Los Angeles, the more Ray had thought about the immigration hall. He's assumed for years that he would be on the files of MI5 and thereby American intelligence, originally through his association with neighbour Carl. Apart from being very much of the left and a shop steward in a defence-sensitive industry, Carl had been a leading light in Cruisewatch, an organisation dedicated to thwarting the Pentagon policy of deploying US Air Force mobile nuclear missiles, aimed at the Warsaw Pact countries, in the British countryside. The action of concealing weapons and combatants among a civilian population is one that western governments are rightly eager to condemn when practised by real or potential opponents, but for some reason was expected to go unremarked-upon when imposed by the US on the English. Indeed, few people did pay much attention, the majority having been successfully conditioned to believe that protesters and objectors, even if they were men of the cloth or respectable elderly ladies, were siding with 'the enemy'. Cruisewatch monitored the missile convoys and at times obstructed them, despite their being protected by considerable numbers of British police. The group's aim was to prove that the movement and location of the launchers could not be kept secret and that the entire concept was flawed, as well as being immoral and illegal. Ray was sympathetic to that view. Carl, anxious as ever to thwart and embarrass the establishment, took up the cause with enthusiasm and would spend nights on end lurking about and chasing the convoys across Salisbury Plain. Ray was never active as a protestor but did venture out on a few occasions to observe the fairly spectacular events. His vehicle details, name and address would have been taken by the Wiltshire Constabulary and passed to the Ministry of Defence Police and thence to MI5 which would unquestionably have shared details of suspects with its American counterpart.

Having said that, Ray had never up to now had any difficulty when travelling to the United States, but since the Cruisewatch time he has always assumed his home telephone could be monitored and that this would in more recent times extend to e-mail traffic. For this reason he's been exceptionally cautious about discussing *One-Zero-Three* using either medium. There is little doubt though, that anyone, seeing a list of websites he visits and that he regularly exchanges e-mails, however non-committal, with people like the avid Lockerbie-watcher, Dick Leigh, would be convinced that Thomas Raymond Scriver has become involved in some investigation into the crime's darker secrets. Given the extraordinarily clumsy and transparently vindictive activities of the FBI and other agencies in their dealings with people like William Chasey, Juval Aviv, James Shaugnessy and Lester Coleman, Ray knew that having lifted the Lockerbie stone, he had to be prepared for literally anything, if he planned to step over that red line.

He would have gone to New Zealand by another route entirely, had he not desperately wanted to see Eve. He couldn't justify blowing a chunk of his dwindling resources on this speculative trip without taking the risk, whatever that might be, of travelling via California and visiting his wife.

The queue shuffled forward by one more person and he nonchalantly slid his computer bag forward across the shiny floor with his instep. Two to go. He hoped that he was acting sufficiently coolly not to arouse the interest of the unseen agents behind the viewing panels. He filled the time recalling visits here years ago to work on commercials for British television and always being told by companies to say that he was travelling on holiday. For to engage in work here, even when being paid for it back in London, was not legal. American technicians could and did work in the UK without difficulty, and post-Mrs Thatcher's prejudiced and counter-productive anti-union legislation did so entirely without restriction, yet British technicians without hard-to-get Green Cards were prevented from doing the same in reverse, and so had to tell lies to Immigration. One friend of Ray's flew into a US airport in a city that was fortunately well away from the main centres of film production. To the IO's question about reason for his visit the friend had given the advised, holiday response. To his horror the officer said in reply,

"Ever heard of an English outfit called Ashwell Matthews?" (the very company with which the chap was due to work for the next two weeks).

"They're in town to make a big TV commercial. Funny, I've had nothing but British film technicians flying in here for the last three days, and do you know, they're all here on holiday. You any idea why that should be?"

The friend had looked interested and puzzled, and said nothing.

"Have a nice day," the officer had said, stamping the landing card. They weren't all as sympathetic.

It was Ray's turn. He crossed the symbolic line and took the few steps to the booth. A very large Mexican American woman was perched on the tall chair in her glass box. She took his passport and landing card and did some typing. Trying not to appear too interested in watching her, he turned his head away so without staring attempted to look sideways and detect any reaction to what she read on-screen. She was probably a better actor than he was, he decided. She betrayed nothing but asked the standard question.

"Just visiting some friends on my way to New Zealand," he answered.

"How long you stay?"

"Five days planned; a week at most."

"I give you to 21st."

"That's plenty, thank you."

"You're welcome. Have nice visit to United States."

That went well. He was in.

In the luggage hall he was slightly surprised to see no sign of DB. He was more interested though in the lack of evidence of his two soft bags on the carrousel, but this was a false alarm and they appeared from the far side with that slinky, caterpillar-like motion that always reminds him, for some reason, of an old-time train clattering along an ill-maintained branch line. He was already bending over, reaching for the floppy straps, when he became aware of the man upstream, also fielding the same catch.

"We'll take those for you, Mr Scriver," said another voice.

A second man was to his other side and, briefly distracted by the use of his name behind him, Ray was completely outplayed in his luggage retrieval. The upstream man, in a short-sleeved shirt bearing some form of ID badge, now swung Ray's bags round towards him, which assisted the similarly-attired downstream man to take his arm lightly but effectively and turn him away from the belt.

"You just need to come with us for a few moments," said Downstream. Any instinct Ray felt to contest the matter was smothered at birth by the sight of a huge uniformed police officer facing him four paces away, arms folded although they were really too podgy to fold properly. How this trio had approached him without his being aware of it was a matter of complete mystification. Within seconds the small group had reached a handleless door that opened silently and automatically on their approach. They were joined by a second uniformed cop who had been observing things from a distance away, hands on hips, one very near his firearm, just in case the target of the lift somehow had armed accomplices protecting him. The door closed firmly behind them, immediately instilling in Ray an overwhelming feeling of the removal of that assumption of safety that derives from the mere fact of being visible to ordinary citizens in a public place. Just as he had, less than two minutes earlier, crossed a physical line representing the boundary between America and all other nations, he now felt he had, with a single step, made another transit between everyday reality and his friend, Dick's, 'Secret World'; one where virtually anything can and does happen.

Downstream showed Ray into a small interview room.

"We'll just have these officers check that you're not carrying anything that could harm any of us," he said, as Ray noticed that the man was carrying his computer bag. In the surprise of the arrest he had forgotten it completely. He reached to take the carrying strap from the man's shoulder but the latter stepped back and the second police officer, hardly smaller than the first, interposed himself definitively between the two. Upstream had already disappeared somewhere along the corridor with Ray's checked luggage, and now Downstream left the room with the precious third bag. The whole kidnap of his person and appropriation of his belongings had taken less than twenty seconds; he was only a matter of yards from the public bustle of the baggage hall and yet his isolation and helplessness was complete. In England he would have had a fair understanding of the legality of his situation and his rights. Here he had no idea, but as he quickly analysed his status, he felt he could safely assume that whoever Downstream and Upstream worked for, they had been given the powers they were exercising in that post-9/11 period when Americans fell over themselves in their haste to give up their civil liberties. What they were doing to him might be repressive and offensive, but it was almost certainly allowable according to some hastily-drafted law.

The two police officers carried out a thorough pat-down check and investigated his clothing with great care, with the huge one standing off, watching and ready to cover this time, while the slightly less huge one did the necessaries. The contents of his pockets, including his passport, wallet, house and car keys, loose change and mobile phone were all placed on the steel table, before being scooped into a polythene evidence bag.

"'Fraid I'll need your watch, buddy." Compliantly, Ray removed his Breitling and handed it to the cop.

"And your belt and shoes."

Taking with them every shred of evidence of his identity, contained in the clear plastic envelope, they left the room. A terrible quiet filled the space as Ray realised that it was totally and utterly sound-proofed. Despite his tiredness, he remained surprisingly alert and the lack of sound gave him a clue. The room would of course be bugged, probably for video pictures as well as conversation. He started to think how he might use that to his advantage. The likelihood was that the interest was not so much in him as in his luggage. He surmised that already Upstream, the silent one, would be taking his screenplay apart and placing its pages in a high speed scanner and photocopier. They would follow that procedure with all the script copies he was carrying, just in case the top, obvious one had been doctored for content, to appear less critical of the US and so offer the analysts fewer contentious passages to find, and their sponsors up the command chain less cause for concern. Thoroughness would be one of their many obsessions.

Within minutes, an analyst in far-away Langley, Virginia would be having the first copy of the screenplay electronically filtered for key expressions, words, names and abbreviations, of which list the letters 'CIA' would have been in the top ten, if not actually at number one. There would be so many keywords in *One-Zero-Three* to trigger the computer's response that its alarm lights would be positively dancing and they'd have to turn off the audio alerts. A decision would be swiftly made that a full reading was needed, and the pages would be passed to another specialist. Ray knew it was highly possible that they wouldn't let him out until the speed-reader had completed work. Then it would be: 'We're very sorry Mr Scriver, there seems to have been some mistake and we're sorry to have inconvenienced you. Please accept our apologies and enjoy your stay.'

At least that's the outcome he expected; the one he was now focusing on and hoping for. He knew, though, that people who had been taken out of circulation in the clinical fashion he'd just experienced could suffer a myriad of different scenarios, many nowhere near as comfortable. If there was an upside to his present position, it was that they didn't need him any longer; his threat was effectively neutralised. Now they had the script, they had all the information they needed to suppress it. If by good fortune he in future managed to interest American backers, it would depend on securing a distribution deal. And both studio chiefs and heads of distribution companies were easily called up, when the time came, by someone they would probably know reasonably well, taking the line that: 'Everyone on the Hill is very keen – and they know you'd agree with them – that this sort of unsubstantiated garbage is not the sort of impression of America that should be pedalled round the world.'

The project would be dead in the water.

The only way it could ever get a green light, against that sort of not-too-subtle pressure, would be if some producer with real guts became convinced that the selfsame explosive content that would so infuriate the inner establishment – the real seat of power – was so exceptionally sensational that everyone, but everyone, would want to see the movie. If a player like that could enthuse and convince a quorum of necessary, influential people that they couldn't afford not to make and distribute it, the film had just a slim chance of getting to the screen.

As he sat there in the sparse, silent space, Ray pondered that every adult on Clipper 103 would have been happy enough to be in his position at the end of their flight; alive and breathing in a warm, lit room, however intimidating, rather than torn, crumpled and lifeless on a pitch-black, rainsodden, freezing Scottish hillside.

Ray has a great deal of patience where time is concerned. It comes from spending years standing by the side of a camera, waiting for other people to make things ready (or God, in the case of the weather). Injustice is a different matter. His fuse is very short when that rears its head. So although waiting an hour or two, with nothing to do but think, presented no problem to him whatsoever, the knowledge that the apparatus of state was, as he sat there, using its limitless power to subvert free expression, supposedly one of the supporting principles of its very existence – that was the sort of thing that could make him lose his temper.

Yet again the Lockerbie victims were, at this very minute, potentially being denied their platform, their turn with the microphone, their right to be heard. He felt an overwhelming urge to make his hand into a fist and bang the unyielding table. Logically he knew there was nothing possible to be gained from the act and that the likely result would be an injured hand. He also understood that to reveal to the watchers and listeners that they had, in some way, got to him, would be to hand them a small advantage. Knowledge is power and to learn that your adversary can be made to boil over is a valuable piece of information to file away.

These very sensible objections survived a microsecond before the irresistible compulsion won the day. He raised his fist above head height and slammed it down on the grey surface.

–ooOoo–

25   The Power of Suggestion

There was a surprising sensation of his fist hitting something unexpected as he lifted it. This was followed, even more oddly, by virtually no pain in his clenched hand but a moderately hard blow to his thigh. He opened his eyes to see why the steel table had proved so soft that his hand had passed through it to punch his upper leg. The passengers across the wide aisle were looking at him in slightly amused shock.

"Sorry. Bad dream," he apologised quietly, so as not to wake DB who dozed to his left, between him and them. The columns of figures in the pile of production budget papers on his friend's knee had proved predictably soporific.

"I think you'd better have this back," said the man nearest, standing to proffer the copy of *A Forest Beat*. "It came down like a meteorite." Ray's hand had caught the edge of the book on his lap as it had risen so sharply up into the air, sending the hardback spinning and arcing across the cabin.

"I do so apologise." Even half-awake, he was conscious of his attempt to exhibit conspicuous English politeness.

What on earth was going on? He hadn't been dreaming, he was sure. For him, dreams are generally surreal. They unfold in an illogical fashion, rarely much connected with what is physically possible and rooted in an alternative existence where the settings are familiar but the ground rules are different. Progress, achievement and satisfaction are typically unattainable and frustration is the dominant experience. Although what he had just been experiencing at LAX had some of these elements of his typical night-time adventures, it had felt totally rooted in reality – no dodgy physics, no impossible situations, no jump-cutting from place to place without rhyme or reason; it had been as lifelike and credible as the rest of the day; an apparently conscious procession of events that had been thoroughly plausible. He wondered if he was truly back in the 747. The screen in front of him indicated a position close to Billings, Montana, which he remembered as being around 1000 statute miles from Los Angeles, meaning arrival in something like two and a half hours. Had he been drugged so that he just believed he had yet to arrive in LA? Was he awake before and sleeping now? Every screenwriter has seen *Groundhog Day*, where the same twenty-four hours are enacted endlessly over and over, until the hero manages to break the pattern. Had he been inserted by hallucinogens into some such cyclic existence? He pinched himself surreptitiously and gently slapped his face. He seemed to be fully awake and, thinking about it, he hadn't been aware of a needle jabbing him in the baggage hall. He doubted whether agents would actually dare to inject detainees with regular airport police officers looking on, so on balance he could discount that one, as he had never, that he could recall, been alone in the interview room with Downstream.

If he thought he'd been face to face in the room with the two agents, he would have been more worried. Injection might be a concern, but far greater would be the fear of hypnotism. Ray knows that a relatively simple technique exists to implant ideas under hypnosis. This takes place during an interview, quite unknown to the victim. The unfortunate target then goes on with normal life until one day he or she receives a telephone call. The call contains an implanted phrase that triggers an associated response, and the response can be anything from spying, up to the big ones, killing someone else or committing suicide. A considerable number of otherwise inexplicable deaths of employees in defence-sensitive industries have been attributed to this practice, when perfectly happy people have suddenly taken their own lives, often in bizarre ways. The common link seems to be that they wanted to change jobs, either leave the industry or change company, and the inference is that someone decides these people have knowledge that is too secret and too important to be allowed to leave the influence of the employer. Effectively they are murdered by the pre-implanting of an instruction to hazard themselves. Many people speculate that such was the fate of Dr David Kelly. Whether they can hypnotise you to forget the whole interview, as well as the hypnosis part, Ray doesn't know, but assumes they can. If they had done that then he could be in real trouble.

He decided that, on balance, he was probably still in the real world; or at least in a 747 some way above it, if that can be called real. He decided that he hadn't yet landed in LA and that Upstream and Downstream were part of an unusually vivid dream, manifestations of his natural concerns about the screenplays in his luggage. He felt extra-pleased that DB would now be carrying one copy through immigration and customs. Did that halve the risk, or double it? He was not really wide-awake enough to work that one out.

—ooOoo—

The immigration hall had nothing much of *Groundhog Day* about it at all. The lines were plenty long but there were four booths open for Non-American passport holders. DB stayed in the same queue instead of joining another. Their continued conversation removed all thoughts of nervousness over the contents of his hand-luggage, and the Immigration Officer, when reached, looked like Burt Reynolds or maybe Tom Selleck.

DB went through first and then, just like his Hispanic counterpart earlier, Burt or Tom processed Ray with the minimum of formality. There were no crewcut men or immense police officers in baggage reclaim and both sets of bags were revolving ready for collection, admittedly though, moving like branch-line steam trains. Also, on their way to the exit to customs, Ray couldn't help noticing and quite possibly reacting mildly to a door with no handle.

Before he can remember the part about being met by Winston, the chauffeur, and making their way to the car park to find DB's midnight blue Cadillac, Ray finally falls asleep.

–ooOoo–

26   Really Out of Control

Ray is almost through his morning routine when two room phone bells sufficient to arouse an entire fire station give him quite a start.

"Doctor Scriver.   Good morning.   Peregrine Sharpe.   Are you awake, dear?" The contrast between Perry's beautiful English tones and some of his London grandmotherly phraseology never fails to amaze.   Nor does his habit of using his full name, when they've been friends for the best part of thirty years.

"Lord Sharpe. How the devil are you? Yes, I'm up and refreshed; I seem to have acclimatised to LA time quite well."

"You don't acclimatise to the time – you adapt to it; and you may have done so, dear, but I assure you, you won't have acclimatised. It's effing hot already and it's only 8.15."

They are due to meet for lunch so this call is a tad earlier than Ray was expecting, but nevertheless mightily welcome. Perry Sharpe is one of those people who cheer you up, whether things are going well or horribly badly, so is a great asset on any film set. He's also a supremely competent and greatly experienced camera assistant.   There couldn't be a better combination for a producer or a camera crew, which renders his struggle to obtain due recognition in the last few years an unfathomable absurdity. Perry very sensibly takes the attitude that the reason he isn't getting much work is not because he isn't very good at his job, but rather that the people whose task it is to employ him aren't very good at theirs.

"Where are you?"

"I thought you'd never ask. I'm in the lobby. I'm taking you to breakfast. We can't have you rattling round on your own. I've got my wheels and I'm totally at your disposal. Whatever you've got planned, I'll run you around in air-conditioned luxury and then disappear when you want me to. Just get out here! I'm hungry. I've been up three hours."

"Top man! I'll be right with you."

–ooOoo–

They sit in a diner somewhere off Third Street, looking out at Perry's enormous, immaculate, ten-year-old Lincoln gleaming in the car park, its brightwork reflecting the fast climbing sun. As they eat, Perry recaps his recent hopes and disappointments. He is legal; he has a Green Card and belongs to the union. He has spent a small fortune in securing the right to work in California, another one in having a base and transport here, in addition to keeping on what he has back home in London. He has an excellent CV, having worked with famous-named cameramen, directors and stars; and he knows many British technicians – DPs and operators – who are busy and highly regarded here in Hollywood. They meet him for coffee; they talk about their next projects; they promise to put him in the frame or keep him in mind – and then won't return his calls. For a man who doesn't know what he is going to do, he remains the most congenial and cheerful companion that anyone could ever spend time with.

"But how about you. What's happening with the script?"

Perched on stools at the counter, facing away but not eight feet removed from them are two LAPD officers in their all-black uniforms and with so many items hanging on their belts that it's a wonder their trousers stay up. The pendulous paraphernalia of course includes holsters with handguns. Reminded of what **didn't** happen yesterday afternoon, Ray discreetly indicates them and puts his finger to his lips. Perry nods, not at all understanding why. Neither, really does Ray.

"You'll never guess who I bumped into at Heathrow; who got me an upgrade and who I spent the journey with – DB Hollingsworth."

"Christ! That was a stroke of luck. I didn't realise you knew him."

Ray explains and keeps the conversation away from the subject of scripts, while they remain in the eatery. Later, as they ease into the Town Car, the two cops' black and white sidles through the palm trees, out of the parking towards the street.

They're a mile or two from the diner before Ray finds an opportunity to break into their chat to apologise for the secrecy and his apparent paranoia.

" . . . It's just that there's a security aspect to the subject. I feel the need to be ultra-cautious. I actually didn't remember you knew about it."

"I don't, really. I just recall your mentioning, last time I saw you in London, that you were working on a screenplay, about what you didn't let on, and that you planned to show it to Gerald Logan, when it was ready. When you e-mailed that you were calling here on the way to see him, I just put two and two together."

"Ah – fine. Well it's about Lockerbie."

Lockerbie is one of those events that for the vast majority of the world's population need no further amplification. You don't have to say 'Lockerbie, the air disaster' or any such addition, at least for anyone over about 25. Perry, like Ray, would have an extra personal interest in the crime. As film technicians they've jumped on and off jets in the course of their careers with a familiarity that British people in other professions might have with the London Underground. Both were well aware at the time that the random dictates of work could have found them, or colleagues, booked onto PA103. It has happened. There were technicians on the ill-fated Turkish DC10. They were returning from a job that Ray's AD friend, Patrick, could easily have been booked on.

"OK," Perry says. "I'm not going to ask any more."

"No, you can ask anything you like – just keep it all under your hat until it's in production." There is a pause while Perry joins the Hollywood Freeway northbound and threads the big Lincoln into a comfortable lane.

"So what do you do? Show the story behind why the guy did it and how?"

"No. It's a story about trying to find out who really did it and how the guy in prison was framed."

"Wow. And who did do it then?"

Ray starts off – explaining about the shootdown of the Airbus; how the Iranians let out a contract for revenge to the Popular Front for the Liberation of Palestine-General Command, headed by Ahmed Jibril, and backed by Syria – and Perry listens, taking it all in. Until he isn't. Ahead the traffic is slowing, and as he's keeping a more sensible distance than most on the US 101 that morning, he's slowing down too – except again that he isn't!

"Fucking brakes have gone!"

With Perry's shout, Ray leaves the Bekaa Valley and is back in its San Fernando counterpart in a flash. They're closing uncomfortably quickly on a massive artic with brake lights showing. There's no gap in the next lane to the right but it's open to the left so Perry swings across and begins to overtake the eighteen-wheeler. Missed that one at least! Ray hits his electric window button and the noise and fumes of the monster's engine and tyres, close alongside, fill the Lincoln. They're in lane five, which is slowing ahead, as is lane four, but there seems a decent gap between the truck and the cars ahead, and lane three now looks even more welcoming, if they can clear the front of the truck. To do that they might have to speed up, which isn't quite the idea. Perry has already selected the intermediate speed on his autobox, but nothing much seems to have happened.

"Go right when I say. You'll need a bit of gas." Perry guns the motor and they gain on the truck, for whose driver they are largely invisible. Ray judges when they are just clear of the vast slab front. The slowing traffic in both their lanes is getting horribly close.

"OK. Go one lane and stand by to go again." Perry complies. "Shit! Stay where you are." A pick-up is coming up fast in formation with them, overtaking the Freightliner on the other side. Fortunately the big truck is easing off even more, now not entirely from choice.

"Hoot! Go when I say!" Ray waves his arms to engage the pick-up driver's attention. Perry's use of the horn is superfluous as the enraged trucker hits his own, thinking he's been cut-up by maniacs. The pick-up driver realises that Ray means business and gives way. Perry slots into lane three. Ray waves a thank you; that will have to do for the Freightliner too. The truck's lane four is coming to a stop not far ahead. The trouble is that the last car in the line peels right into three and now the Lincoln is heading for a relatively slow-moving Volkswagen. Ray's arms get busy again, indicating to a driver that he can almost touch in an open Alfa Romeo alongside in lane two, that she needs to give way or she will be definitely be sideswiped by two tons of elderly luxury motor car. It takes a while for her to overcome her indignation. Rather than slowing she moves ungraciously into lane one – not a moment too soon. She still keeps station with the Town Car, despite Ray's gesticulations and useless, incomprehensible mouthings. She thinks they're everyday LA nutters, trying it on. As is the way of things, lane two is also clogging up fast and in seconds Perry will shunt a Buick in a big way. Ray mimes a foot going to the floor with his hands and, with yards to spare, she gets the message and slows.

"Go, go!" Perry takes the cue and cuts straight across lane one and onto the hard shoulder. He changes into L, which again seems to make not one whit of difference, and after a few hundred feet the big car, fortunately on the flat, rolls to a near-halt. Perry cautiously tries the parking brake and the ride is over.

"Bollocks!" he fumes. "I'm so sorry."

"Never mind that. We did well. Thank goodness we didn't use I-405 and have it happen on the hilly bit, or go over Laurel Canyon."

"No, but this is really going to fuck up your morning."

This sort of thing is all very funny when it happens to Mel Gibson or some other comedy cop, but not so amusing when it's you and you realise that many of your fellow road-users would rather risk a multiple accident than give away half a second.

Ray gets out of the car as first the pick-up and then the Freightliner growl past in the hold-up. He tries the same 'pedal-to-the-floor' gesture that eventually worked on the Alfa driver and thinks he conveys the sense, but the trucker is still shaking his head. But then they do. Perry is on his mobile to someone about recovery. That exercise couldn't really have worked much better if they'd had one of those magnetic emergency *Kojak* lights on the roof.

The alternate arm waves, imperious and directing followed by apologetic and thanking were learnt long ago from French CRS motorcycle police who used to escort film units from location to location at high speed across Nice in the rush hour. They would ride, blow a whistle and hold up traffic simultaneously. Come to think of it, they went in more for the imperious and directing and were not so big on the apologetic and thanking. Quite why the National Riot Police should be persuaded to come and help representatives of a commercial film company stop traffic on mountain roads and assist them shift location, Ray never totally understood, but presumably even France couldn't provide enough riots to keep them in constant employment. Obviously the officers had a good relationship with the local production manager, 'Willie', reputedly really an Austrian Count, for on arrival each morning these burly moustachioed men would park their giant BMW R70/8 bikes and greet the elderly aristocrat with a hearty kiss on both cheeks. *Vive la différence. Vive la France!*

Perry apologises for the fifth time.

"Honestly, it doesn't matter a cow. I had no plans for this morning in case I couldn't wake up, so we're losing nothing. We were only going for a coffee."

It's true that a scrubby embankment flanking Highway 101 is not the best place in the state to enjoy a relaxed talk. The noise, even with the traffic snarled and slow, is pretty horrendous. There's grass of a sort although they dare not sit on it due to the enthusiastic insect life. There's some degree of shade too with some stumpy trees to lean on, having checked them out for spiders and other crawlies. And Perry was right about it getting hot. It must be over 80 degrees already.

"I have to say I got a bit preoccupied and haven't really taken in all you were telling me just before it happened," Perry says.

A major understatement. Ray checks that his friend really does want to hear more. And so, in this unlikely setting, two Englishmen abroad discuss the subtleties of the darker side of late 1980s Middle Eastern politics.

"OK. Both Iranian politicians and media openly called for revenge against the US for the 290 lives lost in the downing of their Airbus; Tehran radio memorably predicted 'blood-spattered skies' – a clear threat to retaliate against aircraft. It's known that almost immediately, Ahmed Jibril, the leader of a terrorist group that has made a speciality of bombing civil airliners, was in contact from Damascus with Iran's Revolutionary Guards and within a week he was in Tehran offering his services."

"His is the outfit with the very long name."

"That's right, the Popular Front for the Liberation of Palestine-General Command, or PFLP-GC for short. It had broken away from the old PFLP way back in 1968 and, as breakaways often are, it was more aggressive and ruthless than the original. So there were further meetings and negotiations over the next three months or so. Jibril was apparently recorded discussing possible targets and prices with the Iranian Interior Minister, Ali Akbar Montashemi, so the intent to avenge was coming from the highest level of government. The Airbus was downed on 3rd July. By September the deal for retaliation had been done and Jibril's people in Europe, and particularly West Germany, started to be very busy. They'd already made two attempts to blow up American troop trains there, and now they finally came under the scrutiny they deserved, largely due to Mossad, Israeli Intelligence, who'd been taking them rather more seriously then the Germans had. A very large surveillance operation, called 'Autumn Leaves', was put in place, and the West German Federal Police, the BKA, watched as Jibril's cell prepared for some form of operation. The biggest clue to what that might be was the arrival in Germany of his aeroplane bomb expert, a man called Khreesat. He, they later found out, immediately started building several bombs in domestic electronic equipment, including Toshiba cassette radios."

"Ray. Sorry to interrupt. Just remind me, this cell, these terrorists, they're Palestinians, yes?" He pauses. "Not Libyans?"

"Not Libyans," confirms Ray.

"OK – r i g h t," Perry says, slowly. Peregrine Sharpe, film person, has just said 'right'. Although he's something of a captive audience at this point, Ray deduces from that a growing degree of interest in the story so far.

"You want to hear more?"

"Absolutely!"

"So! After almost four weeks of watching and intercepting phone calls, the German police decide that an attack is about to go down. This is towards the end of October, and they arrest everyone they can. The bomb-maker is caught with the leader of the European network, a guy called Dalkamoni, and in their car is a completed aeroplane bomb built into a Toshiba radio cassette player. Apart from cell members, the raids also net the bomb-making apparatus and elsewhere what is described as the largest quantity of illegal arms ever seized in West Germany. What the BKA fail to find for now, bizarrely, are three other devices built into audio-visual equipment and a stack of unconverted Toshibas. There is also apparently at least one other radio bomb that was taken away before the arrests, so even though the cell is shut down, bombs have been made and no one really knows how many may have gone undetected."

"Don't I remember that the one on the Pan Am flight started from Malta?"

"That became the prosecution case, you're right, and the basis on which they convicted the Libyan, Megrahi."

"So could one of these missing bombs have been sent somehow to Malta, for him to put on a plane?"

"Well it could, but why take the extra risks of sending an explosive device from one country to another just for it to come back again? Germany – Malta, Malta – Germany. Why would anyone do that? And especially why select an airport like Malta's Luqa, where security was hot, when you could just drive it to Frankfurt, where the security was awful. And anyway that wasn't what the prosecution said. Their case, such is it was, described it as an all-Libyan operation."

"So how was the bomb got onto the aircraft?"

"The CIA was protecting drug deliveries out of Lebanon into Europe and on to the US on Pan Am out of Frankfurt, it's thought by a switching of suitcases. The easy conclusion, although I don't think it's necessarily the right one, is that on the day in question, one switched suitcase didn't have heroin in it."

Perry shakes his head, vigorously. "I don't believe it."

His reaction is interesting, thinks Ray, because to Perry this feels like an entirely new and outrageous revelation. Of course he may well not have heard it before, even though a similar story first ran on networked news in the States as far back as 1990, and this one was made public two years later. The trouble is that today there is so much news, so many articles constantly available to us on every subject under the sun, many of them sensational in content, that we're quite likely to miss items; and even if we see them, they're quickly forgotten as other equally mind-boggling stories take their place. It doesn't help when often one article completely contradicts previous assertions. This happened with Lockerbie a lot, as the intelligence services fed their journalist contacts 'exclusive' leaks supporting the latest version of the 'truth' that their governments, or more realistically, they themselves, wanted the public to accept.

It would be nice, Ray thinks, if news items could come with ratings for accuracy of their content, like nutritional information labelling on food – five stars for the whole unvarnished truth, four for the best possible extrapolation, three for some basis in fact, two for an educated guess, and one for pure unadulterated propaganda. Perhaps it should be a six-star scale, for there needs to be a category for idle cynical invention, which is somewhat different from the last and also quite in fashion.

Ray wants to say all this to Perry, but where do you stop? Ray finds the facts and the myths of Lockerbie supremely absorbing. He has on his computer a database that lists every known significant development in the plotting, the execution, the investigation, the cover-up and the trial as well as every major revelation and item of disinformation in the media. The events can, in seconds, be ordered chronologically or sorted according to numerous criteria. For several years the walls of his office have resembled those of a crime squad incident room, with the suspects appearing on diagrams, and lists analysing their possible motives, their access to the means and their opportunities. He could talk through aspects of the case for hours on end.

But he can't expect his friend to absorb these mind-taxing complexities: Perry, this eccentric Englishman boulevarding his way round Tinsel Town from place-to-be-seen to place-to-be-seen in search of a start on a movie on which to apply his formidable technical and inter-personal skills in exchange for the wherewithal of survival. Like nearly everybody else, but currently with more urgency than most, Perry is trapped in a cyclic contemplation of his own circumstances and prospects. Anything outside that circle can only be a brief diversion. All his friend wants really to hear him say is: 'The film is on and you're on the second camera.' Yet they both know that Ray has no more control over the latter than he does over the former.

Essentially the writer realises, as they stand in the stifling LA summer heat assaulted by the roar of Kenworths, marooned in this narrow strip of non-place in which humans rarely set foot, that in the bigger picture of the outside world which they're temporarily separated from, they're both in the same boat – or actually they're really out of it, treading the same water, each waiting for someone to throw a life-belt.

–ooOoo–

27　Patriot Games?

There are two messages for Ray at reception. The name scrawled in the 'From' line near the top of the first means absolutely nothing. He has never heard of 'Halton Chambers'. Fortunately the caller thought to leave a more meaningful name at the end: 'Hal'. The film nerd from last evening. The receptionist who took the details has the handwriting of a psychopath. Ray deciphers it.

> DB asked me to look at your screenplay. I think there is
> a problem with length. I think, and DB agrees, that you
> should think about cutting the Lester Goldman scenes.
> Call you tomorrow.

His crafted screenplay is being criticised by a man who uses 'think' three times in 16 words. And there are no 'Lester Goldman scenes'. There are scenes involving someone called Lester Coleman and Ray has himself thought long and hard about doing without them. But he doesn't believe for a moment that Hal has actually read more than the title window of *One-Zero-Three*. Ray imagines Hal's idea of 'looking at a script' is finding a space on a reader's desk on which to drop it from waist height.

The second 'While You Were Out' blank on which the potential axe-murderer has left more evidence is from Eve, confirming their evening arrangement in minimal terms. She will collect him, which is why his volunteer chauffeur has been given the rest of the day off. Ray has time for a rest before getting ready.

–ooOoo–

Of course Perry had wanted to know more about the CIA and the drug-running. But first he had stepped down to the Lincoln to find in the boot an English gentleman's straw hat, which he passed to Ray, and an orange day-glo Panavision baseball cap for himself, in an attempt to fend off the sun's heat. They now looked a very ill-assorted couple, even by Los Angeles standards. Ray found himself cutting the story to the bone, almost as if brevity would speed the rescue truck's arrival. Boiling down the whole mass of evidence for the script had been a feat of compression, equal to forcing a whole pig into a buffet pork pie. To précis it yet more to avoid giving his friend information fatigue was a greater challenge, but perhaps useful practice if, just suppose, at some future point he had to give interviews. The popular media aren't happy with anything longer than two- or three-sentence answers.

He picked up the thread with the question of American hostages and how the shadow of those seized from their Tehran embassy by Iran's revolutionaries blighted the Carter administration. He left out the fact that during the presidential election that ended Carter's term, some of Reagan's campaign people went to Paris, met with representatives from Iran and agreed that the luckless embassy personnel, patriotic Americans all, wouldn't be released from their illegal and uncomfortable captivity until after the poll, lest it give some boost to the otherwise doomed electoral fortunes of incumbent Jimmy. Genial Ronnie may or may not have known of that wicked act of supreme political cynicism (which came to be known as 'October Surprise'), but his campaign manager, William Casey, later to be Director of the CIA, planned the inhuman collusion – and his running-mate, former CIA Director and eventual presidential successor, George Bush Senior, was right in the evil loop.

If you mention this sort of thing in conversation, people tend to believe that you're a fantasist extremist. In fact they generally accuse you, quite quickly, of being a CT.

Hostage matters eventually hurt the old film star's presidency too when details of the Iran-Contra affair came out. That was the cosy arrangement whereby the USA ignored trivial impediments like United Nations resolutions to sell arms to Iran, for their eight-year-war with their neighbour, Iraq, in the hope that the Ayatollah's people would intercede with their proxies to release the survivors of a rash of westerners kidnapped in Lebanon. These transactions couldn't be shown in the accounts, so the black money earned was channelled in the direction of the military-industrial complex (no surprise there) to buy yet more guns, these to support one of the CIA's many interventions in other sovereign countries. In this case it was to enable a particularly bloodthirsty right-wing guerrilla organisation to wage war against a popular and effective government, namely the Sandinista administration in Nicaragua; one that was too far to the left to be permitted to remain in office by the people who matter in the States and clearly think that the world is theirs to run as they wish.

Ray sketched for Perry the merest outline of this meddling episode, characteristic of so many others, just to move the narrative along. In the screenplay, he has had to soft-pedal Iran-Contra. Its complexity, plus the presence in Lt. Colonel Oliver North of a major figure well worth a film of his own (surely George Clooney should play him, before it's too late), mean that it must receive little more than a mention. There was also the fact that, when the money from Iran ran out, all-action-hero Ollie was quite happy for the Contras to pay with money from drug production, and eased the importers' worries by smoothing the delivery path. Again, if you allude, over a glass of sparkling, to the possibility that any American official would collude with the twilight world of wholesale drug supply, people generally smile disbelievingly and spot someone else they have an urgent need to talk to. Memory, Ray knows, can be short and selective.

He explained that it was other incentives taken to free the hapless, solitary-confined individuals plucked from the streets of Beirut that have direct bearing on the story of Flight 103. The Mediterranean city had for generations enjoyed the soubriquet 'Paris of the Middle East' until political factionalism, civil war and outside intervention ripped out its heart and soul, leaving it one of the most dangerous places in the world. This was indicated when a CIA station chief, William Buckley, drafted in to help with the extrication of the hostages, became one himself and was eventually tortured and murdered.

It was proving far from easy to convey the subtleties of this story, as the stop-go traffic regularly interrupted the flow when particularly raucous giants were halted or crawling past their refuge and made communication near-impossible. Ray had persevered.

"Lebanon's Bekaa Valley is the country's main focus for agriculture. One of the crops tended there makes it also the centre of Lebanese drug production," he heard himself shouting.

In parallel, he explained, it has become a stronghold of the hard-line Islamist organisation Hizbullah, as refugees from Palestine increasingly pack the country. "It was card-carrying affiliates of Hizbullah that were holding the hostages in the cellars and backrooms of the capital."

It seems more than possible that there was already protected transit to the United States for some Lebanese drug production, organised by the American DEA, the Drugs Enforcement Administration. Faced by an overwhelming volume of narcotics heading to the US, the DEA had reportedly adapted the old maxim to read 'If you can't beat them, co-operate'. The idea of protected deliveries is that if you set up safe routes for compliant traffickers, you know where the drugs are. By following them along the trail, you're led to the major importers, whom you leave alone, but in turn this leads to some of the mid- and lower level distributors and suppliers. A selection of these can be caught and some drugs intercepted, so the agency has some successes to show for its budget allocation. This keeps everyone happy, apart from a few dealers (and the addicts of course, and those who care about the latter). The cynic would say that closing the conduit down totally and arresting the known big players, which is clearly theoretically possible, is not pursued because too many micro-economies and mini-empires on both sides depend on it. As Carl says (or was it Ray who said it to him?) 'What agency needs to be so successful that it puts itself out of a job?'

To be totally fair, though – and what a surprising concept fairness is, in this class of company – the drugs trade has very much the character of the Hydra of Lerna: as Heracles found, for every head you cut off, two more sprout immediately. Ray had been pleased that he mentioned Heracles, as it led to the surprising discovery that one of Perry's better-kept secrets is an extensive knowledge of Greek mythology.

It seems that, becoming aware of the familial link between the heroin lords and the kidnappers, a small CIA unit came up with the idea of its own protected conduit. There is intense rivalry, sometimes bordering on hatred, between America's various clandestine agencies, and the idea of co-operation is not one that appeals much at all to them, as intelligence blunders continue to prove. It's also not completely known how far up the CIA's command chain the knowledge of this operation was shared. Juval Aviv's report for Pan American came to the conclusion that it was supervised in Washington but not necessarily approved by Langley headquarters. Again, there can be no surprise at the latter, but the state of preparedness for the Lockerbie crash, judged by the speed of reaction to it when it came, can only suggest that London station was at some point beforehand put in the picture. Equally clearly, every transit-point on legs of the drug route or routes would have required local CIA supervision. This meant that elements in Germany must have been involved, with others further back along the line; one place seems to have been Cyprus. At whatever level it was sanctioned, in practice the drug clansmen of the Bekaa were offered safe passage for their products, if they agreed to work on persuading their city cousins to give up the secreted Americans.

This all would have continued to work until news of the pipeline for dubious suitcases reached the ears of Ahmed Jibril, who was of course looking for a way of getting just such an item onto an American jet. Jibril is persuasive and, after brief negotiation, fates began to be sealed. In the horse-trading, the Lebanese would have been keen to ensure that the downing of an aircraft would neither expose nor cut the drug supply line. Also, they would not knowingly have sacrificed a valuable consignment of heroin. The fact that both a bomb **and** at least one drug suitcase were on 103 indicates that Jibril ignored their interests and found a way to outmanoeuvre them.

Yet another eighteen-wheeler, this time drawn by a massive Ford, tries to censor the story with engine and freezer-compressor noise. Ray battles on.

"A legacy from the division of Germany into occupied zones after World War II was Pan American's German network," he continues.

He explains that he remembers wondering, as a teenage aircraft enthusiast, why a US airline was flying what appeared to be internal or inter-Europe services, when European carriers of course could enjoy no such privilege in the States. "America has never been slow to seek commercial advantage from her involvement in war." Ray would argue that his whole life to date, along with those of millions of others, has been moderated and impoverished by that stark truism.

Pan Am was not really the USA flag carrier, but bore that mantle in effect. Frankfurt was Pan Am's European hub. There were direct flights to US destinations from its Rhein-Main Flughaven and the network linked to other transatlantic flights leaving from capitals such as Paris and London. In the case of flight 103, the early evening departure for New York from the latter, there was a feeder flight from the German airport, numbered 103A, for which a Boeing 727 was what airlines call the 'equipment'. This is a medium range three-engined airliner, much smaller than the giant 747 that would perform the Atlantic crossing to JFK.

Ray had paused after giving Perry a potted version of all this. It really was getting very warm now and he wiped the perspiration from his face with his handkerchief. Overhead, on its way into Van Nuys Airport, a light aircraft, free in the blue sky above, seemed to mock them by its contrast with their trapped state. Ray envied the occupants for a moment and then changed his mind. Flying at around fifteen hundred feet over a hot city is most uncomfortable. Convection currents rise at different rates from all the various heated surfaces – roofs, asphalt and concrete make the air bubble up, while earth and vegetation cause it to it rise more slowly or even descend. The result is a rolling turbulent sky as these different, invisible, moving columns of air mix and interact. A light aircraft will lurch and pitch through the bumps, feeling unstable and skittish. One of Norman, the flying instructor's, many implanted aphorisms related to flying always as high as possible, for better safety margins and to keep out of the 'bleeding turbulence'. English pilots would refer to such flying conditions as 'rough as old boots'.

Ray and Perry, who started the morning cool and tidy, are now starting to look a bit 'rough round the edges'.

If what Ray had told the rapt camera assistant in the last few minutes had plumbed the nastier depths of human nature, what he had to move onto now suggested treachery that was many, yet many times more shocking. He had barely begun to relate the saga of Major Charles McKee and his colleagues when the tow-truck swerved from lane one onto the hard shoulder, and with much shooshing and hissing of hydraulics reversed back to the metallic beached whale. Their rescue mission was playing out. McKee's wouldn't for now, and in reality never did.

–ooOoo–

The bedside phone blasts out. It's DB.

"Sorry not to have called till now. Been quite a day and I've been up to my eyes."

"No problem. I've actually been out most of the time."

"What did you get up to?" Ray gives him a précis, omitting their car adventure.

"I've heard the name. Don't think I know him," DB says, referring to Perry. "Look, I'm also sorry about Hal last night. He's a sort of mole of mine and it can be worth catching up with him as soon as I get here, before I see anyone else. He's great because he will ask anybody absolutely anything, but I shouldn't have let him loose on you. Obviously you didn't want to talk cold to a perfect stranger about your script. That was a mistake on my part and I apologise."

"No problem. I need people to get interested in it."

"Well yes, which is why I gave it to him to read today. He's quite a good barometer of what's happening here, and his general opinion can be useful."

"Yeah, actually he left a message. It wasn't a general opinion. He just said it was too long and suggested an area for cuts."

"Really. I wouldn't worry too much about that at this stage. Hal is more the big concept rather than a detail man. He's not the world's most sensitive creature, but he has his uses – that sounds bad – he has his strengths and weaknesses, like the rest of us. I'll call him and see what he thought generally. He's no guru. It's just that he's got quite a good nose. You busy tomorrow?"

"Few meetings." Ray exaggerates somewhat.

"Good. I'll catch up with you sometime during the day. Bye."

Ray is confused, or 'Kung-fu' as E always says. Hal, the 'big concept' expert, didn't mention in his message the acceptability of the script in the current market, which Ray assumes is what DB means. All he's done is mention the length, supposedly with DB's agreement, while DB says Hal is not the one for that type of comment and to take no notice. Not that Ray was about to get on his laptop and start editing anyway, at this point in time, but it is all slightly vague and mysterious.

Welcome to Hollywood.

–ooOoo–

28   Cold Table

Ray makes a special effort to be ready on time and is actually reading the *Los Angeles Times* on a sofa in the lobby. People passing in and out mean that he doesn't register Eve's arriving, but the moment **she** sees **him**, he senses she is there. He folds the paper and stands up before he looks round. He navigates round the sofa so he can approach her.

"Hello, E."

"Hello, U."

It seems a lifetime away that they last impromptued their version of the Abba song with the chorus, 'Hello, E. Hello, U. A-ha-a' inspired in part by *I'm Alan Partridge*. They move together and hug, not altogether awkwardly.

"You look good," Ray says into her hair.

"You don't," she answers into his shoulder. "You're too thin." They separate and step back.

"Well, that's . . ." he starts to say, and thinks better of it, tailing off and making that facial shrug that people do by pulling the corners of their mouth down as far as they can go. On the stage he'd have to amplify it with a spread of his hands or even work the shoulders. In life, as in a film close-up, half a look is all that's needed to say everything.

"Shall we go?"

She turns and, dangling car keys, heads for the door. He follows three paces behind. It shouldn't be like this.

In the car, after the small talk about the flight, during which he deliberately doesn't bring up the encountering of DB, there is a short silence before she mentions 'it'.

"So. You finished it." She doesn't call it 'the screenplay', 'the script' or by its name. Just 'it'.

"Yep. For now. There'll be endless re-writes, I expect, if someone picks it up but I'm happy with it. I wouldn't want to change too much."

"Good." There is another pause that is slightly too long. "And you're taking it down to Gerald." She knows. It's a statement; not a question.

"Has anyone else seen it yet?"

"Tom Couper has seen a few pages. He read the crash. Typical editor."

"He like it?"

"Considering it was Tom, the response was lyrical. Yeah, he wants to read the rest, which is a result."

"Good."

"The other news is that I bumped into David Hollingsworth in the terminal at Heathrow. I travelled over with him. He read it cover to cover in more-or-less one hit and is very impressed with it. He might just do it, although he can't really fit it in."

"What does that mean?"

"Well it means he's interested and I think would do it like a shot, except that he's got projects already on the go, that he's committed to, so he's thinking now if he can fit it into his schedule."

"Would you not be better off with someone who has time to concentrate just on your film?" Eve is always one to pose the challenging question.

"In an ideal world, yes. But if fate has put me in DB's orbit, I think I'd rather have 25 per cent of his backing than 100 of most people's. Anyway it's all down to finding the right director, after which it's not really my film any more."

"Do you think Gerald will do it?"

"He would do it beautifully. We all know that. But I'm not sure the subject grabs him – well, I know it doesn't, but my belief is that the screenplay will change that."

"Good." There is another of those pauses.

"Did you get any more hope into it?" It's the question he's known is coming at some point in the evening.

"No. Not to speak of. There's not really much to be found. The hope lies in what the film can do. Not in its content."

"Well. You know what I think." Another statement.

"Yeah," is all he can say.

If the car journey equates to a light dusting of snow, the meal feels like the approach of a hard winter.

In the restaurant it's as if the screenplay, and by extension the disaster itself, divide the small square table between them, like a six-inch-thick transparent curtain suspended from the ceiling, filtering out the possibility of real communication. They can see each other but this jelly in the air prevents reaching out and touching in any sense, physical or otherwise. The gelatine insulation has been hanging about for a long time, growing – displacing oxygen.

A small part of it is that E has never really accepted that Ray is now once again a writer. It has become his day job, although enthusiasm will often see him working late shifts, double shifts and even all-nighters. When employment mostly meant leaving the house at 5am and being away for a few days, or several weeks, or even sometimes months, there was never any doubt that the assignment, whatever it was, came first. The only illness that ever stopped him getting to work was the one that imprisons you in your own bathroom. Even funerals of friends and colleagues had to be missed. Holidays were rare, generally short and had to be snatched or fitted round the work diary. Occasionally, even then, they were curtailed by a phone call. Such is the free-lance life.

Working at home is dangerous. People grow into the idea that because you're there, you're doing nothing important and can be interrupted, as if you were on a day off. Friends with well-paid jobs and pension schemes sit, bored in their offices, and ring up to talk about aeroplane matters, for all the world as if you're retired, and don't have a living to earn. Eve has always been keen for Ray to earn money, but has never seemed to connect that necessity with what he does in the office above the dining room. She will call up the stairs at the moment anything enters her head. Ray can be delicately occupied with the extrication of a young woman's broken body from a freezing Scottish bog, only to be interrupted by an enquiry about the whereabouts of a first-class stamp. Because it can sometimes be welcome to escape the contemplation of sombre matters by perhaps going outside and mowing the lawn, he knows that he has contributed to this blurring of the line between work time and the rest of life. However much he's tried to instil the idea that at his desk he's concentrating and will respond when he comes to a convenient stopping place, there is always the assumption that he will indeed soon stop and have time for whatever E has in mind. He is particularly conscious of the irony, when that which E has in mind, quite often, is that he should check something she herself is writing.

He realises that he's thinking all this in the present tense, which hasn't applied for some time.   .

Because the script has been mentioned in the car, he has no reason to bring it up again, and anyway he doesn't really know whether he wants to speak more to her about it or not.   But there are other topics also hanging in the air around them; items of AOB - which have to be at least acknowledged by mention, even if the main agenda business remains undiscussed.   These topics have to be approached as if by ritual eastern dancers facing each other in slow-motion, on a floor made of eggs.

He lifts a leg to begin a step.

"So what's Dorian up to?" Phew! It's out. That wasn't too difficult, eventually.

There are actually two questions being put under the disguise of these five or six innocuous words.   To the first, straightforward one he suspects the answer will be probably nothing; and to the second, to him the more interesting one, he imagines that there will be no answer forthcoming this evening.

"Well, you know. Not a lot really. He reads a bit."

Ray does know. Dorian doesn't need to do much. Nor, as far as anyone is aware, ever has he.   He is an undefined relation of E's — some sort of distant cousin. The second, unanswered question refers to the status of his and E's current relation**ship**, which is also undefined, at least as far as Ray has been informed.   So apart from, apparently, at the moment taking a moderate interest in some of the things that E studies and works with professionally, which is what Ray has already heard about how cousin Dorian spends some of his days, the big unspoken, unanswered question number two is what cousin Dorian is 'up to' at night.

It may, of course, be absolutely nothing remotely concerning.   In many ways it will be quite surprising if there is something 'going on' between vivacious Eve, the enthusiastic, even voracious learner and Dorian who, while a handsome man still, fritters away his quotient of attractiveness by achieving next to nothing in his life. He was extremely well provided-for as a young adult and lapsed into a not-particularly-active and extremely undemanding social round that has occupied his time for well over thirty years, avoiding both marriage and scandal, and, one suspects, much contact with human warmth at all. The idea that he should have developed an attachment to Ray's wife is not at all impossible; that she might reciprocate is almost laughable. But unhappy women can form wildly unsuitable liaisons.

There is only really the repeated extension of her stay in California to suggest anything out of the ordinary. There was already talk of further courses when she left for the first one of three months. Staying at Dorian's was, as Aunt Cat said, a 'no-brainer'. Aunt Cat is another undefined relation, a sparkling near-octogenarian with a strange penchant for the latest jargon and trendy phrase.

Ray once had a dream in which Aunt Cat's conversations were inscribed on stone tablets, and he had a pneumatic drill and chiselled out the offensive expressions. He broke up the blocks where she used 'no-brainer' and 'gutted' and 'gobsmacked'. Then he was at the BBC, probably the TV centre, although there were radio people and even Classic FM faces around too. And his jack-hammer had turned into a gun and he was rounding up all the presenters and traffic reporters and news readers and sports pundits and the people who write *East Enders*. He was ordering them into the BBC Club Bar, where apparently all the misuse of language was plotted and invented. He was making them put their hands up if they'd used 'ahead of' instead of 'before' or 'in advance of'. Or 'take it off' instead of 'take it from' and worse 'take it off of' to mean the same. All those traffic people who interminably use 'closed off' when just 'closed' will do – and then the advertising copywriters were there too, admitting using 'for free' instead of 'for nothing' or just 'free' and confessing to all the awful split infinitives. Terry Wogan was suddenly at his side, arguing on his team with those who were putting their hands up to using 'sat' instead of 'sitting' and 'less' when they meant 'fewer' and 'infer' when they meant 'imply'. Richard Allinson was in the crowd and he was encouraging them to chant back derisively: 'unfeasibly! unfeasibly!' just as if it were the proper negative and not an absurd way of saying 'very', as if another one were needed. Ray knew he was losing and his gun had turned into a water pistol and the crowd in the bar all had rocks from the broken jargon tablets and they started throwing them at him and Wogan. They'd had to run for it and set off along one of those curved corridors, with Aunt Cat's voice cackling after them. 'You're legging it. I told you! I told you it was a no-brainer.'

It was because the accommodation **was** free, convenient, safe, easy and convivial that to stay with cousin Dorian was such a 'no-brainer' and no one thought any more about it. Until the second course turned into a third, with an optional field trip and then there was an opportunity for a fourth and then another. And perhaps the phone calls half-implied, by what Eve didn't say, rather than by what she did, that she and Dorian had slipped into some comfortable, undemanding but unspecific alternative domesticity. That thickening curtain began to apply to the phone calls and e-mails too and her return began not to be mentioned, even under 'any other business'. Ray is unsure what line of probing to adopt.

"It's a terrible waste. All the things he could have done, still do, with his life with all that money."

"I don't think he's got as much as we all imagine," Eve says.

"Anyone who manages two European trips a year, plus four or five other holidays in the best places can't exactly be on his uppers. And I bet he'll leave it all to a cats' home or something, when he goes. It's amazing how people who never have to worry about a thing their whole lives, have an amazing reluctance to give their relatives even a fraction of that freedom from concern about the future, when they're not going to need it any more themselves."

"What he does with his money is none of our business."

"It's none of mine. I'm not really related. But I would have thought you'd have an interest. It's your family."

"What I think doesn't matter. He makes up his own mind. I'm just grateful for somewhere nice to stay."

Ray notices that she at least chooses the word 'stay', not 'live', but equally that she doesn't quantify the stay in any way. He finds the fact that she doesn't add something like 'while I'm here' or 'while I'm studying' confirmation that no return is in prospect. She seems too to be defending Dorian, quietly. Time for a different tack.

"Has he got a girlfriend at the moment?" He tries to soften the question; to make it less obviously pointed by continuing, "I thought he was so silly to get rid of Marilyn. I thought she was really good for him."

"Everyone liked Marilyn." Not only is this not new ground, but his elaboration has given E the chance to ignore his question; and to deflect it. "Did you know she's gone back to London?"

"No, I hadn't heard that. Be nice to see her. We should catch up with her when we're there."

"That won't be for a bit; will it?"

Ping! That seems to be it. Eve has said something that is not non-committal.

"Won't it? I don't know. I don't seem to be told of your plans. I have no idea what's happening. Why won't it be for a bit?"

"Because I can't come back until you start seeing some good in people; until you start being positive about things." She's let the genie out. The serious stuff can begin.

"I am positive. Haven't I just this second been positive about Marilyn, for God's sake? There are loads of people I like and say good things about and I feel really great now about the script and very positive that it's going to go. Yes, there are a lot of things wrong in the world that need pointing out and someone's got to do that. You believe that things will get better by just ignoring the bad and thinking good thoughts, and I wish I could believe that too, but I just know that we can all think as positively as we like, and it's not going to stop the bad guys. If no one has a go at them and at least tries to wake everyone up, then the bad things are going to get worse and worse."

"I've heard all that. But you never stop complaining. You're always criticising something or someone."

"That's not true, but I am lucky enough, or unfortunate enough, it could be either, to have the ability to recognise things that maybe other people don't see or can't be bothered with. As I've been given it that gift, I think I should use it. Yes I do criticise, but apart from occasional neighbour niggles, the things I discuss and follow up are all about people we don't personally know, whereas you are forever criticising someone you do know, and that's me. It's pot calling kettle, except it's not because I would never dream of saying the sort of things to you that you endlessly say to me, even if you can't see that you do."

This is not the way he wanted the meal to go, the two of them hissing under their breath, not to alert the other diners to the total discord on table twelve.

The waiter, who had introduced himself as 'Your service host, Cruz,' which combination of sounds had persistently defied all meaning for Ray, now returns with their drinks. Ray takes advantage of the short truce to look around the restaurant. There is nothing wrong with the place. It's very agreeable in an earnest, holistic, organic, wholefood, vegetarian sort of way. He's quite used to that, even if its matter-of-fact worthiness, as personified by Cruz, is slightly too intrusive to provide quite the right atmosphere for a quiet reconciliatory supper. Well, that doesn't seem to be remotely on the cards now.

Arguments with Eve follow a typical pattern that has probably been familiar for centuries to those who observe the mechanics of disagreement. The first stage is the mutual disclosure of views, in which by the very nature of things, one of the points of view − in Ray's opinion, normally his − will seem to be the more logical of the two. This traditionally causes the owner of the more shakily-founded standpoint to become more assertive, rather as an army in danger of losing a battle calls up reinforcements. Further exposition follows in the second stage at which there is a tendency for whatever logic had existed on the weaker side to desert the battlefield entirely, although it's not unknown for the stronger side also to suffer from this to a degree.

The third step might well see the battle joined on one of the flanks as the losing side commits to the fray a counter-argument or a series of them that has little or nothing to do with the original subject.

The next level will see the time-honoured stratagem normally adopted when a combatant finds him or herself unable to refute the content of the opposition's case. The often automatic ploy is to attack ferociously the manner in which the opponent is conducting themselves. Politicians do this all the time in interviews: 'I will answer that in a moment, but there's no need to be so aggressive, Jeremy'. In E's case her voice will become quite strident, not to say raised, but if Ray's voice betrays in response so much as a degree of frustration or indignation, which it will, he will be accused of 'shouting'.

It should be noted that to point out any inconsistencies, whether in the argument's substance or to do with any assessment of its conduct, is, at this or any stage, a fruitless exercise. 'I'm not actually shouting. But you are,' is going to earn no points whatsoever.

We are now set for what, Ray remembers, psychologists call the displacement gesture, where the side that is losing the argument, almost certainly in close company with their temper, will physically leave the scene of the scene in the belief that in doing so they have prevailed. This usually involves the slamming of doors, running upstairs or loud off-screen mutterings and unidentified crashing about.

Cruz has gone.

"I didn't come six thousand miles to have a row."

"Don't have one, then. Just listen for once."

"Yeah. Who am I, to have an opinion on anything? I'm listening. Tell me what to think." He's trying hard to keep the sarcasm out of his voice, but it's in the words anyway. At least he managed not to add 'as always'.

"Every time I think about the prospect of coming home, and I really want to, all I can visualise is you in your office, seven days a week, immersed in air crashes and murder and spies and torture and injustice. The feel of the house has got heavier and heavier; it's lost its spirit. Whatever I do to counter it the vibrations are terrible. It's affected you, whether you realise it or not, and it certainly affects me. I know you say that someone has to take up the sword to fight all the demons and that it's all for the good, and that the rest of us are looking the other way so we can have happy little lives even if they're all a delusion. Well, at least with my way of looking at things I've got a life, but I don't think you have any more. I only hope you can get one back when this burden you've chosen for yourself is all over. I can't live with you like it is now, so when things come up that I can do here, the choice isn't hard."

In one way Ray's choice is hard, looking at his wife across the table, with her serious, sad, beautiful face. But in another way there's no choice at all. He's started something that he must see through, for better or for worse, or he's finished – in his own eyes, which is where it counts most. There's something else. That same compulsion to karate-chop the steel table in the dream LAX yesterday makes him stand up quietly. No fighting that either.

"Sorry. We seem to be wasting each other's time. I'll get the drinks."

He finds Cruz, settles the bill and tells him to cancel his food, if not both orders. "Check with the lady." Cruz is confused. He thinks the bill is the check, so if Ray has now paid, why has he got to give another one to the lady? Ray walks out into the hot night to find a bar with beer and a phone for a cab.

He's just made the mother of all displacement gestures.

–ooOoo–

Ray will have another dream tonight. Like most times, he probably won't remember much of it tomorrow. It'll be another of those where he's trying to run a totally unorganisable film unit, again with difficult people in an impossible location, and he'll keep being in the wrong place and not be able to get back to the camera where he should be. He has so many dreams like that. The difference with this one is that out of somewhere or nowhere, a make-up assistant, or an actress, or a PA or an extra, he won't be sure, will be generous with affection, offering the promise of warmth and intimacy. Sexual adventures of any sort are rare in Ray's dreams, so it'll be unusual by any yardstick. But this one will be even more unique. Although it will be the up-to-date him, the feeling will be that of those far teenage days when even the prospect of being at all physically close to a girl was an almost unimaginable goal. Single-sex schools could impose that sort of barrier, at just the wrong time. The notion of having someone sitting on his knee, or holding hands or even just standing closer than an understood minimum distance, seemed forbidden, exciting and an extremely remote possibility. He hasn't even remembered the concept – let alone what it was like to feel it, and what intoxicating promises those small steps seemed to represent – probably since he was seventeen. To experience that again, despite the mad surroundings, and have the prospect of those steps being gloriously fulfilled and exceeded will be so good that he'll want it to last forever. And of course dreams don't and they usually stop at the last place you'd like them to.

But even though this one will and in the morning only a half-memory of something will remain on the cranial hard drive, Ray will wake feeling a great deal better about himself than the events of the evening might have suggested he would.

–ooOoo–

167

29   Room at the Top

The first hours of day two of the California odyssey are, in essential terms, a retake of day one, without the stunt sequence. Perry's landlord is away in Hawaii, and so his less imperial but newer and infinitely more practical Toyota stands in for the in-disgrace Town Car which is languishing in the repair shop in Sepulveda. Sepulveda! It was strange, cooling down in the rescue truck yesterday, finding that Sepulveda was their destination. Ray's known the name, associated with the Boulevard, the Dam and the Recreation Area, all the time he's been going to LA, but it was only relatively recently, since his last visit, that he's read of its significance in the story of the Spanish conquest of America. He knew that Perry had noticed him smile and shake his head at seeing the name on road signs, but he hadn't really felt it fair to go into details of why it provoked this reaction. Bending his friend's receptive ear about the Lockerbie case was one thing: subjecting him to a discussion of the 500-year-old mindset that allowed Lockerbie and its cover-up to happen was another thing altogether.

Most of the continent's European colonisers used the concept of 'natural slaves' as an excuse to steal the land and its resources from the owners, the indigenous peoples, who naturally enjoyed their ownership communally, without title deeds and boundary markers. The argument was that, because the semi-nomadic societies that the newcomers found in place did not conform in virtually any respect to patterns that Europeans lived under and could recognise, their peoples were therefore lesser humans who could not have rights, such as those of property or liberty, and thus could be dispossessed without conscience. The fact that they made their spiritual communion with the land, the elements, with animals and all of the natural world, instead of with Jesus Christ, identified them as primitive heathens, deserving the displeasure of God, meaning that the Almighty himself could be confidently cited as approving their loss, by force, of their land, their liberty and if need be, their lives.

Juan Gines de Sepulveda was one who prominently spoke to that motion in the public debates in Spain. Even his principal opponent, Bartolomé de Las Casas, who advocated the equality of man, still reserved for the Indians a lesser status that has been described as 'natural children', in need of instruction and nurture. Those of the small proportion of natural children who were coerced into embracing Christianity, rather than face the mass-murder that was rampant, were still treated as grossly inferior beings.

Ray remembers being taught without any hint of question at school, both regular and Sunday, that missionaries were engaged in noble work, bringing simple deluded people to respect proper values and the one God. Meanwhile Saturday Hollywood, and later everyday television, in their endless 'Cavalry and Indians' sagas, followed the lead of the Declaration of Independence which referred to 'merciless Indian savages'. The real Americans were cast as athletic, blood-crazed murderers whose word could never be trusted, fit for nothing other than to be shot or otherwise disposed of out of hand. It's taken much of a lifetime for Ray to recover from this brainwashing; to become aware that the spiritual beliefs and respectful practices of those 'savages' were probably a far more appropriate blueprint for life than the so-called civilised code of behaviour that takes its guidance from a basket of other religions, whose common denominator has been violent disharmony.

That Christianity, the religion of the 'Lamb of God' and the 'Prince of Peace' can be invoked to dignify and legitimise genocide is one of the great paradoxes, he thinks. A euphemism for genocide is 'ethnic cleansing', and a parallel form of cleansing involves the wiping out of awareness and understanding by rewriting history, by the substitution of cultural myth for recorded fact. When thinking about the populating of America, several generations, including people who absolutely know differently, still have to overcome the equation implanted so decisively: 'Missionaries, settlers, cowboys and cavalry good – Indians bad.' It's always there, to some degree, at the back of the mind and has to be reassessed, re-rejected every time the subject comes up. It's part of the American creed, the list of things that America believed about itself and taught the world to believe too, using literature, music and the medium in which Ray has made his living.

Most Americans and plenty of others beside will dismiss the assertion that Americans connived in the massacre that was Lockerbie, because of that list. Belief in the Constitution and the rights of the individual makes it impossible to consider that any true citizen could play even a passive part in the wilful random murder of 172 of their fellow countrymen, women and children. Every principle that civilised people cling to, would argue that they are correct. But history says that they could hardly be more wrong. They have been misled, by waving flags, patriotic anthems, by speeches like President George W's on 20th September 2001, eleven days on from 9/11, batting on about freedom of religion, freedom of speech, freedom to vote and to assemble and to disagree with each other. He read fine words from the autocue; he may have even believed them, perhaps knowing no better; but whether he did or not they were essentially spin, product of the cultural myth. For when the first colonist encountered the first native American there were, in what would become the United States, estimated to be between 20 and 50 million established inhabitants. By the time the so-called Redskins had given up the unequal fight for their own land they numbered about a quarter of a million. Taking even the lower of the two initial estimates, 98.75 per cent of the original population had been wiped out as a direct result of governments' policies and actions. Over several generations a population could have been expected perhaps to grow. It shrivelled. Whether by 19.75 million or 49.75 million, the numbers are inconceivable; either figure betrays a scale of decimation never equalled on this planet.

People generally take the actions that their culture decrees necessary, whether it's the culture of their nation, their locality, or some form of organisation. What is held to be necessary defines what deeds are acceptable. Ray knows that few races or states, alliances or religions can truthfully claim that their representatives have never acted unacceptably; that their culture has not at some point, licensed wrong behaviour. Certainly the United States is far from having a monopoly in wrongdoing, even in genocide, although the numbers are startling. What disturbs him is the difference between the values that the country claims to uphold and those values' very denial in much of what is actually done. For example, Bush rhetoric about 'the worst leaders having the worst weapons', setting aside the gorgeous unconscious irony, happily ignores the fact that his 'nation under God' chose to drop an atomic weapon, not on a remote military target as a warning, but on a teeming civilian city – and then not one, but two. Again, noisy, self-satisfied pride in the rule of law and responsible international behaviour contrasts with the reality of the later carpet-bombing of a country with which the US was not even nominally at war. The sad list of discrepancies runs to page after page.

When the Land of the Free murdered its own people in their millions and confined the survivors, 'the lesser-beings' mentality was on hand to legitimise theft disguised as economic necessity. Taking and exploitation are essentials in the culture of colonisation. Here the victims had little choice but to resist, playing into the hands of the usurpers both physically and in terms of propaganda, as the Indians' desperate defence of their own land could be so readily misrepresented in course of its translation into the new nation's cultural myth. But Ray thinks there was a side-effect to the massive scale of the subjugation on which the nation was founded. The means by which 'the west was won' – self-interest, gross injustice, cruelty and force of arms – became the genuine, the essential culture of the nation, the blueprint for how she would conduct many of her future affairs. The musket, the carbine, the canon and the Gatling gun were pointers to her preferred means of persuasion. And it was a preferred means that by definition showed little respect for human life; the fundamental right that was so proclaimed as underpinning everything. Nothing demonstrates this better than the Civil War that saw mainly white Americans slaughtering each other on an epic scale. Later a multitude of overseas military adventures of dubious legality and often suspect motivation proved costly in casualties among the enlisted adventurers as well as their foreign adversaries. The cynical sacrifice of lives for far-from-transparent reasons can hardly be a shocking suggestion, when history shows it to be a national stock-in-trade.

The indigenous Americans and the millions following-on whose lives were forfeit, nominally for Uncle Sam's principles, certainly didn't share in those much-trumpeted freedoms. In theory at least, liberty had been bought with their blood, which should serve to make it that much more precious. But many wonder how much liberty actually continues to exist. Ray's convinced it's mostly lost – mainly through people being asleep in front of their televisions. With the ever-present box and rolling selective news, it's all-too-easy to rewrite history today, often even before its episodes have actually taken place.

With the moral superiority of their particular way of life firmly cemented, the Americans have not surprisingly taken a skewed attitude to everything that is not American; 'not invented here'. It has been argued by academics Sardar and Wyn Davies that the United States élite continues to regard most of the inhabitants of the rest of the world as being somewhere in that range between murdering savages and natural slaves. Even Europeans can come to the conclusion that they are perhaps considered as natural children, needing some instruction to understand their proper second-class rôle in the Order of Things. As Secret Sam's front-men treat most developing countries under much the same principle that the warring colonists held towards the Native Americans – namely that their peoples are expendable and can exist only if prepared to be exploited – then the message from the Big Top should be clear for all, Ray thinks, Europeans included. Being that: the present Order of Things is super-colonialism through culture and economics, take it or leave it.

–ooOoo–

Today Perry and Ray have lunch with English cameraman, Nick Lightman. It's an event that for Ray is amiable and uncomfortable in about equal measures. Ray was already a first AD when he first met Nick, then a young camera assistant. Before Ray met Perry, Nick worked fairly consistently for a couple of years as Perry's clapper-loader. Whereas the two friends had worked their way up through the ranks in the then-traditional manner, Nick had been one of the new breed of technicians who, in the freer, less formal structure of the commercials side of the film business, had leap-frogged grades and reached the top job (it was a more noticeable feature in the camera department) at an unusually young age.

Despite the cordial banter and the recalling of tales of locations and characters long past, Ray is acutely aware that although Perry had provided Nick with several years of valuable training, experience and profitable employment, there is zero likelihood of the debt being repaid. For whatever reason – Perry's appearance, his outspokenness, the existence of too much history, or his recalling for Nick a time when he was less like a hot Hollywood DP than anyone imaginable – Ray's friend won't be on any sort of a shortlist for a Lightman camera crew, even just a few days on a second or third camera for an action sequence. In fact, all three at the table know it, without anything remotely being said, and Nick doesn't really try to disguise the fact. Underlying the whole meal is an unspoken truth that seems to apply more even in the States than it does at home, where it's bad enough. The fact is that people who are working, or who habitually go from job to job, are considered hot and find themselves generally in demand and get more work offered than they can cope with. The converse rule is that a technician who, for whatever reason, appears to be looking for a job is regarded as 'cold', viewed with suspicion, looked down on and is less likely to be hired. Because Perry needs a film, and his old assistant, Nick, knows it, there is a gulf between them that is almost palpable, despite the joking and the bonhomie.

Even Ray is on the other side of the void. Nick has known Ray only as an assistant director. So because Ray's not in Hollywood to do a movie as a first AD, he's not hot. He's second eleven. In a way, Ray saying that he's gone back to writing these days makes it worse. 'I'm writing' can be taken as code for 'I can't get work in my usual grade'. Many technicians when asked what they're 'up to' will reply that they're writing. Too often the assumed decode is accurate.

Nick has a 2.30 meeting and has to go. They all stand up and there are hugs and earnest, clasped handshakes.

Sadly, neither Perry nor Ray will be bothering to contact their old chum Nick Lightman again.

–ooOoo–

30   Company Travel

Leaving the restaurant's overblown columned portico and taking the minimal few steps to the waiting car, it had been noticeably hot. The valet parkers, as they might put it, but Ray would try his best not to, 'really know their shit' and return the cars with the aircon wound up to volume 11. The interior of the Toyota sounded like a taxiing biz-jet.

Outside now it looks as if it's half as hot again. They've reclaimed the Lincoln from Sepulveda and it's the Town Car's blowers and pipes and vents and nozzles that have to cope and keep the immaculate Cartier interior survivable. They pass the massive painted sign for the Eternal Valley Memorial Park, which Ray always thinks of as his personal symbolic point where the LA conurbation finally gives way and lets the rest of America happen. Or Los Angeles' Boot Hill on the edge of town, from where the spirits can drift up and out over the seemingly endless wide open spaces. The 4.6 litre Ford V8 motor is having to climb – as well as move them along and keep them cool, and it's doing the job admirably, purring up the winding, scenic Route 14 towards the Mojave Desert.

It feels a strange choice of day to be deliberately heading for a desert, but some people will go anywhere for a party.

A CHP patrolman, astride a Harley-Davidson parked commandingly at a lonely intersection, watches them pass, panning his sunglasses. Shades of *Electroglide in Blue.*

"I always expect to get pulled," says Perry. "You know why." He assumes Ray does.

"Tell me."

"You don't know? They call this model the 'six body trunk': the boot is so vast that you could get six full-sized men laid out on its floor. They say the mob used to employ it routinely for dumping people they'd stiffed. Not this one of course, or if they did they made a good job of cleaning up the blood."

Ray has seen the boot. It's perhaps even more pristine than the interior, which is near-perfect.

He notices that Perry said 'You don't know?' with almost an American intonation. It's as if, with leaving the confines of LA, he's showing a tiny sign of throwing off his normal archetypical Englishness. He's already told Ray, to the latter's surprise, that he should buy a cowboy hat and even some boots to go to this bash. His own boots are sliding around in a plastic bag, in the cavernous space for half a dozen men with rigor-mortis, and his leather hat is already on the equally leather back seat, ready for deployment.

Not that there are any plans to stop and get out in the blazing sun. This Town Car isn't going to the High Country to find a secluded place to unload dead people, although there are some moribund memories, from last evening in particular, that Ray would be happy to leave with the snakes and the tumbleweed.

There hasn't been an opportunity to return to the subject of Flight 103 since the arrival of the breakdown truck yesterday. On this journey they have metaphorically buried Nick Lightman, and for the rest of the time Perry has been briefing Ray about the evening's entertainment, about his American girlfriend Pippa and some others of the cast of disparate characters they are likely to encounter later. This will be after their proposed visits to the liquor department of a drugstore for a stock of beers and a western shop to investigate required sartorial accessories.

Ray has actually determined to take the same attitude over his screenplay as he did at Heathrow two days ago with DB. If Perry asks to hear more, he shall. If he doesn't, Ray won't mention it. He doesn't want his friends to feel trampled by his large herd of hobbyhorses. He and Eve are hugely telepathic and are often thinking or come out with the same things at the same time. Ray can't imagine anyone less likely to have that sort of semi-spiritual link than Perry, yet even as he finishes with the thought, his companion shifts in his seat, exercises his elbows and says:

"Tell me some more about Lockerbie. You were saying there were some really dirty dealings with – was it a Major McKee?"

Well, I'll be darned.

"Yes. Right. Well. Yes. Where had we got to? Major Charles McKee. He was US Army attached to the DIA, that's the Defense Intelligence Agency. If you imagine that the CIA is powerful and well-funded and it is, then it's a surprise to find that the DIA, which we hear little about, is even more so: I've seen a budget five times that of the CIA quoted. And like most intelligence organisations they don't in general get on; actually that's a big understatement. There was though, as I started to say yesterday, a plan to recover the Beirut hostages, and it required co-operation between them. It was sanctioned at the very top, by the

President, because this was a matter of national prestige and could not go wrong, after the Tehran hostage rescue attempt, the one which sank Jimmy Carter."

"Yeah, I've been remembering things about that. Didn't a helicopter crash in the desert?"

"Hit a support Hercules; eight killed, I think it was. An awful tragedy. But this was to be a similar military operation, involving Delta Force personnel, based on locations established by CIA intelligence. McKee was a communications specialist and co-ordinator of the mission, and he was working with a CIA counterpart, Matthew Gannon, the deputy chief of station at the Beirut Embassy who had succeeded, it's believed, in unearthing the hostages' whereabouts. We know that the rescues would have involved several complex, simultaneous operations, each as daring as the London Iran Embassy raid, with distraction tactics, loads of vehicles and air evacuation. Planning was at a very advanced stage with men already on the ground, when it was called off, again at the highest level – the Oval Office."

Perry, like DB before him, has to ask who was president at the time.

"At some point McKee and Gannon had learnt, with horror, of the unofficial 'drugs for hostages' incentive being run by the unknown CIA unit. McKee had a passionate hatred of drugs, **and** he knew the connection could compromise his mission, so he complained to Langley, CIA HQ. For whatever reason – his tone, inter-agency history, CIA pride, who knows – they didn't come down hard on the drug run, but instead used their influence at the White House to have his rescue attempt aborted, again potentially putting his men in danger. A DIA source said that McKee was livid and travelling back unauthorised to the States to blow the whistle on the drug link. Leaving your post without orders is serious and at least **he** was apparently doing that. Gannon and two others of the team accompanied him."

"They weren't just going home for Christmas, then?" Perry asks. "I mean, it was just before the holiday, wasn't it?"

"It was, but I'm certain they had another motive, because they all changed their travel plans from various other flights, specifically to travel on Pan Am 103, even though regulations meant they couldn't actually sit together. They did this after a known drug courier with family connections in the Bekaa Valley was booked onto 103 via the feeder from Frankfurt. There's no doubt that their action in this was entirely deliberate, with some specific aim in mind. I think they received word that there was a protected consignment going on the flight, and so McKee planned a confrontation on arrival in the US that would provide evidence of his allegations. I'm convinced they planned to shadow the courier through immigration and customs, noting anyone who assisted his passage, and at some point, ideally in the presence of one or more of the facilitators, and probably pre-arranged DIA witnesses, expose what was going on, by intercepting the courier, and opening his cases. This would have been a huge embarrassment for the CIA and indeed the government, if it had come out. McKee wouldn't have intended publicity that would hurt his country. He would have just wanted the rotten apples dealt with."

Ray sneaks a look at Perry, whose body-language shows he is keeping up — a signal to continue.

"They must have decided to confront the drug carrier, a young Lebanese-born Arab named Khalid Jaafar, quietly in advance, because on the flight Matthew Gannon, an Arabic speaker, had gone from Clipper Class, where he and McKee were separately seated, back to tourist class where Jaafar was travelling. We can be sure of this because the front part of the fuselage, where Gannon's seat 14J was, separated from the rest of the plane early in the break-up and his body wasn't found where other bodies from that area fell. His was found quite near Jaafar's. He was without doubt down almost at the rear of the Jumbo, about 40 rows back, when the bomb exploded. I imagine his message was that the game was up, but that they were not especially interested in him but after bigger fish. He would have told Jaafar that he could improve his situation by co-operating, and was probably in the process of describing exactly what he required him to do after landing so that they could stage the exposure to the best effect."

"My God, can you imagine just sitting there at the back having a conversation and seeing it all happen in front of you?" Perry shivers noticeably.

"I know. It's just beyond anything . . . "

There is an interlude, as each of them deals with their own vision of the scene. After a while, Ray picks up the thread.

"The Jaafar shadowing plan was probably icing on McKee's cake. He obviously felt he had enough evidence already, because he had reserved to travel to the States anyway. So it could have been just a terrible coincidence that they re-booked themselves onto a drug flight that had been targeted independently. But there is major suspicion that their new travel plans were betrayed." He hears Perry sigh at this. "There are various possibilities as to by whom and to whom. A straightforward attempt to warn the drug runners to avoid sending a consignment on this flight, so that Jaafar's luggage would be clean, doesn't seem to be the answer, because there was a shipment on board. Any other motive for passing their flight details had to be much more sinister. It would have had to be to encourage the flight to be interfered with to prevent the team's arriving in the US to carry out whatever exposure plans it might have had. In short any message passing the flight details of McKee and Gannon, and O'Connor and Lariviere has to be viewed as potentially inciting or procuring their murder, along of course with those of their fellow passengers."

"Fucking hell," Perry says, but he's not really consciously commenting. He's away in a 747; he's in every one of the dozens of 747s he's been in – flying thousands of miles, over tens of years – imagining what it would be like.

Ray accepts another long pause and concentrates for a while on the shimmering road and the strange stillness of the white-hot scrubby landscape.

–ooOoo–

31   Fatal Attraction

Ray is very familiar with this desert. Its remote tracks and salt lakes have played host to many a TV commercial for all sorts of unlikely products. Getting to California was priority number one for ad agency creative teams and much ingenuity went into convincing their gritty clients that the far-fetched ideas, however inappropriate to the product in question, would up their sales. Of course the gritty clients had to be on the shoot too, so the merits of filming in Santa Monica or Mohave, vis-à-vis St John's Wood, were not lost on them either. Ray remembers that the first time he ever drove a car from the passenger side was on a sandy backroad up here. Actually it was a joint effort. John Tunnel, the director-operator, sat behind the wheel hand-holding the 35mm Arriflex, the descendant of the battle camera built by the Nazis to record their Blitzkreig. He operated the Buick's pedals while Ray attended to the transmission selection and the steering, taking care to keep his hands out of the shot. It was easier in those days, when large cars had a full-width front seat for three. There was no thought of lateral support at that time, and in the era before seat belts you could often, in normal spirited driving, find yourself sliding about on the polished leather or shiny rexine. Such cars were also much more accommodating of amorous adventures than their segregated successors, which generally provide a veritable Maginot Line to defend the passenger – or driver – from surprise advances.

It's Perry who breaks the silence.

"If you're saying that the flight could have been targeted to prevent McKee and party spilling the beans about the drug conduit, and also that the drug people weren't in the loop, then who are you saying told the bombers? There's only one other party involved."

"Exactly! I mean there is an alternative scenario: that the bomb plotters knew the team's travel plans already, because they, themselves, had deliberately fed them the information on the narcotics run that lured them to re-book onto the doomed flight. Which fact, of course, again wouldn't have been shared with the drug network or their courier. That's possible, but doesn't seem too likely – Jibril's contract was to destroy an American airliner; who might or might not be on it was of no particular concern to him. You could say that taking out a few intelligence people would be a bonus, but on the other hand, their whistle-blowing wasn't going to cause him a problem, and added risk for his operation was the last thing he needed. And as we've seen, he clearly wasn't worried about the interests of the Lebanese traffickers, which just leaves . . . "

"The CIA cell! But that makes no sense. Gannon, is his name? He was CIA. They're all on the same side."

"I think the expression is 'supposed to be'."

"And why would they know about the bomb plot if their local accomplices in the drug-running didn't?"

"Well, they were in Beirut, presumably doing other work too, and they did have the word 'Intelligence' on their notepaper. The likelihood of tit-for-tat retaliation for the Airbus shootdown was circulated by the US State Department just four days after it happened. Jibril was under surveillance almost immediately and it was known inside the community that he had taken the Iranian offer. Anyone in the trade had to be aware an attempt was coming and be looking for clues."

"That would go for McKee's team too, wouldn't it?" Perry has a good point.

"True, but if you have to travel, all you can do ultimately, whoever you are, is take your seat trusting that the appropriate professional people have done their utmost to keep you safe. However cautious and astute an operator you are, you can't search an airliner yourself." Perry agrees. He seems, Ray thinks, to be engaged in examining the alternatives rather more than might have been anticipated. Ray decides to lay them out.

"You agree we can count out the drug people as far as complicity in eliminating McKee and his people goes? They didn't know 103 was going down, otherwise they wouldn't have had bags of heroin on board. If they'd signed up to the idea of doing a baggage switch, they wouldn't have been prepared to waste a consignment, or want knowledge of the conduit blown. They might have been prepared to sacrifice a courier, if the price was right, but not the rest. I'm sure that if that sort of bag exchange was ever planned, it never got to happen. "

"Makes sense."

"And we've talked about where it's pure chance. You know – the team re-book on 103. 103 happens to be the target; they're not. The bombers don't know they're on it – or they find out at some point and obviously do nothing."

"That's certainly possible, but it seems a bit of a coincidence."

"Agreed. So what's left? We've got them enticed onto the flight by someone, which means essentially either the bombers, which we feel is not too likely, or the CIA cell or whatever we call it, whose people have a real vested interest in McKee not getting back to Washington." Conscious that Perry is going to contest that one again, Ray keeps going.

"Now there's one more set of alternatives that apply whether the party is on the flight completely by chance or tempted by the terrorists. There, the CIA cell people get to hear about it and they do nothing. Take your pick. I don't see any other variations. Oh yes, there is," he corrects himself. "There's one where the CIA outfit sends a message to alert the drug lords to the group's presence on the plane, which somehow gets diverted to the bomb plotters instead. The spooks might not know this had happened, which would sort of put them in the clear – or they might have found out too late – or they might have heard in time but done nothing. All I will say about any of these options is that my money is on the CIA knowing that 103 was going down before it did, because they appeared there so quickly when it happened."

"I still can't believe it," Perry declares.

"Which 'it' are we talking about?"

–ooOoo–

It now being 3.45, Perry, the Englishman, is taking afternoon tea. Plainly he is a regular client in this very typical roadside establishment, greeted with genuine warmth by the elderly waitress, whom he has trained with her colleagues, he confides, to source proper boiling water to make the beverage, rather than the merely hot, the US norm.

Ray has told him in the last couple of miles what many serious Lockerbie watchers believe. That the aircraft, its crew, the passengers, and four, perhaps five, intelligence personnel were all sacrificed to keep the lid on the secrets of a tawdry drug-running operation which was of course misguided, but may even not have been well-intentioned and, judged by the efforts taken to cover it up, may have had some element of criminality and corruption about it. He has described the suspiciously fast arrival of CIA operatives in the town, and outlined their illegal activities over the following days, blanket denial of which served to convince many observers that there was a major cover-up in progress.

"These agents had to be there to conceal something and everything fits the drug-run scenario," he'd said. "To be fair, if their colleagues on the plane had been 'terminated' as a result of activities of other colleagues, it's unlikely that the people on the ground – or more than a few of them – knew anything about it. That sort of information would tend to be compartmentalised. Most of them would have thought they were just housekeeping, tidying up a mess, keeping company secrets.

"There is also the undeniable fact that if the large body of manpower that was obviously available in London to swing into action so quickly when the jet went down had actually been deployed at Heathrow three or four hours earlier to protect the plane, then Lockerbie could have been prevented. Yet it wasn't. The flight got no special security, despite the fairly pointed warnings. The facts taken together lead the proverbial 'reasonable person' to conclude that not only was 103's fate expected – but also that it was allowed to happen."

Perry had spoken for the first time in several minutes, only to declare that he was speechless. He was already, with some relief, indicating to turn into the carstop.

The liquid in Perry's mug looks like tea and Perry vouches for it, but Ray remains unconvinced and stays with coffee. He does succumb to a doughnut. Perry's 60-year-old fan has reluctantly left the table, giggling at his effusive compliments and his accent. After his personal version of the tea ceremony, he offers his conclusion in lowered tones.

"I've listened to everything you've said," he says, "but I still can't get it into my head that anyone but terrorists and criminals would knowingly let innocent people get on a plane and go to their deaths. They would, yes, but government employees, no. I can't see it."

"I totally understand the fact that you can't accept the possibility, because it's horrible. That alone actually assists a cover-up, because it seems too unbelievable. But how about this? The entire prosecution case, when someone was eventually brought to trial, was that the guilty parties were government employees – two seemingly respectable guys in suits who the indictment said were intelligence agents, just like the CIA. In fact neither of them were anything of the sort. But say they had been. The only material difference between them and a CIA or SIS person would have been that they worked for a different government. And if you say, OK, that government is one known to sponsor terrorism and the United States doesn't do that, I will have to say bollocks. What about the best-known two examples, El Salvador and Nicaragua where the CIA funded guerrilla armies? What about the CIA-backed coups in Guatemala, Indonesia, Chile and Panama? What about invasions like the Bay of Pigs? What about propping-up a catalogue of sleazy dictators who've used kidnap, torture and mass murder on their populations? The documented list of places where the US, through the CIA, has been responsible for thousands and thousand of civilian deaths runs to a small book.

"If you work for an organisation where the culture is that the end, which is supposedly the promotion of America's best interests, justifies any means, including taking the lives of innocents, your senses have to become dulled. If you have a family, the only way you could ever justify being complicit in the killing of other people's children is by convincing yourself that you are doing something that is necessary to protect the future security of your own kids. The fact that all you're probably doing is ensuring the continuing profits of some American-owned multinationals becomes something you'd rather not think about. If you can connive at the deaths of foreigners by the thousand, it's not a particularly big step to convince yourself that in the service of the greater good, a few Americans have to die too. And because you can't help but become inured to the whole disgusting business, you could ultimately convince yourself that colleagues had to go as well, if their agenda happened to conflict with the one that you were following. It's by no means a far-fetched scenario."

"I suppose the guys who dropped the atom bomb, or flattened Dresden, believed they were doing it for their children," Perry says.

"Sure. The SS were probably good husbands and fathers. Torturers go home to their mothers for dinner."

"Stop the world! I don't want to play any more."

If Ray didn't know better, he'd think that the irrepressible Peregrine Sharpe has been repressed.

"Look," Perry asks. "Is there anything else you need to tell me? You know – Tony Blair's actually a Martian. Anne Widdecombe's a KGB Colonel?"

"How long have we got?"

"Oh, fuck off!"

–ooOoo–

32　Party Lines

Parties are odd things. They either go or they don't. That can mean generally, or from an individual's point of view. This Friday night gathering of horse people and stunt artistes in a rambling community of small, not particularly up-market properties on the edge of the Mojave is noisy enough, even if no one is dancing yet to the Garth Brooks on the hi-fi. In Ray's opinion it hasn't taken off in general, and it certainly hasn't for him. Perry seems happy enough. His ladyfriend is part of this place and he knows a few people. Most up here work on movies or TV at least some of the time. It's a two-hour road commute into LA.

There is a well-trodden progression from stunt player to action co-ordinator to second unit director, and there are apparently at least a couple of those likely to be in the talkative throng tonight. A second unit is a small film crew, subsidiary to the main unit on a production, whose job is to shoot scenes that the latter may not have the time to do. The scenes that a main unit director will be persuaded to hand over to a colleague are likely to be the subject of fierce negotiation between director and producer – the one with the vision and the one with the purse-strings. Directors don't really want sequences shot by other people cut into their movies, but the pressures of time and budget generally win the day and they have to agree a list that they will relinquish to someone whom they will brief, but ultimately have to trust. Often the list may include action sequences or elements of them, which explains why quite a few second unit directors are one-time stuntmen.

There are female stunt artistes, and Pippa is among their number, but to Ray's knowledge one has yet to make it to the director's chair. Perry hopes that one of the directors here tonight will 'put him in' for a picture at some point. He's introduced Ray to several of the stunt players already and frankly Ray has found it pretty heavy going. Garth, plus the volume of chat in the house make it hard to hear, and then there's the matter of the jargon, which is constantly overhauling British terminology. Also there's a lot of horse talk, which is fairly much a mystery to him.

Being technicians and being American mean that most people here want to talk about themselves and their movies and their film anecdotes and Ray hasn't found anyone so far who wants to hear him talk about himself and **his** movies and **his** 'war stories' – his normal party repertoire, so he's tended to apply himself to the cold beers slightly more dedicatedly than normal. Actually he'd prefer to drink red wine, but imagines that wouldn't go down too well in this company. The other slightly unsettling thing is that everyone is firmly camped in the single-storey house with the air conditioning roaring away. Outside the desert night air is still surprisingly heated and the form seems to be to stay indoors where it's cool. Yet another factor is the boots. They're comfortable enough standing around, although he wouldn't want to walk more than a minimum, but it's years since he wore cowboy heels and when he moves he's slightly off-balance and he feels too tall. If he ever wears these at home he's going to crack his head on most of the doorways in the cottage.

Even if he could make himself heard, he wouldn't want to talk about the screenplay or its politics to anyone here, and as the other matter occupying the forefront of his mind is his marital situation, he's not really in conversational mode. He would rather like to go back to his spare room at Pippa's place and read a book and sleep, but there's no chance of that for hours yet. Perry and Pippa are hardly in their stride, and it's way too far to hike, assuming he could remember the route they drove here. And he hasn't even considered the influence of the boots in that equation.

After a few minutes more he slides a nearby screen door and slips out. The aircon is slightly too fierce for his thin European blood and actually it's quite pleasant outside now. Given a choice he'd always rather be too hot than too cold. He follows the still-warm paving slabs round to the front of the building, strutting and swaggering in his new boots in a slightly eccentric dance to the muffled rhythm of Alan Jackson from within. Perry wanted him to buy a cowboy hat that felt the size of Jackson's, but he settled for a more modest one that won't be too out of place walking the Ogre on the Wiltshire downs. There's a park bench on a patch of coarse grass, with a low table for his drink. He's the only person here drinking beer from a glass. Even Perry, who would do no such thing on principle in LA, is following the mannerless practice of necking it, up here tonight with the celluloid cowboys.

He looks out from the garden except it isn't really one; they'd probably just call it 'out front'. Beyond the white horse fence and the cars, actually mostly pick-ups and a few 4x4s, there's more horse fencing, only natural wood, and then a paddock and then presumably the desert begins. The newish moon in a cloudless sky is lighting all this adequately enough. Ray knows that in the general direction of the moon, maybe 30 miles away, is that air base with the incredibly long runway in the desert. Chuck Yeager broke through the sound barrier for the first time, flying from there in 1947 when it was called Muroc Army Air Force Base. Later renamed Edwards, it became famous as a touchdown site for the Space Shuttle. From there the amazing craft would be flown back to Florida for the next launch, piggybacked on top of a NASA Boeing 747 – the combination being one of the stranger sights in aviation.

Ray's never been that taken with space, astronomy and all that stuff, perhaps because he's had a problem since childhood with the concept of eternity. He remembers being frightened by it in bed, on Sunday evenings especially for some reason. It amuses him that some people have suggested the moon landings were faked in a hangar turned into a film studio. He's never been particularly convinced by that theory, despite the Stars and Stripes waving in an apparent wind where in theory there shouldn't have been one, and the kicked-up dust falling back to earth rapidly when the much lower gravity means it ought not to have done. He doesn't go for it mainly because he can't imagine such a deception being robust enough to stand the test of time, with too many people involved, which is pretty odd since he is quite certain that Oswald didn't kill Kennedy, yet the authorities have bluffed that one out for 43 years. The more he learns about American power, the more he can believe it capable of faking the Apollo Programme, if it felt it needed to. For some reason though, he thinks that in this case it didn't.

Long before the days of the Shuttle piggyback, Edwards, over there in the blue sandy wastelands, featured in the 747 story when one of the prototype ships went there for the rejected take-off trials. Test pilots have to do extreme and unsafe things to aeroplanes, to see if things break or go wrong, before a new type is certified as sound enough to carry the general public. The RTO involves loading a craft to maximum take-off weight and accelerating almost to the point of leaving the ground, before aborting the take-off and applying maximum braking. The distance taken to stop is patently critical in determining the length of runway required for safe operations. The trouble is that the brakes are likely to become so hot in the process that they catch fire. Regulations stipulate that any fire must be allowed to burn for 300 seconds to simulate the reasonable response time of an airport fire brigade. The flight test crews who, to obtain the necessary signature, are prepared to sit inactive on board for five long minutes with their out-of-sight undercarriage bogies blazing away beneath them and their full fuel tanks certainly earn their money and deserve the respect of all subsequent occupants of their new model.

Ray's aerospatial train of thought is interrupted by the approach of headlights up the dirt track to the property. It seems at first to be another pick-up truck but then resolves itself into a sports coupe. After the normal on-and-fade sequences of interior lights and door slam, a single figure starts a walk up to the house. Before Ray has so much as identified the walker as female he has an overwhelming conviction that it's the girl from last night's dream. Not that he can remember her face or anything about her other than her intoxicating affection, yet he's sure that it's her.

"Good evening," he says as she draws level with the seat.

His accent – and his formality – cause her to stop.

"Hi. It can't be much of a party if you're out here."

"It's fine. Just a bit too cool in there for my taste."

"You must be Ray, Perry's friend, right? Pippa said you were coming up. I'm Deborah."

He stands up and they shake hands. Deborah had been lightly trailed, as clearly he has been.

"How do you do?"

Eve has taught him never to say 'pleased to meet you', which he quite liked as an alternative until he was told it was common. Deborah just says "Hello" at the same time, while he continues.

"Yes, I heard something about your getting delayed at work. Good journey?"

"Awful. I won't even start."

She raises her hands and looks up, arcing her head to approve the silver sky. They could almost be on a Hollywood set.

"I'm here now though and I've got the entire weekend off to do what I want."

"And you're staying at Pippa's?"

He's gathered this rather than actually been told as fact. Maybe Pippa had been allowing her friend to keep her options open.

"Uh-huh," she nods.

"Good."

'Good', used on its own, has a galaxy of meanings. In Dorian's Mercedes last night, Eve used it several times and it had connotations of reserve and censure. It was, he felt, as if she was saying 'I hope it works out but I won't be the least surprised if it doesn't, so the best of luck – you'll probably need it.' That's quite a burden for one little word. Tonight's 'good' is very different. He hardly says it with any conscious intention. It just comes out, almost involuntarily. There is certainly no reserve involved.

Deborah and Ray both know what it means.

It's quite often been like that with women, since he finally threw off the emotion-smothering fire-blanket of seven years at the Grammar School for Boys and dealt with his mother's habitual comment that 'Tom doesn't bother with girls – there's plenty of time for that,' in the only way possible. There has been some history of prediction; of uncanny foresight. The television was on every evening at home and he would sometimes see episodes of a long-running series that his parents watched. There was a particular actress in it with a sensational low voice. She was stunning but he didn't have a crush on her, in the way that he imagined many contemporaries would on film stars and singers; he just knew that if they ever met, they would fall in love. It was as straightforward as that. When after several years they worked together, on a tale of smuggling and other dark deeds, shot in dazzling early autumn on location in North Cornwall, it was a foregone conclusion. Without his doing anything particular to precipitate it, within days they were inseparable, if only for a few months.

Much, much later, in Wiltshire, Carl just happened to mention in passing a name of someone who was doing some research for him. Ray knew from that moment that he had to meet her. He went to the pub with his neighbour and it led to the longest-lasting relationship of his life, next to Eve.

Coincidences and consequences again. Tonight, if he hadn't decided to go through the screen door at virtually the moment that he did, he and Deborah wouldn't have met 'out front' and the evening and the weekend could have panned out totally differently. As it is, by their walking in together, assumptions are made by everyone else there; assumptions that, effectively, the two of them have already begun to half-make themselves.

Had Ray spent another two or three minutes watching proceedings from his corner, or struck up a conversation with the scruffy but interesting-looking scenic artist, it's conceivable that they might not have encountered each other at the party, or perhaps ever at all. Deborah could have entered through the front door alone and within seconds of arrival met a stunt arranger destined to become the love of her life, or equally the eventual instrument of her death – or even perhaps both of those things.

Because of Ray's impulse to move, such particular opportunities or perils that the other people at the party might have to offer are denied her, probably forever and irretrievably.

It puts his high-heeled totter round the outside of the house into some perspective.

Talk about 'small steps for a man'.

–ooOoo–

33   Bad Dreams, My L-A-X

There's nothing to be seen but asphalt, on which shiny aeroplanes move left and right, criss-crossing each other like bright tropical fish in an aquarium. On the grey, unusually smooth bottom of this one, advancing like the water snails and newts, are those mysterious and odd-shaped vehicles mostly unique to airports that converge on an empty aircraft stand in advance of any arrival. Actually at that point they seem more like crocodiles hanging round a waterhole, waiting for something promising to turn up. Otherwise it's pretty featureless, throughout the entire available angle of view. There's just more asphalt — and a few areas of concrete, to ring the changes. Most airports have some grass, at least paying small homage to the time when planes used very large fields, like the Croydon of Ray's youth. Some places where aircraft come and go, especially the military type, are still called airfields. They too can be fairly tarmaced over, but most of them will have some of the green stuff. But not LAX: not any more. It has four parallel runways, high-speed turnoffs, many parallel taxiways and lots of crossing ones too. So not much grass would be left anyway — and it can be a nuisance, especially where the climate's dry. Constant jet blast and parched vegetation aren't a good combination. The grass dies and the soil that's left is stripped and blown around as dust; the last thing you want in your engines and systems if it can be avoided. The grass at LAX has been replaced by concrete painted different colours. Although there's plenty going on to watch, the visual effect is a little too drab for Ray's taste; mildly depressing.

He continues to take in the scene through the triple-glazed window. Is he perhaps actually in an aquarium? The seats face inwards so he has to stand, but he doesn't mind; he's got about thirteen and a half hours of sitting down to come. He likes looking out of windows. Given the choice between observing something close by and something a long way away, he'll always go for distance, for the panorama, for the long view. Psychologists would deduce something from that. He wonders what? He must ask Eve. She'll know, or if she doesn't she'll find out. That's if she'll be speaking to him, which is by no means certain.

He remembers standing at a window, quite like this one, at this selfsame airport in early 1991, waiting for a flight to be called; he can't remember to where — maybe Phoenix. A Boeing 737 belonging to US Air was embedded in a small airport building just the other side of a taxiway and the accident investigators were moving around its burnt remains, doing their patient work.

That was not the whole story. He had flown in from England two days earlier, arriving in the evening. It had been dark for some time. Everything at the airport seemed normal and it was not until he was in the cab on the way to the hotel that he knew anything of an accident. The driver was full of it. Taxi drivers like dramas to relate. Apparently the 737 had been landing and hit a small 19-seat commuter aircraft waiting for take-off part way down the same runway. It later came out that a controller had instructed the Metro III to line up at an intersection and then become distracted by other events. She cleared the US Air to land on runway Two-Four Left, forgetting that ahead of it the Metro was stationary, a sitting duck, still needing her permission to depart.

In the dark, with all the competing lights, the pilots of the 737 had no chance of spotting the stationary commuter until a moment before impact, in the very act of their touchdown at 145 mph. The two aircraft, locked together and already burning, slewed off the runway and across a fortuitously empty taxiway and impacted the small utility building, ironically a disused fire station. All 11 in the Metro and 22 on the 737 lost their lives. Ray's particular interest was that if such a mistake had been made something like an hour later, it could have involved his own 747 flight from London, which would have been a different class of accident altogether. That one was a rather closer call than was comfortable. It didn't help to discover later that several procedural failures in the LA air traffic control system had contributed to the incident, and that, as he suspected it might, the use of unofficial and casual radio procedures by controllers and pilots had also played a part.

He remembers another coincidence: that the commuter plane was working a flight to Palmdale, only fifteen or so miles from the party house and from Pippa's tiny ranch, where he's spent the weekend.

The weekend! Several times during the course of it, he had a feeling that he'd travelled back about thirty years – to another life where he usually went to parties alone, normally hoping for but in sober reality not really expecting sexual adventure. In those days, when things of that sort occasionally presented themselves it was always a welcome surprise, and generally the main moves came from the other party. For someone who thought about such encounters a good deal, he did surprisingly little to bring them about. He had not been one to pick up the phone or organise anything, just as he never chased work. By and large, letting things happen to you as if by fate is not a considered a good life strategy, but in most respects it's one that's served him reasonably well.

When Perry had first mentioned that Pippa's friend Deborah planned to come up for the party, Ray certainly hadn't had one of his instant premonitions; one reason being that he was long out of the market for new intimate liaisons. Over twenty-five years and two long relationships he had never, as police slang has it (in London at least), 'gone over the side'. He hadn't regretted this in the least: there was far too much evidence around to underline that any excitement involved was far outweighed by the potential dangers. The spread of AIDS and the message of *Fatal Attraction* were the sort of disincentives that had made him pleased to be no longer single and available.

What happened on Friday night was an enormous surprise to him, even if everyone else in the know seemed to take it as absolutely normal.

"Ladies and Gentlemen, Air New Zealand flight Zero-Zero-One to Auckland is now ready for boarding. Would those passengers needing special assistance . . ."

The PA cuts across Ray's thoughts and reminds him of the similar announcement that he hasn't actually included in his screenplay, but might do later. He won't be boarding yet; not with his seat number. But he'll have plenty of time to replay the weekend in the course of the next few hours. He watches the ritual of his fellow-passengers approaching the departure lounge door. He notes there are no wheelchair passengers; they and the helpers they need can fatally delay the progress of an evacuation, when split seconds can count. Neither do there appear to be any very young children, whose crying and shrieking can turn a long journey into an awful experience for anyone in range. What is he thinking – 'awful experience'? A bawling infant doesn't really register on the true scale of awful. Wheelchair passengers have as much right to travel as he does.

In truth, whatever the problems, be it noisy kids or major delays, Ray has never had anything that could be described as a really bad flight. Flying is an activity that he's predisposed to enjoy, come what may.

–ooOoo–

191

34   Legs Overwater

You always feel it more in the back. A moment ago someone situated on the floor above and at a distance of a couple of cricket pitches ahead will have called out 'Rotate'. That will be the non-handling pilot for the current leg, who is monitoring the build-up of airspeed. At a carefully pre-calculated figure of around 160 knots the handling pilot, who may or may not be the captain, complies by pulling back on the control column, firmly but carefully, just the right amount to give a nose-up angle of 15 degrees. Pull too hard on many aircraft and the bottom of the fuselage near the tail can hit the runway. It happens. It was a landing tail-scrape, badly-repaired by Boeing, that did for Japan Airlines 8119 and 520 souls.

The rotation is more noticeable if you're sitting towards the rear of the cabin because you feel and you see that the aircraft in front of you is clearly taking to the sky. But **you** don't seem to be. Well, you're right. You aren't. For a moment you're actually nearer the ground than you've been since you got on. This block of flats, this mobile cinema, this metal whale or however you see it; this unconvincing-looking edifice that surely must be too heavy to fly, is pivoting around its main undercarriage like a see-saw in a kids' park. The further back you are, the more you go down, which is why it feels so odd; why your senses tell you that your part of the plane is going to stay firmly on the tarmac and not join the rest.

It stays that way until the aerodynamics add up. The thrust overcomes the drag, the increasing speed produces enough lift to overcome the weight and away you go. It only takes a second or two and your stomach tells you it's happened because at one moment you're at around 180 miles per hour travelling parallel and apparently far too close to the runway and the next you're climbing at an angle to it, and the tummy especially notices these changes. The angle isn't the same as the nose-up figure, but hell, who cares? You've 'slipped the surly bonds of earth' – you're airborne.

Lovely, Ray thinks, that some of the English could still measure things in cricket pitches. Should British aircraft perhaps climb at 23 pitches per minute?

Runways can provide some fairly disconcerting bangs; it's the tyres hitting dome-shaped light lenses; but the ones that really claim notice are the thumps under your feet of the five different elements of the 747 undercarriage hiding themselves away behind their hinged doors. The aim is to get these stowed and so avoid the extra drag they create, just as soon as it's safe to do so, when it's certain they're not going to be needed again until the destination. If an aircraft is going to settle back on the ground on take-off, and it's rare that professionally-flown ones do, wheels are considered desirable.

Already they're over the dunes and the highway and in moments there's Dockweiler State Beach and then the Pacific. The water and the sharks will be beneath this flight's track for the next 6,400 miles. You pay more attention to the lifejacket and life raft stuff on this one.

Ray is definitely 'in the back' for this leg of his journey and looks round the broad cabin with its two aisles and its ten-per-row tourist class seating. Even now, after years of travelling in them, he still regards the 747 as a miracle. They are even more of a wonder when it's remembered that design work began just sixty-two years on from the Wright brothers' first powered flight. Inside three generations and well within a single lifetime, aircraft had gone from a flimsy assembly that could lift just one man for a matter of yards, to this leviathan that can carry hundreds of people thousands of miles. Never mind that larger aircraft followed; indeed the Jumbo project briefly paralleled a competition for a military transport that Boeing lost and was won by the Lockheed Galaxy, which had considerably greater dimensions. It was the 747 though that revolutionised international air transport and captured the limelight and the affection, from its entry into service in 1970.

Ray remembers working on a British Airways TV commercial at Heathrow, when the airline had recently been formed from the merger of BOAC and BEA. That well-known player of oh-so-English eccentrics, actor Robert Morley, was the presenter, and the huge body of the first 747 to wear the new company's livery was, for some forgotten reason, dotted with hundreds of travel posters. Standing under its bulk, Ray could only marvel at the sheer audacity of the design concept. That this was a flying machine was hardly comprehensible. Keeping the charming actor's also huge body comfortable in the heat was one of Ray's many concerns that day.

The aircraft destroyed over Lockerbie was only the tenth example of the type. It was part of Pan Am's first order of twenty-five. When, in 1969, N739PA was being assembled at the giant, specially-fabricated facility on Paine Field at Everett in Washington State (itself the largest structure by volume in the world), just three production stations away was sister-ship N736PA, slightly ahead by about nineteen days in the build process. Their construction numbers, too, were three digits apart. In 1977, ten years and nine months before the outrage over Scotland, 736 was involved in the world's worst-ever aviation disaster, when two 747s, the other belonging to KLM, collided in fog on a runway at Tenerife airport with the loss of 583 lives. The two Pan Am sisters would become reunited in infamy.

More poignant trivia lay under the surface of Lockerbie, awaiting later discovery. As the longest night, literally, of 1988 eventually gave way, the first proper pictures could be taken of what remained of *Clipper Maid of the Seas*, including those shots of the nose section that would become the incident's icon. There was an irony, of which no photographer or anyone else observing the pitiful scenes, now revealed in the grey dawn of the shortest day, would have been aware: the *Maid*'s original name had been *Clipper Morning Light*.

–ooOoo–

Looking back over his shoulder – for he always tries to wangle a window seat – Ray can see the California coast slipping away from view. This flight is departing to the west, more or less straight out over the ocean. If it had been one heading north or east, those seated like him at the cabin windows on the right-hand side would have had one of those views where they could take in a whole conurbation in one eyeful. He finds such panoramas irresistible. They set him musing about the number of people alive in the finite urban area under his privileged gaze. So many lives; so many stories; too many ever to know, even if your whole lifetime were devoted to researching just this moment and even if the details were accessible, they could never be sifted through and assimilated. God must have quite a workload. As you look at a complete mighty city, how many acts in any randomly-chosen category are taking place? How many people are praying? How many committing crimes? There will be people dying as you watch and babies being born. This thought can lead you further, if you're so minded, to speculate on the number of people down below currently engaged in sex. And what fraction of those metropolitan orgasms will actually lead, in about 250 days' time, to new life?

Ray realises that his giving so much concentration of late to life being extinguished in a wholly arbitrary fashion means that he has forgotten that the manner of its creation is also massively random. He has had little reason for quite a while to open that particular subject file in his head, and although he has personally never associated sex much with the biology of procreation, Friday night had lifted that closed curtain slightly once more and brought the link into at least peripheral focus. It had all been totally unexpected, yet had seemed entirely natural, normal and thoroughly nice. The very surprising thing is that, so far, there has been no guilt whatsoever.

Finding himself taken with the statistics game, he wonders how many people in Greater Los Angeles had sex on Friday night. You can play this on a smaller scale too. How many people in this aircraft section did? That's when it can break down. It's OK to speculate at ten thousand feet when you can hardly see cars, let alone people. When you can actually view the people in your sample group, the very thought of some of its participants making love can be so unlikely that the experiment may need to be terminated before nausea sets in.

Noting that some of the larger of the burger and cola brigade occupying their own seat and a percentage of someone else's in this cabin look as if they would have severe difficulty in achieving anything approaching congress, he narrows his sampling to the flight attendants, now moving about. He is sure that they, without exception, did. Well, everyone assumes that flight attendants of either sex are constantly at it. His final subject is the guy two seats away who looks like Tom Hanks. Ray thinks he didn't, or if he did, no one enjoyed it. So much for rigorous scientific enquiry.

Ray is struck that the guy two seats away — and how pleased he is that with few spare seats available on this long flight, one such lies between them — also reminds him of Hal — Halton Chambers, studio executive of unknown function and attachment to the word 'think'. But then he remembers that Hal looked like Tom Hanks too; in fact half the men in the departure lounge looked like Tom Hanks. The job that Ray has now stopped doing would often require him to meet and attempt to memorise the names and faces of fifty, sixty, seventy people at 0800 in the morning and have most of them, the key ones at least, nailed by 0845. He made a personal point of doing that. Assistant directors have to call loudly for stand-by members of the crew when they're needed. Some of his contemporaries, he knew, would never bother to learn all the names on a job lasting only one or two days. Ray disliked having to shout 'props please!' or 'stand-by painter!', and a delay to look up the names on the call sheet or unit list meant that precious seconds would be ticking away. So when possible he prepared in advance so that 'Terry props!' or 'John painter!' could roll round the set, calling the initiates to perform their rituals at the camera's altar. He felt he was giving the technicians a degree of recognition which would help to bond the individuals into a unit. He wonders whether doing this so much over time has filled up all his brain capacity available for face and name recognition for he now finds it difficult to remember new ones unless there's any special reason for doing so. Hal provided no special reason whatsoever. Oddly he can still recall those of people he worked with dozens of years ago.

Sensing Ray look in his direction, Tom Hanks looks up from *Time Magazine*.

"I guess we're gonna be here a few hours. We might as well introduce ourselves. Denzil Kozlowski."

It's a reasonable point. He extends a small, pudgy, warm hand.

"Ray Scriver."

"What puts you on this flight, Ray. Work or pleasure?"

"Bit of both really. I'm going to see an old colleague and we may get to work together again."

"What line of work is that?"

Blimey! Denzil not only looks like Hal but he has the same enthusiasm for direct interrogation.

"I'm a writer."

"Technical? Journalist? What?"

"I write history for obscure magazines."

Ray has decided to change the metaphorical points on this conversation, as he knows from experience that if he says 'screenwriter' he can predict the next four questions at least. For some reason he can't yet explain, he doesn't want to go down that particular track with Denzil. He opts for a partial truth. The history that he writes for obscure magazines hardly contributes to his living. In fact it doesn't pay so much as his own magazine bill, but there's no need for the slightly overweight businessman to know that.

"Here in LA?"

"No. I live in England."

"You English? Gee, I thought your accent was Australian."

How often has Ray heard that from Americans? Where have they been, that they can confuse the two?

Mentioning history, Ray thinks, is tactical. He imagines the very word will make Denzil lose interest in filling more boxes in his questionnaire. He needs to be careful though, for he doesn't want to be forced too early into reciprocal questions. If he's going to have to feign interest in plastic injection moulding technology or the latest developments in veterinary dentistry, he's going to want a glass of wine or two inside him and so far there's been no sign of the bar service.

"So what history do you write?"

Bluff called. This is Hal's twin brother! Ray is open to a conversation; not the Spanish Inquisition.

"I cover the history of most kinds of transport, anything with wheels. And police history; that's one of my specialities."

The true list is rather longer, but he doesn't want to give Denzil an array of topics that could last him all night, going through them heading by heading, like a detective. Even these are probably too many.

"Police history. What's that? The history of perjury and corruption? Goddam police! No offence, I mean you weren't a cop were you? I know they're different in Britain, honest and all that," he backtracks vainly. "Not like here for Chrissake."

Denzil seems to have an issue with the police that Ray will do well to steer the conversation away from.

In Ray's experience, generalising about 'the police' makes about as much sense as generalising about 'moslems' or 'women' or just 'people'. People are different, whatever category or job description they occupy and that's certainly true of the police officers of his acquaintance. He knows one who is by far and away the most unprincipled liar that he personally has ever encountered, so it's conceivable that if Denzil has crossed paths with an American equivalent of Ward Vestwoode he might well have formed an unfavourable opinion of the entire fraternity. However, the vehemence and speed with which his travelling companion reacted to the very mention of the word 'police' leads Ray to suspect a degree of obsession or instability that he'd rather not have to make polite allowance for. How often do you find that? That you hear yourself mouthing platitudes or saying nothing so as not to disagree and incite to further excess someone who holds suspect but forcefully expressed opinions.

Temporary respite, at least, is afforded on this occasion by the arrival of the bar trolley.

Why is it that some people are so insensitive? Why do a foolish minority have to act up when faced with someone who they know can't be rude to them, like waiters or flight attendants? They don't try it so much with bar staff on the ground because bar staff on the ground will remember awkward customers and next round serve everyone else first. Pursers and their like don't have that luxury. Denzil takes two minutes, having the attendant go through the list of all the beers and then all the red wines on offer this evening. In the rows ahead it's like *Airplane* with the passengers rolling their eyes, their tongues and much else besides, desperate for a drink, while this imbecile self-importantly monopolises the beverage cart and wastes everyone's time, because he can. For what? Denzil opts for a Bacardi and Cola, as his neighbour predicted he was likely to choose all along. I'm glad he's drinking poison, thinks Ray, imagining that the sentiment is shared by the patient flight attendant.

Ray has seen a lot of this sort of thing, especially way back, with a big table full of crew at a decent restaurant, where the production company was picking up the bill. Usually the person making the biggest fuss and getting nasty and over-critical about the food, with a waiter or waitress trying their best, was the one who you just knew that if they were paying for it themselves, would be eating a microwaved TV dinner or a cheap takeaway without a thought of complaint.

Ray hates the word, but no other one will quite do. He's got thirteen more hours to spend in the company of someone he's now decided is an arsehole.

–ooOoo–

35   The Eye of the Beholder

There are people, not too many, most of them domiciled on the west coast of America and earning their living in the movie industry, who would describe **Gerald Logan** as an arsehole. Essentially they would be wrong to do so, but then again, if you've seen someone behave like one, the definition is accurate from your perception, which is the only one that counts in the circumstances. Gerald told Ray, after he had directed several films in Hollywood, that he felt he had become a 'bit of a monster in California' simply, he said, because American crews 'somehow expected it'. Gerald has the most extraordinary drive and enthusiasm and like most perfectionists, pursues his quest sparing no effort and no person, least of all himself. On the series way back, he would go to the studio at five in the morning and spend two hours alone on the stage, pacing around the sets, thinking and planning his shots so that by the time the crew arrived he knew exactly what he wanted to achieve. Such rare dedication takes its physical toll and he would always finish a job looking drained and aged. But his on-floor energy and disposition always remained at peak levels, and for 99 percent of the time his set was a delightful and entertaining place to be. Like anyone else's, it could become slightly tense on occasions, but as to monstrous behaviour, Ray could recall just a few very rare instances amounting to nothing more than slight petulance; fairly unsurprising when his grand design, in which Gerald invested so much effort, might be being frustrated by some silly circumstance or thoughtless person.

Knowing Gerald's brass-tacks attitude and actually, rather considerate nature, Ray finds the concept of his acting like a big-time, unreasonable beast of a cartoon film director hard to visualise. He suspects that Gerald's description of a monster is more in the nature of being insistent and suitably forceful in order to get what's right for his movie at any given moment. Ray's own experience of working with American crews has taught him that though, as you would expect, there are many superb technicians in all grades, there is a tendency towards casualness.

There is nothing wrong with informality in itself. Ray believes passionately in a relaxed atmosphere on set, and wholly disagrees with the theory practised by some directors and their assistants that good work only comes out of tension and that people need to be frightened into concentrating. Ray's and Gerald's sets have always been totally focused, but otherwise quite the reverse of intimidating. The mood is light and there is constant humour. People pay close attention, not through fear, but because around the camera is the fun place to be. The trick is not to allow the relaxation to become counterproductive. Easy-going and informal is great; casual is bad. American technicians could not always recognise the difference.

There was too, he remembers, an almost instinctive tendency stateside to treat a request or an instruction as something to be discussed rather than acted upon promptly. It often felt as though the supplementary questions and the offering of alternatives, the 'we can do this for you if you want(s)', were a way of putting off actually starting, in favour of a few minutes chat. Ray had seen lesser directors get suckered into this sort of 'directing by committee' and it could drag progress to a virtual standstill, with half the crew giving an opinion. This would be an anathema to a supreme technician like Gerald, whose preparation was always so complete that the likelihood of there being an alternative he hadn't already considered and rejected was extremely remote. That's not to say that good ideas from crew members were not welcome, but they would need to be really well-thought-through·to get Gerald's attention.

From the time they met on the first series, Ray had done virtually all Gerald's work for the UK, both TV series and advertising, and that had taken them to a wide variety of places, including the director's native New Zealand. The first time Ray wasn't on a major Gerald job was when the latter landed a series with the BBC. In those days freelance technicians didn't get near a BBC production. It was the critical success of this series that kick-started Gerald's feature film career, but that was not to be in Britain. Like many of his talented contemporaries, a lot of them having made their names shooting British TV commercials, Gerald had to go to the States to make movies, and it was years before he would make a feature film in England. In fact the car launch that they shot in New Zealand was one of the last commercials he made for the UK, and he was on the point of becoming permanently based in California at the time.

This was bad news for Ray, being cut off from his rising star director. Ray could not work on movies in the USA, as there the trade unions retained their ability to control access to employment in the industry. Such control is entirely necessary, to ensure stability in an arena that too many people will always be attracted to work in. In Britain this protection had been swept away wantonly. Mrs Thatcher, who, even some of her erstwhile closest team members admit, governed almost entirely according to her own prejudices and obsessions, had a hatred of unions and used her majority in parliament to decimate them, the good along with the bad, the baby with the bathwater. In many cases the associated industries were destroyed with equal contempt. It was odd. In the USA, apparent bastion of free capitalism, organised labour prospered, even though, or perhaps because, there could be strong links to organised crime. In the UK collective bargaining was reviled because Communists were supposedly exploiting a natural tendency to idleness among the British workforce in the hope of causing chaos and driving the country leftward. Watching Thatcher, eviscerator of his own union, courting and fawning over Lech Walensa, leader of the Polish shipyard workers, had been one of those episodes that had seen Ray screaming abuse at his TV.

The effect on his industry had been to open the floodgates; anyone could work, and charge as little as they chose in order to get a job in films. There was little chance of continuity of employment or the maintenance of conditions, and all the power went straight to the producers and their accountants, who rapidly marched working practices back towards the dark ages. The 'standard' sixty-six hour shooting week meant that many on a unit worked more than eighty hours in six days, and often there could be shooting on Sundays too. American companies loved to shoot in Thatcher and Major's Britain. A chief electrician who had long before been one of the sparks on David Lean's *A Passage to India* told Ray in a memorable phrase that, in his view, the 'Yanks' now treated British technicians like 'White Mexicans'.

The sweeping away of all the sensible protections, including the rules about British technicians being employed on commercials and other material for domestic TV, meant that – now bean-counting had replaced a broader view of a self-sustaining industry – producers would crew their productions overseas, using local technicians trained by Ray and his ilk over the years. In the end, Ray and his contemporaries felt fortunate if they got to work as far away as Scotland. And though working on a Hollywood movie with Gerald would be close to impossible for the average British technician like Ray, those from America and indeed of every nationality were freely entitled to accompany their directors if and when they came to shoot in the UK.

Gerald had been very loyal to Ray in as much as he could, and insisted that his production managers call him every time the director needed to visit England for 'extra scenes' shooting. There was – perhaps still is – some devious financial advantage, way beyond Ray's understanding, available to the producers of films made in the USA and elsewhere if they shot in the UK any afterthought scenes that needed to be made subsequent to main shooting or 'principal photography'. He always enjoyed these jobs; they could be planned to the same sort of fine detail that would be accorded to the average commercials shoot, plus it was always great to renew his working relationship with Gerald, whose confidence and assurance as a director grew with every film. Filming is always pressurised, with so much money being spent in very short periods of time, but running these jobs was about as much fun as it could get. There was generally also some socialising and an invitation to a meal at a smart restaurant to look forward to. On one of these brief visits, Gerald had said that he wanted to do a 'picture' in the UK following year and that of course Ray would do it with him.

A first rule of the freelance film technician's life is never to believe a job is going to happen till you're actually on it. The second is never to assume that you're going to survive to the close of the production until you're eating canapés at the end-of-picture party, and the third is never to rely on being paid in full for work you've done until the last cheque has cleared into your bank account. It's sensible, in short, not to become too excited about promises. In the event, Gerald did shoot a movie at least based in and crewed from the UK the following year, but it was one of those international megafranchises that use basically the same crews time after time. Gerald was new-boy-on-the-block and Ray was never going to get near that job in a hundred years for a whole variety of reasons.

That film was barely mentioned when Gerald came back the following year for another two days of extra shooting. These went as smoothly and congenially as ever, despite the selection by someone of a stage too small to accommodate properly the size of set that the designer built. There is nothing worse than working in cramped conditions: it will slow down a shoot and start tempers fraying. In this case, with an amiable crew and plenty of good will, it didn't put too much of a damper on the weekend's schedule. It had to be shot at the weekend because the star was working on her next movie in the adjacent stages at Pinewood. It's amazing how, with all the thousands of actors available to cast from, so often schedules have to be rigged to allow one to earn two salaries simultaneously. On a notable location film Ray did in the deepest Cotswolds, one of the important featured artistes was appearing on the West End stage and had to leave by car for London, half way through each afternoon's work, to the obvious detriment of efficient scheduling and use of time. Directors and their assistants really need to keep their minds focused in such circumstances.

This is one of the great bonuses of working with someone like Gerald, who knows his precise shot list for the day at seven in the morning, if not much sooner. He hadn't always been as easy to work with, only for the reason that his boundless commitment and enthusiasm in the early days could be counterproductive because he wanted to do everything at once. On the first series, it took patient work by Ray and the cameraman, the calm and urbane Tony Lutyens (whom Gerald called 'Hattie' on set and ragged mercilessly about really most things that he did or said, for no particular reason), to teach the director the advantages in efficiency of doing things in a consistent and logical progression. Gerald gradually took the message, and as a result eventually became one of the most disciplined directors ever. He was probably one of those rare individuals who could almost handle a set without a first assistant, thanks to his surfeit of nervous energy and total but apparently relaxed concentration. Ray has never been sure whether having a director who could in theory do your job alongside his own is an advantage or a concern.

The weekend at Pinewood was the last Ray heard from Gerald; a rather sad note after years of feeling a valued, albeit occasional, part of the director's team. The last, that is, until he learnt of the accident and tracked down the hospital by ringing a mobile number he happened to have for Evan Harris, Gerald's favourite producer.

It has always been Ray's intention to show the screenplay to his old colleague first, whenever it was ready. If pressed he couldn't totally rationalise this, given the decided lack of enthusiasm its past mention had inspired. Perhaps part of it was a desire to prove his creative credentials – to demonstrate the side of him that has always been suppressed while working in a grade that calls for perhaps 95 percent organisation and not overmuch artistry, in the accepted sense at least. He will argue that there is actually great art in being an AD, combining personnel manager, actor, diplomat, stand-up comedian, counsellor, mainframe computer, slave-driver, and much more besides, without showing any joins. By contrast, graduation back to the simple world of writing he has found relaxing and blissful.

He's always assumed that he would have to go to California to get Gerald's attention. He is now assured of that alright; it just means going an extra 7,000-plus miles to achieve it.

—ooOoo—

36   Repeat Performance

Ninety-nine percent of air passengers wouldn't have noticed it, but a tiny sensation in Ray's internal balance mechanisms tells him that his second descent of the day is starting, and he looks outside, remembering that this one is likely to be very scenic indeed. Today he will be seeing less than half the view – the best you can hope for from a passenger cabin; but this journey is bound to invoke memories of one of his most spectacular flights ever, taken over fifteen years ago.

He'd been coming to the New Zealand Alps to find locations for one of Gerald's commercials. Just as this morning, he'd arrived in Auckland from Los Angeles. Then, unable to find a shuttle bus, he'd run with his luggage trolley from the International to the Domestic Terminal, a distance that felt about a mile but was no doubt less. He'd just made his connection with his Ansett New Zealand flight to Wellington. It was the first flight of the day on the route, and far from full; indeed he was the only customer in business class. Having dealt with his second breakfast in two hours, he asked the stewardess, who had no one else to look after or talk to, whether he might, as a pilot, be permitted a visit to the cockpit. These were times in which such things were possible. The two youngish men on the flight deck were very welcoming, clearly as keen as the flight attendant to relieve the routine by chatting to a Brit.

Looking at the aircraft at the time of boarding, he'd recognised a very early Boeing 737. It rang a bell immediately by virtue of its dumpy appearance, caused by the short length. The first batch of Seven-Threes always stood out as unusual because only thirty of these 100-series had been built before a lengthened 200 model seating about thirty more passengers became standard. All the initial aircraft had gone to Lufthansa and had spent years plying round Europe, always looking rather fussy and self-important as they bustled round the inner and outer taxiways at Heathrow, to and from Terminal Two, reminding him of farmyard chickens. Now this twenty-plus-year-old small Boeing was working for Ansett. Like all the 737s built until 1984, it had those signature cigar-shaped engine nacelles under the wings. The engines weren't originally expected to be there; everyone at Boeing thought they would be mounted on the rear fuselage, like the Sud-Est Caravelle, and the Douglas DC9. But what worked well on the twins and the so-called three-holers, like the British Trident and Boeing's own 727, didn't add up on the short, stubby 737. There were too many downsides, not least the engines' getting disturbed, turbulent airflow coming from the wing. The man who came up with the fix was the same engineer who later defined that ten-seats-abreast, twin-aisle cabin in which Ray had just spent another night of his life. That too was a surprise to Boeing – and the manufacturer's lead customer in that instance, Pan Am. In the case of the 747, everyone had been expecting a much narrower-bodied, full-length double-decker until Joe Sutter weighed up the pros and cons and specified the layout that made history. That morning in 1989, Ray had got off the aircraft that was Sutter's long-running masterwork and onto one that also bore his hallmark of innovation but which was, by Boeing standards, a representative of a tiny production run.

Externally, and in the passenger cabin, this short, fat 737 looked like a new aircraft; only in the cockpit, the place that hadn't been repainted and refurbished for the new owner, did the elderly craft betray her age. It was not untidy; merely that everywhere you looked, the paint had been worn away and the metal polished by generations of contact with pilots' fingers, hands, trousers and shoes, touching the yoke and the levers, the switches and the panels as they had gone about their tasks. Only commercial use does that to control positions. No private vehicle is subject to a fraction of the use, and thereby a fraction of the wear and tear that is sustained through operation on a semi-continuous basis. Ray wondered what dramas had played out in this cockpit. No aircraft flies for maybe eighteen hours a day for twenty-two years, even operated with German meticulous attention to the rule-book, without encountering some tight situations. What secrets would be revealed if the sound-insulating material covering the cockpit walls could absorb speech, to be played back to us on demand, like a magic version of a cockpit voice recorder?

Auckland to Wellington is a mere 300 statute mile hop; by chance, very close to the distance from London to Lockerbie. By the time Ray was sitting on the jump seat, the South Island was already in clear view ahead and to the right. To the left of the aircraft, the North Island's western coastline was curving towards it, and where the Cook Strait, separating the two, was at its narrowest point, Wellington would eventually appear clustering round the sheltered Port Nicholson, a natural harbour at almost the North Island's southwestern-most tip. Wellington Airport is aligned approximately north-south across the neck of a peninsula that extends out into this body of water. With the two bays that constrict the neck at each end of the single runway, Evans Bay in the north and Lyall in the south, the airport is squeezed into a valley between rising ground on both sides. A residential street runs parallel to the strip on the west side and because of the rising land is markedly higher than the runway. The control tower is actually found on a plot of land along this quiet street, sticking up incongruously between two bungalows. With the mountains of the

Rimutaka Range backing the eastern side of Port Nicholson and the land to the other side of the city climbing to the cliffs of Cape Terawhiti and Cook Strait, plus the seemingly inaccessible coastline of the South Island jutting out of the sea fifteen or so miles across to the west, the approach to Wellington is inherently dramatic.

The pilots that long-ago morning were quite happy for their visitor to stay in the cockpit for the landing, and so he had enjoyed this sensory feast as the old 737 flew a visual approach, in a continuous descent, leaving the airport to the left and passing it, on what's called the downwind leg, and then gently turning, for about a minute, left through 180 degrees to join final approach from the south: an approach to what looked throughout the entire sequence to be an exceptionally tiny runway, but which was of course sufficient.

He'd thanked the pilots profusely for their hospitality. With the refuelling stop at Papeete, Ray had now clocked up three flights and some fifteen hours of flying with less than two on the ground, since leaving Los Angeles the previous evening. There were still two more legs and more than two hours of sitting on airliners before the final destination of Queenstown, but the last twenty minutes of that flight seventeen years ago had been for Ray one of the experiences of a lifetime.

He knows it's inconceivable that today's identical leg will rival his earlier trip for memorability, simply because a passenger window can only provide a fraction of the pilots' view (although even that is surprisingly restricted). Choosing his seat he had been torn between port and starboard. He can never forget that where you sit on an aircraft has implications for more than the panoramas available. Obviously some seats have poorer visual characteristics than others; seats above the wing for example can restrict the view, especially that downward, to a considerable degree. But some aircraft locations can offer a compromised outlook in terms of survival in relation to others, and Ray knows that where you sit can save your life or in some cases sign your death certificate.

The anticipation of the coming approach means that Ray abandons all considerations of the seat allocation mortality lottery, and ceases his exploration of his relationship with Gerald Logan, concentrating on the converging coastline and looking as far ahead as the window frame / head and shoulder interface will allow. What he soon sees disappoints him. A bank of fairly soggy-looking cloud stretches out ahead and below the steadily descending flightpath. He guesses that once today's newer and longer 737 enters that, little will be seen in any direction until about 500 feet above the sea on short finals. The best-laid plans!

Entering the cloud for some reason gives him the shivers. If he had a blanket, he would be pulling it up over his shoulders. He's reminded of Saturday night, snuggling under the Navajo weaving on Pippa's spare bed as Deborah looked for a lock on the door on her return from the bathroom. Deserts can become surprisingly cold places at night. She needn't have bothered: there wasn't a bolt and the last thing Perry and Pippa were about to do was come calling, if the muffled sounds from the other end of the house were to be believed. When he tried to tell her not to worry in exaggerated sign language, they both laughed uncontrollably in the way that first-nighters do. Once, in his thirties, in the early days at the cottage, Ray had been forced to halt an entire proceedings to find a can of oil, his old metal bedstead making such a graphic noise that he feared it would awaken the other guests in the house. That had caused the same class of giggles.

As he'd looked at Deborah, clad fetchingly and solely in a long poncho-like garment, trying to find something to wedge the door, and contemplated a second act of lovemaking, he'd found himself for a moment thinking about Daniel Weiss. Because the lead character in the script had lost his partner, flight attendant Tanya, in the outrage, there had to come a time when he was faced with the possibility of new emotional closeness and sexual contact. Ray had found it quite difficult to put himself in his character's place at this challenge. Daniel had decided (or Ray had decided for him), after some considerable heart-searching by them both, to deflect the advances of the solicitor to whom he had become attracted, feeling that to follow his instincts would be an act of disloyalty to his dead lover. Having forced Daniel to make this sacrifice following many months of loneliness, here was Ray, his creator, being unfaithful just twenty-four hours after his own partner had done nothing irreversible – all Eve had done was to impose what he saw as impossible conditions for her return.

There was another incongruous aspect to this. For five months the only female Ray had taken out when his wife was 6,000 miles away had been his neighbour's dog. He had accepted some possible degree of risk in order to see Eve and having briefly done so was now in bed with someone else a mere fifty miles, as the crow flies, from where she was. He couldn't blame the beers. He'd hardly drunk a thing after Deborah arrived and they hadn't tarried long at the party, both aware of better ways to relax on a Friday night. Deborah had barely touched any alcohol at all, so he regarded the fact that she made a clear-headed decision to get a doorkey from Pippa and drive them swiftly back to the ranch as more than complimentary. He certainly wasn't the least disappointed in missing the rest of the party, and if she was, she gave no sign of it. There had been too much laughing for it to be bad, especially when they heard Pippa's truck and pantomimed keeping the noise down. It was too late not to go with the flow and he didn't want to apply the brakes anyway.

Deborah had located a small wooden trunk and was sliding it along the floor to keep the door closed, unintentionally exposing a very proportionate bottom as she did so. She reminded him, physically and vocally, of Jane Fonda in Alan J Pakula's *Klute*. Anyone able to suggest an image of Jane Fonda, he thought to himself as she slipped in under the Navajo blanket and divested herself of the poncho once more, cannot be anything but good news.

He listens to the whirring of the flap motors and the different tune of the gear doors and the wheels thumping down and locking. How different this bumpy, grey, rainy and very British descent is from the bright blue approach earlier in the 747 into sub-tropical Auckland. Ray doesn't know how he got through that tortured overnighter.

If ever a journey taught anyone a deserved lesson about telling lies, it was that one. Denzil had quickly turned out to be a world-class bigot. His hatred of the police, because he came from Boston, was apparently tied in with a more general dislike of the Irish, also all Catholics – somewhat surprisingly, for despite his name, Kozlowski was a Lutheran. His religious intolerance was generously spread, though, in that he hadn't taken long to express his contempt for Jews, but that was small beer beside his next-avowed loathing of all Moslems, a section of society he would have deported without a moment's hesitation; while Hispanics, and not just the illegals among them, seemed to be at the very top of his list for immediate despatch to the border. This catalogue of contempt was fully disclosed in the relatively brief interval between the drinks service and the arrival of dinner. Ray found it strange, this vitriolic ethnic grading of immigrants, in a country peopled overwhelmingly by incomers. Unless your name is something like Running Wolf or Three Rivers, you are inevitably from immigrant stock; the only question is from how far back. Ray imagined that the name Kozlowski indicated that Denzil's forbears had been in the US for probably two or three generations. How the man could square that relative short tenure with his general denial of other settlers' legitimacy, especially when some of his targets' communities had been established many years longer, was a mystery; one that Eve might have been able to get to the bottom of, but which was way beyond his own understanding. He certainly had no intention of debating the matter through the long night over the Pacific, and he had already realised that his neighbour's questions, which had tailed off, replaced by lectures, were really only a means to introduce subjects that he wanted to air. Hence the lie.

To escape Denzil's monopoly, he had told him that he had a lot of work to attend to after supper. The trouble was this meant that he would have to appear to do some. The businessman was already assuming the form of tormentor and would fill every silence with new monologue. Ray suspected that he would be watched, and that any sign of inattention to his 'work' would unleash a new round of random complaint and provocative comment. His problem was that all-in-all he didn't feel up to doing anything much. It might have been useful to get out his screenplay and think broadly about cutting the Lester Coleman sub-plot, but he had told Denzil that he wrote historical articles and the man was no fool; not in that sense at least. What Ray had really felt like doing after supper was more or less what he was doing now, only with that blanket round him – to close his eyes and enjoy a mental rerun of the weekend, the edited highlights, selecting the images that might go into the long-term memory and be there still in thirty years' time, the Navajo blanket, maybe the trunk, certainly the poncho. Damn Denzil had stopped all that. Ray had had to get out a pad and pen; he'd tuned his entertainment centre to a classical channel and written mostly gibberish for what seemed like hours while his gaoler flicked annoyingly through magazine after magazine, tutting audibly, even through the Brahms in the headset, and sighing and scratching his head. Finally the man had dropped the *New Yorker* and his head had lolled unattractively. Strangely, within three minutes, Ray too had fallen asleep.

Something causes Ray to open his eyes. Grey nothingness changes briefly to grey, flat sea, passing at an astonishing rate. Then there's land and a bang and a roar and a strong deceleration and something comes loose in the galley and makes another violent noise. Why does that happen so often? He's not at all alarmed but is disorientated and he looks round, for some reason fearing to see Denzil, even though he'd been on the other side of him. Back to the window and that street's up there on the hillside with the houses and the out-of-context control tower. Wellington.

Got away with it again! Two more flights to go.

–ooOoo–

37   A Not-so-Special Relationship

Ray is not particularly surprised that New Zealand television doesn't seem to have become any more watchable in the last fifteen years. Then again, maybe it's a cable channel playing in the airport cafeteria. Rolling news networks, in whatever country they originate, seem to have inherited that awkward timing and off-putting presentation that he remembers from last time he was here. The headline items are not totally audible, but one story involves Tony Blair and George W and plays footage of their cosying-up to one another in the manner that nauseates so many of the British who voted for Blair. People expected such a sea-change after his victory that most are bound to be disappointed, however much or little that his government achieves. Ray at one point wrote a piece for a regional paper in the form of an open letter to the PM, asking how he thought he could be the world's policeman and sort out the problems in Kabul and Basra when his feeble administration couldn't so much as control litter in Keighley or manage drunken anti-social behaviour in Brighton. That 1997 win at the polls was of a magnitude always referred to as a 'landslide'. Odd that, because landslides are such unpleasant, disruptive events. No doubt one or other of these discredited politicians will be burbling platitudes during the clips about the 'tight bond' or the 'strong link' or the 'united resolve'. He's grateful that he can't hear the trite nonsense. He notices that no one in the room appears to be taking the slightest notice of the supposed leader of the so-called free world or his compliant sidekick.

Will and Hannah's marriage was the unlikely event that led to Ray's real enlightenment on the subject of Anglo-American relations. It was one of those weddings where the entire cast of characters takes itself off to a large country house in the middle of a remote part of Scotland for several nights. Ray, who feels that living in a Scottish castle is either what he should naturally be doing, or what he perhaps did in a previous life, takes to such a transportation like a duck to water.

Eve hadn't met Will, who is a generation younger, until he was in his late twenties, but was introduced through Aunt Cat, to whom he also is somehow distantly related. He, Ray and Eve had got along famously, and soon Will announced that he was adopting them as his parents, he now being without any. When he met his soulmate in Hannah it was a foregone that the couple would be invited to join this promising wedding party.

Hannah's father Brian, they learnt, was a retired history professor from a major university and he and Ray too hit it off instantly. On the wedding eve, after a memorable and high-volume communal supper the two men and Will were to be found in deep armchairs in a corner of a vast, baronial sitting room, sharing a low table with a bottle of brandy, the conversation flowing relentlessly, while those of the party who were more concerned about either looking good or talking sense on the morrow progressively made their exits.

"You said earlier you work on films," Brian had said, after a pause for refills, "but Will says you're writing a script."

"And he won't tell me what it's about," complained Will.

Ray looked around the room. There were still around twenty other people present. He didn't know all of them by any means and any one of their number could have walked over and taken one of the several spare places on the chairs and sofas round the table. He decided to play safe. With the work perhaps a quarter complete at the time, there was still a long way to go.

"And I still won't," he said. "It's a dangerous subject. Even the walls have ears."

"Ooh, I like that! 'Careless Talk Costs Lives.' That sort of thing? Not even a clue?" Brian pitched in enthusiastically.

"OK," Ray conceded, smiling. "It's a modern story about crime and politics that deals with a real event and involves probing some of the links between Perfidious Albion and her one-time North American colony."

"Crime and politics," interjected Will, an avid amateur inquirer into global economics and strategy. "Many say they're the same thing."

"As generally practised, that's not far off the truth," the old academic retorted. "So you'll be plumbing the murky depths of the dreaded 'Special Relationship!' One of the biggest cons ever perpetrated, in my view. It has to take the 'all-time best award' in the history of rewriting history. It's become such a successful myth that I'm sure even the politicians who rattle on about it so garrulously actually believe what they're saying. The trouble is that few of them bother to learn the first thing about the past, so they mostly make the same mistakes that their predecessors have been making for the last two thousand years. But have you any idea just how much the notion of a close historic bond flies in the face of the facts?"

Ray's research to date had given him a small inkling. Begin with the obvious, he thought.

"Well for starters, the much-trumpeted idea of 'America standing shoulder to shoulder with us through two world wars' has always rankled, when you look at the dates and realise it took them nearly three years to join the Great War and what, twenty-seven months – more than two years – to become involved in the Second, and that was only grudgingly when Japan attacked them."

"Not altogether surprising though, looked at from their point of view," Brian responded. "The average American doesn't bother with anything much beyond his own town, let alone the other side of the world. Of course they had no stomach to fight and die in wars they knew little about taking place more than 3,000 miles away, and there were millions of votes to be lost by any politician suggesting they should do so."

"Isn't their narrow view of the world deliberately reinforced by the education system and the policy of the media?" Will asked. "I mean, I read that the Hearst press were not only anti-war but stridently against offering any help at all to us against the Nazis; in fact all his papers were rabidly anti-British prior to Pearl Harbour."

"So they were," Brian agreed. "But every nation's teaching and media-reporting are tailored to the country's self-image to some extent, ours no exception. Plus there's nothing wrong with being anti-war. It's illuminating, though, that the States would later go on to appear absolutely paranoid about potential Communist totalitarianism and yet remained remarkably relaxed while the Fascist variety was actually overrunning a continent before their eyes."

"But it wasn't, was it?" Ray ventured. "Like you said, it was 3,000-plus miles away. It's easy to turn your back at a distance; to concentrate on the things that matter; and only worry if changes happen to something that you notice, like a tiny rise in your ridiculously cheap petrol. I do find it extraordinary though, the lack of interest in the world beyond their borders, considering nearly all of them are only a handful of generations descended from forbears who came from somewhere else."

"You can't write them all off as ostriches though," Brian warned. "There's quite a lot of residual intellectual antipathy towards Britain because of what she did as a colonial power in her North American possessions – and equally some distaste at what she did globally when her power was at its height and she manipulated and ran much of the world in her own interests, just as the USA does now. America certainly had a good tutor. Britannia, with the largest navy ever seen and the economic muscle to dictate terms to all, wrote the original manuals on how to be a superpower. I bet you're probably not aware that early on in the Great War, there was anxiety in Whitehall that America might actually side with the Central Powers, the Germans, the Austro-Hungarians and so on, because of envy and resentment over Britain's Imperial past." Both the younger men confessed to not having heard that surprising snippet before.

"But hold on," Will objected, tapping the table. "Don't I remember reading that the US deployed troops abroad something like thirty times before the First World War, and not just to the Caribbean and Central and South America? Didn't they fight in China and the Philippines, and don't they still hold some of the places they invaded like Hawaii and Puerto Rico? Not to mention loads more actions between the World Wars and since."

"True, but the thing is that they were all undeclared wars. It's much easier when these adventures start off as 'peacekeeping exercises' or 'limited interventions to protect US assets'. Half the time the public doesn't know anything's happening until the bullets are well and truly flying. In the case of the covert wars, which have mainly taken over, they aren't **ever** supposed to hear about them. But I bet there are a dozen or more things about even the two world wars, where what you and almost everyone else believe is the absolute, complete reverse of the truth."

"Try us," one of them said, responding for both.

Brian set off, starting with the Great War, explaining that Britain was obliged to buy arms from the US, when what was supposed to be a short and sharp campaign became protracted, stalemated trench warfare. The first surprise he had for them was that mighty British industry no longer led the world and could not service the military requirements, thanks to thirty-five years or more of decline through underinvestment. His second was that America and her financiers extracted punitive conditions for the settlement of the bills arising from what was being supplied. With Britain becoming liable for her allies' purchases too, she began to run low on gold and assets to sell for dollars, so the pound fell in value, at which point the US banks increased the interest rate on loans to maximise their profit from the fighting. As he elegantly summed-up the point:

"Lovely people, bankers. They tend to deserve all the alliterative epithets that are bestowed on them."

The next shock he had for his rapt listeners was that the enormous British Empire, which on the face of it appeared to be such a treasure box of riches, was in fact a net drain on the balance sheet, because of the cost of garrisoning and administering it. Few could believe, he told them, and the majority never knew, that this proudest of nations was going bankrupt fast, largely at the instigation of the USA. By 1917, Britain, now spending £80 million per week, had seen her reserves dwindle to the point where she could afford to fight on for no more than another ten – two months and a half – after which she would have to make peace on whatever terms a penniless nation could get. Still the United States didn't help, only entering the fight as a result of some acts of terrorism on her soil plus the German Navy's resumption of all-out submarine warfare. Following the sinking of some US merchant ships, Woodrow Wilson, who had actually campaigned for re-election as president on not becoming involved in the conflict, proposed a declaration of war, which took effect on 6th April 1917.

Britain's problems were far from over, but with America now an ally, loans had to be made available. Britain borrowed $180 million every month from the summer of 1917 to the end of the war in November 1918. While it was obvious, Brian continued, that it was American manpower and resources which ended the First World War, the little-appreciated corollary was that the extended delay and the intervention only when it suited America's financial interest rather than Europe's survival, meant that British pre-eminence in the world was over. Ending the war with a national debt of £7,435m and owing America £1,365m, Britain had to budget 40% of its GDP for repaying interest alone after 1918. A signature on a treaty had cost the country a generation of its young men, as well as everything it had achieved economically in two centuries. Both Britain's wealth and her position as the centre of power of the developed world had been appropriated by America, he said. He ended his summary of World War One with another of his clusterbombs.

"And talking about not learning lessons, just over twenty years later Britain was to go through exactly the same process a second time, with even more devastating effects. I also happen to think, we're doing something pretty similar at this very moment."

Ray was the first to respond.

"Well, I came to realise that we were bankrupt at the end of the Second World War, because I'd grown up in the austerity that lasted for years afterwards. I had no idea that we could have lost the Great War because we were boracic," he offered.

"What you won't know is how bad our position actually was in World War Two. Hardly anyone realises that Britain came perilously close to making peace with Hitler in 1940 because she simply couldn't afford to go on." Both Ray and Will were wide-eyed at this latest revelation.

"Really?" said the latter.

They would have to wait for more details of this, the greatest of his disclosures, as the professor's inbuilt concern for the progression of cause and effect insisted on first taking them through a fascinating overview of between-the-wars politics and the causes of the Second World War. The two listeners would have found any point in his narrative inappropriate for interruption, but there were several as a succession of guests made their not-always-steady way to the table to bid their goodnights. Hannah, at least two bridesmaids, and eventually Eve were numbered among the steadier of the sample.

At each departure, Brian, now in his stride, was clearly delighted at this opportunity to be doing what he most loved. As Eve took her leave, he shifted in his chair, impatient to progress to more revelations.

"OK. Special Relationship again. What do you understand the level of closeness to have been in the 20s and 30s, given that Britain and the US had been involved together against a common enemy in 1917 and 1918?" Ray tries a response.

"My instinct tells me that it was good – close – co-operative. America is usually never mentioned without the word 'ally' being around somewhere. Now I'm assuming that it wasn't?"

"You assume correctly. Did you know that we defaulted on our war debts in the United States in 1931?" Ray looked at Will, given it was his field. Will shook his head.

"No. I didn't know that," Ray admitted.

"And so you won't have heard that Congress passed a bill, the Johnson Act, in 1934, that denied further credit to countries which had failed to settle their accounts. There were also Neutrality Acts in 1935 and 1936 to prevent a repeat, as some saw it, of America becoming involved in a war through supplying arms to one side. These Acts meant we couldn't buy arms from the States, even for dollars, in the event of a conflict."

"God, no. So when did that change?"

"1941, really, only shortly before Pearl Harbour. Roosevelt was already finding a way round it to some small degree, after the almost total loss of our equipment at Dunkirk, but he was facing an election for a third presidential term in the autumn of 1940 and could only offer very moderate support if he wanted to return to office. Other than that, in the build-up to war and all through that crucial year, America in the main didn't really want to know. Try this. How often do you think Churchill and Roosevelt communicated before the US entered the war?" Ray left this one to Will, but would have given the same answer.

"No idea, but I would assume pretty regularly."

"Very little. Incredibly little, considering the enormity of what was happening in Europe, and the plight of their so-called allies. After Winston took over the Admiralty on the outbreak of war, they exchanged a few routine telegrams – nothing of substance. On becoming PM in May 1940, he sent a detailed plea for assistance. Roosevelt's reply completely ignored all the specifics. The following month, Churchill sent ten messages and received only two replies, the second of which coldly stated that the US did not intend to provide military materials to the allies. The president was sitting firmly on the fence, seeing which way the wind blew. As I say, the impending fall of France did see a trickle of arms consignments, but nothing at all like the scale and variety of Churchill's shopping list."

"So we were really on our own. That bit is true?" said Ray, eager for some solid ground.

"Well yes, but it's fascinating to see the 'Britain standing alone' image and the 'shoulder-to-shoulder, side-by-side' one existing at the same time in the public consciousness. They can't both be right."

"I suppose what people think is – yes, we were isolated and in danger, but they imagine that America was helping us behind the scenes. But from what you've told me, she was barely speaking to us."

Brian moved around energetically in the large armchair again.

"I think you could say that's a pretty fair description."

–ooOoo–

38   Bacchanal in a Fermentation House

The next target in the crack marksman's shooting gallery was none other than Winston Spencer Churchill.   Brian dissected Churchill's career and contribution, first in the inter-war years; then as First Lord of the Admiralty in the wartime coalition where, in his personal orchestration of the Norway campaign, erratic decision-making, - not helped, it's thought, by his alcohol intake – contributed to the humiliating disaster.   When that, almost by accident, precipitated a vote of no-confidence in Chamberlain's government, Churchill, against the wishes of almost everyone, including the King, benefited by default and became PM.

For Ray, this particular passage of exposition was like a six-round battering of every solid fact he thought he knew about 20ᵗʰ Century history.   When he'd said as much, the professor gently reminded him that history is written by the winners, which often renders it suspect.   What's more, much of what everyone now believes about Britain was penned by Churchill himself.

The tutorial moved on, to Ray and Will's mild surprise, to the TV series, *Yes, Minister*.

"It paints a picture of government completely emasculated; unable to take virtually any incentive or follow any coherent plan because of the need to pussyfoot round sacred cows."   He broke off and chortled.   "I like that metaphor – I must remember it!   The Minister in question is a total slave to compromise because of the need to maintain image.   His freedom of action and his desire to be radical and use his position usefully are permanently thwarted.   His power is essentially an illusion, chained down by bureaucracy and by the establishment's adherence to accepted ways of doing things that are rooted in centuries-old dominance by a ruling élite.   The impression given by the series is that the inertia preventing change is equally effective, whatever the political complexion of the government involved.

"We can laugh at it and love it, while at the same time we're horrified because we know it's true.   In peacetime this unequal power struggle certainly affects people's lives, but it is so essentially ridiculous and farcical that it can be turned into a popular comedy.   Put into a wartime context it becomes deadly serious.   The Second World War, on the best evidence, could and should have ended in defeat for Britain because of the establishment's absolute determination to guard its petty empires and to cling on to its traditional ways.   This didn't just affect countless lives, it cost countless lives; and as I say, by rights it should have cost the war too.   And there wouldn't have been much that was funny about a Nazi-occupied

Britain."

By now Ray was ready for the sting in the tail at the end of every Brian paragraph, so he listened spellbound as their tutor rolled out, like credits, a list of detailed reasons why British actions and, more particularly, inaction, should have lost the war. As throughout the evening, every one of them seemed to contradict a generally accepted and often much-cherished belief about the era. Even without the writer's close interest in things aeronautical, his ears would have pricked up at the next of them.

"For all his faults and mistakes," Brian said, "one of the cleverest things Churchill did was to put Beaverbrook in charge of aircraft production, taking the responsibility away from the Air Ministry. It's salutory that a newspaper proprietor, refusing to work in Whitehall and operating at first from home, managed to double the output of fighters in a way that the bureaucrats could never have done. Even in the direst passages of the war, certainly the early war, civil servants in vital ministries were working their normal 'gentlemen's hours', five-day weeks and the top brass were still going on leave and enjoying the usual social round, undeterred by the news from Europe. Had Beaverbrook not used unconventional methods, upsetting nearly everyone in sight, the RAF would have been terminally under-equipped and the Battle of Britain would have been lost for sure."

Ray and Will noticed that they were shaking their heads as if choreographed.

Brian had another RAF example, but warned that this sort of thing was repeated throughout all tiers of government and industry; not just the services. He reminded them that during the Battle of Britain, the air force repeatedly claimed to be dangerously short of pilots. What they didn't reveal, he said, is that there were masses of experienced aviators not assigned to flying because of a policy dating from the founding of the service, that all executive positions would be filled by promoted pilots. Engineers, air traffic controllers, training establishments, all were supervised and managed by qualified pilots doing desk jobs. Young recruits, 'the few', were being thrown into the air battle with far too little training and experience, and dying, while men with hundreds or thousands of flying hours totted columns of figures and signed leave chits.

"The British establishment in so many ways didn't deserve to win the war — well of course in truth, they actually didn't. It was won for them."

Ray tried to sum up, mainly in an attempt to come to terms with what they had heard.

"So this is fascinating. You're telling us that the British government were completely powerless externally, internationally, because the nation was bust and our only ally outside the Empire wouldn't help, while at the same time, they were inhibited internally by people who were not taking the situation seriously and bothering to change their ways. So much for the popular idea of the entire nation buckling down and pulling together."

"Another illusion, I'm afraid. There was also the fact that, being politicians, at least some of the leading players made such decisions as they could with an eye firmly on their own future careers. Given how Churchill manoeuvred to become PM, I think if things had somehow been reversed and he had been in Roosevelt's position, he would have behaved exactly the same as the president did. OK. Churchill becomes PM in the evening of 10th May . . ." Ray was conscious that Brian had slipped into the present tense beloved of professional historians. ". . . while just this very morning the German offensive into the Low Countries and France has begun. Within six days the British Expeditionary Force is in retreat. The Dunkirk evacuation is over by 2nd June. France fights on for two more days. Hitler now controls most of the North Sea and Atlantic coasts of Europe, and is twenty miles from Dover, which he can in fact now shell. He can't invade because he doesn't have invasion barges. While a plan and an armada is assembled, the Luftwaffe are tasked to destroy the RAF, radar towers, aircraft factories and the London Docks, a shifting group of objectives that are not consistent or followed through. This is the Battle of Britain for air superiority over south east England. It's badly managed on both sides."

Ray naturally had to question this.

"Really? You mentioned the pilot shortage. Was there anything else?"

"Well, yes — for example, the Spitfire was the best aircraft we had, but there were squadrons with Spitfires stationed at airfields too far away from the south east to participate in the action, while some squadrons right in the battle zone were equipped with inferior and older planes. And because of another RAF tradition under which resources belonged to squadrons rather than stations, every time a squadron moved airfield it was not operational for a whole week while all the personnel and equipment and paper clips were physically transported. Yet, despite all this inefficiency and the terrible attrition rate, enough damage was done to the Luftwaffe that Goering gave up daylight bombing and Britain survived."

With the three of them sitting there, Ray suddenly had a vision of his younger self as one of a small attentive group crammed into a small mediaeval first-floor sitting room with the sounds of a Cambridge spring drifting in through the tiny leaded windows. He hadn't actually gone to university at all, let alone Oxford or Cambridge; in those days it was far from the norm it now is. He could probably have read geography at Durham, but the idea of attending an interview was so intimidating at that stage in his life that he's sure his lack of study and his disastrous A-levels were in some subconscious way deliberately engineered to avoid the need to face one. This conversation was, for a stimulating hour or two, a brief and golden glimpse of the experience he had missed.

His mind could only wander for a few moments: there were more rocks of misconception for Brian's relentless steamroller to pulverise. That the Battle of Britain victory could only grant the most temporary breathing space was clear enough. His bullet point was that ironically, it brought the prospect of capitulation through lack of money ever closer. Still facing invasion, Britain resigned herself to the fact that the United States would not enter the war, nor would there be any financial or material help until after the presidential election in November.

"Then, even though Democrat Franklin Roosevelt wins his third term in the poll, the Congress remains Republican so the re-elected president still has hardly any freedom of action to help Britain in a meaningful way, even if he wants to, and he shows little real sign of wanting to. He does the minimum, other than behind his hand, to encourage Britain to keep on resisting. What he's doing by that, apart from keeping astride that fence, is buying time while his own country gears up its armaments production to deter aggression against herself and her interests, with Japan as the prime suspect in that regard. All through this period Britain is telling America that she is running dangerously low on gold and dollars. I think one of the problems is that the Yanks think the Brits are exaggerating the case. They look at what has been a powerful Empire and still has the appearance of one and they can't believe that it's on its uppers."

"They knew Britain defaulted though, you said, was it, 1931?" Will had taken this on board.

"True, but for all that, Britain still continued to behave like a great world power between the wars, and most of the population of the earth couldn't see through that. Much like now, and for the last half century, really," the professor added, ruefully. "There were also elements in American business who were eyeing Britain's plight with great interest, because if Britain fell, there would be a vacuum in many parts of her empire. There would be new opportunities for trade with the white dominions, if those in the eastern hemisphere weren't snapped up by Japan – and who knew what would happen in the other colonies and dependencies? There could be all sorts of openings for American investment and profit.

"What it would have been harder to appreciate, and it's possible that a few of the cannier people advising Roosevelt spotted this, is that by keeping Britain afloat in the war, they could actually go on to make an ever bigger killing. And by golly, they did."

–ooOoo–

39   Global Positioning

The ATR punches out through the ragged cloud tops into the sunshine. The not-unpleasant slight shuddery feel that the gentle turbulence has been imparting to the airframe ceases and after a few more minutes of climb the angle flattens, the engine-notes ease back into the cruise and the big propellers screw the air away, driving this cigar tube, hanging below its thin wing, across the grey deck below. This is Ray's first time on an ATR. Austin was a co-pilot on these for a while, until he got a job on the Airbus 320 and said goodbye to turboprops. When he was doing the ATR ground school in Toulouse, a second example had, not long before, been lost with all on board as the result of wing icing. The French instructor said to Austin's group 'You will, of course, read ze manual, and you will learn ze manual, and you will know za procedures it specifies, but you should **also** lissen to me. And if you want to stay alife, you will do what **Ah'm** goin' to tell you.' Even air safety has its internal politics, it seems.

It looks as though there will be little to see on this flight; unlikely even that any mountain tops will break through such cloud cover. It's always easy to forget that when you leave summer in the northern hemisphere, you'll be going to winter in the southern, just as it's hard to get used to the sun being in the north here and traversing the sky the other way round.

The thought sets Ray considering navigation and how he's always loved reading maps and charts, but how he had been deterred from the subject as a career option because of the astronomical aspect. When he was leaving school, ships and airliners over most of the globe relied on readings taken from the sun, moon and stars to find their way around. It was called celestial navigation, and Ray was thoroughly convinced that he'd never master it. By contrast, when he'd learnt to fly, he'd relished pilot navigation; the combined use of the chart, the weather forecast for the wind speed and direction, and the identification of ground features, to reach the destination. He'd also very much taken to radio navigation, the use of different types of beacon and beam, vital for instrument flying when the ground can't be seen. Now glass cockpits provide a moving map and if you press the right buttons, finding your way through the sky is a breeze. Even the Piper that Ray flies has a colour, moving-map GPS as a bolt-on accessory, although he tries not to use it. It's best to be able to manage without these things if you can, because sooner or later you may have to.

747 *Clipper Maid of the Seas* had been built when such exotica were well to the future. She, like her contemporaries, had an inertial navigation system

or INS, apparent in the cockpit from three units looking not unlike electronic calculators mounted on the centre pedestal, one set for observation and access by each crewmember. The route would be entered in the form of waypoints, defined by their co-ordinates of latitude and longitude. The progress of flights was not monitored by geostationary satellites in space in those days, but by an on-board system with a computer comparing information from three independent sets of gyroscopically-stabilised accelerometers. To initialise such a system before flight, the aircraft's exact location, in latitude and longitude, has to be entered painstakingly in all three memories, at least thirteen minutes before the aircraft begins its taxi to the runway. Initially one set of co-ordinates sufficed for all the passenger stands at an airport even the size of Heathrow. In the early 80s, for greater accuracy, more precise co-ordinates for every individual parking stand on an airport began to be displayed on boards, visible from the cockpit. INS was accurate enough to take an aircraft across any of the world's oceans, and with the autopilot coupled to it, could fly the 747 from shortly after take-off to just before intercepting the final approach.

At Anchorage Airport in Alaska, the new co-ordinate boards were painted with the decimal points in the wrong place. Shortly afterwards a Korean 747, leaving there for Seoul on the unfortunately-numbered Flight 007, strayed 365 miles off course into Russian airspace and was cynically and casually shot down by the Soviet Air Force with the loss of 269 lives. This was a death toll just one fewer than the official Lockerbie total, and the 747's plunge to the Sea of Japan will have been similarly terrible for those on board. The navigation error was never satisfactorily explained. Just five years earlier another Korean Air Lines passenger flight had also been blown from the sky by Russian jets. A 707 from Paris to Seoul over the North Pole went off-track by 1,000 miles. In that case it was an all-too-easy mistake in astro-navigation that caused the deviation. Identifying and taking sightings of heavenly bodies and reading tiny measuring scales at night in a cramped moving cockpit is far from the easiest of tasks. Remarkably, that aircraft was force-landed and apart from two passengers killed by cannon shells, all on board survived. The 747 was ruthlessly denied that good fortune. Both attacks arose from the US Air Force policy of scheduling routine intruder flights into Soviet airspace, for the linked purposes of intelligence and provocation. As a result of the second Korean Air shootdown, President Reagan authorised the availability of the wonderfully accurate, satellite-based, military global positioning system, for civilian use. That of course was GPS, now taken for granted.

The co-ordinates of radio beacons can be used to define waypoints for the

INS, but these facilities may also be used in their long-established way, especially on departure and on nearing the destination. They too can be coupled to the autopilot. Clipper One-Zero-Three would have been flown on autopilot coupled to beacons from shortly after take-off and subsequently coupled to the INS since well before the Trent or TNT beacon, situated in the Peak District near Buxton. The next waypoint stored in the three INS units was another beacon, Pole Hill, or POL, also on the Pennines, north of Manchester. Given that the second waypoint after the POL was the GOW on Glasgow Airport, the more direct routing of two possibles would have been via Dean Cross, DCS, on the northern fringe of the English Lake District. For some reason the computer had picked a slightly more dog-legged route. Instead of the DCS, One-Zero-Three's flight plan took it over a reporting point called MARGO, twenty-three miles east of the Dean Cross. It was the MARGO to GOW routeing that caused Lockerbie to be on the doomed plane's track. Ray has estimated where the explosion would have taken place had the flight plan specified POL → DCS → GOW instead. According to the calculations, the wreckage would have fallen in open countryside south of, close to but probably clear of, the rather larger town of Dumfries. Had that happened, the disaster would have been given a different name and that of Lockerbie would not have resounded around the world.

Even on the more easterly routeing, the flight crossed the eastern tip of the Solway Firth, the lonely, shallow, treacherous estuary marking the border between England and Scotland. On its Cumberland coast near to the track is Silloth, with its long-abandoned wartime airfield, where the father of Ray's friend, the Mystery Flyer, had been stationed. It was after a period measured only in seconds after landfall on the Scottish, northern side of the unseen Firth that the unauthorised electronics that the *Maid* was carrying executed their foul work. 'Landfall' is a word that doesn't convey the best image under the circumstances.

Ray shivers, as he did on the approach to Wellington. He settles back in his seat and reverts to a more comfortable image of the Scottish borders, the castle fireside. What Brian, the professor, had gone on to disclose next about Anglo-American relations had also been, in its own way, explosive.

–ooOoo–

Even Will had decided it was time to do the responsible thing, the otherwise deserted room having reminded him of his central rôle in the proceedings that were now today's. On his departure the two historians, pro and amateur, master and novice, had moved to chairs flanking the fine log fire, for what Brian had called the last lap.

Ray had asked him whether he believed that Britain really had been straight with the Americans in 1939 and 1940 about her inability to pay her mounting wartime bills. In the course of the evening he had become so alerted to dishonesty at every level, as Brian, far from pussy-footing around the sacred cows of belief, to adapt the phrase that had so pleased the old boy, had been confronting and indeed slaughtering them by the herd. Ray now wondered whether tactical exaggeration had taken place during the diplomatic contacts. Brian thought the evidence proved not; the figures that he quoted painted an incontrovertible picture of financial gloom. For Ray, figures wipe from memory as quickly as raindrops drying on a Mombasa pavement, but he accepted his tutor's assertions. As 1940 wore on, Britain was facing imminent fiscal collapse – no question of it.

"So what happened? If the money was about to run out, why didn't we have to make peace with Hitler?" Ray asked. "Or did we just keep buying on credit, like everyone seems to do these days?"

"Funny, that was exactly Beaverbrook's eventual suggestion to remedy the problem. He said if we kept ordering steel and all the other things we needed from American companies, the US government would never allow these suppliers to go to the wall, so they'd have to settle our bills in the short term, when we couldn't pay. Of course there hadn't been very much land fighting up to that point – just the very limited landings and withdrawal in Norway and then twenty-four days of mainly retreat in Belgium and France – but just making good the losses being sustained by the navy and the air force and attempting to re-equip the army, who'd lost all their vehicles and most of their weapons at Dunkirk, was running up an enormous tab. And even so, all that could do was offer some prospect of survival, not victory."

Having answered Ray's second question, the man who, in about twelve hours time, would become Will's father-in-law, addressed the first.

"Obviously something had to change, and that was the American realisation that there were advantages to be gained whether Britain was defeated or not." Roosevelt, Brian thought, was moderately sympathetic but even he had concluded that Britain was probably going to go down, and told the Canadians as much. Another good reason for not helping with weaponry was that it was likely to fall into German hands; far better to keep it for the defence of American interests, if the conflict widened. On the other hand, all those British orders were crucially putting America back to work, for she hadn't yet fully emerged from the great depression of the thirties, and as the munitions industry had to be got going again anyway, it would be highly advantageous to the United States if Britain paid for it. But still America's voters-at-large had to be persuaded that 'helping' was in the nation's best interest, and if the customer couldn't pay cash on the nail, then something had to be exchanged to convince them that they were getting a good deal.

He explained that it came down eventually to three matters. The first was naval bases. With a German Navy roaming the North and South Atlantic, forward facilities in some of the British possessions in that ocean and around the Caribbean could offer improved protection of US soil and for US interests. The second bargaining item was the future of the Royal Navy if the British Isles were to be overrun. The last thing the Americans wanted was for whatever might be left of the fleet after a British surrender to be added to German strength. They demanded an agreement that the navy would sail for North American ports in advance of defeat. Worse, they insisted that this humiliating commitment was made public. These two concessions were part of a very lop-sided deal for a number of obsolete World War One destroyers that, in theory, could be used for convoy escort. Churchill privately fumed that he had had to strike such a poor bargain, but he had no choice. During the negotiations he told Roosevelt that the US government's conditions were effectively 'a blank cheque on the whole of our transatlantic possessions'. This perhaps was overstatement at the time, Brian thought, but it would soon become reality. America's blatant looting of their supposed ally's remaining resources was underway, as he went on to expose.

"The third concession we made, although it couldn't be announced and so was not part of the transaction for public consumption, ultimately represented what was probably the most costly surrender of all. Effectively the United Kingdom made over to the US, freely and without conditions, the substance of all the country's recent technological breakthroughs and inventions."

"God. I'd forgotten that!" Ray cannot help but interrupt again. "My father used to complain about it when I was a teenager."

"Well, so he might. We gave them the lot, munitions research, microwave radar, the jet engine and even showed them the Enigma code-breaking machine, which was letting us read all the important German communications. Roosevelt also got an intelligence digest from the middle of 1940, which considering he still wasn't committed to helping us meaningfully, was a bit rich. So in handing over some territorial and strategic rights we gave away the fruits of our past, and in sharing all our new technology we effectively mortgaged our future. America was merciless. When it was finally realised in December that Britain was not crying wolf about running out of money, one of Ambassador Kennedy's London staff wrote that Britain would 'in the last analysis, stand and deliver'. His choice of an expression connected with highway robbery, was totally appropriate for what they set out to do from that moment.

"The US Secretary of the Treasury was a man called Henry Morgenthau. He demanded a complete breakdown of British assets worldwide to see which companies and investments could be sold to America at knock-down prices. He was especially interested in supplanting British influence in South America and was absolutely determined that he would winkle every last brass farthing out of our coffers and into those of the US. He announced in January 1941 that British citizens had pledged to sell every single asset that they held in America (they hadn't) and then in March, when there had been natural reluctance to sell holdings at give-away prices, he demanded that Britain sell a major business within a week's deadline, ironically to 'show good faith'. We did, and a major Courtaulds subsidiary company was snapped up at half of its true value by American rivals. The most incredible act, amounting virtually to piracy, was the sending of a US warship to South Africa, unannounced, to collect the last £50m-worth of gold held there. When continuing production mined and smelted some more, a second warship was sent for more looting. History says that America came to our aid because they appreciated our stand for justice and freedom. In reality they did just as much or as little as they needed to, in order to fleece us rotten. That, I should say, is an historian's technical term."

They both laughed in a resigned, ironic way.

"Don't I remember," Ray said, "that Britain acquired most of those Caribbean Islands by what was more-or-less state-sponsored piracy too, so I suppose it's a question of what goes around, comes around."

"Except that you could perhaps expect an apparently sophisticated nation to behave in a little less openly grasping fashion three hundred years on from the British example, given that we were supposed to be their allies and English-speaking kinsmen."

Following the voicing of such observations, Ray decided that there was no reason not to disclose to Brian the subject matter of his screenplay. He outlined the framework and now it was the academic's turn to be wide-eyed. His questions moved the clock on another 45 minutes into the small hours.

—ooOoo—

40   With Friends Like These . . .

Ray is clearing up loose ends.

"Now, the destroyer deal you were talking about – was that Lend-Lease or did that come later, when America entered the war?" .

"No, we couldn't wait another ten months, we'd have been sunk within a few weeks. This was the beginning of the financial straightjacket that they put on the UK to set up Lend-Lease. There was no negotiation, or even consultation: we were just told what help they would give and what we had to allow them to do to get it. And that was to give them total control to manipulate our economy to their eventual, post-war advantage. They literally decided the maximum value of the national reserves we could have and the minimum level to which they could fall; what they would take and what we could keep at any given time. They dictated what markets we would be allowed to compete in after the war and how we should handle our future trade, including our arrangements with our own sterling area."

"God! And we're still paying for Lend-Lease, aren't we?"

"Yes and no. We're not paying back Lend-Lease as such. It came free, because it had to; we could never have repaid it, because we'd already been overcharged twice over and taken for everything we had. The aid amounted to about 30 billion dollars. What we were obliged to do was return anything that was left in terms of capital equipment like ships, but as I say the true price we paid was our status as an independent nation. What we have been settling, and I think the last instalment of about $83 million is due this year, is the bill for what was already ordered when the war ended, because Lend-Lease was stopped within days of Japan's surrender. We only had to pay about ten per cent of the cost price, although I don't know who calculated that – if it was people on Morgenthau's team I can imagine it would have been fairly inflated. The other thing we've been repaying is a separate loan of $3.75 billion dollars at two per cent interest that we had to ask for in 1945, just to exist. To get that we had to join the General Agreement on Tariffs and Trade which automatically worked in America's favour, and we also had to make sterling a convertible currency which only strengthened the dollar and made the pound even weaker.

"The funny thing is that even after all that we still carried on pretending that we were a great world power, and continued to blow money on the selfsame things that had all but bankrupted us twice within twenty-three years. Yet I bet today there are at the very most only a handful of people in Parliament and the Civil Service who are aware of anything we've discussed this evening, even though we're currently following a very similar path."

At this point there had come the noise of irregular footsteps, and someone who was either one of the wedding guests or an extremely resourceful gatecrasher materialised, making a weaving progress to the fire where he stood between the two armchairs. A late arrival, he'd missed the evening meal and was now making up for it, carrying a large plate of cold leftovers that he attacked, not entirely successfully, with a fork. On the drinks side, he seemed to have more than caught up. Dealing with the plate and the whiskey glass that stood on it, tidily amidst the food, seemed to occupy all his available capacity and though amiable enough, he was broadly impervious to attempts by Brian and Ray to make polite conversation. It was almost enough to encourage them to head for their beds, but after a further minute or two of silence, apart from slight eating sounds, he departed in the same fashion he had come.

"So there it was, Lend-Lease," Brian continued, when the itinerant diner had gone. "Publicly Churchill said it was 'the most unsordid act in the history of any nation', which was quite an odd phrase to choose, and obviously one that that didn't stand up, if he was trying to imply selfless. Privately he knew full well that the manoeuvrings that took us to he point where we needed Lend-Lease, and the conditions forced on us for getting it were the opposite of selfless and really actually **were** pretty damn sordid." He paused. "That's why for the whole of your life and most of mine we have been kept considerably poorer, materially anyway, compared to our transatlantic cousins."

"What used to get me in the 60s," Ray said, "was that we didn't only have a lower standard of living than the Americans, but that it was also below that of the Germans, well – the West Germans certainly. That was very hard to swallow."

He stood up and poked at the logs in the grate, sending sparks up the chimney into the black Scottish night and encouraging some renewed vigour from the embers. He stopped and turned round, poker still in hand, with a perplexed expression.

"Brian. Why don't people know all this? Why haven't I heard about this exploitation, this downright bloody robbery? How can this special friendship nonsense be so pervasive?"

The older man set his brandy glass down on the hearth.

"Well, mainly because from 1939 and onwards, like most nations do in time of war, Britain progressively set aside the democratic principles that she was apparently fighting to uphold. I mean you name it, she did it. Censorship; disinformation – Churchill himself was prone to issue false figures when it suited his purpose. Surveillance, in the opening of mail and tapping of telephones. Control of resources and direction of labour, in a way incidentally that impacted far more on the poor than it did on the ruling classes. We had concentration camps for aliens and random deportation, which saw proven anti-Nazis treated identically to possible Hitler sympathisers and housed in far worse conditions than known British would-be collaborators like Oswald Mosley. We even formed a Special Operations Executive that in one case, – Yugoslavia – interfered in a sovereign country and caused a change of government. In that respect we predated the CIA, which of course has since turned the practice into an art form. Once an administration has taken fresh powers, there's always a reluctance to relinquish them; and once a wartime image has been created, or once a particular circumstance, like our near-bankruptcy in 1940, has been hidden from the people, there is never any stomach to reveal it at a subsequent stage, so the propaganda becomes history. Because all the main political parties had been involved in the coalition, each was implicated in what had been said and done during the war – so none of them had any capital to make out of exposing the mistakes and the lies and the things that were never publicised.

"Did you know, for instance, that the government appears to have decided to hand over the Falklands to Argentina – and for strategic reasons it offered the Dublin government a united Ireland, even though it was something they couldn't actually have delivered? Or that avenues for peace with Germany were being explored from the start of the war through until the summer of 1940, with Halifax, the Foreign Secretary and Rab Butler, his deputy, both very keen to end the war and at times putting out feelers to Berlin that went beyond any authorised by the PM? Or that Churchill, for his part, was far less single-minded about continuing than his speeches and his recollections would have us believe? While he was famously saying 'We shall never surrender,' he was actually calculating that it would be necessary to make peace in a matter of months, if no substantial assistance was forthcoming from the States, so that the Battle of Britain was fought essentially to get a better settlement from Germany if she could neither invade nor hold air supremacy over south east England? Your expression says you don't, and why should you, because officially most of these things remain in closed files, but diaries and other countries' records reveal enough for us to know that all these things went on.

"Most of what we believe is what the Ministry of Information wanted people to believe in 1939 to 1945. That's how a winning country's propaganda becomes accepted history. You can imagine, for example, what history given a German perspective would have said about Churchill and about Hitler respectively, had we caved in and made peace, or been occupied in 1940."

Ray had another question.

"Let me ask you this. Do you think that we know the full extent of America's demands on Britain in 1940 and 1941? Is it possible that concessions were forced, maybe on rights, obligations or sovereignty issues that were secret then and that we don't know about even today? Things that maybe even a Prime Minister doesn't get to hear about until he lands the job, and then is not allowed to tell anybody?"

"I suppose it's theoretically possible. If only a tiny group of people were in the know, and all the papers were closed permanently and those involved didn't note anything in diaries or whatever – and that would be unusual. What sort of things do you have in mind?"

"Well in a sense, I may half-know one or two of them." Ray told Brian about the more than 160 places in the UK that he'd learnt in the 1980s could, on just the signature of the incumbent president of the USA, be occupied by the American military. "These places weren't just the American airbases and military installations here; the list included Heathrow and other major civil air and seaports, and I seem to remember other locations of supposedly strategic significance. And it wasn't just the perimeters. For defensive purposes, troops could dig in and control several miles around the installation, and in that zone they could take over property and even demolish people's homes to create arcs of fire. Oh, and they could summarily arrest and apparently in extremis execute people too. I mean, have you ever come across this and if you have, do you know who, if anyone, on the British side signed up to it – actually it was probably unilateral and we weren't even told – and is it still in force?"

"Goodness, no. I've never heard anything about that. I'll have to try and find out. I'll ring some of my more radical former colleagues and acquaintances."

"Well, be careful about the telephone and e-mail when you do."

"What do you mean?"

Ray outlined the bald facts about Menwith Hill, the listening station of the

National Security Agency; that's US national security, not the UK's, he stressed, explaining that the base disfigures acres of North Yorkshire, near Harrogate, one of the numerous tracts of Britain still turned over to be little pockets of America. He told him of the site's capacity for intercepting and analysing the private communications of states, corporations and individuals; how its scope and capacity for intrusiveness ever-widened from radio to international phone calls to fax to e-mail, and that its ears know no boundaries and are subject to no state laws so that domestic traffic is now as easily monitored as the international. He described how, at one point, Mrs Thatcher wanted to know what two of her own cabinet were actually thinking, and used Canadian resources – that country being one of the five partners – to evade the tiresome restrictions of British law so that transcripts of their telephone conversations could be provided.

"It's reckoned they can now get into your computer and watch you type the words. And probably not just the e-mails"

"Are you serious?" Brian almost choked. "I don't believe it! I mean . . it would make you go cold, thinking about what you might have said and written over the years."

"Wouldn't it just."

At this there was a lull. Both men looked into the fire for minute or two. Each had heard plenty that they would need time to digest.

From deep in the house came the unexpected sound of laughter and then briefly two or more voices in animated discussion, although no words could be understood. The noise stopped as quickly as it had begun and silence, an almost unnerving silence, descended again. It was impossible to tell whether the people involved were upstairs, in the distant kitchen, or even in the cellars where Ray certainly hadn't explored. Beyond the influence of the comforting fire the remainder of the castle was far from sinister, but the interruption could not help but remind both men of the history, of the personal and political dramas that inevitably had been enacted in these panelled rooms and stone passages. It was suddenly impossible not to feel watched and overheard by spirits from the past.

"I think," Brian had said, "that if we don't call time-out for tonight, we'll still be sitting here when it's time to start the wedding."

–ooOoo–

41　A Mad World, My Masters

For the fourth time in twenty hours, Ray is sitting in a departure lounge, surveying prospective fellow passengers – this time somewhat blearily. It's a job though, that has to be done. If you're going into a life-or-death situation with people, and you surely are, it's certainly worth your while checking to see if any of them betray obvious signs that they might, if it came to the crunch, make matters worse. It is, of course, virtually impossible to predict how an individual or a group will react in an emergency. Because people's behaviour has been modified by what they see on films or television – 'life imitating art' – it's inevitable that panic and hysteria are more likely than formerly. They've been depicted so often, it must be what people do. Of the prime enemies in a life-threatened evacuation, panic is the obvious number one. Order is important. It employs precious seconds efficiently, whereas the chaos otherwise caused can waste them big-time. More haste: less speed.

But if your part of the cabin is burning and another one isn't – so far – waiting your turn is a difficult option, particularly if the second enemy, thoughtlessness, is playing a part. People ignoring instructions and wasting time trying to collect their hand luggage can hardly expect gentle treatment from people with their hair and clothes on the point of catching fire. Who knows how any of us would react, looking death in the face, or faced with monumental stupidity? When the 737 landed on the Metroliner at Los Angeles International, a woman seated by an emergency window froze and refused to move. A survivor found his way to the exits blocked by 'fighting frenzied people' and two men actually argued at an exit, preventing others from leaving. Meanwhile, ten passengers and a flight attendant died from smoke inhalation, waiting to get out, all within eight feet of the escape window. We know that the practice evacuations, carried out for aircraft certification and for cabin crew training, are undertaken by fit young people, whose life is not under threat and who do as they are instructed: the elapsed times achieved reflect these favourable factors. The reality, we can assume, will usually be very different.

Ray understands that the exercise of passenger-vetting is largely futile, in that the apparently most solidly-grounded citizen can turn out to be selfish and irresponsible and that the individual whose demeanour betrays the potential for trouble can prove to be a hero. Any revue of valour soon reveals that people who become identified as heroes are usually unremarkable and ordinary until the moment when they perform their heroic act.

Where there any heroes on PA103? The sad fact is that there wouldn't have been time. Allowing for the inevitable delay in reacting, there would have been left little more than a heartbeat in which to make perhaps the beginnings of a helping, protective or compassionate gesture, destined never to be completed. If there had been space for heroism, it is as good as certain that Elisabeth Nichole Avoyne, or Siv Ulla Engstrom or Elke Etha Kuhn or Paul Isaac Garrett or any other of the flight's thirteen pursers and flight attendants, of average age 38 years 4 months, of nine nationalities and domiciled in six different countries, would have exhibited it.

In the months to come, one of the hundreds of things Ray will have to justify – one of the arbitrary talking points thrown into the ring by a roll-call of people with nothing more useful to do than think up objections – is that he has invented a victim, the flight attendant Tanya Oaken. And someone will make the predictable suggestion that, as an important character, she should do more, and be shown perhaps trying to protect an infant, or make some other effort, however ultimately futile, to address the awful situation. Ray will have to argue the timescale and the overwhelming physics over and over again, trying to make the point that everyone on board was rendered helpless, and those who were standing up or otherwise unsecured were doubly so. Within three seconds from the moment of detonation, every flight attendant about their duties would have become like a rag doll, vigorously shaken in an empty box by a heartless child. Whatever their inclination, they could do nothing for anyone, including themselves. Such was the reality of their last moments. Having the Tanya character represent all of them and die in this pointless way, untidy both visually and dramatically, is, in Ray's view, not only necessary but also perfectly respectful and proper. The sacrifice that they were called upon to make deserves accurate depiction; nothing more and nothing less.

A group of late-teenage boys has trooped into the lounge. They are in high spirits but in comparison to most British counterparts, their behaviour is mild, relatively quiet and orderly. If this were a Spanish airport and such a party was on its way back to the UK, Ray can imagine the language and the loudness; the general lack of taste and scant concern for the image they would be presenting. Drink aside – and safety is a good reason for excluding drink from airports and in-flight (some hope!) – how would the two squads compare in a crisis? You can guess, but you can never know, until it comes to it. The fact is: human beings never fail to surprise, one way or the other.

Checking out his next set of travelling companions, Ray feels a bit like one of those agents behind the one-way glass, watching the immigration queues. In this line-up no one is giving anything away by standing out too transparently, so he's just going to have to get on the aeroplane and hope.

The same as always.

—ooOoo—

Standing on the desk where the ground stewardess checks and tears the boarding passes, there's a Motorola two-way radio. At the door of the plane, a ground agent has one. The employee placing the final catering items in the aircraft has a hands-free set-up. So many chattering radios; so many messages radiating out, unseen in the air. As Ray waits in the aisle, in the inevitable queue to find his seat and deposit his hand luggage wherever he can squeeze it, he thinks again about Menwith Hill. Menwith Hill, Fort Meade and the rest, plucking all those conversations and documents out of the ether and scanning them for content. He wonders about the list of key words that trigger analysis. The expressions chosen must, he thinks, reflect precisely the interests, obsessions or ambitions of any individuals charged with drawing-up the list. He wonders what his selection would include.

Carl had once made an unexpected point on surveillance. They'd been talking about the military-industrial complex, and the radical neighbour recalled a one-man sketch that Ray had written and performed for the village cabaret. He'd played a civil servant involved with arms procurement, and the cartoon-like one-sided phone call that he was having pointed up the fact that it didn't matter a scrap whether the expensive weapons system that they were ordering actually worked. In fact it was rather better news if it didn't, because that could involve a long and expensive redesign and refurbishment. The important thing, the character reminded his unseen junior, was that the infernal thing was ordered and paid for. That's what made the world go round. Carl had applied this to surveillance, GCHQ and Menwith Hill. Even he admitted the right of a state to defend itself from attack and from terrorism by eavesdropping. He was prepared to be indignant about America using SIGINT commercially for the unfair advantage of American industry, but he was surprisingly relaxed about the widening of electronic snooping to include activists like himself and to people posing far less threat to national security than he did.

Ray couldn't understand this, but Carl's theory was that all this extra expensive apparatus didn't really matter, because one, it wouldn't really reveal anything important and two, anything learnt could scarcely be acted on because to do so would give the game away and expose the extent of the snooping. His view was that the pathetic empires could grow as much as they liked, because, apart from costing the country a goodly sum, they were doing no great harm and even providing jobs.

"There speaks a true devotee of the Soviet way of life," Ray had said. "OK. So it seems unlikely now that we we'll ever get an ultra-left government in this country, but the way polarisation is going we could conceivably elect a far-right one at some point – or maybe further down the line, with demographic changes and maybe the daftness of positive discrimination, we could have a Moslem-dominated administration that might be hijacked by fundamentalism. How would you feel then about the existence of all this technology and this army of people able to spy on what every Tom, Dick and Harry was saying and thinking? There wouldn't be any reluctance to use such information to snuff out free expression and make dissidents disappear if you had regimes of that sort in power. And if that isn't George Orwell's prediction come true, I don't know what is. It shouldn't happen in any future, it shouldn't be happening now, it shouldn't have been happening all the years it has. It makes the West's claim to be free and better than your Soviet paradise a complete sad joke. And that we let it be done, to us, on our soil, with the full protection of our police and our secrecy laws, and that no one, not even a Member of Parliament, can get anyone even to discuss it, I find utterly nauseating. You may consider it just another example of harmless empire-building and job-creation, but I think it's dehumanising and a threat to mankind."

It hadn't really given him much pleasure to be able to argue Carl into silence again, but from long experience he knew the scores would soon even-up again.

–ooOoo–

Ray finds there is an experience common to most airline legs. Because the getting onto an aeroplane, even if it's the third or fourth flight of a series, can be such a business with its series of hurdle-like rituals, once those are all accomplished there is such a calmness about being in the air, where there is nothing to achieve and no decisions to make, that he's almost reluctant for the flight to end. After all, landing only brings its own fresh allocation of procedures and hassles. It's an odd concept; being happy to stay up, balanced in those precarious and inhospitable surroundings by nothing more than the flow of air around a few metal surfaces, rather then return to the human's natural location in the great scheme of things, our stamping ground.

It's not quite the same when he himself is doing the flying. However pleasant or spectacular the cruise segment of the flight might be, the landing to come is always, to some small extent, at the back of his mind. Yes, there are times when it seems a shame to have to start the descent, but for Ray as a pilot, probably because of the captaincy thing, until the aircraft has been landed and is taxiing off the active runway, any flight is open-ended and incomplete.

For the better part of a day, although it's been one hopelessly distorted by chasing the rotating earth and tinkering with its time zones, Ray has been a creature of the sky, save for his few brief interludes on three New Zealand landing grounds. He hasn't seen his baggage since Auckland. He's been in a state of privileged irresponsible limbo, where virtually everything has been organised and provided by people paid to do so. It must be like that for people who have servants, he thinks. The experience is certainly seductive. But the physics dictate that no flight can go on indefinitely, whatever a passenger's inclination. 'What goes up . . . ' and all that. As the tell-tale signs betray the approach to Dunedin, he knows it will soon be time to return to reality and start taking responsibility for himself again, however little he for the moment relishes the idea.

The plan is to go to the hotel, sleep for a couple of hours and go to the hospital later. The last thing you want to do in any encounter with Gerald Logan, sick or not, is arrive drowsy and below par.

–ooOoo–

Who can ever get rest when they feel they really ought to? Ray's body clock has no idea where it is, but although his brain says that some shut-eye would be sensible, now that he has the opportunity the rest of the senses flatly refuse to co-operate. There's only one thing that is guaranteed to make him drop off when sleep is a necessity and it seems a strange prescription for a writer – reading!

He hauls out of bed and fishes in his computer bag for a copy of the screenplay. This familiar old thing will do the trick.

–ooOoo–

42   Chips at Everything

Ray opens the booklet at a random point, and looks to see whether the page chosen holds out any hope for a temporary insomniac. It's numbered 31. He reads the top scene heading and the first lines of the description.

```
INT GARRICK CLUB LONDON - PRIVATE DINING ROOM          DAY
(16 3 1989)

PAUL CHANNON MP, Transport Secretary in Margaret Thatcher's
Conservative government, sits down to an amiable working
lunch. Joining him at the table are ROBIN OAKLEY of the
Times, JULIA LANGDON of the Daily Mirror, . . .
```

In real life it was exactly twelve weeks since the morning newspapers had blazoned the sickening details of the Lockerbie outrage to an appalled public. The early part of the new year had been far from comfortable for the minister. His entire tenure had been plagued by major transport disasters, and on 8th January there was another, when a British Midland Boeing 737 crash-landed across the M1 motorway killing forty-four in a totally unnecessary accident. One engine had failed and the hapless pilots shut down the functioning engine in error, a mistake that would have been virtually impossible, industry-watchers would say, with a traditional flight engineer in the cockpit; a third pair of eyes and another brain to analyse the problem.

But for Channon there were problems closer to home when details began to emerge of the existence of strong warnings pointing to the Scottish tragedy; warnings that had not been sufficiently acted upon by his Department of Transport. In early January he had, in the House of Commons, appeared to discount the first of them, the Helsinki warning, as merely one of a deluge of hoaxes received by his ministry, ignoring the fact that the amount of detail it had mentioned had been highly unusual and, in the event, remarkably prescient. A mystery caller had referred to Pan American, to a flight from Frankfurt to the US, and to an imminent timescale. What's more, he had named possible participants and their organisation, and described a process of inserting a bomb into hold baggage.

When some of the bereaved discovered the specific nature of the content, they had publicly demanded the minister's resignation. They were incensed to learn that a notice, summarising the warning, had been displayed in the US Embassy in Moscow, for one, and that many staff and visitors there had changed their Christmas travel plans. The fact that PA103 was so lightly-laden, at a time when it could have been expected to be full, seemed to suggest to them that far more people had been deterred from using it than was ever admitted. Their dead friends and relatives, ordinary members of the travelling public, had been denied information that had encouraged others to make alternative arrangements. Those 'in the loop' had left seats available that in many cases the eventual victims, ignorant of the threat, had been happy to take up.

Channon's implied assurances that he and his officials were on top of their jobs were not helped by the shadow Transport Secretary, John Prescott, being able to castigate the minister for jetting off, two days after Lockerbie, to his property on Mustique in the West Indies for a family holiday.

So it was, just two months on from the crime, that the first politician was accused of being less than truthful over the events of Pan Am 103. He was the precursor of a long line, few of whose political careers met the swift conclusion suffered by Channon's. Ministers in all governments are continually obliged to play down the importance of certain events, and in another context, his deception might have been considered relatively mild. But under the shadow of 270 deaths, his insistence was categorised as unconcern.

Forty-eight hours before the lunch, he was still peddling the 'hoax' line in the Commons. But the next day, information about a second mishandled warning became public. The DoT had been given even more time to respond to this one and had equally failed. The German BKA had promulgated details of the 'Autumn Leaves' raids, including the nature of the Toshiba bombs and the possibility that some of them were in circulation and might be deployed. This had been known in Whitehall on 17th **November** at the latest. On the 18th, a Friday, civil servants received a copy of advice that had already been sent to US airlines by their Federal Aviation Authority. No doubt the weekend's social pleasures were considered more important, just as they had been so often during World War Two, and it was Tuesday 22nd before a telex went to UK airports. If a six-day delay in disseminating life-or-death information was par for the course, it was nothing to the bureaucratic lethargy displayed in preparing a poster for distribution. That took over a month to produce and was then consigned, two days before Lockerbie occurred, with outstanding lack of vision or forethought, via the seasonally overloaded Royal Mail. It would not, in the main, arrive on the desks of airline security heads until about a week after the downing of Clipper 103.

Straight back in the firing line, Channon decided on the meal, at the Garrick Club, in pursuance of a standard politician's strategy. New news always supplants the previous headlines and shifts the magnifying glass, so something will always come along to take off the heat, if you wait long enough. But if you have some news yourself to release, you can turn attention away all the more quickly. If the new news is nothing to do with you, it doesn't matter whether it's good or bad; but if it's good news about your existing problem it can add to the relief and may be of extra help in cutting the fuel to the flames. Channon had some good news about Lockerbie – information that it was fair to assume might help him wriggle off the hook.

The venue, the London club of the acting profession, was appropriate for a former Minister for the Arts. Millionaire Channon could move comfortably in any circle from Royalty to the Bohemian: it was in the blood – his father had been a noted socialite. Henry 'Chips' Channon was an Anglo-American, born in Chicago in 1897, who had rejected the USA and energetically embraced London society between the wars. With family means, he had written some books before entering politics, where he served in both Chamberlain's National Government and Churchill's wartime coalition. He was parliamentary private secretary to Rab Butler, then a junior minister at the Foreign Office under Lord Halifax. This had placed him in the midst of a group of High Tories who were, in private, far from enthusiastic about war with Germany and virulently opposed to Churchill's premiership and his policy of fighting on. They saw Bolshevism as the greater threat and a strong Germany as bulwark against the proletariat taking over Europe. They were under no illusions about what would happen to them and their comfortable way of life in a future Britain governed by the workers. Though they were in Churchill's team, they, like Chamberlain and his PPS, Lord Dunglass – one day himself to be Prime Minister as Sir Alec Douglas-Home – were far more interested in finding an accommodation with Hitler than was their new PM, and Halifax and Butler would make unauthorised overtures to the Germans through third parties. Ray remembers what Brian had said about Churchill, and how, despite his House of Commons rhetoric, privately his initial policy, once economic reality had been accepted, was also not to fight to the bitter end — to the 'last drop of blood' — but for Britain to remain undefeated and so obtain better peace terms.

Just as son Paul would be accused of lacking the necessary urgency over the Lockerbie warnings, it can be assumed that father Chips, who wrote of

Churchill's taking over as 'perhaps the darkest day in English history', would possess a heart not altogether in his government job. His boss, Butler, was even more critical, and also showed a singular lack of confidence in the USA. 'In my political life,' he wrote in 1939, 'I have always been convinced that we can no more count on America than Brazil.' Channon's scathing opinion of his birthplace was well-documented. He had written of the USA as 'a menace to the peace and future of the world', detecting, in its culture and its economic growth, forces that could and would swamp the customs and taste of the older civilisations. Not too many would have shared his concern at the time. Nevertheless, there was a widespread view of the war that Britain's continuing sacrifice would benefit only the United States and the USSR. History, to a not inconsiderable degree, would bear out this prediction, certainly in respect of their military-industrial élites.

Meanwhile, it was business as usual in Westminster and Whitehall. As an indication of priorities, even as Holland and Belgium were being overrun by the German army, in London attention was found to be entirely distracted by the formation of the new coalition government, and the inter-party and personal horse-trading that always attends such an event. The vulnerability of Britain's situation caused no great concentrations of mind or changes of behaviour in the people who were supposedly running the country. The war was more than a year old before the Foreign Office changed its traditional start time of 11am, and the fact that 10 Downing Street began work at 9.30 was thought 'disgustingly early' by a private secretary, John Colville, joining its staff in late 1939. For those among the nation's governing class, like Colville and Channon, the sparkling social round continued, very little dimmed. Holidays, weekends and midweek engagements were enjoyed much as normal, with little or no reference to the tide of war. The high-living Channon could write of consuming large numbers of champagne cocktails with Robert Boothby in the bar of the exclusive Dorchester Hotel, while a handful of miles away bombs were falling on the docks and the homes of East London.

The sons and daughters of the well-to-do were despatched abroad in droves, mainly to the safety of Canada or the USA, not to return until the prospect of invasion had disappeared. The younger Channon, an only son, had been sent to stay with the Astors in the States.

Now however,– forty-seven or so years on – he was engaged in his own fight: one for his political life. Ironically it was a fight both occasioned and doomed by the very American dominance that his father had foreseen. His guests in the private dining room that day were five leading Westminster journalists, lobby correspondents. They were there to hear his glad tidings that the Lockerbie case had been solved; that the perpetrators were known and would soon be in custody. Most tellingly, Channon revealed the name of the group responsible for the 270 murders – the PFLP-GC. These disclosures were made under so-called 'lobby terms', and as such should not have been published, although it is hard to see the advantage to the minister of releasing the information if he had not wanted it leaked into the public domain. In the event, the news would flash round Fleet Street and many front pages the following morning would run the story. Surprisingly (or perhaps not), *Today*, the paper of one of the journalists at the lunch, would print the invention that a bomber was in custody. In truth, the bomb-maker actually **had** already been arrested – and then hurriedly released, before the crime had taken place; but the story was about an enticing headline rather than such niceties of detail.

As he left the Garrick, Paul Channon must have felt that he had, by a clever manoeuvre, probably saved his career. In reality he had just torpedoed it.

ABC Television in America may perhaps have been engaging in smokescreen tactics of its own when on the following day it named the minister as the source of the reports. Not included in the lunch briefing, there was no need for the company to adhere to the professional conventions. They had new news; the story of Channon leaking information eclipsed that very information he had leaked. The Transport Secretary was back in the roasting pot and most people instantly forgot about the guilt he'd attributed to the Jibril organisation. It might as well have been a fantasy; some will have assumed as much, because of the use to which he was putting the information. His revelation, which happened to be essentially right, was damned by association with an unworthy cause, his self-extrication. If at that point ABC had been acting in the interests of people who didn't want the identity of the true perpetrators to be more widely publicised – and Ray has no evidence to indicate that they were – they could hardly have done a better job. The fact that no arrests of PFLP-GC associates followed the back-door announcement and that there was no confirmation of progress in the investigation by anyone in authority connected with it, could only add to the impression that there was no substance to what Channon had briefed, especially when he denied being the source, was branded a liar by the *Daily Mirror* and could make no response.

–ooOoo–

43　Friday on the Phone with George

What is clear is that even at this relatively early point, there were already people who were anxious to encourage the idea that Channon was talking nonsense, because they had their own reasons for not wanting to see the real conspirators named. The best-known of these was George Herbert Walker Bush, recently installed as 41st President of the United States. Another about to join their number was Margaret Hilda Thatcher, Prime Minister of the United Kingdom.

To conduct the hot war, between 1941 and 1945, Churchill and Roosevelt had been obliged to rely on diplomatic telegrams. A secure telephone link between London and Washington was eventually installed the better to manage the cold one that followed, although on what grounds that war was being fought, and to whose benefit, Ray thinks, remain fertile subjects for debate. The so-called Hot Lines became a necessity once life on the entire planet could be ended with a couple of keys and a few button presses -- a situation which we all tend to forget, still obtains.

It isn't of course absolutely documented who picked up the handset and called whom, but Pulitzer Prize-winning investigative journalist Jack Anderson, who broke the story, said (and therefore the smart money is on) George Bush Senior. The new president would have had several things on his mind in the middle of March. The exact date of the call also isn't known, but it is highly likely to have been shortly after the duty staff at the US London Embassy in Grosvenor Square had their first sight of the morning editions during the night of 16th and 17th – the daily papers with the headlines shouting that the Lockerbie case had been solved.

Theoretically, at the top of George's list of worries there was the matter of the American and other western hostages in Lebanon who remained confined in their anonymous Beirut hiding places. The prospects for success of any moves made on their behalf by diplomatic channels would scarcely be enhanced by the naming or prosecution of the perpetrators of Lockerbie. Syria would not assist if her backing for the murderous PFLP-GC was held up to the world's gaze. Iran would not be disposed to help in any circumstances. Exposure would hardly concern her, as she had publicly promised a Lockerbie-style retaliation (indeed someone apparently representing the Guardians of the Islamic Revolution had proudly claimed responsibility), but any action was likely to incite her to further acts of terror and her associates possibly to take more hostages rather than releasing any. On the ground, the drug-producing cousins of the hostage-takers would have wanted a swift return to business-as-usual without any unwelcome publicity about their trafficking arrangements. Potentially, a deal keeping their involvement with 103 under wraps might convince them to continue dialogue with their Beirut clansfolk. Bush would, it's assumed, have omitted discussion with Mrs T of the drugs aspect, but the hostage welfare angle would have been persuasive enough.

The president had another relevant situation report to share with Thatcher; one that related to a monster they had created. More correctly the monster (many-headed and many-bodied, as it turned out), like so many tyrants since WWII, had been given life by George's old company, the CIA. The offspring's name was Saddam. Having been in 1968 assisted to murder his way to power and thereby control of the abundant oil revenues, Saddam Hussein had since been courted by the arms manufacturers of the United States and Britain, plus those of Germany, France, Spain and anyone else who could climb on the spendthrift's bandwagon. The eight-year Iran-Iraq War coincided with the unholy conjunction of the Thatcher and Reagan administrations. With UN resolutions forbidding the sale of arms to the combatants, both western governments were heavily compromised by assisting their arms traders to circumnavigate the ban, mainly in Saddam's favour. Neither administration raised a peep at the Iraqi dictator's wholesale use of poison gas on the battlefields, and in 1988 he turned it on his country's own Kurdish minority. The war had ended in the summer of that year, and any intelligence agency worth its salt would have been evaluating what mischief an armed-to-the-teeth psychopath might turn to next. A quick look at recent Middle Eastern history could hardly fail to point to Kuwait as a possible flash point.

In the official account, Saddam's invasion of the tiny but rich neighbour on 2nd August 1990 was unpredicted and would take everyone by surprise. Ray finds that contention laughable. Given the number of people employed by and the amount of money ploughed into the CIA, the DIA, MI6, Mossad, and the intelligence agencies of every other nation under the sun, it's hardly credible that the potential at least for major events such as invasions cannot be predicted. With the communications and satellite surveillance available, it has to be possible to see and hear signs of planning and preparations. The list of events where these expensive organisations admit to being caught out is long enough to be highly suspicious, he would argue.

A lot of people besides him think that events are expected right enough, but that there is a preference for allowing some of them to take their course so that the response, when it comes, can be bigger, more symbolic and, importantly, more expensive. In many cases an opportunity is also provided for munitions to be tested on living targets, no matter that they might be retreating and offering no threat: the *General Belgrano* and the Baghdad Road are but two horrific examples. It is inconceivable that Saddam's eye's turning towards Kuwait was not being predicted in early 1989. Certainly by mid-1990 the National Security Council would be happily pointing to Iraq as the replacement for the Warsaw Pact countries as the main justification for maintaining high levels of defence spending, grateful that there would thus be no post-Cold War peace dividend. One recipient of the torrent of tax dollars that therefore continued to flow – the US Army – would actually wargame an exercise that exactly mirrored an Iraqi attack on Kuwait, while the US Ambassador in Baghdad would pass messages encouraging Saddam to believe that the Americans would not intervene should he take such a course, a stance also expressed openly in a Washington congressional committee. Far from his invasion not being predicted, it would actually be provoked. He would be encouraged to try it. A vain and greedy man would be set up.

Those now contemplating future military action against him realised early on that for physical access it would be necessary to come to an understanding with some of his neighbours and of the short list, Syria would be near the top. So for a second reason, to drag Syria's name through the Scottish courts as a sponsor of 270 murders would not make sound sense internationally; certainly not if there was a good, profitable war on the horizon. And if all went well, there was.

There was another very serious subject area over which Bush would have been less than open with his ally. As President-elect and a former Director of the CIA, it's inconceivable that he hadn't received a briefing on 103 very shortly after the occurrence and, given Bush's own track record in dirty tricks, it's unlikely that current Director William H Webster would have held back anything known for certain by Langley at that time. Given that the rapid and targeted response at the scene by the agency had to have been authorised, at least part of the reason for it must have been known at the authorising level, wherever that was. Then at some point the decision to commit resources would have had to be explained upwards. Ray had discussed this with his contact, Dick Leigh, who as a former detective knew that someone is carrying narcotics on most flights, and even a large hidden consignment would not be that unusual. It would normally be a pretty standard police matter to collect, investigate and destroy the drugs: a suitcase of heroin was hardly a matter to mobilise the élite intelligence agency of the world's most powerful nation. No one would dispatch a group of agents merely to collect some smuggled hallucinogenic substances and then deny that they had done so. Whoever sent the CIA detachment to Lockerbie knew there was something else, more important, to keep hidden.

They either had to pass details, or a decent concocted cover story up the command chain. Which makes it likely that Director Webster knew and former Director Bush would come to know just how ensnared 'the company' was in the fall of Flight 103. This would not be information to share with the British Prime Minister.

But Dick Leigh had reasoned that Thatcher must have been put at least partly in the picture within hours of the flight's demise. It was the command chain thing again. No police officer – certainly no British police officer, he had corrected himself – would accept that anyone at all, be they an ally's intelligence agents or even the very Prime Minister herself, could interfere in the process of evidence gathering, override lawful orders or impede an officer in the execution of their duty. The immediate response to any attempt at of these things would be to report the matter to the nearest accessible superior officer. Each rank, faced with such a circumstance or such a report, would refer the matter higher. Despite the chaos, news of the interference encountered would reach Chief Constable level in double-quick time. From there it would pass to, in this case, the Scottish Office and thence upwards still. Such an unprecedented and fundamental matter would have to go right to the very top for a decision. Anyone lower down would take the attitude, as film director Billy Hale jokingly used to say on set, several times a day, **'I'm** not gonna take the heat on **that.'** Permission to accept the glaring irregularities noted at Lockerbie would then have to be passed down to constable level, to prevent any confrontations that might arise. It was the fact that foreign meddling and partial control was being mysteriously tolerated which caused several Scottish police officers to contact their MPs, and some were fortunate in having the clear-thinking Tam Dalyell to listen to their serious concerns.

It seems unlikely that Mrs Thatcher, imperious though she was, would sanction such jurisdictional intrusion without seeking clarification. She will have been moved on that terrible evening to ring her buddy, Ronnie Reagan, still lame-duck president at the time, to offer condolences and solidarity, although she would probably have guessed that he might not know too much about anything going on behind the scenes. For that she, or more likely a trusted colleague, would have consulted 'C', the head of MI6. The latter would have spoken to Langley or someone at CIA London station; indeed, would have already had contact; and on the basis of whatever he was told would have advised: 'I think, under the special circumstances, we should let them do as they wish, Prime Minister'. The justification that Mrs Thatcher would have been given for the intervention already underway would have been the need to secure sensitive documents in the possession of a US agent on board. Politicians seem conditioned to agree to almost anything at the first mention of secrecy. To ask how the plans for a completely dead-in-the-water operation (for it would later become apparent that the PM knew the agent's name and almost certainly the essence of his mission) might be significant enough to warrant the subjugation of fundamental legal requirements, seems not to be the type of question that a head of government is expected to ask of the CIA. In any such situation, it is unlikely that a Prime Minister would ever expect the full chapter and verse.   In politics, or British politics at least, there is a convention on matters of intelligence that senior figures don't want to hear compromising things unless there is absolutely no way to avoid knowing them.

Now, three months on from the bombing, it's likely that Margaret — 'doing her red boxes' of cabinet papers in the middle of the night, as was her custom — would have been quite excited at getting a call from George. For an ambitious daughter of a grocer from Grantham who'd reached the country's top job, there would be a certain frisson at being rung up, confided in and asked for help by one of the few in the world with even more firepower than she had.   According to Anderson, there was a suggestion, doubtless from Bush, that the Lockerbie investigation be 'toned down', and like most British Prime Ministers since Churchill she was keen, or maybe even actually obliged, to ensure that what the President wanted, the President got.

Those requirements of Scottish law had already taken a pasting in the aftermath of Lockerbie. Now they could go by the board entirely if that's what the President felt the bigger picture demanded. The investigation would go on ice, along with the very understandable hopes of thousands of people — relatives, friends, simple well-wishers and indeed investigators, all of whom wanted to see swift and effective justice for the slain. No hope of that now.

   "Goodnight, George."

                                            —ooOoo—

Paul Channon was replaced by Cecil Parkinson in a summer cabinet reshuffle.   Ray thinks there's an interesting point about ministerial responsibility brought up by the Channon case. After researching him, he feels less condemning of the unlucky Secretary for Transport, a man who seemed to be popular and who had piloted some very worthwhile projects in his many posts and especially at Transport, where the sad monsoon of disasters was unfortunate, arbitrary and scarcely his fault. He may have been lacking vigour over the Lockerbie warnings, but how would anyone know one way or the other from the performance of his department? The excellent *Yes, Minister* showed beyond all reasonable doubt the sheer impossibility of overcoming the in-built inertia in the Whitehall machine. We learnt from writers Jay and Lynn that no amount of resolve and determination on the part of the nominal head of a ministry could greatly influence policy, practices or promptitude. Ray has decided that it's probably unfair to blame the minister of a department that's functioning in a totally expected and immutable manner. Nevertheless, Channon lost his job, never to return to government.

Goodnight Paul.

–ooOoo–

44   The Deniable Truth

If they'd left it at that, Ray thinks, it would have been just the one level of dishonesty. The people who apparently control our lives, whomsoever they may be acting on behalf of, are well-practised in the art of misleading us, supposedly for our own good. Things that they decide we shouldn't know, lest we, the simple masses, become too stirred and troublesome, they take it upon themselves to hide, massage or spin. If it had been announced, after a suitable interval, that the Lockerbie crime wasn't soluble; that the tracks had been covered too well, many among the population wouldn't have liked it, but that would, in the fullness of time, have been that. Even major failures don't have to be brazened out for too long before interest wanes. But of course they didn't leave it at that, because an opportunity presented itself that couldn't be resisted. It was a free-shot, something for nothing, a two-for-one offer, too tempting to waste.

103 had closely affected a core group, who were becoming quite vocal. Around them there was a much wider circle of sympathy and interest, wanting answers. If it wasn't now possible, for some reason, to tell them the truth – the facts that Channon had seemed to confirm – and they didn't seem inclined to go away any time soon, something else would have to be said, eventually, to satisfy them. And that of course by definition would have to be a fabrication. If something was to be fabricated, it was going to need to be convincing, which would mean a lot of work. If time and money were to be thrown at the problem, perhaps this alternative story could fulfil another useful function – kill two birds with one stone. The PLFP-GC couldn't be blamed, but was there an alternative around who could be convincingly substituted; someone who could carry the can without any repercussions and whom no one would believe, or worry about if they denied it?

Funnily enough, there was.

–ooOoo–

Ray is always put on his guard when he hears a politician assert that something is or isn't in the national or public interest. It inevitably triggers an evaluation to identify any benefits for the widespread population, or whether the advantages are more targeted, even to the extent of being personal. The process can be illuminating. For example, one of Paul Channon's predecessors, a Minister of Transport who ushered in the motorway-building programme and promoted roads as the future, to the detriment of the rail network, is found to have owned a road construction company and held on to his shares while in office by the simple expedient of selling them to his wife.

This concept of the national or public interest is loved by those in power, because, like the Official Secrets Act, it's awfully handy to hide behind. And they get to define it, which is a great advantage. But there is a degree of danger though, that comes with telling outright lies 'in the public interest'. Our legal system, in theory at least, relies on the use of 'the whole truth', assuming that an opportunity is allowed to present it. The rule of law is the bedrock of society, so if those in charge tamper with the truth, they actually undermine the foundations of the very edifice that they stand astride. If they were to be toppled as a result, they could hardly complain. In reality, they are unlikely to be displaced, but (changing metaphors) they are on a slippery slope, because what happens is that they tend to be forced to introduce more and more measures 'in the national interest' to maintain the status quo.

Big Brother that way lies.

Ray's life has encompassed the entire span of the Cold War, and if he was aware of one thing about it from childhood onwards, it was that the difference between 'us' and 'them' consisted in the beastly Soviet government telling lies, while our Western systems believed in the shining truth. It was a major shock to realise that on the veracity front at least, there was far less to choose between them than anyone had ever imagined possible. In British parliamentary terms, of course, lying does not exist; the word may not be uttered in the chambers of Westminster. There is merely an offence of misleading the House, which has to be expunged by attendance and an apology. In reality the House is misled on a daily basis by the use of weasel-words and carefully selected statistics. One of the reasons that the Commons proceedings are so tedious is that often the response to sustained questioning is the repetition, several times over, of exactly the same phrase: for a masterclass, read the parliamentary answers of Harriet Harman or watch interviews with Peter Hain. There is a reason for this. To deviate even slightly from the rehearsed reply might change the answer from something misleading but technically just accurate, to one that is misleading but actually false. It was such fine distinctions that led Sir Robert Armstrong, Head of the Civil Service during the bulk of the Thatcher years, to make famous the beautiful euphemism 'economical with the truth'. With such smoke and mirror semantics do those apparently toiling on behalf of our nation occupy much of their expensive time.

Many observe that the proceedings both of parliament, in public, and the cabinet, in secret are increasingly irrelevant, when policy is made by a group of Number 10 insiders, most of them unelected, and announced at press conferences, party conferences, in newspaper articles and occasionally on street corners; not to mention through leaks, either unintended or more likely contrived. Churchill was arguably the first PM to govern in a presidential way, by-passing even his small war cabinet and dealing directly with his military chiefs. As if we were in any doubt, we know that the British public have long been misled because most secret cabinet discussions eventually become public when the minutes are released for posterity to see. They are locked away for varying lengths of time, depending on the sensitivity of their content, which we can translate to mean the degree of potential embarrassment they pose. Some documents contain matters deemed so contentious that they are classified as permanently closed, but even so plenty of evidence emerges of many of the agenda items considered best kept from the public.

In Churchill's war, to handle the details of what the nation-at-large should know, not know and believe, there was the Ministry of Information. This new department saw to it that people were not told, for example, of the shambles of Dunkirk until the evacuation was nearly complete and journalists were given deliberately false information laying blame on the French army – a body that actually did, in general, stand and fight, whereas the mass of the British army was ordered to retreat. Miracle there may have been, but gallant undefeated fighting withdrawal there wasn't, in the main, despite the legend that was planted and became the accepted account. Likewise the relative aircraft casualty figures of the two sides in the Battle of Britain were shamelessly exaggerated at the time. And so it went on. Manipulation of the news had become acceptable – 'in the national interest'. Once it was begun, who was going to stop it?

A cabinet discussion that certainly wasn't for public consumption was the creation of the SOE, the Special Operations Executive. Terrorism had been around almost since the beginning of time, and professional, salaried spying in Britain dates from around the turn of the 20th century – Sidney Reilly, so-called Ace of Spies, is thought to have been the first. The idea behind the SOE was to combine the two, whereby agents acting for one country would instigate in other occupied states or enemy homelands, resistance cells that would engage in terrorist-like behaviour. What a precedent that set. While the aims were in this case entirely legitimate, state subversion of other sovereign entities moved insidiously into the repertoire of the Free World. The American OSS, Office of Strategic Services, forerunner of the CIA, was waiting in the wings, ready to refine the concept.

–ooOoo–

Ray had stayed awake just long enough to read the names of the journalists gathered at the lunch table.

—ooOoo—

45　Expletives Retained

On a scale of one to ten for fulfilling anticipation, the reunion with Gerald initially only flicks the needle marginally off the stop, to about the two mark, before dropping back. Ray is shocked by his friend's appearance; he is diminished as a result of the pain and has aged almost another decade. The visitor has to make quite an effort to conceal his surprise. The Logan voice and language remain unchanged though, and the greeting is typically flamboyant.

"Good to see you, you old horsefucker."

"And you, Ger."

Ray is the only person alive who calls the celebrated director Ger. One of his wives used to call him Gerry, but the name didn't outlive the marriage, which itself hardly survived a year. It was Florence, an art director on the long series and for a while Ray's girlfriend, who had started shortening the name. She and Gerald had a great rapport and she was one of those confident souls who could say whatever she felt to anybody if she was right. And she mostly was. It's strange to think that Florence has been dead now for over ten years.

"I can't get up so you don't get a hug or any of that bollocks. Come and sit down here."

I wouldn't have got one if you'd been on your feet, Ray thinks as he pulls up the inevitable metal chair. The first half hour or so is taken up with serious medical matters; a description of the accident and the agony and a half-explanation of why Gerald, after several weeks, is still in Dunedin and hasn't gone back to Los Angeles. After all, he could easily afford a private ambulance jet. There is obviously something more serious to keep him here, although he seems not to know, or perhaps want to know, exactly what it might be. Ray doesn't seek to probe but he is quite upset at seeing this normally vibrant, energetic man in such a bad way.

"Eve can help you with pain control – far more effective than drugs. She can do it over the phone. I'll give you her number in LA. You should ring her. She's expensive, mind." The latter is not altogether true and said as a joke.

"I'll try anything," Gerald says resignedly, without laughing, and they leave the subject, moving to the trivia of the trip so far. As he did with E,

Ray holds back the story of meeting DB. He also has decided not to mention the rocky state of his marriage, and of course he will censor some other aspects of the California stopover.

However poorly he might be physically, Gerald remains irrepressibly obsessed with films and film-making, so having disposed of the necessary pleasantries in the minimum decent time, he is impatient to start discussing the advertised reason for Ray's 28,000-mile round trip.

"So. You've brought me the famous Lockerbie script. You finished it." Gerald pauses and Ray elects to say nothing but wait for more. "Remind me, or tell me, because we haven't really talked about it a great deal, why you've written it – what your aim is – what you hope will happen as a result of it."

"I suppose it's because all my life I've had a big thing about injustice, so seeing someone conveniently convicted and sacrificed in order to hide the real story and the really guilty has made me angry since I first took an interest in the subject. The more you find out, the worse it gets. You realise not only that Lockerbie was preventable, but that it was precipitated initially by cavalier activities by Americans, made possible by cavalier activities by Americans, covered-up by cavalier activities by Americans and the eventual trial shamelessly manipulated by cavalier machinations of Americans." Gerald has nodded throughout the list, so Ray continues. "I am also quite convinced, as a logical deduction from the mass of known facts, that Lockerbie was actually permitted, allowed, sanctioned if you like, in an equally gung-ho decision by one American – or a small group. If all that wasn't bad enough, the British authorities, whoever they are (if there really are any, and that's a question in itself) fell over themselves to facilitate the cover-up. Worse again still, the media, more or less en-masse, both American and British, have either been persuaded to look the other way, or in some cases to publish disinformation much like the old Soviet news agency – what was it called, TASS? This crime still raises enormous passions and intense public interest, and it's so frustrating to see all the anger directed at one scapegoat who sits in prison while all the people guilty of everything from perjury, to perverting the course of justice, to murder, are drawing fat salaries or comfortable pensions. I obviously think that this is a scandal and a story that the public should know. Most of the information is out there in the public domain, in newspapers and books, but it doesn't get mass exposure. For supposedly free societies, the censorship can be quite effective. I think it would make a fascinating film which would bring the subject out into the open again."

"And?"

254

"And it would be nice if it made a bit of a stir – got people talking – asking questions."

"Do you think it might do that?"

"I hope so."

"Do you believe that films ultimately change anything?"

"Well they certainly help to form attitudes. I was just thinking, on the way over, about how Westerns implanted a version of history that everyone, me included, took for gospel. Then I remember seeing *Soldier Blue* and *Little Big Man* which looked at the Cavalry versus the Indians from the opposite side to usual – and either the films or the publicity they got suddenly opened people's eyes to the propaganda we'd been used to. And we know that American Second World War movies have given the world a completely skewed version of who did what in that conflict. So just as films can spread false history, they are also capable of representing the proper stuff."

"I'm not so sure that's true now," Gerald asserts. "I think that because of information and entertainment fatigue – there are so many TV images, so many movies – nothing sticks like it used to. I think that people walk out of a cinema and they might be moved or angered or whatever by what they've seen, and they might even have heard something revelatory and shocking, but in today's world they've forgotten it by the time they've got to the pub, where's there's football or something on TV. It's not as if there aren't plenty of films taking the line that governments and spooks get up to all sorts of dirty tricks. Look at Tony's *Enemy of the State*. People lap up these movies, but they don't go and demonstrate in the street about the abuse of surveillance."

"Maybe you're right, but that shouldn't stop us trying to surprise them with the truth. What's that quote journalists love? 'Write the truth and shame the devil'."

"I suppose what I'm asking – what I'm interested to know, is whether you've written it as a piece of entertainment or as a vehicle to get a guy released from jail?"

"As an intriguing and watchable film of course. If you try and write for a result like the second, you're going to fail, on all counts probably."

"Good. In which case I look forward to reading it."

Talking about movies, even a prospective one, has already visibly restored Gerald's aura to a small degree. He continues.

"I should say that since I've known you were coming, I've done a little bit on the internet, just to remind myself of what I'd forgotten and so as not to appear too stupid and uninformed. There's certainly plenty on there. Obviously I only could read a tiny amount of it, and I know next to nothing compared to the research that you've done, but a couple of things struck me from articles I read – sensible serious pieces, not the wilder, off-the-wall stuff. One, that the evidence offered in the trial seemed so poor in every respect that in any ordinary court on an average day it wouldn't have secured a conviction for shoplifting, let alone nearly 300 murders. There didn't seem to be much of it, and what there was gave no real indication as to who made the bomb, where, when, who else was involved and what the defendants were actually supposed to have done. What little evidence there was seems largely circumstantial and its interpretation highly speculative. There was the identification evidence about Al-Megrahi being the man who bought the clothes for the bomb suitcase, where the shopkeeper had changed his mind so often that his testimony wasn't in the least credible, and there were two other very key witnesses whom even the judges, I think, said they didn't believe. Plus, it said, several of the forensic investigators on the case have been exposed as being biased and unsound.

"The other thing is that – I'm assuming you believe the Jibril group actually did the bombing, right?" Ray nods. "If you're looking at two sets of supposedly ruthless, murderous terrorists and their capabilities, comparing Jibril's gang with these two Libyans – it seems to be a bit like comparing an SS Panzer tank regiment with the Warmington-on-Sea Home Guard, Dad's Army. I can't believe that they did it, because they don't seem to have been up to it. If they had been of a calibre to do what they were accused of, they wouldn't have left the clues they are supposed to have left. And even the so-called clues didn't prove anything concrete. So I'd have to agree that it looks like a set-up. The trouble though, with all that, from a dramatic point of view, is that it's all negatives – it's all what the two Libyans, or one really, as the other one was found innocent – it's what they didn't do. I'll be very interested to see how you handle that. If they didn't do anything, their story won't be very fucking enthralling."

Ray smiles.

"I hope you're not disappointed, then. I'm very heartened that you seem convinced about the miscarriage of justice at least. That's a good start – better than I hoped. I remember that when we spoke about the subject briefly, a year or three ago, you felt it wouldn't be of great interest to the public – I think you used the term 'old hat', which I couldn't understand. Like I said, I think there's still massive interest in the case and as to there being no story, if you just précis the bones of the case . . . I mean, listen to this as a synopsis: Two passenger aircraft are blown out of the sky, causing the deaths of 560 people. There are cover-ups over the reasons for both and the link between them – cover-ups that involve two US presidents and a British Prime Minister. A massive amount of evidence points to the ⸱ involvement of several states and various official and unofficial agencies of those states, yet the guilty are publicly exonerated and others blamed, and there's a unique specially-constituted show trial where false evidence is allowed to convict an innocent man. You could hardly get a story that was more sensational."

"Yeah, well. I hope you're right. I'm no writer but I tried thinking for an hour or two how it could be put over, in an understandable form, that is, and I don't mind telling you it made my head hurt."

"Oh, it can do that all right. No doubt at all." Guessing that Gerald would be keen to have the script in his hands a.s.a.p., Ray has brought one in a plastic bag, now augmented by some fruit from the hospital shop. "Let's hope this doesn't have the same result. I mean the script – not the peaches," he says, as he hands over the unorthodox package. "Fingers crossed."

"Thanks, darling," Gerald says, placing the duty-free bag on his bedside cabinet. "I'll read it as soon as you've fucked off. Now. . . have you seen the new Steve Martin picture?"

Ray's jaw drops in disbelief.

—ooOoo—

Eating alone in a restaurant or a hotel dining room is far from a favourite experience. It takes Ray back to a time when he had to do a great deal of it, in the era when he was regularly tasked with finding locations. If you were abroad, there would generally be a local contact to share your car journeys and mealtimes, and it could be amusing. But Ray had spent sometimes weeks at a time alone in the remoter parts of the British Isles, taking pictures and noting the passage of the sunlight, if any was to be seen. The days were rewarding as he looked at the OS map and then followed his instinct to search out suitable roads and tracks, fields, castles or coastlines; whatever the scripts demanded. It was the evenings that were generally the downside, and the isolation did wonders for his reading. But location-scouting could have occasional highlights. His friend Patrick tells how he was searching in the Border country and one evening after supper a Scottish rugby international walked into the hotel lounge with a friend. With the annual Calcutta Cup match against England due at the end of the week and the final training on the morrow – this was before the days of professional players – Patrick had slipped into conversation with the pair, and as a patriotic Englishman ensured that the drink and the stories flowed. The speedy centre, known for his elusive jinking, left the bar very late that night and much the worse for wear, with a pronounced weave to his walk that was totally involuntary. Practice the following day would be a fairly pointless exercise.

Ray doesn't any anticipate any jolly social interaction of that nature this evening. He has walked down the hill into the city centre (6 minutes down – 10 back up, the hotel's info claims) for two good reasons; one to take some mild exercise after too many hours in a seated position; two because his very new boutique hotel does not serve dinner.

'You old horsefucker!' Ray almost chokes on his blue-lipped mussels as he remembers Gerald's greeting. This was typical Gerald – inventive and outrageous. Gerald's film set was not a place for the fainthearted or the politically correct. 'Get over here Martin, you little poof,' could ring across the stage, as likely directed to a leading actor or director of photography as to a standby propman or stagehand, and quite irrespective of sexual orientation. He also claimed to have actually given the famous two-word note 'Act better' to some celebrated thespian. Ray had never seen anyone offended by anything Gerald said; people always seemed to revel in the very slightly manic atmosphere that he managed to conjure up. Ted, Ray's old first assistant boss and early mentor, was another of those who had the gift of being able to say anything to anybody and occasionally inject a degree of inspired euphoria into proceedings. He seemed to know personally every actor who walked onto the set of *The Avengers*, and though he no doubt had worked with many of them, he couldn't have been acquainted with them all. You would never have guessed this from his approach, yet he too got away with astonishing familiarity.

In his day, openly swearing on set was rare and even an expletive 'shit' from Ted could raise eyebrows. The ultra-urbane Patrick Macnee was the first person that Ray heard use the F-word on a quiet stage, and on that occasion he quickly followed it with 'Sorry Diana,' as though Miss Rigg had been the only woman present. In a very short time even actresses took to saying 'Oh, fuck it,' when they mucked-up their lines. Ray, having spent time on building sites, was well used to swearing in a variety of accents, but there was enormous novelty in hearing such words uttered in cultured tones. Later his amorata, the actress with the phenomenal speaking voice, used a remarkably colourful vocabulary which only poured oil on the fire of his attraction.

Ray's favourite story on swearing came from a client on a Tourist Board documentary. An older man, he had been a young officer of some rank in the Second World War, elevated enough to have a staff car. One day the inevitably poor wartime maintenance caused it to break down, and on asking his Scottish driver the obvious question as to what was amiss, he'd received the comprehensive reply, 'The fockin' focker's focked, sor'.

When Ray's trip had been mooted, it hadn't been expected that Gerald would still be in hospital. The plan had been that he would go back to his mother's place near Queenstown, with a private nurse and a physio-therapist, to convalesce sufficiently before undertaking the journey home to LA. None of this had happened, so Ray was in a Dunedin hotel instead of one of Mrs Logan's chintzy spare rooms. This had put a totally different slant on things. Instead of more or less 16-hours-a-day access to Gerald, whereby they could talk as and when they felt like it, Ray was now locked in the always uncomfortable ritual of the hospital visit. At the house, the default position would have been contact. In a hospital the expectation of everyone – staff, patient and visitor – is that the latter is an intruder who will shortly leave.

The circumstances of the accident had been typically Gerald. On a duty visit to his mother he had, as always, quickly become bored to distraction. By chance, he'd met a couple recently moved to a nearby property. They keep horses and invited him over to ride. Although he hadn't ridden for upwards of twenty-five years he had confidently chosen the most spectacular horse on offer – with the inevitable outcome. The horse's Ferrari-like responsiveness coupled with Gerald's coarse inputs very quickly resulted in a spectacular parting of the ways, and in the human's case a split pelvis and other sundry injuries. Eve says that even the most horsey people, including the famous ones, generally have not the slightest inkling of what their animals think and feel. Treating them in the same way as we do our mechanical transport, she told him, discussing Gerald's mishap, generally breeds dissatisfaction or worse for both horse and rider.

The restaurant is not particularly busy but even the lowest volume setting on Ray's ring tone would feel to him unacceptably loud. It's way up on that but no one apart from him seems concerned. It's DB.

In Ray's most optimistic moments in LA, after the supper on the first evening, he had gone so far as to wonder whether he might have to think of delaying his onward flights, if the producer had maybe wanted to schedule a meeting. This certainly hadn't happened and apart from a couple of almost-courtesy calls, there had been no significant exchanges. Ray had tried not to read anything negative into this, telling himself logically that whatever DB had gone to LA to do, it wasn't to progress a script that he didn't know about until he was on his way there. This is different. Whatever his high-flying friend has to say that's caused him to ring Dunedin after midnight Los Angeles time should be more than interesting.

"Mr Scriver! How's New Zealand?"

"Pretty bloody wintry actually. I should have brought warmer clothes."

"What news of Logan? Have you seen him yet?"

"Yes. He's not at all good. He was fairly cheerful when I left, after talking films for a bit, but he's certainly not mending quickly. I was shocked when I saw him, and he didn't say but I think there's some complication. No idea what."

"He like the script?"

"I left it with him, so I don't know yet. He doesn't seem as flatly against the idea as he was, but I'll know more tomorrow when he's read it. Fingers crossed."

"Well my news is that I had dinner tonight with Arran Samson and I mentioned your property. He was highly intrigued and wants to see it."

Arran Samson is a bankable star. He's been box office for maybe ten years, one of that group of English actors that Hollywood has embraced and nurtured in recent times. Most importantly in the context of *One-Zero-Three*, he has acquired the status of a movie radical, a major name prepared to take controversial rôles and be critical of establishment practices both in his work and outside it, following in the footsteps of Jane Fonda, Vanessa and Corin Redgrave, and more recently George Clooney and Julia Roberts, to name but some. Having Samson on board certainly could kick-start the project, although Ray will have to do some hard thinking to visualise him in either of the possible parts he might play. This is not something he is about to voice at this moment. It's highly positive progress, which is not in any way to be discouraged. He is torn between saying 'brilliant' and 'fantastic'.

"Erm. Brantastic," it comes out. DB fails to notice the cobbling.

"So, I should have asked when you were here, is it OK if I have some copies made? It's getting hard making do with just the one. I'll obviously only pass it to proper people."

"Of course. You don't need to ask. This is really exciting."

"Well you know how he likes good causes. I thought he'd be interested, at least. It's early days but at least the ball is slightly rolling."

"Is this something I can mention to Gerald?"

"I think you should keep this between ourselves for now. If Gerald likes it, he'll start to have his own ideas about cast, and to plant an idea about Arran might colour his thinking and stop him having a better idea. But when do you think he's likely to be back in harness?" They both laugh at this unfortunate expression.

"Back in the saddle, you mean?"

"Ouch!"

"I can't say, but no time soon, I suspect."

"Yeah, I mean, as you know he was due to start prep on the Tom Cruise picture quite soon, but I hear on the grapevine they're looking to replace him. You'd better not mention that either, in case it hasn't got to him yet."

–ooOoo–

46   Gerald's Cross

It's got to him. It seems to have arrived shortly before Ray has. The private room is blue with expletives. Gerald moves agitatedly in the bed rattling the adjacent trolley and its saline bag by the tube attached to his arm. If he could plug in a poison drip to the phone and pump it through to kill a boardroom full of studio executives he would be doing it. And the person on the other end is actually on his side. Ray turns as if to retreat to the corridor but the director, in his oversize pyjamas, motions him to stay and fills him in succinctly.

"The fuckers are trying to bump me. I'll nuke the bastards – flatten the fucking studio."

His attention returns to the phone and his unfortunate agent, who is soaking up his client's anger like the sand behind the targets on a firing range. Edward is well used to Gerald's ways but won't have had to cope with his being sacked from a film before. This is new territory.

The diatribe lasts for five minutes. Although the man is deadly serious and there will be millions of dollars involved, Ray senses that there is, even in this extreme, just the slightest degree of tongue-in-cheek, a hint of theatricality, a faint suggestion that it's all really a game. Jim, the grip – a man with a host of film sayings, mostly unprintable – used to say that in America there was a film industry but for the British it was a hobby. Hobby it might be, but the likelihood is that Gerald will net a fee that would represent a fortune to most people, just for being replaced.

It's just as well that the patient isn't at the moment connected to the monitor behind the bed, as his blood pressure would be jumping off the screen. One of the factors in its super-elevation, he tells Ray, is that Edward has dropped the news that the studio, although he is safely under contract to make the Cruise movie, is trying to avoid his cancellation fee by claiming that by exposing himself to such an accident, he has breached it. Breaking a pelvis, a wrist and some ribs is one thing; a contract is another thing entirely. Gerald Logan this morning is not a happy man.

Ray can hardly be anything other than acutely aware that this is not the best moment to seek a wholly-balanced opinion of his hard-wrought screenplay. He reminds himself of Gerald's great powers of concentration, but set against the pain the man is suffering, and the unwelcome news he's just had, they're unlikely to be enough. In his state, it would take near-superhuman detachment to focus on the subtleties of a very complicated script. The writer desperately tries to manufacture a credible reason to absent himself from the room and get as far away from the hospital as he can, for at least the rest of the day. But he can't think of one, and his lame offer of giving his friend some space to rest and sort out his new problem is waved away. Ray can sense exactly what is likely to happen – he's seen it before, as a third assistant on a horror film. The Six Day War had broken out during the production and the normally charming cameraman, who was Jewish, became thoroughly distracted by the events in the Middle East. He vented his anxiety in an escalating feud with the sound department, to the extent that many on the unit truly felt that he began to see sound's Fisher boom, a cumbersome, wheeled, elevated platform carrying an operator and a microphone on a gun-like arm – something that he was obliged to take into consideration in his lighting for every set-up – as a symbolic Egyptian tank. Now Ray worries that his screenplay will similarly take the flak that the frustrated director would like to send the way of the company stooges who have so enraged him. Shit! He's come a long way and invested valuable time and money in this trip, and it looks like being sabotaged by the politicking of a bunch of Hals.

Providentially, Gerald's surgeon walks in and Ray takes the opportunity to scurry off for a coffee. In the queue, through the café windows his eyes light on his hire car parked outside. He's tempted to make a run for it and head for the hills, in the form of the Pisa Range or the Remarkables, a hundred miles away as the crow flies, but he still can't think how he'd explain his disappearance. He hopes the interlude will perhaps stabilise the mood of the man in the orthopaedic ward.

After half an hour, the meeting reconvenes, one of them fortified by caffeine, the other by extra painkillers. Ray pulls out his notebook and pen; an essential screenwriter's ploy that he's used since reading William Goldman's *Adventures in the Screen Trade*. Goldman's assertion is that by being seen to take full notes you cut down not only the number of observations and suggestions for changes that producers and execs are inspired to offer, but also limit the extent of their mind-boggling idiocy. This will not be a problem with Gerald; Ray just wants to make sure he doesn't forget anything the man says.

"I haven't written in the screenplay, because you'll probably want to keep it for someone else after you've heard what I have to say. I've just made some notes on paper," Gerald begins.

Ray is stunned. All he can see is a fruit machine flashing 'GAME OVER' in large ornate letters. He checks the Logan profile as, half-glasses on nose, the director turns the first few pages. There seems to be no sign of that tongue-in-cheek. This may not be too pleasant at all.

"Right. The Star Wars-type credit sequence. It's a twist on a theme, certainly, but it doesn't grab me. I know you've got the tension there and that you want it for scene-setting, but I'd hope for something more punchy."

Ray decides he's going to respond to each point as it comes rather than store them for later discussion, and he has a ready-made answer for this first one.

"OK. Well for you I could start with Jibril's European cell trying to blow up American troop trains in Germany. It's a good piece of crash, bang, wallop that establishes that side of the story. There were two that took place in the eighteen months or so before Lockerbie. I thought about using one as a pre-title sequence but I left it out because I need the screentime later. The group also raided Israel at night using microlights, you know, motorised hang gliders, almost exactly a year before. That's your sort of thing."

"That I like. I could do something with that."

"OK, I'll give that some thought."

"Now we come straight away to the nitty-gritty. Daniel Weiss. He doesn't work as a main character. I know why he's there and that you need him and what you're trying to do but all he does is talk. He talks in some interesting places, but that's about all you can say for him. He **does** fuck-all, for two and a half hours. It's worse than *JFK*. At least the Kevin Costner character eventually stops just talking and prosecutes someone. Your guy only watches the trial. Costner – what was he called – Garrison, he was still just talking as a prosecutor of course, but at least he was **in** the action."

"And what a great film. With the greatest respect, your point about Weiss is bollocks, Ger. He falls in love. He loses her. He grieves. He gets angry. He immerses himself in an investigation. He comes out of the grief but still not enough to have a new relationship. He arrives at a conclusion about what really happened, and so on and so on – he's developing all the way through. I think it's a great leading rôle a lot of people would give their eye teeth to play."

"I think he's boring as arseholes."

"You think he's boring because all your leads these days carry a weapon and survive a murderous attack every five minutes. This isn't that sort of story."

"So I guess it's not my sort of story." He looks up from the play and regards Ray over the glasses.

"I don't understand that. You do a great job with this type of material. I remember two of the series that we did – I mean, *Clapham*, that was all politics and plotting, implied evil and suggestion – not an explosion or a car chase in sight. I can't remember any stunts at all, but I suppose we had some. And *Thumbscrew* had some war sequences and a few bangs, but it was really all in the character and the dialogue."

"*Clapham* was more than twenty years ago and it was for television. You can't make feature films like that these days – not successful ones anyway. *Thumbscrew* was even longer ago. And I've done my share of cerebral movies that did no business. It's not something I can go back to."

"You used to love plot and story. You've got hooked on fast-pace and stunt-porn. It's a phase. It will play out, like any other. No amount of spectacle will keep a poor plot afloat."

"That I agree with. The story has to mean something or you're fucked."

"Well this story means â hell of a lot."

"Then let's find a way of telling it without Daniel Weiss sending everyone to sleep."

"Can't you see him played by someone like Ralph Fiennes?"

Gerald shrugs.

"If you want. For my money, Weiss is not a leading character and his mate Brad is just a sounding board. You've written Brad nicely and he's actually somewhat more appealing than Weiss, but dramatically, he just talks and listens, mostly listens. You can keep them in as supporters but is there no one else you can hang it on, like an intelligence guy or a cop?"

"They'd have to be invented, because there's no real person that's done this, as far as anyone knows."

"How about Juval Aviv?"

Gerald **has** read the work carefully, or paid attention to what he's seen on the net, thinks Ray. Aviv was the ex-Mossad agent who investigated Lockerbie for Pan Am's insurance company and first uncovered the likelihood of a drugs-for-bomb switch.

"If you go down that road, or use Lester Coleman, it becomes the Juval Aviv Story or the Lester Coleman Story, because they've got their own beginning, middle and end. All these stories are intriguing and frightening but they lack the universality of the main event – these characters can't follow the story all the way through. They're sub-plot material, really. Also, to be honest, their experiences are not that much more action-packed than Weiss's. There are a number of journalists who've followed the subject, but exactly the same applies to them."

Ray is really thinking now – Gerald has thrown him a major challenge. He's been over all this ground many times, but obviously it needs to be done again.

"I feel that it's one thing to invent one of the bereaved, because sadly there were many of them and so you can hide someone to represent all of them discreetly in their midst, if you like. Also Daniel Weiss does what a lot of the bereaved actually have done, which is to try to figure out what really happened. I think that's different from inventing a maverick policeman or an agent and having them do things that apparently none of the real ones did – that's openly or covertly to question their agencies' behaviour and then investigate the cover-up – because that involves also inventing a lot of scenes that didn't really happen. Then the film becomes an action adventure and the purity, if you like, gets diluted; inevitably then the message of the film gets lost and people can say that it's a fantasy – you know, like *Braveheart*. It would be great dramatically if Weiss or someone could go to Amman and confront Khreesat, the bomber, or find some over-the-hill CIA guy and squeeze some information out of him, but it would be hokum because these meetings haven't taken place. Any explanations or confessions coming out in such scenes would be worthless and confusing."

"I'm interested that you say 'message'. I asked you yesterday what your aim is and you said that it's to make an entertaining film, but from what you're saying now I think you really want to make a documentary, you know, an exposé."

"I don't agree at all. I just think we may have a different definition of an historical film. Any movie worth watching takes some form of attitude to its setting in time and place, but when I say 'message' I guess I mean credibility, I want people to know this one is being straight with the facts. Look, the whole subject matter concerns a real-life massive manipulation of the truth, so the last thing the film should do is engage in the same practice itself, or it loses all chance of belief. I think that the events that did take place were so extraordinary and so revealing, that there's a fascinating enough story without any need to invent anything."

This point gets through to Gerald, who softens for the first time this morning.

"OK. But that still gives you the problem of making it entertaining; you've got to make the lead character way more charismatic and powerful or no one will want to play him."

"All right. Give us a minute and I'll re-write him."

"What?"

"Joke, Ger."

Gerald retorts using an appalling, over-exaggerated impersonation of director Tony Richardson that the two of them have traded for years.

"'If that's your idea of a joke, don't write any fucking comedies.' Do you want to get us some coffees?"

"Should you be drinking coffee?"

"Don't **you** start."

From the café, the car still sits tantalisingly in the parking lot, but despite the grilling, Ray feels less like fleeing than he did. He's come for an opinion, and a very firm one he's getting. He can't complain at that. He disagrees about the title sequence, and he sees a lot more variety and depth in the Weiss character than Gerald does; maybe it's the pain and the drugs making the man read quickly. But in at least some respects he has to admit that the little sod in the bed is right. And he suspects there's more of the same to come.

–ooOoo–

"There's something I haven't told you."

"Am I going to like it?"

Ray describes meeting DB and the producer's enthusiasm for the screenplay. Gerald brightens visibly at the mention of their old colleague, but when it leads to a few reminiscences of their involvement on *Thumbscrew*, he becomes quite wistful. Talk of those days so long ago when they were all young and he was so unbelievably charged with energy, provides too much of a contrast with his present tethered state getting his fluids through tubes. He compensates by questioning DB's acumen.

"He didn't mention the weakness in the structure – the Weiss syndrome?"

"Not so far. As far as I know he likes the Weiss and Brad interplay."

"It's a miracle he's done so well then. So is he actually interested in doing it?"

"He's just saying he wants to but doesn't know if it will fit in."

"Right." Gerald has said 'right'. Ray wonders which meaning he has in mind. Gerald answers his question after a minimal pause.

"Probably means no."

"When did you take your Masters in cynicism?"

"Well before I left school."

"The courses are better now."

"Don't you believe it."

Towards the end of the afternoon visit Ray informs the impatient patient of a small plan. He doesn't say so, but he can only take this hospital bedside stuff in small doses and has made a decision.

"I won't be in until late afternoon tomorrow. I've booked to do some mountain-flying up in Queenstown. I'd always planned it, when we were going to be up there. It means a bit of driving but it's worth it."

"Are you addicted? You've just spent God-knows-how-many hours in the air getting here and the moment you arrive you can't wait to risk your arse some more."

"I guess so. It's what happens. But in my book the drive there and back is the far more dangerous bit."

"And books never lie," Gerald says with an attempt at amused sarcasm.

"Absolutely. They're just like governments and film producers.

Always tell the truth."

"Solid as a rock."

–ooOoo–

47   Show and Tell

When he'd arrived at the Brothers Hotel yesterday there had been a message waiting for him.

Missing you already. Deborah xx.

He'd scored the message ten for timing, ten for sentiment and not, it has to be said, an enormous amount for originality. It was, however, in the prevailing climate, warming to be remembered. He must call her back. He's promised himself he'll do it this evening.

Today on his return, there's one from Perry. One of the hats at the party has turned up trumps; is shortly photographing a second unit, and has become convinced – on the evidence of the Englishman's hilarious film anecdotes and a subsequent, rather more sober meeting – of his experience and capabilities. Ray is pleased that Perry's immediate problem is dealt with and hopes that this will prove the breakthrough that his friend so needs. Now he just requires one of his own.

Last night he promised DB that he'd let him know how Gerald had reacted to the script. He won't be able to settle to anything until he's tried to do that, so calculating the time difference, he locates his phone and dials LA . He has to leave a callback message at the Beverley Wilshire. That's put off telling Hollingsworth for a short interval, but it's got to be faced.

In truth, there are many sequences that Gerald is enthusiastic about, unsurprisingly those with suspense and action and spectacle, and he likes the handling of the trial, but he has taken a thoroughly fundamental dislike to the characters that Ray uses to sift through the evidence and filter out the truth. He can't stand Daniel Weiss and his friend Brad and no amount of pointing to similar, successful relationships in other movies will make him give ground.

When it comes to characterisation and structure, Gerald is no fool and has got to be listened to. No one is infallible and Goldman's famous assertion that nobody knows anything, not for a certainty, where movies and their appeal are concerned, has to be largely true. But there are people with a track record suggesting some insight and Gerald is one of them. His opinion may be a little extreme, but there's no smoke, etcetera.

Things don't look extraordinarily promising and when DB rings back, they don't improve. Ray gives him a potted version of his bad news and then the producer discloses his.

"I was in a meeting with Joe Wyzell today, you know, the head of Galactic, and I took the opportunity afterwards just to mention the bones of *One-Zero-Three*. His reaction was , well . . . it was basically if someone came up with the best package that there had ever been, you know, hottest stars, happening director, dialogue to die for, you name it, he would never, ever, ever greenlight a movie with that content, having the Libyan guy innocent. It was quite unbelievable how fired up and angry he seemed at the very suggestion. I'm afraid we can forget that avenue. Fortunately others are just as likely to take a diametrically opposite view. In fact one or two are more likely to take an interest if I let it slip that Wyzell hated it. They love having successes that their rivals have turned down – you know how it is."

Ray makes an affirmative noise and a knowing "Yeah". In fact he has very little idea how it is. He does however find it extraordinarily strange that the decisions about what films are made or are not made in the entire world in the English language, are in the hands of six or seven Joe Wyzells, who incidentally continually exhibit, on the evidence of the output, a remarkable lack of judgement in their choices.

There is the famous industry story of a director discussing a script point with one of Wyzell's famous, or infamous, predecessors. The mogul seemed enormously reluctant actually to get the script out and read the section over to himself. When there was finally no alternative, the director realised to his astonishment as he watched, that for this mighty man, reading involved following the words with his finger and silently moving his lips. They control the world's most popular and influential art form, but men of culture and letters they mostly 'ain't'. These days they're from business school or they're former agents. They can read better but the other constraints can apply.

"It's interesting about Wyzell," Ray says. "By denying the possibility of any debate, he's reinforcing the propaganda that's convinced him in the first place."

"I suspect that a lot of people over here are in that boat."

"But not many have the power to suppress ideas that they've closed their minds to."

"That, we're not going to change, I'm afraid."

Ray knows DB is right; after all, the man has dealt with these people for years, while Ray has, as far as possible, deliberately avoided all contact with the upper echelons of the industry. He's always been mindful of the in-joke about Wardour Street, the backbone of London's film quarter, having shadows on both sides.

–ooOoo–

48   Take it to the Ridge

The light aircraft, to anyone watching, would appear to be about to crumple itself against the rockface. It isn't of course. It's considerably further away than even the pilot imagines.

It's highly unlikely that anyone is here to see it in this empty, otherwise silent valley, but if there is the Cessna 172, against the bulk of the sheer mountainside, will seem an insubstantial and insignificant speck, doomed like a fly heading towards an insectocutor in a fish shop. In the left-hand seat, Ray is remarkably calm under the circumstances. The voice in his ears gives him what can only be described as lunatic instructions.

"Just maintain a constant wingtip distance to the terrain, level flight, as close as you feel comfortable. Be aware of your clearance below too, in case of sink or turbulence."

As close as you feel comfortable! When he'd first heard these words, more than fifteen years ago, he thought the instructor in the seat beside him must have been away with the fairies. How could anyone ever be comfortable, placing an aircraft at what feels to be few feet from a potential impact that would tear the wing off and mean certain death? Today he's been expecting the phrase, waiting for it, knowing that it's just part of the exercise. In the normal way, Ray avoids any suggestion of extreme flying like the plague. He dislikes the idea of formation, feeling it's a risk that you don't need to take. He doesn't care for aerobatics, never getting beyond the second lesson. If he had tried a more capable aircraft, it might just have been another story, but a tired 150 Aerobat was never going to do it for him.

Mountain flying is different.

It's different because what he learnt here all that time ago and is recapping today could just save your life over Wales or the Lake District, if you happened for some reason to find yourself in a really dire situation. Of course your whole training should prevent your ever doing that, but as Austin, moved on from the ATR and the A320 and now a 340 co-jockey, often says, 'Shit happens'.

Knowledge is power. Having the techniques to escape from the otherwise inevitable makes a lot of sense. Ray knows that two sorties in fifteen years aren't going to make him a real mountain pilot, but it's valuable nevertheless. Carlton, the original instructor, likened it in the debrief to a first parachute jump – a total sensory overload. Only with practice could you achieve realistic depth perception and appreciation of safe operating space. The first time out, he said, a pilot was at the illusion stage; everything would appear much closer that it really was. Be that as it may, the rocks had been close enough and the picture changing rapidly enough to make it thoroughly challenging and stimulating. It's also seriously good fun, the more so because back at home most of this flight – instructive, enjoyable and mildly terrifying – is effectively illegal, for anyone who's not a military pilot and specially authorised. In theory you could fly this exercise in Snowdonia. Technically you could do more or less all of what Ray and Neville are doing this afternoon, but if you rounded an outcrop only to come upon a group of walkers eating their packed lunches or a stick of climbers clinging to a face, and the chances are that in Wales at some point you would, you'd be committing an offence. The UK Civil Aviation Authority, the CAA, likes offences. Not for nothing is it known throughout the light aircraft fraternity as the Campaign Against Aviation.

In the South Island of New Zealand, if you're planning to pilot an aircraft anywhere near the Southern Alps, and if you're going far you don't have too much choice in the matter, it would be foolish not to have tucked away for reference the wisdom that Neville is today reimprinting on Ray's grey matter. This is chapter and verse for flyers in this part of the world.

The Cessna breaks left away from the cliff and makes a brisk 225 degree turn which brings it gradually towards the mountain again, closer and closer, until Ray eases a little right to fly the skimming manoeuvre in the reverse direction. This time it's Ray's, left, wingtip that seems to be twenty or so feet from the unyielding Haast Schist Metagreywacke. Travelling in this direction it's harder for Neville, on the right-hand side of the cockpit, to see the relationship between the wing and the dull rock; more difficult to judge if and when to add some control input to save their bacon. That's why they flew in the other direction first! Ray divides his scan between the terrain ahead and the wingtip margin. One direction he doesn't look is down as, strangely, he is not keen on sheer drops.

This is not a place Ray would want to be in strong wind conditions. He's thankful that the air is calm and stable and feels nice and thick. After a few passes in each direction, when Neville is happy that his student's performance is within tolerable limits; calculated and accurate, without veering towards the foolhardy; they move on to ridge crossing. They've been following this valley, with the Lochy River winding through it, since leaving the shore of Lake Wakatipu. Starting wide, the valley floor has gradually narrowed and risen somewhat to meet them and now they need to climb up nearer to where the stratus hangs round the higher slopes, masking who knows what? Pilots call the cloud formations in mountains cumulo-granite.

Neville's experience leads him to suspect that further up they'll find what he's hoping for – a letterbox. They've been gaining altitude for a few minutes with the right wing again tracing the shape of the mountain, displaced by maybe once to twice the aircraft's span. By now this is starting to feel perfectly normal. Rounding a steep jagged outlier they see a gap below the cloud, still slightly above their level. The greyness shrouds the upper parts of the massif they've been skirting and does the same to another wall of rock ahead. That's the far side of the valley, which has now curved round to meet them. Ray remembers the terms from school geomorphology, the cirque, corrie or cwm, the classic bowl-like blind head of those 'U'-shaped valleys formed by glaciers in the last Ice Age. In parts of these Southern Alps, of course, the Ice Age is still alive and well. With or without glaciers, many a French cirque, Scottish corrie and Welsh cwm have lured pilots into navigation errors and a meeting with an insurmountable and all-too-solid wall.

But two of these features back to back give you a ridge. Ridges can connect two peaks or groups of peaks in a chain and the good thing about ridges is they're lower than the summits. The tops may be in cloud but, in extremis, the bottom of the cloud and the dip of the ridge may provide that letterbox, enough clear space between mist and rock to transit safely from one valley into another. That's assuming you want to. Letterboxes can be too tempting by half. For if you're minded to cross a ridge and go into a whole different valley – one that may well have its own weather and especially cloudbase –, if said second valley is full of cloud and grot at a lower level than the one you're about to leave, doing so is more than inadvisable.

It's a fact that conditions can worsen behind you; a truism that no pilot should forget, mountains or not; but you certainly don't want to press on and substitute reasonable conditions in one valley for impossible ones the other side of that rim. You need an escape plan, and unwisely crossing the ridge can void that plan in seconds. So the next apparently mad exercise that Ray will practice is all about knowing how to avoid traversing until the pilot is absolutely sure that it's safe to do so. Obviously if it's clearly OK you can fly over the lip at any safe height and angle and start to descend into the next valley. But if there is any doubt – as a catchphrase that Ray often used on set goes – 'You don't wanna do that!'

Crossing at right-angles is dangerous because if you need to turn and come back to the original valley, there may not be enough room, or you may enter cloud and probably encounter that cumulo-granite while trying to complete the reversal. You need to keep your options open, and for that you need to approach the ridge obliquely, always with an eye to turning back into your first valley. What Neville now has Ray do, is decide how late he can leave that manoeuvre – how long he can safely delay the decision to go either way, but especially back, all the time bearing in mind that tight turns mean increased risk of stall, so must be avoided, especially in case of sink or turbulence. And ridges are exactly where those conditions can be expected. There's a lot to factor in. While you're deciding, you will be more or less heading for solid rock that's rearing up into saggy, soggy cloud not far above you.

They've come along the face with the mountain to the right, so the ridge appears also to the right, dropping out of the cloud. Ray is now using two stages of flap to fly more slowly without fear of stalling, but this close to the landscape outside, things are still happening very quickly. Neville has briefed that he will, at some point say 'Clear across' to simulate the moment when it becomes visible that the weather is suitable on the far side of the ridge. Already it's obvious that in reality it is, but the exercise assumes the reverse, until the instructor calls it. When Neville does so, Ray has to decide whether enough room remains to make the crossing safely, which in this case needs a right turn. If not, then a timely left one is going to be needed to avoid the lump of landmass ahead. The same applies if the instructor doesn't make the call. He wants to see Ray make his decisions correctly and as late as safely possible. After a few goes at this, they try an approach from the opposite hand, left to right, and when Neville eventually calls "Clear across" and the Cessna at last growls its way over the ridge, they shoot some from the other valley, also from both angles of approach.

Neville gives Ray a heading to steer and conjures another ridge out of nowhere, and they do a few more passes on this one with different topography, just to reinforce a realistic appreciation of the variables affecting the timing of the decision to cross or not. It's important to know when you are approaching the point when the escape, the return, option is about to be lost. This is not the type of flying that Ray would normally relish for a moment but the adrenalin is flowing so freely that he feels he could do this for hours more. Of course he couldn't and he will sleep like an infant tonight.

Suddenly the calm instructor's headings have put them in another, rather tighter valley. There will be no letterbox at the head of this one. He now tells Ray to fly up it, close to its right-hand edge and decide when he thinks its narrowing profile is approaching critical for a 180 U-turn; then he should make the manoeuvre. Ray complies conservatively leaving a third of the valley width unused, and so they double back and he tries another a little further along. Neville now takes control and returning to the same point, he demonstrates a technique that has the aircraft round, under perfect control and not at all alarmingly, in a fraction of the diameter Ray's reversal took. Ray repeats the pattern, a couple of times, very pleased to be reminded of this tool in the box. At this moment, when they've changed direction enough times to disorientate a perfectly adjusted homing pigeon, Neville asks Ray if he has any idea in which direction Queenstown Airport lies. Ray's been waiting for this too, because when Carlton Campbell had asked him the same question on a similar day in 1990 or thereabouts, he thought he knew, but also thought he couldn't possibly know, so told the instructor that he didn't, rather than give a wrong answer. Carlton had pointed in exactly the direction that Ray sensed, and the fact that he hadn't come out with it when asked has rankled ever since. Today he has been paying better attention to the matter of headings and is able to suggest a fairly accurate direction for their return. As before, there's been no help from the sun today.

The last exercise, almost, is the minimum radius descending turn, which can be used to drop down through a small hole in a cloud cover, if it happens to be the only escape course available. It's another potential lifesaver, but because of the rate of descent, it needs plenty of height above ground for safe practice, and can't be started until the valley floor has dropped down to give a reasonable working clearance below the cloudbase. There are no actual holes in the stratus today. You can't do any of this in a 747, Ray finds himself thinking.

Now they're leaving the serious mountains.

And then just as Carlton did, after the last spiralling descent, Neville pulls the throttle of the 172 and gives Ray a practice forced landing to deal with. This time round, Ray manages to aim the aircraft at a piece of firm pasture and not at what, Carlton had informed him, was effectively a bog – albeit, by English standards, a well-disguised one. For some bizarre reason he'd been reminded of the knife line from *Crocodile Dundee*. 'Bog! I'll show you a bog!'

They head back across the lake to Frankton and Queenstown Airport. The writer feels elated and alive from the weaving and soaring among the rocky giants. You can never tame the mountains and you are foolish to imagine you can try, but you can confront them boldly and thoughtfully, and come back the better for it. It's been an interlude, a transfusion that Ray needed. He briefly identifies with the gliding sequence in *The Thomas Crown Affair*, to the singing of Noel Harrison and his one hit, *Windmills of Your Mind*. What would be a suitable musical accompaniment for the last hour? A bit of Wagner perhaps? He'll give it some thought later.

There is a message from Gerald waiting for him in the Wakatipu Aero Club. The little director hasn't been idle with his pen and paper in his Dunedin bed with the drips.

Get back here a.s.a.p

I think I've solved the boring Daniel Weiss's problem

And yours!.

–ooOoo–

49   Structural Defects

Gerald is pleased with himself. Like most directors, he enjoys improving writers' work. In fact it's not only directors; all sorts of people think they can improve something once it's written. Only some of them can. Working on so many TV and cinema commercials, Ray became slightly acquainted with plenty of ad-agency copywriters, and he remembers one telling him that at some early point in his career, he'd totalled up the number of people, just within his firm – forget the legions working for the client or a few later at the production company – who would be waiting, vulture-like, to pounce on his work. With a few exceptions these were people without a creative bone in their bodies, who could produce nothing themselves, but felt themselves eminently qualified to say what was wrong with his scripts and in what ways they didn't work, within minutes of his completing them. He'd stopped counting at twenty-four.

The man in the plaster cast like a corset looks a lot better this evening. Applying himself to script revisions seems to have worked something akin to magic and he looks much less like a shell. After some unspeakably offensive greetings he comes straight to the point.

"Right, well it's not rocket science, but I think one way you go wrong is having Weiss break off with his lawyer lady-friend as soon as the relationship gets anywhere near the sack. If you allow their intimacy to go somewhere eventually, then he becomes far more interesting. Most of the audience will then be rooting for him; everyone wants a romance to flourish. So while they're doing their investigating, they are getting closer personally. You can still have him decide to call it off at some crucial point, but that shouldn't be the end of it and she should come back and take over a lot of the scenes from the Brad character. I think it gives you far more scope if it's an involved man and woman wading through all the stuff they do. You get options that you don't have if Brad is the only character he can discuss things with."

"Yeah, I see that. I suppose I was trying to make him very loyal and single-minded."

"Loyal and single-minded is all very well, but characters who go too much that way in movies can get on everyone's tits."

Ray is aware that for real people in Weiss's position, such matters are the very opposite of amusing, yet in spite of himself he can't suppress a smile. This is what Gerald does. His irreverence is incorrigible and totally seductive. He has more to say.

"I mean, it doesn't stop the piece being very talky and you're still going to need some more tricks to address that. I like some of the devices you've used so far, but you're going to need some more. Oh, there's another thing. It would be better if the lawyer, Jane, is someone he already knows, before Lockerbie. You understand why?"

Ray does. It brings a leading character into the script earlier, which makes the part potentially more appealing to an actor. It's another one of William Goldman's points. 'Stars count pages,' his book says; the sooner their character appears in the story, the better they like it. Also having her change from friend to would-be-amour to rejected woman and eventually to lover would make it a more substantial and satisfying rôle.

"Yeah. Yeah. I can do that," he says. "She can have a boyfriend at the start and they could be another couple on Brad's boat, or at least in their circle of friends. Then there can be a split that leaves her single so she can be around and available when Daniel Weiss needs support. I'm slightly worried though that having to accommodate extra relationship stuff will eat up screentime – and take attention away from the meat and potatoes."

"In my view," Gerald says, "there's no choice. Leave it as it is and you ain't got a movie, well not one that I'd want to make – or even watch, come to that."

"Don't mince your words, Ger. Say what you mean."

"When did I not?"

The changes Gerald has suggested are all eminently sensible if *One-Zero-Three* is going to be an all-out major movie. With the heroine dying in what used to be called the 'first reel', the script was quite unbalanced. Her part is one that Ted Lewis would have called 'a spit and a cough' – not many scenes and not a great deal to say. Although her contribution to the story is pivotal, the actual part of Tanya is supporting. If the likes of Gerald, DB Hollingsworth and Arran Samson are going to be involved in this picture, then it needs a proper female lead rôle. Ray mentally kicks himself for not taking that into account until now.

Strangely, driving back down to the coast from Queenstown, after his powerful flying fix, with the renewed confidence that the mountains have wrought, he was thinking about his film without Gerald. It's always been a long shot that the Kiwi will direct it, and as the canny devil's first assessment has hardly been over-encouraging, Ray has taken advantage of the journey to engage in some 'what-ifs?' DB, like Gerald, can only be involved in a big bucks movie, so if Ray has to interest a lesser producer, and settle for a more frugal budget and for hungrier, up-and-coming talent both behind the camera and in front of it, so be it. In that case, without the need to attract star names, Gerald's structural changes would be less necessary. Even as he's promising the man that he'll get down to starting a fresh draft at the very first opportunity, like this evening after supper – at the back of his mind he's wondering which of the two versions, his or Gerald's, would truly make a better *One-Zero-Three*. At this moment, he's inclined to the former.

Already he can feel that his precious project, even as it begins to bob on the tide, starting to float, is stirring to currents that will soon carry it away from him.

–ooOoo–

Travelling westwards as he has, Ray has nominally lost a day this week and already it's Friday again. At the flying club they were talking about the weekend's programme, and now back at the hotel there's that indefinable Friday evening atmosphere of anticipation. The trouble is he's not sure that he can survive a weekend in Dunedin. He's no great lover of towns at the best of times and there are few in the world where he could remotely contemplate living. It wouldn't be too disrespectful to the place to reveal that Dunedin is not on that select list. Hospital visiting too is a miserable business and now that he and Gerald have dissected the screenplay at length, they don't have a lot to discuss until Ray has sketched out a new draft. Gerald, on form, is an amiable companion, but he wins no prizes for small-talk. When there's no work to focus on, there is only so much conversation possible on the new releases and the industry gossip, and Ray's always way behind on both counts. It would probably be a relief for both of them if he disappeared until Monday. But where?

He reaches for a phone.

–ooOoo–

For the second time in about sixteen hours Ray is cleared to land and crosses the Shotover River in a Cessna 172 on short finals to runway Two-Three at Queenstown. Fortunately Neville was free and willing to make an early trip across to Dunedin. At this moment Ray is not sure how he'll get back tomorrow afternoon or Monday morning. Something will turn up. It usually does, if you don't worry too much about it. As Ray taxies the craft up to the Aero Club, Jack stands on the grass, arms folded, watching them park. After a few minutes for the paperwork, Ray's small bag is tossed in the back of an untidy pick-up and they head in search of breakfast.

When the New Zealand trip had been mooted, contacting Jack had been at the back of Ray's mind, but when the plan changed and the main event moved to Dunedin, it was in the natural way of things that the thought wasn't carried through. Jack had worked on the big car launch with Gerald and was one of those interesting people who do a job for which they are quite manifestly over-qualified. Set-building and painting were clearly by no means the limit of Jack's capabilities. Everything shouted this, from the accent and the vocabulary to the approach which was confident in the extreme, and as with so many people in the film business, very slightly off-the-wall. Also, it seemed unlikely that the occasional free-lance daily rate supported the lifestyle. For example, Jack was also a pilot and the day after the job finished had hired a 172, steadfastly refusing a contribution from Ray. The pair, with two other members of the crew in the back along for the ride, had done some more mild mountain-confronting. What Ray had either forgotten, or perhaps had never noticed at the time, was that Jack was an exceptionally attractive woman.

It's over breakfast that it hits him. When he'd called out of the blue last evening, it was the first time they'd spoken for fifteen years; yet the moment he'd announced that he was at a loose end in Dunedin's fair city and was thinking of coming back up to Queenstown, the invitation to stay was instant. Ray's encountered a few people over the years who, after meeting for only a few minutes, seem to have been lifelong friends; it probably happens to film technicians more than in many walks of life. But Jack wasn't actually one of that number. He had never thought about that past invitation to go flying before now, but the alacrity with which this weekend was arranged was remarkable. She had even tracked down Neville in town and sorted the early morning pick-up. If any of this indicated that she bore some form of unsuspected interest in him, that hadn't exactly been taken into account in the plan.

He needn't have worried. Over the café's eggs and toast, there are soon several mentions of Kim; Kim who is male, clearly a few years younger and not without problems. With the revelation comes a reversal and Ray is now slightly jealous and mildly miffed that his just-formulated assumption is off-mark. He is aware of his own conceit. How could he for one moment imagine that someone might have been carrying a torch for him and not having a proper life for all these years, awaiting a chance phone call one winter's Friday?

Fifteen years need a lot of catching-up and catching-up requires mutual disclosures. Then he had been in a long-term relationship; now he's married to someone different. He wasn't even aware of Jack's status when they worked together and shared an hour and a half in their log books. Their joint experience had been one of those typical film friendships; real enough while they last but unlikely to survive the combination of distance, time and subsequent preoccupations. For Ray, the hundreds of open-ended friendships like Jack's niggle at the back of his mind. Really he wants to contact every one of those past colleagues, to prove to them and himself that his intentions were good and that the bonds of amity they shared weren't convenient and shallow. He wants to, but knows that in most cases he won't. It's nice to tick mentally the occasional one on the list though, which is why he hadn't hesitated for a second to call Jack. They had been mates and there was no reason why that should have changed.

People say you should never return to somewhere that holds pleasant memories, because it's never as good. Ray disagrees. He generally finds that to be back in a place without the crushing weight of responsibility that you carry when working, has to be rather better. Certainly if you're an assistant director, you in any case rarely truly enjoy a place, however idyllic, when you're there to make a film.

After breakfast they drive some of the familiar roads to adventures past and he's able to appreciate the spectacular scenery without the stomach-churning anxieties that would have travelled with him on the commercial. He's reminded that much of the moving about was done by helicopter. He's already spotted some of the high locations in the distance on the flight over this morning.

Jack no longer flies, but she still works sporadically in the film industry. Ray still occasionally flies and effectively is no longer an AD. Strange that for years he was defined by those two activities, and thought of the pattern as a permanency. Everyone moves on eventually. No one escapes that. It's the one single thing that you can guarantee.

—ooOoo—

They sit on an outcrop, looking down on a tumbling river, he bundled up in a padded jacket borrowed from the deep litter on the floor of the truck cab. And he does something he's never done before, ever, especially to someone whom he hardly knows.

He tells her everything.

283

On the rocks and in the pick-up and in The Café in Arrowtown, he explains about Lockerbie and the screenplay and Gerald and about Eve and even about Deborah. He can't say why he's doing it, but the need to give someone the whole picture is suddenly compulsive and inescapable.

"I'm the last one to offer any advice on relationships," Jack says, about two hours down the line, now back in Queenstown at 'Joe's Garage'. "With my track record of disasters, you'd need to treat anything I might have to say with the strongest suspicion." She outlines a succession of inadvisable liaisons and elaborates on the current unsteady arrangement with Kim, whose inability to concentrate or settle to anything is hardly assisted by his ambitious intake of drink and smoke. She lowers her voice to a semi-whisper during these confessions, which take up the space of two more coffees. This is a small town; she wouldn't wish her words to be heard, even though the substance of what she says is well enough known by the pretty waitresses and most of the clientèle.

Jack's potted survey of her life and loves reveals something Ray had suspected; that she was originally from the UK. She's from a well-to-do Scottish family, of which she is undoubtedly the black sheep; a label confirmed when she'd taken off for the other side of the world at the age of seventeen with a New Zealander twice her age. What she has to reveal at the end of the summary of bad experiences, though, brings Ray very much up short.

"You should meet my brother," she says, "with your interest in intelligence and all that secret stuff. He was some sort of spy. He's out of it now and hates them, but he knows a lot and is quite open about it. It might be useful for you to talk to him."

Once again Ray is left almost speechless by this apparent coincidence. He couldn't work out exactly why he'd come to Queenstown and now he knows. There is a reason for everything. Very little really ever turns out to be just by chance.

−ooOoo−

The wind whistles round the corrugated eaves, making something somewhere rattle, and what could be sleet spatters quietly against the window. The room and the bed are pleasantly snug. Ray contemplates an extraordinary few hours and his remarkable good fortune at finding himself in this unlikely place. There was a moment when it looked as if he might not be staying at Jack's after all, when they'd got back to the house in the late afternoon. Kim was still sleeping off his Friday night session, dead to the world, stretched out on the sofa with the TV tuned to a rugby match. Waking, he'd eyed Ray suspiciously and there had been some confused sentences that try as he might, Ray couldn't turn into a coherent exchange. Then came one of those embarrassing, repetitive 'Can I talk to you?' conversations and the younger man insisted on taking Jack upstairs to discuss something requiring privacy. Ray wondered whether the questions pertained to **his** identity, but later decided that they must have related mainly to the financing and logistics of Kim's Saturday evening, as on reappearance he shuffled out of the house with a cheerful and dismissive "Seeya, mate," and an apologetic Jack followed, explaining that she was just going to run him into town. As far as Ray knows, as of approaching 1.30 he hasn't yet come back.

Taking a look at the kitchen area while she was away, Ray had decided that eating out would be safer on health grounds and his proposal was readily accepted on her return. Jack said she wasn't the world's greatest cook; a fact that he'd not taken long to work out. The state of the house, like the truck, was in character and tuned with his abiding memory of this woman in a paint-splodged boiler suit or dungarees. She wouldn't have dressed like that for the post-shoot flying, but that day he hadn't registered the difference. If he'd looked at her with new eyes this morning, tonight when she came down changed to go to supper, she was different again – a real revelation. Kim, he thought, must be crazy!

The evening by the fire in the intimate house bar of Eichardt's Hotel had been easy. They'd slipped into a replay of the events and characters of fifteen years ago; what members of the crew had done since – their individual stories of success and failure, as far as they were known to them. They'd mainly kept clear of their own – these had been well enough aired over much of the day. Ray can't recall talking and listening so much for a long time. The enjoyment had been slightly moderated for him by a small worry that at some point their quiet tête-á-tête would be raucously interrupted by a red-eyed, jealous Kim, bursting in dramatically to claim possession of Jack by demanding her attention. She seemed to think this sort of incursion unlikely, but nevertheless had gone along with Ray's suggestion of trying for both a restaurant and a table that were not too obvious. There are only so many choices in Queenstown, but they had made a sensible one on all counts: the food was good and the feared intervention hadn't taken place.

When they'd finally lapsed into silence he'd asked for the bill and the drive back had stayed wordless, but it was a contented, comfortable silence, so unlike the recent journey in LA with Eve. They had no baggage. They'd hugged enthusiastically outside his room, as they had at the airport this morning, and bang, the evening was over. Now, of course, he can't sleep. The very thought of Eve makes him think of Deborah and the thought of Deborah makes him think of Jack. And the very act of considering Jack alone in the next room, in the same breath, as it were, as Deborah and Eve, makes him realise that he's approaching dangerous ground, one of Carlton's bogs, and should try and turn his mind to something else.

To divert him, there is another matter to address; quite different, and more than a little worrying. Gerald had said something else, while Ray was gathering up his notes from the bed yesterday evening. Talk about a throw-away exit line!

"Before you go too far with the girlfriend rewrite, have another think about Juval Aviv and what's-his-name, Coleman? Or anyone else who's got a bit more action and involvement about them."

'Christ, Ger,' he'd wanted to say, that's like going right back to square one – a complete rethink and potentially a total rewrite from the ground up.' He hadn't of course. Gerald is a friend, yes, but he's also a big league international director who from habit feels he has every right to ask people to do such things – and so can. Ray has put this comment out if his mind for more than twenty-four hours but he now realises that before he goes near the laptop or writes a word of a new draft, he needs to talk to DB and find out exactly where he stands, if indeed he stands anywhere.

As he's already told Gerald, he's been through and rejected all the alternative possibilities many times over. For goodness sake, he'd even at one point sketched out an outline on a page of A4 notebook in which the main character for the film was Marwan Khreesat.

–ooOoo–

50   Darkling Plains

Marwan Khreesat!

The first time Ray really thought about Marwan Khreesat in depth was when he paid his initial, landmark visit to Dick Leigh, whom he'd encountered through the internet.   Leigh is a man immersed in the Lockerbie mystery to a degree that in a lesser person might be considered obsessive.   In his case though, it equates to a perfectly logical retirement project.   Arriving in the early afternoon of a hot September day, Ray had waited in a sumptuous garden while the retired Lancashire detective dealt with a phone call in the house.   Dick lives on the western slopes of the Pennine Moors.   Beyond the dry stone wall a field of rough pasture dropped steeply to a wood of arguing rooks way below.   There was a magnificent view; to the left the Cheshire Plain stretched towards the mountains of Wales, quite clearly seen, sharp in the unusually dry air.   Panning slowly right he was able to look across the Manchester conurbation, looking surprisingly green from here, and beyond that, much of the rest of Lancashire in all its variety, with the Cumbrian hills of the Lake District as the limit in the very far shimmering distance.

The panorama encompassed whole passages of English history in the simple turn of a head.   Distant Wales was the permanent boisterous irritation on the English rump that was nominally tamed by Edward I with the naming of his son as Prince of Wales in 1301.   Long before that, standing on this spot 935 summers ago, you would have seen the air over Cheshire thick with fire smoke as William I's bloodthirsty followers burned every village, mill and grainstore, and took the lives of animals and humans, old and young with equal contempt.   The Norman Conqueror's so-called 'Harrying of the North' was mindless but self-defeating ethnic cleansing that Hitler's SS Generals advancing through Poland and Russia would have been happy to use as an inspiration and blueprint for their devilish work.   The new king had ordered his henchmen to lay waste to the northern third of the country.   Their unimaginable savagery didn't cease until seven of the largest counties, to that moment civilised and relatively prosperous, were left 'populated only by ghosts'.

There was a strong likelihood, a statistical certainty even, that ancestors of Ray's would have been here, somewhere within this field of view, this sweep of flat terrain, at the time these terrible events were taking place.   Ray asked himself whether they would have been numbered among the ranks of the oppressors or the oppressed.   Possibly the answer was both, but because the survival rate among the latter was poor, the circumstances would favour the former, which was an uncomfortable thought.

As Cheshire was to Wales, so were Lancashire and the Cumbrian counties to Scotland. The border was elastic for centuries as monarchs, liegemen and ambitious freelancers ranged, raided and raped over northern English and southern Scottish counties in a seemingly endless round of extortion, destruction and bloodletting at the expense of those unfortunate enough to be born there. The often ungovernable English border counties became palatinates, semi-independent provinces officially controlled by princes or Dukes who were appointed from shortlists containing generally the names of the most callous or ruthless. Their rule, nominally on behalf of the King, was as absolute as monarchy, until at regular intervals evidence of outrageous personal greed or infighting would bring temporary intervention from the south. Society here was now modelled more along Afghan warlord principles and Mafia-like practices rather than the simple citizenship enjoyed in earlier Saxon times. Yet for Ray's entire life, first the film newsreels and then television have presented, on a virtually daily basis, evidence of people somewhere on the globe behaving to others in similar exploitative, callous and wicked ways as the Conqueror's thugs, those sidekicks of the man nicknamed the 'Butcher of Calais'. In few places would this be more evident, even in the first decade of the third millennium AD, than in those blighted territories at the eastern end of the Mediterranean, whose enmities and inhumanities lay behind the reason for today's visit.

The sight of Manchester was a reminder of more recent English history. Lancashire's landscape bears witness to the whole expansive process of the Industrial Revolution, then its decline and replacement by unsustainable consumerism. The machine age, when this view would have been smudged and soft-focussed by the smoke erupting and streaming from thousands of giant chimneys, now mostly felled by Fred Dibnah, was fuelled by the riches of Empire. It's by no means clear to Ray what's going to pay the national shopping bill in future – to keep the lights on and the motorway box surfaced, save for a return to our old practice of international bullying and helping ourselves, but we've probably disqualified ourselves from a place in the small gang able to do that; funnily enough by becoming too civilised and no longer sufficiently ruthless. According to Colin Powell, George W's Secretary of State and supposed liberal, he wanted his country to be the only 'bully on the block' in future. Ray is convinced that the rate at which we're spending our dwindling resources pointlessly trying to impress and keep in with the rich tough, pretending we have that special friendship, fooling ourselves that we have commonality of interests, means the British aren't going to be in any position to deny the USA that ambition for much longer. Bullying has a cost though, as even the biggest one is coming to realise.

Bringing Ray back to the business in hand were the condensation trails and the tiny darts that headed them, some directly above him and some over his shoulder, plying in this day's sunshine that same more-or-less south-north airway that Clipper 103 had followed on a nasty, cold, wet, windy night that would in a few months now be eighteen years past. Eighteen years it might soon be, but it remains, thankfully, the greatest recorded single act of unsolved mass murder seen in the UK.

'Unsolved' is an odd concept when a trial has found someone guilty, but Judith Ward, the Guildford Four and the Maguire Seven provide the best known of numerous examples in fair and free Britain where legal guilt turned out not to be guilt at all. And it's an even odder concept still when a US Senator could tell a UK victim's relative, almost as many years ago now, that his government and theirs both know who was responsible, but that he's sure they will never disclose the truth. Lockerbie is solved all right – it's just that the real solution is another official secret.

Sir Humphrey in that so-true-it was-almost-not-comedy series *Yes, Minister* said that the Official Secrets Act is not about keeping secrets; it's about keeping reputations. There's our democracy in a nutshell. We're free (as far as we know, for the present) to discuss contentious matters and we can make even make jokes and poke fun at obsessive secrecy, but no way can we actually change anything important. The party in opposition will often promise to make government more open and reduce the Big Brother-like all-enveloping scope of the Official Secrets Act. Then, when they get into power they not only forget the pledge, but usually become even more inclined than their predecessors to take refuge behind it, using it to mask their own mistakes, their own waste, and their own inadequacy. If our 'elected masters' can keep secrets about 270 violent deaths, to preserve the reputations of a few foreign spies and double-dealing politicians, have we really come very far, since Royally-licensed murderers roamed at will across beautiful Northern England?

Just maybe, Ray thought, something might come out of the discussion today to shine new light on dark landscapes.

–ooOoo–

51   Enigma Variations

His phone call completed, Dick had appeared and started crunching the facts almost before his rather younger wife had brought out a tray of tea and left them to talk. He was a slight man, so slight that it was difficult to imagine him in a police uniform. In some countries investigators are recruited separately, which makes sense as they require different skills and attributes from those of the regular police officer. In Britain they have to come from the ranks, so every detective starts as a uniformed constable. This man was as far from an imposing figure of authority as it was possible to get. In the days when Dick would have been starting out, forces had minimum height requirements. The lowest for men was 5 feet 8 inches. Most of the short females who seem to make up a large proportion of forces' personnel today would never have got near 'the job' in those days. So how had Dick become a bobby and coped with yobs and drunkards twice his size? Then Ray remembered another slight Pc that he'd met through flying. He'd wondered the same thing about him, until he visited his house and saw in a corner glass cabinet, insignia and artefacts from service in the SAS. Obviously the police height rules had been sometimes waived for applicants who'd gone through that toughest of selection and training processes, and whose service would have required strength and resourcefulness of every possible kind. Ray decided that Dick, this razor-sharp and totally organised, bird-like man, had military experience as well as his long police career. If he had served in the SAS, he wouldn't be entirely unacquainted with what, Ray would learn, he always called the 'Secret World'.

"Whichever way you look at it, the starting point in any review of this case has to be Khreesat," Dick began. "Because of his history, he has to be considered totally central, even if we eventually reject him as the bomb-maker. Whatever he did or didn't do, his influence is absolutely fundamental and it has to point our way."

He barely paused for breath, before launching off enthusiastically again, like Peter Snow, the TV presenter on General Election night.

"OK. What do we know? You're Marwan Abo Rezak Mufti Khreesat, Jordanian, aircraft bomb-maker for Ahmed Jibril's Popular Front for the Liberation of Palestine-General Command. All the literature describes you as the master bomber – the veteran and all that sort of stuff; but the facts don't really bear out that reputation. Mind, there isn't a big field of competitors. You start in 1968 when Jibril asks you to build an

290

altimeter bomb. You do so, in a safe house in Sofia, Bulgaria, and two devices are tested, on top of a mountain in southern Germany apparently, although why they should be taken across borders when there are plenty of higher mountains near Sofia is a mystery. You'd only be testing the switching of course, so you wouldn't actually need to set off bangs, and you could do it using a car and a light bulb if you could find a high enough road."

"That's interesting," Ray interrupted. "Did you know that years later Jibril tried rather ludicrously to claim that altimeter bombs weren't necessarily for use against aircraft and that they could be used in cars against hilltop targets?"

"Yes, I saw that" replied Dick. "It's about the daftest attempt at a misleading explanation that I've ever heard. If you've got to drive the car, you can either detonate it as a suicide bomber or leave it and disappear, in which case why bother with an altimeter, when a timer will do just as well?"

"And if you're going to put it in someone else's car, covertly, you're never going to be able to set it accurately enough to make sure it blows when the car arrives at the target, and anyway how many strategic places are found conveniently up mountains?" Ray added.

"Exactly! So, on one day in early 1970 two of your new devices are used against aircraft. This is a real attempt at what's since been called a spectacular, demonstrating the competition that exists among terrorist groups as much as anything. One explodes on an Austrian Airlines flight bound for Israel via Vienna, a Caravelle with thirty-eight on board, climbing out of Frankfurt. The barometric trigger device seems to have been set fairly low, or perhaps you didn't combine it with a delay timer, as you will later, for the bomb goes off at 10,000 feet, where the decompression isn't as potentially critical as higher up. Despite being holed, the aircraft and its human cargo survive, mainly because the mailbag that the bomb's in is surrounded by other bags full of newspapers that absorb a lot of the blast.

"The other aircraft this day, a Swissair plane – a Convair 990, much bigger, a four-engined job very like a 707 – also bound for Israel, leaving Zurich, isn't so fortunate. It's destroyed with the loss of all forty-seven on board. That bomb explodes in the rear hold after nine minutes climbing through 14,000 feet, and the damage eventually becomes unsustainable. These bombs, hidden in – guess what? – transistor radios, had simply been put in the post in Frankfurt addressed to places in Israel, because security was lax on mailed parcels at the time. The PLFP-GC claim responsibility for the Swissair attack."

"So I'm not that good so far," said Ray. "That's only a 50% success rate."

"True, but it's untried technology. And it is a first. Prior to this, hijacking has been the standard method that Middle East terrorists, at least, use against aircraft, so this is a new departure. These two incidents lead to immediately increased scrutiny of cargo and parcels, so another way has to be devised to get bombs onto planes. Jibril comes up with mules or dupes, whatever you want to call them. And they choose them carefully to avoid all the profile characteristics of the terrorist – they go for women, and women holding passports from what you might call 'safe' countries, and women that don't look at all Middle Eastern. What's more they don't know they're carrying anything bad, so they can't betray any guilt to anyone watching or questioning them.

"The next summer there are three attempts, two successful, to get bombs aboard Tel Aviv-bound flights using this method, so you've probably been quite busy, as aircraft IED builders go. For the record," (Ray was scribbling notes, just in case Dick mentioned a piece of background that he hadn't heard before) "the departures were from Rome again, New York, although there was a question mark over that and it may not have been one of yours, and London. Neither of the two that flew exploded. The bombs were probably sent unprimed to Syrian Embassies in diplomatic bags."

"Because the main sponsor of the Jibril group is Syria."

"Correct. The next year, 1972, you build a bomb into a record player and in Yugoslavia pass it to two men who later give it to two British women they've groomed because they are shortly to travel to Tel Aviv. This one explodes at 15,000 feet yet this El Al aircraft out of Rome lands safely."

"So I seem to be calculating the altitude too low, unless the pressure switches have a limited range, or they're just not accurate enough at that time."

"Well, we don't have access to the technology, but don't forget that when luggage holds are pressurised, and most of them are, then the air in them is going to be the same pressure as in the passenger cabin and that only goes to an equivalent of around 6,000 feet, or we'd all start to get breathless from lack of oxygen. Cruising at 35,000 feet or whatever, the cabin and hold will be at 6 and the altimeter device will think it's at 6. There would be some capability to set the pressure you want, but whatever the range you could set, it wouldn't be as accurate as if you were able to pick the actual altitude at which you wanted it to bang. You'd have to guess where the cabin pressure might be at the height you choose and that's normally done by the aircraft automatically according to a simple programme. The danger from the bomber's point of view is setting too high an altitude, because if the cabin pressure doesn't go that high, the device isn't going to function. That's why you'll eventually go for a modest pressure setting plus a timer to ensure it doesn't go off until the plane is up at cruise levels."

"You know, I'd completely forgotten the point about hold pressurisation, and I'm a pilot, although not on pressurised aircraft," said Ray.

"Well then, you'll be aware of another complication. As I say, I'm not technical on this stuff, but you'll probably know – I think everything I've said has to be considered in the reverse sense, because the higher the altitude, the lower the pressure – and I believe that you'd be setting a pressure on the device rather than setting an altitude. You can't actually go to a B&Q or the aviation equivalent and buy an altitude switch for a bomb, so I imagine you'd be adapting what is presumably the innards of an altimeter or a barometer. You'd have to do a calculation to see the atmospheric pressure you wanted it to trigger at."

"Which let me tell you from experience would be very easy to get wrong. These things are very hard to visualise, it's easy to calculate in the wrong direction, plus the fact that the pressure varies a great deal with the weather, or the other way round," laughed Ray. "Actually the pressure causes the weather – I think – whatever. We're agreed that it's all-too-easy to make a Horlicks of setting the altimeter device."

"And that may well explain the malfunctions," concluded Dick.

"Very true."

"I saw a pressure of 950 millibars quoted as the setting on the radio bomb that the German BKA seized when Khreesat and Dalkamoni were arrested. That was given as the equivalent to only 2,500 feet, but a pilot friend I asked said it could be a lot lower, more like 1,200 in low pressure conditions, plus he said, that's above sea level, not airport; something to do with the difference between height and altitude, which I can never remember."

"Height is measured above an airport or the ground," Ray responded helpfully. "Altitude is above sea level and there's a third option which is

Flight Level, used for instrument flying above 3,000 feet when we use a standard pressure setting of 1013 millibars. But none of that strictly matters because here we're talking about the actual air pressure being experienced by the pressure sensor. The only thing to think about is that under low pressure conditions at a high airport, you could get a pressure of 950 on the deck. I mean, I seem to remember that Zurich is about 1,400 feet above sea level."

"So you're saying with that setting on the bomb with low pressure over Zurich, the bomb's timer could conceivably start ticking away on the ground?" asked Dick.

"I'd have to check the figures, but in principle, yes." He'd later looked it up and found his recollection about Zurich was accurate enough; the elevation was indeed 1,416 feet.

"So then to be honest," came back the old detective, filtering out the facts, "it seems the only real value of a home-built pressure device is probably for the fairly coarse task of stopping the bomb going off on the ground before the plane takes off. Once it's in the air and at really any height that registers a decent pressure change, it can be allowed to trigger the conventional timer, and that can run for as long as you like. And don't target high airports."

"Indeed, don't do that, if you can help it. Nairobi would be a bad choice at 5,300 feet. Now Dick, all this raises lots of questions about the bomb supposedly being involved in more than one flight – three according to the Crown's case and the version accepted by the court – and also why the timer wasn't set for longer than it was, so that the aircraft should fall into the sea."

"So it does, and we should go on to discuss all that. I suspect you like me, are of the opinion that the bomb suitcase only went on one flight or two – not three, but can I suggest that we stick with Mr Khreesat for the moment and come back to that?"

"Absolutely," agreed Ray. They were both organisers by trade but instinctively he was happy to defer to the policeman.

"Right, so the bad news for you after the 1972 Rome attempt is that the two Arabs you hand the record player to, cough your name under interrogation. You're added to the list of most wanted international terrorists. I mean, you're a murderer forty-seven times over; potentially you could have killed several hundred by this time, so you are a serious player.

What do you do? You go into hiding in your home country, Jordan, and what's your main worry, wherever you choose to go?"

"That's an easy one. Mossad."

"Exactly. Because you've been attacking Israel flights and now an El Al, the ladies and gentlemen of Israeli Intelligence would be most keen to have either a long and very painful interview with you, or an extremely short one with a totally one-sided exchange of views. And they are very, very adept at finding people, wherever they hide."

"So I need protection, which presumably I get from the Jordanian Secret Service."

"The Mukabarat, yep. Now remember that by going to them, or accepting their 'offer you can't refuse' if it happens that way round, you've effectively changed sides. Jibril is Syrian-based and Syrian-backed, and Syria has close links with the Soviets and sided with Iran during the eight-year Iran-Iraq War. Jordan is aligned with and has covertly backed the West in that conflict, assisting with their secret arming and supply of Saddam Hussein and Iraq. Remember the Teessport Supergun and all that?"

"Of course. Work took me to a Saudi Air Force base while that war was on and I noticed parked Iraqi freighter aircraft that could only be seen from restricted areas. That connection was kept nice and quiet."

"Blimey," said Dick, "you weren't a spy yourself, were you?"

"One of the few outdoor careers I didn't consider," said Ray.

"One thing I've been thinking about this," Dick continued, now really beginning to enjoy himself. "When do you, Khreesat again, become an asset — now or much earlier?"

"You mean was I working for Jordanian Intelligence when I was building the bombs from 1968/69? Astonishing idea!"

"Not that astonishing when we know that's exactly what you **were** doing from 1986 to '88. I don't suppose we'll ever find out, but it's food for thought."

"OK." Dick was off again like a terrier. "Nothing comes for nothing, so if the Mukabarat are going to look after you, and if they're going to persuade Mossad not to kill you, both are going to want something in return. It probably won't be now. They may ask you to feed them tit-bits but they would probably be happy for you to 'sleep' until someone, and that would most likely be one of your old friends in Syria, contacts you again."

"So I appear to retire as bomb-maker."

"You live quietly in Amman, making a living repairing electronics – TVs, radios and cassette recorders; plenty of opportunity to keep your hand in with the old soldering iron and the inside of all your favourite toys, and no doubt copping a Mukabarat salary as an agent at some level or another. Now we've got to remember that they have very close links with the CIA, which helped get them set up, so we've really got to think of one as the local subsidiary of the other."

"Which means the CIA know about me?"

"They may not know exactly where to find you, but they know you're there somewhere.

"Bom, bom, bom – the years roll on – we don't know exactly what you're doing. I was about to say: 'but what we **do** know is', but it would be a nonsense, because except where there's corroboration, we don't know much for a fact. Mostly what we have is what you choose to tell the FBI when they get to interview you in 1989. What you actually say may not necessarily be true. The FBI may well edit what you tell them, plus long before the FBI are finally allowed access to you, the CIA will have rehearsed you and told you what to say and what not to say, again based on what you yourself decided to tell **them** in the first place. So how complete the truth is in some of this is basically anyone's guess, but it's the best we've got. You say that in 1985 you're in Syria; you buy five Toshiba single speaker radios, including the one that will be seized in the car with you in Germany in 1988. On the instructions of Ahmed Jibril, you build a bomb in each, but then, most bizarrely, you say you take them apart again. God knows why, or if you really did. You leave three in Syria and presumably take two home to Jordan, where you actually convert one back to a working radio.

"Then in April, 1986, comes the famous Nezar Hindawi case, where a Jordanian who later confesses to working for Syrian Intelligence gives his pregnant Irish girlfriend a suitcase to take onto an El Al flight out of Heathrow. He's going to join her in a couple of days, she believes, only he's really booked on a Damascus plane the same day. And it is of course a suitcase bomb and fortunately it's discovered. The plot uses the classic PLFP-GC dupe method, and as there's no terrorist organisation leader closer to Syrian intelligence chiefs than Ahmed Jibril, it's got to be suspected that he, and you as bomb-maker, are involved. There are so many pointers to GC and Syria that some believe it's a Mossad false flag operation to finger the Syrians and highlight their undoubted support for terrorist groups."

"Do you think that's possible?"

"In that murky world anything's possible, but whether it's true in this case, I can't say. Anyway, you obviously go to-and-fro to Damascus a bit because you say you first meet Dalkamoni, Jibril's European Mr Big, there in '86. He's got, probably among other things, an active cell in West Germany that in '87 and early '88 carries out two railway track bombings against US troop trains. In September '88, Dalkamoni calls you to go to Krusevac, Yugoslavia where you meet Mobdi Goben, alias Abu Faud, who runs a PLFP-GC safe house and explosives store there. Whatever happens there, on 13th October with your wife, you fly from Amman to Frankfurt. Not only that but you are actually carrying the Toshiba radio that was converted to a bomb and then converted back again, supposedly as a present for your wife's brother who's in prison in Germany. I don't know if you have spotted the significance of that; not just the radio but the travel, full stop."

"Enlighten me," said Ray.

"Well, you are a named suspect in bringing down an airliner and causing forty-seven deaths, by means of a bomb built in a transistor radio, plus other attempts. You've never been caught so you should still be wanted for questioning. Yet here you are, flying into an airport about 150 miles from where the poor innocent souls that you killed met their end; you're even blatantly carrying a radio that has been a bomb and restored back again, and yet nothing happens – you're not stopped, interviewed, arrested, nothing. Doesn't that say that something about who is protecting you?"

"Got you. Christ – yes. It wouldn't just be Jordanian Intelligence."

"Exactly, I can't see them having that much pull with the German authorities. The fact that you are allowed to sail straight into Germany unmolested has got to involve one of the heavyweights, and top of the list would be the CIA."

"You know, one of the questions that I wanted to ask you is whether you believed that Khreesat told his intelligence controllers that he was coming to Europe, or whether he came on his own, relying on the arrangements that Dalkamoni would have to make to get him into Germany. Obviously he couldn't tell Dalkamoni that he had, what did you say they were called – Mukabarat protection, much less CIA?

"Well certainly I don't think Khreesat would have dared to fly into Frankfurt, bold as brass, if he hadn't told his handlers and got some assurances for his safety. There would be no point, if he got arrested, in claiming that he was a Jordanian agent, as he obviously did later, if Jordanian Intelligence didn't know he was there. He had to tell them, in order to get in, I reckon, as well as out again. But as to who knew what in the PLFP, I mean this is where it gets really interesting. Jibril, if not Dalkamoni, must have wondered about Khreesat's survival, why he didn't get liquidated by Mossad after being named in 1972. Given that Khreesat's only real chance was to get official protection, Jibril might have guessed, accepted or even suggested that he go to the Jordanian authorities."

"But that implies that Jibril could have expected the CIA to be in the loop about Khreesat, and so bring them closer to him and the rest of his organisation. Surely he couldn't have allowed that. It would have been better for him to let Mossad deal with Khreesat, or better still have him killed himself, rather than give the Americans access to his own activities," said Ray, pleased with the logic.

"Unless one of two things," Dick came straight back, returning to the present tense in his enthusiastic analysis. "One; Jibril is happy to have Khreesat run as a double agent and feed disinformation to the CIA, while pretending to have changed sides. Or two; Khreesat's supposed defection is immaterial as Jibril himself is an asset of the CIA."

Ray had been in the process of biting into another of Mrs Leigh's exceedingly good cakes when Dick dropped this bombshell, and he almost ejected it into his tea cup.

–ooOoo–

52   Divided Loyalties

"You can't be serious," Ray had almost choked. "Everything I've ever read about Jibril paints him as the arch-terrorist, absolutely implacably opposed to Israel and the US. The record of the GC; the operations they've carried out; the things he's said. What was that statement in 1986: 'From now on there will be no safety for any traveller on Israeli or US airlines. We do not have planes, ships or radars, but we will know how to strike.' You don't honestly believe he could have been working for the USA?"

"All I'm saying is that it's a possibility, however unlikely. In these dirty games, you have to consider any angle before you discount it. Let's face it: if the CIA, to achieve some objective or other, wanted to be able to point to a credible threat to US citizens, Jibril and his outfit, bombing planes and threatening more filled the bill perfectly in the 70s and 80s."

"Just like Ousama Bin Laden was godsend to Cheney, Rumsfeld et al in the new century." Ray well understood the point. "Just the bogeyman they needed to persuade the American public to support their military adventures and expenditure, not to mention the way people fell over themselves in their haste to give up their civil liberties."

"Yes. Commentators have said that if Bin Laden hadn't existed, someone would have had to invent him," Dick contributed.

"In a sense it's true; the CIA did, in the first place, by backing and arming him against the Russians in Afghanistan. Some are even convinced that he could remain their creature."

"But we're getting away from Khreesat again," they both said, virtually in unison, and laughed.

"So to recap, you think that Jibril knew that his bomb-maker was reporting to the Mukabarat, and so by extension, to the CIA?" said Ray, picking up the thread again.

"I'd be surprised if it were otherwise."

"If he did, then he had to be confident of Khreesat's loyalty, and sure that he was not betraying anything serious, just enough to keep the spooks happy." Then a penny dropped. "Hold on – that doesn't wash. The only, only reason any of the intelligence agencies would be interested in Khreesat would be to learn what PFLP-GC was doing. But look what would be bound to happen. If Khreesat told them he was going to be reactivated, then he would be watched and that would inevitably lead the authorities to every member of any cell that he came in touch with, which is exactly what happened in Germany with Operation Autumn Leaves – and Dalkamoni for one went to prison as a result. There's no way that Jibril could have known and gone along with that, because to know would have been to expect that sort of result – basically the loss of his German network."

"But you're forgetting two things. Flight 103 did go down, which if it was Jibril and Khreesat's doing, then the network had done its work – GC could count that as a major success. Until that, the European arm hadn't achieved very much of significance since the Swissair bomb in 1970, so it wasn't actually seeming to do too much for the struggle. It wouldn't have been a great loss; it was expendable. Yes, there was collateral damage in the loss of some cell members, but, as we know, it's a filthy game. History is full of people being sacrificed in the name of a cause. This wouldn't have been the first time nor will it be the last. Actually one of the odd things is that the network didn't really get destroyed. Despite the damning evidence, most of the suspects were released very quickly. As a sidelight on that do you remember that even the two who did go to jail, for the earlier troop train attacks, were let out early and that was as part of a deal with Iran, not Syria, which is very revealing?"

Ray thought that he was pretty well-informed about this case, but Dick was beginning to dazzle him; the old boy seemed to have all the pieces of this ridiculously complicated jigsaw filed away in his head, with all the threads that link them, ready to recall at will.

"And as we know, the Autumn Leaves raids failed dismally to get hold of all the IEDs that had been built; that was either really poor work or allowed deliberately, but we'd better not go there at the moment. No, the thing I was getting to is that the mindset for betrayal that you reject for Ahmed Jibril was exactly the one demonstrated by Marwan Khreesat. He definitely knew that telling his handler he was off to Germany to make bombs would have repercussions, and as far as he knew, he was the only one in the plot with a 'Get Out of Jail Free' card, which he didn't hesitate to use. The rest could take their chances. If the bomb-maker was self-centred enough to think that way, why not his boss, Jibril?"

"I see what you mean. It's funny; I'm as open to ideas as anyone, but I still find this one really unlikely . . ."

Dick poured him some more tea.

"Well, think about this. According to Khreesat, the Mukabarat clear him to go to Germany on the understanding that any devices he makes should not work. Well you'd expect him to say that; you'd expect them to say that; but do they and their American sponsors really trust him not to double-cross them? I doubt it, but they let him go anyway, and what happens? He makes five bombs and then, surprise, surprise, he finds an excuse to make them viable."

"Yes, I spotted that. That's such a lame one. He pretends he's scared that – what was his name, Abu Elias? – who's introduced as an expert on airport security, and nothing to do with bomb-making, is going to realise that the bombs are rigged not to go off."

Dick powered on:

"Yeah, so what's this security expert going to do, what's anyone going to do, even if they are suspicious – take the radios apart and poke around, assuming they know what they're looking at? It'd be a very good way of blowing yourself up, I should think. I mean, Khreesat can even say they're booby-trapped to foil intervention, if he wants to. Who's going to argue with him? In fact one that he built did explode and kill a BKA technician who was dismantling it. Make no mistake. He wanted to make functional bombs and yet have a let-out for doing so, and the story that one was taken without his knowledge while he was taking a shower was, I imagine, just another little ruse to distance him from anything that might be done with them. So was he running rings round the two intelligence agencies, as he might have thought he was doing – or was he doing exactly what they expected him to do and hoped he'd do – that's to say the reverse of what they'd instructed? Or then again, had they told him just to build whatever he was asked to build but if questioned later bring up the matter of the 'instructions' and the excuse for disobeying them?"

"Bloody hell," said Ray. "My brain hurts!"

"There are a few permutations and combinations, aren't there?" agreed Dick. "Especially when the Ashton and Ferguson book says that a number of sources in Western intelligence informed journalists that the bomb-maker was 'an asset of the CIA, the German foreign intelligence service BND, and Mossad.' I think that some of the 'sources' were playing the disinformation game there, myself. I mean, CIA possibly but more likely through the Jordanian proxy. The BND, well why? I can't see that one. And Mossad – I would have thought, never in this world. I'd almost stake my reputation that he wouldn't work for the Israelis; not directly anyway. I mean when all is said and done, the Palestinians and Arabs have plenty of reasons to hate the Israelis; rather more on balance, I think, than the other way round."

"So where does that leave us? I think I've lost the plot," confessed Ray.

"Well, where we've got to is that Marwan Khreesat, with or without the connivance of his boss Ahmed, betrays the German cell, but in doing so makes what is acknowledged to be an unknown number of aircraft IEDs. Although they are supposedly monitoring events, whether together or separately, the massed assets of the CIA and the BKA manage, by error or even design, to overlook and lose track of a number of these devices, and some at least disappear for good. I think it's time to introduce the first rule of the Secret World."

"The first rule of the Secret World?" repeated Ray.

"Mm. What you must never forget is that in the Secret World, if you kill someone, or betray someone, or you steal some information or you give some information away, or if indeed you act on information that you've got by covert means; whatever you do, you always try to lay a false trail that points to someone else. That way you protect yourself and your contacts, and anyone who then tries to find out who did what, especially anyone with retaliation in mind, looks elsewhere and probably takes revenge on someone entirely innocent. And those who're really clever at it don't make the false trail too obvious, so that the investigators, whoever they are, think they've been very astute in working something out, when in fact all they've done is walk straight into your elephant trap."

"So the question is, are **we** being really clever, or are we about to drop in with the elephants?"

"Even when we think we've worked it out, if we get that far, we may still not know one way or the other."

"What are you saying, then?"

"What I'm saying is that everyone involved in 103 at any point, including this particular one — after the arrest of Khreesat and before the fatal day itself — will be covering their own tracks and trying to divert attention onto others. All we can do is look at every party one at a time, decide what they could have done using the standard old CID tests — motive, opportunity, and means — and then also look at who they could have used to muddy the water and take the blame. Who, how and why. I've done you copies of these, if you want to take them away and think about them; see if you can find any holes or anything to add or change."

He'd taken some A4 sheets from his pad and handed them to Ray. They were paper versions of those suspect wallboards that are often seen on TV in documentaries and dramas about murder investigations. There was one for every individual or agency suspected in having a hand in 103. This was fascinating and exciting, the solution to the mystery was in there somewhere for the finding, but suddenly Ray felt very tired. He felt like a detective must feel after working on an unyielding case for months. He had come to see Dick Leigh in the hope than the number of possibilities and permutations could be significantly reduced. What had happened was that the variations had considerably increased. He felt he couldn't say so. He went off at a tangent, just to relieve the pressure for a moment.

"You know the thing that gets my goat is that the authorities have lied about so much; they can't be open about things that everyone knows about, like the drugs on the plane and the cash – oh, loads of things that there's no point in denying but they do."

"Actually it helps us," said Dick. They think that by denying every little thing, they're growing a dark impenetrable forest where the truth will never be found. I've always felt that the lies give us clues, starting points to probe, because they indicate areas that worry the powers-that-be."

"I wish I felt as confident as you do."

"We'll get there," said the older man, still bubbling with energy. "Let's try and finish with Marwan.

"So there are bombs in circulation, but you aren't. You are firmly in custody. You know you were recruited for an attack on an airliner. You may even know of a target flight and date, although you never say so, but clearly it's in your interest to be released before anything happens. To this end you're allowed to make a phone call to Amman on 5th November. You talk about the need to speed up legal matters in Germany and whatever you say works because on the 10th you are taken to the Federal High Court in Karlsruhe for a hearing to keep you in custody. What should be an automatic remand goes completely out of the window when the Judge . . ."

"Christian Rinne", interjected Ray. "For some reason I always remember that name."

"The very one. He goes into a convoluted speech that basically says that black is white, that there's no evidence to hold you and bang, he sets you free!"

"He must have been livid, being forced to sit in his court and spout the most ridiculous possible nonsense."

"Absolutely. This is what happens when the spooks run our lives. The whole system, politics, justice, the police, the judiciary, everything gets compromised and subverted. For the judge to say there was no proof that Khreesat was complicit in any planned crimes flew against every known fact; not least that Khreesat, Dalkamoni and Ghandafar had confessed there was a plot and that he had made bombs and that a completed airliner bomb had been found in the very car he was arrested in."

"How can a judge live with himself and carry on pretending to dispense just decisions, once he's been made to do something so fundamentally perverse?" asked Ray.

"From my long experience of judges, I think that the moment they've made a determination, right or wrong, they move on and forget it; otherwise it could easily make life impossible for them. Don't forget that a lot of the time they're forced to free people who they're pretty certain are guilty, either because the evidence isn't strong enough, or because the defence has managed to sow enough seeds of doubt, even when there shouldn't be any. I spent half my career in court watching people I'd caught doing bad things walking out of court laughing at me. It's the fault of our poxy adversarial system, which isn't about finding out the truth – it's a contest between lawyers where the barrister who's the best prepared and gives the slickest presentation will usually win the day. The lawyers might as well have played squash or snakes and ladders to decide the verdicts of some of the cases I was involved with, for all it was to do with establishing the truth and dispensing justice."

'Our poxy adversarial system.' Ray would have many discussions with Dick over time, and this was the only time he ever heard the man come close to swearing – and it was in the course of describing the system of criminal justice that he had served for most of his working life.

"All right." said Ray. "The sixty-four thousand dollar question. Do you think one of Khreesat's devices brought down Flight 103?"

"On the balance of probabilities – yes, I do."

"Why?"

"Because if I accept the trial prosecution case, that it was an all-Libyan operation, then I have to believe that there were two airliner plots in progress quite independently at exactly the same time. That is not impossible. But I am also asked to believe that these two completely separate plots both involved building bombs in, not just radios, but Toshiba radios. Now I believe in coincidence as much as the next man, but that to me is stretching credibility way too far. We know for certain that the Jibril plot existed, and that there were IEDs built. The obvious inference we draw is that the plot involved getting one or more onto aircraft. That could be correct; it could be wrong. Taking into account the habits of the Secret World, it could simply have been designed as a distraction for something else, perhaps so that the arrests could occupy everyone's attention while a real attempt could proceed without scrutiny. Not too likely that, but certainly not totally impossible. Or the plan could have been simply to produce bombs that 'others' would use, having been 'accidentally' allowed to 'disappear'.

"What I don't buy is the idea of someone in Libya, or Malta, or London, building Toshiba bombs at the same moment as Marwan was soldering away at his table in Neuss. The only way that would be a likely scenario was if they were part of the same plot, and you'd have to say why, and there would be no reasonable answer – why would that ever be necessary?"

"Interesting idea though, Dick. Several cells building their own bombs for simultaneous deployment at the same time – a spectacular like 9/11. I mean, it's akin to what Jibril tried with two aircraft on the same day in 1970; but this way if some cells get discovered, or some bombs don't go off, you still stand more chance of getting a result."

"I'd maybe agree but it didn't happen. One, because Khreesat built four or five devices in Germany, so what were they for? If there was to be a spectacular, it was going to be Europe-centred. And two, because no flights other than 103 were attacked from other places. Admittedly, perhaps, it had to be a one-off because a cell had been uncovered, but there was only one bomb in the air that day."

"And you think that was Khreesat's from Frankfurt?"

"I didn't say Frankfurt . . ." Dick began.

At this point Sally came out into the sunshine on the subject of more tea. Ray, head now really spinning, was glad of the interruption and thought that until the tea appeared, he might interrogate Dick a little about his time in the police, for something else he was writing. But before he could action this, the veteran investigator had a most perceptive and highly relevant question for him.

"What I want to know is how are you ever going to make a film out of all these different possibilities?" he asked, fixing him with an intense policeman's gaze the younger man could almost feel on his skin. What he replied was largely true.

"Do you know – at this moment I haven't the least idea," he had said, although what he was actually thinking deep down was that he hoped, like Baldrick in *Blackadder*, he had a cunning plan.

–ooOoo–

Ray wrestles with the intertwined intricacies for the umpteenth time, as the wind lashes the freezing rain at the glass with more extreme force. This has not merely been about writing a screenplay; this is effectively about solving the case. He truly believes that between them, over the months, he and more particularly Dick have got nearer to the truth of Lockerbie than anyone outside the cover-up. All it needs is just one or two more connections – the last leaps of deduction that must be there for the making – the final pieces of the jigsaw, lost for now under the table, in the basket of the dog with the sharp teeth. They've come so far. He's excited that Jack's brother could just provide the crucial links. Plenty of people in the intelligence community must know what happened to Clipper 103. It will only take one with a grievance to break the cloying, arrogant silence. He toys with the idea of switching the light on and making yet another of those 'Whodunnit?' charts.

There is another sound; one he hardly hears above the noise of the wild night, so intensely is he concentrating. It must have been a tap on the door, for it opens and he catches a brief glimpse of an almost idealised female outline but carrying two mugs, silhouetted by the light of a faraway bulb.

"I brought you some tea," Jack says. "I knew you weren't asleep." The door has swung shut and the room has returned to pitch black.

"Great – thank you. Too much thinking."

He hears and feels the mattress react as she sits on the bed. She is only a couple of feet away and he can see nothing whatsoever.

"You shouldn't always think too much." He can feel and hear her shivering too: there is a tiny chattering of her perfect teeth in her perfect mouth. He almost believes he can detect her heart beating, but it's probably his own. He doesn't know what, if anything, she's wearing or how she is sitting. He dares not put his hand out in case he contacts something inappropriate. But exactly what is inappropriate or appropriate in these circumstances? What are these circumstances? Twenty years ago, fewer even, he might have understood the ground rules. After a day like today, even with all that frankness, or especially with all that frankness, he has no idea what the rules are. Does she really mean you shouldn't think too much?

"You're cold?"

"Mmm."

Somehow, even in the utter darkness, their movement is mutual; the moment they choose identical, which is just as it needs to be.

–ooOoo–

53 Spare Room

Ray is feeling like a film spy. He sits with a drink only half-reading a newspaper at a table on the terrace selected for its view into the hotel office. There will be a certain extra piquancy in watching a stunning woman checking in for the purposes of a secret liaison in a building that was formerly a Catholic seminary. Ray doesn't care at all for the Roman church, but when he voices his objections to it he feels as if he's in the 'What did the Romans ever do for us?' sequence in *Monty Python's Life of Brian*. He dislikes everything about the institution apart from the architecture and the music and the art – and the theatre, and the bells and the incense! He even quite likes the obvious decency and downright niceness of some of those soft-spoken priests. But there's no doubt that basing an affair within these walls will provide a certain irreverent gloss – a tiny payback for the Spanish Inquisition and the Conquistadors.

Not that the secret liaison needs any further spicing. On the basis of this morning's small hours it could hardly be more seasoned and nourishing. Over the *Sunday Star Times*, he spots Jack entering the room . Very sensibly she's insisted on making her own reservation and appearing to arrive separately. As she signs in, with her slim back angled towards him, he again feels extraordinarily fortunate. There is the excitement that not a soul in the world can imagine that inside ten minutes he and this obvious free-spirit, now taking her key, will be in each others' arms. He'd wondered for a moment if she would actually appear in the hotel. It wouldn't have been totally impossible that she'd change her mind and drive away into the late afternoon. Free spirits do that. They've done things of that nature to him in the past. And if he's honest, he too has occasionally behaved in such ways – and sometimes to spirits that were not noticeably free.

Earlier he hadn't been able to avoid seeing the note in her artist's hand that she left on the table for whenever Kim might next appear.

> Gone to Dunedin. Given Ray a lift down. I'll do a
> few things down there. and be back mid-week. – J.

Very straightforward and non-committal. No lies.

She says Kim won't even notice her absence.

It's odd. Ray should have spent this entire weekend grappling with matters of the highest levels of power-abuse and political dishonesty that it's possible to imagine, and he's chosen instead to concentrate on things at the complete opposite end of the spectrum, the totally personal and by comparison trivial and irrelevant – friendship, enjoyment of landscape, food, drink and unexpectedly, sex. But that's what normal people do with their weekends, he argues to himself. These basics may or actually may not be the whole reason we exist, but if we're lucky enough to be able to savour them now and again, then we darned well should.

In a way this dichotomy is exactly what he's dealing with in *One-Zero-Three*. This contrast, he knows, rears its head every time you add the prefix 'historical' to any film or play or novel, because the certainty is that the background will be some major event or epoch, and the writer then has to tell its story through the experiences of individual people, even if they might be members of a group of any size, caught up in the particular circumstances. Applying themselves to this task, authors and screenwriters can attract criticism almost automatically. It's such an easy line for a critic or detractor to take and will almost certainly happen to this film at some point. It's virtually inevitable that one executive or another will pronounce the opinion that the balance between the broad canvas of the underlying historical events, the background, and the depiction of its effect of individuals and small groups, the foreground, fails in places to work.

This conclusion will no doubt be expressed in rather cruder terms. Goldman describes how the Hollywood executive in-crowd affect an all-knowing nonchalance by invariably referring to product, even their current endeavour (in as much as they do any endeavouring), as a 'piece of shit'. If *One-Zero-Three* gets into production Ray assumes that some people will confess to be working on 'this conspiracy theory piece of shit'.

The broad brush/fine detail balance is undoubtedly an elusive one to achieve, and the more awful the event in question, the harder it becomes. Disaster films are different, because they are conceived to focus on the protagonists' stories. It's the true historical movies, especially those dealing with wars, where it can really get tricky, or close to impossible.

The reason is that inevitably the experiences and concerns in the individual lives can seem slight and almost meaningless, compared to the events that are impacting people in their thousands. It's hard to mix the macro and micro. Ray remembers noticing this in *Battle of Britain* and finding it almost embarrassing that screentime could be devoted to the conventional emotions occupying the thoughts and hopes of the Susannah York WAAF character, captivating though she was, when the Luftwaffe was trying to pulverise London and its people to dust with high explosive.

But the reactions of individuals are necessary to an understanding of the big event. If a battle contains ten thousand people, there are ten thousand individual stories, each one unique. In fact the battle doesn't really exist as anything except those separate experiences, be they of triumph, tragedy or something else entirely; even if most of them can never be known or depicted. Conflicts are enormous monsters, started and orchestrated by a few important, or at least influential, people – and the actions of those few are naturally worthy of note. The lives affected though, can be numbered in millions, and the doings of most of those caught up in these tragedies of élite making may not seem significant. But yet they are. They're the very essence of every conflict. They are its sum. The task, as Ray has learnt, or tried to learn, is to select the right stories for your narrative and balance them with all the tight-rope-walking skill and sensitivity that you can muster.

Lockerbie was one incident in a different sort of war: an 'occasional series' sort of war with many other episodes. Gerald fancies to start *One-Zero-Three* with Jibril's commandos making their James Bond-like motorised hang-glider raid from Lebanon, flying over the border into Israel, although Ray has neglected to tell him that it was only a two-man operation. There were just eight dead, including the two fliers. 'Just eight dead'! A phrase of dismissal, as if eight wasn't a figure of real consequence, not a meaningful degree of loss. You could as easily start with heavily-armed Israeli soldiers shooting a single stone-throwing child. Out of the micro comes the macro. One small individual tragedy affects a few. The repercussions resound until a bang kills 290, then another one kills 270, that's 561 in three incidents, three of thousands. And for every deceased name on the casualty list there are innumerable stories, their own plus those of the people they leave behind. Back to the micro. Have sympathy for the screenwriter whose job is to grope around the catacombs and memorials and unmarked graves with a clipboard, a pen and a pin, to select a few representative deaths to bring to life, waiting to be shot down himself.

Ray won't be doing any selecting or any rewriting this evening. Having given Jack a few minutes' start, he heads for his room to wait for another of her taps on a door. For the moment, all the concentration is going to be on the immediate foreground.

–ooOoo–

DB Hollingsworth doesn't know it, but the moment he chooses to make his call to Dunedin could hardly be less sensitive. Fortunately Ray has no compunction about ignoring the demanding rings of telephones when circumstances demand. It's a point of principle about the ownership of his personal time. He has technology-slaved friends who feel compelled to respond to buzzes and whirrs and bing-bongs, whatever they're doing. Eve may be watching a TV programme to which she's looked forward for days, but if the phone goes, she does. He will never understand that.

Ray manages to resist DB's second attempt, for reasons similar to the first, and it isn't until the third go that he decides an intrusion may now just be tolerated. It is, after all Monday morning; there is work to do as well as pleasure to seek, and the likelihood is that any call to the Brothers for himself will be of a professional nature. He hopes to God that it's neither E nor Deborah. He manoeuvres to take the handset whilst reserving another limb for tightly enfolding and gently appreciating Jack's firm contours. The aftermath is, in many ways, as important for romance as the other phases of sex. Switching straight to everyday configuration is possible for a man but is not much appreciated by what used to be called 'the ladies'.

In LA, thanks to the International Date Line (which Ray always thinks sounds like an up-market lonely hearts service for high fliers), it is neither morning, nor is it Monday. DB is hoping to speak to Ray before becoming involved in a Sunday lunch.

"Ah, Mr Scriver you are there. How's it going?"

"Good, thank you." Ray knows he should say 'Well' and hates himself whenever he lapses into the fashionable 'I'm good', but he can't help himself sometimes. "I was going to call you later to give you a sitrep and get some advice." Just listen to himself – 'sitrep'. Has all this unaccustomed sexual activity softened his brain?

"What's new then?" Ray relays Gerald's last comment from Friday. He confirms that he's very happy to take up the suggestion to rewrite the Daniel Weiss/Jane Maddox relationship, a major task in itself, but that he's disturbed by the director's hankering after a complete reappraisal of the film's essentials.

Ray is totally unaware that his comments will force a decision from DB, completely reversing one that had precipitated the call – probably.

"Right, well. Here's where I'm at. I told you on day one that I've got work stacked up like a traffic jam, and essentially that hasn't really changed. As you also gathered, I was and am very impressed; I love the script. I'm convinced that there needs to be a film about Lockerbie, exposing the things that you do. I can also see that it needs to be made soon, because of the poor sod in jail, and I'm very keen to see that happen. I half-formed an idea of how it could be done, given that I don't really think I can do it.

311

Have you heard of my son, Ralph Hollingsworth?" Ray hasn't, but never admits things like that when he doesn't have to. He doesn't have to. DB continues: "He's only twenty-four but he's produced a couple of small British films . . ." He mentions two names, neither of which mean anything to Ray. "Now it strikes me that your script isn't that big or expensive to do, relatively speaking." He quotes a ball-park figure, a number of millions of dollars that his listener instantly forgets. Such sums are so way beyond his understanding that DB might as well quote the currency of Saturn. "I've been wondering if *One-Zero-Three* might be something he could take on, with the old man at the end of a phone with advice in the background, if he needed it, and obviously other good help. It would be a step-up from what he's done, sure, but I think he's ready. However, while I think that, my only worry would be putting him with a heavyweight like Gerald Logan. If everyone were singing from the same song-sheet, it would be possible, but when you tell me that Gerald really wants much more of an action movie, and that he's in full demand mode, I realise that I don't think the pairing would work, not now. A couple of years down the line maybe, but lovely though Logan is, we both know he can be a handful."

"So, what are you suggesting?"

"I think you should make the changes that **you** want to make, or at least say that's what you're going to do before you leave. If he's still interested, great, he'll probably have someone in mind to produce it anyway, Evan Harris I expect, and you could put a deal together with them. I'm slightly worried that, because all this so far is being done on the basis of friendship, with nothing formal, you're slightly out on a limb, as more people inevitably get to hear about the script. You really need to get some form of agreement with Gerald before you go much further. On the other hand, if you want to explore the idea of going with Ralph, then you'll be looking for a director and you need to get together with the Boy-Wonder to kick ideas around. The advantage of that, if it is an advantage, is that you get me as a backstop – sort of 'Buy One; Get One Free.' The reason I bring this up now is that Ralph's in LA at the moment and I'm just going for brunch with him and his girlfriend, so I'd love to mention the project to him, if there's any chance you think it could work."

Ray is somewhat deflated. For the last week and a half, Logan and DB have been up there on the billboard in his mind as an ideal combination, a dream team, and although he's always been prepared for it, hearing that his dream team is a non-starter has to put a downer on the start to the week. Decide one way, he might get Gerald, if Gerald wants to play; take the other course and he in reality gets neither of them.

"Can you give me a few minutes to think about it? I mean, mention the film by all means, but I'd like a mo to just take in all that you've said. I'll ring you back on your mobile, if you're just setting off."

That's how they leave it and Ray replaces the handset. Obviously he doesn't have to make a final decision instantly, but when he does, it could prove to be the most important he'll ever take in his life. That thought represents quite a tall order at a few minutes past eight on a wet Monday morning in Dunedin, snuggled close to a warm, fragrant, naked woman who, he now realises, reminds him of Marion Cotillard.

There's another choice to make. On the one hand, the pair can get up, shower and go to breakfast, discuss DB's suggestion over the cereals and fruit and call him back. On the other hand, they can do none of those things except the latter and carry on in the same absorbing fashion that they have for the last couple of hours. No contest. After two minutes' earnest deliberation, Ray gets through to DB's mobile and agrees that the idea should be floated, without any commitment, to Hollingsworth Junior. That's crossed off. This is some spectacular way to conduct a business meeting! Having dealt with the main proposal, he and Jack move down the agenda to Matters Arising – which has been held over.

—ooOoo—

People who run and work in hotels are no fools and generally know if anything is going on almost as quickly as those involved. There is probably no earthly reason to suppose that the charade Ray and Jack adopt is in the slightest way convincing. She goes to breakfast, obviously not long before the service finishes and shortly he comes in, 'spots' her in the nearly empty dining room and politely asks if he may join her, as though they are strangers.

Mind you, it can work the other way. On one fortnight-long commercial on location, Ray and a stunning production assistant were, as it happened, always first into breakfast at 0630 and shared a table, to the extent that everyone on the unit and no doubt the hotel staff were thoroughly convinced that the pair were 'up to no good', as Aunt Cat would say. 'If only they had been' was Ray's single observation on the matter. The fact that they very nearly were, and almost certainly would have been but for an unfortunate misunderstanding, was something that no one ever found out.

Ray goes back to his room with the hope of compressing maybe three days' work into as many hours. Jack takes off to attend to some chores and errands around the city. Just the fact that she'll be back at lunchtime makes

313

him work better, as he makes notes about which scenes require alteration to accommodate the newly-elevated Jane Maddox LLB. He's now actually looking forward to the cut-and-paste exercise, because he's become convinced that the script will benefit. And it's fulfilling to be engaged in the writing process again. It's been a few weeks.

After all, this is what he does.

–ooOoo–

54   Free Transfer

Ray almost springs into the hotel. For the third day running he's had a good brainstorming session with Gerald, who seems at last to show signs of improvement. The small surgeon sought Ray out earlier and said that whatever alternative medicine he's brought from the UK, appears to be working. The man didn't have to do that and it made Ray feel slightly emotional. Now he's looking forward to yet another evening, the fifth in a row, of well-prepared food, a few glasses of decent wine; to becoming more acquainted with Jack's interesting mind and later to renewed contact with her remarkable body.

There is an envelope waiting for him in the reception office. An empty feeling opens up in his central core, long before he takes it to his room and reads any of the words in that flowing hand on the paper.

> Ray. This has been too wonderful, but I shouldn't inflict my chaotic life on you, and I <u>would</u> do, if I stayed around much longer. I know you'll be sad, but I promise you that yours won't be nearly as big a sadness as mine is. We'd have to say goodbye in a day or two anyway, and I hate that and you need to concentrate on your important stuff before you leave. Do good work and be happy. What you're doing matters a lot. And you're going to be rich and famous, if that's what you want. Come and see me when you're passing through Queenstown next time. Try not to make it fifteen years.
>
> Much love, J.
>
> PS I <u>mean</u> be happy. And remember not to think too much.

It was always on the cards. Just as Ray could not truly believe that Jack would check in at the Brothers until he had watched her filling in her guest card; for some reason he had felt each time they had kissed goodbye since; that it could easily be the last, whatever arrangements they had made to the contrary. Not that he doubted her word or her good intentions; her commitment even. It's just that on a handful of occasions he has seen in her eyes a fear of fresh complexity, a concern about the strong possibillity that she was inviting another, major layer of influence into that 'chaotic life' she admits to. Although what she's now done might seem to confirm the free spirit label he assigned her, he thinks it suggests she isn't one at all.

–ooOoo–

He sits, eyes closed. In the headphones Steve Knightley's words duetted plaintively with Polly Bolton touch several contradictory chords.

I'm searching rumours with my hollow plans

When all I want is what's mine

Lost and lonely in a foreign land

I'm left too far behind the lines

I want to tear down the walls between us

But I can't do it all alone

A million spaces in the earth to fill

Here's a generation waiting still

We've got year after year to kill

But no going home

There's no going home.

The song is about exiles. Jack is one, certainly. Tonight, Ray too doesn't know where in the world he belongs.

–ooOoo–

55   You Don't Say

The lights of Scotland Island, out to the right, and Bayview to the left, reflect picturesquely in Pittwater.   There isn't a breath of wind, and although the temperature is far from hot it's a good deal warmer than Dunedin.   Ray sits, somewhat incongruously considering that it's dark, feet up, on a sun lounger, nursing a vast gin and tonic.   On another one beside him rests Annie, still wearing her Qantas uniform, complete with topcoat, while the third is empty, vacated by Des, who as he speaks prowls round his 'deck' in shorts and a summer shirt.   He also bears a serious gin and is gesturing with his free hand.   Des, like those American TV attorneys, believes that moving about adds weight and emphasis to what he has to say. And Des always has plenty to say.   One of the delights of seeing Annie and Des – and this is Ray's first-ever visit to Sydney, their home for a dozen or more years – is going to be to catch up with Des's unique take on our life and times.   Almost entirely self-educated, he is one of those rare individuals who approach every subject from an unexpected angle, who uncover items that everyone else misses and who make connections that the rest of us fail to arrive at.   Ray told him on one occasion, 'You don't just think outside the box.   You live outside it'.

Sometimes Des's razor-edged candour has not won him friends.   It seems to be a trait of the film industry that some of the best technicians are largely fearless about what they say.   Gerald and Perry are certainly two such; Tom Couper another; there are, or were, many more.   Examples from the camera department included the late wonderful David Watkin, who while being interviewed for the cinematographer slot on *Yentle* that Barbra Streisand was about to star in and direct, allegedly leant close to her, sizing-up and pointing at her nose and said 'What worries me is what we are going to do about **this**?'   Not surprisingly, assistant directors, who are in any case 'licensed to rile', are well-represented in the ranks of the outspoken, as in not suffering fools – even those warming the chair with 'DIRECTOR' on the back.   Bert Batt, Ted Lewis and Roger Inman are listed as masters of that art whom Ray had watched in action and there was the legendary Bluey Hill.   Ray had, unfortunately, never met Bluey but, along with everyone else, has heard the stories.   Like when at MGM, Borehamwood, on *The VIPs*, Elizabeth Taylor was being difficult over something and refusing to come to the set, despite entreaties from all-and-sundry.   Leaving the camera and the stage, the redoubtable Bluey made his way to the foot of the stairs leading to the star dressing rooms.   To his booming 'Taylor!   Get your fucking arse down here!' came the distant, compliant response, 'Coming, Bluey.'   Ray suspects that real characters (as opposed to self-promoters) in all grades are a dying breed. As with other industries, outspoken comments, however perceptive, and even sensible suggestions seem to be less welcome these days. As in so much of life, the ruling assumption is becoming that those 'at the top' know what's best and everyone else should do what they're told and keep quiet.

Keeping quiet is not a concept within Des's comprehension. Annie, who has smiled through his theorising since they met by chance at Heathrow thirty years ago, gets up to go and change for the restaurant.

Ray looks to this Sydney visit as an opportunity to get the cameraman's reliably idiosyncratic perspective on one or two separate questions that his Lockerbie research has forced to the surface. He has no idea when he might get the opportunity to introduce the matters: with Des, you have to bide your time. Ray has been here just over an hour and already Des has entertainingly outlined the first half-dozen reasons why the couple will not at any point be returning to live in the UK, plus his preferred solutions to the deficiencies implied. Des's controversial solutions generally veer in the direction of zero-tolerance. Anti-social behaviour, in Des's logic-based dictatorship, would invoke penalties on an uncompromising scale. Des has seemed unimpressed by Ray's counter that his system had to a great extent been tried from the 1700s, one of the extreme punishments seeing many minor criminals from Britain landed to serve out their life sentences just a few miles from where they are having their conversation.

When wishy-washy toothless government is mentioned, Ray gives Des a two-sentence outline pointing towards those in whose interest he thinks British society is currently organised. In his endearing way, Des shows no sign of having heard his friend's opinion, although Ray knows that it has gone into the mill for consideration and will be brought forward again at some point. For now, Des is on the trail of more obvious beneficiaries of the state's decision-making. Ray regards this level of politics as a sideshow. His view is that the policies which the population-at-large believe come out of Westminster and which the sharper knives in the box have decided originate in Downing Street and Whitehall, are actually designed somewhere else again. The day-to-day decisions, he has told Des, are important in as much as lives are affected by them, but essentially they are a distraction, a smokescreen behind which the really important power games are rarely glimpsed.

"I don't believe the politicians have anything to do with it." Ray repeats his conviction, as it had no reaction first time out. "I think that party politics is a façade to convince people they've got a democracy, but I don't think the politicians actually run things. They tinker, but really only provide a public mechanism for the exercise of real power. You know, just as no one believes for a moment that George W runs the USA – a man who couldn't manage a country filling station with no customers. If he's not a puppet with his strings being pulled, just what would one look like?"

"Don't you think," Des says, "that even half-wits can get by if they surround themselves with more competent people? We've both seen that tried dozens of times on jobs."

The voice of an unseen Annie from somewhere above cuts through their further consideration of the suggestion.

"Are you two getting ready or am I going out on my own?"

The two men drain their G&Ts and Ray stands up. Des takes his glass.

"We'd better comply with orders." He exaggeratedly mouths the words at half his usual volume. "But remind me later; I want to know who you think really runs the world." It has gone in, as Ray knew it would.

"Yeah, and I'd like to hear who you think does . . . apart from Annie, that is."

–ooOoo–

Des, like Perry, is one of Thatcher's refugees, one of perhaps hundreds of film emigrants forced to hawk their cinematographic skills at the other ends of the earth, as a result of the cartoon schoolmistress's resolute meddling in their industry. Odd that her administration, like any other, guarded unto itself the right to train the numbers of soldiers, police, firefighters and so on, that it deemed to be correct and necessary, but yet legislated for change to allow an unsupportable torrent of people, swamping and destabilising, into a cottage-sized fragmented business that could never absorb a fraction of them. How her beloved 'market forces' would resolve this situation, she neither thought about nor cared, having happened to take a dislike to British TV technicians in the course of giving her always-condescending interviews. Even as she was lecturing and pronouncing her platitudes, she was making instant judgements on the number and the work-rate of the people being employed to help project her self-image of superior being, despite the fact that her understanding of their industry was non-existent.

Ray calls her reign a regime, rather than a government, in that it progressed to be, according to some of her closest associates, a one-woman-band. There were other instrumentalists, but they were mainly unheard because they rarely sought to disagree with the band leader, however inharmonious her selection of strident music. Her style, if you believe some of their memoirs, eventually became one of arriving at firm and absolute decisions – all-too-often based on superficial information or existing prejudices – and steam-rollering them through, sweeping aside discussion or dissent.

It was an approach that should have brought her down, according to Carl, in that she refused to face the fact that the far-from-transparent means by which her son amassed and concealed a considerable fortune could hardly not have been linked to her own position and her apparent endorsement. That he was deriving commission from trade deals which her government was sponsoring propelled her into an unacceptable conflict of interests that was obvious to everyone who was aware of his involvement. Everyone that is, apart from her. There is, however, no mechanism for disciplining a prime minister other than the exercise of popular opinion, and the media, whose function is to mobilise public outrage when necessary, mysteriously failed to report her selective myopia. In letting her off, they exhibited what can only be described as criminal negligence. There was scarcely a peep from them when she asked John Major to create her husband not just a knight but a Baronet – the first for many years; a move designed to ensure that in due time her discreditable offspring would become 'Sir Mark'.

While she could forgive Mark anything, other people could find her very unforgiving, especially when she 'took against' them. That she secretly had the telephone conversations of two of her own ministers, whom she suspected of being off-message, tapped and transcribed, indicates how dangerously paranoid things could be in Number Ten, Downing Street. Ultimate self-assurance and total conviction of the superiority of one's own position, despite often ample evidence to the contrary, is a familiar trait in political leaders. You can see it in Robert Mugabe, Saddam Hussein and Muammar Gaddafi among a host of others including, many agree, Maggie's most recent successor, the Right Honourable Member for Sedgefield.

Coincidentally, in a modified form, these are also well-known features of Des's character; indeed this was but one of the considerable list of factors that propelled Des and Annie to live where they do. Another of those was Barclays Bank, whose salesman had dutifully informed them that 'investments can go down as well as up' while assuring that in a lengthy recorded history, they never had. How that changed in the course of a very short time as the institution's wizards managed to fritter away a third of Annie's modest inheritance, naturally charging handsomely for every unwise transaction and no doubt still collecting eye-watering bonuses as the couple cashed-in what still remained and abandoned Britain in disgust.

Before departing, Des had famously confronted a senior executive in the

City and told him that the only people who had treated banks in a manner they deserved, one that equalled the contempt that they showed for their customers, had been those characters in the 1960s with the Mark II Jaguars, the stocking masks and the sawn-off shotguns.

–ooOoo–

"So!" Des begins when the formalities of ordering are out of the way. "What's this screenplay about?" Ray has been expecting this to come up, sooner rather than later, and has decided to use one of his small repertoire of standard responses.

"Well, it looks at a real event, a major crime, in relatively recent history and reinvestigates it and exposes a high-level cover-up. That's about it, really. I can't at the moment tell you what the event is because it remains quite politically sensitive and though many, many people will be delighted to learn what the film will present, there will be some who will be very keen that it isn't made. All in all, it's better for everybody that they don't know anything until the film is well underway."

"How intriguing," Annie says, approvingly. "A mystery on top of a mystery."

Ray knows that Des will be less happy at his secrecy and will inevitably spend a few minutes probing. Ray can't think why he's not prepared to tell all to his old colleague when he was perfectly open about the project with Perry, and also with Jack, whom he really hardly knew at the time. He doesn't for a moment thinks Des will discuss it if asked not to and there should be far less worry about airing these matters in Sydney compared to LA. But for all that there's a niggling reluctance and he's therefore quite prepared to stonewall as Des tries to find holes in the fence. It's Annie who gets him off the hook by changing the subject and asking about E. At which point he realises that, for the second time in a row, his response to a question will be less complete than it might be.

–ooOoo–

They are well into what, in the last few days in New Zealand, Ray has known as the 'mains'. Des has not been noticeably silent or at all preoccupied but now he puts down his knife and fork.

"I think I've got it. Knowing your speciality it's likely to be aviation. A significant aviation crime – boils down to two – 9/11 and Lockerbie. You said event in the singular and relatively recent history rather than recent history, so I think it's Lockerbie."

"Your talents are wasted. You should have been a detective. Now you see why it's sensitive stuff."

"Yeah, I won't ask what conclusions you came to but I can probably guess the sort of thing, and why you need to be cautious. I mean, if a country can let a group execute its own president and get away with a cover-up, what chance does anyone else stand? It's funny – America must be the only nation to have had three coups d'état that its citizens never noticed."

"Three? Kennedy's assassination – one. George W and brother Jeb stealing the presidential election of 2004. What's the other one?" Ray's surprised that he can't think.

"Kennedy did something similar to George and Jeb; or at least his father, Joe, did. He swung JFK's election by a vote scam organised with the Mafia. That's why Bobby Kennedy was killed and one of the reasons for Dallas, too."

"Because the Kennedys were making war on the people who had helped make Jack president. Of course."

"You got it."

"Mind you, does election-rigging actually count as a coup d'état? It seems to be as old as voting itself. Where hasn't it happened?"

"Well, if the people are minded to choose one administration and a faction intervenes, by whatever means, to subvert the democratic will and substitute their own preference, that's a coup in my book."

"Yeah," concedes Ray, "although I've become very sceptical about the democratic will. I don't actually believe any more in the principle of one man– sorry Annie – one person one vote."

"Well; that makes two of us," Des agrees, not altogether to Ray's surprise.

After all, Des does live well outside the box.

–ooOoo–

56   Parting Thoughts

Ray has enjoyed the evening, but he's glad to back and ready for sleep. For some reason he's never until this trip taken in the existence of a two-hour time difference between New Zealand and Australia, so for him it's now 3am. He's glad that they went local, to the Newport Arms, rather than trek all the way down to the Sydney Harbour waterfront district, as had been the original plan. Exploring the city can wait until daylight and tomorrow. Des proved as entertaining as ever, spending much of the meal in a clinical dissection of the question of republicanism versus monarchy. Ray, being a Queen and Countryman to his last breath, was more than happy to throw in his own favourite ambushes when Des's coach and horses seemed to be heading straight into the republican camp. In Ray's opinion, the apparent logic of the abolitionists always underplays the significant dangers and heavy costs of all kinds inherent in electing heads of state, while ignoring the great bonuses, tourism not the least.

"People don't spend their life savings crossing oceans in order to catch a glimpse of Angela Merkel," he had said, at which image Annie had nearly fallen off her chair. "Why would we need yet another party politician telling lies to get elected, breaking all their promises and treating us with complete disdain once they're in the job, except the secret ones made to their cronies and backers?" he'd gone on, getting into his stride. "Where's the book called *Lives of One Hundred Great Presidents*? I tried an off-the-cuff count-up a few months ago and I got up to about seventy-five, and apart from about three or four, I remembered the names because they were associated with bad things – you know, scandals, corruption, human rights abuses, starting wars, going mad, genocide; that sort of stuff. The trouble with living down here in Murdochalia is that your media is about as free and diverse as Russia's. I love the way the Digger shamelessly employs the principle of dynastic succession in his own empire, while apparently reviling it in his attempts to undermine the House of Windsor. Oh and by the way your argument about Royal patronage makes no sense, because the complaint is that it's misused by politicians; not that it's necessarily an evil in itself – so it makes the case against electing dodgy prime ministers, not the existence of a Monarch."

Ray thinks that one of the strange things about Des is how he turns his total solidity into an endearing quality. Whatever arguments you throw at him, you know you will never, ever, change his mind, and yet you love him for it.

It was interesting that when he had deduced the subject matter of Ray's script, Des had made an immediate assumption that its conclusions would involve criticism of the US; as though he too was convinced of American implication. Ray wonders what his self-taught friend has read or seen to lead him to that, inevitably firm, conclusion. Maybe he will discuss it with him after all. For now the priority is to get some rest.

–ooOoo–

There seems to be a rule that the first night in a new bed is highly likely to be disturbed, whatever the level of fatigue at bedtime, even or perhaps especially when the changing of time zones has piled the fall-out from extra hours of wakefulness on top of normal tiredness and could be expected to induce sounder sleep. But then there's plenty going on in Ray's brain in these early hours to kick the senses back into life after an hour or two and deny the necessary repose. It's only seconds after waking that the strong physical feeling of emptiness makes itself felt in his centre. There follows a few microseconds of combing through the mind's files to search out its cause. How must more acute must this sensation be at every single waking of anyone who has lost someone irrevocably? He hasn't felt even this lesser form of loss for many a year, but its onset in the last couple of days has given him renewed sympathy with those forced to cope with the real thing. The Lockerbie bereaved must have returned from every sleep for the last eighteen years wondering why they are feeling so ill-at-ease – and then, even worse, remembering. For some, mercifully, the immediacy will have diminished, but for others it will remain as sharp as ever.

His feeling of bleakness is keen enough but hardly comparable. Set against death, the degree of finality involved cannot begin to register. Theoretically the void in front of him could be bridged with little difficulty. He wasn't actually 'dumped', to use the currently popular but ugly-sounding expression; Jack merely said goodbye before he was obliged to. In response, he could have chased her back to Queenstown; or he could have overcome his fear of awkward telephone conversations and called her. He had done neither, giving her the space she'd sought. Instead he'd spent hours contemplating every course of action, including that of offering to sell up in Wiltshire and move to take up disordered residence with her anywhere in Otago or Southland. Very soon he'd realised the scale of the assumptions he was making on the strength of one short and hasty note. After all she theoretically has an existing partner in the errant Kim, and she's always referred to him as a settled fact, not a transitory feature of her life. For another thing, Ray is hardly a free agent. It has surprised him though that suddenly he has been prepared to embrace contemplation of a whole range of radical alternative futures in a way that is most uncharacteristic and mildly disturbing, especially given the extremely short length of their relationship.

Yet it is also a degree encouraging. He has tended to think that his life is in a established pattern which will now continue until overpainted by infirmity or his own encounter with the Grim Reaper. To admit even the possibility of major changes is rather liberating. He knows he shouldn't really be surprised at this, absorbed as he is in his work by the fact that life is unpredictable and subject to instant realignment through pure chance.

He begins, in that light, to think about this whole trip and realises that virtually nothing so far has gone as anticipated. Apart from a certain amount of looning and tyre-squealing around LA with Perry, and a predictably stimulating first evening here being treated to Des's insights, both of which were givens, everything else in this venture has deviated wildly from the half-formed script that played at the back of his mind in the days before he set off. First and foremost, Gerald has not been won over by the material he's been shown, to anything like the extent that Ray had assumed he might be – though the disappointment over that had been largely cancelled out by the unforeseen reunion with DB and the enthusiasm and progress that's come from that chance encounter. In the second major objective of the foray, he would never have believed that his meeting Eve in LA would go so badly, and when that happened, that he could remain so relaxed about it.

As to the rest, he certainly didn't expect to have the chance to do quite so much piloting; and never in his wildest dreams could he have predicted becoming involved in a hot affair, let alone two of them. These latter aspects rather smack of a man in a mid-life crisis, but if this is what one's like, Ray Scriver is not altogether disinclined to be having one.

Nevertheless, just thinking of Deborah causes him almost to break out in a rash of embarrassment. This round-the-world Odyssey has developed something of the character of 'a girl in every port', which was never his style even at the height of his globe-trotting. He should have been so lucky! Although he never saw it, he remembers what must have been at the time a quite risqué farce with a plot along similar lines being produced for the West End stage in 1960 while he was still at school. Ironically called, in the light of his present study, *Boeing-Boeing*, it revolved round a Paris architect who balanced the delights and demands of three fiancées at the same time. The ladies in question were all air stewardesses of different nationalities working for their respective flag carriers, flying into the French capital and receiving his amorous attentions in turn, according to their duty rosters and their airlines' timetables. His meticulous planning naturally suffered inevitable disruption, caused by a number of factors, not least of which was the introduction of a faster aircraft, the Boeing 707, which entered service in late 1958.

Ray had, in fact, at a short interlude in his life run two girlfriends simultaneously, one actually the only flight attendant that ever occupied the girlfriend slot; but that was only because the principal object of his affections at the time was so impossibly blow hot, blow cold (in truth blow lukewarm, blow cold), that he never knew where he stood from one day to the next. The FA, who was actually a friend of a friend, just happened to invite herself down at a Bank Holiday weekend when GF1 was being even more cruelly blow-cold than usual and had gone away to visit an old flame. After a few weeks of *Boeing-Boeing*-like juggling, when they both uncharacteristically arrived unannounced on the same sunny afternoon, he still managed to choose the wrong one and stayed with the uncommitted incumbent who didn't appreciate him. The latter phenomenon and the double-tracking were one-offs, until now. Two at once never became a habit; let alone three.

Unlike the total disclosure to Jack, he had not made Deborah aware of the existence of Eve, though he was sure that she had been briefed on his status by Pippa in advance. Even if she hadn't, he thought it wouldn't be a matter of concern for Deborah. It was those ground rules again; he sensed they had been understood even before she had found him waiting in the silver moonlight.

He had responded to her waiting message during his stay in Dunedin, fortunately before the Queenstown weekend and its surprises. Their exchanges had been warm and in keeping with their story-so-far, with no undertakings offered on either side other than to speak again in similar vein at an early opportunity. He's nervous now about the definition of 'early'. His relationship with Deborah he can perhaps now rate as stable and civilised. At present he can find no adjectives suitable to ascribe to the one with Jack. It is possible that the one with Deborah has run its course, although she may not yet know it. Lying there, he has to accept that the one with Jack may also have done so and that he may be the one who isn't at present fully in the picture.

–ooOoo–

As if the personal questions now keeping him awake are not insistent enough, there are plenty of professional ones gnawing away like mice in his attic.

It was unfortunate that Ray's perturbation at the sudden melting away of Jack had affected his concentration in the few remaining days of his stay in New Zealand. Far from allowing him to focus on reworking of the script, as her note had suggested, he was more than a degree distracted and out-of-sorts. Nor was Gerald on best form. His recovery had reached a plateau; the marked improvement had slowed and his frustrations understandably made him slightly tetchy. He was still smarting over the loss of the Cruise film, and the fee that went with it. In fact there was a second fee also lost; he was also contracted as a co-producer, and when he complained of his extra misfortune in losing another undisclosed sum, no doubt enormous, for which it's certain he would have had to assume virtually no additional duties in order to pocket, Ray had to work hard to try, and probably fail, to keep the sarcasm acceptably light.

"My heart bleeds for you, Logan. Tell me, what do you actually have to do extra to get the producer's salary on top? No, don't tell me. I'll get too sodding depressed. All I've had for my entire career are production managers telling me that for some unexplained reason they can't pay me what I'm worth this time, but if all goes well they'll have more work in the pipeline with proper money next time round, which never actually comes. Usually I end up without enough staff to do the job efficiently, while there are people swanning around calling themselves producers earning God-knows-how-many-times my salary for doing, as far as anyone can tell, absolutely naff-all.

"I mean, what qualifications do you need to get one of these producer jobs? Have they all got forty years of experience and loyal service to the industry? Because, if they have, why haven't I heard of a single one of them before they pop up on the credits? I've spent years getting producers, good and bad, out of trouble with my ingenuity and sheer hard work and not one has ever said 'Wow, you saved us a fortune on this one – have a producer's fee or even so much as an extra day's money'. Or on a commercial, 'We made a complete killing on that one so please accept this token of our appreciation, to make up for all the times you got less than you should'.

"Do you know what I was given as thanks in forty years? One short note, two long-playing records and one smart bottle of scotch – and they were all from directors – not so much as a bottle of wine from any of the thousands of producers. Except one had some t-shirts made that read: 'I must work harder, longer hours for less money!' and the joke was on us, for that's what the company, nice though they were, really meant and expected. No, it was always, 'There's no budget on this one, can you help us out with a deal?' When the money was tight, if it ever really was, the problem was shared with the technicians who had to take a cut; when the job made a bomb the idea of sharing didn't come into it – that was the producer's good fortune. Remember Beth Warren? Mean as arseholes and she always had a brand new Mercedes convertible and would virtually drive it onto the stage so all we proles could see how much money she was making out of her jobs: jobs that never, of course, had any 'budget'.

"In the time that you've done two massive features and earned several lives' fortunes, I've had four days' work – three for Neo-Mega which was a deal, even with them, and one other where the company wanted to pay me half what my rate was ten years ago, and when I queried it, they contrived not to pay me at all. That might well prove to be my last ever job as an assistant director – it'll be a pretty fitting close to a long and dedicated career if it transpires that I got bilked for my final day's work. No doubt when I come to sell this screenplay they'll be some blip, some technicality invoked so that I'm only offered a fraction of what anyone else would get. Do me a favour. Don't complain about how badly done by you are and how much you're losing when I'm about. I might get so depressed I'll go and jump off a bridge!"

He thinks now that he was probably the first person for years to talk like that to Gerald Logan. Big directors, like big stars, can become insulated from reality. The bigger they get, the more the people round them tell them what they want to hear. It won't have done Ger any harm to know the financial realities of the life of his one-time lieutenant – he won't have given a thought to what Ray has actually lived on since America beckoned and their ways were parted by that nation's drawbridge mentality. His old collaborator doesn't feel in the least that he's taken advantage of the director's captive status to set some of the record straight. He's also realised that while he was close to 'going into one' or 'blowing his top', he was also consciously putting down a marker that says he won't be giving his screenplay away at a bargain basement price. The Old Pals' Act is very useful for everybody, but for once it's going to work in Ray's favour. Several years' worth of serious research needs to be paid for.

Gerald pretends to be totally insensitive but Ray has learnt that, as with Des, anything said to him will always be taken on board, even if there's no sign of it at the time. The only apparent response to the outburst had been typically disarming. Adopting the cod Tony Richardson impression once again he had merely said,

"Are you going to stand there all day whinging, or are we going to do some fucking work?"

And work they had despite their separate preoccupations, going through the script scene by scene, line by line, with Ray noting Gerald's comments and making his own notes, pointers to whether he might later make individual changes, or maybe not. It had, though, become a singularly uninspiring, nuts and bolts exercise; there were few flashes of insight or sudden new avenues. He was glad that Gerald had not mentioned the concept of a total re-think again, although it wouldn't have been forgotten, and Ray knew he would at least have to go through the exercise of reading all the notes and eliminating those alternative lead characters once he was back in his office.

By the second day after Jack's farewell, Ray had begun to feel that he could be achieving just as much, if not rather more, on his own. He'd always found collaboration difficult. Though he was very glad to have Gerald's interest and input, he was beginning to wonder whether what they were doing was not more in the nature of therapy for the casualty, rather than adding much to the screenplay. He would still have to do the actual re-write and that's when the magic happens for Ray; when he sits at the computer and the words flow and lead him in unexpected directions. He was now becoming impatient to get on with that process and the hours in the hospital began somewhat to drag. They were a highlight, though, compared to the remainder of his day, and in reality, when his time was his own, progress was minimal. Not surprisingly, he found it virtually impossible to work at the hotel, where his thoughts were inevitably seduced by associations. All in all, the first leg of his journey home could now not come quickly enough. There was just another day to go. He'd had to steel himself and try to forget that it was once again Friday. The coming weekend gaped like a chasm with no way across, every time he thought about the events of the last. He had consoled himself with the thought that by Sunday night he would be far away from Dunedin.

It wasn't until the last meeting in the small sterile room that had almost become as much of a cell for him as for Gerald, that he could overcome his normal reluctance to discuss business aspects and attempt to get his friend to show his cards.

"Look, it's big question time. I'm sorry to have to ask, but this film's going or not is rather vital to my future and I'm the world's worst negotiator, but I rather need to know before I go back how serious you might be about doing it."

Gerald's voice and manner had become unexpectedly and touchingly kindly.

"Yes, I understand that, sweetie. The honest truth is I won't know until I get out of here. I can hardly think beyond tomorrow at the moment. Look, I'm really grateful that you've come all this way to see me. No other bastard did. My mother's the only other person I've seen since I arrived. I'm very flattered that you've shown me your work and that you want me to direct it, and I honestly think that the effort we've put in together on it will make the script a whole lot better. But, will I want to do it when I escape from this place? I don't know; I can't say. I'll certainly think about it very carefully: I know that much. But as to what I might feel when I'm up and fully running, I'd be lying if I said I could tell you today. I know that's not very much use to you."

"No, on the contrary, that's absolutely reasonable and I much appreciate your candour. I'll try and progress it and keep you posted as to any success I have. The news at the moment is that DB thinks now he can't do it but is suggesting his son, Ralph, who's produced a couple of cheapies. Oh! And he's sent a script to Arran Samson who heard about it and expressed interest, but there's no word back yet."

Ray had noticed a small change come over Gerald at the mention of Samson. It was nothing you could put your finger on but it was as if from the moment of that revelation he was suddenly taking the whole subject thirty per cent more seriously.

"You wouldn't want a rookie producer on a picture with Samson," is what Gerald had actually said.

"Funny, that's what DB said about you."

"Quite right too! I have people who're wet behind the ears for breakfast."

"It's odd. I taught you everything you know about the floor, but I never told you to do that."

"You cheeky fucker," Gerald had laughed. "Actually you're absolutely right. You did. You and Hattie."

"Be fun to do it again."

"It would." He'd paused, far away for a long moment. "Arran Samson. That's quite interesting casting."

—ooOoo—

All in all it had been quite poignant, bidding farewell to Gerald. Ray found it strange because there were two such distinct possibilities for the future. In one scenario the diverse paths their careers had followed for many years might soon merge dramatically again, with all the certainty of railway lines converging at a junction. On the other hand, it was equally possible that from that rather remote station with its bleak waiting room, smelling of disinfectant, two tracks would separate and head in very different directions, probably never to come back together.

Before finally lapsing back into sleep, Ray makes two decisions. The first is that he's going to have a producer's credit on the movie, whoever produces and directs it. The second is that, true to his newly-determined job title, he's going to engage in a spot of double-bluffing himself.

–ooOoo–

57   Out Lunched the Swag-Men

When Ray doesn't have an appointment to meet or a plane to catch, his morning routine can seem infuriatingly leisurely, even to himself. Almost inevitably, because much of his working life has been tightly focused on making the most valuable use of every second, no such effort is applied to his personal existence. There is no suggestion of idleness; he is always fully occupied; it's merely that deciding what to select from the list of things to do can be a protracted process. It's better for him when there are no options and no decisions. On the set he can make choices on a wholesale basis, virtually instantaneously. At home the uncertainty verges on the agonising. It's fairly uncharacteristic that this trip is happening at all. Ray is one of those people who are not good at holidays and leisure.

This morning proves the point. With Annie gone hours ago for an early shift at the airport and Des committed to something or other for most of the morning, Ray should be taking the opportunity for some Sydney sightseeing. But he isn't. He's still sitting at the dining table at 10.30 turning the pages of the guidebook that Annie has thoughtfully interleaved with post-it notes, trying to come up with an efficient plan to use the dwindling time left before he meets Des for a late lunch.

He is surprised when the creative process adds further to his delay and requires several minutes of serious note-making. He has realised, with a flash from nowhere, that his dodgems experience on the freeway in LA with Perry can be used in the revised screenplay as a new and possibly crucial scene between his two lead characters. As in the real incident, they can be discussing some aspect of the case on a car journey. After the spectacular evasions, when calm resumes, they too can be stranded in some inaccessible spot. It could even be the moment and the place when they both finally realise what they mean to each other. In earlier times in an English film the star would express it in clipped-toned Noel Coward-enunciated dialogue: 'It wasn't until I came to the very point where I could have lost you, Susan, that I knew how much I care for you.' On today's screen it will be ninety per cent played with subtle looks and meaningful silences, with any dialogue understated and disarming: something like, 'Can we agree not to make a habit of this?'

This has taken Ray into more dangerously time-consuming territory as images of Trevor Howard and Celia Johnson in Coward's *Brief Encounter* set him thinking about music in films, in their case the haunting Rachmaninov. This leads him to Richard Addinsell's manufactured *Warsaw*

Concerto for *Dangerous Moonlight*. What a title, thinks Ray, as recent memories of the two nights in the Mojave Desert briefly cross his mind. He returns, though, to the music theme and, as so often, to the Parry that he's envisaged for Flight One-Zero-Three's plunge to earth. There's another piece of music that he's proposing for the following morning when the full horrors of what has happened in the night become revealed with the dawn. As it was in reality, the obscenity of the crime will be most acutely expressed by the presence of the bodies of the dead.

Aircraft seating is modular and is constructed in rows of two, three or more seats, the feet of such sections located in tracks on the floor, to allow blocks of seating to be fitted or removed, or the pitch, the distance between consecutive rows, to be increased for comfort or reduced for greater density. In an accident rows of seats are likely to stay intact, and on 103 many fell with their occupants remaining belted-in, exactly as fastened by their own hands before take-off from Heathrow. Amongst the wreckage on the ground, in displays framed by these seat backs and cushions, were found some unutterably moving final tableaux, showing passengers reaching for the comfort and reassurance of bodily contact in their final moments, grasping for or holding on tightly to those in the next seat. This and the expressions left on many of the faces provided ample evidence that there was time for them to be all-too-aware of their imminent deaths.

Those who not been secured in their seats at the moments of disintegration were spreadeagled on roofs, or draped in trees, one man apparently sitting up in the centre of a field, with astonishingly an unbroken bottle of scotch in front of him. These were the corpses that were intact. There was luggage both completely undamaged and burst open, spilling intimate content. There was every other imaginable item associated with a great flying liner, the familiar and the unknown, the normally unseen, and there was the added pathos due to the seasonal nature of many of the articles on view, it being just days from Christmas and its exchanges of gifts. This appalling mass-littering was apparently scattered randomly, but in reality had been sorted by the wind according to the laws of physics across several counties, the lightest pieces drifting furthest, some into Northumberland even to the English east coast.

Ray has envisaged the use of slow pans and long tracking shots to accentuate the total apparent incongruity of the scenes and has them accompanied by Elgar's *Sospiri*, a slow, haunting, orchestral piece entirely appropriate for the sombre revelations.

This would be in total contrast to the hellish chaos of the previous night, where the natural sounds of fires burning, sirens approaching and instructions being shouted and relayed would be interplayed with the muted snatches of conversation and the otherwise shocked quiet.

He feels compelled to listen again to *Sospiri*, a relatively short work, so he sets it up and pipes it through his headphones. He's brought with him all the music that he's referred to in the script, with the original intention of playing it over to Gerald, and though he'd mentioned this prospect in Dunedin it had not actually happened. The director had never seemed in the right receptive frame of mind for a musical interlude.

As the piece, which took eleven years to complete, fills his ears, he is conscious that events in Lockerbie and the surrounding countryside had already now for some hours begun to take an even stranger turn than the unique circumstances themselves might have mandated. But even as he is being tempted into contemplation of, for example, the strange story of police surgeon Dr David Fieldhouse, he fortunately catches a glimpse of a clock and as the music dies away, he gathers himself for his solo advance on the centre of Sydney.

—ooOoo—

Annie and Des differed entertainingly on their suggestions of route for Ray's drive into the city, and having noted the bones of both versions and consulted a map he uses a judicious combination of the two. It's no surprise that having arrived in the centre, he makes no attempt to park the hire car and visit any of the attractions that Annie has highlighted, but rather goes with the flow, following where his inclination and the traffic carry him, taking the pulse and gaining a feel for the city in a random fashion.

It's an approach he's long used and it has over the years seemed to lead him rather more often into fascinating places and rewarding situations than it has into dull surroundings and unpleasant experiences – although there have been exceptions. And you have to be careful with it. Most cities in the world have areas into which it's better not to stray in a shiny new motor, however near bottom-of-the-range it might be. Today the experiment comes out on the positive side of mid-scale. Anyway, it's not too long before it's time to stop, get the map out and devise a route to the Botanic Gardens and the Andrew (Boy) Charlton Café.

Ray supposes it's being an Aquarian that attracts him to water. For him, Des's suggestion is perfect. There's no one swimming in the pool but the view across to the Navy Yard is full of things to look at, not least the largest hammerhead shipyard crane in the Southern Hemisphere. Ray remembers working on one of those, in Newcastle, with a director who was so petrified of heights that he had to wear a harness clipped-on to the nearest handrail and physically held by the unit rigger every time he wanted to move his position.

When Des sweeps into the airy café, it is with news that he has just been offered three days' unexpected work starting tomorrow, covering for a cameraman who has gone sick, but that he plans to turn them down to undertake the socialising and sightseeing that had been planned for the next two, with Ray actually due to leave on the third. Ray will not hear of this. They might not have seen each other for a year or four, but he can't have his friend losing three lumps of DP's daily rate on his account. Work is hard enough to come by for free-lancers without opportunities to earn being thrown away. He is·more than capable of touring the city on his own. He senses that Des, although he protests to the last, is in truth relieved that his visitor is adamant that he should accept the job. Ray is pleased to see that the cameraman gets on the phone with alacrity to confirm his availability.

With their time together now massively compressed, this will be a much shorter lunch than planned and what remains of the afternoon will become a great deal more whistle-stop in nature, as Des selects some highlight features of Sydney that Ray probably wouldn't find alone. This means that no opportunity presents itself to pick up on any of the unfinished topics from last evening. Resigned to this, Ray throws himself into tourism for a few hours, very happy to let Des do the thinking and worry about logistics. It's not until they are back at the house and hitting the first gin and tonic that their discourse returns from local to global considerations.

It soon becomes clear that Des has no special insights into the Lockerbie mystery. Quite surprisingly, it has not been a subject that his enquiring mind has lighted on. His assumption that Ray would have found cause to criticise the USA over it in some way was just that – an assumption; one based on his own predisposition to question American intentions, given that they, on his reading of topics that he has looked into, are not infrequently suspect.

One area that troubles him a lot, he says, is the matter of business standards and their decline in pursuit of the bottom line, the mighty dollar. Corporate greed, he asserts with a fine selection of gestures from his repertoire, overtakes concern for employees: is indeed frequently seriously exploitative. Businesses lobby strongly against regulations on everything from safe working practices to financial oversight, and when rules exist, they are routinely ignored. Sometimes companies' behaviour is plainly criminal, leading to major scandals like Enron and Andersens.

"Whichever business sector you care to look at in America – energy, food production, the nuclear industry, petrochemicals, pharmaceuticals, the motor industry, banking and finance – you come to the conclusion that corporate ethics are out of the window, that practices are either treading the fine line of legality or more likely crossing it. And with big business behaving more like organised crime, you have to ask whether there are links. We know in some cases there are. There are 'legitimate', well-known companies with household names that were set up to launder crime money and there's one thing that you can be sure of, however legit and independent a company seems to be; once Mafia-controlled, always Mafia-controlled; the mob still manipulates them from deep cover, behind the complicated corporate structures.

"The only question we can't answer is how large a proportion of American business has been affected like that through takeovers. There are certainly billions of dollars to launder every year. We know there are mob lawyers and mob accountants who've been sent to the best universities. I even read an article suggesting that there will be mob-sleepers working normally in many sectors of government and its departments, working, being promoted upwards to positions of more and more influence, but whose ultimate loyalty is somewhere else entirely."

"Scary. The Russians are supposed to have done that, aren't they, in the Cold War? Moles. Some of them could be quite high up now," Ray offers.

"Indeed. 'The enemy within' is always especially frightening. Historically, people have become unbelievably paranoid about fifth columnists in wartime, and just look at the madness of the Macarthy purges in the Cold War – every liberal was a red under the bed, according to the fixated senator, but sleepers and real subversives are genuine threats that always need to be considered. You'll remember, we suspected it in our own union in the 70s. But in business the evidence that keeps trickling out about Corporate America's behaviour doesn't do a whole lot to dispel the impression that these days, for whatever reason, it has very questionable standards. It certainly doesn't offer a business model that anyone would wish to see imposed on their own country, yet clearly the UK is, through multi-nationals and simply following trends, adopting a more and more transatlantic approach to commercial practice every day."

"Well, I've become firmly convinced that powerful elements in America have a firm intention to dominate the entire world economy using every form of coercion that exists. That's reason a-plenty to despise them, but I had no idea that they might be as corrupted in the conventional, criminal sense as you're suggesting."

Ray is these days normally accustomed to opening the eyes of others to startling and uncomfortable disclosures. It's unusual for someone to tell him that things are potentially rather worse than even he has hitherto imagined. He knew he could rely on Des to give him something to chew over. He has a thought.

"The crime connection is fascinating. I've read very little about the Mafia, but I found it astonishing that the CIA and the mob worked together over Cuba against Castro, with all sorts of weird assassination plots, and that they're strongly suspected of joint involvement in the murder of JFK. Certainly Jack Ruby, who conveniently silenced Oswald's denials and helped cement the lone-gunman fantasy – he was undoubtedly a Mafia player. The mind boggles to understand how a government agency gets into bed with organised crime."

"You obviously don't know that the US Army virtually resurrected the Mafia during the invasion of Italy in the Second World War." The cameraman likes to play high cards.

"No I don't. Why? How?" Des has done it again!

"Well, Mussolini was quite successful in suppressing organised crime, but his efforts were wasted because, when the American forces were liberating towns, they had to replace Fascist mayors, but they found people reluctant to step in. There was a vacuum and the civil administration was in chaos. No doubt townsfolk had been warned not to become involved. There was a major racketeer called Lucky Luciano, who was in prison in the USA and still happily running from jail his empire that included the New York waterfront. The government had already had to approach him, cap in hand, to get the docks running properly to support the war effort. He suggested that he could have the word spread in southern Italy that the populace should co-operate with the Americans. And of course those who came forward as a result were people approved by the Mafia. Under the principle that 'my enemy's enemy is my friend', the American military were supplanting Mussolini's hard men with local dons or their appointees and Luciano was freed long before he'd served his full sentence.

"So on two continents, the US establishment had been coerced into actions that renewed or strengthened the mob's grip. It's no surprise they have co-existed ever since and that the less savoury arms of government have collaborated when it's suited them."

"Certainly the Kennedy murder makes it clear how alike they operate," Ray comes in.

He realises how much Des's revelation colours the matters he's been thinking about all these months, although he doesn't want to mention this aspect now.

"When you look at what both parties were doing in Dallas – trying to change a regime for the benefit of shadowy big business interests and big money, you realise they were equally corrupt and ruthless – and so why wouldn't they still be? The ends they were working towards for sure weren't to the benefit of the average hard-working American then, and won't be now. 'One nation under God' it hasn't been for a long time."

–ooOoo–

58   "Brothers and sisters, I bid you beware . . ."

Ray has risen at an uncomfortably early hour in a spirit of solidarity with Des, off for his day of meetings and a pre-light in a hot studio. Neither of them has accorded similar courtesy to Annie, who left the house much earlier for the hour-plus drive to Kingsford Smith, Sydney International, named after Sir Charles of that name, the Australian pioneer aviator. Ray was at first confused over talk of Mascot until realising that this is the Sydney-dweller's usual name for the airport.

Even over breakfast, Des manages to raise several contentious subjects with his accustomed individual and challenging perspective, making his points with gestures and by roaming the kitchen area whilst simultaneously dealing with coffee and toast. At this hour, Ray is content to listen, offering little except monosyllabic replies and what he hopes are intelligent expressions. Des's adrenalin is up and running. Ray's isn't.

The only topic that Ray can recall when Des has sped off along the street is the one about the apparent intelligence of the average member of society. To précis Des's argument, not too many people can in reality be as brainless and stupid as they manage to behave, and if they can't be bothered to use the intelligence they've got to better themselves, stuff 'em. Those who don't try should be exiled to an island and left to fend for themselves.

Have a nice day, Des.

At a point that feels to be soon after Des's departure, but actually is much later, Ray is finally forced to snap into intelligent mode. The phone rings, and having earlier cleared with his hosts that he should answer calls, as important ones are possible, he hears the voice of someone called Edward, whom he apparently knows slightly. Ray is grateful that this mystery Edward quickly identifies himself as Gerald Logan's agent, speaking from New York. Beyond shaking hands a couple of times many years ago, they are not really acquainted.

"Sorry to ring so early. Gerald asked me to call. He tells me that you have an interesting film script . . "

–ooOoo–

Des is still at his pre-light when Ray gets back from his solo sightseeing. Annie is sitting alone reading in what they call the lookout room.

"Hiya.   There's a message for you from England, someone called

339

Richard; said to call as soon you can." Something in his stomach drops ten feet. Ogre! Richard is looking after the dog. He would never call Australia unless something was wrong. Annie gets up and finds the post-it note. She's helpfully added the dialling code for the UK.

"Do you want a tea?"

"Please, Annie." She heads to the kitchen, tactfully leaving him to it. She'd heard something in Richard's voice.

Dialling seems to take an age.

"Rich, it's Ray. How are you, mate?"

"I'm fine, I'm fine, thanks." Ray hardly dares say it and almost knows the answer already.

"How's the Ogre?"

"Well that's it, that's why I called you. I don't know how to tell you this but – he's dead, mate. When I came down this morning he was stretched out. He must have been gone a few hours. He's been a bit quiet this last week. Jane said she thought he was missing his Dad a few days ago, but we had no idea it was serious – perhaps he thought you weren't coming back."

Ray takes a long time before he can actually speak.

"I told him Rich, I told him over and over that I'd be back. I told him the date, the day, the number of nights I'd be gone, everything." Ray has trouble in getting the words out. "We always did."

"I know. I know, and **I** did. I kept saying to him that his Dad would be home in a few days." He pauses. "I should tell you that Eve knows. I got hold of her about an hour ago, when I couldn't reach you. She's devastated of course. She said she'd call you later. She said to say not to worry; that it's not your fault – she knows you would have told him that you weren't leaving him. She thinks that perhaps sometime in the past, before you had him, when he was with that family that couldn't cope, he was told lies, and that perhaps because of that after a month he'd stopped believing you." There is another long interruption before Ray can make words again.

"Where is he?"

"He's still here. The vet's coming later this morning to pick him up. They asked, will you want to see him, when you get back?"

"No. No, I couldn't. I don't . . . Just let them do what they need to do. I'm so sorry this has happened to you, in your house. You don't need all this."

"Listen, we've always loved having him. Normally he was the one cheering us up. It's never been the other way round till now. We're as sad as you must be, but don't worry about us. Go and have a brandy – it must be about that time of day there – and think of the good times."

"No shortage of those. Oh Rich, I do want to see him. Will you ask them to hold him for me? I've got to go. I can't speak. Thank you. Thank you. I'll see you in a couple of days, or whenever it is. Bye."

E has taught him that we aren't the owners of our animals, especially our dogs, and that really, we are theirs. That they don't exist to bolster our image or make us feel better about ourselves. We're there to make their lives happy, and if we manage that, when they die we've done a good job by them and we shouldn't be unduly sad. That's the theory, but he always knew the last bit wouldn't work when it came to it.

All the time that Ray has been writing *One-Zero-Three* and living in the shadow of intolerable sadness, sometimes feeling that he alone has been carrying the hopes of 560 tragic lost souls, he's coped, in the way that professionals do, by keeping it shut in a separate compartment, even if Eve would say that he hasn't. When E herself left for California on an open-ended ticket, not a tear was shed, however empty he felt. Now, for the Ogre, everything comes pouring out . . . in reality for all of them.

–ooOoo–

An hour later, he emerges from the guest bedroom. He looks awful. He'd told Annie the news before taking his tea and disappearing with his sorrow. Now Des is back and they both look at him with concern and sympathy. Ray does his best at a smile.

"I'm taking you to dinner," he says "except I'm not driving because I expect to get very, very pissed."

–ooOoo–

341

59 " . . Of giving your heart to a dog to tear. "

Ray cannot believe that he is sitting on a jump-seat in an Airbus A340 cockpit as the flight approaches the English Channel. All the rules put in place following 9/11 should render his present location impossible. Fortunately there are still captains like the independent individual occupying the left-hand seat immediately in front of him who reserve to themselves the right to substitute common-sense for blind obedience. As Chris Parlour said yesterday evening, about twenty-four hours ago now, at the street restaurant in Singapore, after he'd issued the invitation:

"What is the purpose of the rules? To keep terrorists off my flight deck. Are you a terrorist? No. Then the rule is not appropriate – doesn't apply. I don't see why we all have to stop doing perfectly reasonable things that we want to when there is not the slightest thing – no advantage to be gained by anybody, just frustration and inconvenience. If we can't carry on living and doing normal things just taking sensible precautions, the buggers have won. Anyway," he grumbled, "we're all getting more and more like the old Soviets – regulations for everything and obeying them becomes a religion, even when no one can remember what they were designed for."

He had gone on to say that he couldn't be seen to be accepting requests for cockpit visits from random punters, as was the custom in the old days, but while he remained a captain he would continue to invite occasional people like Ray that he could see were transparently bona fide. Ray wondered if the fleet manager might have a view on that, but naturally kept his thoughts to himself.

What he offered instead was that the same applied to the governments making all these rules. Governments, he'd argued, exist at the discretion of nations' inhabitants as their agents and servants and not, as all too many involved in them seem to assume, rightful rulers. Captain Parlour had warmed to that thought, adding that the only exception, the only place where absolute power should be exercised was, in his view, the cockpit – specifically his. This had raised laughs from all the licensed pilots at the table, who knew that the modern mantra was Cockpit Resource Management which encouraged collaborative rather than hierarchical conduct on the flight deck. The aim was to prevent co-pilots feeling inhibited from questioning the decisions of the captain, especially if they were bad decisions. Certainly the senior aviator had a point: the two human beings at the front of a passenger aircraft wield the power of life and death throughout every flight in a manner that its immediacy makes unique.

Austin had arranged the Singapore meal not at all with the possibility of the present outcome in mind, but rather because he'd found on the outbound trip that Parlour had a huge number of hours in the dim and distant past as a flight engineer on the Classic 747, of which *Maid of the Seas* had been a very early example. The friends' meeting-up on Ray's journey back had been long planned, but here was a bonus. If anyone could answer some of Ray's few remaining technical questions – things he, Austin, couldn't himself definitively answer, about the 747 emergency lighting, for example – he'd realised it would be the genial and approachable Chris Parlour.

In every respect, the evening could be counted a great success, helped by the attendance of a few of the cabin staff, inevitably adding glamour and good humour. Austin, Parlour and Ray had met in a quiet corner of the hotel bar an hour before the others had come down and Ray had set out his stall. At the mention of the Iranian Airbus, Parlour had thrown in a bombshell of an anecdote. He related that after the shootdown, British Airways, his employer at the time, not surprisingly instructed crews to maintain, without fail, simultaneous monitoring of one-two-one-decimal five, the international distress frequency, when using airfields in the Gulf.

"Of course the extra task was dumped on the Flight Engineer, so I'd be listening to that as well as Approach and Tower, while I was reading the checklist, and monitoring the flight and my panel – so plenty to do. This one night we were over the sea on the ILS into One-Two Left at Dubai when I picked up a call on one-two-one-five from that goddamned ship of fools. The *Vincennes* was still out there, after everything she'd done, looking for more trouble, now hanging about under the runway extended centreline. Her radio was demanding the aircraft closing with them, that was **us**, to identify itself and change course. Failure to comply could incur the use of lethal force. My response was to tell them to look up in the sky where they would see a BA 747 with a big British flag on its illuminated tail. I also suggested they get a copy of the current BA timetable and that they should take it and play (I didn't put it so nicely) somewhere other than final approach for Dubai International. The thing is that those aggressive cretins might just have done the same thing to us as they did to Iran 655 if I hadn't been on frequency. I suppose they would have got more combat ribbons if they had." He'd shaken his head and repeated the word 'combat' with clearly heartfelt contempt.

Parlour proved to have the definitive answer on the 747's emergency interior lights. Even on the early 100-series ships like N739PA there were quite a number, he confirmed, positioned at each door, aisle and cross-aisle and they had batteries that automatically charged during flight. They would illuminate as soon as the main electrics failed. Mostly they would have worked, while the mouldings they were fixed to remained in place, which would of course not have been long. For that limited span of seconds there would have been some degree of clarity to the confusion. The director of photography will have his solution: no one else had theirs.

Before the party broke up at the end of the evening, the grey-haired four-ringer had asked if Ray had any sort of appropriate ID badge he could wear on board. He did; in his wallet – one that he uses when passing through a regional airport like Bournemouth when clearing the aircraft through customs. Airport security staff can just occasionally be somewhat reluctant to allow transiting light aircraft pilots and passengers back to their aircraft, and a badge generally helps. He'd put it on in the Changi departure lounge and it was one of the flight attendants from the meal who had, at an appropriate point during the flight, come to find him and whisper the captain's compliments and would Captain Scriver like to follow her? Captain Scriver certainly would.

In the right-hand seat, Austin is flying this sector of the non-stop. In a few minutes it will get very busy and he won't be able to turn round, as he has on an off throughout the last couple of hours, to point out features on the array of colourful information display screens that are the most striking elements in the pilots' panel. As they approach Heathrow, Ray will feel fortunate just to watch and marvel, as he has on every occasion that he's been allowed to sit in on a jet approach. This will be his first one in an Airbus, with a 'glass' cockpit and flown with small sidesticks instead of the traditional yokes on columns. For Austin, having his old friend behind him in the cockpit is going to put the pressure on for a tidy approach and landing; it will be something not too far short of having a line-check captain watching over his shoulder.

Ray is glad to be getting home and he's terrified of getting home. There is no better way than this of taking his mind off the next few hours and days.

–ooOoo–

"I have to explain that Ogre unfortunately won't look as you might be expecting. Because they have to be frozen, they're obviously cold and stiff and the coat can be icy and matted."

The vet has a sympathetic manner. Ray thinks that she looks little more than schoolgirl age. How time passes. Thinking back, he'll notice she has carefully avoided emotion-triggering words like corpse and body and dead, and be grateful.

"That'll be in character, then. He preferred to be scruffy."

He is being brave; trying to be light and matter-of-fact, but for him this will be as near as he will ever come to viewing a dead son.

The green-overalled figure leads him into the treatment room and steps to one side. On the high table four thin legs issue from what seems to be an impossibly small pile of clammy fur. He steps towards it. He remembers from the chaotic attempts at bathing him that underneath the bouffant coat, the Ogre, although a large dog, has a much smaller body than would be expected. It's as though he's been in water; something he resolutely avoided in life, and has then lain down and gone to sleep outdoors in a frost while still wet through. At the mouth, there is a slight baring of the teeth, giving something of a disturbed look that belies the typical sleeping pose that the dog is otherwise in. Ray wants to touch the head. Actually he doesn't but feels he has to. He can't bring himself to do it with one hand and has to use two, cupping the grey muzzle. He finds it impossibly hard and cold and moves up the face to find those so-expressive ears. They're flat and stiff and icy. Despite much of the hair on his head being stuck down, Ogre still retains a trace of his normal look. Even in death he has kept the air of a dissolute canine version of Rod Stewart.

Ray cradles the beloved head for a long moment and then it is done – enough. There is nothing here. Corpses without life and spirit are just chemicals. He's believed that for years and hadn't viewed the bodies of either of his parents for that reason. He doesn't subscribe to closure because the spirits are always with us. He'd thought he needed to do this today, but he was probably wrong. This is not a memory that he wants. He turns to the young veterinarian.

"He's gone. Thank you. Thanks for all you've done."

He takes one final look. This is now ceremony – ritual. He can't wait to get out of the building. He has one more thought though and turns back in the doorway.

"Did you come to any conclusions about what might have caused it? I mean, he was getting on a bit but he was very fit."

"No. There was nothing obvious. Do you want us to try?" she replies, searching his face. He already knows his decision.

"No. We'll let him be. I think I've an idea what it was."

–ooOoo–

345

With his sad task accomplished, Ray knows that his first priority should be to knuckle down to the rewrite. Without concentrating overmuch on the question, he's quietly come to the conclusion that Gerald's main critique is valid, and needs to be implemented come what may. But there are all manner of factors conspiring to prevent his settling down to work in the untidy upstairs office, not least the prospect of meeting Jack's brother. Ray rationalises that if he completes or near-completes his revisions and then meets the former spy, and through him learns something that cries out to be incorporated in the script, he'll be wasting time; doing work twice. It would be much better, he thinks, to hear what the man has to say first. Eve often accuses her husband of procrastination. She may be to some extent right. It tends to come with the job.

There are other matters to attend to. Edward Argent's call to Sydney had, like so many experiences recently, held a mixture of promise and disappointment. The agent had dropped the bad news first. Gerald had made some phone calls, asking acquaintances about Ralph Hollingsworth. The impressions he'd picked up through the grapevine suggested that Hollingsworth Junior might have a drug habit. There had been a third, ultra low-budget movie, as yet unreleased and probably unlikely to be; word was that the producer and the director had made one of their priorities on location the taking of cocaine with one or more of the actors, with a predictable effect on the rate and quality of the work. As all the crew were working on deferred payments, several key technicians were thought to have walked in disgust, adding to the overruns. Argent had made his own enquiries, and though no one was saying it in black and white, there had to be some degree of truth in what Gerald had learnt. One person who hadn't so far heard about it, a reliable source had stated with complete conviction, was DB.

"Obviously, Gerald was keen that you shouldn't get into any sort of arrangement with Ralph, without knowing about this." Ray was naturally grateful to receive the tip-off and said so. What Argent revealed next, however, had only added to his confusion about next moves.

"Reading between the lines, I think Gerald's quite interested in directing your script. I think warning you off Hollingsworth Junior may not be entirely without some personal motive."

Thinking about it later, Edward's suggestion seemed to be somewhat indiscreet, unless Gerald was having his position conveyed obliquely, keeping his option alive or sending a degree of encouragement without commitment. At the time though Ray took it at face value and couldn't see the question to ask.

"What would you do, in my position?" was all he could come up with. It wasn't a bad alternative, as it happened.

"Let your agent do the worrying."

"I haven't had one for five years." Jeremy had died young and unexpectedly. Indecision and, yes, some procrastination had ensued.

"I know. That's why I said it. I think you need to get one again."

Which is how Ray comes to have an Qantas phone message slip as his second scrap of paper with a name and telephone number scrawled on it, in the depths of his wallet, awaiting attention. Argent is recommending a young former colleague, who has recently set up on his own in London.

"How young?" Ray had asked.

"Twenty-eight."

"And no coke habit?"

"No coke habit."

"Then I'll call him."

—ooOoo—

For the third or fourth time there has been no reply from the number on the piece of paper written in the stylish handwriting. Rather to his own surprise, Ray has spoken to the name spelt on the more carelessly-written note, and a meeting has been arranged. Perhaps in a few days he will once again have what some call 'representation'. It can't come a moment too soon: he is a hopeless negotiator and the thought of juggling his own interests with those of the directors, producers and actors who are starting to circle round his film makes him feel way out of his depth. Too late! As he presses the clear button, the handset rings out in his hand. The tone is someone's computerised approximation of *Pachelbel's Canon*. He's got to find time to change these settings!

It's Ralph, now also back in the UK.

"I need to tell you that Arran Samson is out. I just got hold of him, a few minutes ago."

"He give any reason?"

"Yeah, it's odd. He implied that it's a bit too dark for him, which is a bizarre reason to give when you think of some of the films he's been in."

"So what does he want in a script about mass murder, loss and perfidy; the cast and chorus of *The Most Happy Fella*?"

"I spoke to Dad, sorry – DB, and he wonders whether the man's gotten a bit close to some people in politics out there – rumour is he's socialising with one or two senators and congressmen recently. Odd that someone known for taking many a swing at the establishment should find himself courted by it, and he's apparently has taken to it. I didn't know that much till I rang an American buddy just now."

Ray wants to say three things. One is: 'You're English, so why use that awful word 'gotten' which we expelled from English usage aeons ago on the grounds that it sounded so ugly. Two, why on earth did DB show this sensitive script to someone who seems to be changing sides? The third thing of course is: 'Are you a coke-head?'

What he actually says is rather different:

"Don't be worried about referring to DB as Dad. It's not a crime to be related to someone."

"Oh no, right. Thanks. Sometimes it just slips out."

"Don't think about it. I will know who you mean."

Ralph is keen to talk about other players to whom *One-Zero-Three* might be shown. He starts to list some directors and actors that he would like Ray to think about. Ray has to tell him that he doesn't want anyone new seeing the screenplay until the rewrite is complete. His justification is reasonable enough. Strengthening the part of lawyer, Jane Maddox, will promote that part to first female lead and should interest an A-lister. The change cannot help but give that of first male lead, Daniel Weiss, considerably more range and appeal too, but it must reduce the size of the rôle of Brad, Daniel's friend. Any prospective actor reading the existing version of the script with a view to playing Brad is going to be somewhat disappointed by the new draft that's in the pipeline. The part will drift from second lead to supporting and may no longer attract an actor big enough to form part of the package; someone 'bankable'. Like most things in films, it's a matter of swings and roundabouts.

None of this is the real reason that Ray wants Ralph to hold his fire. He doesn't want the enthusiastic producer to be any further involved until it's clear whether or not his reputation is about to be shot to pieces. It seems likely that it is, whether he is guilty or not. People tend to think in terms of 'no smoke without fire'. If the rumours are unfounded it will be a tragedy for the youngster of course, but not one that can be allowed to take the *One-Zero-Three* project and Ray down with it.

–ooOoo–

60   A Week is a Long Time in Polemics

The call from Ralph has convinced Ray that there is real urgency now over the rewrite. As if to underscore the decision, the prospective agent's secretary shortly calls back with the news that her boss has gone down with summer flu and the meeting will not now be this week. That means no trip to London. Jack's brother's mobile continues to go unanswered, which equally means no assignation at some perhaps exotic, James Bond-like location, or more likely Glasgow.

In desperation Ray has even called Dick, on the excuse that the ex-detective hasn't yet seen the screenplay in any version, to try and put off the inevitable start with a day excursion to the Cheshire-Derbyshire border, but the Leighs' phone is another that just rings and rings. Eve's conclusion in such circumstances would be that these are signs that he is meant to stay where he is – and so he does.

Against his every inclination to get away from the leaden atmosphere, he settles down and concentrates, and within a few hours is magically changed and totally engrossed. Soon the only time that he notices the quietness of the house is when he stops, and that encourages him not to. He probably achieves more in four days than at any time in the whole *One-Zero-Three* writing process. The adrenalin is flowing; he is totally in the zone. Despite the travelling he's done and probably not yet really recovered from, he's able to put in long hours, fully alert without feeling remotely tired, which explains why at the end of a long session, he's practising instrument flying in the small hours of Friday morning when the mysterious woman calls.

–ooOoo–

After the unsettling conversation he goes to his bed, where inevitably he finds sleep highly unlikely. He thinks through her angry comments maybe a dozen times, his mind and body both turning over and over, unable to get comfortable. By chance, trying to fathom how this woman has found him finally does the trick.

He begins trying to tick off and list in his head all the people who have seen the screenplay document. Of course there are more of them than he has been imagining. But counting is a cert. He's never found that it works with sheep, but visualising a list of identifiables, like holidays, or countries visited, or girlfriends' names will generally send him off before he's reached ten. Fortunately he doesn't start to take into account people who've seen the work at one remove, and those who might just have been told of the existence of it. If he begins to wade into consideration of those categories, anxiety will very likely dictate that he'll not be getting any sleep tonight at all.

—ooOoo—

The timing is nothing short of uncanny.

Despite the late night and the troubling American woman, Ray makes an unaccustomed early start. There is of course no mid-morning dog-walking to interrupt. On the Date Modified information panel referring to the folder titled *One-Zero-Three - Version G* (for Gerald) on the Documents page, the time segment reads *12:58* as Ray stretches, stands up and goes down the steep stairs to make a coffee. The revised draft is complete! By the time he has come back up with his mug, there is an e-mail. The interval has been not much more than three minutes.

> Dear Ray Scriver,
>
> I hope you will excuse the fact that I'm perhaps not really supposed to know about this, but I can't contain myself and wouldn't want to maybe miss an opportunity by being cautious. I hear you have an exciting screenplay about a subject that interests me keenly. Is there any chance we could discuss it at some time convenient? I'm pretty free at the moment. I'm based in Bucks but more than happy to meet somewhere down your way.
>
> Look forward to hearing back,
>
> James Metz.

Ray assumes this message is due to networking by Ralph, but given the number of names on the wider list that he could have used to get to sleep last night, this may not be a correct deduction. He hasn't actually given other directors for *One-Zero-Three* much thought, having remained emotionally locked-on to the notion of Gerald, but if he had made a shortlist, he realises that the name Metz would certainly have been on it. With a body of work going back some fifteen years, James Metz has successfully tackled any number of genres, the common thread being that his work always brings a fresh approach and a believable tone. It might be contemporary crime drama; it might be an historical farce, but if Metz puts it on screen, you tend to think that you are seeing something very much based on the truth.

His First World War film, *Pass It Down the Line,* is profoundly moving and offers a powerful indictment of inadequate and callous decision-making, while his black comedy about the rise of materialism in the fifties and sixties, *But You're Having None of Mine,* is a genuine social document underneath the abundant laughs.

There are two question marks in Ray's mind. One is that though Metz's pictures are liked by the critics and he enjoys a loyal fan-base, he has yet to have a major box-office success. Probably not dissociated from this is the fact that he, like many directors, has a 'repertory company' of actors that he tends to work with on a recurring basis. While this in itself is no bad thing, it tends to mean that there are rarely star names in Metz movies. And like it or not, stars do put bums on seats.

Then again, pictures without stars are cheaper to make and can involve a lot less hassle and waste. It's those swings and roundabouts again. And such films can become popular and even make money at the ticket-booth. Naturally he will be meeting James Metz at an early opportunity. He decides to e-mail back later on, so as not to appear instantly available.

He sets up his computer to print some copies – one for himself; one for Metz; he'd better send one to Gerald via Edward Argent's London office, and a couple of spares. He's got to risk the post now, even if he still won't send any mention of *One-Zero-Three* by e-mail. He's checked and re-checked the revised scenes, of which there are plenty, on the computer, but he still has to read the dialogue out loud to make sure it works. He also knows there will be more minor changes to make, once he sees the words transferred to the printed page. But it's tidy enough to go to Metz or any other director; after all, the dialogue remains subject to revision right up until the moment of shooting, and even then the final version entirely depends on how accurately actors remember their lines. Ray has watched some noted thespians consistently blunt sharp dialogue by paraphrase, and others who through the same process breathe apparent meaning into drivel.

Satisfied with a productive morning's work and noticing that the weather has become quite enticing, Ray leaves the printer whirring and takes himself for a walk.

It doesn't take many minutes from leaving the hamlet for Ray to realise that without the Ogre, however beautiful the day, every step he takes is torture. Wherever he looks he sees an unfinished, unbalanced frame. The big dog used to appear somewhere in every one of these scenes and without him, the sequence means nothing. The transition from wood to ridge, normally glorious, is merely painful. He turns on his heel and sets off back. He can't do this. If nothing changes, he runs a high risk, he thinks, of becoming overweight and round-shouldered, probably in a short timescale.

—ooOoo—

Ray arrives early at the Bibury Court and having parked the Saab, wanders across the wide lawn and for a while watches the trout lurking in the clear water of the River Coln. He makes his way back, finds the bar and orders a large tomato juice with the trimmings. Rather than settling, he finds a place to stand and view the drive and sweep of parking area. Bang on time an Aston Martin growls across the gravel and a tanned and well-groomed Metz steps out of its wide, heavy door. Then the one on the passenger side opens. Reflections had masked the presence of a second occupant. An elegant and well-dressed woman, probably a few years younger, joins the director and, tellingly, makes minor adjustments to his hair with her hand and flicks his jacket's shoulders and lapels before they set off towards the door.

Damn! Metz could only have had the script just over a day before telephoning to arrange the meeting. He'd been so enthusiastic and impatient to see it that he'd sent a motor-cycle courier to the cottage to pick up the copy. Ray now wishes that he had spent a little of the intervening time doing some more intense research on the man. He was expecting him to come alone and now he's arrived with a companion whom Ray might be expected to recognise and doesn't. She could be an actress or someone in the business whose career he should know about, and if she is he'll be left with the proverbial egg-on-face.

It's rather bad form of the director to spring someone on him at this first meeting, he thinks. All Ray had done Metz-wise was indulge in an hour of speculation as to who in his regular troupe of actors might be considered for *One-Zero-Three*. Versatile they all might be, but Ray could see no obvious castings.

He goes outside to meet the couple, rather grandly, he feels, as if he is the owner of this spectacular Cotswold manor house, or at least as if he lunches here three times a week. He enjoys the moment. Metz introduces the woman as 'Karin Clements, my producer.'

"I'm sorry to inflict her on you without notice, but she became free just as I was leaving, and it was such a lovely day for a drive that I couldn't not bring her."

Well, that was disarmingly done, thinks Ray, and decides that on first impressions they are both quite pleasant.

As ever, it's small-talk about the respective journeys and where exactly they all live that's allowed to fill the time while the drinks are sorted and until the lunch orders are taken. Metz can't wait to get going. He is really excited, he says.

"I have to say that Karin is less taken with the subject, because she's been rather hoping that I'm going to do something musical for the next picture."

–ooOoo–

By the time they are in the conservatory restaurant, tucking into their starters, all three of them really know, despite the director's earnest questions and the writer's comprehensive answers, and however many more discussions may follow in the coming weeks, that the next James Metz film will have musical content, and that they're not talking Parry, or Elgar, or Show of Hands or *Little Town of Bethlehem.*

–ooOoo–

61   Timers, Gentlemen? Please!

The lunch conversation, when Ray thinks about it later in the day, tended to suggest that Metz, like his producer, has a thematic idea in mind for his next project.   He appears to have become intrigued by forensics programmes like *Silent Witness* and the American *Crime Scene* series. If he wants to make a movie about old-fashioned dogged police work assisted by clear-thinking, detached scientists, it's a mystery why, having read Ray's pages, he bothered to make the journey to the Cotswolds. If the Lockerbie trial had been a pantomime (something that, of course, numerous commentators feel it was), the scientific investigators would have been be the recipients of many of the audience's boos. The attitude the writer has taken to their determinations and their evidence at Camp Zeist very much follows on from Dick's instant and economical summing-up when Ray had first mentioned the subject.

"Forensics?" he'd said. "I don't believe a word of the forensics."

Nor did almost anybody who troubled to look behind the headlines.

Firstly, people found the apparent survival of just one piece of circuit board attributable to the bomb's timing device to be strange, especially as it was a fragment that lent itself to identification rather more readily than almost any other segment might have done. The circumstances of its discovery added to the sense of disbelief, in that it was reportedly found at a late date hidden in a piece of shirt, which had originally been recorded as 'cloth' – the label at some point changed by a police officer, in a non-approved fashion, to read 'debris'. There were so many accounts given at different times as to which investigator had made the discovery, and when, and at what point it had been linked to a specific model of timer, the MST-13, that suspicion as to the veracity of any statement about this now crucial piece of evidence could only intensify to the level of general disbelief and rejection. Yet this tiny shard of material formed one of the main planks of the prosecution case, being one of several scraps of highly dubious physical 'evidence' that, even if they were genuine, could only be thought of as connecting the accused to the crime with the help of an enormous leap of faith; a degree of surmise and speculation that the wildest of conspiracy theorists would hesitate to accept.

The trial judges embraced those unproved and inconclusive connections in reaching their verdict, as well as wholly accepting the authenticity of the mysteriously-found fragment. This was unfortunate and surprising for many reasons. The defence had been able to suggest that the prosecution's behaviour had not been above question on a number of matters. One of them, crucially, was that there was much evidence available to show that the leaders of the forensic probe had a nasty history of influencing important trials in an adverse fashion, by presenting unsound testimony.

Responsibility for the forensic investigation into major terrorist explosions in the UK was in 1988 handled by a section of the Royal Armaments Research and Development Establishment (RARDE), a Ministry of Defence organisation that would later become the Defence Research Establishment and, by the time of the Camp Zeist trial, the Defence Evaluation and Research Agency (DERA). Two years after Lockerbie, but with nine to go before its criminal proceedings, Appeal Court judges in respect of another terrorist case, the conviction of Judith Ward, would say of RARDE's witnesses: 'Forensic scientists employed by the government may come to see their function as helping the police. They may lose their objectivity.' They determined that the head of the laboratory, Douglas Higgs and his senior colleagues suppressed test evidence, 'took the law into their own hands' and 'knowingly placed a false and distorted picture before the jury'.

Higgs and his successor, Dr Thomas Hayes, who would later head the Lockerbie Forensic Team, were involved in another miscarriage of justice involving the Maguire Seven. The only evidence offered in the case was forensic and an independent inquiry eventually determined it to be severely discredited, only after the unfortunate defendants had all served long prison sentences. Hayes and his eventual successor-in-turn, Allen Feraday, went on to give biased testimony in the prosecution following the Hyde Park bombing, and Feraday did the same in another terrorist case in 1982, both of which were overturned on appeal, with heavy criticism of RARDE input. In 1988 Feraday's evidence at the inquest of a three-man IRA team shot dead in Gibraltar by the SAS helped to obtain the 'lawfully killed' verdict that the Thatcher government wanted, despite some of his key assertions on remote detonation betraying an elementary misunderstanding of the technicalities, according to experts.

Doctor Hayes was not the only chief forensic explosives examiner credited with having made the vital identification of the piece of Lockerbie circuit board. His counterpart at the FBI, Thomas Thurman confusingly made the same claim on American network television, becoming ABC's person of the week in the process. But Thurman suffered from the same habit as his British counterparts and left the FBI after complaints that he regularly revised reports written by scientists in his unit, changing emphasis and sometimes meaning, usually with the result of strengthening a case for the prosecution.

Discussing these events would see Dick holding up his hands in despair and frustration. He had seen too many miscarriages of justice in his time to find this anything other than deeply depressing. His experience had been, as far as he was aware, of guilty parties going free, which he hated. But evidence being manipulated to convict the innocent was many times more repugnant in his book. Ray became aware that Dick was all-too-conscious that it wasn't just the scientific investigators who had subverted justice; case detectives in the forces involved in the Maguire Seven and the associated Guildford Four miscarriages had been guilty of the type of activities that everyone is taught to believe happen in other, less enlightened, countries. The man felt that these people had shamed his profession.

For many years the 'fitting-up' of criminals, whereby the CID would plant evidence or invent confessions to convict habitual criminals was an abuse, but an abuse that was tolerated by the few who knew about it. It was part of the game: criminals didn't like it, but it came with the territory. There was a degree of justice involved in convicting people who were known to be guilty of strings of offences that couldn't be laid at their door in court. The danger of the practice is exactly the one that Ray and Dick see in the growth of the Secret World: dishonesty becomes the norm. Some in the CID began to plant and 'verbal' people they **thought** were guilty, instead of those they **knew** deserved to go down. They'd lost the plot. They'd forgotten what they were there for. Dick thinks that likewise most people who descend into the Secret World soon lose a proper sense of proportion and direction: their moral compass can become deflected.

By the time their meetings had got as far as consideration of the forensics, Dick was somewhat more tuned-in to what Ray was trying to accomplish, and he was led to rephrase the question that he had raised the very first time they'd met.

"I still can't see how on earth you'll make all this complexity understandable for the average cinema-goer," he'd said, shaking his head.

Ray had admitted that it was a tough job, but outlined the bones of his strategy. He didn't want to be pressed too far as the detail was still evolving in his mind at the time, so he ducked the question somewhat by pointing out that if the 'discovery' and apparent identification of the single piece of timer seemed a hard story to get across, the extraordinary tale of the man whose company probably made the switch in question represented even more of a challenge. When you added to the equation the fact that both Ray and Dick had very strong doubts that this wholly unsuitable piece of apparatus was actually used in the radio bomb at all, the writer's task at the time had assumed Himalayan proportions.

He was looking forward to showing the old sleuth how he'd coped.

—ooOoo—

The probable manufacturer of the possible timer had links to Libya, and to defendant al-Megrahi; facts that had undoubted appeal for the investigation when it was attempting to put together a case against two sacrificial Libyans. The fact that one of the partners in the Swiss firm of Meister and Bollier, trading as Mebo, seemed at times to be doing his utmost to cast doubts on the accuseds' guilt did nothing to deter the prosecution. It would not really be until the trial that the story – although it could never be described as the full story – emerged. The partner in question was one Edwin Bollier and everything about him and his statements tended to require clarification, which was generally not forthcoming.

The basic facts about the MST-13 timer at first seemed very straightforward. Only twenty had been made and they had all been delivered in 1985 to the JSO, the Jamahirya Security Organisation – the Libyan intelligence service. Later the certainty was diluted when it was revealed that Mebo supplied a small batch of prototypes to the Stasi, the secret police of East Germany. That country was, like Libya, an active supporter of terrorist groups internationally, including the PLFP-GC. Later still, Bollier revealed that a number of burglaries had taken place at his firm's Zurich factory, clearly using skeleton keys, during which the only apparent missing items were a few unused MST-13 circuit boards and some technical diagrams.

Later still, it became apparent that a firm in Florida, Mathews and Associates, who manufactured electronic equipment for a client list that included the CIA, may have made a very similar, even a replica, timer. This last fact was not revealed at the trial, however, as the Crown seemed casual to the point of reluctance about investigating this information or passing it to the defence. In any event, the CIA had had in its possession, since 1986, an example of an MST-13 recovered from Togo, West Africa. Also, in early 1988, similar time-switches had been found in the luggage of two Libyan agents arrested in nearby Senegal. According to evidence from CIA officers at the trial, they were inspected by both themselves and the FBI, but there was some vagueness about the date and the fate of these seized MST-13s.

Extraordinarily, Bollier, despite spending many hours with the Scottish police, was not allowed to see the found fragment; only, eventually, a photographic blow-up. Perhaps they had learnt enough to decide to treat him with caution by this time; but more likely they had been told that his assessment might not help the case-building. The image, though, had been sufficiently revealing to persuade him to go public with his conviction that the piece was not from the Libyan batch, which were machine-cut boards, but from one of the prototypes supplied to the Stasi. These were hand-made with rougher edges and other visible detail differences. But already it was possible to cherry-pick Bollier's statements, choosing according the version of the truth that you wanted people to believe.

Summing up the case for the defence in respect of al-Megrahi, William Taylor QC would later describe the Swiss businessman as: 'an illegitimate arms dealer with morals to match'. The court had by then heard a great deal of evidence about Bollier's conflicting statements and loyalties. He had been covertly supplying agencies of the East German government with prohibited exports since the 1960s, and was considered to be an asset of the Stasi and assigned a cover name, 'Rubin' and a handler. He also supplied directly to terrorist groups including the IRA and significantly the PLFP-GC. The Stasi believed him to be a double agent for the CIA, such was the apparent ease with which he could procure and ship banned sensitive items. Whether that was true or not he had, astonishingly, contacted that organisation by letter a mere fifteen days after Lockerbie, citing Libya as responsible.

It would be many months before the name of that country would figure in any leaks or statements as a suspect. The identification of the fortuitously 'discovered' single timer fragment was always represented as a long and patient task; only at the trial it was revealed that the CIA had, just days after the crash, been told, in effect: 'I make the MST-13, and have sold them to Libya. The bomb timer could be one of mine'. At the very least the investigators should have been put especially on the alert for pieces of MST-13. As Dick says: 'Maybe they were. They certainly did find one, at some point that's rather vague, when they needed to. My question is **where** they found it. I don't believe it was in that piece of shirt, and why should it have been the only fragment to survive? It would take a lot to convince me that it wasn't fabricated evidence – planted.'

Bollier said that he wrote his letter under threat from a mysterious unknown agent who appeared at Mebo's Zurich premises nine days after the disaster. Many thought this was a cover story and that his motive was to get on the CIA payroll, now that his sources of income from Eastern Europe might be drying up under the spread of glasnost. Certainly, having pointed the finger at Libya, he and his partner, two years on, made a blatant approach to that country's Minister of Communications offering to 'discover' another recipient, in Beirut, of a consignment of MST-13s, so potentially taking the heat off the Gaddafi regime. This may have been a dangerously self-incriminating move and wasn't proceeded with, but certainly Bollier had at least some legal expenses met by the accused Libyans' lawyers.

Another assessment of the man came in his cross-examination by Lamin Fhimah's counsel, Richard Keen QC, who pointedly alluded to scenes from the post-war black market classic *The Third Man* as a means of ridiculing some of the arms dealer's evidence. But however contradictory and water-muddying Bollier's association with the Lockerbie saga might be, his activities, both true and fantasized, provide some excellent scenes for the screenplay, with Daniel Weiss and Jane and sometimes Brad going over the events and picking his stories apart in commentary while the cloak-and-dagger events are portrayed.

As an example of how excerpts from his story provide welcome colour in terms of action but probably the reverse of clarity in terms of plot, there is no better than the coverage of a trip to Libya which Bollier says was undertaken literally a matter of hours before the death of Flight 103.

Because of the complexity of the whole script, Ray has followed an unusual, maybe unique practice of putting an-as-accurate-as-possible date on all the scene headings in the film. Year headings are relatively common, but he has never himself encountered months and days. Also, because the action is obliged to jump so much backwards and forwards in time, in an attempt to bring logic to the storytelling he has made use of screen devices as used in TV sports coverage to go to replay from 'live' and back again. Flashback action has been denoted by many devices over the years: a long-popular and rather over-used example was to break up the picture with ripples like the surface of a pond. The devices Ray has in mind are a tad more dynamic.

```
EXT MAIN ROAD - ENGLAND              DAY   (22 DEC 1993)

DANIEL'S car speeds through curves on a spectacular
section of road.

                                              Cut to:


INT DANIEL'S CAR                     DAY   (22 DEC 1993)

DANIEL drives alone.  The carphone rings.  He lifts the
handset.

                                              Cut to:
```

INT JANE'S OFFICE   DAY (22 DEC 1993)

JANE, on phone.

> JANE (excited)
>
> It's me. Brad just called. Get a copy of today's
> Guardian! Apparently there was a thing that we all
> missed on BBC Radio last night with the Swiss guy,
> Bollier, whose company supposedly made the timer
> for the bomb. Well you know the story **was** that all
> of that particular type had gone to Libya but last
> night he said that a few were delivered to the East
> German Stasi, which means they could easily have
> gone on to Jibril and co.
>
> Anyway Brad says that the Guardian piece – I
> haven't seen it yet but I've sent out for it – he
> reckons they're still saying it's Libya because
> someone from the guy's company was in Tripoli with
> timers just a couple of days before Lockerbie.

Cut to:

INT DANIEL'S CAR   DAY (22 DEC 1993)

DANIEL on carphone.

> DANIEL
>
> Blimey! Listen, I'll find a paper and call you
> back.

Cut to:

EXT MAIN RD WITH JUNCTION – ENGLAND   DAY (22 DEC 1993)

DANIEL'S car signals and turns off towards a village.

Cut to:

EXT VILLAGE STREET WITH GENERAL SHOP DAY   (22 DEC 1993)

Open full screen on Guardian page upside down. Pan up
to reveal newspaper on.roof of stationary car. On far
side of the car, DANIEL reads the article, carphone in
hand. The village shop is seen behind him.

DANIEL on carphone.

> DANIEL
>
> So they ask him to fly from Switzerland to Tripoli,

two days before Lockerbie, taking 40 bog-standard
commercial timers . . . (Sound continues)

Flashback device to:

INT HINSHIRI'S OFFICE JSO - LIBYA   DAY (19 DEC 1988)

CAPTION OVER: "Office of Izz al-Din al-Hinshiri

Senior operative of JSO - Libyan Intelligence
Service."

A typically North African sparse room. BOLLIER sits on
a sofa being poured a small glass of tea by a SERVANT.
HINSHIRI is at his desk, on which are a few Olympus TM2
timers. He plays with one while he talks, shaking his
head.

The sound in the room is not heard. Instead the
telephone conversation between DANIEL and JANE continues
over.

DANIEL (V/O)

. . . that they could have had bought anywhere in
the world and put in a diplomatic bag. Do we
believe that?

JANE (V/O)

Er. Probably not. But he says they didn't want
the timers he took anyway.

DANIEL (V/O)

In which case, why did they want someone to go
there? That's if someone went at all.

BOLLIER reacts to HINSHIRI, slightly surprised.

JANE (V/O)

Do you think the someone was Bollier himself?

DANIEL (V/O)

You're right. Had to be, didn't it. You're so
clever; that's why I love you.

JANE (V/O)

Apparently, it says that later that day he went to
a second meeting. . .

Cut to:

INT   AL-MEGRAHI'S HOUSE - LIBYA   NIGHT (19 DEC 1988)

 Sound of telephone conversation continues over as
       before.

     JANE (V/O)(cont)

 . . . at al-Megrahi's private house

     DANIEL (V/O)

 I see it! Where he spots two big wheels from the
 JSO that he happens already to know. I don't
 believe this.

BOLLIER again waits on a sofa, drinking tea. You can
spend hours doing this in the Middle East, but this
seems to be excessive. He is alone in the room apart
from a LARGE MAN who stands by the side of an archway.
Bollier looks at his watch, stands up and walks casually
round the room approaching the archway.

Bollier's POV. Beyond the man, in a room through the
archway, are seated on a carpet HINSHIRI, AL-MEGRAHI,
SENOUSSI, ASHUR and a group of 3 other men. Senoussi
looks up towards the arch.

Closer on the sinister Sennoussi as he and Bollier
exchange a look.

Bollier makes as if to enter the room but the large man
makes the slightest of gestures to indicate it would be
a very unwise move. Bollier moves away and looks out at
activity in the courtyard.

     DANIEL (V/O)

 I don't think he was there. I think he's invented
 the visit himself to put the black spot on Megrahi.
 If he **was** there it would mean that Hinshiri or
 someone higher was offering up Megrahi, trying to
 incriminate him and this is **before** the bombing, for
 God's sake! That doesn't make sense.

Another LARGE MAN comes out through the arch, joins
Bollier, takes him by the arm apologetically and leads
him out into the courtyard. Bollier seems not to want
to leave. They cross the yard and Bollier looks back.

Bollier's POV: The meeting has broken up and al-Megrahi
is dimly glimpsed in the outer room, bidding farewell to

the remainder of the group.

                    JANE (V/O)

    None at all, that I can see. Why would anyone do
    it? Whereas Bollier has the greatest incentive to
    make it up known to man . . .

                              Flashforward device to:

EXT VILLAGE STREET WITH GENERAL SHOP - DAY (22 DEC 1993)

DANIEL on carphone by his car.

          DANIEL and JANE (V/O) together

    Money!

                                        Cut to:

INT JANE'S OFFICE   DAY (22 DEC 1993)

JANE on phone. She is now opening a copy of The
Guardian.

                    JANE

    It looks bad though. The Libyans apparently
    looking at timers 48 hours before Lockerbie.

                                        Cut to:

EXT VILLAGE STREET WITH GENERAL SHOP - DAY (22 DEC 1993)

DANIEL still on carphone, gathering the newspaper and
getting onto the car.

                    DANIEL

    It's intended to look bad! That it tries so hard
    to look bad proves for me that it didn't happen; it
    isn't credible. Are we really expected to believe
    that proper serious terrorists would be still
    acquiring fundamental components for their bomb a
    matter of hours before it supposedly flew from
    another country entirely. I know people can be
    disorganised but that's just too ridiculous.

It had been Dick's point, and it was a fair one. It had swayed a decision for
Ray. He's worked in a few countries in North Africa and the Middle East,

and for him the story of Bollier's visit (for it was later admitted that he was indeed the 'Mebo representative' in question) did sound fairly bizarre, but not especially untypical. Ray has on repeated occasions been treated not dissimilarly. He feels some of the story of the visit could be true, but that because of Dick's observation on the timescale, he's sure that Bollier's journey, if indeed it actually took place, was nothing to do with Lockerbie.

The way he has written the visit it leaves questions open. He is much more inclined to the view, as he has Daniel Weiss imply, that the account was a deliberate piece of disinformation, the standard practice of the Secret World. That the Guardian got the story of the Bollier trip by way of a police report leaked by the Foreign Office rather confirmed that – and suggested an official manoeuvre to counter Bollier's Stasi disclosures. A statement putting Abdullah al-Senoussi – Gadaffi's brother-in-law and, at that time, deputy head of the JSO – together with other heavy intelligence players, at al-Megrahi's residence at such a significant date, whether invented or true (Senoussi was also related distantly to Megrahi, both being members of the large Megarha tribe) would have been also useful in cementing the impression of the latter's guilt, once more blatantly pre-judging any trial to come.

By the time Bollier's allegations became public in late 1993 another aircraft bombing had taken place, for which Senoussi and five JSO colleagues would in their absence be deemed by the French to be responsible. This had been the 1989 downing of UTA Flight 772, a DC10 blown up over Niger with the loss of 171 lives. In that event too, as with Lockerbie and 103, there may be matters that do not quite accord with what meets the eye

–ooOoo–

62 For What It Was Worth

The Guardian's revelation either implicated Libya, or else it showed Bollier attempting to do so (as we were to learn, not for the first time). Soon though, he was again publicly expressing doubts that the North Africans were to blame, so his position was never very well-grounded, and at the 2000 trial, his lack of credibility was much exposed. He became one of a rare class of witness that is given a rough time by both prosecution and defence. But if the story of his December 1988 visit or some details of it were invented, as seems irrefutable, the question has to be asked, for whose benefit? Bollier's own, certainly, for payment but as to the paymaster, who, Ray asks, could look a more likely suspect than the organisation the dealer tried to link up with just days after Lockerbie – acknowledged world leaders in disinformation, the CIA?

As to the man's frequent apparent changes of allegiance, was he motivated by improved recollection, a sudden attack of conscience or merely a changed (or perhaps additional) generous sponsor? By the time of Camp Zeist, Bollier seemed to have come down on the side of the Libyans' not being the responsible party. This adds colour to the trial's screenplay depiction, since he was called as a Crown witness. This was inevitable as the prosecution was steadfastly chained to the theory of the MST-13 timer – and Bollier was the only witness who could speak to the link between maker and customers. They had to produce him, warts and all.

Certainly in pointing out that his MST-13 was a bad choice for incorporating in a Toshiba cassette radio bomb, he was stating the obvious. It was so bulky that its outer case would have had to be removed to fit the small space available. His other stated drawback; that it had to be set for a specific number of hours between 1 and 1,000, did not really bear too much examination. He claimed that the bomber would have to calculate the actual number of hours required to elapse after arming until detonation. So he would, but this, if anything, would be less complex than setting a commercial timer, where the present time and the explosion time have to be set correctly. In both timers any allowance for differing time zones must be made, and this is probably easier to visualise when making the single calculation, as on the MST.

In one sense, Bollier was a distraction. Dick had drawn attention to the wildly improbable coincidence of two independent plots choosing to build bombs in Toshibas at essentially the same time. He and Ray are totally convinced that the Lockerbie bomb was made by Marwhan Khreesat, whomever **precisely** he was working for, and incorporated his tried pressure capsule plus time-switch principle, and that no Mebo MST-13 was anywhere near Pan Am 103. The fact that no trace of a pressure capsule was found (something brought up at the trial) was because it was blown to smithereens, just as every piece of the supposed MST-13 apparently was, except one easily recognisable fragment which, according to the Crown's wobbly case, miraculously survived.

Yet Bollier was also crucial, because he was so associated with the prosecution's case, whether the Crown's legal team liked it or not. He was central to the trial because he himself, or someone else, had projected him there. He had to be heard, but what he had to say would need careful auditing. He gave evidence, which no one could prove or disprove, that he had attended desert tests of air bombs using the MST, and that a person who figured in them was a man named Nassr Ashur. Nassr Ashur, conveniently, was someone else he had claimed to have seen at al-Megrahi's house hours before Lockerbie.

The trial judges would, in their judgement, rate Bollier, as well as his partner, Meister, and Mebo's chief technician, Lumpert, as unreliable. The evidence of these three was nevertheless accepted in part. The strangest thing is that the very evidence that the judges accepted was that which showed there was real doubt that if an MST **was** in the bomb, it had to have come from Libya. For a reason known only to themselves, they then rejected the normal principle of 'proof beyond reasonable doubt' and accepted Libyan provenance. Indeed they went further and took that in turn as demonstrating al-Megrahi's involvement, as if the latter were one and the same thing. These were remarkable leaps of assumption, the likes of which judges normally caution juries against making.

In this case there was no jury to caution. The defence lawyers would have assumed the judges were well aware that the evidence did not prove any of these links or justify such leaps. That assumption would prove to be unfounded to a remarkable degree.

To get to this point the judges had already failed to see any reasonable doubt that the contentious and vital timer fragment was genuine. Given that the police officer who had done the re-labelling was characterised as giving explanations for his actions which were 'at worst evasive and at best confusing', their view that evidence had not been tampered with could only be a subjective one, in which it should have been impossible to be totally confident. In this context too, Allen Feraday's Thatcherine habit of clinging limpet-like to a personal opinion whatever strong currents of reason there might be motivating a move to a different position, when it was amply demonstrated to the court, should have alerted their lordships to at least the possibility of something amiss. Tellingly perhaps, the phrase they chose to dispel their own caution was 'nothing sinister'.

The court was never given the opportunity to hear it denied that either of the defendants were operatives of the JSO, the Libyan intelligence service, because of their respective teams' decisions that they should not go into the witness box. Dick has satisfied himself that neither belonged to the JSO and that al-Megrahi, as Head of Security for LAA, was involved with the organisation solely by virtue of being responsible for the assimilation training of armed sky marshals, who **were** initially JSO assets, to make their presence and practices acceptable to airline crews. But as Dick points out, even if he had been an agent, that in itself would not be a crime, however repugnant aspects of the regime might be. Several of the witnesses at the trial fulfilled or had fulfilled similar functions in the agencies of their own countries.

There was no dispute that al-Megrahi possessed a second identity and passports, for an explicable reason, unconnected with intelligence work. But again, this too in the opposite circumstances would have been a shared experience. It was claimed that his airline employment was cover; it wasn't, but again, many of the CIA agents who poured into Lockerbie were pretending to be Pan American engineers. It's the sort of thing that raises suspicion and rightly prompts questions but is not in itself automatic proof of wrongdoing. Like most able Libyans of his class, al-Megrahi had other business interests. The indictment claimed that the trading company he was involved with, ABH, was a front for the intelligence service. Again untrue, but equally a device that many agents, Britons and Americans included, become involved with at some time or another, just as surely as the so-respectable foreign service includes both genuine diplomats and out-and-out spies.

ABH, word has it, was involved in sanctions-busting, and not state terrorism. It rented an office from Mebo, in their Zurich premises. Mebo and more particularly one partner, Bollier, had a record of supplying dubious material to dubious organisations. If the picture of Megrahi painted by the indictment and in the Crown's case had been accurate, and it wasn't, none of this would have remotely indicated guilt of the crime, yet all-too-many, judges included, allowed themselves to be so persuaded. And on those slender links, apparently stemming from one single distortion of fact, the first accused was found guilty of 270 counts of murder.

As Dick has been moved to say, more than once:

"If there aren't grounds for appeal in that, what chance is there for British justice?"

—ooOoo—

Ray had asked Metz, as he and Karin settled into the Aston, how he had heard about the *One-Zero-Three* script. The answer **was** from Ralph. Ray asked them not to tell Ralph that the rewrite was complete, giving as the reason that his copy wouldn't have reached him yet. He hoped that he would very soon have someone to handle the tricky question of the would-be producer's association with the project, and until then wanted to keep the young man at arm's length.

—ooOoo—

63   Agent – Travel

He needn't have worried. When the ding, ding, ding, ding-a-ding of *Spring* from Vivaldi's *Four Seasons* catches him in the bathroom, the voice on the other end is the one that's going to solve the problem of the errant Ralph.

"Ray. It's DB." Ray can tell that he's not his usual self by the way he doesn't call him Mr Scriver. "Listen, I'm **so** – sorry. I can't tell you how angry I am." Ray waits for more.

"You know what I'm talking about?" DB says in response to the pause.

"I think so," Ray replies cautiously. "But I don't know exactly. You'd better start from the beginning." DB takes the advice. He has just today learnt what Ray already had been told, thus putting him on an equal footing with half the industry. The father is now engaged in the humiliating process of apologising to everybody he's recommended Ralph to in the recent past.

"Look, we hadn't actually gone too far down the road yet, so I don't think there's much of a problem," Ray says. "I'm waiting to sign up with a new agent really, so I can't move anything forward until next week at the earliest. It's on a kind of hold, although I've finished the rewrite."

"Have you. That's good. Any chance of sending me a copy? Only, I reckon the next *Land of Kings* is going back nine months or so, by the look of things. If it does I'll be looking for something to do. I love your project, as you know, and as for landing you with my dick-head of a son, I think I owe you, so have a ponder about it, but I'd like to hope we can put something together."

"Brilliant! How likely is it that it's going back?"

"About ninety per cent plus, I think. I'll know in a couple of days at the latest."

"What's happening with Ralph?" It's funny. Ray feels concern, even though they have not actually met.

"He swears he's cleaning up his act. He says he doesn't need re-hab, but I've told him he's really got to take hold of himself and get right off everything. There won't be any more chances."

"But what's actually happening, work-wise, for him?"

"I've got to have a couple of meetings, but I may be able to put a package together. He says he needs a two-day shoot to make his movie editable. He has to finish it and sell it and pay the crew before anyone will look at him again."

"Well, when he's done that, if the timescale works at all, I know it's early days but if you wanted to use him on this and he stays clear of the rubbish, I just liked his style and enthusiasm."

"I'm really touched you've said that," says DB with something in his voice that confirms his words.

"No. Don't mention it. By the way. Whoever does *One-Zero-Three*, I'm having a producer credit."

"Of course."

Well, that was easy.

Once he's put the phone down, Ray has no idea why he said what he did about Ralph. It's one thing to feel it, but to offer it is quite a different thing. It's living dangerously. All in all though, he's rather pleased that he did.

—ooOoo—

Within twenty minutes, Ray is almost sweating with worry. He had not the least intention of setting a trap for DB, but now thinks that it may well appear that he did. The producer could conceivably feel that Ray's generosity towards his son was deliberately expressed as a prelude to staking the claim for his own producer's credit. Ray agonises for a while and comes to a decision. He will handwrite a personal note to DB and attach it to the script copy that he's promised to send. It will explain that he had made the decision to insist on the credit after seeing Gerald in New Zealand (which is the truth, and he could even obliquely blame Gerald without actually saying so), and that he had resolved to raise it at the earliest moment with whoever took on *One-Zero-Three*. The juxtaposition in their conversation was entirely coincidental and certainly not contrived. He only hopes DB will accept what he says. God. You have to be so careful! That could be another 'most important phone call' of Ray's life and he may have messed it up with one sentence.

Once again, Ray needn't have worried. DB, who has spent years now navigating the alligator pools of Wardour Street and Hollywood, watching the overloaded boatloads of bluffers and chancers, can recognize devious when he sees it. He knows full well that Ray is not of that world.

—ooOoo—

In completing the new draft, Ray notes that he has in part taken the advice of Hal, DB's mole in Los Angeles. Hal's day job, he has learnt, is at Joe Wyzell's Galactic Pictures. Hal's only suggestion had been the deletion of some scenes related mainly to what was essentially a sub-plot. Ray had included some elements of this story, the tribulations of journalist and one-time DIA agent, Lester Coleman, for two reasons: firstly because the episode offered the most extreme and ugly example of US agencies moving to silence one of their own whistleblowers; secondly because Coleman's testimony seemed to offer first-hand confirmation that Khalid Jaafar was indeed a drug mule.

The only Arab on Flight 103, Jaafar was the passenger whose suitcases are suspected by most commentators of holding the large consignment of heroin on the aircraft. Some of those same commentators also conclude that one of his suitcases, or one substituted for it, contained the bomb. Jaafar was a Lebanese-born American citizen. One of the many mysteries about him was his dual passports. His US document, which a witness noticed on check-in at Frankfurt, was not listed as recovered at Lockerbie – probably being one of the items, including his drug consignment, removed by the CIA cleaners during their illegal interference with evidence. His Lebanese passport, suspiciously, had pages missing. On that he had, just five months earlier, been issued with a multi-entry visa for the States (which he clearly didn't actually need) at the US Embassy in Beirut, which had a policy of only issuing such to officials of the Lebanese government and internally to embassy staff. This seems to confirm that Jaafar had a connection with some arm of the US government.

Coleman's undercover work for the DIA involved getting a job with the DEA, the Drugs Enforcement Administration, and reporting back from the Middle East on the activities of that organisation and the CIA. The concept of one branch of the US Secret World spying on others was both frightening and illuminating. While based in Cyprus gathering information on Lebanon drug production, Coleman had insight into the protected deliveries that the DEA was running into Europe and the USA, and knew Jaafar as one of the heroin couriers. The analyst left the Middle East before Lockerbie, and it was only some time afterwards that it came to his attention that the young man had died on Flight 103. Coleman's eventual going public with his endorsement of the story that a bag switch might have facilitated the murders would change his life, with the DIA setting him up and then abandoning him, leading first to exile, then through Judge Thomas

Platt's court, to prison. Fascinating and shocking as Coleman's saga is, it tended to add extra complication and eat up valuable screentime, so has now been much curtailed. Coleman still gets mentioned, as does Joe Miano, a 'real' DEA analyst who encountered not dissimilar treatment for questioning the official line on Lockerbie. Ray feels he can't leave out at least a passing reference to these two government servants who suffered malicious prosecution, fines and prison, just for speaking their mind, a right supposedly guaranteed under the first amendment of the US Constitution. Miano had even been coerced by the FBI into an attempt to entrap Juval Aviv, but was punished anyway.

Aviv was number one on the US establishment's Lockerbie hate list, and it is virtually impossible to probe the events without referring to Aviv's contribution.

Very few months had passed after the outrage before Pan Am faced a compensation suit from the families of the bereaved, on the fairly obvious grounds that their poor security had permitted its occurrence. The airline and its insurers, USAIG, had to decide, with their lawyers, whether to settle or whether there were any grounds to contest the suit. The lead attorney, James Shaugnessy, decided to commission an inquiry into how the terrorists had introduced the device. He chose a company called Interfor that had an impressive record of investigation work with a client-list that included several government agencies. It was Aviv who had founded Interfor in 1979. Prior to that, he had been a Mossad agent for ten years, although the Israelis would later deny this – not especially surprising, given the closeness of Mossad to the CIA and the latter's horror at what Aviv's three-month investigation uncovered. Seen from their point of view, it would be necessary to discredit Aviv totally so that his findings would not be believed. The lid, however, could no longer be put back on this fiercely bubbling saucepan. When Aviv's impressive unattributable sources in the field revealed to him the existence of the CIA-protected drug deliveries, and the likelihood that one had been appropriated to blow up 103, Shaugnessy determined that the US Government should, at the very least, be sharing the burden of compensation with his clients.

As with some other aspects of the Lockerbie narrative, Shaugnessy's battle with government agencies and the various legal actions that followed merit a major television film of their own. The obstructions that were strewn in the path of the lawyer and his team as they tried to access information and then present their case in Judge Platt's New York courtroom provided truly dramatic evidence of the way every assumed principle could seemingly be swept aside in what could only be read as a concerted, ruthless attempt to allow secrecy to triumph over truth. Shades of things to come! Shaugnessy and his firm were threatened with damages, merely for subpoenaing evidence, and a Grand Jury Investigation was begun against them, simply for doing their job. The default position of the American establishment is to side with business, especially big business – and there was hardly an enterprise of much higher profile than America's de facto flag-carrying airline. The attack on Pan Am was therefore probably unprecedented. It is hardly credible that it represents a sudden shift of conscience; a new sympathy with ordinary people. Dick's logic said that the more the US Government mobilised its overwhelming fire-power against the airline, the ever greater the likelihood that what Pan Am was alleging was correct. He cautioned though against avowing any great sympathy for the company: its security had been independently demonstrated to be inefficient, any conspiracy notwithstanding. If the Interfor report and other sources, such as UK Customs, were right, bags were being injected into the luggage stream undetected, possibly with the connivance of some of the airline's own employees; circumstances that could only compound its responsibility, rather than diminish it. Again, if Pan Am was being used as a regular channel for drugs, it seems unlikely that such knowledge in the company was confined to a small number of baggage handlers.

Juval Aviv was the first but not the only investigator to whom individuals in the intelligence services confirmed the existence of the drug run – the national scandal that required such heavy-handed attempts at censorship. James Shaugnessy conducted further probes. Roy Rowan, a highly-respected journalist, was told the same for a piece in *Time* magazine; Allan Francovich heard it when researching for his TV documentary; and John Ashton and Ian Ferguson had it confirmed for *Cover-Up of Convenience*. Strenuous attempts were made to prevent both the filming and the showing of Francovich's *The Maltese Double Cross*, and when it did air, unprecedented steps were taken to discredit it. Bringing the story to a wider audience could not go unchallenged by the establishment, and within days of the transmission, both Juval Aviv and John Brennan, president of the company that managed Pan Am's insurance, were charged with fraud, in old cases unrelated to each other or, in theory, to Lockerbie. The charges arose not from complaints but from two cold investigations by the same FBI agent, which strongly suggests that they were manufactured. The prosecution of Brennan and his company revealed that the ethics of elements in the aviation insurance business were far from perfect, but large fines for both and Brennan's prison sentence were overturned on appeal.

Neither Pan American, their insurers, nor even ultimately Shaugnessy himself, emerge well from the Lockerbie episode, but that shouldn't be allowed to mask or at all justify, Dick had argued, what seems to have been blatant state interference with the normal process of law during their legal action.

Aviv was eventually acquitted of his bespoke charges, but by that time his reputation had been comprehensively destroyed – by the FBI, who had simply contacted his clients and informed them that he was under fraud investigation, and by newspaper articles, including one in *The Wall Street Journal*.

That such a large number of commentators in the print and broadcast media have been prepared to dance to governments' tunes and wield generally rather blunt but injuring hatchets on those people, including their journalistic colleagues, who have approached the facts more openly and critically, has been a worrying feature of the whole Lockerbie saga. It's a tendency that shows no sign of abating, Ray feels.

–ooOoo–

The next few days see dramatic activity and apparent progress. Ray and his prospective agent, Jake Baring-Smith, take to each other instantly and Ray surprises himself by signing up on the spot. The ink is barely dry before DB is on the phone to Baring-Smith, wanting to option the screenplay. The *Land of Kings* series of films is confirmed as going on hold after several years of almost straight run, and the producer can barely wait to start raising interest in *One-Zero-Three*. Ray is mildly euphoric at the prospect of some actual income for the first time in many months, and is able to celebrate by telling Jake that he is about to take a short holiday . . .

. . . at the Scottish seaside!

–ooOoo–

64   Intelligence Tests

As far as he knows, Ray has never met a spy before, so the coming experience is festooned with question marks, some of them terribly predictable.   Stereotyping in films has long established strong preconceptions about how spooks might look, speak and behave and it will be interesting to observe how much these are borne out in reality.   The voice on the telephone had been non-committal but not overly-guarded, and as soon as Ray's first line cast the bait that the overture was being made at the suggestion of 'Jaquetta, your sister', its owner had positively relaxed, almost as if a password had been uttered.   The former intelligence man had obviously been briefed to a small extent and was expecting a call on his mobile at some point.   A surprise had been the strong but cultured Scottish accent.   His sibling's speech carries not a trace of the tones of the Kingdom of Alba.

Ray had shivered, hearing the ringtone finally answered.   For a brief second he had been transported back to Queenstown with the sleet lashing the window and the encouraging secret whispers close to his ear.   It's weeks on now, yet there remain two gnawing voids in the region between his heart and his stomach, and one of them is named after Jack.   He's known that this encounter is likely to stir brittle memories and in a way he's quite content that it will.

As Fraser will later confide to Ray, it's only the fact that Jack had met Ray several years ago that made him agree to a meeting; gave him confidence that Ray is not any form of plant associated with his former colleagues or their extended family.   Ray will echo the sentiments.   Had it appeared to him in the slightest that a meeting with someone currently intertwined with the Secret World was being engineered, he wouldn't be going anywhere near Plockton this weekend.

He doesn't know where Fraser lives; merely that he said he would only meet him in north-west Scotland.   Given the habits of intelligence operatives, Fraser could in reality be resident anywhere at all, with the Highlands and Islands probably the least likely of any option.   Ray wonders whether the man uses the same surname as Jack.   He knows what it should be, having looked up their family in Burke's Landed Gentry.   But the name he goes by is of no significance and Ray's certainly not going to use it.   Jack had given him just 'Fraser' and a single mobile phone number.

Ray has been intending for years to return to Plockton during the regatta. He fell upon the place and the event by chance years ago when scouting and then shooting some car commercials in the vicinity. The company had needed to move heaven and earth to find accommodation, and when the reason for the scarcity became apparent it had come as some surprise. A fortnight of sailing, racing and partying in the Scottish Highlands seemed an unlikely concept, although the palm trees pictured on the waterfront in Ray's recce stills gave evidence of a location somewhat out-of-the-ordinary. Out-of-the-ordinary indeed! The Gulf Stream donates a benign climate that allows the palms to flourish – and enables a small Scottish village each year for two wild weeks at the turn of July and August to emulate, in a very individual way, the rivers and harbours of the south of England and even the fashionable bijou boat-magnets of the Mediterranean. Suggesting Plockton to Fraser was, for Ray, a sound case of 'three birds with one stone' and on reflection made some further form of sense – with the waterborne activities and the gathering of spectators providing what seemed to him, as a dramatist at least, rather effective cover for a contact that neither party would be keen to be observed.

Helping in this respect, the village has a second, almost surreal quality attributable in part to its being on a peninsula with just one road giving access. Such cul-de-sac places can assume the air of separate Kingdoms – almost like independent states with their own rules and customs. To a degree Ray's own hamlet comes into the same category. When Ray worked in Plockton he was told that 'the authorities' (the exaggerated winks of his informants telegraphed that they meant 'the polis') tended to leave this unique settlement to its own devices. If, for example, over-the-limit drivers crossed the railway bridge to the 'outside world' they might well be stopped and dealt with. But within the village everything was in walking distance anyway, and it comprised mainly the one single, curving waterfront street. It was like a frontier town; but one with no real need for a sheriff, probably never more so than during the revels and celebrations of King Neptune.

Fraser had been happy with the venue of the lochside village inasmuch as he had a good friend, he said, living nearby, with whom he could stay. Ray secured a room at his previous, friendly B&B, situated at the extreme far end of the village, even though it wasn't actually providing B&B any more. Armed only with a telephone number for Fraser's local buddy, given that mobiles would mostly not work in the mountains, Ray has simply taken off, literally, for the far north-west.

–ooOoo–

65   Borderline Traces

In fact this is Ray's third flight of the day. The first was a twenty-minute hop to Gloucester to call at the Staverton Flying School to buy the current Scottish chart, it being not legal to fly without the latest information. He's very particular about preparing his laminated charts (pilots and sailors insist on the term 'chart'; maps are for everybody else). It's very important to ensure that the folding converts the relatively large sheet into a readily-accessed concertina of sections that can be turned almost like pages of a book as the journey progresses. The last thing you want to do is a major re-fold of a chart in the air; it's awkward to accomplish and it would distract from other rather higher priority tasks such as controlling the aeroplane and looking out for conflicting traffic. Ray's meticulous pleating is worth the time it takes. With updating the weather picture and then equally careful journey planning, plus some social catching-up with Jennie the CFI, who arrived back from a sortie, the flight had tarried for well over an hour at Staverton. Happily though, two hours and five minutes more had seen him on the ground at Carlisle, for a quick bite and more importantly the purchase of fuel for the coming legs.

The buying was the easy part; working out how much to load was trickier. The point is that Ray knows there is no Avgas available at Plockton. Airfields and air strips are few enough north-west of Glasgow, and of them only Benbecula and Stornoway, out on the Hebrides, sell the fuel that Ray's aircraft uses. Echo Bravo has to carry enough fuel to get to its destination and then on to either Inverness, which is 55 nautical miles (if the weather allows a crossing of the mountains to the east coast), or a return to Glasgow or Prestwick – 97 and 116 miles respectively. In addition to the fuel for the basic journey, an extra allowance needs to be carried for weather diversion or return. If the easy answer seems to be simply to fill the tanks to capacity at Carlisle, that is emphatically not the solution due to the length of the runway at Plockton. Although it's asphalt and not grass, its 597-metre length dictates that a full and complex calculation is required to determine the maximum weight at which the Piper can safely take-off after the visit. The fuel load remaining at Plockton is critical. Too little and you're going to be stuck on the ground until someone, somehow, can be persuaded to convey some from Inverness at vast expense. Too much and you're going to be searching for cans to drain some of the precious spirit from your tanks and giving it to anyone in Plockton who wants it; otherwise you could, in the worst case, reach the end of the runway without becoming airborne. This is not a popular option.

Ray always does his calculations in the grandly-named Imperial gallons, notwithstanding the fact that uploads are sold in litres and that the aircraft's fuel gauges are calibrated in US gallons; something different again. This is an exercise designed to focus the mind and accord the subject the degree of attention that it warrants. As he'd paid for the fuel at Carlisle he had been aware that despite the careful mathematics, there was some degree of guesswork involved. Rather more than usual in aviation the venture bears some hallmarks of a gamble, although here one involving inconvenience rather than danger. The window of success is smaller than Ray would prefer, but the compensations are proving to be more than adequate to balance any unease. This flight is becoming increasingly spectacular.

He can never transit through Carlisle Airport without imagining those secret agents arriving in the specially-arranged Pan Am 727 during the horrible evening of 21st December, 1988 – a night that was raw in every sense. He was aware that the crew of that flight would have made, at Heathrow before setting off, exactly the type of calculations he has just carried out, due to the main runway at Carlisle being considerably shorter than those normally used by the trijet. The 'three-holer' is known for good short-field performance, but this represented a very different order of magnitude for the two pilots and the flight engineer. They too had to calculate their payload of fuel and passengers to keep their gross weight within limits for the length available. There are occasions when Ampsey's 770 metres feel short in a light aircraft approaching by day at 70 knots. The concentration in the cockpit of the Boeing airliner aiming for a declared landing distance of 1,469 metres at around twice that speed must have been commensurately high. Arriving at a completely unfamiliar airport equipped with only basic navigational and lighting facilities and a short runway on a wet, gusty night would have been challenging even for highly experienced professionals; and that's without the pressure of intruding emotion flowing from what had happened to their colleagues earlier in the evening. The cockpit and cabin crew of the feederliner would have deservedly been very happy to be on the ground at Carlisle and more thankful still to be safely on their way back to the familiarity of Heathrow.

Ray knows that the 727 crew did their fallen countrymen and women proud that night and is saddened that numbers of the people they transported on the flight ended up doing exactly the reverse.

Walking out to Echo-Bravo, he had recalled those other agents, filmed by a local Border Television news crew at the very spot where he now strode, unloading the coffin from the luggage hold of the second special charter that landed at Carlisle the following day. Whoever or whatever that coffin was intended to, or perhaps did, spirit away from Lockerbie is potentially one of the key questions hanging over the whole mystery. Some at least on that flight will know why they brought it. If just one of them provided that answer, the whole cover-up might well be exposed and crumble, like the one crucial move that often resolves a whole game of chess or patience. Ray actually thinks the cover-up is exposed, well enough. It's simply the details that remain unexplained. How possible is it that Fraser might supply the missing jigsaw piece? Probably unlikely, but stranger things have happened.

The take-off and the initial climb-out on departure is undoubtedly the most critical phase of any flight, and not a time for permitting distractions or allowing the mind to wander. However, Ray was very well aware that the line of Hadrian's Wall, the celebrated frontier fortification that for more than two centuries marked the northernmost reach of the Roman Empire, passes just to the north of Carlisle Airport and is crossed shortly after a departure from runway Zero-Seven. Not surprisingly, given his interest in the turbulent and bloody history of the borders that followed the relative tranquillity of that Roman occupation, Ray was determined to spare a second for a quick look at the significant feature as it slipped under the nose of the Piper. In fact the structure at this western end was never as spectacular as the stone switchback, reminiscent of a mini Great Wall of China, that is found further east, but the general line stands out well from the air and is impressive enough. The Romans did go further into the wildness of Scotland and even built another defensive wall, the Antonine, between the Clyde and the Forth, but they only garrisoned that for approaching sixty years.

Tonight after herrings in oatmeal and over a few glasses of single malt in the Haven Hotel, Ray will ruminate further on the historical certainty that any period of relative peace and stability is always followed by violence and upset. Ages of enlightenment have always given way eventually to upsurges of self-interest and ruthless exploitation. England and Scotland are unlikely to fight each other again, but both have seen no war on their soil for sixty-six years now – which probably just means that the next major bloodletting in the UK is merely sixty-six years closer than it was in 1945.

Des would have an observation to offer on that for certain, but these uncomfortable thoughts could be pursued this evening. Ray had a flight to accomplish first. In theory he had been going to turn left and intercept the one-six-zero degree radial from the TLA or Talla navigation beacon – meaning a course, once centred on the beam, of three-four-zero degrees or put another way, twenty degrees west of north. This would take him bang over the town of Langholm, the only settlement of any size on the first leg, or indeed in the area, which would therefore provide a good fix and timing waypoint. In 1988 Langholm was right at the centre of the Lockerbie debris trail and he's never flown over it. Nor did he today, in the event opting instead to head 25 or so degrees further left with the object of passing roughly half way between the two towns. He had no intention of flying over the more famous of the two, much less circling or anything so intrusive. He has actually flown by in the past, with Eve, and it wasn't that he wanted to look at it today so much as rather to pay his respects, especially having failed to spot the grey settlement from the Los Angeles flight with DB.

Approaching the Lockerbie to Langholm road he had been struck, as so often when flying, of the privileges and the freedom of the private pilot. He was permitted far more discretion and liberty than his professional counterparts plying the airway Alpha One several thousands of feet immediately above him. They couldn't decide to alter course at will to look at a town off their route. They had flight plans to comply with and air traffic controllers to answer to. Ray, provided that he kept below 5,500 feet in these parts, could do much as he liked. He had looked down at the place that had occupied so much of his thoughts for such a long time, tranquil and ordinary-looking, five miles or so off his left wingtip. Nearer was Tundergarth church and the field opposite it where the nose section had come to rest so symbolically.

"Rest in peace, good people." He had said it out loud.

Looking to the right, he had found Langholm, already slightly behind the trailing edge. It was a signal to get his professional hat on. About ten miles beyond Talla, just after the town of Biggar, he'd be entering the Scottish TMA or Traffic Management Area, where he then **would** have to be in contact with controllers and watched on radar. He would request to route from the TLA to Cumbernauld at 4,500 feet, thus slotting neatly between Glasgow and Edinburgh and ideally keeping out of the way of any traffic bound to and from either. They would almost certainly approve his request, but he'd have to fly accurate headings and keep his level carefully. He knew they would probably ask for an estimate for his time overhead the beacon, just to see if he was on the ball.

He'd re-centred his VOR needle, read off the new heading to Talla, remembering somewhat tardily to tune in the audio and check the Morse identifier to prove that he was indeed receiving the beacon. The thin beeps spelt out T-L-A: identity confirmed. He'd cheated by reading his estimated flight time to Talla from the GPS display and adding it to the present time, ready to give the controller his ETA. He'd used the seconds saved to have one last look over his shoulder at Lockerbie, receding fast, looking much as it must have done before 21st December, 1988. Life goes in circles. All good things come to an end, as do, fortunately, the bad. Duty done, it had been time to call Scottish Information.

All that is an hour past. Everything had gone according to plan until, skirting the northern edge of the Glasgow Control Zone and approaching the margins of Loch Lomond, Ray had realised that the weather was not as 'bonnie' as had been forecast, and that it would not have been wise to route straight across the mountains of Argyll to Oban. He had taken a decision to fly west-south-west towards Loch Fyne, where it looked much less gloomy. In fact, the further west he had gone, the brighter it had become, and Echo Bravo had soon found sunshine and perfect visibility, turning north to follow the coast, then traverse the Firth of Lorne and shave the eastern tip of the Isle of Mull.

Now Ray and the Piper are crossing the sinuous Loch Sunart, heading for the wireless mast that marks the last scheduled heading change. Thirty-five nautical miles and twenty minutes to go! And the fuel gauges, rough and ready blunt implements that they are, are showing just the sort of quantities that Ray wants to see. The engine sounds sweet and the scenery is simply sensational. The sense of freedom that Ray acknowledged over the Borders has now been overtaken by a feeling altogether more epic and spiritual. This is the viewpoint formerly reserved for eagles and Gods. We are used to a limited form of this magnificence available through our window-seats in economy – many of us have become blasé about such sights and ignore them, to the consternation, even anger, of fellow-passengers who have failed to secure a window but would like to enjoy them. But to be here alone, in sole unfettered control of where to go, what to choose to see, from which height and from which angle, literally adds dimension beyond measure. Echo Bravo may just be pieces of riveted aluminium and cast metal but, under Ray's light guidance that is almost more thought than touch, expressed by that Knightley phrase, 'gently in my hand' – the trusty craft is capable of taking him – **is** today taking him – to the very gates of heaven itself. How could he begin to contemplate giving this up?

He remembers Austin's sister, Annette, saying that she envies her brother's job, because it always takes him into the sunlight, whatever the weather being experienced on the ground. Ray envies Austin less for his work taking him to that mad and dazzling landscape above the clouds – more that his friend's 'office window' daily offers such panoramas as this. How dare he, and almost every flightcrew professional he's ever met, complain about the job? Everyone moans about their lot though. Ray remembers spending and resenting thousands of bright and balmy days in hot, dark studios. When the work had been slow and tedious, how often his thoughts had drawn him out through the heavy doors and up into the sky, waving imagined farewell to his addiction to film-making.

The famously-named islands of Eigg and Rum punctuate the blue sea to the left, while ahead, across the Sound of Sleat, rises the even better-known and romantic Isle of Skye. As with Mull, Ray's track will take him across its far eastern extremity. The mainland coast to the right is a series of dramatic drowned valleys — sea lochs mostly supporting little or no habitation, just spectacular, empty grandeur. Ahead and on each side of track there are peaks less than a thousand feet below Echo Bravo's present altitude. If this were New Zealand, Ray could take her down on such a day and contour the valley sides and skim the ridges by tens of feet, rather than hundreds. It won't happen. For him the Piper is an airliner that just happens to have four seats — and anyway this is the regulation-ridden, risk-averse UK. He won't start to descend until he's over Skye and can see Kyle of Lochalsh, at a point from where he could glide to Plockton if he had to, with the Broadford strip on the island as another option in an emergency. All these mountains are impressive but none equal the needle-like Cuillins, 15 miles off the left wing, beyond Broadford's grass.

However faultless any progress over the earth's abundant wonders, some feature to signal the harsh realities of life will always appear eventually to intrude on the reverie. Ray's cue to reduce power a fraction and re-trim the Warrior a degree or two nose-down is his sight of the new Skye Bridge; the first time he has seen it from the air. The concrete arc represents more than a mere in-flight timing point. Environmentalists might consider its impact on its matchless surroundings to be inappropriate and discordant, but for those aware of its significance in the conduct of local, Scottish, British and international affairs, such mild criticisms are wholly insufficient. Everything in the planning, financing, building, operation and administration of the structure, the first-ever Private Finance Initiative, proved, he knows, to be a shameful indictment of modern ethical standards in politics, the civil service and in corporate behaviour, tarnishing the institutions involved almost without exception.

Touted as a way to provide infrastructure at minimal cost to government and the taxpayer, this trail-blazing PFI saw almost the reverse. The taxpayer in fact greatly funded the project, providing the fortunate operator with a means to extort massive profits through swingeing tolls from users, over an apparently undefined timescale, with the ferry service immediately withdrawn. Both major British political parties, in concert with the Scottish Office, exhibited a poisonous combination of inefficiency, oversight, appalling negotiating acumen and apparent duplicity. As one example, a bank employed as a consultant to advise ministerial departments was actually part of the PFI consortium, standing to benefit from government's acceptance of its own recommendations. With the advice accepted, setting the project under way, it proved to be bad, based on skewed figures, so astonishingly the consortium, including the bank, demanded and got compensation. This contaminated process delivered the islanders, representatives of one of the poorest economies in the UK, into the hands of predatory companies who used the government-rigged monopoly to 'print money' – mostly theirs.

Even more shamefully, when the islanders, although denied any form of assistance or legal aid, challenged this burdensome tax on their right to basic mobility in the only ways open to them, and repeatedly uncovered facts proving the whole PFI administration had been riddled with deceit and illegality, they were criminalised and punished, intimidated and harassed, and their sound legal points peremptorily rejected. It was abundantly clear that both the police and the Scottish Courts system had been instructed by the British government to neutralise and wear down the objectors' very resolute and justifiable opposition. One of the campaign's more revealing discoveries was that, through a process of acquisition by transfer that was specifically forbidden in the PFI terms, the sole owner of the bridge – profiting both from the unwitting generosity of the British taxpayer at large and the misery of Skye's hard-pressed inhabitants in particular – had become that very bank of bad advice, the Bank of America, formerly known as the Bank of Italy!

For once it was a scandal that eventually had one redemptive feature. In 2004 the Scottish Government bought the bridge and abolished tolls. The islanders had won, but so had the dubious consortium. £33.5m had been collected in ten years; it got another £27m for the bridge, for an outlay calculated as £28.5m – profit of £32m, maybe more. The larger point, for Ray, is that given the legal authorities' clear willingness in the Skye Bridge saga to bend any concept of right and justice, at the behest of British governments of both complexions, to the advantage of unacknowledged overseas interests, there can be little surprise that in the Lockerbie trial which paralleled its darker phases, the reputation of the Scottish legal system for demonstrable independence and detached judgement would again take such a comprehensive nose-dive.

Beyond Kyle and the Crowlin Islands on the Inner Sound, Ray spots a warship, a destroyer or frigate, with what must be a Ministry of Defence Police launch in attendance. He suspects that the hourly costs of running the pair probably exceed the monthly value of the entire Skye economy. Whom, he asks himself pointlessly, are they defending us against this afternoon? Certainly not young men on underground trains with rucksacks.

He crosses Loch Alsh, with the railhead town to port and the unmistakable fairy-tale tower of Eilean Donan visible rather further off to starboard. In 1719 the castle was involved in a Spanish invasion in support of James Stuart, the 'Old Pretender' – one of several failed landings by European powers since 1066 which for some reason British history rarely acknowledges. Perhaps the grey frigate out in the Sound is waiting in case Spanish reinforcements arrive. At the mainland shore he realises the geography of the last few miles of this flight is almost a mirror image of the situation of Wellington Airport seen so spectacularly from the cockpit of the elderly 737 all those years ago and hardly glimpsed at all on his recent trip. Plockton even has both approaches over water – just, although only one is across open sea; the other crosses a small bay but is not far from some hilly terrain. Enough! Every airfield has differences. Every let-down and landing is unique. The one big difference between Wellington and here is that Ray himself will be flying this approach. He must have done something good to deserve this!

There has been no response to his position reports on the Plockton frequency. No one is at the airfield. With his preliminary checks complete he aims for the overhead at 2,000 feet to check the windsock. He savours a brief picture of the familiar settlement fronting the curving shoreline of the inlet that provides the safe harbour; with the profusion of moored boats, buildings and trees looking like one of those perfect architect's models, not dissimilar to the one in *Local Hero*, part-filmed not far away. What little wind there is favours runway Two-Zero, meaning a descent and approach across the main loch, from just east of north. Wonderful!

As he unhurriedly teases the control yoke to bank the aircraft left, he experiences, for the ten-thousandth time in his flying career, a sense of wonder that his subtle hand movement can translate into a magical three-dimensional shift of the windscreen picture, as Echo Bravo's nose responds, sliding across the scenery, to point in exactly the new direction he wishes. When the DI approaches zero-two-zero, he stops the turn, by now heading out across the shimmering sea for the downwind leg, announcing his position and intentions again on the radio. He will fly a continuous descent from here, rather than a conventional circuit join. You can only do this at an uncontrolled airfield and when there's no one else flying anywhere near. It's close to certain that there's nothing airborne within miles.

With the throttle back to give around 1,800 rpm, a quiet burble, the descent is stable, close to 400 feet per minute and soon he is pulling gently back on the yoke to reduce speed, checking the airspeed indicator until the needle settles below the flap limiting speed of 103 knots, the figure above which the anti-stall devices must not be deployed. He pulls up the flap lever that

385

sits like a car handbrake between the front seats; it even has a rachet button at its top, but unlike its motoring counterpart there are four positions from no flap to full. Ray selects two stages and a touch more throttle and retrims the Piper to 80 knots; it feels like walking pace! Almost immediately he begins another gentle, rate one turn to the left. If he's got his positioning right he'll completely reverse direction in exactly one minute and find himself in line with the runway.

The elation he feels at caressing the controls to achieve what he needs is akin to that he still gets from using a steering wheel to place a car exactly where he wants it on the road, all those years on from the circular piano stool at his parents'. The magic remains – the better if everything is working out nicely, as today! He calls finals, and looks carefully at the runway to assess his elevation in relation to it. The altimeter reads 600 feet, which will be his approximate altitude, his height above the lazy swell. The runway lies at 80 feet above sea level, so all seems good. The water is not greatly helpful in judging height and he ignores it, concentrating on keeping the appearance of the runway in constant proportions; if it gets too flat in aspect, you're too low; if it becomes more plan-like, you're high and overshooting. The hill, rising beyond the not over-long runway helps the concentration. Now, he's at about 200 feet above the threshold altitude, having slowed to 65 knots as there's little wind and he could still glide in from here if the engine failed.

He selects full flap and bleeds the speed further with slight back pressure and trim, aiming to be at 60 knots and about ten feet at the start of the runway. At the threshold, the so-called round-out stops the descent with more back pressure on the yoke with his left hand, while his right simultaneously closes the throttle. The Warrior II will float if you allow it, so ever more easing back is called for, to stop the efficient wing flying and to plant the wheels on the tarmac. Pull too much too soon and the Piper will wallow up towards the sky again and plop back down very uncomfortably. That's one reason not to land too fast in any aircraft, but especially a Warrior. Today Ray manages it admirably, with no obvious juggling. With a slight squeal as the tyres touch the asphalt, he's down, smoothly at 47 knots and so a very short ground roll ensues with little need for braking.

Welcome to Plockton! Almost unbelievably, the parking brake goes on in the north-west highlands only two hours exactly after it was released in Carlisle, England. Even Clarkson, Hammond and May couldn't match that. Magic! The sense of achievement is total, however often you've done something similar. The moment that the concentration stops and the realisation of the enormity of what has just been performed clicks in; that you have effortlessly crossed mountain and moor, marsh and ravine, settlement and sea, travelling so far, so directly, so fast, so successfully; most pilots have but one reaction:

'Time for a drink.'

The old adage that pride comes before a fall is nowhere more applicable than aviation. It's mighty galling when having completed what seems to have been a faultless flight, you discover that you made some form of error or omission. The discovery can take various forms. You might receive a letter form the CAA telling you that you mistakenly infringed controlled airspace. It has been known for light aircraft to blunder into a Temporary Restricted Area, set up to protect an airshow. More than once the Red Arrows, for example, have broken off their display and gone home due to airspace incursion. Occasionally Ray has overheard pilots being requested to report to a control tower or telephone an Air Traffic Supervisor after landing. There is usually little question but that the pilot is due for a severe dressing-down for some demonstration of poor airmanship. Today Ray is about to find out that he has missed something – nothing serious or safety-critical; and a lapse that no one else need ever know about. The tellings-off that you give yourself make you feel just as embarrassed.

Ray has flown into Plockton before, about ten years ago with Eve for a few days' break. Then, the ultra-careful fuel planning he has carried out at Carlisle today was needed. Today it wasn't. Then the airfield had a tank and a fuel pump only for Jet A1, the diesel-type fuel used by turbine-powered helicopters. Today as he begins his walk to the village with his soft bag, he notices there are now facilities for dispensing **his** grade of fuel, 100 Low Lead, known as Avgas. His pre-flight preparation has failed to notice this, rendering a good proportion of his calculations unnecessary. He still needed not to have arrived with too much fuel in the two wing tanks, because of the take-off weight, but with Plockton selling 100 LL his consideration of having too little for his outward flight had been superfluous. In flying, you never stop learning lessons. And fortunately most of your mistakes, like today's, are ones you get away with.

Carlisle's border air had definitely been of a different character from Ray's accustomed, West Country variety, but marching down the lane to Plockton, the change is of another order again; he can almost taste the peat and the pines and the seaweed and the salt. Flying also makes you hungry. He's ready for a beer certainly but despite having eaten a decent breakfast at home and something with chips at Carlisle he's glad that supper will be available at the Haven by the time he's walked to the B&B, nattered to Frank and Helen, and retraced his steps along the full length of the seafront. He's glad he's kept his luggage to just one light bag; it wasn't just his runway length considerations that made him keep the weight down. Of course he had plenty of leeway really: after all, when he flew in and out of Plockton before it was with Eve and she isn't famed for travelling light. Which reminds him of course that Frank and Helen are going to ask after Eve, and for the hundredth time this year he'll say, 'She's very well. She's studying in America,' and then move the conversation somewhere else.

It's not until sipping the third single malt and water in the Haven's comfortable lounge after supper that Ray realises another mistake from earlier. The notion that the three countries of Albion – England, Scotland and Wales – have enjoyed uninterrupted peace since 1945 is more than questionable. Terrorism in pursuit of several causes has certainly visited Great Britain on numerous occasions, with major losses of life, and what about Lockerbie? It may not be as clear to everyone as it is to Ray exactly who had been fighting whom – indeed of course the British government has gone out of its way to point to the wrong aggressor.

Nevertheless, by most definitions it had been a serious act of war.

–ooOoo–

66   Borderline Insanity

Ambling along the sea front, Ray feels very comfortable; well-suppered on herrings and pleasantly warmed by the whisky. Even at this time of year in Scotland there is generally a slight bite to the air of an evening. People are overflowing onto the road outside the tiny Plockton Hotel and there is the sound of a folk group playing reels in the bar. Ray is tempted to step in for a final nightcap but he remembers that he needs to have his wits about him tomorrow and so had best get back to his bed. Leaving the chattering drinkers and the warm light and moving to the quieter and darker part of Harbour Street, a dramatic change comes over him. All the confidence wrought by the day's flights and the high adrenalin totally drops away as if he's removed a thick cloak. Suddenly he feels astonishingly vulnerable.

What is he doing here? Meeting up with an apparently whistle-blowing former spy is the logical progression from the research he's been involved with these many months, and the opportunity to meet Fraser came out of the blue as if it was something meant to be. It was a gift that had to be accepted and he hasn't given much thought to what is potentially involved, having been totally preoccupied with the logistics until now. The point is that assignations between writers and disaffected members of the intelligence community have historically been dangerous, actually all-too-often terminal, for one or both the participants.

As so often during Ray's rather bloodhound-like, somewhat haphazard sniffing along the Lockerbie trail of evidence, it had been Dick who'd given him what the old detective liked to call the 'heads up'. Dick's practised CID mind had methodically followed and meticulously noted literally hundreds of internet links in his own hunt for clues. Ray had soon discovered that the net can take you very quickly into some quite bizarre areas, and Dick's disciplined trailblazing had been indispensable in sifting the wheat from an almost infinite amount of chaff. What he had distilled was far from reassuring for both of them. Ray had long known, from reading *Cover-Up of Convenience*, that delving too deeply and perhaps getting too close to the truth of Lockerbie could bring all sorts of trouble down on your head. Even if you didn't propose to delve at all, you could fall foul of concerted dirty tricks, as William Chasey for one had found out when he was harassed and attacked by multiple agencies. Many people who did real digging experienced the same. The individuals involved in Pan American Airways' defence of its liability lawsuit, when they produced evidence that pointed to scenarios suggesting the involvement of intelligence agencies and drug couriers, not only saw their professional attempts blocked at every turn (including a series of court rulings that bordered on the unfathomable), but also their personal lives affected. The FBI would start completely specious investigations, and any official body from the local sheriff's office to the IRS might join the party, while banks could mysteriously foreclose on loans or freeze accounts. Actual whistle-blowers like Lester Coleman and Joe di Manio could find themselves unemployable and in some cases incarcerated in prison on trumped-up grounds. The hand of the US Department of Justice could be detected behind much of the activity, with clear violations of the rule of law and denial of individuals' constitutional rights seemingly the preferred options rather than any actual dispensing of proper justice.

All that was well-documented, but Dick had come upon a scandal with some similar themes: a rambling saga continuing the heady mix of drugs, arms, millions of dollars in dirty deals and misbehaviour involving shady companies and government agencies or personnel at all levels. Centred around the US Government's alleged piracy, use and sale of proprietary software in a case known as the Inslaw Affair, its story had significance for Dick and Ray – not just in the familiar pattern of justice being obstructed and investigations being consistently delayed and thwarted, by for example the sacking of prosecutors who looked like taking their task seriously – but much more sinisterly, in the wholesale slaughter that had apparently been visited on those trying to uncover the scandal and people suspected of being about to assist them. An incredibly long list of list of people – some forty-five, including would-be whistle-blowers and attorneys had met violent deaths, culminating in the murder of Danny Casolaro, an investigative journalist together with a National Security Agency operative, killed in a room at the Sheraton Hotel in Martinsburg, West Virginia, with the whistle-blower's body actually being covertly removed from the scene without acknowledgement of its presence. In many cases local police and coroners had conveniently accepted deaths as suicide, to the extent that followers of events had introduced the expression 'suicided' to indicate their contempt for the determination.

Dick's discovery of the Inslaw case had come about while doing a search on a British man, Ian Spiro. In early November 1992, a woman named Gail Spiro and three young members of her family were discovered murdered at their rented home in the highly exclusive community of Rancho Santa Fe, near San Diego, California. After four days her husband was also found dead, in his car, parked in a lonely desert spot seventy miles away. He appeared to have taken his own life by swallowing cyanide. The authorities came to the easy conclusion of murder followed by suicide. But Ian Spiro was no ordinary businessman driven over the edge by company collapse and debt. His brother and his wife's family are adamant that all five were murdered by others, citing the CIA or Mossad as their prime suspects. For London-born Spiro had been based in Beirut for some two decades, and his business interests had included dealing arms to Iran, thus making many contacts with the Shia radicals of Hizbullah. He was an acknowledged asset of the CIA and – his relations assert – had done work for British intelligence. He is known to have been involved with the discredited Lt-Col Oliver North during the Iran-Contra affair and was an intermediary in some of the negotiations to free the western hostages in Beirut. Spiro seems to have been sidelined after the 1986 exposure and symbolic sacrifice of North, despite the fact that other British arms dealers like the Aspin brothers kept the supply going as late as 1988 – largely, it is thought, at the behest of George H W Bush, long after the whole business had been officially disavowed by the US Government.

Spiro had apparently retired to California in 1988. Enmeshed as he had been in the darker reaches of Middle East politics, the idea that he might share his secrets with a wider public would have caused consternation in a number of camps. When it became known that he was preparing to go before a Federal Grand Jury in connection with the Inslaw case – a move that would undoubtedly have at the very least involved shedding light on some of his reclusive employers and clients – and that he was also contemplating the sale of his story to ease his financial situation – which could be expected to do the same for some of his unorthodox contacts – it was not altogether surprising that he began to complain of receiving death threats, mentioning the CIA, the DIA and Mossad.

The murder of his family – his 41 year-old wife, his daughters of 16 and 11 and his son of 14, each shot in the head – had the hallmarks of an execution with very much the signature of Lebanese extremists, but as Dick had pointed out, that detail may not have meant much, other than that the perpetrators wanted to make 'someone else' look responsible if the 'depressed, bankrupt father slaying his family before killing himself' scenario failed to convince the necessary authorities. As might have been predicted, given the track record, the necessary authorities **were** convinced.

The reason that Spiro is believed to tie into the Lockerbie story is that he, as acknowledged in testimony by a former US Ambassador to the UK, Eugene Douglas, had used perhaps five false passports and aliases (including, surprisingly, John Smith), one of which is thought to have been David Lovejoy. This is a name clearly meant to be the one identified in an extraordinarily frank interview given in May 1989 to the writer of an article in a Lebanese newspaper, *Al-Dustur*, by a senior cleric very close to the heart of the Iranian establishment. The Mullah gave the name of Lovejoy or Love-boy as the person responsible for tipping-off – via the Iranian

Embassy in Beirut – to the group poised to plant a revenge airliner bomb on Iran's behalf, the information that Major Charles McKee and members of his hostage rescue operation would be travelling on Pan Am 103. The article implied that the flight was selected specifically in order to include in its victims five (it stated) US intelligence operatives, and that the bomb was infiltrated into the baggage system at Frankfurt.

Spiro's arms and hostage dealings in Beirut would have undoubtedly brought him into contact with Lebanon's drug exporters, these being some of the diverse facets of the same organisation, and thus inevitably onto the radar and very possibly into direct touch with the CIA cell running the protected drug conduit. The likelihood is therefore that 'Lovejoy' either personally or at one remove also alerted the 'rogue' Company men to the travel intentions of McKee (from the rival DIA) and his 'regular' CIA associates, who were Washington-bound with the intention of blowing the conduit operation wide open. Any thought that Spiro might be intending to confess to being Lovejoy and to a part in that murderous betrayal, could have inspired a preventative strike on him from a number of quarters. It could even have been a question of which organisation got to him first.

In an almost unbelievable twist-of-fate, in May 1997 an inquest on Gail, who was also British, and the youngsters was held in Whitehaven, Cumberland. That town looks out on the Solway Firth across to the Scottish coast and is a mere fifty miles from Lockerbie. *Clipper Maid of the Seas*, which seems likely to have been targeted for destruction on the strength of a phone call from her husband, had flown very near to Whitehaven just five minutes before ceasing to exist as an airliner carrying families just like his. Now five more names could be added to the Lockerbie toll; four completely innocent; one perhaps partially responsible.

Had anyone entertained any doubt that the official line on the Spiro murders was remotely feasible, a fortnight after the deaths, Jose Aguilar, who did contract gardening work at the expensive properties along Avenida Maravillas, was also shot dead with a bullet to the head. Whether he had seen something in the course of his work or if he had possibly even reported seeing something is not known. The inescapable conclusion is that he was eliminated in case he spoke of activity that some party did not want discussed. Whatever motivated his death, the unfortunate 44-year-old tree-pruner certainly could not have been killed by Ian Spiro. Three days later, as if to reinforce the warning, 25-year-old Jorge Aguilar and 23-year-old Francisco Arredondo, who many believe may have been told by the older Mexican of his suspicions, were also executed in the same familiar style.

Ray has stopped, looking out at the dark waters of Loch Carron. The music in the bar can be half-heard, now and then carried on the night air. It's as if he is reluctant to leave the open sweep of the promenade and walk up the dark stretch to Camus an Arbhair. He is getting jumpy and needs to pull himself together; meeting a spy for the first time is certainly getting to him. 'Come on,' he thinks. 'This is rural Scotland, as isolated and safe as you could be anywhere in the world. People don't get murdered in Britain to protect murky intelligence secrets; do they?' 'Yes!' answers another voice, as quick as a flash. 'Of course they bloody well do. What do you think your screenplay is all about? Isn't that exactly your conclusion? It's part of why One-Zero-Three went down, for God's sake.'

One article that Dick has shown him explains how the US Justice Department has its own covert intelligence agency that operates out of the Criminal Division's Office of Special Investigations. OSI is known to employ scores of agents of diverse nationalities, as well as individuals employed in jobs in other US government departments and agencies. Dick has came to the conclusion that the OSI, like the CIA and others, can impose their version of justice pretty well anywhere in the world that they choose, using local free-lance enforcers known chillingly as 'outside contractors' or 'mechanics' for whom a killing means nothing more than a cash transaction. Any meaningful investigation of mysterious deaths, he says, is normally swiftly terminated on receipt of telephone instructions citing the 'national interest' or simply issuing authoritative threats. A similar blanket has been thrown over numerous unexpected and bizarre suicides in the UK, many being employees of defence and electronics contractors involved with secrets. Dick has naturally compiled extensive lists. This is a far from comforting thought.

Ray is also aware that while Lockerbie and Inslaw may both have happened a fair while ago, it is less than two years since Pulitzer Prize-winning investigative journalist Gary Webb met his premature death. There too the local police and coroner were quick to accept the cause as suicide, despite the fact that he had received two gunshot wounds to the head. A vastly experienced homicide expert subsequently determined that it would have been totally impossible for the victim to have fired both shots, yet the official fiction stands. Webb's investigative speciality was the misdemeanours of the CIA, with strong emphasis on arms and drug trafficking. He was quite obviously murdered and, friends and sympathisers point out, while the suicide verdict may close the matter as far as mass public interest is concerned, those who committed the murder must be happy that thinking people will recognise it for just what it was and take it as a warning not to follow Webb's path and meddle where attention is not appreciated. The practice of suppressing unwanted investigation with use of lethal force by no means seems to have stopped.

Ray sets off at a jog towards the short dark wooded hill, now really spooked for the first time since he was ten or eleven. His feet pound up the lane until his chest hurts. He hasn't run this fast in years. Every tree seems capable of hiding an assassin with a handgun and silencer. Out of the wood he doesn't feel out of the wood and keeps running when the lane opens up and becomes oddly suburban with a pavement. He trips on the unseen kerb and goes sprawling, rolling over several times before getting up in one movement and running again to reach one of the modern bungalows incongruously clustered at the end of the road, overlooking the open sea-loch, unseen below. The house is unlocked and he gets inside, trying to be quiet and control his noisy breathing as he shuts and bolts the door. He leans on the back of it. He's never believed that action when he's seen it in countless films, thinking it to be one of those cinematic clichés – something that people don't really do. Tonight he realises for the first time that they might well have no option, other than collapse on the floor. The house is uncannily quiet, but suddenly a door down the corridor opens. This could be it!

"I thought I heard you," Helen says. "I'm making some tea. Do you want a cup?"

–ooOoo–

Out on the loch, a Juniors' dinghy race is in progress. A gaggle of brightly coloured craft are crewed by figures, many of whom are so slight that they are barely seen over the gunwhales and when they are, seem like small Michelin people in their fluorescent and bulbous lifejackets. The safety boats, in the charge of serious-looking adults and far-from-serious teenagers, bustle around, attending to the capsizes, for this racing is as cut-and-thrust, to Ray's eyes, as the grown-up version and the gamesmanship and upsets make for moderate entertainment in the light breeze. Many of the watchers along the esplanade and the foreshore are proud relatives urging their junior selves to greater endeavours.

In the garden of the Plockton Hotel, squeezed between the road and the sea wall, there are no free seats among the palm trees, so Ray stands with a pint of orange juice and lemonade in his hand, taking in the action and the fabulous views across the loch to Duncraig Castle and the mountains of the interior rising to the east. Fraser had asked him to describe his appearance, which he had. When Ray had responded in kind, the ex-spy had simply said 'Don't worry. I'll find you.' Of course he would – how silly of Ray to imagine otherwise. The thought makes Ray turn to look over the roof of the hotel and its adjacent terrace of cottages, up to the fields beyond and the quiet track that he knows runs behind and above, overlooking Harbour Street. He has the thought that someone up there might, from the cover of the trees and walls, get a clear headshot of him in the garden with a sniper's rifle and a sighting scope. Him or Fraser. There wouldn't be a chance to guarantee taking out both. He's aware of the 'Judas Kiss' whereby an agent identifies a victim to a watching gunman by greeting in some visible way, before stepping back. Logic tells him that Fraser isn't leading him into such a trap, but logic isn't always quite reassuring enough.

He turns back to the water with a dismissive frown. He'd recovered from last night's jitters quickly enough, but now he's at it again, jumping at shadows. Maybe he should just go up to the airstrip and fly home, forgetting the meeting.

Of course neither he nor Fraser is going to be shot in the midst of a crowd watching a sailing event. Something much more inventive and discreet would be on the cards. Ray knows there are sophisticated poisons now, a single small drop of which can kill in moments, or others with a delayed reaction, and yet evaporate from the body within hours of death and so be undetectable at autopsy. These days the assassins have got it made. Ray has been very careful to tell a few close friends like Carl and Austin and now Jack, as well as to leave a letter to the same effect with his solicitor, that if he is ever reported as taking his own life, it will under no circumstances represent the facts. It would be unlikely that the most dogged attempts by friends might get anywhere officially, as in the cases of Webb, Casolaro, the Spiro family and all the others, but at least his nearest and dearest would know at least part of the truth.

If his years of work as an assistant director have nurtured one attribute, it's that of being grade one observant. It is not very surprising then that in his occasional casual glances at the street he spots a potential Fraser making his way along from the direction of the Haven and the car park. In truth, it's not that difficult because very few among the modest-sized crowd moving up and down the promenade are on their own, most being attached to family groups or walking with at least one other person. When Fraser One, in a tweed jacket and cloth cap, having almost arrived level with the hotel disappears between sweeps, Ray decides that he has gone into the bar to buy a drink. On the telephone, the instructions were quite clear. Ray is not to do anything to indicate that they either know each other, or that they have **not** met before; no shaking hands or any such sign. Fraser will simply strike up a conversation, appearing to any watcher to be simply chatting to a random person in the crowd in the garden. That is exactly how it plays.

Ray has contrived to stand at a maximum distance from any of the tables filled with holidaymakers or any of the standing spectators. After a few minutes he becomes aware of someone who has bisected the space between him and his nearest neighbour, whilst remaining slightly behind him.

"Not always the greatest spectator sport, this," a voice says, and Ray senses rather than sees the lifting of half pint glass to mouth.

"I can think of more exciting," Ray replies, without looking round. It sounds exactly like agents using challenge and response phrases to verify identities, he thinks, although no such niceties have been pre-arranged. There is a pause. Ray assumes it's for the man to assess whether anyone at all has reacted to their making contact. In the garden the families continue being families and the couples maintain their quiet conversations or continue their silences exactly as before. Clearly the voice is satisfied.

"You'll be Ray."

"That's right."

"I half-wondered whether you might have my sister in tow."

"Sadly not." The owner of the voice has now stepped closer and in line with Ray who, as he's expected, sees tweed in his peripheral vision. Both men continue to look out towards the water.

"How do you do? I'm Fraser."

"Well. Thank you."

"I apologise for the pantomime aspect, but one has to be cautious these days."

"I understand."

"I doubt you do. I wouldna say I understand entirely myself, but its better to waste caution than court wasting, as a smart friend o'mine once said." This is exactly what Ray doesn't want to hear. He notices that Fraser has turned round, taking in the entire surroundings.

"Can I ask exactly how dangerous this is, for you or for me?"

"You can ask, but I'm no sure I can give you an answer. I'd prefer to discuss that later. Do you have a car here?"

–ooOoo–

67   The Bank of Revelations

If Fraser has ever been taught advanced or defensive driving, Ray decides, he has forgotten every single piece of instruction or advice that the course might have offered. Ray clearly didn't have a car at Plockton so now Fraser is pushing this scratched and unwashed Mondeo through the blind bends of the back road to Balmacara as though the likelihood of anything coming the other way is zero, despite occasional evidence to the contrary. So far all the oncoming challengers have been avoided, although Ray is unsure quite how. The man is dressed for a Range Rover or a Discovery at the least and looks quite out of place in the Ford's grubby and littered interior. Ray wonders if it's his. It certainly isn't a hire car, which Ray would have expected.

"Jackie says you're writing a film. She didna put about what."

"It's Lockerbie."

"Why are you doing that?" His accent makes the word 'that' last as long as the other four. Ray slips easily into what has become his standard response, although few have ever posed the question in quite as direct a manner. He chooses his words carefully, especially when he talks about the Secret World setting up an alternative morality and rewriting the rule of law and constitutional rights to suit its own objectives. Ultimately though, there can be no fudging of his position. He has been told that this man has himself rejected that world's excesses. They are either on the same side or they aren't. He can only wait for the Scot's reaction. He comes to the end of his pitch.

"Aye," says Fraser. "There's no' much I would argue with in that."

Ray hadn't exactly stopped breathing, but now he relaxes a few notches. As far as he can, that is. It's rare that he is driven and it seems fated now that when he is, it's often by someone with no concept of self-preservation.

—ooOoo—

Fraser doesn't stop until Glen More. It is an inspired choice for an unobserved talk. No one could have concealed themselves anywhere on this valley's sides in advance and no one can now move into position without being spotted. The place selected affords a commanding view of the only road in both directions, giving several minutes' warning of the approach of any vehicle, of which there has only been one since they left the main road at Shiel Bridge, six miles back or more and five hundred feet lower.

Now, finally, when they're out of the car and looking down the Old Military Road – in fact a single track lane traversing its way across the valley side in a spectacularly straight long descent back to sea level and the Kylerhea ferry and Skye – Fraser introduces himself properly. They shake hands and Ray notes that his driver uses his correct surname.

"I figured that I'd have to see you. Having two messages and a call from my sister in the space of a week, which normally would have been a year's worth, it was clear you were OK – and also that she wasna' going to give up till I'd agreed to meet you. She can be very persistent if she wants something." Ray smiles. He can see a trace of family resemblance, and talking to this man slightly bridges the 12,000 miles.

"Excuse me for asking, but how old are you?"

Ray tells him.

"You're a weebit older than her usual taste, since the dreaded Patrick, of course. Did you meet the awful Kim?"

Ray nods.

"I won't ask. But if ever there was a loser. Still – it's her business," he says before dismissing triviality and turning to the matter in hand.

"Now – I rather doubt that I can tell you anything about Lockerbie that you haven't already found. I have no special knowledge: I had no involvement. Did Jackie tell you I was Military Intelligence – not the Security Service or SIS?" She hadn't; this may not be looking too promising. "Yes, I was originally a soldier, for my sins."

Fraser outlines his career, in terms only of where he went, rather then what he actually did. It's effectively a list of countries, mainly in Europe, the Middle East, the Balkans and Northern Ireland. The last of the roll seems to have been his final posting. In December 1988 he had been in Berlin, so probably saw less, he says, of Lockerbie than most Brits will have seen on their televisions. To Ray's questioning he confirms that he'd known about the two Hedemunden attempts on troop trains, because the second one had happened in April '88 shortly after his arrival and naturally his American counterparts were very exercised about security of their military personnel. They hadn't forgotten the La Belle Disco bombing in the city two years earlier, that also had targeted American service people. He remembers security for British forces in Germany too being stepped-up following the railway attack. He reminds Ray that Germany and Berlin were both still divided at the time.

Ray responds to mention of the discothèque incident with another question.

"You remember that Libya was blamed for the La Belle attack and that was used as justification for the US to bomb Tripoli and Benghazi, when the UK was, I think, the only country that provided approval and assistance. Did you know that although Libyans were later convicted, in shades of Lockerbie, it was originally thought that a Syrian agent, Ahmed Hasi, was responsible and that the 'messages of congratulation', supposedly from Gaddafi, that were 'intercepted' after the bombing and seized on as proof by the US, were widely believed to be false and some said originated from a Mossad transmitter putting out bogus 'Libyan' traffic?"

"I've no information on that. And if I had I'm no sure I'd be telling you. I'm no too keen on having the Mossad looking for me."

"You recall that the two Hedemunden incidents were PLFP-GC, Syrian-backed?"

"I would have known at the time, I suppose. Funny, it all seems less important now."

If the intelligence man has forgotten details, he remembers hearing of the Autumn Leaves raids, although he has to be reminded of the operation's actual codename. As to the details of the German BKA's operation that saw Khreesat, Dalkamoni and others of Jibril's PLFP German cell rounded-up, Ray has far more at his fingertips than Fraser, to whom the names mean nothing. He is, though, far from surprised when Ray describes the wanted aircraft bomber, Khreesat, being released by the Karlsruhe judge for 'lack of evidence' despite being found in a car with a complete Toshiba aeroplane bomb.

"If he was a double agent as you say, or any sort of an agency asset, they'd have him out of there. The judge would just do as he was told – end of story."

"Did you see that sort of thing occur yourself?"

"It would happen."

Ray waits, but Fraser is not sharing any personal stories on that score. Ray tries another approach.

"How did you get on yourself with the CIA?"

"I didn't care for 'em. They seemed to feel they had a God-given right to do anything, anywhere. America's interests came first and everybody else could put up with it."

"You felt it was different from the way your colleagues approached things?"

"I think we trod a little more sensitively."

"Did you have much to do with them, the CIA?"

"Enough."

There is another long pause, giving Fraser time to add more if he wishes. He doesn't. Ray searches for another question; desperate for anything that will get the man to open up.

"The attitude you describe is very much what was reported by some of the police at Lockerbie with the CIA contingent seeming to take control and dictate the focus of the search and recovery at first."

"They would. I'm no' surprised. They seem to wield enormous power. I'll rephrase that. They **do** wield enormous power. They ask: they get."

"People were surprised how quickly the first American agents got there; inside three hours."

"There's a lot of them." Fraser almost smiles. "It's a big employer."

"So where would the nearest ones have been, to get there so soon?"

"Oh, my guess would be Menwith Hill, near Harrogate. There would be a decent intelligence presence at a listening facility the Americans have got there. They'd probably do it in under two hours, with the M6."

Ray can't imagine why he and Dick haven't come up with that before, they've discussed the place often enough in a different context. It was inevitable there would be a CIA detachment at the National Security Agency's main European eavesdropping station. It was 50 or so miles of far-from-easy road to the motorway, but then a mere 70 to the crash site. Of course that didn't explain the large party that was ready, many of them equipped with Pan Am clothing and identities, to board the special flight from Heathrow within around three hours of One-Zero-Three going down. Pan Am's London-based Head of Corporate Security for Europe,

Jim Berwick, who was on the 727, had no idea who they were or how they had got their wardrobe items. Ray asks Fraser about them and for the first time the response goes beyond the minimal.

"Well he wouldn't know anything about that. Uniforms for cover purposes is a standard thing. It'll have been arranged in America years before and way, way above his level; indeed it's just conceivable that no one in Pan Am even knew of it, and the stuff was just copied and made up by the agency and imported and stored by them. Then again, the airline was the major international carrier and was very co-operative with all arms of the US government, so there was almost certainly a special office hidden in Pan Am somewhere where those sort of things were organised. The CIA will have rails of every uniform you could ever imagine, and they won't have got co-operation for all of them; some they will; some they won't; European and British Military, Police, Airlines, Gas Board; you name it — just hanging somewhere ready in case one day they're needed for some covert operation. They'll have their own vehicles too — ambulances, looking like civilian jobs — that sort of stuff."

"Did you have such things?"

"What do **you** think?"

Jack's brother now seems intent on a return to vapid answers.

"And how about their being ready, as if they were expecting the crash?"

"Well you've probably got more idea on that than I have, if you've been researching it."

"But would the idea surprise you, if they were?"

"Nothing would surprise me, I mean, presume you've read *Plausible Denial?* You said earlier that you believe these agencies are outwith the control of governments. I didn't disagree. You think there was a protected drug channel. How can anyone say there couldn't be, when there's the evidence of Iran-Contra? You say that the agency or people in it let it happen because someone in another service was going to expose whatever they were up to. I don't know if they did, but I know they could have — inter-agency hatred, inter-section warfare, personal vendettas, they all go on, and people get caught in the crossfire. You've decided it could happen, and you're just an outsider who's done a bit o' digging. You wouldna believe me anyway if I said 'No — it could never occur.' Literally anything is possible. Whatever you can imagine, somebody's done it or is doing it."

"And are the British as bad as the Americans, or the Israelis, or the Russians?"

"Not yet. But they're working on it. If they needed convincing, your industry as much as anything has persuaded recent generations that life is cheap and expendable."

Their exchange is interrupted by the sight of a vehicle approaching from the west, climbing the long gradient towards them. According to the map and logic, a threat from this direction should be 99 percent impossible, but Fraser nevertheless moves them up off the road to a place above a stone wall that provides both cover and some possibility of escape on foot. It's also a reasonable ambush position and Ray wonders if his companion is armed. He won't find out. A Land Rover rattles and clatters up and past without slowing. Now a car is coming down from the Shiel Bridge direction and the pair wait, trying to appear like holidaymakers taking in the magnificent view, as two tourists potter harmlessly by.

Ray cannot help thinking that this is rather a lot of security for not a great deal of information. Clearly Fraser has serious concerns about personal safety, but Ray doesn't know whose – Fraser's, his or both of theirs. He's already raised the subject, so he'll see if there are any more nuggets to come before mentioning it again.

"Do you know much about Menwith Hill?" he asks as they scramble back down to the road. "I know it pretends to be an RAF facility, and then a branch of GCHQ, but that it's really controlled by the American National Security Agency."

"Not only is Menwith Hill NSA, it's the largest electronic monitoring station in the world, one of a whole international network of such places that transmit gathered material back to their headquarters at Fort Meade, Maryland. What they collect is Electronic Intelligence, ELINT, and Signals Intelligence, SIGINT. In layman's terms that means computerised, industrial-scale eavesdropping on phone calls and radio traffic and intercepting fax messages, telex, e-mail, you name it. And we're talking the ability to access most of it and we're talking world-wide. Obviously it has to be selective; they can't read everything so they have to use key words to tell them what to analyse, but basically they can get whatever they want."

Ray knows the substance of what Fraser is telling him but is desperately trying to implement a new policy of keeping quiet, in the hope that the intelligence man will move on to things he hasn't heard of. In this case the policy works: Fraser is continuing.

"What's more, if you write any document on your computer, even without any intention of sending it electronically, the chances are they will be able to copy and read it, if they want to; certainly if you open it while your modem is switched in and you're connected to the net or e-mail." Ray realises that, in that case, the spooks could have had a copy of his screenplay before he left for New Zealand, and that they could have the rewrite too. He hopes they appreciate the improvements. He wonders whether communications were Fraser's speciality, like Charles McKee's, as the subject has certainly brought the former soldier to life.

"Menwith Hill was originally set up in the fifties as a field station of the US Army Security Agency, in co-operation with our War Office, but the agreement to share intelligence came out of secret Second World War agreements." Ray thinks what Fraser is saying makes sense, remembering that, according to Brian, President Roosevelt was getting British intelligence digests from 1940, when the help he was giving beleaguered Britain was minimal. "They were formalised," Fraser continues, "in an ultra-secret treaty called BRUSA in 1943 and another called UKUSA in '46. Later the Canadians, the Australians and New Zealand joined in. The task of all the stations in the network was to monitor international communications of citizens, companies or governments for information of political, military or commercial value to the USA – note the last bit. The NSA was formed in 1952 by Presidential decree, without any debate. It didn't take over the Yorkshire site until '66, I think, at about which time a big cable, thousands of lines, was laid to the Hunter Stones Post Office tower, a few miles away, to get access to the British long-distance microwave telephone network. In 1975, interception of satellite messages began and then in 1992 they went fibre-optic with another huge cable that can take 100,000 simultaneous calls, so basically anything using a telephone cable to or from Europe passing through Britain can be analysed."

Now there is no stopping the man. "Then you've got the information coming down from the spy satellites, like the Keyholes and Lacrosse, which if you've come to their attention can show them what you're reading in your garden or the address on a letter you put in the pillar box. If you think they're after you, never work on anything in the open air." Ray thinks of those outdoor sessions at Dick's house. He clamps his mouth closed and nods his head vigorously, willing Fraser to carry on. "I mean this stuff gets more sophisticated every day; goodness knows the things they've developed since I knew something about them. The beauty of it all is the deniability. Our government continually maintains this façade that it only uses strictly controlled surveillance in specific, serious circumstances and not randomly and routinely. The American government says the same. It has to, because that country has a Constitution which makes such things illegal. But if some other country spies on your citizens for you, as a politician you can say that you're not doing it and convince yourself you're not telling a lie – in the unlikely event that such a thing would worry you. So the Americans monitor the Brits and in theory the Brits and the Canadians are doing the domestic spying for the Yankees, with the Aussies and the Kiwis in on the act as well. In reality it's an American operation, ultimately run in Uncle Sam's interests. They share what they want to share and no more, especially in the commercial area. Did you hear that the European Parliament held an inquiry into all this?

Ray shakes his head. This has passed him by. Fraser is on a roll.

"The whole process gets referred to as ECHELON, and when our good friends in Brussels learnt that the UK was spying on them on America's behalf, they formed the Echelon Committee in 2000/2001 to look into it. It's worth reading, especially the evidence of a New Zealander called Nicky Hager, who wrote a book called *Secret Power* about what he found down there. One thing that had upset the Europeans was that they'd lost a big Airbus contract because the Americans leaked that Airbus had been bribing people in Saudi Arabia. Well, for a start, everyone bribes in the Middle East: God knows how they sold all those Boeings out there if they didn't. It's like a standard part of a contract, you have to pay a percentage to a local agent, who's usually Prince So-and-So – they call them the Black Princes. Two, an ex-Director of the CIA, James Woolsey, actually let the cat out of the bag when he justified the bugging by saying 'We have spied on you because you bribe.' He'd obviously forgotten the Lockheed scandal involving Prince Bernhard of the Netherlands, which nearly destroyed the Dutch Monarchy, and he also had a strange notion of chronology – I mean Airbus didn't even exist when these worldwide surveillance facilities were set up. And as for bribery, just read about how America is securing co-operation in Afghanistan – it's with millions of dollars in suitcases. Oh and needless to say, Boeing got the Saudi contract instead. Equally needless to say, Airbus doesn't get to hear of anything significant that's intercepted about Boeing's commercial or technical secrets. One of the reasons I left was that I didna join the British Army to work for the likes of ITT and Raytheon."

"What you're telling me," Ray interjects, rather to his own annoyance, "is very much what I've believed for a long time, but it's still uncomfortable to have some of these things confirmed. The day of Big Brother has certainly arrived."

"It arrived about 40 years ago. It makes me laugh when I see people jumping up and down about a bit o' telephone tapping. They don't realise that they've been living in a surveillance state for a couple of generations and no one's done a thing about it. Read Antony Thompson's *Big Brother in Britain Today* and you think, 'This is hellish frightening,' and then you realise that it was written in bloody 1970!"

Ray comes back.

"I mean, I'm very happy with eavesdropping on bad people. Obviously there's no problem with surveillance of criminals or terrorists but then you read that virtually anyone who opposes something that the government does or wants to do can get the treatment. Be it cruise missiles or backing foreign dictators or building new by-passes or nuclear power stations, it's quite horrific that heavy government resources are used to counter dissent, of the most innocuous kind too – remember Hilda Morell, the elderly woman who was murdered just before she was to speak at the Sizewell power station inquiry?"

Ray stops himself. He has only now remembered that some commentators thought there was evidence pointing to possible involvement by military intelligence in her bizarre abduction. Fraser, if he is aware of it, does not take the unintended bait and continues as if Ray had not mentioned the Herefordshire rose grower.

"You've got to remember that when the Cold War ended, there was panic in the West's armed forces, the defence-dependent industries and the intelligence agencies. For them the fear of the Eastern Bloc that had been built up had provided the largest gravy train that the world had ever seen. Ordinary people were very optimistic. They were pleased for the people who lived in the freed nations and happy that more resources in their own countries would now be released, available for worthwhile things – the so-called peace dividend. But a reduction in spending on arms and armies and hi-tech surveillance was of course the last thing wanted by those whose comfortable livelihoods depend on such things, and they set about finding new threats and new enemies to justify the continuation of 'business as usual'. I remember in my lot, there was suddenly the feeling, 'Hell, we're gonna be out of a job!' In the UK, it didn't take long for there to be an announcement that MI5 were going to add some areas of interest to their portfolio. You remember they got organised crime and cross-border offences like money-laundering and people-trafficking added to their remit."

Ray is tempted to come in, to tell the Scot, if he doesn't know, that many in the UK's police forces bitterly resented this 'muscling in' on their territory and inevitably the diversion of some of their budget. They rightly thought that combating crime was what they were about, and that to introduce another organisation could only cause duplication and inefficiency. It was the reverse of what was generally a trend to amalgamate and to combine resources, not fragment them. And that was before the overnight invention of the British FBI – SOCA. He decides though that it's best to let Fraser continue, now he's in expounding mood.

"You didn't have to be a cynic to realise that everyone was contriving to see any hope of a peace dividend neatly thwarted. Far from their being downsized, everything about the security and intelligence services multiplied, except bizarrely, a little of their secrecy. In selling the idea that their growth was vital to the health and well-being of the nation, they had to venture much further out of the shadows than ever they had before. Top people started to be publicly named; Stella Rimmington wrote her memoirs; we now even have a sympathetic BBC drama series telling us that MI5 is full of nice people who pay a terrible personal price for trying to keep us all safe."

It's a firm belief of Ray's that MI6's moving into a massive and sinister-looking headquarters by London's Vauxhall Bridge is a part of this new public face that has gone horribly wrong. Transferring from anonymous office premises to openly avowed, showpiece accommodation was always going to be a risk. The new structure might be impressive but is, appropriately he thinks, brutally ugly and totally lacking in humanity, in the manner of much Soviet architecture. Its riverside location mimics that of the House of Parliament, not far downstream, and some feel that this could be deliberate. The edifice shouts total permanence; it clearly identifies itself as a centre of extreme importance and gravity, but could another message also imply rivalry – an alternative seat of power? Those who spend any time examining the minimal amount of influence wielded by the hob-tied elected inhabitants of the older institution two bridges along, might readily conclude that it does. Looking at the blank and austere face of Vauxhall Cross, even though the SIS is concerned with overseas intelligence, people can easily feel themselves looking at Orwell's Ministry of Truth, and imagine that from behind its reflective windows their lives are being scrutinized, assessed and controlled. Perhaps, in some perverse way, that is what they are intended to feel.

Later, when returning to inter-agency rivalries, Fraser will drop the interesting plum that the name used by the Security Service, in their HQ on the north bank, for their international opposite numbers in their new south bank palace is 'Tsars'. It stands, he says, for 'Those Shits Across the River'.

It is the closest that Fraser will approach to a light tone throughout their entire meeting.

His whole stance, Ray notices, is increasingly one of total detachment from the Secret World. More and more he speaks as if he had never been an agent, not been part of it. This is strange. Intelligence had been his career for what clearly had been a considerable length of time. Surely he must have believed in what he was doing for a good proportion of his employment? Maybe it's the same syndrome as with former smokers who, it's often found, can become the most fervent haters of tobacco smoke.

For all that, the amount of hard new information is minimal. Fraser seems to think he is imparting valuable material; he probably underestimates the breadth and depth of the research Ray has already done. The writer soon comes to the conclusion that not only does Jack's brother not have the magic key to unchain Lockerbie's remaining secrets, but that what he does have to say is insufficient to require any changes to the screenplay whatever. On one level, Ray is relieved at the last realisation. It's not going to mean another major re-write. When he and Dick discuss the Scottish adventure in cautiously-worded e-mails, their different professional 'takes' on Fraser's minimal contribution will be noteworthy. Dick, the investigator, is well aware that promising avenues of inquiry all-too-often turn out to be blind alleys; sometimes in a case they all do and the file is labelled 'unsolved'; disappointment is routine – par for the course. Ray from his standpoint will remark that he would have difficulty in using such an episode in a screenplay. His audience would be expecting the meeting to yield more tangible results. It's a shame, he will say, that real life is rarely as obliging as it needs to be portrayed in drama.

This may not be a bad thing though, in terms of personal comfort. Recapping the flow of the conversation this evening over another solitary meal in the Haven, Ray suddenly finds himself wondering what extreme dangers and discomforts might have been encountered if his and Fraser's meeting had been a scene in a Gerald Logan picture. Being slightly disappointed is much preferable to being definitively slaughtered. Still, he's enjoying the break and even the believable worst hasn't happened. In the words of one of his favourite acerbic songs from Loudon Wainwright III:

> Walked out of my door – and I didn't get shot.

> It's a pretty good day – so far.

–ooOoo–

68   Deleted Scenes

DB has been far from inactive during Ray's absence in Scotland. There are several messages waiting on the all-singing answer machine. They suggest progress.

Beep. "I know I can't reach you in the land of moor and midge, but ring me when you get back. I may have got Warren Hanson interested." Beep.

Beep. "Me again. Warren Hanson **is** interested. I think he might be good for Weiss. What do you think? Talk soon. Bye." Beep.

Beep. "Holidaymaker not back yet? OK, well. Hanson is definitely keen. Asking about directors – correction – suggesting directors. We need to talk some ideas. He's saying 'How about Larry Ralston?' Not sure about that myself. Speak to you soon." Beep.

Beep. "Ray. It's Jake. Listen, DB is desperate to talk to you. Please call him as soon as you're back." Beep.

The flight back has been delayed two days by poor weather, fulfilling the pilots' tongue-in-cheek maxim: 'Time to spare – go by air'. Ray has been out of touch for longer than planned. He hadn't, though, been expecting such a pace of developments or his absence to present any sort of problem. He notes, somewhat ruefully, that every message on the machine relates to the *One-Zero-Three* project. Such is the effect, he laments, of single-mindedness on your social life.

–ooOoo–

He explains his delayed return to a fraught-sounding DB Hollingsworth. The man can't just be working on the Lockerbie film to be under the degree of pressure that almost permeates down the phone line. Ray continues, undeterred.

"Anyway I got your messages. Very interesting. I have to ask though – about Warren Hanson – he's American. Daniel Weiss is an Englishman. I can see that he looks right for Weiss, but can he play English?"

"I doubt it," DB says. "But if we can get him, it would be worth a few tweaks to accommodate his accent. Look, I wouldn't worry too much about it until it happens. I just thought you'd be excited. I've gotta rush. Are you going to be there later?" He's gone almost before Ray has grunted some form of affirmative.

'A few tweaks.' Ray is against the idea of an American star playing Weiss on so many levels that it almost hurts.

Presumably DB imagines that Weiss can be re-written as a US citizen without anything being lost. This may possibly be true, but he has been created as British for very sound reasons, and to change his nationality would upset a number of carefully thought-out balances. Weiss is English, because his flight attendant girlfriend, Tanya, who dies, is written as an American. Reasonably enough, Ray wants his two lead characters to represent the countries that lost the highest number of their nationals on the flight. The victims from the passengers and crew were from 32 countries in all, but of these, 20 lost one single casualty and ten had numbers in the range of two to six. The remainder of the dead, as might be predicted, were Britons and Americans, with 33 of the former and 170 of the latter. And Tanya's nationality makes sense for other good reasons. Although it's true that Pan American cabin crews were multinational in make-up, and that there were indeed ten nationalities working on board 103, there was only one Briton, one of the two pursers, Mary Geraldine Murphy, and three American flight attendants, of which one was a male. Ray's strong conviction is that for obvious reasons the Tanya character should not be directly identifiable with a real victim, which certainly therefore rules out the possibility of re-writing Tanya as British. In any case, because the airline was American, some form of explanation would then be required – an unwanted complication, especially as the script calls for the early Weiss-Tanya relationship to be played in the shorthand form of a montage without dialogue.

Ray thinks that the balance is made clearer by having the couple live, initially at least, on their respective, opposite sides of the Atlantic. It helps to keep the story simple. In fact the real crew lived in a variety of countries, in several cases not that of their own nationality; one of the American female flight attendants actually made her home in London. There are sound reasons too for making Weiss UK-based; it's where the disaster takes place, where many of the meetings and later the Fatal Accident Inquiry are held, so that he is in the right country to see things for himself and to do his digging, without having to travel backwards and forwards. Of course an American can live in London, but to give the balance Ray wants, Tanya would then have to be British and live in America, which wouldn't be at all easy to explain and would lose for America the victim character that the statistics rightly call for. In short, changing Daniel Weiss to a US citizen would cause a domino effect, requiring innumerable changes and, in Ray's view, unnecessary compromises.

Little does he know that in meetings to be held in the coming weeks – many of which he will not be personally involved in – numerous people will casually and sometimes forcefully propose American nationality for every possible combination of the principal characters, Weiss, Tanya, Jane and Brad. There will be more than one call for all four to be made sons and daughters of the US of A. Ray will learn enough though to make a blunt observation to his producer: 'If I'd made him American, some non-entity would have found a reason to suggest he should be something else. They seem to fulfil no useful function, these people! They have to invent work for themselves, and they do it by finding something to change. They'll make a huge palaver about the first thought that comes into their head, because otherwise they've got nothing to do.' DB will listen, smile and move on.

Ray has always thought of *One-Zero-Three* as a British movie. As his research progressed and revealed more and more about the Lockerbie case, he reached the view that, in all probability, episodes that the film needs to depict will not be conducive to obtaining American backing. Joe Wyzell's reaction has already indicated that this might well be true. Ray has assumed that if the film is to be made at all, it will be with British and European money, perhaps with the participation of BBC Films or the Channel 4 counterpart. It has only been the resurrection of his friendship with Gerald, and his fortuitous meeting with DB, that have permitted him ever to consider its promotion to an international picture with major stars, and all the attendant bells and whistles and razzamatazz. Until then his assumption was – if made at all, British picture on mainly British locations, using predominantly British actors, with Americans where required.

Under strong interrogation, Ray would probably admit further reasons for his preference; reasons connected more with chauvinism than with objectivity. They would stem from his indignation, from his very earliest days of cinema-going, at so many films set in the British Isles having one or more North Americans parachuted in to take leading rôles for no discernible dramatic reason. Indeed, usually they seemed to have been dumped incongruously and unconvincingly in a British environment, where their presence, as far as he was concerned, was just distracting. He had actually worked on such films in the early days of his career and just couldn't understand the practice. It didn't always seem to be financially motivated, because sometimes the actors involved were not well-known enough to influence the takings at the box office, yet there they were – flown in and put up at great expense – often adding nothing to the movie and merely depriving British actors of work. There was an early TV series, *Dial 999*, in which Robert Beatty, who was a decent enough Canadian star of the era, played a Scotland Yard detective. Theoretically such a character was possible, but to depict one was wildly unrepresentative. TV viewers, who were not that numerous in the UK at the time, happily accepted this misleading scenario.

Strangely enough, had the public only known, there was at this very time in real life a rather prominent Canadian at Scotland Yard. This was Pc Bill Rutherford, who was a radio operator in the new Information Room. For many years 'Canada Bill's' presence on duty would mean that one of the voices directing London's wireless cars to their assignments had a strong North American accent. Had this been put in a film, it would have been derided as wholly ridiculous – by Ray's father for one.

Gratefully, Ray is more than aware that in the last few years the trend has been rather reversed, with British actors becoming very popular in American movies and TV. He's quite happy to accept this, seeing it as making amends, balancing the books and some recompense for the travesties that he had to watch while growing up.

He will share his analysis but not be discussing his prejudice in this matter with DB or Gerald, or new agent Jake. Unlike Ray, they are obliged to strut a more cosmopolitan stage where, as Eve would deliberately malaprop 'The world is their lobster'.

−ooOoo−

For Ray's taste, the bar is too crowded and noisy, but then he's become less and less enthusiastic about bars, full stop, in recent years. Nevertheless the invitation to join Will for a drink has come as very welcome and he's actually been looking forward to some mild social interaction, the first really since his return from Plockton (and Fraser had hardly been a bundle of fun). Will, after all, is effectively family and with Ray's family numbers seeming to have dwindled to virtually zero, he can't imagine not taking the opportunity. As Will's tipple is bitter, Ray is drinking lager; also a rare event, and as he's staying over at Will and Hannah's, with no driving involved, there is nothing to stop the pints flowing, in parallel with the conversation.

Ray hasn't seen Will since well before New Zealand, so with that and the Scottish trip, there are plenty of adventures to recount. He has to be slightly careful and remember at all times that Will and Hannah are very close to Eve. There are traps that he can fall into on that score, if he becomes incautious. But he thinks that there is no longer any need to be secretive about the subject of the screenplay, and he assumes anyway that father-in-law Brian will probably have mentioned the barest bones at some point after the long session on the night before the couple's wedding. Naturally the script is going to come up at some point, it being the motivation for the New Zealand foray. 'Further research' can also be used to justify the second excursion. Flying off alone to Scotland for a few days is hardly typical Scriver behaviour and some explanation will be called for, to keep things tidy.

Will's study of international affairs inevitably takes in the exercise of military power, so he is fascinated by current events in Afghanistan and Iraq and there's plenty to discuss on those scores. When the screenplay comes up, the younger man asks some perceptive questions and Ray finds himself, once again, giving in a low voice a very potted summary. Will seizes on the idea that it was the over-aggressive behaviour of one military commander, Captain Rogers of the *Vincennes*, that precipitated the whole sad Lockerbie saga. As they discuss it, Ray realises for the first time the coincidence involved in that a US warship also played a part in bringing the story to its present imperfect conclusion. The Crown's star witness against al-Megrahi and Fhima, one Majid Giaka (pronounced Jacka), was illegally spirited out of Malta by speedboat and transferred to the *USS Butte* and eventually into the US Witness Security Program.

Star witness Gaika might have been, but his performance proved to be far from Oscar-winning and his 'producers' in the CIA and the FBI must have been very unhappy with the millions of dollars they spent on securing this most unconvincing actor.

His contribution to the story in dramatic terms is another of those complex sub-plots that are too long and convoluted to deal with in totality in the screenplay and again one which could well stand up as a TV movie in its own right. It wouldn't be a very uplifting one, though, and the audience would not find much to like and very few characters with which to identify. Ironically (given current public perception of them) the 'convicted bomber' al-Megrahi and the acquitted Fhima would come out as the only protagonists with whom a TV audience might find sympathy.

Majid Gaika was a low-achiever who joined the Libyan Intelligence Service, the JSO, in 1984 and worked as a mechanic in the motor transport department for two years before being sent to Malta to work under the cover of a post as Assistant Station Manager for Libyan Arab Airlines, where his boss was Lamin Fhima, who was not an intelligence operative. It is thought that the embezzlement of funds intended for aircrew expenses and some smuggling, plus an involvement in gambling, were the activities that occupied Gaika's spare time. Some four months before Lockerbie, his superiors ordered him to return immediately to Tripoli. For whatever reason the recall, and there are several possibilities, he was concerned for his future and contacted the American embassy. Inevitably the CIA personnel there recruited him on condition that he stayed in place, which he did and so began to report to them on the JSO.

He continued to work in Malta, and was there at the time of Lockerbie and through the year following, 1989, but clearly was not supplying American intelligence with information of any value whatsoever, inasmuch as the CIA decided to cease paying him after December of that year, unless he could start to produce worthwhile material. So throughout the crucial period, during which he would later claim to have seen the two eventual defendants in possession both of explosives and of a Samsonite suitcase, he mentioned none of this; he mentioned none of it for a year; he even apparently had no such knowledge when first questioned by the FBI on the warship, nearly two years further on. It was only after a series of 'interviews' that his recollections of these events magically materialised – and materialised in vibrant detail.

Will picks up the point that, given these raw facts, it's a mystery that anyone could consider this man a credible witness at all, let alone one of star status. Ray provides him with the explanation. The intention had been that only Giaka's later, detailed statements fully incriminating his two colleagues would be presented: information pertaining to the poor quality or non-existence of any viable intelligence from him had been suppressed by the CIA. In a large amount of evidential material relating to the witness and his statements, everything that cast doubts on his character or the value of his evidence had been redacted (a fancy word for blacked-out or obliterated, ostensibly on the grounds that they contained matters of 'national security'), leaving only that which served to make the defendants appear guilty. Originally neither the prosecution nor the defence had seen this material without the obliterated passages, but quite surprisingly (and as it happened, fortunately), early during the summer recess, some members of the Crown team were shown versions of the documents with many fewer redactions. Ostensibly this was to enable them to check that the hidden paragraphs did not contain anything that might help the defence case. Even if there had been no material casting doubt on Gaika's truthfulness it was, of course, outrageous that one side should be deciding in secret what was or was not relevant on behalf of their adversaries.

None of this might have come to light, but for the steadfast honesty of a member of the Crown team, Advocate Depute Alistair Campbell QC, who realised that the hidden material weakened the Crown case and was indeed of remarkable significance for the defence. In contrast to the laissez-faire attitude of his colleagues, he informed representatives of the latter that some of his colleagues had seen the less censored documents.

Even when this was brought to the court's attention, the Crown were happy to give assurances that nothing of importance was being suppressed, despite the existence in the newly revealed material of passages suggesting that Gaika had seen nothing at the time but was later either encouraged to invent damning evidence, or more likely coached to give a version concocted by his new protectors and sponsors. Eventually the defence was shown sufficient of the material to enable their cross-examination effectively to cut his evidence to ribbons, none of which stopped his tainted and damaging account being aired in court and entered on the record, however large the question marks that might hang over his every utterance. Ray knows from bitter personal experience that mud can stick, even when flung by a demonstrable liar.

In the throbbing bar, Ray by no means trades pint-for-pint with Will, but going onto Scotch does nothing to improve a deteriorating position. They are still discussing Majid Giaka as they toddle home to Will and Hannah's, eating fish and chips.

–ooOoo–

A new package has come into the frame. So much seems to have happened in the last few days that Ray's brain feels as if it has gone into overload. For the moment he exists in such a fug that all he can be sure about is that DB has told him that Hollywood-based Welshman Rod Pembrey now wants to play Weiss. Pembrey worked with English actor Jill Gault on *War of the Oracle* and they are both keen to perform together again. Such a proven pairing would go down very well with the money people.

By modern convention, actors' names in synopses of movies now are followed by brackets in a halting shorthand: 'Oscar®-nominated* Ruth Bloggs (*Witches and Damons*) and Joe Belch (*The Long Wait*) (*Racing to Reno*) reprise their wheeler-dealing partnership from *The Discreet Charm of the Borgias* in this story of betrayal and infidelity set in the mid-layers of corporate finance. When Rose Virtue (Bloggs) discovers that her boss, Carter Blank, played by Franciso Forbes (*Easy Money 3*) (*The Termite Eaters*) is breaking US treasury rules and tells colleague Bill (Belch) the scene is set for a succession of side-splitting adventures! This is a roller-coaster romp best described as *White Trash* meets *Johnny and Eddy go Fishing*.
   * Best supporting actress – *Rules of Endearment*.'

That sort of thing.

Rod Pembrey and Jill Gault certainly have plenty of brackets. So much so that director Barry Patron, who is not himself bracket-free, is soon reported as keen to join the party. DB suggests that Pembrey might be keen on Patron because he can dominate him – they have worked together before, and there was a suspicion that the actor was over-influential in the decision-making. But DB has played some big fish and seems to think that he can handle this one. Patron is a competent enough director and his brackets suggest that he could make a success of *One-Zero-Three*. If the package can draw out the finance, and DB thinks it certainly should, they could be go.

Then it starts.

"Pembrey is insisting his girlfriend comes on as a producer. She's done that on his last couple of pictures," DB informs Ray.

"And what contribution is she going to make to what appears on the screen?"

"Well, with luck, none. That we could cope with; she wouldn't actually have to do anything more demanding than bank her cheque. But there is something else – the bit you won't like is that she's a writer and he wants her to look at the script with another guy that she writes with." Ray is stunned beyond belief.

"What you mean is that they want to dick around with my script and each take a credit and a heavy fee for screwing up my work."

"No, hold on, Ray."

"No you hold on. No way is this right. Jesus! The time I've devoted to this project is measured in years. How much time has this woman spent researching Lockerbie – ten minutes? Fifteen? Twenty? They're going to tinker around writing more scenes and more lines for Pembrey, taking out stuff we really need in, to make space for building up his part and they're going to take two co-writers' credits. No fucking way!"

The best producers, like assistant directors, could all have alternative careers as diplomats, so used are they to smoothing feathers and massaging egos. DB practises his skills on Ray.

"Look," he says. "They can't make his part any bigger; there's hardly a scene he isn't in already. We don't have to use any of their stuff. We just let them go through the motions. Don't worry about the money. It won't come out of your fee. We just ignore it and they don't even get a credit if we don't use it."

"You're telling me that Rod Pembrey is going to let that happen, with her showing her version direct to him and then complaining to him when we don't use her 'improvements'." His tone is high sarcasm. "And Patron will roll-over for Pembrey; you told me as much."

"Come on. Like you say, you know this story inside-out and backwards. There is no way she can come up with anything that can top what you've done. Let's just see what they turn in, if anything; I mean it's that complicated I can't imagine them really daring to try, once they actually look at the scale of it. Honestly, I wouldn't worry about it. I have to give them the rope to hang themselves."

Clearly it's a done deal.

Again, Ray loses track of the time that elapses before the doctored version of the script appears. DB was essentially right: they have added virtually nothing, because clearly they don't know anything that they could add. Beyond that, they have done what is known as a 'polish', a superficial make-over of an original writer's material. They have deleted a few scenes for no definable reason; they have juggled the order of a few others to no worthwhile effect. In many scenes they have changed a few words or the odd line 'just to show they've been there', as Ray puts it. Few of the changes contribute anything; in the main they are less illuminating than his original. What really gets him though, are the two extra scenes.

Pinky and Perky, as Ray calls the two writers in his conversations with DB, have picked up on the rift that grew between the two main factions among the bereaved. There were those who were convinced, like the woman who had telephoned Ray, if she was genuine, that the investigation and the Camp Zeist trial had found at least one perpetrator; someone they could label 'the bomber' and vilify accordingly. Others, to varying degrees, expressed reservations as to whether justice had been done and the truth revealed. Clearly Ray has created in Weiss someone from the latter camp who reflects his own total distrust of the official version. Pinky and Perky's little piggy snouts have sniffed out this divergence of views as an excuse for two angry confrontations involving Weiss. They have written scenes, exactly as Ray predicted, which they feel will allow Rod Pembrey full dramatic rein and the chance to dominate what they will see as powerful and revealing exchanges. Ray differs, seeing the scenes as unnecessary and unconvincing.

What makes matters worse is that the style is quite different; the two polishers have failed to replicate the way Weiss speaks throughout the rest of the work (except possibly where they have also meddled). They have also fallen straight into what is one of the most common and fundamental traps of screenwriting, the error of over-nomination – too much use of characters' names or titles during dialogue. 'Look, Chief Inspector.' No one ever says that in real life. People holding a conversation do not constantly use the names or ranks of the people they are addressing, yet time and time again screenwriters have their characters do so in line after line, in a way that drives Ray to expletives when he hears it. He calls it the *Thelma and Louise* syndrome' or 'The bad thing about *A Good Year'*. The new scenes in the Pinky and Perky version are peppered with 'Mr Weisses' and 'Daniels' and other much-repeated appellations.

Worryingly, the pair seem, as their one piece of research, to have been on the internet and have actually written Weiss arguing with characters using the real names of actual people on the far spectrum of the families' groupings; an intrusion Ray has avoided like the plague, however much he deplores the way they seem so oblivious to the obvious – and the tendency of some to howl their hatred for a man who isn't guilty and is, like them, a victim.

As he re-reads the new scenes, he feels that anger rising again. Suddenly, uncontrollably, he is trying to break the back of the revised screenplay. Finding this impossible, he resorts to an attempt to rip it in half. This too is to no avail and as each assay fails he roars as he braces and contorts to destroy the offensive card and paper in his hands.

"No. No! NO NO! NOOOO!"

His shouting wakes him up; Hannah too, he will learn in the morning – although not Will, perhaps unsurprisingly, given the uplift of Uley Old Spot Bitter. He has also attempted, fortunately unsuccessfully, to tear the duvet apart.

It's been one of those plausible nightmares again. He knows from reading William Goldman that the experiences he has just suffered are commonplace; part of the regular lot of screenwriters; even those at the highest level with strings of successes. Now fully awake, he accepts the dream as a warning to harden up and expect the worst. He is at the point of stepping over the barbed wire into the scriptwriters' minefield. It has reminded him that his opinions now carry only limited weight and that he has to be selective about the occasions that he chooses to be forceful. He can only afford to get 'out of his pram' over really serious issues where he definitely needs to get his way. A writer who starts to argue every point and resist each single change that he or she dislikes is not likely to have a long future on any project. As Goldman makes clear, once a certain amount of money has been invested in pre-production, if something the writer thinks is right strongly conflicts with what the director or producers have decided they want, the only loser, the person going off the picture, is going to be the one who created the blueprint. Even nice people – and they can be personal friends of the writer, as Gerald and DB are of Ray – will feel that they have no choice. The movie will have become bigger than individuals; certainly bigger than the originator who, once the script has been delivered, is wise to regard himself as expendable.

Indeed writers can be sacked, and their vision soon changed out of all recognition, without their putting a foot wrong or saying a word out of place. Some directors are known for axeing writers almost as a matter of course. Interesting weeks may lie ahead.

Ray resigns himself to the fact that he may well have to rewrite Weiss as an American, with all that entails. Compared with having to accommodate the demands of a Rod Pembrey, reconstructing the script to fit Warren Hanson's accent would be a small price to pay.

–ooOoo–

69   The Stuff of Dreams

If Ray, now back at home, is still feeling strangely disembodied, when he puts his phone down after this call the sensation of disconnection with reality will have magnified tenfold.

It's DB.

"Are you ready for this?"

"Probably not," Ray starts to say, but his words are carried away by the caller's anxiety to spill many beans.

"Right here we go. Hanson's out. That will please **you**. Arran Samson's back in again, because, and this is the bit you won't believe, Gerald is up for it; in fact he's as good as in. He's back in LA – and walking, albeit with a stick, as of yesterday, by the way. Gerald brings Evan Harris, who's got access to some Fivestar money so we'll do it together – I can cope with that, and there's more. Evan met Ralph in LA and they got on so we're hoping Ralph will be AP, oh and we think we've got a Jane Maddox – Jill Gault." Ray, bowled over by everything so far, is truly dumbfounded at that revelation. "It's coming together, Mr Scriver. And – best bit saved till last – guess where the major money looks as though it's coming from?" He doesn't pause, even a beat for a guess. "Remember Joe Wyzell didn't want to know at any price?" Ray does indeed remember that the head of Galactic had been adamant that he wouldn't go near the subject. "He's totally changed his tune. According to Hal he's seen the light and he'll be very surprised if he doesn't come across with the dosh as soon as we've put some new figures together. What do you think?"

Ray is beyond the point of expressing any opinion other than mumbled gratitude and pleasure. What he actually thinks but doesn't say is that he needs a hair of the dog, and that it might just be a glass of fizz, by way of cautious celebration. He's streetwise enough to know that today's highs are all-too-likely to turn into tomorrow's lows, but that you should enjoy the sunshine while it's there.

When it doesn't happen, it doesn't happen. When it does, it can come as suddenly and be as simple as that.

–ooOoo–

70   The Tracks of Her Tears

Ray's eyes roam round Dick's familiar garden. It is as immaculately tended as ever. But this time it's Sally who sits opposite him across the tea tray placed in the centre of the hardwood table.

A lone long-distance hiker had seen Dick's accident. From his path on the bare, domed moor the other side of the broad U-shaped valley, he had noticed a car following a similar trackway that ran more-or-less parallel along the next ridge maybe a mile away. He was surprised by its speed. Even at that distance he could see the bouncing caused by what had to be serious ruts and potholes. Tractors and quads were rare enough up on these lonely heights: cars, never. It had to be stolen, he'd thought – joyriders with no concern for damaging it. Then it had made the turn that concerned him. It left the worn path on the crown of the moor and raced across the sheep grass, coming broadly in his direction. But the slope that lay ahead of it has that frightening characteristic of these hills, becoming steeper and steeper until the valley side is nearly vertical, dotted with rock outcrops but mainly scree. Concern had turned to horror. He will answer at the inquest that he was sure the driver had made no attempt to slow or stop, but if anything accelerated to the point where gravity did what gravity does.

He'd seen the car in free-fall, before his view of its deadly trajectory was blocked by his moor in the foreground, so deep was the valley between. It had taken him over half an hour of scrambling and panting to get down to the stream at the bottom and up the paddocks on the other side, to where the wreckage had been brought to a halt and mostly contained by a meeting of two dry-stone walls. It had not exploded or burned; it was just impossibly and unsurvivably compacted. The walker was the only person aware of the incident, and, being a stubborn traditionalist who would not carry a mobile phone, he had then to walk five miles to raise the alarm.

The verdict will of course be suicide.

Ray had seen nothing in the media of either the death or the opening of the inquest, and had been intending to contact Dick with an update on progress and a few minor questions when he'd had the call from Sally.

Apart from simply informing him, she obviously had some things that she wanted to say to someone face-to-face. The fact that she'd tracked down his number because of the interest that he shared with her husband had given Ray a chilling idea of what she might have on her mind. When she'd mentioned on the phone that Dick's laptop and address book were both missing, Ray had not been any further surprised.

Sally Leigh is carrying herself very well. The womenfolk of police, like those of soldiers and other risky trades, must have a secret place at the far back of their minds where they half-prepare for the worst. She would, though, have relaxed since he retired, distanced from daily concentrated exposure to the fall-out from Care in the Community. This was deeply unfair.

"He shouldn't have been anywhere near where he was. He was going to the library in Bolton, to look something up. I've no idea why it was Bolton or what he checking. He may have said but it didn't sink in. It was totally the opposite direction to where he went."

"And you said on the phone that he was his normal self when he set off."

"Absolutely. There was no hint of anything remotely wrong."

"Did he have any visitors – unusual visitors – in the last few months, or did he go to any meetings or interviews that you know of, that were at all out of the ordinary?"

"That's one of the reasons that I phoned you."

"Ah," Ray breathes, involuntarily. He'd hoped she wouldn't say that.

"He had a call about a cold case – you know, one of the jobs that he'd worked on in the past that are being looked at again. It wasn't the first one – it's happened before. Except this time he told them that he was happy to talk if they came here, at least I think he suggested it. He'd had hassle before with parking and passes and he thought why should he schlepp down into Manchester at his own expense. So they came to him. I think they were a bit surprised to see me – I don't know why. The thing was, I've been around detectives, professionally and socially . . " She stops and almost laughs in her voice though her features are too strained to participate. "That sounds wrong – bad. I should tell you I was in the job myself, though in uniform of course, for about five years. That's how I met Dick."

For a moment some distant memory almost makes her crumble, but she hangs on and regains herself.

"Yes. I've had a lot to do with the CID for going on thirty years, but these three weren't like any detectives I've ever known. One could have been, I suppose, one of the new breed, I don't know – he did all the talking. He was a Scot, but the other two didn't say anything in my hearing. Even when I offered them coffee they said no by smiling and mouthing 'no, thank you' and one gestured with his hands, as if he couldn't speak. It didn't strike me till later that they didn't want me to hear their voices."

Ray takes the bull by the horns, because it's so obvious what Sally is going to say. In court he would be leading his witness. Here it doesn't matter. In Dick's garden, a fragrant Court of Appeal where the Camp Zeist trial has been painstakingly reviewed, tested and dismissed as unsafe, they both know the answer.

"Because they were American?"

"Because they were American. I think they were." She nods with increasing animation, in the way that people do to stop breaking down. "They'd tried to look British, but it hadn't quite worked. I can't say why."

"What did Dick say about their visit?"

"Almost nothing. He just said that he hadn't really been able to tell them anything, but what the case was supposed to be, I never knew. That wasn't unusual: we almost never talked about the details of his work at home; the organisation and the office and the police characters, yes, but he never wanted to expose me to the nasty stuff he had to deal with. Even though I'd seen my share in my time in the police, he liked to protect me from all that." There's another twitch and a pause that Ray decides best to fill quickly with another question.

"Did he seem affected or changed by the interview?"

"Not really. Nothing that I noticed, and I think I read him pretty well. No, not changed at all. No signs of being worried or depressed."

"Had you ever seen him frightened of anything – in the past?"

"No. I've always thought that you couldn't frighten someone with his background and training. You know he was special forces before the police?" For some reason, Ray nods, even though Dick had never actually said anything more than that he had been in the army. Sally is confirming what has long been his assumption. Looking back, Ray will wonder why he does this. Saying 'no' might have elicited more detail, not that more detail would change anything relevant. Dick's questioners had no need to frighten him in a conventional way.

"Do you remember anything about what happened while these people were here?"

"Only that the Scotsman disappeared. I guess he went to the car, because when I looked out of the window Dick was just with the other two. The third man, I feel, didn't come back until they were standing up to go."

"Could you see Dick when you looked out of the window? Did you see him talking, for example?"

"No. He was facing away from me. He was here. They were there and here." She indicates their positions by pointing and tapping the table. As she does so, the memory becomes too much and she comes to the edge of crumpling again.

"And you were?"

"I looked out once from the kitchen. Then I went upstairs and saw them from that window. But that was when they were on their feet ready to go."

"Did you get the impression that he was fully awake, when he was at the table?"

"Awake?" She almost shudders. "Awake. What do you mean?"

"Did you notice if he was moving; you know, moving at all – arms, head, shoulders, hand banging on the table? Or was he still?"

"I honestly can't remember. I'll try and think back and let you know. I think he was just sitting up straight."

"And how long did it all take?"

"Hard to say. Ten minutes – maybe fifteen, twenty. I was doing things. Time flies. I just can't tell you very accurately."

"Have you talked to anyone else about any of this?"

"No. Suddenly I'm not sure who I can trust."

"But you're talking to me. Which means you have a strong suspicion what this is all about?"

"Am I right?" the widow asks. This time she doesn't quite hold it together.

"I think you could be."

"They hypnotised him, didn't they?" she says, through her tears.

"You've heard of this before?" Ray says, more than a little surprised.

"Dick had a book. I happened to pick it up and read a few pages. They prime you to kill yourself when you hear a coded phrase."

"Did he have a phone call the day it happened?"

"Again, I don't know, because I was out before lunch. He was here on his own all morning."

"Which is when it would have been. Did you have lunch together?"

"No. He was keen to get off and he said he wasn't hungry. I tried to give him some chocolate and fruit to take but he said he didn't need them."

She pauses for what seems a long time, suddenly looking exhausted and empty. Ray reaches across the table and takes her hand, before she continues.

"Well he didn't. Did he?"

—ooOoo—

71   Dare, Truth and Consequences

Ray is very aware that he shouldn't be on this motorway. The M6 southbound is thick with fast-moving afternoon traffic, and it's no place to be distracted. Yet try as he might, he can't help replaying the meeting that he's just had, as well as fragments of his previous visits to the dark stone house and especially the long discussions at the table in the garden. So immersed is he in his thoughts that he has become the driver most likely to cause a multiple accident in Cheshire this rush hour. He is always telling Eve that she shouldn't think about other things while she drives. He remembers Graham Hill saying once in an interview that driving on the public road, as opposed to the race track, was when he did his thinking and his problem-solving. Ray has never understood that, believing that you need active concentration to be safe. Relying on automatic reactions, with your thoughts elsewhere, is a principal cause of serious trouble, he thinks, though he has to concede that it was a mistake in an aeroplane and not on the road or the track that ended the life of the popular racing driver. It is not long before he regains his senses, takes his own advice and leaves the motorway at the next exit. It'll take somewhat longer to get home using A-roads, but there will be more obvious and forceful incentives to stay focused on the driving.

Sally has now confirmed that her husband was ex-special forces, presumably SAS. Although Ray long ago deduced this, he remembers Dick talking about the interface between special forces and the Secret World.

"Virtually any country you can name," he had said, "has now got its own élite forces, which means that dozens and dozens of nations are training people to be killing machines; to dispense death in every possible way, normally without giving a second thought about the people whose lives they are taught to extinguish like snuffing a candle. Worldwide, thousands of expert killers are being trained every year and equally, thousands of them come to the end of their military service. Now most of those will be entirely responsible citizens who will happily resume normal civilian life, but inevitably there will be a small proportion that for reasons of economics or reasons of temperament can't do so. After they've held the power of life and death, some people can never settle to being a plasterer or a scaffolder or a delivery driver, even if there are jobs to be had – and in too many countries often there aren't. So just think, even a small proportion of thousands equals quite a lot. So what we've got is an ever-growing pool of people with all manner of skills, most of which outside the armed forces are seriously anti-social, who are on the market, looking for paid work. Some go into security and some become mercenaries, but there are plenty available for hire by the players in the Secret World who need arm's-length deniable assets to carry out their enforcement, their black ops, their sabotage and their assassinations. I don't see that situation is going to get any better, with so many killers in the marketplace."

He had gone on to speak of people employed as bodyguards in Iraq shooting at cars and killing innocent drivers solely for amusement.

It's clear, though, that a different class of operative was complicit in ending Dick's life. Why fake a murder-suicide or a traffic accident when the victim will do the job for you, on demand? Dick and Ray had shared a discussion as to the likelihood of down-on-their-luck film stuntmen being recruited by the dark forces to organise the highway mishaps which figure so prominently in the statistics of mysterious deaths. Plenty of people are knowledgeable about road crashes and their prevention but few outside films and TV have any experience of staging them and then surviving them. It would be an obvious field to trawl for expertise. The appeal of motor smashes for the employers of the 'outside contractors' is easily appreciated. Crashes are commonplace and so rate less investigation than other forms of unexpected violent demise. Morgues have a semi-industrial throughput of corpses arising from travel. Sudden death from other means is noteworthy and has to be explained in a way that is at least slightly convincing. The downside for the Secret World is that setting up an execution using vehicles, such as that of Karen Silkwood, is by nature a difficult and complex business, with the inherent random factors always liable to bring about exposure. Having all the elements in place at the right moment in a suitable location free of witnesses is demanding enough. The imperative to remain mobile, without leaving clues at the scene and without sustaining damage that members of the public might notice and remember during the escape, imposes a whole extra set of constraints on the perpetrators. All in all, it's a very coarse and unpredictable instrument; an equivalent, Ray thinks, of that spiked ball on a chain and a staff, used in mediaeval battles – dangerous to use. He's surprised that the method remains so favoured.

Ray remembers another comment his friend had made in relation to the armed forces.

"Have you ever found it strange that, in our country at least, we claim to hold the sanctity of human life in the highest respect, to the extent that we won't execute even the most brazen and brutal and unrepentant of murderers, yet we have an army, navy and air force whose sole reason for existence is to kill people; and with the use of missiles and especially nuclear weapons the targets, intended or not, are all-too-often going to be innocent civilians? I know I'm on shaky ground here, having been a soldier, but there does seem to be a serious philosophical inconsistency. If it's morally OK in the course of wars to kill people who actually represent no threat to our safety and welfare, why are we so reticent about meting out proportionate retributive justice domestically, when there are people who offer a real threat?"

Ray had suggested it might be because of the high incidence of miscarriages of justice, Lockerbie included: a pardon and compensation are no good to someone who's been executed. Also, and it was a big also, a great deal depends on who is defining the way of life that is being threatened and the activities constituting a danger to it. Dick had said that he was referring to criminal cases of murder in which there was absolutely no doubt.

"I came into contact with people who had no respect for anything or anyone and had taken life in the full knowledge that if they did get caught, the worst that could happen to them would be a relatively short jail term. Some quite openly said they would do the same again, given the right circumstances. I can tell you, there were a few where I would have volunteered to pull the trap-door lever myself!"

He was fond of throwing up these conundrums. He'd said on another occasion that he couldn't understand why, if your profession was war, you got invited to the highest councils in the land, whereas people who espoused peace were derided, obstructed and ignored. He'd done a spell with special branch and he'd found it thoroughly distasteful that the Secretary of State for Defence at the time, Michael Heseltine, had run a campaign that branded thousands of genuine, patriotic people from all walks of life, including churchmen and the elderly, as subversives. Dick, like Ray was a monarchist, but he couldn't avoid being critical of the Royals' total immersion in things military, to the extent that training to kill people seemed to be the only acceptable career choice for a male Royal, and all the females were Colonels-in-Chief. Ray could understand that, both historically and practically. The rallying cry is 'Queen and Country' and the sovereign is nominally the commander-in chief, even if no ruler has gone anywhere near the battlefield since George III at the 1743 Battle of Dettingen. Portraying the armed forces as the symbolic bodyguards of the sovereign as well as defenders of the nation is a powerful motivator to great endeavour and heroic deeds. The caveat is that the aims need to be worthy, and often they haven't been.

Another conversation with Dick plays on Ray's mind as he threads his way past Coventry. They had returned to the subject of pre-emptive elimination by murder of potential whistle-blowers.

"The rule seems to be," the bright, wiry man had said in his garden, he then as full of life and vigour as his luxuriant shrubs, "that you are more likely to get whacked if you have direct evidence of something corrupt. If you look at the people who have been taken out, you find that it's mainly those who have personal involvement and are thought to represent a risk of disclosure, or someone who has been a witness, or someone who has some concrete evidence like a letter or a tape. Alternatively you are a lawyer or an investigator or a journalist who is about to get their hands on either some physical evidence or a taped or written confession. Any of those things seems to bring out the heavies. Just repeating theories and second-hand information is not quite so dangerous."

Ray wonders if Dick has been 'suicided' because he had crossed the line into one of those more serious categories. Had he become a target because he'd made contact with someone, or been passed information or evidence that had brought him too close to be tolerated?

If he had, then whatever it was would likely have been tabulated somewhere in the hidden recesses of the hard disc of his missing laptop, but he would also have kept a copy, Ray is sure. Neither of them had believed themselves to be high on the list for termination, but both were sure that their inevitable opponents would be interested in any progress they made, and that they needed to guard against theft of their notes. Despite this, they had not actually exchanged information about hiding places; perhaps because to have done so would have admitted just how close the secret forces might be; how far down Big Brother's road the United Kingdom has slid. Once again, Ray kicks himself. He'd asked Sally whether she knew if Dick had a safe or some other place away from his office where he might store copy discs or papers, but she hadn't been told of any such, presumably in line with her husband's practice of saving her from worry. She is sure that his workspace is exactly as he left it and is equally certain that the house has not been searched. Ray thinks this indicates that the opposition has got whatever they need from his laptop and any papers in his computer bag, but he felt obliged to tell the brave woman to secure Dick's research to the best of her ability and to be very alert for intruders and take all precautions for her own safety. This had done little for her peace of mind, but her regained composure had remained remarkable. Waving from the bloom-bedecked porch, she had looked very small and vulnerable as he had driven away.

She and her husband had both served the establishment well, Ray had thought angrily, remembering this image as he drove off the hills, and yet some state within a state had done this to them without hesitation. Dick wouldn't have been that surprised. They had talked about John Stalker, whom he had of course known at Greater Manchester Police. If a Deputy Chief Constable could be fitted-up and hung out to dry, as Dick had put it, because he wouldn't do what was expected and produce a whitewash report, what chance did a retired detective-sergeant stand against the dark forces? As with so many things, he'd had an interesting take on the Stalker affair.

"John Stalker was appointed to conduct an inquiry into whether the RUC had been running a shoot-to-kill policy against IRA terrorists, but there was a whole assumption in setting up that inquiry that said that such a policy was wrong. My point," he had continued in the enthusiastic way that was so often at odds with the solemn subjects being dredged, "is that the assumption was nonsense. Society has a perfect right to kill when confronted by people who proclaim themselves to be fighting a war and are content to murder innocent people in pursuit of a minority cause; people whose methods of waging 'war' include shooting policewomen in the back. What was wrong about the RUC policy is that it was inefficiently and clumsily carried out and that they too shot innocent and unarmed people, making them just as reprehensible as their opponents."

Dick had been horrified at the way the police establishment connived in the trumped-up charges against Stalker, effectively ending the career of a 'good copper' despite the fact that he was completely exonerated and the specious allegations against him eventually exposed for what they were.

"They went for him because he wouldn't be fobbed off and say that there was no shoot-to-kill. No one, on either side of the water, could believe it when he insisted on doing a proper investigation and tried to get at the real truth."

The short blip on a Whelan yelp alerts him to the blue lights in his mirror. Despite his best intentions, he's been doing a Graham Hill, on auto-pilot, and hasn't noticed the silver-grey BMW.

"We've followed you for more than a mile and a half, and your driving has been very good generally. You obviously know what you're doing, but with your straight-lining you've come very close to crossing the double white line at times. You need to be careful about that."

Ray knows he has been driving exactly as normal, but with active concentration as the missing ingredient, so he has been deservedly caught out. He apologises, but in his pre-existing indignant state of mind can't help observing that the white lines are a blunt instrument and their application is often inept and unnecessary, getting in the way of safe decision-making, rather than encouraging it. He's fortunate perhaps that the officer is in an amenable mood.

"You may be right, sir. It is hard to see why they've been put down as they are in some cases, but we have to enforce what's there; not what we might think should be there. We have to realise that most people's standards of decision-making, and concentration," he adds, not pointedly, although it strikes home, "they're so low that they can't be trusted to think for themselves. It has to be done for them. Do mind how you go."

–ooOoo–

Ray stirs his coffee in the Tesco café. The Tesco café! What is he doing here? He couldn't be more opposed to this place. In the projects file on his hard disc there is a barbed article, unsold naturally, inveighing against all supermarkets and their destruction of the essential fabric of the high street by the theft of trade from the traditional staple businesses, bankrupting the grocers, the fruit and veg shops, the butchers and the bakers and going on in their insatiable greed to undermine the local garages, the newsagents, the chemists, the dry cleaners, the bookshops, the tea-shops; even the insurance brokers and the photographic dealers, in fact virtually all the retail enterprises that you can think of. They rarely offer the full range to be found in specialist shops; they just skim the popular lines, leaving their competitors, who can offer a wide selection of products and knowledge, denied their staple income, so they fail and close, to everyone's disadvantage except the invader. Yet here he is, working his way through a cafétière, as guilty as everybody else of succumbing to the ease of accessibility. He's not altogether sure what town he's on the edge of, but all he had to do was follow the 'Superstore' signs, chose a vacant parking space and stroll in. At least half of him hates himself.

At Lockerbie, a vast Tesco store now overlooks the Sherwood Crescent crash site, so dominant that many locals call the old burgh Tesco Town. The town centre lost whatever bustle it had retained, and boarded-up shops for a long time gave the main street the air of a ghost town, not altogether inappropriate in the circumstances.

The idea of making the stop is to clear his mind and get his concentration back to standard pitch. The policeman had been more right than he realised. He'd been correct too in what he said about the public on the road; they're in the main much too unskilled, unaware and distracted to be permitted to make many of the more serious decisions any longer. Ray realises that the same applies in the wider, civic, political context. There is a fiction maintained that people's opinions matter, and that they participate in how society runs by casting their votes at elections; exercising their democratic rights, as politicians love to trumpet it. Ray loves fairness for all but he has precious little confidence in democracy as it's practised, given that democracy should be about the making of informed choices.

He remembers being horrified at a campaign fronted by Brian Rix, the former farce actor, who as Chairman and President of Mencap wanted the franchise extended to people with severe mental impairment. Given the myriad ways in which someone who suffers in that way could be influenced by others in the use of their vote, Ray was incredulous that the concept of informed choice could be so disregarded. More mature reflection told him that it made little difference, since the vast mass of the population could hardly be less informed on most of the issues of the day and in truth place their votes according to an extraordinary wide spectrum of influences, few of which have anything to do with serious evaluation.

Most votes, he had long decided, are given either as a result of a politician's image, in fact usually that of a party leader, rather than of the person actually being voted for; or cast to fulfil the voter's own self-image, whatever that might be. In any event, free choice has been rendered irrelevant in recent general elections by the proprietor of the *Sun* newspaper telling the readership which party to vote for on the day, having first softened them up by months of selective reporting and dedication to personalised trivia.

Of course Ray's view is that the election of a government of any complexion is itself largely an irrelevance. New Members of Parliament, even those on the winning side, soon run up against the close limits, indeed the virtual non-existence, of their ability to influence anything. Ministers on their first day step into the deep, cloying mud spread in their path by armies of Sir Humphreys, while one or two Super-Humphreys, one being the Cabinet Secretary, quietly brief an eager new Prime Minister as to the bounds of his or her power and open their eyes for the first time as to who is actually in charge of the country. What a shock it must be to find that it isn't them! It's from this point that many of the admirable promises that have been made prior to the election are consigned permanently to the back burner. Undertakings to hold inquiries into obvious scandals and injustices; pledges to make government slimmer, less wasteful, more open and accountable, less centralised; vows to reform the all-embracing Official Secrets Act, all go the same way; are brushed away with the same polite terminology: 'Unfortunately, Prime Minister, there are factors that render such a course of action most inadvisable.'

The Labour Party, in opposition, promised a full inquiry into Lockerbie.

New Labour came to power in 1997. Nine years on now, in 2006, veteran Labour MP Tam Dalyell, and thousands of other interested parties, are still waiting for the commitment to be fulfilled. Ray is not holding his breath for developments on that front.

He drains his remaining coffee and heads for the very convenient car park.

–ooOoo–

72   An Interview with Parky

Of course, the prospect of an independent inquiry had appeared and vanished, mirage-like, under the Tory administration too. The British Government effectively ignored the concerns of the families of the bereaved for at least six months after the downing of 103, but in September 1989 (ironically on the very same day that UTA Flight 772 was bombed out of the sky over the Sahara), Cecil Parkinson, Paul Channon's successor as Transport Secretary, finally met a representative group and seemed to take on board their anger and frustration at the way their very apposite questions had been ignored or brushed aside with glib answers. Overall this would not change, but that meeting at least and at last provided brief hope that someone was listening.

Ray has written this important apparent turning point into the script, with a sympathetic Parkinson offering to recommend a full judicial inquiry. In a DoT conference room, he can do little else but respond to the plight of this group whose individuals have lost so cruelly and who have irrefutable logic in the points they raise so earnestly and yet with such dignity. The action cuts to the delegation's spokesperson, Dr Jim Swire, being interviewed for television afterwards, and referring to an impression of progress. Reacting to Parkinson's apparent sincerity, he describes him as 'a fresh face and a fresh mind'. Daniel Weiss stands in the group behind the actor playing Swire, or perhaps he can be digitally inserted into the original video footage, in the manner of *Forrest Gump*. All of their faces show marginally less turbulence than they have worn at any time we have encountered them since the night of 21st December last.

In the detached, self-contained world of political opportunism and powerplay, fresh minds coming to bear on the subject of Lockerbie were the last thing that was wanted. A few scenes and a few weeks later, the relatives learn that Parkinson's suggestion of a judicial inquiry has been quashed, not surprisingly by 10 Downing Street. Ray would have liked to suggest 'or somewhere higher', but the Daniel Weiss character is at this point in time only stepping towards the threshold of such contemplations.

He flicks over a few more pages. Now in the quiet house after the long drive, he sits with a large glass of Rioja. He's picked up the buff-covered booklet deliberately. This evening, for a few minutes, he wants to consider, by way of tribute, how very different this piece of work would be if fate hadn't chanced to place him in touch with the short policeman. Small man: big contribution. Without Dick, *One-Zero-Three* would have slightly the character of a Victorian penny dreadful; conclusions reached through a combination of deduction, supposition and conviction. Dick's detective skills had put the evidence through a fine mesh screen and given the piece the authority and the edge of a CPS brief to counsel.

Or something like that. He smiles at the perhaps dubious comparison.

Ray raises his glass and toasts his lost friend. Surprising himself, he breaks the silence.

"Thanks mate. I won't forget you."

There are two cases in which Ray is accustomed to speaking out loud in the house; a good and a bad, and the good one no longer applies. That of course was the Ogre. Everyone talks to their animals, or if they don't they should; it's great therapy as well as a good excuse to be eccentric. It's an outlet the lack of which is currently painful in the extreme. The bad reason would be to swear at some inanimate object impeding his progress by being in the way or not functioning as expected. Eve calls his outbursts of impatience 'getting wire coat-hangers' or 'having hosepipes', for obvious reasons. Incidences are on the increase. Now, not just surprised but shocked at the sound of his own voice, Ray returns to the document, mildly embarrassed and also slightly unnerved. Ogre had been a good house-dog as well as a devoted friend. The silence around the house is so profound there is an element of threat to it.

Ray has become even more than usually cautious, very mindful of one of Fraser's more unsettling remarks, referring to the vague and unspecified 'them' among which the Scot had apparently been long numbered.

"If they're interested in you," the spy had said, "they'll likely have as many keys to your house as you have yourself."

How he wishes the dog could be dozing on his bed near the front door.

—ooOoo—

However strongly Parkinson had or hadn't conveyed the feelings of the Lockerbie families to his political mistress, he must certainly have emphasised a conviction that these people were not going to give up and melt away. For although his judicial inquiry plan was quickly vetoed – in mid-December, just a few days short of a year on from the bombing – it was announced that there would be a fatal accident inquiry. Although this had the appearance of offering something of what they wanted, the relatives quickly recognized what was a smoke and mirrors move by the UK government. Under Scottish law, an FAI equates to an English inquest, and the terms of reference of an inquest preclude discussion of virtually all of the matters that could provide the answers desperately sought by the bereaved.

A further ten months elapsed before the FAI began. In the run-up, both Margaret Thatcher and Paul Channon sidestepped moves to have them give evidence by claiming parliamentary privilege. Politicians are ever-ready to accept power from the populous but notoriously reluctant, not to mention arrogantly dismissive, when asked by any of the people to explain their exercise of it. The government put other obstacles in the inquiry's way, to ensure that it stayed within its narrow boundaries. Nevertheless, even in this emasculated form, the proceedings couldn't avoid once or twice turning back the corner of the carpet to reveal that there was more than a suspicion of dirt, the dirt that many were coming to believe had been swept under it in serious quantities. As this hearing constituted the first and indeed only formal public forum on Lockerbie that would be held on British soil proper, it was a significant event in the story and has to be covered in the script, yet in itself it has little to offer in dramatic terms. Even the later criminal trial with its accused and its quota of dubious witnesses doesn't really make the grade as courtroom drama; Ray has been forced to cover that, too, mainly through characters' reactions and their interpretation of what were extraordinarily lengthy and generally turgid deliberations, and the plodding, earlier FAI cannot be allowed very much screentime either, for fear of totally frittering away the film's momentum.

Perversely, Ray thinks that one aspect of the Scottish inquiry, the curious slander of Dr David Fieldhouse, is one of those Lockerbie stories that would make a very compelling TV movie. Unfortunately it would not be a vehicle that could carry the whole extended saga; otherwise the police surgeon from Yorkshire could have been the involved, leading character that Gerald had so argued for in the feature film script. As a minor piece, exploring the edge of the conspiracy, and serving as a prompt for further questions, the self-contained Fieldhouse saga has much to recommend it, especially as it involves some of those rug-turning revelations. If *One-Zero-Three* doesn't go as a feature, Ray thinks he may have to rapidly put together a TV script on those lines, in an attempt to remain solvent.

With long experience that included dealing with multiple victims of the Bradford City stadium fire, the doctor offered his services to the Dumfries and Galloway Constabulary immediately upon hearing of the disaster. Not surprisingly, he was asked to set off at once. Assigned a search area and an accompanying police officer, he then worked through the night and the next day in atrocious conditions near Tundergarth, finding bodies, certifying them dead, labelling them and recording all details including descriptions and precise locations. He dealt with 59 victims without any real break or refreshment, reporting his activities to an inspector in charge of his search area after nightfall on 22nd December. When on the following morning it became clear there was no further call for his services, he returned home and wrote and posted his report.

A few weeks later the doctor was asked to attend the Police Incident Centre to assist with the identification of the bodies he had certified and logged, and spent some days matching his records to passengers' details; a process made no easier by the fact that the police had, perhaps forgivably in the confusion of an unprecedented incident, but nevertheless rather unwisely, relabelled the victims with their own serial numbers without recording the numbers assigned by him. This may or may not have been connected with the fact that the services of the FBI Identification Division and Disaster Team had been offered to the Scottish police, and had been accepted. The FBI at Lockerbie were impressed with the *Holmes* major incident computer software used in the UK and rather surprisingly admitted that it was way ahead of anything they had available. However, it was eventually possible to reconcile confidently all but two of Dr Fieldhouse's bodies with names on the passenger list. For this remaining pair, none could be matched. In the case of one of them, DCF 50, a male in his 20s wearing Union Jack boxer shorts, it is unclear if he was ever identified. According to information given to radio reporter David Johnston and later detailed in his 1989 book *Lockerbie – The Real Story,* if he was, his body was not returned to his relatives. In a coffin-labelling mistake, a casket containing miscellaneous unidentifiable body parts was sent to them and cremated in the US before the mistake could be rectified. This meant that the one containing the probable DCF 50 was quietly and anonymously dealt with in the UK. Johnston's trusted source stated that a second body, that of a woman, befell the same fate for similar reasons. Not surprisingly, efforts had been made to keep these mistakes from the public; Johnston was vilified for making the revelation, and like so many other facts that had leaked into the public domain, these were also strenuously denied by the authorities.

At best this was unpardonable negligence; at worst it may have been the result of an attempt by some party to conceal something more sinister. The eventual response to the book certainly indicated that the account touched nerves in the Scottish police and judicial hierarchy. The reason for such sensitivity might be illuminated by the even more startling case of David Fieldhouse's second unidentified victim, DCF 12, who simply vanished without trace from the police records. This total disappearance led some commentators, including Ashton and Ferguson, to speculate as to whether there were one or possibly more extra passengers on the aircraft whose presence and naming might be embarrassing in influential quarters, and who had perhaps therefore been removed from the passenger manifest before its release. Ray hasn't forgotten that the American agents on the second Pan Am charter to Carlisle brought a single coffin with them and were angry at being filmed unloading it. It had to have been there for some reason, and as coffins automatically draw very particular attention to themselves, it's unlikely to have been procured and transported to remove anything other than a body. Whose body and why it might have merited concealment by the CIA, seemingly aided and abetted by the Scottish police and judiciary, are questions whose answers could clearly turn the key in the stiff mortice of the Lockerbie cover-up.

Doctor Fieldhouse's Lockerbie story was not over. In mid-April he was asked to provide the police with formal details of his work on the night of the disaster and the day following. He responded with a lengthy statement including annotated maps, effectively duplicating his earlier report. He might well have assumed that despatch of the new document would mark the end of his involvement, but there was another twist to come.

The parents of Bill Cadman, a 32-year-old sound engineer, had been given two conflicting dates for the date that his body had been found. Although the police, Bill's death certificate and a confirmation by the Procurator Fiscal stated 24th December, a policeman returning his effects had with him a document indicating the 22nd. On day five of the FAI, Martin and Rita Cadman were given a formal schedule indicating that the latter was correct and that Bill's death was one of those registered by David Fieldhouse on that day, but that his body was not photographed and removed until the 24th. Naturally the Cadmans wanted to know why there had been such delay, and also why they had been given the wrong date twice and – when they had raised the matter of the constable's document mentioning the correct one, it had been categorically dismissed as a typing error. Again, Ray feels, making allowances for the complicated situation and the bureaucratic workload, perhaps the confusion might be slightly understandable, except for what happened next.

The small Dumfries and Galloway Constabulary had from the first hours gratefully accepted assistance from its neighbours, including the English Cumbria Constabulary and more particularly Lothian and Borders Constabulary, centred on Edinburgh, and Strathclyde Police, headquartered in Glasgow. It fell to a detective-sergeant from the latter force to present five days of detailed evidence relating to the victims and their identification to the inquiry.

Soon there was an opportunity for Brian Gill QC, representing the Lockerbie Air Disaster Group, to ask the officer the question that had so disturbed the Cadmans and other families as to why the recovery of the bodies had suffered over 48 hours delay. Astonishingly the policeman began an account of Doctor Fieldhouse's activities that misrepresented his contribution, impugned his work practices and made him appear entirely responsible for any delay and confusion. The testimony suggested that he had gone out on his own without the 'officer in charge' knowing the area he was covering, a version at total variance with the truth. No one having any evidence to the contrary, the sergeant's version was accepted by the presiding Sheriff Principal and all assembled, to the extent that from then on, every time a victim certified dead by the Bradford surgeon was introduced, there was likely to be some disparaging reference to his lack of professionalism.

The victim of these slurs may never have become aware of what was being written into the record, but providentially his son read a newspaper account of the FAI. This led to the doctor himself attending to give evidence that established his work had been carried out in an exemplary fashion with full liaison with the appropriate police officers. He had submitted a verbal briefing on completion, a written report in confirmation by the fastest means then available, and a formal statement later when requested. It is hard to see how the sergeant could be unaware of the first two of these, as he had been one of the team involved when Dr. Fieldhouse had returned to the Incident Centre and spent many hours assisting with the identification of his group of victims. Anyone paying attention might too have questioned how an officer collating for inquest all the data relating to the dead bodies in what were by then known to be 270 murders could possibly be unaware of two, fully detailed statements made by the police surgeon responsible for pronouncing life-extinct in nearly a quarter of them.

No one could be more sympathetic than Dick to the position of a detective sergeant giving evidence in an important hearing, yet he could offer no explanation other than that the officer was 'riding to orders' as they say in horse racing. Dick, like others, had become convinced that it was the mysterious American agents in trench coats or in Pan Am jackets with false engineering department name tags who had been calling the shots and dictating the priorities in those first hours. And their priorities had not been the removal of bodies; perhaps with the exception of one. Dick was confident of this, principally because fellow police officers had said as much. Many of the rank and file, both the local and the drafted-in had been scandalised at the apparent takeover of the response by these anonymous Americans, and a few risked their careers by saying so. Some passed information to radio reporter David Johnston and some contacted their Members of Parliament. Those in the Lothians and Borders force found a ready ear in the person of the Honourable Member for Linlithgow, Tam Dalyell MP, a veteran campaigner for truth and a scourge of dissimulators of all parties, including his own. He would go on to take a close interest in the cover-up, raising the subject often in Parliament.

Dick knew from his long experience that the abuse of normal procedures must have been very serious to motivate the few who complained to the likes of Johnston and Dalyell. The police service is by instinct self-contained and inward-looking; to go outside with trouble is not part of the culture, however discreetly it might be done. In the past, complaining about something too openly, even internally to the wrong ears, had all-too-often led to an unwanted posting or career disadvantage. The reaction of the vast majority of the police at Lockerbie, however much angered by what was being done, would, he said, have been to look the other way and keep their heads down. If you wanted to continue to enjoy your chosen career there was little choice but to do as you were told. Once the direction to comply with the Americans' wishes had been confirmed, and filtered its way back down to the troops on the ground, there was no future in becoming a martyr. If, for example, the sergeant at the FAI had been told to suggest, if asked, that the delays in recovery of bodies had been the result of undisciplined practices by an outside volunteer doctor, and that sergeant held any aspirations to becoming, in due time, an inspector, superintendent or higher, then he had one course and one course only open. Do it!

As with the judge who released the real Lockerbie bomb-maker from custody in Germany for reasons that flew in the face of the facts, Dick thought that the attempted blackening of the reputation of David Fieldhouse, in another solemn legal forum, was just another indication of the inevitable price we pay for permitting the Secret World to gain its stranglehold on all of us.

—ooOoo—

When Fraser had mentioned *Plausible Denial* in connection with the CIA, Ray had been prepared to ditch his principle of not admitting to ignorance unless directly challenged. What had won out though that day had been his resolution to keep silent, when he could manage it, in the hope of encouraging a useful flow of information from Jack's somewhat taciturn brother. In the event, the high octane meeting had overcome his intention to ask about what was clearly a book which Fraser had assumed he would be familiar. He had not however forgotten the title itself and in the weeks post-Plockton had sourced a copy. What he read both buoyed him up and perturbed him in approximately equal measures. The work is concerned with the second trial of an action for libel, brought by one of the Watergate burglars, E Howard Hunt, an admitted highly-placed CIA official, against a publisher over an article which placed him in Dallas at the time of the Kennedy assassination. The heartening though appalling aspect was that the jury became thoroughly convinced by the evidence that not only was the article true, but that the agency had murdered the president.

The sense of elation at realising that this determination had been spoken in a US courtroom and repeated by the forewoman of the jury numerous times outside the courthouse to a substantial press-gaggle was quickly replaced by wonder. JFK's murder would be high on most peoples' list of significant events of the 20th century and here was a real verdict bearing on the case, one that completely demolishes the official Oswald lone gunman theory, yet Ray together with the vast majority of the world's population knew nothing of it. The book vividly describes the manoeuvrings by the CIA to use both secrecy and false testimony to prevent the emergence of truth in court. That he accepts as automatic, given the record.

But the truly astonishing and utterly depressing element was that the media largely reacted as if the trial, the exposure of CIA-endorsed witnesses and the finding of the jury had never happened. It was chilling that, although totally discredited, the agency nevertheless held sufficient influence to persuade major respected newspapers and the TV networks to bury news of its culpability in perhaps world's highest profile crime of all time. Barely a word of the determination in E Howard Hunt versus Liberty Lobby reached the American public and the world beyond. So much for the First Amendment and free speech. Virtually every publisher in the US refused to release *Plausible Denial*, the author, Mark Lane, asserts.

Lane also describes how the *Washington Post*, fêted as the breaker of Watergate, sent a correspondent who disparaged Oliver Stone's film, *JFK*, even as it was shooting. If all that were not troubling enough for Ray, Lane has some cautionary words on the competing and perhaps incompatible claims of truth and entertainment in feature film making, deriving from his work on another movie, *Executive Action*, and from discussions with Stone himself. If Ray had begun to feel optimistic about the prospects for *One-Zero-Three*, with the turning of each page of Lane's work, he couldn't help but feel dark shadows of influence capable of reaching out towards his own.

—ooOoo—

73   The Fog of Secret War

The Fatal Accident Inquiry provided one other episode with dramatic possibilities that Ray has been able to use in the screenplay. Again it arose thanks to the dogged determination of bereaved parents.

From very early on after the crash, according to both police and volunteer searchers, it had become clear that the American agents were concentrating their focus on certain specific items, although at briefings they would not, in the main, disclose what they actually were. 'You'll know what it is when you find it,' was all they would offer on one occasion. There is no doubt that the spies were desperate to locate certain of the bodies, and very possibly magic one away. They would have wanted to check the pockets of other targets and go on to locate any hand baggage and hold luggage belonging to these individuals. None of this was conveyed to the British searchers, other than a mention of some documents, supposedly given to Captain MacQuarrie, and a black Samsonite case.

What searchers did soon stumble across in the sodden fields and swollen streams were large quantities of money and also of drugs, notably American dollars and heroin. Such finds would have not excited particular surprise or interest, save for the fact that, prompted no doubt by the tendency of the Secret World to deny everything, the spooks instructed the police spokespeople to refute the rumours of such discoveries. This was very much a self-defeating move, as so many people had personal experience of these finds. Indeed at least one group of police searchers **had** been briefed on the possibility of luggage containing heroin. It was also widely known that a special area of the warehouse used for recovered property had been set aside specifically for drugs. The denials, rather than diverting attention, immediately alerted everyone, including the vast media contingent that had flooded the area, to the fact that the spokespeople were not telling the truth. The inference to be drawn was that there was something to hide, and that it was therefore at least possible that drugs and perhaps covert cash transactions could have some bearing on the aircraft's destruction. This was a classic proof of the argument Dick advanced: that denying the undeniable merely showed sceptical inquirers where to dig.

Over time, when pressed, the British government also chained itself to the fiction that no large quantities of drugs and cash had been on board Flight 103. This was an act that demonstrated to a swelling number of people that any reputation for truthfulness the once-great nation might have retained could now be frivolously subverted, apparently at the behest of some mid-ranking foreign spies.

When, at the FAI, the drugs finds were ignored and then categorically denied by police witnesses, the Revd. John Mosey, who with his wife had lost their 19-year-old daughter, Helga, became increasingly concerned that all was not as it should be. He asked the relatives' group's lead barrister, Brian Gill, to raise the matter. When nothing happened he asked twice more; an approach through their solicitor provoked a refusal and a further direct request was rebutted with some heat. To satisfy his own conscience, Mosey wrote to Gill and others of the legal team, formally reporting a single drug find, on the farm of one Jim Wilson, and noting his attempts to have the subject aired at the hearing.

This produced a remarkably quick result. The letter was passed that day to the Lord Advocate, Lord Fraser, and thence to John Orr. Orr had led the Lockerbie investigation as joint head of CID in the Strathclyde force, and had since been promoted Deputy Chief Constable of Dumfries and Galloway. The same afternoon Fraser and Orr met Revd. Mosey, and assured him that Mr Wilson had confirmed he had no evidence to add to what he had given the inquiry. The clergyman remembers being assured by Orr that Mr Wilson would be interviewed again. Lord Fraser much later wrote that he understood that a further interview did take place. If one did, it was not for more than a year following the end of the FAI. As it was, the hastily organised meeting between Mosey, Orr and the Lord Advocate ensured that the finding of large quantities of drugs was kept out of the record of the inquiry and thus the official line on the matter received no challenge.

Ray remembers that Dick, with his mind like an encyclopaedia for Lockerbie facts, had added to this story, with a quizzical smile:

"Of course, Orr's appointment in Dumfries and Galloway was but a springboard to a knighthood and further elevation to Chief Constable of Strathclyde. Brian Gill became a Scottish Law Lord and ultimately Lord Justice Clerk, Scotland's second most senior judge."

"And speaking of promotions, what happened to the sergeant who gave the misleading account of Doctor Fieldhouse?" Ray had asked.

"Would you believe, I don't know," Dick had laughed. "I must try and find out."

As far as Ray knows, he never had the time.

—ooOoo—

There was one episode, central to the story, where some police officers took positive steps to avoid having their integrity compromised by the CIA subterfuges. As someone having a great respect for the generally proud record of duty provided by so many British police, often at great cost to themselves, over approaching two hundred years, and depressed by having had to demonstrate that the service had been subjected and apparently ordered to submit to intolerable interference and pressure at every stage of the Lockerbie investigation, Ray is pleased he has been able to highlight one small incident where good coppers took the initiative and scored just a few points back from the cheats. As with so many threads in the saga, this event centred around the presence on the flight of Major Charles McKee.

Of particular interest to the CIA men, way above the possessions carried on board by any others on their list of special names (far more important, it would appear, than for example the suitcase that contained the bomb), were the luggage and effects of the army engineer assigned to the Defense Intelligence Agency. If there had been nothing else to raise suspicion of their motives, and had not blanket denials been thrown over everything they are known to have done, it could be allowed that their keenness to recover papers that McKee inevitably would have been carrying, might have been entirely reasonable. It was hardly desirable that military maps, strategic descriptions and code details for a complex hostage rescue mission (even one that could now not take place) should be scattered over miles of the border counties, for anyone to pick up and perhaps publish. Fortunately, at least one British police officer was able to view some such items before they were spirited away. It's also certain that at least part of the very large volume of cash found in the soggy fields was part of the float for the mission. The dispersal of large bundles of dollars as bribes for co-operation is standard intelligence agency practice, as seen spectacularly in Afghanistan, paving the way for the American military operation.

Where the natural quest to draw a veil over secret operations crossed the line was that the anonymous spooks were not merely content for McKee's paperwork to be secured and logged, as Scottish law required. They apparently had motivation to make it disappear, to ensure that it could never become part of the investigation. Ray and Dick had reasoned that the aborted rescue's co-ordinator would have written a comprehensive report detailing the compromising of his sensitive mission, ready to justify the exposure planned at JFK and to defend his own return. A copy would undoubtedly be somewhere in his luggage. Perhaps, for security, another copy formed the mysterious unspecified papers supposedly in the care of Captain MacQuarrie. This document, they decided, was one of the major items that the searchers had really been after. It was to that end, they believe, that Charles McKee's suitcase was recovered illegally, 'sanitised' illegally and then replaced illegally so that it could be later found for a second time, 'legally'.

On 24th December, Christmas Eve, the third full day of the recovery and investigation, the cloudbase was so low that the littered countryside was wreathed in thick mist. To depict this on film will present an enormous opportunity and also a considerable challenge to the director of photography and others. It is always hard to achieve and maintain the required density of fog or mist, and the special effects assistants have their work cut out, running around with their smoke generators. If there is any sort of a breeze, it's usually impossible to shoot until it abates. Indeed the likelihood is that a set of woodland and field edge will be built in a studio. Inside, the doors can be shut and the extracts turned off so that the intensity of the diffusion can be kept constant more readily.

It's odd. When a production designer lays out a set to be constructed on a sound stage, he or she aims to make the built result as realistic as possible. Yet when location managers are scouting for existing backgrounds to offer directors, they are always on the lookout for places that have an element of artificiality or perfection about them – in essence, actual places that look like sets. Whether the decision is to go for location or studio, Ray thinks that the sequences representing the activities on that raw day will be among the most atmospheric and visually telling of all, with searchers and investigators moving in and out of view through this ghostly monochromatic landscape that is still disfigured and draped with aircraft fragments, passengers' effects, and indeed evidence of passengers' bodies, as yet unrecovered from among the sculptural, leafless trees.

Through the mist comes a strange little party, clearly on a mission, led by two American field agents, still keeping up the pretence that they are Pan Am employees. As the pair flounder around trying to find the ridge above Carruthers Farm, near Waterbeck, the remainder of the group, Scottish police officers, hang back; easy enough to do with the mud and the obscuring wet murk. In an interlude reminiscent of a Shakespeare battle scene on stage, without the 'alurums off', they debate the purpose of this trek and realise that they have been ordered along to record and legally certify the finding of Charles McKee's suitcase. These officers though, happen to know through the grapevine that the much-sought case had been found the previous day by a search dog and already removed, by agents, without the necessary legal formalities. They decide that by having anything to do with evidence that has been undoubtedly tampered with, they run the risk, at worst, of an accusation of conspiracy to pervert the course of justice. One deliberately gets separated and 'lost' in the mist and the other two use the worsening weather and his disappearance as a reason to abandon the search and return to Tundergarth. In the coach back to Edinburgh at the end of the day, the group learn from colleagues that eventually a local police dog handler and a British Transport Police officer from Glasgow have been used to locate the case on the hill before nightfall. They have provided the required signatures for evidence purposes, knowing nothing of the criminal interference that has been perpetrated.

It was not only the Americans who were sensitive about Major McKee, as would be proved in a highly dramatic fashion. When David Johnston of Radio Forth contributed an item which was broadcast nationally, mentioning McKee's name, detectives were at the radio station within an hour. The reporter's story disclosed that a team of intelligence officers returning from Beirut had perished on Flight 103, and that investigators were evaluating whether a bomb could have been planted in luggage belonging to McKee or one of his colleagues. The policemen knew who had written the piece, despite its being uncredited on air. They demanded to see him and for four hours pressed him to reveal his source or sources. Eventually he agreed to check with his informants to see if they were prepared to be identified. The police advised him that not supplying the names would render him liable to imprisonment for contempt of court. When the sources declined, the journalist was indeed reported, not to the local Procurator Fiscal, but to Scotland's Chief Law Officer, the Lord Advocate. Proceedings against him were only dropped after Tam Dalyell MP raised the matter in a question in the House of Commons. Of course, if Johnston telephoned his informants, the likelihood is that the Americans at Menwith Hill were waiting to monitor his calls in the hope of identifying them. Presumably this is also how the authorities knew he'd written the piece in the first place.

The revealing part of the episode was that during his efforts to persuade Johnston, the Inspector, Alex McLean, offered to facilitate an immediate interview with any figure to whom the reporter would feel able to entrust the information. The list, he said, included the Prime Minister, Margaret Thatcher.

If Major Charles McKee and his mission were important enough that suppression of their mention could become the concern of the British Head of Government, logic would argue that his presence on the flight and the fate of the flight had to be connected.

—ooOoo—

74   "Speculation is not Evidence"

'Speculation is not evidence' is a blindingly obvious truism, but one which usually escapes recognition by those in the media following an air crash. People who cannot possibly know the cause are asked for their opinions by journalists who are rarely conversant with even the basic facts of aviation. Perhaps the most common ignorance is the misuse of the term 'stall', which in non-aviation parlance usually refers to a car's engine stopping. By simple association the layman assumes that if aircraft engines stop, that is a stall. Having an idea that a stall is something bad implants the idea that if the powerplant fails, the aircraft falls from the sky. It doesn't.

The truth is that stalls relate to a whole range of aerodynamic conditions, and can occur while engines are developing any power from zero to full. They are studiously avoided by pilots under normal circumstances, although they can and must be practised regularly (in the simulator with airliners and in the air, normally without passengers, in light aircraft). This training is designed to be perfectly safe. Stalls can involve considerable and rapid loss of height, so pilots are especially alert not to precipitate one anywhere near the ground. Stalls need height for recovery, but recover you can. An aircraft that loses power does not automatically stall; nor otherwise plunge out of control. It glides. This means it comes down gradually, but pilots practise engine failure so that they can glide, either for the longest time or the greatest distance the physics permit, in order to reach the best option available for an emergency landing. The longest time allows the best chance to restart the engine. One thing a pilot avoids particularly after engine failure **is** a stall. The two are totally different animals, albeit they can be deadly in combination. It will soon be time for Ray to have his two-yearly flight check with an examiner, in which stalls are a required feature.

In the aftermath of an accident, the last thing a newsroom editor wants is footage of an accident investigator saying 'It's too early to speculate' but that's all they are going to get from that source, other than a reiteration of what is transparently obvious. The investigator will be at the start of a process that can take weeks or months and possibly come up with factors totally unsuspected. The journalist wants someone to say 'pilot error' or 'it looks like poor maintenance' for the *Six O'Clock News*, while the public remain interested and shocked.

The phrase 'Speculation is not evidence' was spoken by Prime Minister Thatcher, in Lockerbie on the morning after the disaster. The 'Iron Lady' made a point of appearing at hospitals and at the scenes of tragedies, so much so that some acid wits produced badges and wallet cards, rather like those for organ donation, reading:

If I am involved in a major disaster

PLEASE DON'T LET MRS THATCHER VISIT ME

Ray has always been in two minds about politicians and heads of state insisting on attendance at such events. On the one hand, they may feel they have to go and show concern, but it is incontrovertible that their presence must interrupt and distract from the necessary work on the spot. Lockerbie was visited during the first night by Malcolm Rifkind, the Scottish Secretary; Lord Brabazon, the Aviation Minister and Charles H Price III, the United States Ambassador. The following day came Prince Andrew, narrowly beating Mrs Thatcher, in contrast to the norm where she usually managed to get to a disaster before the less flexible Royal Family. Dick had been very conscious that making arrangements for the planning and security of each one of those visits would have taken up considerable resources in police time and not least in phone lines, which were at an absolute premium. He held that it was inevitable that all this symbolic visiting hugely diverted logistic effort from the tasks of recovery and investigation in hand, especially given the diminutive size of the police force involved -- the Dumfries and Galloway Constabulary, the smallest of any on the British mainland with a strength of only 333 officers at the time. It was perverse that the largest UK murder inquiry ever, in terms of victim-count, should literally have fallen to the police organisation probably least best-placed to undertake it.

Dick and Ray came to the conclusion that VIPs should in such circumstances announce that they are being kept in close touch with events, but are themselves staying away so as not to compromise vital operations. In reality they would be better-equipped to make any necessary decisions in their offices. Personal inspection tours, they decided, were really little better than official voyeurism. They had coined the phrase 'Celebrity Rubberneckers'.

They found it interesting that Thatcher should choose to voice the distinction between supposition and fact. Everyone was anxious to know the cause, it is true. Had the Boeing fallen to earth as a result of structural failure, there would have been panic among the world's air-travelling public and chaos in the travel industry, so embedded and fundamental was the 747 as a vital component of worldwide transport capability. Travellers needed to know what threat was actually to be confronted. If the weighty aircraft had not broken apart due to age and an accumulation of stresses, then there were limited other reasons for its having done so, with terrorist intervention as a prime suspect.

Was there hidden meaning in what the Prime Minister said? The sentence is ostensibly a warning against jumping to conclusions. Was she steering people away from a particular interpretation? Ray thinks probably not, believing that she was just being her usual self and talking down to people; demonstrating her standard capacity for giving voice to simple concepts in her trademark condescending tone that always suggested no one was capable of grasping them without her patient explanation. Dick felt that she probably had no inkling of any of the hidden causes at the time of her visit, but she would have known that the police were, from a few hours into the investigation, treating it as a potential crime.

There may have been no concealed meaning, but there was irony a-plenty. Here was a politician renowned for making up her mind on instinct rather than fact, counselling the reverse. And here was the woman who would soon order that the very evidence she referred to would be firmly obscured and then buried, in favour of other 'evidence', manufactured to suit a different scenario.

Dick and Ray had many discussions about evidence. As one used to gathering and presenting it, Dick could only marvel at the statements of Tony Gauci, the owner of the Malta shop where someone ostentatiously bought a random collection of clothes which apparently found their way into the bomb suitcase. Gauci was interviewed numerous times, and each time parts of his recollection changed significantly. There is a scene in the script where Weiss, Jane and Brad use a whiteboard to review the differences in each statement, with their comments intercut with the scene in the boutique replayed several different ways to highlight the inconsistencies. While writing the sequence, Ray had at one moment felt as if he was penning a *Monty Python* sketch, so comically disparate were the versions. The trial judges elected to believe one that placed Megrahi as the clothes buyer, despite the great contradictions, and compelling contributory evidence that taken together strongly suggested otherwise.

In fact Gauci's testimony could merit attack on the grounds of his many conflicting statements: on identification, on the date of the purchases and on the list of clothes bought, especially the grey shirt in which the crucial piece of timer fragment had reportedly been found. Mention of shirts was absent from his first statement. His second affirmed his certainty that the buyer took no shirts. It was two years before he remembered the buying of shirts, but the colour he described never matched the forensic evidence. It has been said with some justification that al-Megrahi's counsel did not manage to highlight the many discrepancies in this witness's evidence to the degree that might have been expected.

When the indictments against the two Libyans had been issued in November 1991, both British and American governments had officials give off-the-record briefings (highly irresponsible and prejudicial in the circumstances since they pre-judged the criminal hearing) stating that Flight 103 was blown up in retaliation for the 1986 US bombing attacks on Tripoli and Benghazi.

Those who see Lockerbie as Libya's response to that 'Operation Prairie Fire' seem happy to accept that a volatile Gaddafi, bent on revenge, would tolerate a delay of 32 months before unleashing his dogs. It apparently carries no significance to them that the interval between Iran Air 655 and Pan Am 103 was a mere 23½ weeks, less than **six** months.

Mrs Thatcher was Prime Minister when US bases in Britain at Lakenheath, Upper Heyford and Fairford were used to launch those North African raids. Writing in her memoirs of the possibility of a Libyan reprisal she states, 'The much-vaunted Libyan counter-attack did not and could not take place.'

If you are going to start telling lies, it's advisable to do it consistently, or you get found out. Either the government briefers were doing so in 1991, or the ex-Prime Minister does in her book. One statement had to be true; the other false. Ray's money on this occasion is on Mrs T. She did, after all, advertise herself as a woman so sure of herself that she could never make a mistake. 'The lady's not for turning.'

If she wrote it, she believed what she was writing was correct. It wouldn't be uninformed speculation. She, of all people, had the real evidence. Later she sought to 'correct' herself but in her book, even though it was a lapse, an inconsistency on her part to admit the truth, she did.

The Libyans didn't do it. Mrs Thatcher said so.

–ooOoo–

75 Unwanted Baggage

Among Dick's A4 sheets of crime analysis diagrams, there are two pages that he generally referred to as the 'Nonsense Sheets'. Other names include the 'Crown's Comics' and – reflecting his love of football – the 'OFFside Trap Sheet' where OFF stood for 'Official Fiscals' Fantasies'. These contain two diagrams, in this instance effectively timelines: one representing what al-Megrahi and Fhima were supposed to have done; the other what al-Megrahi is supposed to have done alone, given that Their Camp Zeist Lordships, in their wisdom, by correctly finding Lamin Fhima not guilty, removed him from complicity in any conspiracy. Both variations on the story made brief, bizarre and unconvincing reading, but the one in which Fhima was ruled out of the equation, the perceptive investigator argued, saw even any tiny vestige of possible credibility collapse like a sandcastle at the first wavelet.

As he pointed out on several occasions, ignoring the transparent concoctions put into the mouth of the expensive witness Giaka, the only evidence that could even remotely link al-Megrahi to the Lockerbie crime was the purchase of the clothes in the bomb suitcase. If he had bought them, it still wouldn't have proved in most courts that he was the 'bomber' as the bovine headline writers so predictably love to call him: that called for a whole succession of far-from-proven inferences to be drawn. But to get even to that point, the judges needed to be secure in their belief in the soundness of the identification evidence given by the shop owner. In fact they seemed to go out of their way to find reasons to explain their acceptance of impossibly ambiguous recollections.

If they were prepared to go along with identification that was both wavering, undoubtedly contaminated and procedurally deficient, they would hardly be likely to be sensitive to the feel of the evidence. Although they mentioned in their judgement an awareness that evidence might have been massaged and manipulated, they showed no reluctance to accept some portions of it that they might therefore have been prompted to question more critically.

For example, even ignoring the dubious identification, Dick wondered that since the clothes-buying was so pivotal in their decision, why Their Lordships might not have at least wondered to themselves why anyone in al-Megrahi's alleged position, an agent involved in a massive plot, might have behaved as oddly and in such a noteworthy fashion as the actual purchaser apparently did.

As he put it, with his rolling Lancashire vowels:

"You've been given the job of putting a radio bomb in a suitcase, so you need some items to stop it moving about. As a professional you would undoubtedly go further than that; you'd try to pack it with objects that would also pass a casual inspection and appear to be a thoroughly normal and believable set of contents, just in case it should be opened or X-rayed. OK, so the intention is that everything is going to be blown to pieces, burnt and scattered, ideally into the mid-Atlantic Ocean, but things often don't go to plan and it really takes very little effort to do a convincing back-up job, just in case. At the same time, you don't want anything in the case to provide clues that could lead investigators back to the source – either your country or yourself, so you have good reason to think carefully about what you put in. Fortunately you have the resources of a well-funded intelligence service with operatives in embassies, or if you are Libyan, so-called 'people's bureaux' in numerous countries. It would be simplicity itself to have a colleague take a shopping list to any crowded retail outlet or market, and pop the items in a diplomatic pouch to wherever you want to use them. Most goods these days carry identity marks that will indicate where they are made and where they are sold, so good sense dictates that the items in your case lay a false trail to somewhere else.

"Your solution to this hardly taxing task is somewhat at variance with the ideal, according to the prosecution's version. You elect to collect the contents yourself. You buy in a place, Malta, which has very well-established links with your own country. You find a quiet, personal, family-run shop that doesn't normally cater for Libyans, rather than a busy anonymous outlet. You purchase a completely random and disparate selection of clothes, some of which are locally manufactured. Just to make sure that your purchase is remembered and will put Mr Plod on your trail, you could barely make it plainer that the items are unimportant in themselves – mere packing – makeweight, and to cap it all you buy an umbrella because it's raining (a far from everyday occurrence in Malta). If it was you – and of course it wasn't, because the shopkeeper's first description is of someone looking nothing like you – you might as well have said 'I want you to make sure you remember this incident and even the date, because something's goin' on!'"

Dick's hardly earth-shattering conclusion was that whoever bought the clothes was saying just that very thing – following that favourite First Rule of his. They were putting down a misleading scent. Strangely, little or nothing was made in court of the fact that the deliberate and attention-getting purchase of odd and identifiable clothes might have been a typical Secret World ploy to suggest that the bomb suitcase started its journey in

Malta. If it was, it worked hook, line and sinker. But the bizarre shopping expedition proves something else surprising. It shows that it wasn't only the CIA that wanted to put the blame on Libya some time **after** the event, but that someone who it seems must have had some function in the real conspiracy (since the clothes, we are told, **did** go into the bomb suitcase) (or did they?) for some reason may have contrived to do so **in advance**.

An extension of one of Dick's favourite investigative axioms – and one that generally seems to yield positive results – argues that the more vehemently the authorities deny a suggestion, the more truth is likely to reside in it. Trying to adapt this approach to the question of false trails, Ray and Dick had it found sometimes to work, and sometimes not. It was perfectly possible to understand, for example, the potential sources and possible motives behind the appearance of bogus clues pointing to Libyan involvement **after** the infamous Bush-Thatcher 'tone-down-the-investigation' phone call three months following Lockerbie; but harder to understand why someone apparently associated with the actual bomb plot might have been doing so before the event. Far from being reticent, terrorist groups frequently claim responsibility for their atrocities with expressions of pride, and Ahmed Jibril was very much on record as stridently determined to attack American targets. He, of all people, would hardly wish to steer credit towards another organisation in the event of what he would see as a successful operation.

Light could be shed on this apparent inconsistency if it were possible to determine the part that may have been played by Mohammed Abu Talb, a noted and convicted Palestinian terrorist who was on a list of names prepared by the trial defence as potential alternative perpetrators. Despite Talb's being called tactically by the Crown as a witness, and despite there being evidence of a visit to Malta, connection to a Palestinian cell there, and of some Malta-manufactured clothes being taken to his home in Sweden, the question mark remained after his evidence, just that – a question mark. However, Dick had pointed out that Jibril, safely sheltered in Syria, could if he wished afford to be open and bullish about his activities, especially as they now suspected that Jibril was also a protected CIA asset – although such a connection, Ray had suggested, might encourage him to be slightly less publicly exultant about his 'success'. On the other hand, Talb, who for five years prior to Lockerbie had been living 'quietly' in Sweden, would have had, even after his arrest and sentencing for other bombing offences, very sound reasons for diverting attention away from any criminal activities that he might have been involved in. A Libyan 'connection' for the Lockerbie crime would have suited him, just as it later suited a whole raft of players with all sorts of allegiances and suspect motives.

In one of his statements, Tony Gauci, the shopkeeper, who reputedly received $2m expenses for his 'co-operation' with the authorities, (his brother also netted $1m) had happily identified a photograph of Abu Talb as the closest likeness to the mystery clothes purchaser.

−ooOoo−

Of the other analysis diagrams that Ray and Dick had revisited most frequently over many months were the set that charted the various ways that Khalid Jaafar and his fellow mules could have been assisted, to ensure uninterrupted passage for their heroin-filled suitcases. Then there was a complementary set that took all the possible scenarios from the first list to see how each of them could have been used by the Jibril organisation to switch or add the case that contained the bomb radio. There was also the possibility, advanced by a relative of Jaafar's, that the young man had simply been given the radio as a present. Having unwitting travellers agree to convey gifts for others was a standard, regularly used PLFP-GC modus operandi and this was a feasible variation. However the relation insisted that Jaafar was not involved in drug deliveries, which contradicted other seemingly sound evidence and appears not to be true. This example indicated the typical problems and the fascination of the case. So often informants' accounts contained thoroughly credible details, but some of these would contradict assertions within equally plausible information coming from other sources. Ray had been so fortunate to encounter Dick, with his facility for analysing, comparing and evaluating all these competing and compelling alternatives.

It had really been Dick's Inverse Denial Law again which had convinced the old sergeant that the McKee mission and drugs had to have played a major part in the downing of Flight 103. Just as in thousands of interviews he'd conducted in his career, when it had been the topics that suspects **didn't** want to talk about that indicated areas to probe, everything in this case that officialdom had either ignored or denied most strongly had provided pointers to the doors to push at and look behind. Yet despite this firm conviction that the Lebanon, hostages, heroin and the CIA all cast their shadow over this tragedy, he had become sure, as he had eventually told Ray towards the close of their very first meeting, that the primed bomb had actually been sent on its way not from Frankfurt − but from London Heathrow.

He'd joked that you'd needed to be a really far-out conspiracy theorist to believe the prosecution argument and the judges' acceptance that the bomb had been primed in Malta, trusting to luck that it would detonate at an appropriate time after being successfully transferred onto two further flights without being intercepted or delayed. An explosion in an airport baggage area was not an acceptable outcome to the perpetrators. Nor was one in the hold of an aircraft on the ground. The limited amount of Semtex that could be employed would be capable of causing minor to moderate damage and perhaps some injuries in a localised area if that had been the outcome. Neither of these would have provided the spectacular that the sponsors wanted and were paying for, yet given the likelihood of delays, especially at a peak period during this busy time of year, either would have been more than possible. Dick pointed out that it was inconceivable, if plotters in Malta were using the accurate Mebo timer alleged by the Crown, that they would have set it so tightly to the scheduled take-off from Heathrow as the actual time of detonation would imply. A delay to Flight 103's departure of just 40 minutes (not at all an unusual hold) would then have seen the bomb go off as *Maid of the Seas* trundled around Heathrow's inner taxiway towards runway Two-Seven Right. Yet they could have, from their point of view, safely set it for several hours later and the Clipper would still have been over the Atlantic, New York-bound. Even the most incompetent terrorists could not have made such a ridiculous miscalculation.

This alone, without all the other doubts, had been sufficient to convince Dick and Ray that the bomb did not have a Mebo timer, but rather one of Marwhan Khreesat's signature, pressure capsule plus delay-timer arrangements which would fit perfectly the actual take-off and climb plus approximately 30-minute profile, with Heathrow of course as its activation point, as opposed to Luqa or Flughafen Frankfurt Main.

Ray had for a long time been attracted to the theory of German cell – Frankfurt airport. Unlike Malta, the central German hub was known for poor security; the drug route passed through here, capitalising on that fact. Khalid Jafaar was actually witnessed that day, nervous at the check-in, but somehow getting his haul of heroin into the baggage system undetected. But the uncomfortable part of the logic was the question of why a Khreesat bomb would not have detonated on the Frankfurt to London feeder flight, the 103A. This suggested either the use of some further complex and perhaps risky extra electronics, for which there was physically almost certainly not room in the radio case, or that the bomb would have needed to be primed in London. Dick had gone for the latter.

His reasoning might have been the physics, but the nudge had once again been his tendency to note where everyone else had avoided looking and to wonder why. If the authorities had hardly been rigorous in their investigations at Frankfurt, their considerations at Heathrow had bordered on the dismissive. Dick had started to look at London for whatever it was that there had been no apparent will to find. He was not of course suggesting that the suitcase had been dispatched on 103A and somehow intercepted at Heathrow by someone in the plot, opened somewhere out of sight, the bomb radio primed, and then the case placed in a particularly effective position in container AVE 4041PA. This was a possible, very filmic scenario but too full of uncertainty to be of much appeal to the serious terrorist. Opening luggage for the purpose of pilfering might be relatively commonplace and easily accomplished, but being able to identify a particular item and remove it from the baggage stream under the gaze of the assigned unloading gang would hardly be an option. Ray sees the bomb case's contents as making the journey from Germany to England most likely via the unchallenged route of the diplomatic bag; the bag was probably Syrian, but given the known high-level involvement of the Tehran government, the unprimed radio, with or without the clothes, could alternatively have been consigned from Germany to the Iranian Embassy in London's Kensington.

Then again, perhaps the suitcase was delivered straight to London Airport, by special courier. It was revealed at the trial that an Iranian wanted internationally in connection with the 1985 hijacking of the cruise liner *Achille Lauro*, one Armad Jusif, had arrived at Heathrow on an Iran Air flight on the very morning of Lockerbie and departed for the USA via Pan Am at lunchtime. The presence of an active Middle Eastern terrorist at the airport in the hours before a bomb was infiltrated onto an Pan Am airliner at the behest of Iran may just be one of those coincidences, but it is surely worthy of note, especially given that the two airlines, Pan Am and Iran Air regularly used some of the same gates and parking stands at the time.

One of the character Daniel Weiss's most compelling theories, played out in the screenplay, has a Khreesat bomb radio sent to from Germany to Tehran via the Embassy post. Agents of the Revolutionary Guards order Iran Air staff to convey it in the cabin on Jusif's London flight, perhaps in a box, probably now in its Samsonite with the clothes incriminating Libya. After landing, Jusif, concealed in a lavatory on the plane or in Terminal Three airside, arms the bomb with one switch; and either hands over or leaves the case for an accomplice. This person is possibly an agent with a stolen pass posing as a loader or more likely someone employed as such, with a genuine pass – either a cell member infiltrated or an existing member of the workforce, possibly a recruited sympathiser or someone just bribed to carry, hold concealed and finally position the case, as directed, for money. Whoever it is will have worked at the terminal long enough to learn the maze-like layout and know the routes where a loader carrying a bag is least likely to seem out of place. At about the time of Lockerbie, Ray and two colleagues had found themselves forced for very good reason to access the apron of the airport of a major European capital, totally without authorisation or identity, and had simply walked past armed police at a checkpoint to do so. His theory has long been that if you act confidently enough, you can generally get wherever you want to, and this person, or perhaps series of people, would have had the undoubted advantage of wearing an identity pass and a uniform jacket.

Pan Am baggage loaders from both Frankfurt and London airports gave evidence at the trial of the Libyan duo. John Bedford had been away from his station at Heathrow baggage interline, leaving the container in question unsupervised for some 40 minutes. On his return two hard Samsonite-type suitcases had been placed on its floor, in front of those he had loaded before his absence. This was well before the landing of the feeder flight 103A from Frankfurt. Many researchers, including Dick, have become convinced that one of those mysterious Samsonites contained the IED. Very little notice seems to have been taken of this apparent 'wide-open goal', especially as these cases were never reconciled with any of 103's known passengers; nor apparently were they ever recovered with blast damage, unlike the 'actual' and mysteriously identical bomb bag, supposedly placed on top of them.

The lack of interest in evidence relating to Frankfurt had been equally baffling. In defending the victims' liability case against Pan Am, their insurance company's lawyers had conducted lie-detector tests on three of the airline's luggage staff. These polygraphs had suggested that two, named Tuzcu and O'Neill, could have been involved in a bag switch in respect of Flight 103A. When the Scottish police were given this lead, they, their German counterparts and the FBI all did nothing with it, the FBI being more interested in taking action against the polygrapher than investigating what he might have unearthed. Pan Am even flew the men to Heathrow, but the British police ignored their presence and the loaders returned to Germany. Years down the line, shortly before the Lockerbie trial, O'Neill gave an interview that seemed to confirm drug passage and absolutely confirmed minimal security.

Something or someone persuaded him to change his mind before he appeared as a Crown witness at Camp Zeist. Despite his words having been taped by the reporters just a few months before, O'Neill now claimed to know nothing and not to have spoken of controlled deliveries.

Dick, in common with other observers, had become convinced that the investigation was 'steered away' from Heathrow and Frankfurt in the early stages; a distraction that was made easier when the official line became that infiltration of the bomb had taken place at Luqa, allowing the investigation's resources to be firmly redirected towards the Mediterranean holiday destination. Until that point, the British and German authorities had been playing a game of 'blame tennis', each side trying to point to the other's airport as the one with the poor security procedures which had allowed the bomb into the luggage stream. No doubt as part of this, knowledge of an occurrence at Heathrow in the small hours of the day of the Lockerbie attack was suppressed for years. The cutting of a lock allowing access to Terminal Three airside was an event that security guard Ray Manley, with 19 years' service there, described as the most significant break-in. he had ever seen at Heathrow. This breach, plus the existence of some 38,000 airside passes, many of them unaccounted for, made it eminently possible that a rogue bag or bags could have been covertly smuggled airside during the night and concealed for placement later in the day. The Metropolitan Police 'lost' the guard's statement and no mention of this penetration of airside security appeared at either the Fatal Accident Inquiry or the Camp Zeist trial. When the incident was raised as part of Megrahi's 2002 appeal, the judges seemed to clutch at any flimsy straw to rule that the evidence did not indicate that the bomb could have been dispatched from London.

There was yet another compelling finger, pointing vigorously to Heathrow. The bomb case had been positioned near-optimally for explosive effect within the luggage container. A fact glossed over was the extent to which its relatively modest force would have been attenuated if the bag had been surrounded by other luggage on all sides. This device had only succeeded by exploding close to the aircraft's external skin and structural cavities. Had it been masked by layers of energy-absorbing materials, the plane may well not have disintegrated. Just two months and two days after the Lockerbie crime, another 747, United Airlines UA 811, out of Honolulu for Auckland, suffered explosive decompression at around 22,500 ft when a forward cargo door failed. The main deck floor caved-in and 10 seats and one other passenger were sucked from the aircraft through a large hole. Despite ingested material causing the shutdown of both starboard engines and other external damage to surfaces, including controls, the aircraft did not break up but was descended and returned for a safe landing, so suffering just 9 fatalities instead of a possible 355.

This incident emphasised the point that a jumbo jet could survive decompression at considerable altitude and tolerate a large hole in its structure. This should have demonstrated emphatically just how critical the placing of the bomb bag had been on 103. Or more importantly, how allowing a random loading of that bag on transfer, as would have been the case with the Malta scenario, or even the Frankfurt version, would have been highly unlikely to produce the terrorists' desired outcome; that of total destruction.

"In other words," Dick had said, "you would have had to be bananas, given a bomb of that limited size, not to have done all you could to ensure it was positioned where it needed to be in the tin." This was what the loaders called the luggage containers. "That meant someone physically placing it at Heathrow, which would align exactly with what John Bedford reported."

"How about the evidence that it couldn't have been on the floor, but had to be on the second layer of cases?" Ray had asked after further research.

"Well, that was more from our friends, the forensic scientists of DERA, and you know how confident we have learnt to be with their impartiality. I think that was because in theory interlined bags from other, earlier flights occupied the floor and the story they wanted to prove was that the bomb bag was in the baggage from 103A, which was loaded on top of them. In fact, Richard Keen got an expert to admit at the trial that using a different formula it could have been in the lower layer; but even then their lordships managed to avoid seeing the significance of that. One way or another, someone got that bomb suitcase placed near the bottom left-hand corner of that container. I know you love coincidence, but accepting it could get in the right place by pure chance after arriving from Malta and Frankfurt would have been like the terrorists banking on winning a raffle."

"Do you know what all this reminds me of? You know, the so-called trail of evidence. The idea of culpability. It's Anne Robinson, isn't it?"

"What do you mean?" Dick had responded.

"'Mr Megrahi – you are the weakest link. Goodbye.'"

–ooOoo–

The rain spatters the windows of the coffee shop. Outside, holidaymakers in zipped-up waterproofs amble past, stoically determined to enjoy their summer break. It's windy. It isn't cold but feels it. The glass is steaming up as more people come in with wet clothes, taking refuge. Ray had hoped this conversation would be taking place strolling along the banks of the Cam, looking across to the colleges, but they abandoned that plan an hour ago.

Ray isn't altogether sure why he's here in Cambridge. Some weeks ago he sent Brian a copy of *One-Zero-Three*, recorded delivery, wrapped up in so much brown paper tape and a profusion of sticky labels that it would have taken a very brave interceptor to have opened it. But then, he wonders, would they really care if he suspected tampering? He hadn't been truly obliged to send it, for little of what Brian told him at the wedding castle had found its way into the script: there just wasn't screentime to spare. It was more of a gesture to the ex-professor because he had expressed such interest in learning of Ray's conclusions when they had talked through those small hours.

He supposes he has come because he wants someone outside the film business to approve his work; an independent review of the validity of his research and his conclusions. Well – his and Dick's conclusions. That's part of sending it too. Since he heard the news about Dick, he's been understandably distracted and keen to place the script in reliable hands; someone who has a grasp of the value of history and how important it is not to manipulate it for any motive, well-intentioned or evil, or in pursuit of some 'artistic' objective. In film hands, the script may soon become unrecognisable. It's good that Brian has a version the integrity of which Ray vouches for.

He had been in two minds before dispatching it, wondering whether it was fair to involve someone else in the intrigue that he is sure has consumed his northern friend. He had phoned Brian, and in guarded terms gave him the option to keep well out of it – but, as he had suspected, the man jumped in with both feet, albeit expressed in equally cautious language. Today he has been startlingly direct.

"The more copies there are from now and the more people who know," he said earlier, "the less danger there is for everyone involved. They can't eliminate everybody." There should be truth in that, Ray feels, although the evidence of the Inslaw affair suggests they might try.

Ray feels he has something of an apology to make.

"I'm sorry that there was no room – no place to include most of the things we talked about at the wedding. But it was incredibly useful for me to understand how we got into that situation, where elements of one major power could so interfere with the criminal justice of another. Obviously, as you've now read, there is so much else to cram in and going into UK-US history any more than I do would move onto totally different ground; a whole different subject – far more subtle in some ways. I mean you could make brilliant films about 1917 and about 1940, based on what you told me. I think they'd be even harder to get financed than this one, though."

"Yes. You wouldn't get much American backing for dragging those skeletons out of the cupboard. I have to say I was worried that because of our discussion, your script might come out a rather anti-American document. I was pleased to see that it doesn't read as such. You seem to go out of your way to be fair."

"I tried to spread the blame around – made sure that everybody gets their share of the flying dung. And I'm genuinely not anti-American; my complaint is with just that tiny proportion of America that expects to run my country, and the rest of the world, come to that, for its own benefit. I mean – those people exploit most ordinary American citizens just as much as they try with everybody else – we have a common enemy."

"And one that most people don't even realise is there!" Brian sighs.

Ray knows that his work is not primary research as Will's father-in-law, as an academic, would regard it. Some of Dick's would probably rank as such and his deductions very much inform the final offering. For his own part, he has mainly cross-referenced and applied fresh logic to all the reliable accounts he could find. If his work were a thesis and not a screenplay he would be probably be criticised for not going back to original sources, but what he had managed to do had taken several years, for goodness sake; and many of the primary sources would not be open to him in any case.

It saddens him that Dick never got to see a completed draft.

–ooOoo–

Neither of them could drink another coffee if they tried, but fortunately the rain has stopped. To the great relief of their respective nervous systems they retrieve their topcoats from an overloaded and dripping coat-stand and risk an amble towards the river.

"So, you really think it's going to be made?"

"It's beginning to look possible, but I won't believe it until it's at least started shooting. You know – they tell me it's go, but I suspect the odds are still fifty-fifty at the moment. If anyone can get it off the ground it's the producer who's taken it on."

"That's good. Tell me. If it happens, what do you think people are going to make of it?"

"You mean the critics or the public or .. ?"

"Well anybody really – both."

"Well, **if** a decent publicity push is put behind it, that's what gets people into the cinemas, and if word of mouth or word of web gets round that it's worth seeing, interest should spread. Maybe, just, maybe, then people will start to think about the issues and ask questions, not that anyone is likely to answer. I mean – Oliver Stone's *JFK* exposed the total implausibility of the official line on the Kennedy murder brilliantly, but America still goes along with the Warren Report. It's fairly rare, I think, for single films to change very much in the way of entrenched beliefs at any level. If there should be any widespread reaction, our puppet government will be told to say nothing and wait for interest to fade, but behind the scenes there would be effort put in to discrediting the film's assertions. There could be pieces in newspapers and items on television, just like we've seen for eighteen years really, pumping out what the intelligence community wants people to believe. As happened with Stone's film, where the stories claimed his information was inaccurate, maybe they pick just one or two details: they may not even **be** wrong but they use that 'exposure' to dismiss the whole movie and its vast mass of evidence.

"Critics-wise, assuming it does actually turn out OK, I'd expect most to review on merit but it would get some sniping from some of our more predictable columnists and then, as I say, there might well be guest commentators wheeled in who would darkly hint that they are privy to a complete understanding of the entire Lockerbie case, and assure readers that the film's conclusions are off-beam due to wrong information or deliberate bias, and that really everyone would realise that what they have been told by the authorities is correct, if only they could all know the facts, which unfortunately have to remain secret in the interests of national security."

"The old catch-all," interjects Brian. "There's so much secrecy now in this country that it's a miracle anyone can come to a proper decision about anything."

"That's true. You know, my friend Des wants to bring in an intelligence test as a qualification to vote. If democracy is about informed choice, he says if people want to participate in it they should be able to prove they are informed – but thinking about it, how would we ever decide? Yes, you could weed out people who don't even appreciate what the chosen issues are, but anyone who professes to know something, anything – then you'd have to ask if what they know is fact or propaganda."

"And deciding one way or the other would totally depend on who was setting the test and what they too believed. It's just as well it's not going to happen!"

They pick their way through a group of ducks pecking at the path for invisible breadcrumbs. On the river a pair of swans makes a perfect formation approach and landing, dealing instinctively with the crosswind.

"Just supposing," Ray says, returning to Brian's original question, "a groundswell, a demand for answers did happen to be generated. In the unlikely event of government deigning to respond at all – maybe if some MP managed to raise a parliamentary question, HMG would most likely say that the film adds nothing new, and there's no fresh information that hasn't been heard before. They'd probably even try to imply that they've 'dealt with' these allegations over and over again when of course they've actually done nothing of the sort. There's a world of difference between dealing with a question and actually answering it. They've refused to explain even the most innocuous discrepancies, let alone the major and most glaring ones. I mean, the reason that we keep bringing up the same points and asking the same questions is because the points and questions have never been addressed with anything more than doublespeak.

"Did I tell you the example of everyone being so obsessed with keeping everything secret that a widow was informed at one point that she couldn't be told where her late husband had been sitting on the aircraft because it was 'confidential'? Did I say that when the Cadmans were pressing to know how it could have been determined that the Helsinki warning was a hoax – the warning that seems to have meant that would-be passengers from the American community in Moscow avoided the flight – they were fobbed-off and eventually sent brusque, dismissive letters by an official at the UK Department of Transport?"

Brian notes the use of the word 'obsessed' and that Ray has somewhat strayed from the thread of the question he has been asked.

"Raymond. I think you've got to step back and take a break from this now. You've done all you can for the present. There will plenty of convincing to do when it comes out. What are you going to do in the meantime? If you take my advice it will be something completely different."

"And now for something completely different," Ray laughs, but Brian notices how tired he can look at odd moments.

"You're right. I've got a few ideas I've been thinking about. I'll get down to one of those."

"How about a holiday? Why not go out and see that lovely wife of yours and relax in the sun."

"I don't think I'll be going to the States again, somehow. It doesn't seem an advisable move. It would feel like Salman Rushdie planning a weekend break in Tehran."

—ooOoo—

Damn! Ray realises he's breaking his cardinal rule by thinking and driving again. It's a struggle not to. There's much to go over from his talk with Brian and behind every topic he feels the influence of Dick and wonders what he would have made of the discussions. How he wishes that it could have been a three-way conversation. He feels so lucky to have fallen in the way of these two giants in the business of the distillation of facts. It makes him angry they will never meet.

It's fortunate, he thinks, that the cross-country route home from East Anglia is the last one on which a driver is likely to fall asleep either literally or metaphorically. Everything constantly changes: bends, gradients, villages and junctions determinedly succeed each other in random permutations, requiring concomitant reactions from a driver. Anyone properly trained, as Ray was long ago, will be driving to a formula that responds automatically to every unique set of circumstances. Part of that formula requires full allowance for the unseen and unexpected, so there is a built-in safety reserve, but not one that should offer any substitute for full concentration. He wouldn't attempt to justify reliance on this back-up protection, but today the pressures are too strong . . .

As he'd promised at the wedding, Brian had done some digging around on the subject of post-WWII British sovereignty. His prediction that one of the more leftish among his former colleagues would point him in the right direction had proved correct. Ray's receipt some months ago of a slim package of notes with Brian's Cambridge return address had been the result. Again, little of the material had actually found its way into the screenplay, yet its influence pervaded the work, because for Ray it put the rise of US dominance into context; it explained what he and Carl had seen at first hand; the cruise missiles being paraded at night through Wiltshire's sleeping countryside; the Boeing KC135 tankers (based on the civil 707 jetliner) shaking picture-book Cotswold villages like Bibury to their foundations as they took off to support the sneak raid on Libya – and events that the pair had only watched and read about second-hand – such as the aftermath of Lockerbie.

Uncannily, the journey home that Ray is now taking can be seen as providing a virtual road map or timeline of that growth in US assertiveness and decline in UK self-determination. He is leaving East Anglia, home to the bomber bases that had been central to the story. The eastern counties had been Britain's back door through which in 1942, to avoid one invasion, another occupation had begun unnoticed. The flurry of airfield building on flat fields looking towards the North Sea and further, to the dark shores of occupied Europe beyond, had been the earliest visible result in Britain of the entry of the United States to the war. When that conflict ended, almost every base soon fell silent: most planes and servicemen returned home. But there would be a new, unnoticed, dominating influence in their homeland. The US Army Air Force, by wielding the awesome might of the atom in the flattening of Yokohama and Nagasaki, had become credited with ending the World War. Now the Strategic Air Command of the new USAF, separated from the army, with its growing inventory of atomic bombs and B-29s modified to drop them, would have the opportunity to exploit its new powerbase.

Just as the Germans would not have been defeated without the US entering the war, Nazi aims might not have been thwarted by conventional means had Hitler not been unwise enough to invade the Soviet Union. That monstrously expensive diversion allowed Britain to escape her own invasion and granted the time, with the US eventually in partnership, to build and prepare for the recapture of Western Europe. When the tide of war did turn, Russia, never an easy ally, proved herself to be as keen on territorial expansion as the enemy they were jointly in the process of defeating. As German might waned, it became clear that today's comrade was all-too-likely to become tomorrow's adversity, or at least that's what Stalin and the Western leaders were happy for everyone to believe. The example of Japan had suggested that wars could be won with atomic weapons: Russia's seemingly endless reserves of manpower, it seemed, might only be contained in the same way. The air force generals of Strategic Air Command found themselves with a new mission; one that allowed them the freedom to define and implement US defence policy. In their Iron Curtain counterparts, they found ready accomplices with the same idea. The mutually profitable Cold War could begin.

For their revamped rôle confronting the Soviets, SAC would want some of those eastern British airfields back. In 1947, they determined that they would indeed have them, even if they needed, as they put it during their secret meetings, to 'seize and hold' them. US politicians had put an end to the UK's sovereign control of her financial affairs in 1941. US generals, in this new decision, evidenced equal contempt for her territorial integrity.

In the event, they didn't need to take what they wanted by force. They didn't even have to approach the UK Government – all they had to do was ask a fellow pilot. Lord Tedder was Marshal of the RAF. His was perhaps the most crucial decision of any that were made in post-war Britain, in that it put the country in harm's way to a degree that exceeded the threat which had been posed by Hitler and his would-be conquerors, for it firmly located us in the eye of a storm of potential total nuclear destruction, an exposure that persisted for more than half a century and – Ray shudders to remember – effectively remains to this day. Yet Tedder took the initial decision alone as an agreement between military men, with no recourse to higher authority. The government of the day, under Labour's Clement Atlee, was neither asked, consulted nor informed. That back door had been opened, a precedent set, and the entire process put in motion 'on the nod'; a process that would, at its peak in 1957, see 63,008 military personnel, with more than half as many again civilian staff and dependents in the UK, and eventually they would occupy more than 160 sites of all types. As a result, this garrison, together with a vast range of the most up-to-date weaponry, including of course, nuclear bombs, would be imposed on the country, with successive British governments continuing to have little knowledge of and certainly no control over whatever was going on behind the barbed wire fences.

It was only really when elements of the public woke up to the nuclear danger in general, and the extra hazard created by hosting America's forward strike force in particular, that anything was heard from the government. When it couldn't avoid saying something, it was always to claim that the presence of US forces added to British security and that they were here to defend us. Ray now knows that it didn't and they weren't. The theory of the arms race and nuclear confrontation was touted as Mutually Assured Destruction; the apparent certainty that peace was secured because war would inevitably destroy both sides. MAD was truly mad, because it failed to allow for accidents, misunderstandings and human irrationality, but what was being planned by the SAC was even more insane. In their halls of lunacy it had been decided that nuclear war was winnable, if you fired your missiles first. Global nuclear winter, contamination for the rest of eternity, zero food production and mutant survivors notwithstanding, there could be, these contorted minds had come to believe, a winning side. That it might comprise only a handful of generals and their batmen, living out their lives deep underground, singing *God Bless America* night and morning, seemed not to matter.

Meanwhile the so-called Independent Nuclear Deterrent was a sham. The means of delivery might be British-built, but the weapons were bought from America and could only be used with that nation's concurrence. Gradually those who make decisions in the UK, which definition does not, of course, include Parliament, had also embraced the unthinkable and planned for war with 'battlefield nuclear weapons' as though the 'battlefield' was some separate abstract place that did not involve homes, cathedrals, farms and civilian death in a thousand forms.

It was claimed that the bases helped the economy. They didn't: they were provided rent-free at British expense, with the burden of their defence falling on the RAF, and not the USAF. Financially, they were insulated and largely self-contained pockets of America, offering little local employment or outside commercial opportunity, however much the Civil Service was tasked to provide bogus figures apparently proving the opposite.

Of course British governments never admitted their lack of knowledge, much less their lack of control, particularly over the sharing of decisions on the launching of nuclear weapons from their soil. Other European nations admitted US bases only by formal treaty – arrangements that in many cases precluded nuclear material. When France was unable to get agreement on dual control of munitions and their use, General de Gaulle gave the US forces their marching orders – a brave decision that saw many march to the UK, where it continued to be open house. It was only Britain, presumably because of that shaky and unstructured beginning, which accommodated US bases and forces completely without treaty, legality or oversight. This didn't stop British ministers claiming that we had a veto over the launch of attacks from UK territory, always referring to a joint communiqué issued by PM Churchill and President Truman in 1952. Margaret Thatcher and Michael Heseltine were among a long list of those happy to mislead Parliament on this point, but the document was merely a joint statement with no force of ratification and no practical way of its being enforced, especially when successive American officials denied over and over again that it in any way represented a binding veto. The text and the emphasis of their answers varied, but the sense always remained: 'Our bases and our forces are deployed in American interests and cannot be answerable to anyone but the American president.' Ray is sure that no amount of mutual admiration, back-slapping, posing for photo-opportunities or stooging around in golf-buggies – or even military support in reckless overseas adventures – has changed those circumstances one iota.

Illustrating just how everything pertaining to the governance of the US forces' presence was totally unacceptable from the British perspective was the revelation that they were exempted by British legislation, the 1952 Visiting Forces Act, from being subject to UK law, on or off base. In practice this has meant that British citizens have been injured or even killed, principally in traffic accidents, without any redress or compensation being available and without any question of responsibility or guilt being considered by a British court or inquest. Learning that, it had been easy for Ray to understand how American agents at Lockerbie, versed in such a mindset, could dismiss the measured requirements of Scottish law as an irrelevance.

If Ray had decided to travel home using a longer route taking faster roads, he could have, some 25 minutes after leaving Cambridge, passed one place, and would later, nearing home, be driving quite close to another, whose common factor lay in enjoying very public Cold War notoriety. Molesworth near Huntingdon and Greenham Common in Berkshire were the two bases chosen for Britain's allocation of Ground-Launched Ballistic Missiles, commonly referred to as Cruise. The imposition of Cruise did much to revitalise and refocus the opposition to nuclear arms, emphasising as it did the apparent accordance to the American military of the right to ride roughshod over the interests and concerns of British people at every level, including our elected legislators. It was at this stage that the metaphor of Britain as the American's unsinkable aircraft carrier, moored conveniently off the coast of Europe, took hold and the indefatigable Duncan Campbell produced a book of that name, that unaccountably Ray and Carl had missed at the time.

Hand-in-hand with the military build-up were constantly developing facilities for detection, command and control – the radars and a whole panoply of communications networks to fight the war in Europe that American strategy regarded as inevitable, and which we eventually learnt the more hawkish elements considered it would be advisable to start, when the time came. The decision, once again of course, would be made without reference or advice to their NATO and other allies, who were not informed of these plans.

The third element in the mix was, Brian's notes had revealed, intelligence. Ray's route will take him near Bletchley and the country house where from 1939 British cryptologists decoded German military instructions and reports. They didn't break the Enigma code there, as many believe: the Poles did that in 1932 and shared their findings in 1939, but the massive work at Bletchley Park was absolutely crucial to the eventual allied victory. At the end of the war the Government Code and Cypher School was scaled down, moved and in 1946 renamed the Government Communications Headquarters, GCHQ; but for the Americans, eager to eavesdrop on political, diplomatic, military and intelligence traffic in Soviet-controlled Europe, and soon the newly-liberated democracies too, the pliable attitude of the British authorities meant that UK soil could quickly become dotted with facilities dedicated to surveillance of ever-increasing capability and widening scope.

Because he's avoiding the roadworks between Bedford and Milton Keynes, the Sandy to Ampthill route takes him right past 'RAF' Chicksands. Chicksands Priory was the British listening post that from 1941 provided the intercepts of German signals, especially to and from Berlin and further east; messages that were among those decoded at Bletchley Park. In 1950 it was given to the Americans and so became the first of many UK signals intelligence assets. National Security Agency 'defectors' in America have confirmed that the US monitors friendly host nations' communications just as avidly as it does those of third parties.

Having crossed the M1 and negotiated most of Milton Keynes' endless succession of roundabouts, Ray spots a sign to Bletchley Park, which is now a tourist attraction. People have an endless fascination with war – many of the most successful museums and visitor sites are those associated with killing in its manifold forms. Who can resist the sight of a handsome castle, dominating a tract of countryside, but yet how many of us really reflect on the barbaric acts almost inevitably committed in its dungeons, within its curtilage or in its vicinity? Ray has a modern equivalent. As an aviation buff, he enjoyed military airshows, until he was struck by the recognition that families were being encouraged to participate in a carnival atmosphere amidst displays celebrating monstrously expensive killing machines, which they were paying for, and whose effective purpose was the murder, maiming and dispossession of people exactly like themselves.

It's not long before he has the opportunity to see, on the left, two just such death-dealing aircraft, long retired and dramatically mounted as gate guardians at yet another US installation in the heart of England. He also spots two overweight, over-armed USAF security police controlling access to the site. Croughton is a communications centre, responsible, among other things, for the transmission of CIA encrypted traffic. He smiles as he remembers Fraser's deadpan comment on the Company: 'It's a big employer.' There are a few cars on the road with US licence plates. 'Don't get hit by one of those,' Ray reminds himself. Brian had provided, thanks to his contact and Duncan Campbell's research, an answer to Carl's question as to what CIA agents might be engaged in, if they were based full-time in the UK. There was evidence that they had indeed, as might have been suspected, given their track record elsewhere in the world, infiltrated organisations such as trade unions which they deemed to be, in their view, dangerously left-wing. There was no firm evidence that they had attempted to influence the result of Parliamentary elections, but on the balance of probabilities there was little reason to suppose that they hadn't.

Crossing the M40, he's just a couple of miles from Upper Heyford, now like others of the airbases long closed, its Cold War rôle over. In its day it had played host to tactical fighters, then F-111E nuclear bombers on continuous readiness and finally EF-111 electronic jamming aircraft, that had taken part in the highly dubious bombing of Tripoli, in company with Lakenheath's 111 bombers supported by Fairford's Boeing tankers.

A few miles further on there's a sign for Barford St John, another one-time RAF airfield festooned with snooping aerials, feeding back to Croughton. Before Burford, on a nearby hilltop there's the former RAF Little Rissington, site of one of nine USAF, four US Army and one US Navy 500 bed hospitals, built solely to await American, and only American, military casualties from war in Europe. Three more of those are not far from Ray's route. At Burford, RAF Brize Norton is just down the road. Still the RAF's main trooping base; under Cold War plans, it would have hosted Strategic Air Command B52 nuclear bombers moved into the battle zone from California and Texas, as would Upper Heyford and Fairford, not very far away.

Brian's notes, quoting Campbell, said that at its fullest extent the US presence had amounted to 25 major bases or military headquarters, 35 minor or reserve bases and 75 other facilities, plus 30 detached housing complexes, a total of 165 facilities. Ray had noted that the list had not included Heathrow, although it and several additional civil airports were listed as US base requirements for NATO purposes in 1950. 1950 may seem a long time ago, but one thing seems certain; that once the US military have assumed the right to occupy a base, they relinquish it only when **they** wish to, the exception being when they came up against the redoubtable Charles de Gaulle. The UK government, Ray feels, seems to exhibit no more willingness in 2006 to take proper charge of its own civil and military infrastructure, nor indeed the country's very continued independent existence, than it did in 1947. All that's happened is that everyone seems to have become far more reassured and relaxed about their apparent security. In as far as anything has been planned, this is exactly what will have been hoped. Billions have been squandered on devices to destroy the earth a thousand times over and hardly anyone seems to have even noticed – far less be worried about it, because nothing has happened – yet. Everything's fine – so far.

As in Loudon's song.

The small projectile comes from nowhere. Ray doesn't see it because he's in a strung-out line of traffic, the first time he's really seen any to speak of on this journey and this driver is overtaking all of them. So suddenly there's an engine scream alongside and a flash of silver and it's passed, mopping up those ahead, one – two – three. The double white line is solid this side now but that doesn't deter. Ray's always the first to notice when the lines are not necessary, but there's nothing over-cautious about these; there **is** a blind crest ahead – only a fool would be on the wrong side of the road where this maniac is. There's a flash of red brake lights and the projectile pushes in, now the red lights in the line ahead snap on towards Ray as each car starts to close too fast and has to ease off or pile-up. A horsebox growls past in the opposite direction: the delinquent car driver has missed head-on death, for him and others, by a second and three-quarters. What gives people the right, Ray wonders, to take risks with our lives on our behalf? There seems to be a rule that if you control the levers of power – politically, militarily or just mechanically – you can play fast and loose with others' destiny. Being 'in the driver's seat' at whatever level, should require an intelligence test, like the one Des wants for voters. But even being Ray's sort of captain, which demands much study, understanding and, he's always thought, common sense, doesn't seem to guarantee responsible, considered behaviour any longer, as he's been noticing. Those Air Force generals, prepared to go nuclear unilaterally, were all pilots too.

Is nothing sacred?

–ooOoo–

With the rain threatening again, the pair had started to make for the town.

"I've got something else for you that was given to me a few days ago," Brian had said. "One of my more computer-savvy colleagues got hold of it. It's just recently been de-classified by the Americans. Apparently in 1930 the US military prepared a scenario for a war with Great Britain that would have deprived us of the remaining international influence that we held post-

First World War. It involved invading Canada, in the knowledge that the British would have to go to its aid and fight a campaign on a continent the far side of a vast ocean. Fighting enormous odds with impossibly long supply lines, we would almost certainly lose, and the US could impose a peace that allowed them to help themselves to any of our profitable or strategic colonies that they wanted. It was called War Plan Red, because it was a war with all the red places on the world map."

At this Ray had stopped walking and Brian had observed that his eyes were closed and he was shaking his head slowly at this astonishing disclosure.

"Now my friend, who is a bit of a military history expert, says that we shouldn't read the worst into this as, he says, sophisticated armies do this sort of war-gaming routinely, although why they should spend time and resources plotting against supposed allies escapes me – perhaps it just gives them something to occupy their otherwise idle time. I've thought about it and all I can say is that, given the way America treated Britain in both world wars, and the Cold War, and since, such plans would have appealed quite strongly to at least some elements there and I think it probably reveals a more accurate picture of the relationship as seen by the power brokers on that side of the Atlantic, than any one that we've ever believed from this. I think we both subscribe to the view that at least some legacy of that attitude exists to explain many of the things that you've written about."

Ray had made no further response. Sometimes the weight of things that you learn simply gets too great to deal with; at times there is just no further energy left. When the walk resumed, the younger man moved differently, as if he was in some sort of daze, like a rugby player with minor concussion.

−ooOoo−

Before they'd gone their separate ways, Ray had phrased one last question for the old history man; it was one that he'd chewed over with Dick Leigh, and he wanted to leave Cambridge with Brian's view absolutely clear in his mind.

"Is there the slightest chance that I've got it all wrong; that I'm being unfair, unreasonably suspicious – that there's nothing to worry about or criticise at all?"

Brian had looked surprised.

"Good Lord! I can't see how, given the general transatlantic things that we've talked about and the anomalies that your specific research has thrown up. That's a bit like looking over a gate into a field with 100 sheep

471

with 98 of them white and then asking if there's any possible chance we can conclude that the majority are black. My view is that at least since 1914 the default position of the British government has been to mislead the people, even though very often most of the people in the administration in question might not know what they were actually being misleading about, why they were doing it and in whose interests. No, if your film can nudge the public-at-large towards an understanding that we've been ostensibly governed for close on 100 years by people who were either incompetent, or liars, or both, and who usually weren't actually in control of events at all, then more power to your elbow. Just send me two tickets for the première!"

"It's done," Ray had said.

−ooOoo−

77   Through the Ether

Ray has a plan for the day. The weather looks favourable. Somewhat uncharacteristically, he has made an early decision and intends to carry it through. As he makes a cup of coffee, Ken Bruce plays a new song that he can't abide. It must be on the Radio 2 playlist, as Wogan spun it earlier and indeed every presenter seems to be obliged to include it on their shows every day this week. It's not only pretentious nonsense, but the performer can't sing in tune. There's so much of the Emperor's New Clothes about the music business; everyone treats this singer and composer like pop royalty. Pretentious nonsense is fine if it sounds good – plenty of Beatles' lyrics or Steely Dan tracks are patently meaningless, but they're still great songs. Then again, performance isn't everything if the song has something strong to say; plenty of singer/songwriters don't have the greatest voices but their songs hit all the buttons. This is one of those that fulfil neither condition. Oh, for the days of Juke Box Jury, when panellists would say 'This is painful, tuneless rubbish,' and vote it a resounding raspberry-hootered miss.

He flicks to Radio 3, which he can often enjoy, but this morning the music is outside his fairly extensive comfort zone. He's tempted to Classic FM, but knows he will probably be screaming at the set and wanting to smash it, the moment the interminably repeated ads come on. With his career-long connection to advertising, he can't imagine how anyone could believe that the repetition of the same message or the same joke several times an hour and dozens of times a day can be anything but wildly counterproductive. In the same way, the presenters seem dragooned to mention the station's name in what seems like every sentence they utter. If the aim is to make the listeners feel that the station is their friend, don't the bosses consider how people actually react to people who talk about themselves constantly or tell the same story every few minutes?

There is something particularly bothersome about repetition. On '2', Ray cannot stand the constant self-promotion of one presenter, who constantly 'bigs himself up', as he would put it and accords himself canned applause. It seems that he never receives a request message that doesn't include the phrase 'Love the Show'. Even if listeners, who must have become brainwashed, write the nauseatingly trite compliment, what presenter with any taste or due modesty would read it smugly every single time? He might as well say 'I'm good, aren't I?' twenty times an hour. 'No, you're not,' Ray would reply, if he could bear to hear the man's whining voice and sneering references to people of far greater talent. 'You have every reason to be modest.'

He is in the act of switching to Radio 4 when he has a revelation. He will think later that it would have been more explicable had he actually tuned in and heard some word, phrase or scrap of an item that precipitates the thought, but it isn't like that. His finger is literally in mid-air when the recognition hits him. What he realises is that he perhaps has a way to give the script that unifying character that a few people, including himself and especially including Gerald, have been wanting all along. He understands there is no point in being annoyed about not spotting it until now; that's the way things work – you don't see it till you see it. As to whether it's too late, he doesn't know. The film is not yet at the stage of detailed planning, although it will have been budgeted on the basis of the last draft. Without sitting down and seeing what broad implications any revisions might have, he can't really know. His impression is that there would be no great difference, in that roughly as many scenes are likely to be dropped as would be added. There would be one new, fairly straightforward action sequence. The major change would be to the character of Brad. Ray has never been totally happy with the part that was left as a something of a rump when so many of Brad's scenes were re-worked for Jane Maddox. This could be a chance to resolve that and in doing so bring forward a new character that would be a real plum that many actors would be very keen indeed to play. And if the tricky time-transposition could be managed, it would, in **his** mind if nowhere else, honour Dick's contribution in a far more tangible way than just the simple name-check in the "Special Thanks" listing. Dick actually deserves a "Dedicated to the Memory" credit, Ray decides.

After all, in many respects, he died driving to work on the film.

It's odd. So many people have wanted revisions for all sorts of reasons over the last few weeks, and now the man who thought his job was at last done has been struck, in his kitchen, while thinking about radio programmes, by one that could make the script maybe thirty percent better.

He resolves to set about working through this, and will begin this evening, when he gets back from his planned few hours out.

–ooOoo–

Up in his office he checks his e-mails, just before he sets off. There is one from DB describing the latest progress with the finance, which remains a closed book to Ray, and some further ideas on casting, which are of interest and he will look at later. As he is about to close down, a new message pops up in the inbox.

His eyes go the sender's name and he opens it at once, almost shaking.

> Hi Ray,
>
> I hope you're not horribly surprised to hear from me, but I thought you might just want to know. My mother is not too well and I'm coming over to Scotland for a few weeks to give her some moral support. Probably not before time. I don't know if you would be interested in meeting up while I'm there. If you are it would be good to see you. Hope all is well with everything. Let me know and I'll send dates and details when I have them.
>
> Love Jack.

Would he be interested in meeting up? Don't be ridiculous. He's been hoping for a contact like this for weeks. He'll take time to compose a suitable reply tonight.

"Yes!" he says out loud. "Yes! Yes! Yes!"

He looks over his shoulder. He almost expects to see the Ogre behind him, wagging his tail. The dog always loved it when he was happy.

–ooOoo–

78   As the Fall of Silver Leaves

At the airfield, it's one of those perfect early Autumn mornings. Of the several delights of this place, effectively a farmer's private strip tuned into a modest business, the most striking is that it is almost impossibly quiet – most of the time – which is pretty odd for an airfield. You could spend a whole day here, and Ray has often done just that, servicing or fettling the aeroplane, and see just a handful of people; sometimes no one for hours. It took some getting used to, moving here from Staverton all those years ago; Staverton with its three runways (or six, depending on how you view it), with its serious, professional air traffic controllers and its friendly firemen, sitting reading the *Sun*, waiting to save you from your own ineptitude. It's a strange feeling when you land for the first time at a deserted airfield with no firetrucks and no men in silver suits with big crowbars to release you with luck before the flames take hold. You can get used to anything, any degree of danger, if you put your mind to it; look at circus performers, soldiers, submariners. Look at spies, for God's sake.

On such a day, when the air is so clear the sharpness is surreal, you feel that anything is possible. It is a gift, perhaps eight hours in which you may achieve whatever you wish; a day to be approached without a single doubt; with 'No Lurking Negatives', as read a T-shirt once gifted to a unit by a production company that Ray often worked with. People must have felt good just like that on the morning of 11th September, 2001. 'Gin clear', the expression goes. He has never looked up to find what gin has to do with it. Passengers and crews boarded those planes in Boston and New York and Washington in full confidence that they would attain their goals for the day; whatever they were travelling to accomplish, the sunlight and the blue sky flashed messages that it was within their grasp. It was a day with hope, triumph and success written all over it. That it proved to be so for such a tiny percentage of the four planes' occupants was a cruel irony indeed.

However benign the weather, Ray never performs his pre-flight walk-round without the most earnest consideration of the critical dimension of what he is about to do. Just as every car journey is prefaced with contemplation of the possibility of its being his last act on earth, the drive to the airfield is accompanied by deeply suppressed forebodings of the most obvious kind. These background thoughts do not consume him; distract him from his precise driving or from his meticulous planning and his checking once at the clubhouse and hangar. Rather they serve to refocus his concentration and intensify the seriousness of his approach to tasks that he's performed some thousands of times. Do the professionals feel this, he wonders?

How much time does a commercial pilot need in his logbook before these nagging doubts fail to present themselves for inspection in advance of each departure into the blue or grey? He must ask Austin if he still feels vulnerable pre-takeoff, after all his thousands of hours.

The cut-off point for Ray is starting the engine. After that the furies mysteriously depart and total calm and confidence settles upon the cockpit. He announces his intention to taxi over the radio – a completely redundant exercise he knows, as it's unlikely there will be anyone tuned to the airfield frequency this morning; no one to hear his measured, Captain Speaking tones. His door may not be on automatic, but he is. Now every action and thought process is professional and rehearsed. Anyone who does happen to hear him will form the impression that he has a co-pilot beside him and hundreds of trusting souls in a liner of the sky behind him, instead of just three empty seats. This rather-too-long still-dewy grass could be the asphalt of Heathrow's Outer Taxiway; runway Zero Four, with its rather better-manicured turf might just as well be the 3,658 concrete metres of Zero Nine Right.

He turns into wind, stops and lets the engine warm up properly. There is no rush. He takes his time, savouring the privileged experience. Meticulously he goes through the power run-up and carries out all the pre-takeoff checks using the list that he made on his first Amstrad. How long ago was that?

"Ampsey Traffic. Golf Echo Bravo is entering Runway Zero Four for backtrack and line-up."

He enters the last few dozen yards of the runway and taxies the "wrong" way for a few moments towards the fence that forms its limit. Then, with feet on rudder pedals he turns the Piper left through 180 degrees, tightly enough to finish in the centre of the strip; not so tightly that the nosewheel will skid on the grass and make a muddy scar. It's also rather important not to catch the wingtip on the fence. That would be too silly. He loves this manoeuvre. Taxiing well, he thinks, is an unpractised, unappreciated art.

Eight hundred metres of generally flat grass stretch out beyond the nose and the propeller's blur. He checks his watch. Nine minutes after midday. It's strange how he hardly ever gets airborne before noon. He writes the time under 'U' for 'Up' on the minimalist flight log clipped to his kneeboard. Log book entries use Greenwich Mean Time and his watch is naturally on BST. The pen traces the figures '11.09'. Also strange, he thinks.

He checks the temperature and pressure gauges yet again. All OK. The brake-pedals are above those of the rudders and he slides his feet up and plants them firmly to lock the wheels against the coming thrust. He taps the button on top of the stopwatch attached to the control yoke and progressively pushes the throttle fully forward with his right hand. He remembers that sequence of events being performed in a real Concorde cockpit for a simulated take-off on a British Airways commercial that he firsted. Despite the headphones the noise is considerable and the aircraft begins to shake on its wheels in the slipstream. He checks the RPM counter and those all-important temperatures and pressures once again. Finally he scans as much as he can of the nearby sky just in case a helicopter or a low flying RAF Hercules is about to conflict with his departure by flying across the airfield or through the climb-out profile – both have happened. Satisfied, he lifts both feet from the brakes and plants his heels on the floor to be ready to steer with the balls of his feet on the rudders. The Piper begins to accelerate and the vibration stops.

"And Echo Bravo is rolling Zero Four, for a right turn out."

There's a noticeable ridge across the runway after about five seconds, where a hedge used to be before the sheep gave way to aeroplanes. The Piper always lightens on her wheels here, skittishly pretending that she's ready to fly. She isn't. Even lightly laden as today, she will require another few seconds and a few more tens of metres to be ready to lift. The Cessnas that Ray trained on would take themselves off; all you had to do was keep them straight with your feet. Ray still remembers his first time in a PA28, with its need to make a positive pull back on the yoke to 'unstick' the nosewheel and rotate to the climbing attitude. He liked that. It felt like an airliner must, he thought; a 'proper' aeroplane. He was a Piper convert from that day on.

He begins the pull just before 60 knots, or 69 miles per hour, and once more the aerodynamics do their faithful work. Airborne! Ray checks forward to build up speed and establish his preferred rate of climb – gentle angles, predictable trajectories. As with driving, smoothness is the game: imagine it's a 747 with cabins full of punters. Statistically some will be apprehensive; do nothing to give them cause. At a safe speed and a hundred or so feet he makes a small heading change right for neighbourly noise abatement. This increases the proximity to the National Grid pylons closing from the right, but in moments Echo Bravo is higher than their tops and, barring engine failure, they will slip harmlessly away below.

All the while he is checking the engine temperature and oil pressure, RPM, rate of climb indicator and altimeter. He keeps the balance ball in the centre by pressure on the right pedal, so the aircraft flies straight and doesn't skid through the air, as it wants to, due to the engine torque at full power.

"Four hundred feet. Positive rate of climb. Flaps away." Ray isn't actually sure that he says this, and many of the other drills, properly out loud. He does often when he's flying with other members of the group. With passengers who are not pilots, he generally doesn't, although it can be useful to stop them talking, by showing them that he has routines and procedures to attend to and that flying is not at all the same as sitting in a car and chatting. Flying solo, he's not sure. So ingrained are the mantras, and so loud are they in the head, that he can't say whether he vocalises them or not this day.

With the flaps retracted he winds the trim wheel to take the back pressure from the yoke and checks the nose attitude and rate of climb. Looking all round, importantly including to the left, he puts Echo Bravo into a right turn, looking for an initial heading of two-two-five degrees magnetic.

Another routine flight begins.

—ooOoo—

Compton Abbas in Dorset is one of an exclusive list of hilltop airfields. The traditional requirement for a landing ground, a large area offering flat space allowing a virtually unlimited number of directions for operations, means that air installations were originally most likely to be found in wide river valleys and other areas with little relief. Compton, with its single runway along the edge of a ridge of downland with the land dropping away dramatically at one boundary and from one threshold, would not have been considered for an airfield site in the early days of aviation. It's ironic, then, that now it is a place that captures the spirit and energy of traditional flying as well as anywhere that Ray knows. The spectacular setting is exploited to full advantage and combined with the availability of exceptional home-cooked food has made the place a magnet for aviators and their passengers, as well as for a constant stream of visitors by road who enjoy the entertainment supplied by the aerial comings and goings. At about 35 minutes' flying time from home base it is, not surprisingly, Ray's lunch destination of choice.

It's a shame to be flying alone on such a day, not sharing the experience with someone occupying at least one of the spare places. Jack would enjoy this: Deborah too perhaps. How many times has he flown this route with Eve, over the years? Thinking about empty seats reminds him that it was Compton Abbas where they lost Harry. Harry was never a member of the aircraft group and yet he was at its very core. Not a pilot, he was a ground engineer in his seventies who during his RAF service had sent DC3s (aircraft that most would term 'Dakotas', but were properly C-47s) to D-Day, to Arnhem and to the Berlin Airlift. He possessed a phenomenal memory for names, incidents and details and related his aviation stories most entertainingly whenever prompted. To have Harry along on an outing was a bonus and a privilege and it came to be that he would occupy a spare seat on almost all the group's flights. He would always try to insist that he paid the away-airfield landing fees as his contribution to the adventures.

Ray had not been on Harry's last flight. At Compton, as two of the group were securing the aircraft Harry had, as was his practice, hastened along the flight line to the clubhouse, there to slap some cash down on the booking-in counter before he could be out-manoeuvred. He was no longer a fit man and as he arrived at the flight centre his heart stopped and he dropped dead. Many people later remarked that if they had to go, they wanted to go just like Harry, doing something that he loved best. He had just completed a spectacular flight on a stunning day. He was with his mates and anticipating a nice cup of tea at the most beautiful of airfields, with another flight yet to come. What could be better? Harry would ever be missed but the manner of his death, given the myriad of unpleasant alternatives always on offer, was certainly one to be envied.

There is very often a rather strange decision to make when flying to Compton Abbas, indeed if you are cruising at anything below 2,600 feet it is inevitable that you make this choice. It's necessary because the airfield has an elevation of 810 feet. As you approach, you will be flying at an altitude, based on mean sea level, the concept that disciplined Dick always had trouble with. If you are at 2,000 feet, as Ray is today, you are not at 2,000 above the ground below you, but above the surface of the Bristol Channel, just visible away to the west. To make a standard overhead approach to an airfield, you normally need to arrive at 1,000 feet above the height of the airfield's circuit. Circuits are usually at 1,000 above **airfield** level, but in Compton's case it's 800. If you add the 1,800 feet to the airfield's elevation, you require to be at 2,610 feet above sea level in the overhead. So to comply, Ray actually needs to climb a further 610 feet before he gets there. This is the reverse of what you normally expect to be doing as you near your destination. The decision is whether to make that standard overhead approach or join in a variety of other ways -- crosswind, downwind, base leg or long finals. These joins are made at circuit height, thus obviating the climb to that 1,800 foot overhead with the immediate descent to 800 that would follow. At an airfield like Compton the choice is the pilot's; with full air traffic control the choice would be made by the controller. The decider is really the amount of traffic in the circuit. It's bad airmanship and potentially hazardous to 'muscle in' on a busy circuit pattern with a non-standard join, for it can be remarkably hard to spot other traffic, especially traffic below your level. It's often the best option to plan in advance for the overhead join and convert if the other traffic is sufficiently light.

Today Ray has somewhat uncharacteristically chosen to cruise at 2,000 even though there is no earthly reason in this perfect weather why he shouldn't have climbed, to 7,000 feet initially, and once south of Bath to 10,000, about the Piper's ceiling, had he wished. He doesn't recall ever doing that for a transit of this length, but 3 or 4,000 would not have been at all unusual for such a leg. In fact below 3,000 he normally tends to use a tip of one of his old instructors and fly at about 200 feet above or below the popular 1,000 or 500 foot intervals to put a theoretical safety margin between himself and pilots flying the conventional altitudes. Today, unaccountably, he hasn't even done that. It may be something to do with the weather history of Warminster. Warminster is one of those hazardous places created by the powers-that-be, in their wisdom. If you prohibit general aviation from an area, for sound reasons or for mere bureaucratic empire-building, congestion and therefore hazard is inevitably increased around the margins of the forbidden area. Because of the zones created for commercial aircraft using London's airports, for example, GA traffic is banned from what seem to be excessively large tracts and also squeezed into the lower altitudes, creating a degree of congestion and potential conflict that horrifies pilots from quieter regions.

East of Warminster the cause is the military's demanding sterile airspace over the Salisbury Plain training ranges so that their wargames can be practised unobserved and uninterrupted. This means that for much of the time there is a no-go block measuring some 30 miles west to east, requiring a major dog-leg in many journeys heading to and from the south coast airfields and the continent from the western side of England. Much of this impeded traffic therefore routes just west of Warminster, requiring exceptional look-out for conflicting traffic. Also for some reason, due perhaps to the gap between the high plain and the Mendips, there often seems to be lower cloud lurking in the town's vicinity than there might be anywhere else nearby on any given day. Ray has lost count of the times he has encountered tricky conditions near Warminster, which may possibly explain why he hasn't cruised higher today – an expectation of the regular need to ferret around above the garrison town however encouraging the weather elsewhere.

He's cleared Lyneham's radio frequency shortly after negotiating the rat-run without having seen or even heard of another aircraft in the vicinity. Now he monitors the one assigned to Compton Radio with the object of gauging the state of the circuit to determine the approach that he'll propose when he calls them up. He soon hears that the runway direction in use is Zero Eight, close to easterly, as he could have expected. With a left hand circuit and the minimal traffic that there seems to be, he will be quite happy to suggest a left base join, which will mean beginning his descent near Shaftesbury on its much lower hill, trying not to be fazed by the steeply-rising terrain ahead and trying to judge his final turn towards the runway on the ridge just as if it were an airfield in flat East Anglia. This approach is always spectacular with the downs dropping away below, sometimes presenting the challenge of downdraughts – and then there's the fact that the runway descends noticeably after the threshold and if you don't touch down early, you can float and float, especially in a Warrior II.

Most of that's to come whatever join he chooses, but then he makes his unexpected decision – to go for the standard overhead. He suddenly thinks that he could do with the practice as he does them so infrequently; never at Ampsey, the home base, and rarely at most of the places he uses with any regularity. He will climb that 600 feet and report to Compton at 2,600 on the regional setting, for a standard overhead left-hand. He's approaching the east to west railway line and ten miles to run, so he'll go up fairly quickly. He looks around and behind him, as far as is possible, for other traffic. As his hand moves towards the throttle quadrant, he has his second Damascene moment of the day. On a totally different subject from the one earlier, the light at last goes on; two and two finally add up to four. He realises that he knows about that mystery white helicopter hovering over the debris trail at Lockerbie, with the marksman in the open door, ordering people away from selected places. Well, more specifically, he knows who was almost certainly flying it; someone with whom he has worked more than once. Why has it taken him years to come to this so-obvious conclusion?

He selects full power; applies some right rudder to keep the aircraft in balance against the torque and eases steadily back on the yoke to increase the nose attitude, which soon feels quite steep, around 45 degrees, with the horizon gone and the windshield full of sky. He reaches for the trim wheel to counter the pressure and so continue the climb without needing to hold the controls back. 'Let the aircraft fly herself whenever possible,' Norman the instructor used to say.

Behind Ray, past the two empty seats, beyond the small luggage compartment, behind the crawl-through access panel attached with Velcro, in the darkness of the metallic tube that is the rear fuselage, one of the six cables running from the controls to the various tail surfaces parts company with a noisy thwang. It has been interfered with, of course. In normal circumstances these cables never break and their adjusters never become unlocked. Nor do they even in abnormal circumstances, under conditions of extreme turbulence or for any other reason, really. Ray knows what it is from the moment he hears it, despite his headphones. The fact that the control column slides further towards him of its own volition, without any resulting change in attitude felt from the aeroplane is a sure clue as to which cable is no longer functioning. As if to check what he already knows, he pushes the yoke forward cautiously and it moves limply, offering no resistance and imparting no directions to the aircraft. The stabilator, the all-moving, one-piece tailplane and elevator, is now quite independent of his input. His direct means of controlling the pitch attitude of Golf Echo Bravo has ceased to be effective. He has lost one of his primary flight controls. As he swiftly reaches for the throttle to reduce its setting, a fraction at a time, from full climb power, to prevent, he desperately hopes, the nose from raising further and precipitating a stall, from which there could now be no means of recovery, he is under no illusions about the seriousness of his situation. This is unlikely to be survivable.

Who'd be a captain now?

–ooOoo–

The intercom buzzes in DB's London office.

"Mr Hollingsworth. It's Mr Wyzell for you," says the voice of the temporary. "Shall I put him through? And I'm just about to go."

"Please. And goodnight, thank you Anna. – Joe! What can I do for you?"

"David! It's about your *One-Zero-Three*; ya know we were saying how we were worried about dis thing; ya know – about the mixing of the truth and fiction – how it all gets complicated and gets messy? We bin thinking some more and I have to tell ya, bottom line, we come to a decision. I'm sorry to tell ya . . ." The fat executive pauses on the line. DB can picture Wyzell looking away, even on the telephone somehow afraid of the concept of coming eye-to-eye for more than an instant; a man who can seem shifty even on the rare occasions when there's no reason to be so; a true cartoon, a man who has almost deliberately grown into his own stereotype.

DB can hear him breathing; the wheeze of many thousands of cigars. He can even hear him swallowing and wriggling in his seat. Finally some words are formed.

"We ain't gonna make dis picture."

–ooOoo–

Appendix

A small selection of highly recommended further reading, some mentioned in the text, some not, but all providing more detailed examination of topics mentioned.

THE LOCKERBIE CASE

Lockerbie - The Real Story David Johnston 1989 Bloomsbury

Air Accident Investigation Branch Department of Transport Report on the Accident to Boeing 747-121 N739PA at Lockerbie, Dumfriesshire on 21st December 1988 and Appendices 1990 HMSO

Cover-Up of Convenience - The Hidden Scandal of Lockerbie
    John Ashton Ian Ferguson 2001 Mainstream

Tell Me No Lies - Investigative Journalism and its Triumphs
    Edited by John Pilger 2005 Vantage
    (Paul Foot - The Great Lockerbie Whitewash 1989 - 2001)

An' then the world came tae oor doorstep - Lockerbie Lives and Stories
    Jill S Haldane 2008 Grimsay

Megrahi You Are My Jury - The Lockerbie Evidence
    John Ashton 2012 Birlinn

AVIATION AND THE 747

Flying the Big Jets Stanley Stewart 1984 Airlife

Air Disasters Stanley Stewart 1986 Ian Allan/Arrow

The Tombstone Imperative - The Truth About Air Safety
    Andrew Weir 1999 Simon & Schuster

747 - Creating the World's First Jumbo Jet
    Joe Sutter 2006 Smithsonian Books

THE UK, THE SECRET UK AND WHO RUNS THEM

Big Brother in Britain Today
     Antony A Thompson 1970 Michael Joseph

The Arms Bazaar - The Companies, The Dealers, The Bribes from Vickers to Lockheed Anthony Sampson 1977 Hodder & Stoughton

Beneath the City Streets Peter Laurie 1979 Granada

The Right to Know - The Inside Story of the Belgrano Affair (The Reach of the Official Secrets Act) Clive Ponting 1985 Sphere

Death of a Rose-Grower - Who Killed Hilda Murrell?
     Graham Smith 1985 Cecil Woolf

Open Verdict - An Account of 25 Mysterious Deaths in the Defence Industry Tony Collins 1990 Sphere

Thatcher's Gold
     Paul Halloran & Mark Hollingsworth 1995 Simon & Schuster

Captive State - The Corporate Takeover of Britain (Includes The Skye Bridge Mystery) George Monbiot 2000 Macmillan

Who Runs This Place? - The Anatomy of Britain in the 21st Century
     Anthony Sampson 2004 John Murray

THE BORDERS

Kings of the North - The House of Percy in British History
     Alexander Rose 2002 Weidenfeld & Nicolson

AMERICAN HISTORY, POLITICS AND THE 'SPECIAL' US-UK RELATIONSHIP

The Kennedys - Dynasty and Disaster 1848-1984
     John H Davis 1982 McGraw-Hill

On the Trail of the Assassins Jim Garrison 1988 Sheridan Square

1940 Myth and Reality Clive Ponting 1985 Sphere

The Unsinkable Aircraft Carrier Duncan Campbell 1986 Paladin

Plausible Denial Mark Lane 1991 Thunder's Mouth

Why Do People Hate America?
    Ziauddin Sardar & Merryl Wyn Davies 2002 Icon

Tell Me No Lies - Investigative Journalism and its Triumphs
    Ed. John Pilger 2005 Vantage
    (Greg Palast - How to Steal a Presidency and Get Away With It)

Yo, Blair! Geoffrey Wheatcroft 2007 Politico's Publishing

SCREENWRITING AND FILM MAKING

Adventures in the Screen Trade - A Personal View of Hollywood
    William Goldman 1983 Macdonald

Final Cut - Dreams and Disaster in the Making of *HEAVEN'S GATE*
    Steven Bach 1985 William Morrow

AND THE MUSIC

Captains. Written by Steve Knightley Performed by Show of Hands
    Show of Hands - Lie of the Land Isis Records

My soul, there is a country. Music by Sir C Hubert Parry Words by
Henry Vaughan Performed by the Choir of Trinity College, Cambridge,
conducted by Richard Marlow Conifer

Keep Taking the Tabloids. Written by Richard Stilgoe Performed by
Richard Stilgoe and Peter Skellern - Stilgoe & Skellern By the Wey

Can't Get You Out of My Head. Written by Cathy Dennis and Rob
Davis Performed by Kylie Minogue Parlophone

Exile. Written by Steve Knightley Performed by Show of Hands with
Polly Bolton   Show of Hands - Live Isis Records

Sospiri. Sir Edward Elgar

Pretty Good Day. Written and performed by Loudon Wainwright III
    Social Studies Rykodisc

Coming Soon from the Author

The Buses Must Go Through

It's 1966. Last year Priors Boswick almost won the Prettiest Village in England Competition. That near-success has given the villagers two things to cope with this summer – several thousand tourists every day – and a large Hollywood film unit shooting a period drama.

The visitors do what visitors always do: they wander. The film-makers do what they always do: they take over. And the villagers do what they always do: they disagree.

The stage then is set for fireworks (as it happens, almost literally) when the shooting is due to start in the single village street.

To quote from that astonishing art form, the motion picture trailer:

"Things will never be the same again!" "You've seen nothing like it!"

"Now – it can be told!"

"Everyone ready?" "Stand-by." "Roll the camera." "Speed!" "And – **Action!**"

www.paddycarpenter.com

Grey Dog Books

Made in the USA
Charleston, SC
16 August 2014